The Enthronement

Charity Mae

KNIGHTED PHOENIX PUBLISHING

Contents

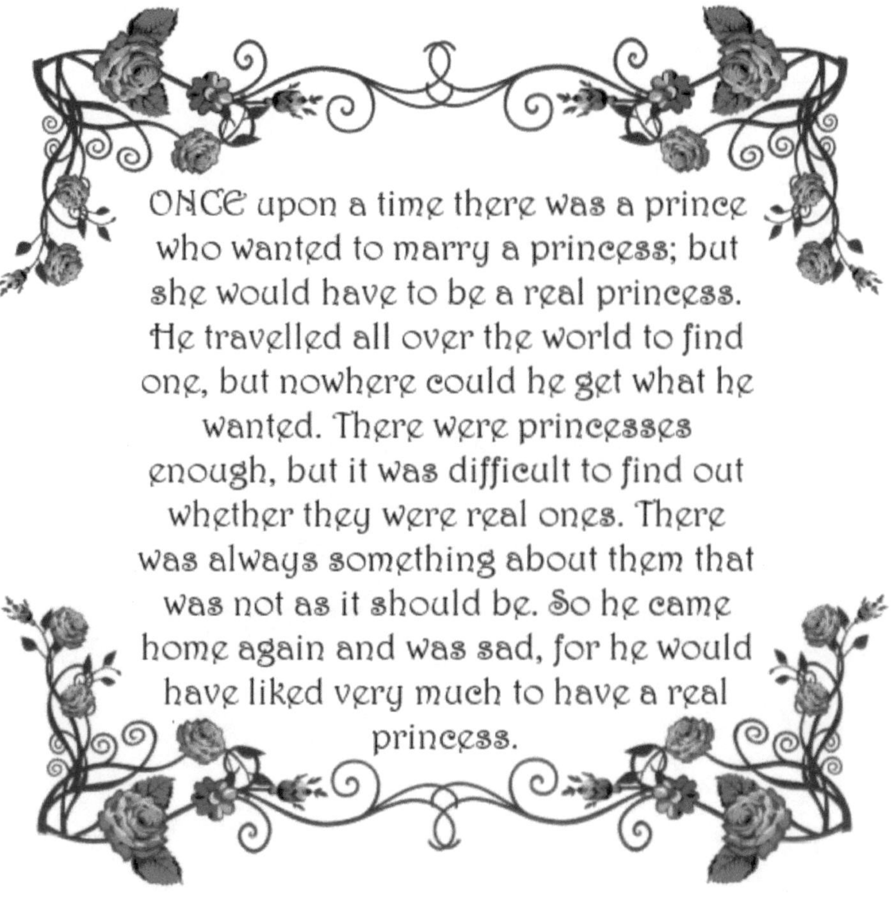

ONCE upon a time there was a prince who wanted to marry a princess; but she would have to be a real princess. He travelled all over the world to find one, but nowhere could he get what he wanted. There were princesses enough, but it was difficult to find out whether they were real ones. There was always something about them that was not as it should be. So he came home again and was sad, for he would have liked very much to have a real princess.

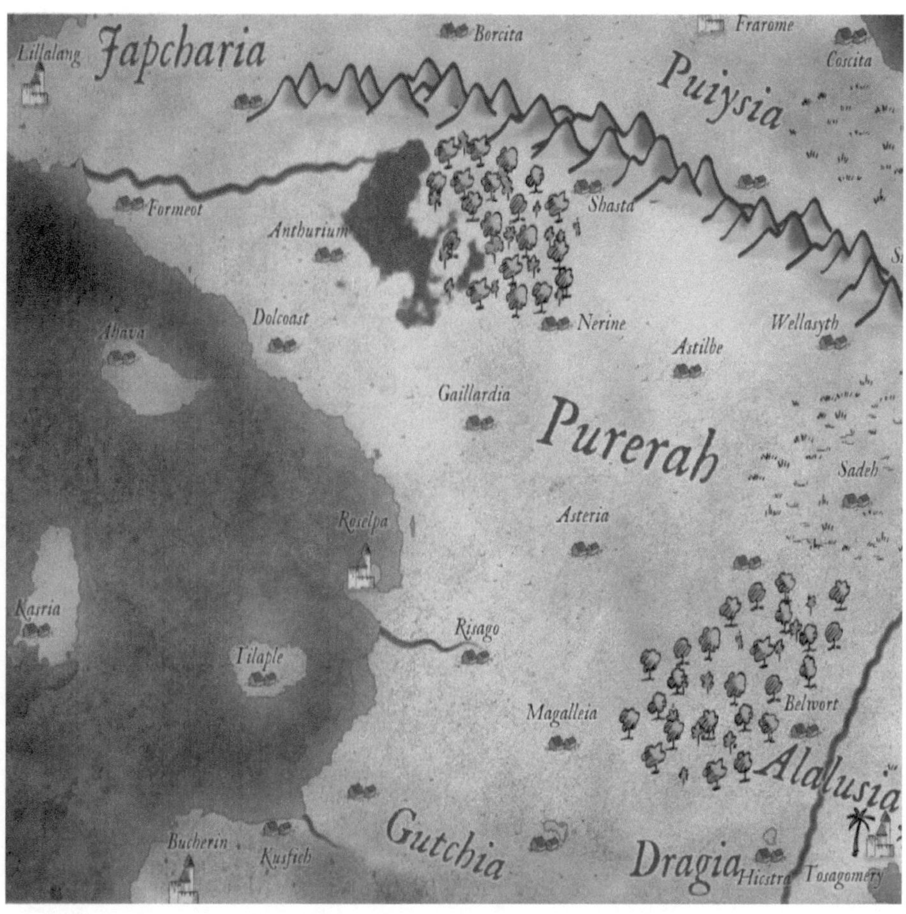
Lillalang
Japcharia
Borcita
Frarome
Coscita
Puiysia
Formeot
Anthurium
Shasta
Dolcoast
Nerine
Wellasyth
Astilbe
Gaillardia
Purerah
Sadeh
Asteria
Roselpa
Kasria
Risago
Tilaple
Magalleia
Belwort
Alalusia
Bucherin
Kusfieh
Gutchia
Dragia
Hicstra
Tosagomery

Chapter 1

I never wanted to be a princess, my Father destined me to be a queen. But today I am a dancer, and that's all I ever wanted to be.

Not that I don't understand why he wants me to be queen. It's nearly impossible for anyone to walk these streets and not understand. The evidence lies bare no matter where you look. Not a soul, no matter how hardened, can miss the battle and poverty scarred souls who live here or how every building and structure in the city cries for relief. With the right queen, relief could be given, and if you ask my Dad, that queen had to be me.

Not even the heavy mist that looms in the early morning air can hide the slowly decaying city from view. Rather, the mist toys with it like sadistic fingers stroking the fur of some demented pet. The mist swirls across the stone street, dipping into the countless potholes, cracks, crevices, and shattered stone gaps it can find. It snakes between the buildings, dipping into and back out of the dozens of cracks and dents inside the stone walls, teasing the broken, splintered, and missing roof shingles. It skips up the slanted roofs and basic coastal stones, adding a shiver to the air that makes me hug my shawl tighter around me, thinking perhaps I should have brought my cloak.

The mist gives the illusion of being alone, but there are plenty of people out and about, even this early in the morning. With the day, most of them are desperate merchants or performers who want to be ready for the activity of the festival, scraping as much of a living out of it as possible.

The mist hides them from view, but each whispering voice makes the chill worse. A small part of my mind debates if it's an innocent merchant, shopper, guard, or a desperate soul ready to do whatever it takes to get by. The mist dims the eyes but enlarges the ears.

"Have you heard?"

"The Enthronement, yes."

"Could such a contest be real?"

Ah yes, of course. I'm already sick of the word, and the rumors had only been circulating for a day or two. No one seems quite sure what it is, but if it's some grand contest to find a princess for the prince — as rumor had it — then it's a waste of everyone's time. Why worry about such a silly game when more real games are tearing our city apart? Tearing our nation apart.

I stop my ears and push through the mist like heavy curtains as I struggle to ensure the sounds roll off my shoulders like rain off a seagull. I'm not successful.

"Have you heard?"

"Yes, a chance to be princess? Every woman in Roseple, oh, for Merlin's sake, all of Purerah will wish they were eligible."

"Just an excuse to waste more money."

There's someone speaking sense. The tax is high enough without them spending money on such a frivolous affair. Can't the prince find a girl on his own? Maybe he's hideous. That's why no one has seen him in public.

But there are safety reasons too, I can't deny. He is the sole heir to the throne in a kingdom whose people have been in revolt for five generations. Five generations of over-taxation that's all but pushed us to the breaking point. It will either crush us, or things have to change. The relief my Dad sought to bring, which he believes I could bring.

I finally reach the cobbler shop and open the door, making the little bell sing into the crisp morning air. The mist vanishes in an instant as I step into the friendly warmth of the store.

The familiar stinging scent of the glue, the rough smell of the fabric, and the coarse scent of leather envelopes me in a familiar sensation and warmth that relaxes me.

I close my eyes to enjoy the feeling as I stand with my back pressed to the door, enjoying this moment of warmth and relief when two women whispering in a corner catch my ear.

"They're calling it the Enthronement," one is saying excitedly.

"That's a strange name for such a contest," the other woman frowns.

I sigh frustratedly. Not this again. Why is everyone so excited?

A man is already speaking with Jashon, so I wait patiently, holding the strap of my dance bag in both hands, wandering the shop, allowing my eyes to skim over the rows and rows of boxes that contain for the most part, example shoes and some sizing shoes. They line one wall, the one where the women are talking. On the other side is a bench, reusable foot tights, socks, and mirrors so patrons can look at how different styles of shoes fit them.

"What do you think the girls will have to do to win?" the ladies jabber on. Curse my dancer's ears! I can't help but listen to the cadence of their conversation with nothing else to keep me busy.

"No idea, but the rumor is we'll find out today. They'll announce it on town square Imaginal."

"Think we'll get to see him?"

"Who knows."

"Kascia!" Jashon calls out to me, making me turn to look and smile at him over my shoulder. "I wondered when you'd turn up. I thought your old ones would have worn a while ago."

My smile grows as I walk over to him, and the last customer leaves, making the bell above the door tinkle once again. "You're getting good on timing," I compliment him. "But it's also because I'm going to be ruining a pair today."

Jashon clicks his tongue, "I should have guessed. What was your last role? Did you even need them? They last longer when you don't use them all day."

"*The Witches* does not require pointe," I smile. "Not that they weren't getting used." I at least did some training in my pointes every day if I could help it.

"Well, you're my best customer because of it. So, thank you." Jashon smiles. "I have your pair right here." He bends down below the counter and pulls out the small delicate box he always puts the shoes in. I love how small and narrow it is.

I take the box with a nod of thanks and open it. I beam to see the soft pink pointes shining in the light. They are really shiny and smell of wood, satin, and slightly of the glue that holds them together.

"Beautiful as always," I tell Jashon. "What would I do without you?" I look up at him in delight.

"Dance demi-pointe," he teases. I laugh. What a shame that would be. "Your Dad already paid for them, so no note this time. I'll see you in a month or two."

I chuckle and roll my eyes as I close the box and put it into my bag. I adjust the strap and look up to thank Jashon, but he cuts me off.

"Have you heard about it?" He nods at the two women in the back.

I roll my eyes with a heavy sigh. "Yes, I can't stop hearing," I say dryly.

"You should try it," he says.

I blink and give Jashon a disbelieving look, "What?" He can't be serious.

"You play such a good princess on stage. Who else would be better to prove herself a true princess?" he grins at me, leaning over the counter. "A contest to win the prince's hand. Sounds right up your alley, Lady Kascia." He mock-bows his head to me.

Perhaps I do play a good princess, but I'm already taken. Not that he can know that. No one can know that. Sure, my friends know I have a serious boyfriend, but they don't know how serious.

"Thank you, but—"

"Seriously though." Jashon's face falls from its joking expression into a softer one. His eyes seem to glow against his dark skin as he looks up at me, "you should."

"I shouldn't."

"Honestly, you should. I don't know many girls who'd be better. You actually care about people. If you won't try it, I hope at least someone with a good heart like you wins that game."

"My heart isn't up for toying with," I tell Jashon. I'd heard enough to know I didn't want it, even if I wasn't fully sure what "it" was.

"Even for your people?"

He cuts me to the quick, but what he doesn't know is I have other work to do for my people. "My people don't want me," I state.

"Hm, maybe they do. I'll ask around," Jashon teases me as he pushes himself off the counter. "I'll see you soon, Kascia."

"Until then, Jashon."

I ensure my shawl is still safely around my head as I turn away and back out the door.

The mist is starting to lift as I walk along the street. More people are awake now, most of the shops up and running, many already have their merchants calling out into the street. I ignore them as I pass, keeping my shawl close.

It's not too long before I step into Governance Square, the largest open area in the city. Anyone who knows what they're doing will try to set up their stalls or performances here. But as the royal theater, we have enough experience to know how to get the best spot.

Sure enough, my fellow troupe members are setting up the tents in one of the lesser-used alleyways and have taken over the area near the fountain. Mom is supervising the stage boys in cleaning up as much as possible.

Normally, this square was teeming with people waiting to meet with the mayor or applying for a slot to have the court see their case. It was rare anyone got either, but some foolishly still have hope their sovereigns care about them.

Some had tried today too, even though no government work is done on the holidays. Many likely have nothing else to do. The city guard forces them out of the way of the incoming merchants and performers. They aren't gentle. I glare at a pair who are shoving a woman with two small children out of the way using the flat side of their spears to push them off the perimeter.

"Kascia, you're going to behave, aren't you?" Mom smiles at me, brushing a loose strand of her blonde hair from her face. Her hazel eyes sparkle in amusement.

"Can't cause trouble when they're just doing their jobs," I reply irritated. Their bosses could tell them to be gentler though.

"Don't focus on that. Today is a happy day: the day we celebrate the independence from the darkness and how our nation, or any for that matter, could be their own," Mom tries to remind me. "It's been exactly two thousand years."

"Hm, lots of that to celebrate around here," I say dryly as I pick up one of the changing tent bundles.

"Let the boys handle that," Mom waves at me to give it to one of the stagehands. "We want to work on the stage." She gives the stagehands a nervous glance. I think she also wants to make sure they're not doing other things instead.

The mid-morning sun has cleared out the mist by the time we have the curtains and tents ready to go.

"We have a long day ahead," Mom calls out to us. "We are doing pieces every half an hour, but that leaves you time to enjoy the festival too. But please stay close and don't be late when one of your pieces is up. We'll start at ten with the rest of the main activities."

"What in creation would we go do?" Max, our premier actor, complains.

"It's a city-wide party. It's a part of the national, honestly worldwide, party going on right now. You'll find something," she smiles, "or you can keep singing for your bread here."

I giggle as Max sighs in annoyance and walks off. Most of the stagehands do too. Mom frowns as they go, obviously worried about what they'll get up to.

"Mom, there are guards everywhere. What are they going to do?" I ask her.

"Cause havoc, I hope." Dad's voice joins us.

I chuckle as Mom stands upright putting her hands on her hips as she faces my Dad. "And ruin my shows? Don't you dare!" She kisses his cheek. "You weren't around to help with any of the setup," she complains.

"I had to get my mask," Dad nods at the bag on his back.

"Which mask?" Mom asks tentatively.

"For our preview," he assures her. "Am I not doing that piece with her today?"

"You are, but with your rabble boys, how do I ever know?" Mom replies.

"I also had to get nice for your shows. You don't like it when my beard is unkempt." Dad points out, stroking his goatee which does look nice, dark and thick and perfectly trimmed, his dark brown hair helping shape his handsome face. They contrast his pale blue eyes nicely, though admittedly their pale color makes it hard for them to pop on stage.

"Well, you do look nice," Mom agrees.

"You aren't dressed up yet," Dad notes Mom's hair is still in its high braided bun, and her hazel eyes are not highlighted by the normal makeup she'd use for a day like today. "Where is your makeup?"

"I have time before I get onto the stage," Mom points out.

"How about my cygnet?" Dad turns to me with a huge grin. I smile back. "How many of today's performances are yours?"

"Um... a lot." I am the prima actress, after all.

"The preview for *Hunchback*?"

"Then our piece."

Dad nods. "When is your first?"

"Ten thirty."

"Want to see the sights before then? I doubt you can wander far once that hour hits," Dad suggests. "We'll be back by ten," Dad promises my mother.

Mom sighs but allows it. Dad offers his arm, and we walk around the square. We see several other performing troupes setting up. A group of acrobats has just come in from the train and is hurrying to find a spot. The merchants are already calling out to us with goods: food, jewelry, art, and even pets.

"Odd to see the city so alive without the normal snapping," Dad comments as I admire a stunning array of island roses.

My stomach drops at the thought. "I don't mind it."

"Who would?" Dad chuckles.

We talk about the upcoming show, what I've been up to, just enjoying the time walking in the spring sunlight as we admire the traditional red, orange, gold, green, and black decorations popping up around the square: red and gold phoenixes, banners, the musicians warming up or starting to play for coins, the general excitement of a holiday.

Raised voices draw our attention as we reach Governance Hall. A group of people has started a shouting match with the guards keeping people out of the building.

"Potentate rebels," Dad mutters disapprovingly as the group screams insults at the guards. "So uncivilized."

"Traitors!"

"Puppets!"

"Murderers!"

The group of about twenty or so people scream at the guards. A few throw rotten food at them. The guards remain patient only until they can't drop their shields for the yelling. They are given the order to disperse the angry crowd.

"It's too early for this," I sigh.

"Let the people come!" a girl shrieks at the guards as they try to intimidate them, drawing weapons and charging them, but not going into their midst yet.

"You don't need to push them around," a boy about fifteen says as he throws a rotten tomato at the lead guard, striking him in the head and making him stagger back now he can't see.

"You would rather people starve than let us in to see our own leaders!"

"That's enough. Go home!" the second guard orders, which only makes the crowd shout and throw more rotten food.

One guard loses her cool and dives at the crowd. They scatter like flies. The guard manages to grab one of the younger boys in the group, perhaps about ten years old. I tense as she violently yanks him back.

"Let go-" The boy calls the guard a nasty name.

"Learn some respect, boy." The guard backhands him.

I move to jump in the way, but Dad holds my arm to keep me back. I frown and look at him. I trust him. He knows better but...

"They're hurting him," I say quietly, studying Dad's face carefully for my orders.

Dad looks into my eyes a moment before he smiles a little. "I trust you." He lets go of my arm.

I look back at the boy, who spits at the guard. She moves to strike him again, but this time nothing holds me back, and I grab her wrist.

"He's just a boy," I object. "You don't need to smack him around."

"That boy needs to learn manners."

"And that's not up to you to teach him," I say calmly. "Are you charging him with anything?"

The guard doesn't answer right away so I go on, "I presume not. It's not your place to teach him manners. Wouldn't that be his parents' job?"

"Because of those monsters, I lost them!" the boy yells at the guard.

"That had nothing to do with us!" The guard screams back at him.

"You made us all broke!"

"I'll take him if you aren't going to charge him," I cut them both off. "Thank you for your service." I give the guard a small curtsy before I take the boy and pull him aside.

"I'd not speak to them like that if I were you," I warn him. "That gives them an excuse to arrest you or worse."

"If that gives them what for then that's fine by me." The boy folds his arms. "That's what they deserve for taking it all."

"I know, but don't make it worse for yourself to make a point they won't even see."

"There are better ways," Dad joins us. I give him a small smile. Dad will know what to do. "Did I hear you're on your own?"

"Aren't most of us?" The boy glares at Dad as if it's his fault.

Dad doesn't bat an eye. "I know that feeling. You know, I think I have some friends you might like."

Dad glances at me to get my permission, and I nod. Dad smiles thanks, puts a hand on the boy's back and walks off with him, talking in a low voice. I'm sure Dad will make sure he's safe with the others. Just another one to protect with what little we can collect.

It's almost time for me to get ready, so I head back to the changing tent to get into my costume. I slip into the red dress that flares when I spin — which I adore — and put on my pointe shoes then start on my hair and make-up, making sure my make-up works for all my shows.

When I'm done, I turn my head side to side, admiring how the golden red/brown tones make my sea blue eyes pop, almost hiding the hazel ring in the middle I inherited from my mother. The same tones highlight my warm olive-toned skin for a smooth look.

The trickiest part is my hair. I got a mix of my parent's hair colors, my mother's blonde and my Dad's dark brown, giving me a dark golden-brown shade that gives off glints of red in the right lighting. But it's my curls that make my hair difficult to manage. I may not have the royal coils that are the envy of so many, but my thick curly hair came with its own unique set of problems.

But for my first show, I just pull it back with a headband to let it flow full, thick, and wild and set a tiara into the headband.

I am stunning as Esmeralda. I'd become her and charm every already uncharmed boy within earshot. I pick up the tambourine and do a few warmups with it before I'm called out to sing and dance the preview piece for the show we'll be putting on in a few weeks, just enough time for the tourists to help increase the revenue. Creator knows we need every gem we can get.

The piece is a hit, drawing more crowds than any of the other stalls so far, and I'm showered with whistles and applause as I bow to them at the end.

I have a half an hour break before we're doing our next performance which is just a group dance number from another show we're planning this season. I enjoy the smell of the dumpling and sea weed wrap stalls, admire the seashell jewelry and stone work trinkets.

Right before we go on, someone takes my shoulders. I look at him and chuckle to see Jake, my long-standing boyfriend, looking around frantically.

"Hide me," he says, his dark eyes darting about the square.

"What are you in trouble for now?" I ask teasingly.

"Nothing, the guards are after me," Jake says innocently.

I frown. "Jake, what were you doing?"

"Nothing! You know how it is. Say a word against the royal family, and they'll call you a rebel and lock you up for being unhappy we're drowning in debt." Jake insists.

I raise a brow, highly doubting that is true. He likely got into a fight with a guard that would make that little boy Dad spoke to blush.

The call for my cue to join the group of dancers comes. The guards in question come into the square from an alley behind Jake. I grab Jake's wrist and pull him, so he's behind me as we start to dance.

I carefully keep an eye on the guards and use the dance to keep Jake out of view. Though Jake is quite a bit taller than me, and I'm not large enough to block him completely, my dancing and flashing skirt certainly could keep them well distracted. It works, and the guards move on by the time the dance ends.

"Thanks," Jake smirks as we dash behind the curtain we're using as a backstage.

Jake leans down and kisses me deeply. I can't resist the little smile that climbs my cheeks as I run a hand along his rough cheek. The foolish boy never shaved enough, yet he never quite grew a beard, looking cutely stubbly all the time. I wrap my arms around his neck, the lighter tone of my skin contrasting his deeply tanned neck. Even this stolen moment makes my heart sing. I adore this man, the one I'd been secretly betrothed to since I was twelve years old.

"Jacek!" Mom snaps at him.

Our lips part, and I giggle. He's always getting in trouble with Mom.

"Jack," Jake insists.

"Your given name is Jacek, and that's what I'll use," Mom says, folding her arms and raising a brow at Jake. "What have I told you about being backstage?"

"Never, ever again. Stop scuffing up my floors," Jake recites.

"Maybe then I'll call you Jake." Mom smiles at his correct answer.

Jake frowns. "Jack." I'm the only one who gets away with calling him Jake. He was called Jake when he was little, but he hates it as an adult.

"Maybe when you stop causing my rehearsals such trouble then we'll get to calling you that." Mom gives me a smile. "You have time before your next piece," Mom says to me. "But be back."

"Am I ever not?" I tease as Mom leaves us alone.

Jake takes my hand, and we head into the main square. "But honestly, what were you doing?" I ask as we join the crowds enjoying the other performances and shopping. I wonder how long they saved to have that luxury. Or maybe they were smart and knew there would be discounts so they used today to do their normal shopping.

"Just talking with some other guys about how we could do something about how much they take. It was nothing."

"And what were the 'guys' doing?" I ask. Jake's group of friends aren't exactly the best examples. Honestly, I dislike all of them.

"Making fun of the guards for guarding the intake booth at the governance building when everyone knows nothing is going on there."

"And they attacked you for that?" I frown, annoyed.

"Well, the guys may have gotten too close to it for their orders to allow," Jake hedges.

I roll my eyes, hugging Jake's arm. I love him, even though he really is an idiot sometimes. "And we all know crossing the line is all it takes. Pretending to sign up for the waitlist, I assume."

"Stuff like that," Jake agrees.

I sigh. It was silly, but a reason to arrest them all? The royals have gone too far once again.

"On the bright side, they didn't fine or tax us," Jake jokes to cheer me up. He does win a giggle.

Jake and I enjoy the sights and smells, talking casually. I notice a few of the beggars have tried to creep into the square to beg for coins. I watch a group of them, using a young boy as a lookout to warn them when a guard is coming so they can scatter away from their view. In our circles of the square, I see it several times. They just want help to get by.

The large clock strikes eleven, cueing me to lure Jake back to our area, so we can watch one of the most impressive showpieces we'll have today where our two best men are performing a piece done at a bar, using the bar, drinks, glasses, and stools as props to perform an impressing singing and dancing number.

I know Jake finds it boring, but I love to watch. Partway through, he spots some of his friends and asks if he can go. I don't mind. It's the one thing I wish I could change about Jake, his lack of interest in the theatre world I live for. The poor man can hardly dance with me.

When the piece is over, I clap with the rest as our stagehands try to hand out flyers announcing this season's shows and that if they bring the flyers when they get tickets, they'll get a discount. When the discount is mentioned, many take them, but many also ignore it or toss them into nearby bins, or just let them flutter to the cracked, decaying street. So few can afford it.

A group of street musicians clear the area around the fountain and invite anyone who wishes to come dance to their music. I smile and can't resist joining in. I may be performing most of the day, but I love to dance, and a good folk dance is irresistible.

I weave in and out with the others who joined in the dance, moving from free partner to free partner as I am one of those who is unattached. These dances are impressive, designed to be danced with a single partner or several

"May I cut in?" Dad joins me for a circuit. "Or are you trying to meet new people?"

I laugh as we clap and spin around each other. "You know me, if I get to dance, I'll dance. I am alone." I assure him as we do a small jump that makes us face one another and do a slight bow, waving our arms down as if in welcome to each other.

"Then I'll be taking your slot," Dad teases as the dance pulls into a basic hold, and we start to step and turn around the line of dance around the fountain.

Though Jake can't really dance with me when he tries, Dad makes up for where he lacks. I'm sure his skill is part of what helped him win Mom. I feel pretty and playful as we dance, laughing and clapping with the proper beats.

When the song ends and everyone applauds the players, Dad hugs me with a smile. "Can't believe it's so soon that this will be over."

"You arranged it," I remind him, smiling at where his mind went.

"Still, in so many ways, I'll miss these days," Dad offers me his arm. "We should make sure you're ready for your eleven-thirty."

"Our eleven-thirty," I remind him.

"Yes, then we'll break for the retelling at noon," Dad recites how the festivals always go.

"Think they'll do more as it is the big two-thousandth anniversary?"

"Of course not," Dad's face darkens. "It would be money spent on us."

He has a point. The royals are as thrifty as could be when it came to spending money on their people, as liberal as possible in collecting taxes, and as wasteful as possible when spending it on themselves.

I change into the white dress that is the signature of this song as Dad changes into his suit and puts on his phantom mask. Mom starts our introduction. "Now a special treat, performing the star piece from *The Phantom* Kascia Thorapple and Peodrick Thorapple!"

The opening notes of the song play as we get on stage, and the crowd gathers around. I'd done this on tour with my Dad a few years before, and it was a huge hit. It's the role I'm most famous for. And it always draws a crowd. That's why I'll be doing it twice today.

The crowd cheers madly for us when it's over, and Dad takes off his mask as we go backstage. "Beautiful as always, Cygnet," he says.

"Creepy as ever," I tease Dad back.

We stay near our area, looking around for an idea for what to do to kill the next half an hour when there's yelling from the north side of the square.

Dad frowns and gets onto the stage for a better look over the heads of the crowds. I follow his lead.

A man dressed in the attire of the palace staff - a long Purerahian blue side button-up jacket with Purerahian yellow collar, trousers, and dark brown boots, topped with a Breton hat with a yellow band - strides into the square with a rather haughty expression. He's making his way to the raised platform in front of the governance building, likely to make an announcement.

The guards are calling the people to make way. When they don't, the guards act quickly. When anyone moves closer to them or refuses to move, the guards bark the command to back away and if the person — no matter the age — does not, they push them back, many so forcefully they fall to the ground. One guard shoves an older man so hard, he not only falls onto the stone stairs but almost knocks over several behind them. I know the man isn't armed. There was no need to be so harsh.

I look at the palace official to see what he'll do. He does nothing, that cold haughty expression still on his face. How could he stand by and let the guards treat us like this? The royal family truly doesn't give a guppy's fin about their people.

Dad takes my arm and squeezes it assuringly, telling me there's nothing we can do to stop it. "Not yet," he reminds me as he has done a million times. This is why I can't carry gems anymore in town. I'm free with giving them out to those who beg and am known to be a bit mouthy with the guards like I had done to protect the boy. But I've never been in any danger of being arrested, at least not yet.

It takes a long time for the official to reach the steps as the guards forcibility shove everyone and anyone out of the way. When he finally gets there, he stands still, watching with those expressionless eyes as the guards form a double ring around him as protection. His blue cloak catches the spring breeze revealing its yellow interior as it waves in the wind.

The guards force more people away from the perimeter around the circle. I spot a few of Jake's friends among those being forced back, throwing insults at the guards.

"They could at least send a member of the court, or as we are in the capitol, a member of the royal family could show their face," Alsmeria, my best friend and fellow soloist in the theatre, grumbles as she comes onto the stage for a good look.

I smile at her and take her hand. I can't help but think the same. We'd never even seen the prince. And the king and queen rarely came out of the castle. We got to see them in reports on the Governance Square Imaginal now and then, but that was the best we could hope for.

Once the guards have their perimeter, the official calls out for our attention.

"Go back to your safety net, royalist!" Someone screams at the official though he is yelling so harshly it is hard for the whole square to hear.

"Where are the royals now!?" A female voice shierks.

"We'll never get to the retelling at this rate," Alsmeria complains.

Dad gives us both a look but doesn't speak. He just keeps his hand on my shoulder protectively.

"Thank you all for your attention," the official calls. He has an impressive voice that carries easily across the large square. That must be how he got the job. He doesn't even have an amplifier. "Before we start the traditional retelling of what happened in the Great War two-thousand years ago today, the royal family has an announcement they will give over the public imaginal systems that will begin in about ten minutes."

"Too afraid to face us?" One of Jake's friends whose name I didn't bother to remember challenges the official.

Impressively, the official ignores these jibs. "The royal family thanks you for your time and attention and wishes you a Happy Restoration Day."

He gets a lot of boos for his trouble, and he goes to sit in an outdoor waiting area in front of the governance building, the guards tightening their position around him. The lead guard goes to sit beside him, and I see them talking, but that's all I see before Alsmeria pulls on my hand.

"We have about ten minutes. I've been busy looking around, but did you want to do something?"

"I could use a break," I smile.

"Just be back here for the announcement and retelling," Dad orders me. He doesn't use that tone often. He must be worried about what they're about to announce.

"Glad he didn't ask to come," Alsmeria says, brushing her stunning coiled braid out of her face.

"Why?" I smile. I have a feeling Alsmeria wants to ask about her latest hunt.

"Do you know Blake?"

"Who?"

"That tall dark guy with the blue eyes that hangs out with your boyfriend all the time," Alsmeria complains.

"I don't like Jake's friends. I don't talk to them or get to know their names."

"Oh," Alsmeria's face falls. "He's kind of cute, and I think he was hitting on me during the dancing. I was thinking maybe..."

"You just broke up with Derek two weeks ago. Are you sure you're ready so soon?" I frown. Alsmeria moves from boyfriend to boyfriend every few months, but each failed attempt takes longer for her to get over. Two weeks is a record for her.

"I know, I know, but it's nice having a guy show interest first, that's all."

"If you stop chasing them so hard and give them time, they'd go for you first."

"Don't want to wait," Alsmeria confesses. "I want to be courted. Is that so bad?"

"Guess not."

"So you think I should flirt back, see if it's worth trying?"

I sigh. "I don't know. As I said, I don't like many, well any, of Jake's friends. They like to cause trouble and are normally rather rude to those they don't like. I may only be judging by how he is around those friends. I mean, I don't like them, but I love Jake. So maybe he is better on his own."

"Maybe." I see the disappointment in Alsmeria's eyes.

"Hey, something will turn up, always does." I hug her arm in mine.

"Yeah," she says half-heartedly.

"You're hardly better than a royalist!" a voice hisses dangerously to our left.

We both jump and turn to see two groups of people glaring down at one another. There are three men and a woman on one side and three men and three women on the opposite side, clearly opposing rebellions.

There are three rebellions in Purerah, the nation I live in. There are the Loyalists, who want to overthrow the royal family and crown a common man to the throne. The Potentates want to overthrow the royal family and put a natural Potentate on the throne. Then the Custod rebellion wants a Custod to change their authority status from a defender to ruler. The first two were constantly at each other's throats."

"Because we respect what the Merlin gave us, that's worked for other nations for two-thousand years?" The lead girl of the second group spits at the first. "Potentates are given authority, skills, and power to rule. It has not failed other nations. One bad line doesn't ruin the whole. We throw it all out, the Merlin will surely reign his retribution as he did to Spearim and Englaria when they refused Potentate rule."

"It's their elitism that has made this nation fall into near ruin. Look around! The city is hardly livable. It's so rotten, walls fall on a daily basis. It's time a man of the people who knows them and their struggles takes the throne. Who needs ancient ways when they failed us?"

"Custods overthrow those rulers all the time. They will bring more war." The Potentate sympathizer argues.

"What will you do about it? Protest? Throw things at the walls?" Mocks the Loyalist.

"You attack guards, doing nothing but destabilizing the little security these cities have. What happens when your warring lands stop trying to take over cities up north and come here with how you ruin our defenses? More of the common people will be hurt, and your droves still can't get into the palace to hurt so much as a serving maid."

"Like you Potentate rebels haven't broken things that caused harm to the people." Sneers the Loyalist.

"You are worse than the royals!"

In the blink of an eye, the two groups rush each other and start fighting. I grab Alsmeria and pull her back as one punch from the lead Potentate girl sends one of the Loyalist boys flying towards us.

We quickly retreat to our area while the guards come in and break up the fighting, though I'm pretty sure it's the guard who breaks the Loyalist boy's arm, not the Potentate sympathizers.

"Isn't it bad enough, the royals cause such harm? These rebellions will cause even more harm," Alsmeria complains.

"But if everyone does nothing, how will anything be fixed?" Dad asks her.

Alsmeria shrugs. "I don't know. But fighting each other doesn't help."

"No, it doesn't." Dad sighs, folding his arms and giving me a meaningful look.

"You want to get chairs out for us to sit on for the retelling? Mom is bringing us lunch." I suggest to Alsmeria.

She happily takes the excuse and leaves Dad and me alone. "You didn't jump in, did you?" Dad checks.

"Of course not. It was just the Loyalist and Potentate group. You know me better than that." I assure Dad.

"Merlin, if the Custod council heard we got involved in that type of fighting," Dad shakes his head. "We'd be in for an earful."

"Some contact would be nice," I mutter.

Dad gives me a sad smile. "I know. But if the royals found out the Custods sent us to help overthrow and replace them, it would be a political nightmare the world over."

"Shh," I look around.

"I'm careful." Dad kisses my head.

A loud shout makes us jump. Dad and I turn to the center of the square where the sound had come from.

A man had climbed onto the top of the fountain. An impressive feat. The fountain is nothing too special apart from the top where the Purerahian emblem is sharped into a globe. The man is holding onto it like the top of a cane as he stands in the top tier, which is pretty small. It's a large fountain, but it's four tiers tall.

"Now is the time to act!" the man yells across the square. "How can we stand here as if we have something to celebrate?"

I frown and look at Dad. "Is this one of yours?" I ask quietly, so no one else can hear.

Dad shakes his head. "I'm thinking this is a Loyalist attempt or perhaps a Potentate."

"Two-thousand years ago, the Merlin rose from the grave to overthrow an oppressive king and his court. Today, we celebrate all that was made possible. How do we celebrate when we're in a situation almost as dire? How can you pretend all is well when each of us struggles to get by for how heavily we're taxed just to survive in this land? How do you celebrate when deep down, your heart is tired of it, tired and angry, ready to take back what is rightfully yours?"

The crowd is muttering, a few nodding assents, others looking frightened and slowly backing out of the square while others whisper to their neighbors. I grip Dad's arm tightly. They're not going to do something foolish, are they?

"Get down from there!" the lead guard stands from sitting with the palace official and barks at the man. "In the name of the king, I order you to stand down."

"A king who's done nothing for his people! A queen who has not tried to look after the domestic interests as is her duty," the man yells at the guard. "I will not submit to the authority that has not been earned."

"Desist this treasonous talk and get down before we are forced to remove you under arrest," the guard growls.

"When the king and queen have earned it!" the man screams back and turns his attention back to the crowd. "Do we let them take all we earn again? Are we going to let them squeeze us dry until we have nothing left? Rise, people! Rise up and show the royals how we feel about their announcements. Just wait. This announcement will mean no good for our people, mark my words. Whatever it is, they will make us pay for it with our coin and with our blood."

"Get down!"

"Down with tyrants!" the man yells back.

The head guard snaps and orders five or so guards to try to remove the rebel from the fountain, but it's so tall, none can reach him. A few try to climb, but it's so wet, it's hard to get a grip. How had that man gotten up there?

"Should we do something?" I frown at Dad.

Dad shakes his head. "Too public, and any fighting here would end badly for the people and do no good for the overall effort. We act, it's over."

I hate to let the guards take out their frustrations on this man who just wants to help his people as we do, but I watch as the man keeps calling for the crowd to rise and show the royals how we feel about them by removing their representative and preventing the casting on the Imaginal.

The guards try to use the blunt end of their spears to knock the man down, but they hardly reach, and the man either impressively avoids them or can stay up even when poked harshly. A few try the pointed ends, and others throw the spears as if to strike him.

The crowd backs away. A few yell in protest; some even throw things, tossing stones, food, or whatever else they have on hand at the guards to stop them. The lead guard is barking orders to take the rebel down as the rebel keeps screaming. "Don't let them silence us! Let them know how we feel! Rise and get justice!"

The crowd has risen to feverish screams, and the guards are having to keep the crowd back by force, using their spears as staves to keep distance between them and the people as they push them away from the fountain.

"Someone has to stop this," I say, but Dad takes my arm to stop me.

"He chose this. He knew what could happen," Dad warns me.

"But he's right."

"His methods are foolish."

I look back at the man as the guards jump up as if to knock him down, jumping, trying to climb, bat him down, whatever they could do.

A powerful twang cuts the air, and a scream runs through the square as an arrow strikes the man through the back of the right shoulder. I cover my mouth in horror as the falling body plunges the square into silence.

Chapter 2

The stunned silence doesn't last long. The palace official gets up to assure us all we're safe and no harm will come to anyone today because of that man's actions. "Please, remain calm," he says. His tone is too even, too calm. How can he be so calm when we just watched one of their guards shoot one of his citizens? How cold is the royal family? "We will start the casting in just a few minutes. Please, remain calm. We are here to ensure your safety from all rebels and rebellions in all their forms. Please, just stay calm."

I think most of us are too stunned to react. I spot Jake and his friends looking more than horrified. They look angry. The one Alsmeria said hit on her moves forward as if to speak his mind. Jake grabs his shoulder and shakes his head. The two get into an argument.

That's how the whole square reacts. The people start talking and arguing with one another. The guards look at the official for direction. How can they break up so many arguments? The official shakes his head. He isn't even going to try!?

But only a few of the arguments escalate into actual fistfights which the guards pair off to handle. I turn to Dad. We are Custods; we have to do something!

"Keep cover," Dad reminds me.

I think of the weapon I hide in my pack, a merlinet style sword that retracts into the handle and is disguised as an umbrella. Dad trained me well with it. We can use that to help stop the fighting. "But if we get—"

"Not now," Dad shakes his head. "Remember time and place."

"But..." My heart breaks looking at my people fighting among themselves when they should come together to defend themselves. I know things are bad. It's why the Custod Council sent us here. The people are ripping themselves apart because the royals care more for their comfort than their people's well-being.

"Are you alright?" Mom comes over to me, putting a hand on my cheek.

"I'm fine," I assure her. "I was with Dad."

The guards break up several fistfights. A few more people are arrested and dragged off before the square reaches any kind of normal. Dad checks all of our cast and crew are fine before returning to the stage. Alsmeria joins us and helps set up seats, so we can hopefully more easily see whatever announcement the royal family is going to make.

She takes my hand when she sees I'm shaking as I help her set up. "Hey, only the one guy was hurt. Everyone else is okay."

"I know." But we're supposed to stop this kind of thing. I'd seen many a rebel fighter, but I'd never seen it escalate like that other than the one raid I'd joined in. I can't believe the city guard shot one of their own people.

We settle in as the city official diverts our attention to the screen thirty seconds before it goes live. Afterward, we'll have the traditional retelling. I just hope no one else takes that as an excuse to try to start another fight.

The large screen that's built into the side of the governance building comes to life and the Purerahian symbol comes onto the screen with a flute trill that comes on every time an imaginal is activated.

"Hello Purerah, and happy Restoration Day!" The familiar face of the royal press courtier, Count Barsat, appears, beaming at us with his huge white-toothed smile. His hair is perfectly cut and coiled, and his dark Purerahian blue suit is as perfect as ever.

"Today, we have a special announcement that will change the lives of some of you forever." His smile is too big. He's trying hard to get us excited. It's not working in this square. "On this special day, the two thousandth anniversary of the Merlin's conquering of the dark one, we're announcing a special event that will change our history, perhaps in similar ways. Starting immediately after this casting, applications to join in the Enthronement will begin."

An outbreak of whispers carries across the square. Really? All this drama and a man dead so they can announce some contest to become princess? The idea makes me angry. I fold my arms and cross my legs, wishing I had anything else to look at that didn't make me so angry.

"The Enthronement is a special event in which the royal family will choose our next princess. Our Prince Gavril still has not taken a bride. Those ladies who are eligible will be given the opportunity to prove themselves a true princess. She who passes all the tests set by the royal family will marry our prince and become the crown princess of Purerah. All ladies eighteen to thirty are eligible to apply."

A few excited squeals, as well as dark mutterings, carry across the square, but everyone is interested and reacting. I glance at my Dad, but his face is neutral as he studies the face of the count. Alsmeria squeezes my hand in excitement.

"Forty-four girls will be invited to the palace to live with the royal family as part of the Enthronement," the count goes on. "There will be several tests that must be passed to reach these coveted spots."

"Why forty-four?" Alsmeria wonders. I shrug.

"Each eligible lady has two weeks to put in her application. The paperwork needed is available at every town center across Purerah following this casting. More rules and details will be released as each girl progresses through the Enthronement. Those who are chosen to come live at the palace as the royal family's chosen guests will receive the title of Lady — if they do not already have a title of higher station, as well as the members of her immediate family. Those who reach the top twenty-five will be given higher titles as suit the court positions the royal family sees fit to bestow upon them. The top ten will be awarded at least the title of Earlaness, and of course, the winner will go on to marry Prince Gavril and become our crown princess and one day queen.

"We thank you for your participation and patience as we take up part of your holiday. Enjoy your Restoration Day and may fortune be in your favor as you apply to be our next princess."

And with that, the imaginal shuts off with another little flute trill.

The square bursts into talking right away. "It can't be real," Alsmeria says, turning her body to me. "Can you imagine getting in? Let alone winning?!"

I give her a look. "I thought you hated royals."

She just laughs, "How many people do you think will do it?"

"A lot," Dad says dryly, nodding at the crowd of girls already heading right for the intake desk at the governance building.

"Wow," Alsmeria gasps.

I roll my eyes. How stupid. Like that many will get in. Then again, it means a life of luxury instead of scraping by for a living as you are taxed out of house and home. I can see the appeal when I think of it that way.

But me join in? No way in creation. Sorry Jashon, but I have a different way to the throne. A throne I don't want.

"Will be quite the opportunity for those that get in," Mom nods, giving me a quick glance. I return the look, making sure she knows there's no way. Besides, they betrothed me years ago, remember?

"Can you imagine? Even if you just got a court title and then came home how many more people would want to see you perform," Alsmeria says dreamily.

"But you hate the royals."

"So?"

I guess that's how the army of girls swarming the governance building feel.

The performers doing the retelling take up their places on the governance building steps, having to work around and ignore the loud chatter of the girls snatching up applications. It sounds like one girl is trying to get two, and the guards are refusing.

"Miss Karen, please, one per girl. Your sister can come to get her own," the governance worker yells so loud the whole square can hear it.

The retelling begins, told by a rather gifted storyteller. But it's hard to focus on his performance though I try. I've heard the story a million times because it's my heritage.

In the beginning, the Creator chose two brothers to look after the world: one to raise his line to be rulers of the peoples of the earth and the other to be their protectors. The Potentates to rule; the Custods to protect. A thousand years or so later, the dark one possessed a young, gifted enchanter and slaughtered all the Potentates and all but one Custod, who raised four children, one of whom was the Merlin.

The Merlin grew in strength and wisdom and when finally ready to help the peoples of the earth break free from the darkness the dark one cast on the world, fought in many battles, helped take most of the city-states back, but in the process, was possessed by the darkness himself and sacrificed his life to stop that darkness spreading further and causing unspeakable suffering to all peoples.

Without the Merlin's power, the rising nation of Emilimoh that he had created struggled to survive the dark one's power. But three months after his sacrifice, the Merlin rose once again as the Creator's phoenix and slew the dark one, ensuring the kingdom of Emilimoh and the other nations of the day were then run as the Creator intended, creating centuries of peace and freedom that persists to this day. It is said the Merlin still interferes to ensure the Creator's will is done in the world.

I'm sure the storyteller did a better job than me at making it exciting, but it was all I could do to pay attention. I should pay more attention. Dad had reminded me many times as a child that I should. "You're a Custod, even if you have to hide it," he'd tell me. "Be proud of the family you come from and your duty."

Even though my duty is to do as one of the Merlin's brothers did, give up the life of a Custod to become a Potentate. That's why I was born here. My Dad was assigned by the Head Custod before I was born to help overthrow the royal family and establish a new Potentate line. But we had to keep our relations with other nations, and if they knew the Custods were planning such subterfuge, we'd be in bigger trouble. I've grown up here, hiding who I am and being the actress I always wanted to be, waiting until the time comes to do my duty. One I dislike but have always known is my fate.

I glance over to where Jake and his friends are laughing at the line of girls trying to get an application. A few are openly mocking the girls. I frown. There's no need to make fun of girls who just want to escape a life of desperation.

Jake meets my eyes and smiles at me in amusement. I shake my head. His friends are not funny. He gets the hint and tells his buddies to knock it off. At least he dares to stand up to his friends. As king he'll need it. And as his queen, I'm going to have to keep him in line.

"So you won't even try? Guess Jack is that cute," Alsmeria teases me after the retelling, jogging me from my thoughts.

I turn to her. "Well, why shouldn't I? You saying I'm not good enough for him?"

"Girl." Alsmeria pulls back her chin. "He's not good enough for you." I laugh. "I'm serious. You deserve a prince far better than him."

But Jake is my prince. I like it that way. I smile at our plans for tonight. I can't wait.

"Come on, the next show is at one. We have only a short time to clean up from lunch and get ready." Mom snaps us to attention, and we get back to work.

I spend the rest of the day dancing and singing for the crowds, even catching the attention of the line of girls trying to get applications. Dad and I do our piece one more time, getting a huge crowd, and we do each of the other songs we'd already done until the sun starts to set.

We quickly clean up and go back to the theater to put away the gear before dispersing for the night. "Shall we make a fine dinner?" Mom asks as she locks the theater doors behind us.

"I was hoping to meet up with Jake," I say nervously.

Mom chuckles. Dad smiles. "Go on, we won't mind a quiet night." He gives Mom a sideways smile that makes her giggle harder than me.

"Thank you, Papa," I kiss his cheek, hug Mom and run off to join Jake.

I skip down to the river that runs along the southern side of the city, outside the walls. It's about a fifteen-minute walk from the theater to this place I know so well.

The setting sun sparkles stunningly across the river as it runs down to the ocean and bathes the area in a golden light that makes me feel giddy and feminine. It's our place.

Jake is already waiting, beaming widely, his teeth standing out against his tanned skin are only outshone by the brightness of his eyes at his happiness to see me.

"Can you believe it's been ten years today?" he asks me as I run to him and throw myself into his arms.

"No, it's so hard to believe." I sigh, sliding down from hugging him around the neck, letting my hands slide down his shoulders to rest on his chest. "But the day will be soon. In the new year..."

I daydream about that moment. I dream about waking up with his warmth next to me, being annoyed by his morning breath and stubbly face. I think about what it will be like to be with him as he learns the ropes of ruling a country, of how we'll tease each other, talk like we do now but about affairs of state. To raise our children safely inside the palace instead of in the dangers of the open cities.

"Ten years ago today, we both hated the idea." Jake smiles. "Do you remember?"

"How could I forget?" I chuckle. "You seemed so old and grumpy to me."

"I was mad at my father for making me do it," Jake recalls. "We'd been engaged three years then. And every conversation we had was a fight," he chuckles.

"I hated you."

"I detested you."

"Do you think we'd have found each other if our fathers didn't want to have an agreement?" I ask.

"No idea, but I know I'd be lesser if they didn't." Jake looks down at me, his dark eyes heavy with meaning.

I beam, "I was lucky." I close my eyes and accept his kiss, my skin erupting in goosebumps.

"I love you," Jake breathes. "I saw how upset you were today. I only wish I could have made you proud and stopped it all."

I sigh. I wish the talk didn't go there. "I'd not seen anything like that since the one time Dad took me on a raid."

Jake's face falls. "Are you alright?"

I nod, focusing on my hands still on Jake's chest. I fiddle with a loose hanging bit of leather on his vest. I smile slightly and start undoing the ties around it. "It was a shock, but I'm alright. Just a reminder on why..."

"Why we have to do this." Jake nods his agreement. "The royals don't care. They kill their own people. Sometimes, I can't believe the Custods let this happen."

"I'm sorry. I know. I wanted to—" My voice catches. I wanted to stop it. I felt I should have. I'm a Custod. It's our duty. It's what the Merlin would have done. But I'm under my Dad, and if he says it wouldn't help, I believe him. He's never led me wrong.

Jake kisses my head. "Sorry, I sometimes forget you still are a Custod. It's not your fault."

"So, it's Dad's?"

"No. I just wish the world wasn't as it is, so the Custods could come in and overthrow the wicked rulers as they did in the past. Isn't it crazy to think they used to be able to do that?"

"With so many nations, and with the fact we are supposed to be neutral to all nations, it's harder," I say, still playing with the ties on Jake's vest.

"So they send you on a secret mission," Jake teases.

"I'm just happy my mission means marrying you." I smile and kiss Jake again, running my fingers up his chest to his shoulders, my right hand going up against his neck into his hair while the other grips his arm tightly.

Jake returns the kiss, wrapping his arms around my waist, making me feel beautiful like I could fly. I love how he makes me feel, how his touches make my skin tingle, how excitement flutters in my chest, and a desire forms in my belly.

Our lips part only for him to kiss me again, and again, and again. I sigh in pleasure as I kiss him back, letting him force me to bend back a little more. Who needs the prince? My king here is far better in every way.

A breeze teases our hair, waking us up from the moment. "Hungry?" Jake asks.

I nod, and he leads me over to a mossy stone that has a tall tree growing around it. It makes a perfect natural bench we've used many times. In front of it is a blanket spread out with some of our favorite foods: noodles with chicken and vegetables, fried chicken, meat dumplings, egg rolls, and little cream cakes to finish.

Jake helps me sit down on the blanket before he joins me. "Happy Restoration Day." He jokes as he pours us some juice. As a Custod, I'm under oath not to drink any alcohol, so Jake accommodates me. "May the next Restoration Day bring us better days, and some wine when you're not a Custod." I laugh as I toast with him and take a drink.

We eat and chat happily, laughing and teasing each other as we talk about all the things we plan to do in the year before we get married and take the throne. I talk about all the shows I want to be in before it's all over. That is the biggest thing I gave up. If I had whatever I wanted, I'd never leave the theater. I'd be like my mother, who married into being a Custod, and run the theater and perform until I'm too old and teach the next generation. But my duty comes first.

Jake jokes he's going to save every morning he can sleep in and goof around. A king can't be too silly, and he wants to let out all the anxious energy.

We finish eating and lie back on the blanket, looking up at the sky where stars are starting to show as the sun sets. The forest around us is dark; only the small lantern Jake brought lights the area.

"The hard part will be taking the castle at all." Jake frowns. "I know our combined forces will make it easier, but I think about that a lot. No one has breached the castle in years."

"They get onto the grounds sometimes," I point out.

"But no one breaches the palace wall," Jake frowns, his arm around me tightening. "I have no idea how to do what they all fail to do."

"That's why you'll have Dad's help. He's great at it. That was what he did as a Custod before being assigned here," I remind him.

Jake shrugs. "I know a king needs help, but I still feel like I should do more."

"Your father isn't much help."

I should have known better. Jake tenses in anger. "No, he's not." Jake and his father do not get along. They haven't since Jake was little and his mother died. I can't blame him. I don't much like Jake's Father either. He's far more calculating and vindictive than his son.

"Do... do you think your father put that man up to his rant today?" I ask quietly.

"I don't know." Jake sighs. "Sounds like him though." He holds me tighter. "I can't wait to have the power to stop that."

"Me too." Even if I don't want to give up my life at the theater to be a princess or a queen, I do want to help my people. Custods are supposed to be unattached to any one nation, but I grew up here. I know no other nations other than those I met on tour. I love my people. I want to help them and stop this pain more than anything.

"And we will," Jake says, kissing me deeply. I sigh in contentment as I return his kiss. "You and me together, as we dreamed," he says breathily.

I beam and kiss him, turning my body more towards him. He kisses me back, running a hand down my arm. I like that and give him more of a kiss in return. He stiffens next to me and then melts into it. I press more into his kiss, wanting to show how much I love him, love this, need this.

His arms wrap around me. Without thinking, I tangle one of my legs with his to help us be closer, kissing him deeper.

Jake sighs contently before pulling back. He sits up a little against the rock and guides me into lying my head on his chest and shoulder. He strokes my hair with one hand, settling the other behind his head as he looks up at the treetops.

I happily follow his guidance and cuddle close, wrapping my arms around his chest. "I can't wait to be free for more of this," I say.

"Not long now." He keeps stroking my hair.

I close my eyes. I wish I could fall asleep, but anyone who knows me knows I'm notorious for having sleep problems. I have a strong tea that induces sleep each night to get me to sleep even on the days I worked hard in rehearsals or the days we did two or three shows a day.

"One day, I am going to fall asleep in your arms." I promise him.

"You? Not until we're married and sharing a bed because nothing gets you to sleep," Jake laughs at me.

"I will," I say stubbornly.

"Not until then."

"Watch me."

"Will you sleep if I'm watching though?"

"Oh, be quiet," I push him playfully before I settle next to him again, fiddling with his vest once more, watching my fingers play with his clothes.

We sit in silence for a while, enjoying each other's warmth as the night around us grows cold.

"Kascia," Jake says after a long time.

"Hm?" I ask, too relaxed to want to speak.

"We're leaving for a raid tomorrow."

I frown. "Why?"

"With this Enthronement business, the palace is going to need to bring in more funds."

"And you're hoping to catch the bigger payload."

"Exactly."

I swallow. I hate it when he goes. Raids are dangerous. I've only done one, and I was no help because I was too scared to kill anyone. Dad never made me do it again, but men died. I always fear for my dad and Jake when they go.

"Do you have to?"

"Only way."

"Be safe."

"I will."

"I love you."

"You know I love you." Jake kisses my head, sighing as I shiver and his arm moves. "But it's late, and most of all, it's getting cold. I should get you home."

I nod my agreement and let him help me up. He packs up the blanket and other goods and puts them into a bag he tosses onto his back. He takes my hand and walks me home. I live in a small house just off the river and about a five to ten-minute walk from the theater.

"Rest well, my lady." Jake kisses me.

"Be safe, my king." I smile, keeping my eyes closed from his kiss.

"I'll see you soon."

"I'll be waiting."

Chapter 3

The next day, we're hard at work doing technical rehearsals to open our production of *The Hunchback in the Bell Tower* next week. It's a good distraction from Dad and Jake being gone on their raid. I like it when we're rehearsing because when we aren't, all the girls can talk about is the Enthronement, who's applying, rumors on what the tests might be, who they think might get in. I try to ignore all of it. It's stupid, and in the end, we'll have to drive the winner out of the castle sooner or later. I hate the idea of having to do that to one of my friends.

Mom notices our distraction and repeats one of the many quotes she keeps on the wall. "No disaster worse than a distracted rehearsal." We're all tired from all the dress and technical rehearsals by the time the end of the workweek comes. Thankfully, we don't have any shows in this week's rest days.

Mom and I stay late to clean and lock up. We normally finish our rehearsals around five, but it takes Mom and I an extra half an hour to close up.

As I wait for Mom to lock the door, I notice Dad is waiting for us. He puts a finger to his lips, clueing me in to keep quiet. But my heart leaps. If he's home safe and teasing, then they had to have been successful. At least no one was hurt.

Before Mom can do more than put her keys away, Dad comes over and wraps his arms around her waist.

She jumps a mile then laughs. "Hello Peodrick," she says warmly though with a hint of exasperation.

"Hello my beautiful Chrisa," Dad says before kissing her on the cheek.

I giggle. Dad has a big smile that makes his eyes crinkle just like Jake's do. Though Jake has the features of someone who is from here, like olive skin and dark hair, my Dad does not. Dad looks the part of a villain so well. It was his main role when he was on stage. He always played the villain. His charming, yet dark features made him perfect for it. But I know better. My Dad is wise, dedicated, loving, and patient. He looked and played the villain well, but inside he is anything but.

"I didn't expect you to pick us up. What's going on?" Mom asks him with a playful tease, but I also hear the faint tremor of concern in her voice.

"Nothing, I just was excited to see you," Dad insists.

"You never see us at the door unless it's after a show," Mom shakes her head, "What are you after, my love?"

"Nothing," Dad smiles so wide his eyes almost vanish. I love it when they do that. "I am seeking nothing from you. Just happy to see you." He kisses her cheek.

He then turns to me. "There's my princess," he says.

I shake my head. "Not this time."

"No? You're not a princess this time?" He frowns, making his brows almost touch in his confusion.

"The lead role is a gypsy, dad," I state. "Don't you pay attention? Wasn't your living also a performer?"

"I wasn't as good of a triple threat." Dad smiles. "I met your mother that way."

"I know. You played Rothbart, and she was Odette," I say with a roll of my eyes. He loves telling that story.

"And she was glad she went with the kidnapper." Dad grins that mischievous, evil smile of his.

"I know." I roll my eyes. Mom loves to make that joke anytime she tells the story. "But I'm not here for romance tips."

"No, Jack clearly is happy with you as you are, my cygnet. Do I need to be more careful with you two?" he grins. I roll my eyes again. It was his plan for us to be engaged after all. It's his own fault. Not that I'm complaining.

"I picked up dinner." The way he says it makes it sound like he's brought home some odd treasure we didn't think he'd ever find. "It's to celebrate I'm back, and to celebrate new and better plans for our future."

Better plans? Something about how he says it makes nervous snakes dance in my stomach, but I can't pinpoint why.

We walk home, Dad beaming in delight, Mom watching him with nervous amusement. But for some reason, I can't quite join in. I can't name why, but something in my gut is scared. I don't know why. My Dad has only once done something I didn't like, and it turned out one of the best things in my life.

"How did your raid go?" I ask. Is Jake alright?

Dad shrugs. "It was alright." But he doesn't give me more detail.

Please, don't let something have happened. Maybe that's why I feel so nervous.

Dad must read my nervousness because he elaborates. "We managed some. But as always, we seem unable to get the deliveries that take the real money. I wish we took enough to give back to those the royals take from. We'd have less begging; that's for sure."

"So then why the good mood?" I ask. The nervousness returns to my chest.

"Well, a new idea, a new plan, came up. We'll talk about it as we eat."

Is this why I am nervous? Why? Dad was always good with plans. "What kind of plan?"

"One that involves more political and... unique tactics," he says with a playful smile.

"Peodrick, what are you up to?" Mom asks, her tone showing a bit of nervousness too.

"All good things, my love. Let's eat then talk," Dad insists.

With the food being pre-prepared, it doesn't take us long to warm it up and set it at the table. I try to get up the nerve to ask, but with Mom feeling unsure too, I'm scared. Why? This isn't normal for me at all.

But then I notice Mom watching Dad. She's waiting to lull him into an even better mood before broaching the topic. Something inside of me relaxes. Perhaps it's just another one of those things Mom doesn't like. I sometimes wonder how Dad got her to marry him when she clearly is not a fan of what we have to do as Custods. She is from Purerah, unlike Dad. He was assigned here and worked in the theater. If it has anything to do with the mission the Head Custod gave us, that must be why Mom is nervous.

"So, what is this new big plan that has you grinning like a cat?" Mom asks him at last.

"A way to get into the palace without all the drama it will take after the wedding," Dad says, his grin as wide as Phoenix bringing out his best gift at Christmas.

"Really?" My eyes light up. That's just what Jake was worried about. An answer to that would be a godsend!

Dad nods, "Yes, and it's simple, brilliant, and allows us to move the wedding up."

I can't stop the smile that spreads across my face. The wait will be shorter?

"What in creation could do both?" Mom asks skeptically.

"The Enthronement."

My brows draw together. "The Enthronement? How? Won't they have more security with so many outsiders in the castle?"

"Perhaps, but not as likely to be successful," Dad smiles at my excitement. "I knew you'd like this."

I wait with bated breath to see what he'll say. I miss Mom's confused and worried expression as she watches Dad with how intently I'm looking at him, awaiting his answer.

"We are going to get a girl on the inside," Dad says. "And she'll let us in during the Harvest ball."

"Why the Harvest ball?" Mom frowns.

"The guards will have a harder time dealing with security with courtiers and other guests arriving. The royal family will all be in one place, and the distraction and spooky atmosphere will make breaking in easier. They'll presume messing with the lights is just part of the show."

"How are you going to ensure a girl gets inside?" Mom asks.

I have the same question. How will he make certain his girl gets in?

"Honestly, I've been thinking it over since they announced it," Dad admits. "I've gone it over and over in my head, and there's only one person who will get in without fail."

"Who?" I ask, oblivious to the nightmare he is about to drop on me.

"You."

My heart stops. All my blood freezes and drains into my toes. "Wha-what?"

Mom is frowning even deeper, looking from my Dad to me and back with a calculating, yet uncertain crease in her eyes.

"Don't worry, you aren't supposed to win."

That doesn't comfort me. My breathing picks up as my mind reels at the idea and what that will mean. I'll have to fawn over the brat of a prince, pretend I adore the king and queen while all the while planning their assassinations? I got sick when I saw the man shot in Governance Square. I throw up when I even think about the time I almost killed someone in a raid. I can't hide my intent from his horrid face when I'm dating the scoundrel prince!

"We just need to get you in the competition to the level that you'll live in the palace. After that you just stay low, out of attention, and stay in until the harvest, then it's all over. We take over. We'll have a harvest wedding, and the rebuilding can finally begin." Dad's still beaming.

But I'm far from smiling. A new horror is filling my heart as I continue to feel like all the blood in my body has dropped into my toes; my hands are shaking. My fingertips feel funny like I'm having an out-of-touch or out-of-body experience.

"We've never gotten anyone on the inside before. If we can get someone inside, we can get into the castle and remove the royal family. We just need to get you on the inside and keep you under the radar so you don't get eliminated before then. If anyone can do it, it's you."

"Me?" I get out. He can't be serious.

"Yes. You're talented, beautiful, and a natural princess. I'm sure you'll have no trouble passing their tests. Then it's over. You get your fairytale wedding, and we'll do our duty and save Purerah as we were ordered. All you have to do is—"

"Pretend to flirt and pretend to want to marry a spoiled little boy and lie," I retort.

I would have to cheat on Jake. I can't do that. Every bit of me resists the idea. I had to fight hard enough to find the pure love we have now. How could I betray it?

Are the royals horrible?

Yes.

I saw how they made my people beggars en masse and whipped them terribly if they just tried to survive. I saw the scars of war on these people as they only tried to free themselves. The royals deserve to die, but I can't play sweet and charmed by the prince. I can't pretend I want to marry him when I'd rather take him out myself.

I would have to stay for months. The harvest is still five months away. I'd have to pretend for a long time to stay in. I might have to... I feel sick at the idea. I couldn't cheat on Jake like that.

"But you still get what you want," Dad says, "Just sooner. You don't have to wait a year. It's only six months — less inside the castle. I'm sure the qualifying rounds will take at least a month or two."

I shake my head. "I can't lie to them or Jake. I can't betray him. We've worked too hard to be where we are."

"Kascia, be reasonable," Dad says, "It's just a full-time role."

"That's different, and you know it."

I turn to my mother for help. She can't like this idea. She hates the subterfuge we live by.

She gives me a sad smile. She won't stand up for me. Just like she didn't when I didn't want to be engaged to Jake. I normally side with Dad on most things, but when I needs Mom on my side she never defends me against him.

I groan and look at Dad, "I agreed to the old plan a long time ago."

He can't take the life I now longed for away when I'd fought so hard for it. I trust him, but this? I'd never doubted him before. Perhaps I'm overreacting. But acting to be in character full time like that? At least an audience knows it is acting. This is much more like lying.

"But Kascia..." Dad tries.

"But what?"

But what? I never disagree with my Dad. My heart pounds as if I'm dancing an allegro. My hands shake a little on my lap. He always knows best, but... My heart aches, making my throat clog with bile.

"What about Jake?" I try. "We can't just throw it all away. I won't stand for it."

I had to give up my dreams of being like my mother, working in the theater, and loving my art for the rest of my life. I gave up getting to have children to raise and hand the theater off to. I gave it up a long time ago. Now he wants to make me give up the old dream and play a liar. I feel sicker, the bile stinging my chest and throat.

"It's just another role, Kascia," Dad soothes me. "Nothing more."

"When it's a role, people know it's pretending." I retort.

I take a final bite of my noodles to try to shove down the bile and put my fork down.

I need space. I need Jake. We always meet in our special spot after he comes home from a raid. I need to see him. I need to know he understands. He can't be happy about this.

"Find another girl. I'm taken. I can't do it," I say with as much finality in my voice as I can, but it's not much. I'm shaking and so is my voice. Am I really going to just say no and turn tail? I never do this. Oh no, what am I doing? I take a deep breath, soothing the sting in my throat. I just need to talk to him first, that's all.

"I already filled out the paperwork for you. You just have to sign it and turn it in," Dad pleads. "We all agreed to it."

That makes me angry. The feeling surprises me. I hadn't been angry like this with my parents in a long time.

"So, the rebel alliance gets to choose my life?" I snap. I trusted Dad. He arranged the engagement, and he'd been right. He'd been right to trust me to help the boy and to stop me at the announcement. But this?

"Not this time, Papa." Why can't what I want matter? I know it's selfish, but... for once? Yet inside, I'm also breaking down. I need my anchor. I need to see him.

"You get the choice, Kascia, but as a Custod, sometimes duty has to call the shots," Dad says.

There, he threw it at me. I know I'm a useless Custod. I'm too timid. I had avoided killing in raids. For Phoenix's sake, I avoided raids at all costs. I did little to defend my people other than agree to escape the Custod duties I feared. I agreed to be their Custod turned Potentate. I agreed to marry Jake even when I disliked him. Wasn't that enough? Why did they demand more of me?

"I've already given duty everything," I squeak out. "Who gets to decide what my duty is anyway?"

"The Custod Council does. And they told us to do whatever it takes to dethrone the corrupted Potentates and get a Custod on the throne. This is what it takes."

"The old plan won't work now?"

"Not as well."

I groan. He's right. Jake and I were just talking about that problem. But… I can't turn on Jake now. I can't. I love him. I want him. He's the only prince I want to win. I can't cheat on him. I can already see the pain in his face as I have to kiss or… or whatever else I'll have to do with that rat of a prince. The idea of kissing that prince makes me sick enough without Jake's pain in my mind. He gets jealous enough when I kiss someone on stage.

"I can't do it."

"You need to."

I shake my head. "No." The word pops out like a sick cough.

I hate saying no to my Dad. I never have before. His approval means everything to me. Now… but I can't do it. I can't have my world stripped away and morphed again.

I bite my shaking lip, biting so hard I taste metal in my mouth. I won't survive it. I don't want to say no to him. I blink back hot tears.

"Kascia. I beg you to think it over." Dad's face is contorted in concern. After all, I never say no to him. It is confusing and hurting him. I swallow more tears. I can't say yes. It feels so wrong to lie like this.

"I can't. I-I'm sorry, Papa. I can't." I turn to go.

"Kascia." Dad tries, but I just shake my head and go out the door. I need time. I need my rendezvous.

"Let her go," Mom says to Dad, "Let her think."

Chapter 4

I shut the door behind me as politely, and yet, as quickly as I can. My feet march on the path I know so well without much conscious thought. I need something concrete. I need an embrace to remind me what all this is for. And I know where to get it.

Normally, it's from my Dad. But as that won't work, I know who can fill the emptiness and fear I feel with warmth and hope.

I hug myself as I push past the trees, old berry bushes, and mossy stones until I reach our spot. Like the other night, the water sparkles in the moonlight and the lantern light.

Beside the lantern, sitting on the mossy rock that is our bench, waiting for me with a smile that lifts my heart like the rising sun, is Jake. I knew he would be. He opens his arms wide to me.

My heart lifts again. The smile escapes before I can process it. In moments, I'm engulfed in his loving embrace. I smile and hide in it. I shut my eyes and listen to Jake's breathing and heartbeat.

In my life, that sound was one of the few things that was truly mine. I adore my music and dance, but they are not mine, but my mother's and the theater's. I relish in fencing and my swordplay, but that's Dad's. Jake's warmth, his embrace, and his love are mine, and mine alone. And Dad wants me to betray the one thing that is mine.

My heart sinks at the thought, but then Jake hugs me tighter, squeezing the despair out of me. He chuckles at my delight, making my heart sing. Oh, how I love that feeling. I soak it in along with the sound of his breath, the tinkle of the river, the distant rush of the seaside. I take in the scent of the evening air on Jake's clothes, the smell of his breath, the mossy scent in the air. I can hide here and enjoy the one thing that is mine. The thing I can't betray. I'm reminded of how I had the strength to reject my Dad though I never had before.

"Even after all your work during the day, your hair always smells so sweet," Jake says. "Like coconut and the sea."

"We do live next to the ocean," I point out, delighting in this banter.

Jake smiles. "Yes, but you are far more beautiful. I can't wait to enjoy it more once we're married."

He entwines his fingers with mine, playing with each finger as I had his earlier. He plays with the ring on my right hand most. It's our secret bond to one another.

It's of two hands reaching for a heart in the center with a crown on the top. I wear it with the heart pointing inward to show I am taken, but wearing it in this manner meant only dating to most. But not to us. We know what it meant. He wears one like it, only his is pure silver. Mine has an opal in the heart. It is a tradition handed down by my family. And it suits our secret engagement well.

I sigh heavily as I watch Jake fiddle with my fingers. I had wanted to talk to him so badly about it, but now, I just want to avoid it. He is too busy kissing the tips of my fingers to notice my mood yet.

He pulls back just a bit, still smiling. "I brought something for you."

I gasp in delight. "Jake, you didn't?" But I hope he did.

Jake grins like a cat over milk and steps back to his bag. He pulls out exactly what I love most, a yellow cake with chocolate frosting, cream in the center, and a small blue flower on top. My eyes pop out in delight. That is an expensive and rare treat for a girl who is on a strict diet and small budget.

Jake laughs in pleasure. "Those blue eyes could outdo the sea for vastness when I bring you cake," he says. "It's worth every gemlet."

"Oh Jake, you're the best!" I kiss him on the cheek in excitement, my heart brimming with happiness. How I love him. How he looks after me. How much he gives up for me.

"I know," Jake sighs dramatically, making me giggle. "Come on then." He sits on the rock, putting his arm out, so I can sit and lean against it.

I sit down and let him wrap his arms around my shoulders. I smile as he hand-feeds me bites, taking bits for himself now and then, but he gives me far more of it. I never let him not at least share a little. But it also means the world to me how he wants to give me the most.

I hold Jake's arm around my shoulders, hanging my hands off his arms almost like I am going to pull myself upon them as I lean against his chest and enjoy our shared treat.

I wish this would never end. The perfect sunset, the glitter of the water, the sweet treat, his warm arms around me. I just want to turn and kiss him, give him everything. But that's not for today. We still have to wait. If I break my oath, we'd be in far worse trouble.

We finish the treat, and Jake puts the box aside. I lean deeper into his arms, holding him tight and sighing in contentment, shutting my eyes. I needed that. I wanted to vent to him when I came, but now, I just want to enjoy the moment.

I close my eyes, taking in all the smells, savoring the chocolate and cake flavor on my tongue, listening to Jake's breath and the wonderful waterworks around us. This is heaven. I can't betray this. I can't lose this.

"How was your raid?" I ask in a relaxed tone, eyes still shut, wanting to forget why I'd come into this magical place so upset.

Jake's exhausted sigh shakes me from my moment. I frown in concern for him. He sounds so tired. I turn to look at him as he lets his head plop back on the tree behind him.

"Not great," he laments. "It wasn't one of the Enthronement loads like we hoped. We hardly got enough to feed those who helped us, let alone help the others."

I feel the sadness and weight that came with those words. Jake is dedicated to the Loyalist rebellion, most of all, in its efforts to feed those in the ranks who want to support themselves. He sounds worn already, and we aren't even on the throne yet. My heart aches for the stress and exhaustion in his voice.

"We'll figure it out." I assure him.

"I just wish we knew how they were transporting all their money. They tax it. It should go right to them, right? How are they spending it if it never gets into the castle?" Jake scowls.

His frustration makes his breath hot, his arms tense, and his movements haphazard as he moves his free hand about. "We tried the sea. It's not coming in there, and what we get in raids is nothing, hardly enough to feed the palace for a day. So, what in creation are they doing to get the money?"

I have no answers. I never do. I don't think anyone does or we'd have tried it by now. I wish I was more helpful, but I feel useless when it comes to this kind of strategy. I would support Jake on the throne, but I feel much more confident in helping with orphanages and schools and programs to help people get jobs than... this.

"I just wish..." Jake sighs, all the anger draining out of him in a heavy sigh, "...we had enough. I'm so tired of looking at the small ones begging for food and... being powerless." Jake drops his head.

I know what that means. They lost another child to illness or hunger or who knows what. Each one strikes Jake hard. We try, but... how can we help those starving children when we can hardly help ourselves?

"H-how many this time?" I ask as gently as I can, trying to comfort him and let him vent.

Jake swallows hard. "Five died in the last month," his voice shakes. "We got three more. I don't know how we'll keep feeding them if we can't find out how to get the money back from the royals." Jake shakes his head. "We tried. It goes into that storehouse, and we attack all the carts going to the palace we can. And it's always chump change. We feed our troops, sure, but that's not the goal." He lets his head fall against the tree, "I just want this life to be over."

Well, I don't want all of it over. I don't want to give up my shows, but I know this means the world to Jake. And for him, I'll give it up. I shut my eyes to dream of what it will be like.

But instead, all I can think about is Dad's plan that would change everything. My heart drops, and I tense as if to defend the one dream I was allowed to have for myself.

Jake frowns. "What's wrong?"

"Nothing," I say too fast.

"Kascia." I hear the hint of a scold in Jake's voice as I stare into the running water. "We both know it's not nothing. Something's wrong."

I sigh heavily and hold him tighter. "Nothing, just..." I try to find the words to dismiss it, "It's not really important right now."

"So are you saying that to assure me or avoid it?" Jake asks carefully.

I have to admit I'm not even sure. I bite my lip. If I don't tell him, does that make it as if it won't happen? Maybe if Mom agrees with me, but she didn't seem to at dinner. Would I ever find a way out of this? Maybe if Jake doesn't agree, I'll have a leg to stand on. Why I felt I had to talk to him at all, but I don't want to lose this magic. "I love you." I choose to say instead.

"Kascia, what's the matter? Did something happen today?"

I nod, biting my lip harder and taking a deep breath to hold in the anger and pain. "Yes, but it's not something we need to talk about now."

"If it upsets you, we do," Jake disagrees. "That's how we got over ourselves, remember?" He smiles playfully.

"I screamed I didn't like you. Then we realized we had something in common. Took years."

Jake smiles. "You were worth waiting for."

He kisses me deeply; I suck it in. Dad can't take this. He can't take the thrill I feel as the energy of that kiss rushes through me, or the intoxicating dizziness I feel at his touch, or the pleasurable press of his lips on mine, and the delightful soft bite of his lips on mine. He just can't take it. I won't let him.

"So, tell me," Jake says when he pulls back, "what is bothering you? Saying it and screaming at each other is always better. You can throw anything at me. I'll take it."

"It's not you," I insist, grunting in annoyance.

"I didn't mess up?"

"No," I kiss him to assure him, "not this time."

I kiss him deeper, harder. He grins and puts his other arm around me as I push myself up a bit to kiss him better, again and again, sucking his lips into mine, turning and releasing his arm to put one hand to his cheek, while I hook my other hand to his shoulder, keeping him close. I run my hand through his hair on the way to the back of his head. I press closer, almost sitting on his lap.

How I adore him. How he looks after me. How he makes me feel. His strong chest so close to mine. His breath against my skin. How his thick lashes tickle my face as I turn to get at his lips. His arm wraps around my waist. I all but dig into him, kissing him harder and harder, encouraging him to hold me tighter. This is what I wouldn't give up.

Jake falls for it. He always does, then again, so do I when he tries it. He returns my intensity and fights for that passion too. We struggle for the feeling, relishing every bit of it we dredge up.

I gasp as he switches from kissing my lips to kissing the round of my shoulder. I shut my eyes and relax a little as he kisses down my arm, inch by inch, until he reaches my hand and presses his lips to it, holding it closer to him. I sigh again, eyes fluttering at his touches. I want more of his touch. I want that touch more than anything.

I leap forward and kiss his jaw, yanking his face to mine, bringing him down with me. Jake returns it, kissing me again, and again. I feel myself tilt back as he gets into it.

"Kascia," he breathes. I love his breath on my skin.

"What?" I ask, kissing his cheek.

"I can't ever get enough," he sighs heavily.

"Have enough," I tease.

"We know better. We'll lose what made our fathers agree," he reminds me.

This floods me with anger. Who cares anymore!? Maybe if we just caved in, Dad couldn't make me lose my whole life again. "I don't care what he wants!" I snap and kiss him harder.

"Woah." Jake pulls away and puts a hand to my cheek to hold me back. "Kascia, what is that?"

I hate him for denying me this. I push him away, turning my back to him. I fold my arms tightly and don't turn around, pulling into myself as if to protect myself.

"Kascia?" Jake frowns deeply. "What's really going on? What did your father do?"

"You don't care," I snarl back.

"Yes, I do." Jake runs a hand down my arm, starting at the round of my shoulder again. I shut my eyes. Yes, touch, his touch it's all I want. Dad can't take it.

I shut my eyes as tears come. "Will you all take it?"

"Take what?" Jake kisses my cheek from behind.

I adore that. I turn to him to kiss him hard, but Jake holds me back. "What is it?" he asks.

I roar in frustration and shove him away. "He can't take it," I insist. "So why must you?"

"What am I taking?" Jake asks. "I love you."

"Do you?"

Jake smiles gently and pulls me closer like a toddler refusing to sit next to her parents and puts his arm around me again, kissing my cheek. I lean into it. I need it.

"Yes, I do," he assures me. "You can throw anything at me."

"The only thing I need to throw at you is me." I don't want to discuss Dad taking him from me. Even if the plan is to go back to him, I couldn't be gone that long. And we'd never gotten into the castle. No rebel had in my lifetime.

"You normally are good at taking no for an answer, just like I do when I get too intense." Jake rubs my shoulders. "I'm not pulling away, Kascia. Just keeping our rule. What's the change?" He kisses my shoulder and neck.

"He wants to end it." I finally admit as hot tears come.

"End us?" Jake laughs.

I turn to him in shock. He's laughing at this?!

"That's not what the plan means," Jake is still laughing.

"Excuse me?" I snap. "You know?"

"He proposed his plan to get us inside, right?" Jake asks, still smiling at me like an overreacting child.

"Which is?" He can't know, can he?

"To use the Enthronement to get a girl on the inside," Jake says. "And as you're the best princess we know. It's why I love you," he adds, "he figures you'll get in, piece of cake."

I gape at him. "What?" I can't believe this. "You knew he wanted me?"

"Who better?" Jake asks innocently.

"Do you not understand what the Enthronement is?" I demand, pulling away to see him better.

My anger mounts, but it's just to cover up the hint of fear. I feel my heart stilling, afraid it's going to have to deal with the hints of a crack that are threatening to form depending on the answer I'm about to get.

"A contest to prove yourself a true princess?" Jake looks at me as if I'm crazy.

"With what goal?" I demand.

"Uh, for you, it doesn't matter. You'll let us in before it's even over."

"And you think courting the prince isn't part of that?"

"So?"

"So!" I clench my fists and stand up as the flood of emotions rises in me, wanting to break out like a stormy tide against a coastal wall. One wave is anger; how could he not understand!? The next: desperation, he had to be thick because if he isn't, the last wave strikes: fear.

It was an old fear I'd not thought about in many years. So buried I'd all but forgotten about it until this moment. That the love we'd built was forced so unreal. Did this mean what I'd feared, deep down, for so long, our love was manufactured, fake, unnatural?

I'd never loved anyone else. I had nothing to compare him to, but I love him. I worked hard for it, and true love was fought for. I love him. I love him... I have to. He has to love me. I need him. I need what we have.

"Don't you know what that means?" I rage. "I'll have to *date* him, Jake. I'll have to *court* him. It will be six months..."

"Three," Jake corrects.

I want to grab him by the throat. "What!?"

The fear in Jake's eyes is familiar to me. He realizes he did a dumb. "Sorry, but they are only just getting started. There's no way you'll be living in the palace with the dog until at least August. Three months."

I take a deep breath as I contain my anger. "Jake..." I force out between my teeth, "it doesn't matter. Six months, three months, it all means the same thing. If I'm going to go unnoticed, I'll have to play along. Do you have *any* idea what that means?"

Jake tilts his head. "That you play along. You do it on stage all the time."

"And you hate that! So why are you alright with me doing it with... him?!"

"Because it will get us where we want to go," Jake retorts. "We will finally win."

"I thought our combined army would win?" I quote what they told us both to talk us into this in the first place.

"Weren't we just discussing how even with that we don't know how to get in?"

"Yes, but..." I want to throw something at that smug face so badly I actually look for something to throw, but there's nothing.

I roar in frustration again and stomp my foot.

"But I'll have to play in love with him. It's not a role. We don't both know it's fake! It's not the same, Jake. It's not. How can you not hate this?" I can't understand. He won't come to my shows for it, but he'll shove me into the brat prince's arms no problem? Does he not care about me at all? Does he not know what this will do to me and us?

Jake's face falls a little. "You said no?" He sounds like he can't believe it.

"Well... of course."

"Kascia, you didn't!" Jake sounds horrified. "If we don't get in, we might never get them. We haven't ever gotten inside. With you on the inside to let us in—"

"So, we'll sacrifice me like some pawn in a chess match?"

"No, you're the queen of the board," he smiles at his compliment, "who has the most power to take the king."

"By playing the starry-eyed girl over that brat of a prince," I remind him. "Jake... it's a contest for his hand. I'll have to do... this with him." I wave at the rock.

"You'll not be there long enough," he waves it off.

"And if I am?"

"You won't."

"But *if* I am?" I know I will be. Three months seems short, but it's not.

"Then... then that's the game." His tone makes it sound like it's bitter on his tongue, but he ate it anyway.

"Jake... I-I love you," I squeak it out as my hands shake and tears come. "I can't lose you."

"I'll be there when the deed is done," Jake shrugs.

He shrugs?! I try another angle. "What if he charms me, Jake? What if he makes me forget you?"

"He won't. We love each other too much."

"You can't tell me you don't hate this."

He shrugs once again. "I don't. You should do it."

My shoulders fall. What if I do? Why can't he see it? "What if I have to kiss him like I do you? What if he demands more? You know the kind of man he is. What if... if I say no, they'll disqualify me and send me home. What if that happens, Jake?"

Jake swallows hard and meets my eyes. "Then stay in."

I gasp as if he'd stabbed me instead of spoken. He doesn't mean that. He couldn't. "Jake..."

"It's about the cause, Kassie," he says, finally sounding angry. "You know that."

"So how I feel doesn't matter?"

"How I feel doesn't matter!" Jake shoots back. "I thought we both knew this."

I glare at him. "What if it was you? What if it was a princess instead of a prince, Jake? What if you had to go and kiss and make out and worse with another girl? How do you think you'd feel when your heart was with me? How do you think I'd feel? Could you really do that to me?"

Jake looks down and scuffs the mud with the toe of his boot. "I'd have to; that's the job."

My mouth falls open. "What happened to the best thing for the throne is being unified? What about the best rulers are united in their rule? What happened to loving one another completely is the best way to prepare for the throne?"

"It's still true." Jake looks up at me, "We just have to be apart for a while."

"Jake... how... Do you not care?"

"Of course I do." He steps closer to me, "but this is bigger than us."

"I thought the biggest thing was us." A hot tear slips out.

Wait, hot? Shouldn't I be more crushed? Shouldn't the fact his love for me is this weak hurt me differently? Is something wrong?

Maybe this is normal. I'd never had this intense of a fight before. Jake and I fight all the time; we scream our anger all the time because it's what drew us close. But it's not working today. It's only making me angrier.

"It is because we're the cause," Jake replies.

"Am I nothing but the means to an end?" I demand.

"Isn't that all I am to you?" Jake yells back.

How dare he?! I use all my acting skills to control my actual reaction. I'm tense from shoulders to toes in hurt and anger. "Get another girl to do it then. I'm not your only choice, I'm sure. Why isn't that something you'll fight for?"

"Because no one is as sure as you. Your father picked you because you are the best choice," Jake states.

"It's because I'm a Custod!" I shriek at him, "Nothing more! The Custods want one of their own on the throne. They want a Custod to renounce their current role and take on a royal one. I'm not the best choice for queen, you idiot. I can't help with your stupid battle plans, or your cursed raids, or even how to figure out the best way to defend or attack or feed them or any of it! I'm not the best choice for queen or princess. I'm just the Custod they chose. You're the one they want to rule."

"Oh Kascia." Jake softens. "Do you not see all that you will bring to the throne? Do you not see what you should be? My dear girl, my sweet, precious Kascia, no. It's far more than that. Why did the Custods pick you of all their daughters?"

"Because they told my father to do the job, and he had me while working the job." I roll my eyes.

"No, it's not. Your father could have asked for anyone else," Jake says.

"So? I'm easy." I accepted this truth a long time ago. I don't mind. I could support Jake as the real ruler. I always expected to. I could do the cute stuff, but I am not the best choice for queen. I'd just not make a mess of it. I'm not terrible, but I'm not as great as Queen Airabelle, Queen Esther, or Queen Emma. "It's not about that."

"Yes, it is. You're the only girl we *know* will get in. Kascia, you have to do it." Jake pleads with me, "We may never find another way."

"And the old plan?"

"Was always a long shot." Jake sighs, bowing his head. "Even if we pretended otherwise. This is sure."

"Jake, I don't want to hurt you or give up what we have. I can't betray you. We've fought for this." I try again. "Don't you see?"

"You really love me so little he can steal you?" Jake asks timidly.

I sigh in frustration, "You love me so little you'll happily lead me into the cursed prince's arms?" I swallow my anger to try to keep my voice steady. "Because if you ask me to do this, that's what you'll be doing."

"If it saves our people." Jake nods firmly.

"This doesn't hurt you at all?"

"Of course not, I know you have to. I won't punish you for it." Jake comforts me. The monster has the nerve to step forward and stroke my cheek tenderly.

I slap it away. "So you'll make me?"

"Never force, but beg." Jake smiles sadly. "Please, it's the only way."

"So you'll hand me to the prince?"

"Against my will, yes." Jake runs the back of his fingers across my cheek. "Don't think I don't dislike it, but sometimes, that's the price we pay."

"And what if he asks everything of me?" I ask, my eyes boring into Jake's dark ones.

He bows his head with a sigh then meets my eyes. "Then you do whatever it takes."

How quickly love turns to hate. How could he? He would sell away the most sacred part of me for the cause?

I try to remind myself what the cause is. Stopping the guards killing their own people, shoving innocent people to the street, smacking the homeless children, stopping more children from dying of starvation, bringing peace so we never have to see the people at each other like I had on Restoration Day. To provide orphanages, schools, and arts back to the kingdom, to bring the prosperity it needs by lightening the taxes and giving back what was stolen. What better cause is there than that?

But selling that part of me? Giving that away to someone I'd never love or marry? To give it away when the one I want to share it with was far away and the one I'd marry in the end? To give it to someone I plan to let my Dad and fiancé murder? To give it away, forever. I fought to keep it special even against the man I wanted to give it to. Now I'd be expected to sell it for a kingdom?

I take a step back. "How could you?"

"Kascia, I know it's a lot to ask. I'd do it myself if I could," Jake promises. "I'm not asking anything I'd not do myself."

"You'd take that from me and give it to the one you plan on having killed later?"

"As surely as I'm asking and begging you to." Jake frowns. "Kascia, please."

I shake my head and drop it. How could... did all we fight for mean nothing all along? Did we not have any real love? Was it all just... a play? Was our love just an act I'd fallen for and come to believe was real?

"I love you." I give it a last try.

Jake bends down and kisses me hard, long and deep. "And I love you more than breath," he states.

"But not more than the cause?"

"Kascia, can we be so selfish?" Jake asks.

Can we be so selfish? Does he have a point? I step back and hug myself. Am I being a spoiled, selfish brat now? Do I even know if the prince would ask that of me? Yes, he likely would. Maybe if I make myself small and meek enough he'd ignore me for other girls who want it more, but I just... he takes and takes. He's never outside the palace. I'm sure he's starved for a woman. His parents gave him and themselves all they wanted by taking it from their people. And after being near him, in and out of his grasp, for three months? He would surely ask it of me. And even if not, I'd have to do the rest. And Jake said "okay"?

That is the real problem. He is alright selling me if we had to. He would sell me. He would betray me in a heartbeat if we were switched. And that... What kind of relationship is that? Are we fake? Was this selfish?

"Kascia, please," Jake begs. "Think about it?"

Yes, time, space... that's what I need. I need to get away from him and the temptation of how badly I need his touch. "I won't say no or yes yet."

"I still love you. I love you with all I have, but..." he swallows, "Kassie, we can't be selfish. We'd be no worse than the royals if we did."

"No worse than them." I repeat quietly. Am I just as bad as the royals? "Please, take me home."

Jake nods. "Always." He kisses my forehead.

I can't bring myself to take his hand. I normally did, but not today. I'm scared, petrified. I need him. I can't imagine longer than a few weeks away from him. Even thinking about it makes me shake.

What is happening? That morning, life was normal. I had hope in my future marriage, my future life even if as a girl I hated it. Is that life suddenly gone? Do I have to sell my soul to keep it? And even if I don't, would my world be the same?

When we get back, I nod my thanks to Jake. He kisses my cheek and goes for a good night kiss. I want to say no, but I need him too badly and let him kiss me. I keep it short though.

"I'll see you tomorrow," he assures me, "I love you."

My lip trembles. "I love you too."

Jake smiles then walks away. To avoid my parents, I slip in through my window and lock my bedroom door. Then I break down and cry hot and bitter tears into my pillow.

Chapter 5

With it being the first rest day, it is easier to hide from my parents in the morning. With my sleep disorder, sleeping in when I am able tends to be helpful, so they let me lie in as late as I like. I use this to hide for as long as I can get away with before I sneak something for breakfast before my parents find out and slip off to be alone. I think better alone.

I escape to a stretch of beach I find by going across the stream and up for about five minutes. It's a lovely beach but not easy to get to so tourists don't often find it.

That's the problem of living in Purerah's capital city Rosepla during tourist season. Without it, our people would have gone broke generations ago. After five generations of this heavy taxation, it isn't a surprise. And the more entertainment heavy your industry, the more heavily it is taxed. In other kingdoms, there is no direct tax on the people. The taxes comes out of high-demand industries, theaters, sporting events, and things like that. It works well there, but I guess five generations ago the king figured they needed more.

And here I was, a Custod tasked with finally ending it all, pushing away the best chance we have at doing so. I sigh and rest my head on my arms which wrap around my knees, curled up to my chest as I sit on the golden yellow sand that stretches to the stunning blue water. It's where Purerah's national colors come from, the unique blue of our oceans with the golden yellow of our sands.

And I had wholeheartedly supported any means of overthrowing the royal family that polluted this wonderful land and its resilient people. But when I have all the power to change it, I recoil?

This thought brings up questions about my life I'd never really thought about before. I chose to ignore them because I was happy with how life was and the plans we had. But now, I had to question them.

I believed in the cause. I know what horrors this kingdom faces because of the irresponsibility of their rulers. But is that enough to sell my soul? Was Jake right and I was selfish? Was it wrong of me to want him to be unwilling to sell me to the devil?

That's the real pain. Not that they want me to do this, but that Jake honestly told me to give the spoiled prince what he wants if it keeps me in the game long enough. He'd give me up for the cause. I was and would be second, always. No matter what else happened.

And what if I said yes? We take the throne, then what? What kind of relationship would we have when I fear Jake will sell me off again? I'll always be second to him. Always. I'd done all I could do to make him the only thing that was mine and my number one, only for this to happen.

What if as queen he felt the best way to help the people was to sell me off to some foreign king?

He'd do it. I know Jake would. After what he said to me last night, I know the truth. The one I'd thought was my one and only, not only wasn't mine, he didn't see me as his. No more than someone saw a tool as theirs.

How do I choose between two paths, one that dries me into the obedient zombie they want and the other that freezes me into a zombie?

Is it really selfish of me to not want either fate? If I wasn't so selfish, would I not feel like I was being made a zombie but feel good and excited like Jake had been? Or is that the reason the Maker had made my "day job" an actress?

I'm a natural. I am one of the best: famous for performances in *The Phantom, The Witches,* and my dancing in *Twelve Dancing Princesses* and *The Phoenix.* Is this why I'm so good? So that for the rest of my life I can play the role of good Custod and good queen when the time comes? The show must go on. That is my bitter pill to swallow as a Custod. The blow I have to take for them.

My sobs tear at my heart like claws ripping out my insides. I know what I have to do, and I hate it. I don't know if I have the strength to do it. My face stings with tears; my hands shake, and my chest throbs with each fresh rip at my insides. I curl up as the pain eats me inside.

"I knew I'd find you here."

I jump and turn as Mom sits down beside me. She gives me a small, reassuring smile to let me know she's not upset.

"I know you better than you think. Believe it or not, better than your father does. He started looking about an hour ago. I thought I'd let him get well enough on the wrong track before I came out to you," She gives me a soft smile. "I have something for you." She offers me a small package.

I look down at it. It's not a package; it's a sheath of paper. It's laid out in a rather stiff envelope with an unbroken seal. I recognize the mark as the Purerahian emblem.

"It's an application," Mom says carefully. "And as you can see it's sealed, your father hasn't played with this one." She rests it on the sand in front of me. "Just promise me, if you agree to do it, you won't use the one your father crafted and you'll actually fill it out yourself?" Mom bends forward a little to study my face. Her hazel eyes crease in concern as she watches me for a reaction.

I hardly heard what she said after "if". "If?" I repeat as a question.

"Oh Kascia," Mom sighs in sorrow. "No one has the right to make the final choice but you," Mom says, stroking a loving finger under my chin, "Don't let anyone else make it for you. Yes, if. I'm not going to force you."

"But you want me to." My shoulders drop.

"Yes, but," Mom looks around to be sure we're alone, "not for the same reasons he does."

"What other reason could there possibly be?" I ask dully, "Other than doing my duty. They're right. What other right choice is there to make?" I start to draw in the sand, not making anything, just playing with the touch of the sand around my fingers.

"Jacek knows?" Mom's brows draw together in a frown.

I nod. "We talked about it last night."

"And?"

"He said if it works..." I take a deep breath to control my emotions.

"What does that mean?" Mom's tone is worried and slightly angry.

I swallow. "It means... he knows I should do it too."

"But he doesn't want you to?"

"No, he does." I keep playing with the sand, watching my finger dance through the soft sand of my country. I'm a Custod. I shouldn't have a country. But I love this place, these people. I'm a failure as a Custod. What rule of my duty do I keep?

"He *wants* you too?" Mom presses.

"Only because it helps the cause. He's right. It's selfish."

I feel Mom tense, and I look up from my fingers to see her eyes are closed. I'd seen that face before, normally backstage before she took the stage. She is getting into character. Why? Is she upset I was being so selfish?

"He told you that?" she asks.

"Yes. He's right. I should be willing to do what it takes as a Custod."

"And what does that mean to you?"

I look back down and start playing with the sand. "I have to do whatever it takes. Whatever he wants, I give it until that night."

"Anything?" Mom's voice is oddly loud.

"You know what they're like, Mama. If it comes to that, I'll have to, won't I?" I love how the sand feels as soft as the water.

Mom is quiet for a long time, and I don't mind the excuse to keep silent.

"Kascia," she says gently, "do you want to do this?"

"No." The word pops out before I can decide if I don't want her to know that. "You know what they're like, Mama. What will they do to me? And

I'll have to pretend to like him?" I swallow down the sick bubbles in my stomach. "And in the end, it's all just to let them be assassinated? I… I don't want to love anyone else, Mama. But he wants me to, and Papa wants me to, and I'm a Custod. I have to do what's best for my people. So I don't have a choice." My voice started shaky and upset but got more firm towards the end.

"So, you're going to do it?" Mom frowns in confusion this time.

"Yes. No. Ugh," I sigh. "I don't know."

"Is it just being afraid of what they'll make you do that makes you not want to do it?"

"Yes and…" I take a deep breath "…and what else it means. What Jake said. I honestly never thought he'd be alright with this. When I told him what the prince might try to make me do, he said don't be eliminated."

"Like what?" Mom's frown grows a little with each question.

"Mama, you know what they're like," I give her an exasperated look, "and he's never been around girls. Sooner or later, he'll try to get someone to do it."

"Then say no," Mom states firmly.

"But if I do, they'll kick me out."

"So?"

I sigh, "Then I can't fulfill the mission, and it would be for nothing."

"Jacek can't want that," Mom points out.

"If it gets the job done," I reply in almost a whisper.

Mom pauses before asking, "And how did that make you feel?"

"Betrayed," I say honestly. "No matter what I do, I'm trapped. So, what choice do I have? Either say no and disappoint everyone I love and watch my people suffer when I could have stopped it, or I have to let the prince have his way and then finally get the life I wanted." The tears return. I don't want that life anymore. I know now it's a lie. "It's a selfish choice to do any different."

"No Kascia, it's not." Mom takes my hand. "Kassie, there is another option."

"Like what?" I demand. "I can't just let Jake go. He's all that's ever re-really been mine." But was he ever really mine?

"Join the Enthronement for another reason."

I look up at my mother with tears in my eyes. "Like what?"

"Kascia, I love you and your father, and you know I support you, but I don't think the life you're trying to lead is the one you really want." She gives me a sad smile.

She's right. It's not. But I don't get another choice. "It is because it's the best I can get with my duty," I say. "Or was."

"What if you didn't have that anymore?" Mom asks.

"Mama, it's what I was born into. I don't get a choice." I sigh tiredly. "I thought the old plan was a good compromise."

"But you do get a choice," Mom says. She taps the application in front of me. "This gives you a way out."

"What?"

"Kascia," Mom says gently. "I know how much you love your father, and I wouldn't change that. But you know so little of the world outside that theater and the bubble he's made for you. Win or not, let them in or not, the Enthronement is your chance to escape his bubble and make your own choice. I believe you should do it, but not his way. Do it for yourself. It's time you made your own choice, Kascia. Remember when I asked if you wanted to work for the theater when you were thirteen?"

I nod. How could I forget? I thought it meant Mama didn't want me there, and I cried for days.

"And what did I tell you then?" she asks.

"That you just wanted me to choose."

"Exactly." She smiles gently. "Your father has never given you a choice. It's always been the Custod path, and honestly, that's not normal. All Custods are asked, sooner or later, if they want to remain a fighter or take another path. You never did. Your father never gave you that option. There are other ways to help the cause."

Those Custods are seen as lesser, weaker ones. I'd shame my father if I did that. I'd shame myself. I don't like being a Custod, but by heavens, I didn't want to be one of those Custods.

"Regardless of that," Mom gives a telling-off look as she reads my expression correctly, "you should have been offered the choice. You never were. And the Enthronement will provide the chance to choose. That's why I want you to do it.

"If you're eliminated for telling the prince no, honestly, I'll be far more proud of you than if you let him have his way. I don't care if you do choose to let them in. I don't care if you run off with the milkman or the stable hand or the kitchen boy, or whatever it might be. I just want you to get a chance to see the world outside your father's eyes and make your own choice." She cups my chin in her hand. "I'd be proud of you for winning if that's what you chose to try to do. The only way you could disappoint me is by not making your own choice. Even if you decide you don't want to join the Enthronement, I'd not mind a bit. As long as you make your own choice, alright?"

I smile and nod, meeting my mother's eyes. A rush of relief washes over me, relaxing the tense parts of me I didn't even know were tense. At least I knew one person would truly be on my side no matter what I choose. It takes a huge weight off my shoulders, even if a lot of weight remains.

"Just promise me one thing." Mom gets me to meet her eyes dead on again. "If you decide to do it, no matter your reason, fill out your own application and not use your father's?"

"But... what if the prince does try to get those things from me?" I ask. "What do I do?"

"What you want," Mom says firmly. "I'd say smack him away, but I know that is overly simple. If you don't want it, don't let him."

"But if I fail, what will Dad and Jake do?"

Mom sighs and gives me a tight hug. "I wish I knew," she says tiredly. "But if you get far enough, you'll be given a position in the court or cities of some kind. You could use that to get away from whatever they want."

"Can... you ask the Head Custod for a different assignment?" I ask. Just because Dad was placed here didn't mean I had to be. My heart ached at the idea of leaving Purerah. I had never known any other home. Even if I don't agree with its government, I love its people. It would hurt to leave them, the waters I loved, but perhaps that could be my safety net.

Mom smiles a little. "I'm sure he'd at least take an audience with you to discuss it."

That meant there was hope in that choice. "So... if it was really up to you, what would you do?"

"Honestly, if I was in your shoes, I'd at least try it." Mom smiles. "I was more into this kind of thing though. You're much meeker than I ever was. I would have had a blast showing off to the palace and the other girls." I giggle. "And as your mother, if I had to make the choice, I'd send you in with no strings attached. I wouldn't expect you to win or let the rebels in, or anything. I'd just expect you to do your best and decide for yourself what path your life will take."

I accept that with a nod. The paradigm made accepting the fate Jake and Dad handed me a bit easier. Perhaps Mom was right, and I could use it to escape. But then I'd lose Jake. But had I already? Or was what I loved an illusion I'd made to survive?

Mom and I stay on the beach a while, just sitting quietly together until late afternoon, and we head home. Dad is waiting when we return, smiling playfully at us. "Sneaking off to the studio?"

Mom nods but doesn't say a word.

"I want to show you something." Dad smiles warmly at me, his eyes twinkling in a way that makes me smile. It's like he is about to bring out the best surprise. "I think it will help you, and it's far past time I told you."

The idea Dad trusts me enough to tell me something important makes me nod instantly.

Dad beams and has me put on my shawl before we head into town.

The city is back to normal after the Restoration Day celebrations. The bright decorations are gone, revealing the worn-down cracked sandstone streets and buildings.

We have to pass the main square on our way. I tense as the first crack cuts the air. I avert my eyes from the punishment row that's here. The line, as always, is long full of men, women, and children awaiting punishment. More than half of them would have been caught stealing food. The rest will be for minor acts of rebellion or sedition.

I hold Dad's hand tightly as I try to ignore it, but each new snap makes me start as if I'm the one being whipped. The cries of those punished doesn't help. There's a line for the adults who are whipped across the back, their crime deciding how many times. The children are stuck across the hand with a crop-like whip. The cries of both make me tense and tears start in my eyes. How do we let this keep happening?

Dad is hardly phased by the sounds. He keeps a grip on my hand as we go through the large town square and across to the other side of the city. I rarely came to this side of the city. The area we're going to is on the northeast side. I don't know what's in this part of town. It's known as one of the worst parts of town.

I start to wonder if I should ask where we are when we reach a place where it's as if someone has drawn a line through the town. The buildings come to a sudden end, leading to a large expanse of an open field.

Dad walks into it without hesitation or fear. I am slower to follow, having to ease into it, slowly rolling toe-ball-heel into the space. It's like crossing into another world.

The silence of the field strikes me dead in the chest. The quiet is eerie, unnatural as if nothing dared disturb it. Far removed from the rest of the city, there's hardly a sound to be heard apart from the rustle of the wind, the ghostly whisper of the ocean, and the eerie cry of the sea birds.

The buildings that "stand" here hardly stand at all, giving me a wide view of what must have been a huge section of the city at one point. The open space is so large I can see where the earth slowly curves down to lead into the ocean in the distance. On my right, the expanse stretches on until I can't see for the mist and ruins.

The buildings that had once stood here were either completely gone or only five feet high at their highest but for a few jutting exceptions that look ready to fall over in the ghostly breeze. They are made of finer stone than I'd ever seen in Rosepla before. But whatever they were made of could not withstand whatever had happened to them. They now stand broken down, ripped up, and smashed. The broken stones on the ground are worn smooth from the mist that hangs over the place, contrasting the charred and burnt sections of stone and wood.

I take slow, uneasy breaths. We shouldn't be here. But I follow Dad, feeling the rotting planks that were once roofs against my feet. I see where the roads used to be, grown over with plant life and rotted wood, most of it with scorch marks. I almost trip on some odd gouge marks in the stone street. More bedeck the tops of some still standing structures.

I have to avoid large outcroppings of stone that have fallen off some structures. The air smells wet from all the undergrowth.

"What is this place?" I ask as I gape in a kind of mystified, frightened awe.

"We call it the Burned District," Dad says solemnly. "It's the first sign that things need to change."

I'd heard the term before, but never realized it was a real place. I thought it meant the worse part of town. I shake my head. "I don't understand."

"This happened about five hundred years ago," Dad says grimly. "When the heavy tax was first laid on the people," Dad says as he follows me as I reverently wander through the old, ruined shops, homes, and offices. My steps are silent and delicate. His footfalls are frim and hard, grinding the broken bits like a painful reminder of all that's shattered around us.

"Even back then, the tax was so high the people could hardly stand it. They objected, and many refused to pay. As punishment, the king sent his men to burn down the homes of those who refused." Dad waves a hand around us as I step into what I think was once the district square. "And that's what you see all around you. That's when the first rebellion started. But then after a generation or two, squabbles about who to put on the throne once the greedy Potentates were out broke the rebellion apart.

"That is when the three factions you know today formed: Potentate, Custod, and Loyalist. Your marriage will aline the two strongest."

"If we're lucky," I say dismally.

Dad nods sadly. "If we're lucky," He says solemnly. "But not anymore. If you can get us in, we'll take out the royal family and put you and Jack right in position to take the throne. We'll get more than half of the population behind us, forming a kingdom and unity faster than we ever predicted, ending the punishments you saw today, ending the wars that this kingdom has known for generations. You could end it all just by playing their silly game and letting us in at the party. That's all it will take."

"I guess it is selfish to say no," I hug myself.

Mom had talked me into it, but now I was seeing why even if I did, I'd still be trapped. It was selfish to run away and leave my people to… this.

"Kassie, I'd never say that." Dad smiles and puts a hand on my shoulder. "But sometimes what we have to do hurts. The greatest Custod had to do a lot of things that hurt. Like killing the puppet king in his sleep and ending his own life, there's so much he had to endure though he didn't want to. It's the pain and honor. Custods have to be the shield.

"I wish I didn't have to ask it of you, but I think it can't be all bad. You get to try out the palace before you move in, learn their secrets, play princess before you have to be queen. You were going right to queen before," Dad teases playfully. "I love you, Kascia, but it's a hard role we play. Please, it's only a few months."

"I know." Though I'd decided, I can't just say yes now.

Yes, I'd seen the current pain, but this? I shudder as the air itself feels colder than in the city as if the ghosts of those wronged are trapped here, making the mist and quiet that hangs around us, hiding in the ruins, begging me to right their wrongs and end the line that murdered them and condemned their descendants to the hell I know today.

Could I really use this game as an escape? Mom's suggestion sounded appealing, but now I'm questioning her wisdom. Perhaps she and I are too alike in our artistic daydreams. I could use them to survive, but if this place says anything, it was that it was time to face the truth.

Chapter 6

I put the application on my desk and sit down before I just stare at the envelope.

It's beautiful. It's easily the finest I've ever seen. It's made from thick paper that feels beautifully textured, yet smooth. It has a strong, yet cool scent like a flower I can't name. It's cream-colored and beautiful. But that's not why I'm staring. I'm nervous. Am I really about to do this?

I flip it over to see the Purerahian blue wax seal on the back, bearing the Purerahian emblem. I study each pattern of the wave splashing up behind the three main items of the emblem. In a color version of this emblem, they would be a creamy white. I look over the stunning dolphin, curved and leaping from the waters, arching so slightly over the island rose in the center. I study the twisting, powerful breach of the great shark, coming up in more of a twist than a curve, showing grace and power, contrasting the smooth, playful grace of the dolphin. I run a hand over the contours of the pedals that make up the centerpiece of the emblem, the island rose. It's similar to a standard rose, but it's found in the Purerahian blue and a dark pink color exclusively and grows wild along most of Purerah's shores.

I take a deep breath, huffing it out hard and fast as if I'm trying to shove all the air into a staccato note. With a trembling finger, I carefully pop the wax seal away from the paper.

The top pops open effortlessly, making it easy for me to lift it fully to show the neat papers folded underneath. There aren't as many papers as it felt like. The fine paper was so thick.

The application is pretty basic, and I fill out most of it quickly. The main struggle is family history. Mom's parents died when I was young. My grandmother passed before I can remember and my grandfather when I was six. I hardly remember him, but I knew their names. But my Custod family? They couldn't visit for fear of being found. I don't know what to put in their sections. I'm sure Dad made up a good excuse in his application, but I made Mom a promise I plan to keep.

I state I don't know and hope it doesn't cause too much trouble. What would happen to me if my application doesn't even get picked for the first test?

I shove these thoughts aside and hastily sign my name before I panic. I clutch the envelope close, twist on my shawl, and head out the door to put it into the drop box that's at the town square.

Sadly, I am not the only one who had this idea. I suppose with how many girls had gotten their applications on Restoration Day, there had to be many who used the rest to drop them off. We are getting close to the end of the first week.

Girls, all dressed up, are going into the room off the side of the governance building to drop off their applications. I try not to look at any of them, embarrassed by my plain clothes in comparison.

I duck into the room as soon as they're gone. A flash startles me, making me jump harshly, clutching my shawl to make sure it doesn't fall.

A handsome young man is standing there, grinning at me with an impressionor in his hand. He'd just gotten an impression of me. They're taking surprise images.

I blush, anxiety bubbling in my stomach. Others must have known. They got dressed up. I must look so silly in mine; my face was mostly hidden in my shawl. Would that make them not pick me?

The young man beams at me with a huge, warm smile. It matches his warm brown eyes. "Thank you."

"For what?" I manage, trying not to think of Jake's annoyance and Dad's disappointment if I don't get in.

"Not throwing a fit." He smiles back. "Most girls see I took an impression and demand a reshoot. Some do need a reshoot, but I'm not supposed to if I can help it."

He gives me another warm smile, getting me to smile weakly back at him. He tosses his head to get his blond hair out of his eyes before he looks back at the impressionor. "But yours is actually really nice," he assures, "and the most honest. You'll save me having to go over budget."

"I'm sorry to hear that. I hope no one else yells at you. Most of all because the royals won't even give you a fair budget. That puts a lot on you. You must have had a lot of fights."

He laughs, "Not too many. I just tell them we want surprise impressions. And honestly, we do. It's why we didn't mention we'd be taking impressions at drop off. Yours is sweet. I'd show you, but I'm not allowed. I hope you get in." He smiles at me again.

"Thank you. And I hope more girls don't scream at you today," I say. "I'll pray for you to be spared."

The man laughs, "And I'll pray you to get in." His eyes meet mine.

His sincerity strikes me like a blow to the chest. I *just* started and I have people cheering for me? I'm not a real contestant. I'm a plant, a fraud, an insurgent, nothing more. A lie hidden under a pretty face and good acting.

I swallow to try to ease the tight feeling in my chest, as I quickly walk home.

The next day, I am happily distracted by our last set of dress rehearsals before opening day the following week. It keeps us busy, and I do my best to ignore the normal gossip from my fellow performers on break, all obsessed with the Enthronement.

Mom stays late to work on finishing touches, but knowing it's been a hard week for me, encourages me to head on home.

I'm just about home when I feel hands on my shoulders and tense to drive my elbow back into whoever has just assaulted me, but as the person flips me around, I recognize the movement. It's the only reason I don't shove him off as strong lips press themselves to mine.

I want to, though. Or do I? Part of me wants to grab his collar and drag him closer, suck him in and forget what he'd said and wanted and get back the warmth he used to bring to my heart. I want to enjoy feeling his strong arms under my hands as I hold him. I want to enjoy his strong lips, the slight tickle of his stubbly face to bring me joyful-annoyance. I want the romance back.

I don't feel it. I let him kiss me hard, long, and deep, but it just doesn't spark as it did. Would this be how I felt for the rest of my life? Would the romance die? Would the spark I'd manage to light and turn into a fire slowly fade?

I can't let that happen. I finally return the kiss in desperation for the flames to ignite. It doesn't work. The ache is still there. I pull back, using all my acting skills to keep the tears in.

"You did it," Jake says breathlessly. "I can't believe it."

"What?" I frown, and my brows draw together as I look up at him.

"After you left the other night, I thought you couldn't do it. I... but your father said you did it. You're in." Jake is beaming at me as if I'd just told him we were expecting a baby.

I can't understand it. It wasn't like this was going to help us. I'd have to play the girl smitten with the prince. I'd do what he asked and be the girl I had to be.

I look down again. "I had to."

"I wouldn't make you. I didn't bug you about it, did I?" Jake asks, caressing my face.

I shut my eyes to stop tears again. I miss this. I hadn't gone that long without it. I want things to go back to what they were. I want the love back. It was like he wasn't the same person. I know he didn't change, but how I saw him did.

Once, I knew he'd take on the world for me. He'd done just that. He'd gone out of his way, defended me, argued with me, done all that I expected and wanted in my partner, even attempted to give me the dance partner he knew I wanted, no matter how bad at it he was. But now, it felt like it was all a lie. Once, he'd slay dragons for me; now he'd offer me to his enemy.

I leap up to kiss him, fighting for that assurance again.

Jake kisses me back, wrapping his arms around my waist and lifting me closer the way I loved so much. I feel nothing. Just my heart sinking at the lack of passion in me.

I take a breath as he lets go and gently lowers me to my feet. His warm breath, smoldering smile, a hint of more in his eyes: all the things that lit me up before are there. He teases me with a kiss just below my ear then lower to my jaw. It used to make me giggle but makes me feel sick now. What is happening to us?

What is worse, he hasn't changed. He is acting the same. He didn't even notice my tears or tension. I make a little sound he might mistake for a laugh, but it's just the pain escaping. What am I going to do? I was going to be with him no matter what. Enthronement or no Enthronement, the only way forward was with him. What if I never get that feeling back?

"Jake..." I fight for words as I put my hands on his chest, trying to get my head around what's happening.

He keeps his arms around me, waiting patiently with a soft, loving smile on his face. How could it all have died like this?

I can't bear to look as I realize he's catching on. His smile is slowly fading. How could I be so cold to him? He still cares about me, right? He looked it. I feel his concern but knowing what he asked me to do makes his love frightening. Was it even real?

"I don't want to do this." I manage to get out.

"Oh, Kascia, I know." He hugs me tightly. "I understand, and I see why, but... that's what true royals do, right?" I feel his twinge of a forced smile against my ear as he hugs me close. "Sacrifice for their people?"

I nod, biting my lip. "I don't know if I can do this." I don't know if I can keep our relationship alive. I don't know if I can play second fiddle to the mission when I could be sacrificed to it at any moment.

But why is that so bad? That had once been a part of him I learned to love. His dedication to the cause, his desire to save those struggling and starving were part of my love for him. I knew he'd give up anything for them. I guess I never came to grips with the idea I'd be one of those things he gave up.

"Just keep a low profile, make sure they like you enough to keep you around, but do your best not to be noticed," Jake advises. "Other girls will battle for his attention. They'll keep him satisfied long enough for you to skate by until the end of October. That's all you have to do. Impress them enough to get in, but then let the others outshine you, so you can get by. That's all you have to do."

That wasn't what I meant, but I suppose his words are good advice. If I keep low, the prince can't desire me, the royals wouldn't figure out my plot, and I could just endure until I got back to him.

Oh, why does that make my stomach knot? What was I going to curse myself to? "Jake..." I fight for words again. My thoughts race through so easily, but the words to say them are so much harder. "What if I don't come back?" What if I don't come back to him?

"You will." Jake pulls back, taking my hands and looking into my eyes, "You're a perfect fit, Kascia. They can't help but see the princess in you that I do. You'll get in. No one will suspect you. I never could." He smiles and strokes my cheek. I close my eyes, fighting the longing again, the ache for him. I feel the ache, but nothing he does soothes it. What is happening!?

"You'll get in and outsmart them all." He smiles. "You're the smartest person I know and the best actress. No one will see through that beautiful face."

Clearly, neither could he. I force a smile though.

Jake kisses me gently, trying to comfort me. I suck it in, trying, begging him to fill me. It doesn't. It's like no matter how much of him I get, it doesn't fill me. Before, it felt like it never filled me up because I couldn't get enough. But now... it's like no matter how much I take it, it leaks out like a hole had been punctured into my heart.

I pull back, unable to keep the tears in anymore. "I-I'm sorry." He hasn't changed, just me, but it is breaking everything for me and my future... for him and his.

"Hey, it's alright." Jake tries to dry my tears. "I know it's hard. I..." He hugs me tight, "I love you."

"And I love you. I don't know what to do."

"Just do your best. I'm out here rooting for you," Jake promises. "And I'll be ready to storm in and rescue you the moment I can. It's just for a time."

"But you know what I'll have to do." I look up at him.

Jake sighs heavily, "I know. I try not to think about it. It's not something I am excited for. I… I hate thinking about it, but it's the only way to save them." He holds me tight. "I am sorry. I wish I could do it for you."

"I wish I could not hate that you have to ask me to."

Jake's face falls. "Oh, Kascia, I…" He pauses.

"I know. It's selfish," I sigh heavily.

"Still." Jake hugs me tighter. "I understand. But I still love you, I promise."

"The mission just means more."

"Kascia, that doesn't mean you don't matter to me." Jake kisses me deeply, "You matter."

"Just… not as much as this," I accept.

Jake frowns, "It's… not like that. It's just…"

"One for the many." I nod. "A Custod is a shield. I understand."

"Kascia, I can't imagine. I really can't, but that doesn't mean you don't matter. I love you, please, don't forget that." Jake holds my hand tightly. "It's just… has to be done. For them."

"I know. It means the world to you."

"If I could, I'd take it for you," Jake assures me.

"It's already done."

Jake kisses the back of my fingers, clutched tightly in his hand. "You're still not okay with this, are you?"

"Would you?"

"If it defended you and them."

"But it isn't."

"Do you not want to help them?"

I sigh heavily. "I do, but it doesn't make it easy."

"I know." Jake kisses my hand again. "I still love you. I respect you're struggling. Is… can I help at all?" His voice is unsteady, uncertain.

"I don't know," I frown.

He bends down and kisses me deeply. "I know what you may have to do. Your father already spread the story about our breakup and asked me to keep back if the royal family's spies come around, but if you want me to, I'll stay close until you go."

"We don't know I'll get in," I remind him.

He smiles gently, "Yes, we do."

"I don't know what's easier," I confess.

"Will you be okay if we keep that distance?"

Oh, how horrible, yes, I'm alright with it. I bite my lips. "I'm sorry."

"It's okay. If you don't want me to hide—"

"It's alright." I cut him off. "It… might be easier."

"Whatever you need." He kisses my hand again. "I'll see you at the end of October then, promise. I'll come for you. I'll be the first to see you once you let us in."

I nod uneasily. "I-I should head home."

Jake nods, and we walk the short distance past the tree line to the house.

When we get there, he doesn't say anything but kisses me deeply one last time. "I'll see you then," he tries to comfort me. "I love you."

I try to say it back, but the words get caught in my throat. Jake doesn't seem to mind. He strokes my hair, studying me carefully before he turns and slips back into the night.

A tension I didn't know I was carrying drops. Tears fill my eyes. I haven't felt tense around him in years. Now it was back. The work we'd both put in was for nothing. My heart longs for him, but no matter how close he is, the comfort is no longer there. How could I ever get it back? I pray the distance makes the heart grow fonder and more forgiving.

Over dinner, Dad goes over plans, but I can hardly listen. I sigh and put down my fork. I really don't want to force down any more food or even pretend to eat. I'll sit through the plans, but I don't want to fake being hungry. I will have to fake so much in my life from now on, I can decide on the few I refuse to pretend on. And this is one that won't get me in trouble.

Mom notices but doesn't comment. The only sign that she took in what it means is a slight crease forming between her brows.

Dad smiles. "And then it's a holiday wedding."

But then I'd not get to be in the holiday shows. Last year was my last. I wasn't emotionally prepared for that. My heart aches to think I won't be back. I'll be done with the Enthronement. I'll likely be married to Jake and ruling a nation. Oh gosh, I should... If all went according to rebel plans, I should be trying or already be expecting my first child by then.

The thought makes me so suddenly sick I push my plate away. "I-I think I'll get to bed early. I-I've been having trouble sleeping." I get up and give my father my normal goodnight kiss on the cheek before I slip off into my room.

Mom watches me. Normally, I kiss her on the cheek too, but I knew she'd see through my sick feeling and ask.

Instead, I shut my door and press my back against it as if to keep her out, taking deep shaking breaths.

Why did that sudden thought scare me so much? I always knew that would be the plan. I'd thought about it before without hesitation. I guess it's just the fact it's so much more real when there's a time frame. One that include it being before this year is even over. I could be pregnant — in fact, people would hope I was — in just over six months' time. And that frightens me.

I put a hand to my stomach as I take deep breaths. It suddenly became that much more real, realizing these things would and should happen so soon. All of that had been in the far-flung future. Now, they are on top of me. Everything has been thrown in my face, and it's real.

If I hadn't had this revelation about Jake, would I mind? I think this over, and it comforts me to realize, yes. I don't mind the idea of having my first child soon. I am more scared of who the father is.

I take several more deep breaths before I prepare for bed, taking double the amount of tea I normally would in desperation, wondering what the next week holds for me.

Chapter 7

A week of worrying was all it was, as much and as little as it was, before I get my first notification about my Enthronement application. It's an invitation to participate in the first test, a "written test" at the Governance Hall. Thankfully, it's on the first workday, the day before our opening night for *The Hunchback.*

I take extra sleep tea again that night. This is all stressful enough without my sleep disorder becoming a problem. Mom reads my anxiety and tries to calm me down by humming *A Little Lullaby* about the kitchen as I help clean up dinner. I'd never seen it written down. It was just a lullaby passed down through the Custod family. It often helped me calm down when my sleep disorder first manifested itself in my late teens.

I don't know if it helped, but I sleep in as late as I can the next morning. It also gets me out of more drills from my father who is desperately trying to help me prepare.

When I step into Governance Square, I'd have thought it was a festival day again. The city has never been so colorful with how many girls have dressed up trying to look as "princess-y" as possible. The colors are bright, mostly shades of yellow and blue with huge skirts, fancy buns, and far too much pink or red lip and cheek colors.

I'm handed a sheaf of paper and told I can sit outside or wait for an opening inside. I opt for outside, knowing I'll think better in the open air with less of a crowd. I don't expect the test to be hard. They're looking for a spoiled pampered girl to marry their son. It's not like the rotten royals are looking for a girl of substance.

I'm proven right for most of the test. There is a basic reading and writing section, then math, science, even magic. I wonder if this test is hard enough to eliminate enough girls when my face falls as I read the next question:

Two naval commanders report pirates are taking all merchant ships coming from the isles. They were unable to capture the pirates upon first orders. The merchants are ready to riot in the streets if their goods and workers are not guaranteed protection. You've already sent your two best naval ships, but it has not worked. What do you do?

My mouth pops open as I read it five times over to be sure I understood it. I'd not prepared for this kind of question. I didn't think they'd ask anything like this. I look around to see other girls looking at their tests with similar expressions to mine. This is testing our ability to judge and think critically as a ruler should. Not the kind of princess we were expecting them to want.

I take a deep breath and answer the best I can.

I'd set a trap for the pirates. Get a ship that looks like a merchant ship. The ship would be manned only by enchanters waiting in a smaller hidden vessel. They then blow up the ship which would destroy the pirates' ship. I would then see how many survivors we can gather and have them stand trial as well as see if there are more pirate ships. If there are, I would work with my council of enchanters to come up with new traps in case the original plan is found out and the pirates no longer fall for it.

My answer feels a bit rushed and corny, but it's all I can think of. I can at least say I tried. The next question is similar, and the next. There are five questions like this in total. I answer them the best I can with a small prayer in my heart, *Oh please Father, let that be a good answer.*

I groggily get to my feet when I finish, feeling like I'd been running my head against my skull. I wasn't the last to finish, but I certainly wasn't the first either. I hand in my test to a gentleman who smiles at me and tells me the next invitation would arrive in the next few days if I passed.

When I arrive home midafternoon, Dad grills me about the whole thing. I tell him his prep made the first part easy, but I tell him everything and he's surprised by my answers.

At least I finally get to lie down in my bed and try to get my mind to solidify. If that was hard, how had I ever expected to rule even at Jake's side? Who am I kidding? I always knew I was just a tool in the game. I fiddle with the heart ring on my finger as a longing for what had been fills me once again. That happens when I'm alone, trying to fall asleep.

I wildly try to think of anything else to distract myself. But only one question comes up. *What are the royals looking for with those questions?*

Luckily for me, opening night is the next day, so we spend the day doing final run-throughs all morning, taking a break in the afternoon to clear our heads before we come back to put on the show.

It goes as well as ever. The theater is only one-fourth full, with people scattered from the better upfront seats and the cheaper further back seats, but it lets me escape into the world I love most. We all forget the drama of the outside world as we make the audience laugh, cry, and ponder the problems the characters face that are so like our own.

When leaving via the backstage door, a few people are there who want autographs or impressions. I love it when there are people who do. I know a few on sight, our rare patrons who always come to the shows. The mayor always came to the opening nights, and he brought grandchildren this time who are bouncing for happiness for an impression and autograph from "Esmeralda".

I perform every night with matinees at midweek and first rest day as our normal routine. We'll do this show for two months or more depending on demand. I come home for a break after my first matinée to the next invitation resting on the kitchen table.

I read it over and immediately am not looking forward to it. It's a fully paid-for physical. The invitation gives me an exact time, place, and date for my physical. It will be on the last workday, at ten AM. Dad is delighted to see the invitation, but Mom gives me a sad smile. At least she knew it would not be fun.

And it wasn't. On the day of, I arrive, and they bring me into a private area, blocked off with curtains. Each room is sectioned into three, so they can handle as many girls as possible. I had two doctors look me over. The first was a male who does most of it until they have to call in an overworked-looking female doctor. It's supposed to help us be more comfortable, but I don't know if I'd be comfortable either way.

They draw blood, cheek swab, urine sample, and other things I'd never had collected before. It is uncomfortable. It takes a few hours for them to finish collecting it all and testing me. They test me for different allergies, do a cardio test, blood pressure, and everything I've ever seen or heard of.

When I'm done, they tell me if I pass, I'll be given a time for my personal interview by delivery. If not, they'll give me the results of my tests. At least a lot of girls get free physicals out of this. I come out of mine feeling like every inch of me has been poked, rubbed, or swabbed.

I go home and sit on my bed awhile, feeling queasy and a bit violated. I shudder a bit and struggle not to cry but end up crying anyway, though I don't know why. After I cry, I feel better and a bit silly for crying at all.

I try to take a nap, but as always, I can't sleep a wink. Instead, I shudder to recall how used I feel. Today reminded me I'm not a person anymore.

I'm a pawn in the game, even if my position on the board is thought of as high as a queen. I still am little more than an object to be tested, prodded, poked, and played with.

The following days are anxious for my father, and therefore, for me. When will I be interviewed? Will I at all? How many made it to this point? Thousands had applied. Half of the girls who applied from our troupe made it to the physical. Would we all make it to the next round? We were all dancers for a living, so you'd think so. But who knew how our reproductive health was?

It's two weeks before we get the next notification. I have my interview next week. Every girl is assigned a day. We are to arrive in the morning or afternoon time slot and await our turn. If they didn't get to us that day, we'd be asked to return the next day. I hope I don't have to come back on a day I have a matinee. We don't really have understudies. Alsmeria would take my place, but then her spot would be left empty which always causes trouble, most of all when it's in the corps dances.

Mom is so excited I get to meet the royal family. Even if I don't get much further, at least I get to meet them. Dad is just happy I am moving on. He seems sure I'm a shoo-in now, but the paper did say there are four hundred of us left. They are going from four hundred to forty-four. I swallow hard.

On the morning of the interview, I wake up more worried than anything. Mom comes in to help me get ready.

She beams and hugs my shoulders, resting her head on my left shoulder as we look at ourselves in the mirror. "You're beautiful, even before dress and make-up," she smiles. "A true princess isn't just beautiful on the outside. But inside." She hugs me a bit tighter. "Remember that. This test will be superficial, but be a true princess inside, and what should happen will. I trust the Maker and Protector on that." She kisses my head.

"Mama, what if I don't..."

Mom shakes her head. "I want you to focus on your interview today. I'll tell you another time. But today, I want your thoughts on being honest in your interview and learning. An interview like this is two ways. You're interviewing possible in-laws."

I nod in my numb nervousness.

"Good, let's get you dressed." Mom smiles.

When I'm all dressed, I put on my flats and attach my side bag to my skirt. It blends right in and doesn't draw attention. I look like a maiden ready to meet her prince in the forest. I hope it is enough for the king, queen, and prince.

It hits me hard. I'd meet them today. I'd meet *him* today. I might be meeting the man who'd take my innocence from me. The man I'd be setting the assassination for.

I step into the kitchen for breakfast, feeling like I'd rather throw up. I hold a hand to my stomach as if that would comfort it enough to eat.

Today, my butterflies are in full attack mode, fluttering around in a panic to get away before having to meet the prince. They'd not been this agitated since I was a girl doing shows for the first few times. They would go mad just like this. They never went mad over Jake! Even knowing I'd be married to him one day. I need them quiet now. I need to eat.

I look at Mom as she turns to me. "Are you sure you're alright? You've never been this nervous," she says. "Not even opening or closing night."

"I just... I realized I'm meeting him today," I say.

Mom smiles. "I know. It's a frightening feeling. Here, I know what might help." She sneaks me some dark chocolate from her stash. "It won't help you not be hungry, but it always makes me feel better." She winks and hugs me.

Oh, I love my mom! She's the best. I return the hug and enjoy the chocolate while she rubs my back.

When it's time to go, Dad offers me his arm. "I thought I'd escort you."

I smile. He's trying to soothe my nerves by helping me feel special and pretty. It helps to know he's trying. Mom hugs me for good luck before we go.

I feel a rush of panic as I leave as if I'll never be back. I take deep breaths, assuring myself I'm being silly.

Dad doesn't notice. He's still smiling to himself as he escorts me like a lady to the Governance Hall.

We join the queue of girls gathered for the interview.

Some girls, like me, have escorts. Most are on their own, waiting: some reading, watching others, some doing nails or chatting it up. Some wear floor-length gowns. Others look like visiting princesses more than a common girl dressing up as one, having kept their fancy dresses from being gaudy.

Oh no, did I dress too simple in a blue and white frock? Would they look down on me? Of course, a selfish king and queen would. I half want to go home and try again, but Dad doesn't notice my butterflies are scattering again.

Instead, he takes me right up to the man in charge. The man just nods and points to where I can sit and wait, dismissing my father. "You stay here until we tell you it's your turn or we call you back for tomorrow," he tells me. "You may get up for refreshments and the restroom is over there. The only other thing is you need to wear this, so we know who is who."

He holds out a name tag. I take it and put it on my dress just over my heart. It has my name on it as well as a little pink rose. I wonder what that means.

I sit in my chair, cross my ankles, and wait. I wait a long time, watching the other girls. A few are already favorites of the people. I can see a few signing autographs. I even have a few ask me.

As the hours drag on, those crowds start to thin. I sigh and go between reading my book, watching people, and doing a few dance steps to keep myself from getting stiff.

There's a big fuss when a carriage goes through town, towards the castle. It looks like an official trip. I wonder who'd be going to the palace with the royals all here for interviews. Perhaps it's another tax run. I wonder if Jake and his team tried to raid it. My heart aches at the thought of seeing a carriage he may have just been working on.

"Miss." A voice cuts into my musings. I jump and look up to see the man in charge. He smiles at me. "They're ready for you."

Chapter 8

The first thing I notice is the atmosphere of the room. It's not what I expected. The room doesn't have a judgment seat or throne-like chairs. Two comfortable chairs are set in front of a long table with stacks of papers. I recognize them as applications, all marked and color-coded. The light in the room is brighter than I imagined it would be. The king and queen sit there, not looking up at me but at the paperwork. They aren't at all what I expected either.

I'd always imagined the king was a large, imposing, dark-skinned man with a heavy stern brow; the queen equally as tall and imposing with dark skin, looking down from her heavily bejeweled mane of hair and narrow, yet beautiful eyes. I'd pictured their crowns huge, bejeweled to the point of being too big and at least four inches tall.

None of that is true.

Instead, the queen's crown is tasteful: interlocking seashells with pointed tops, almost like leaves, placed in a golded circlet around her head with the traditional gem in the center. Hers is the kingdom color, Purerahian blue. The king wears a crown that's a basic golden color with just a Purerahian gem at the front and wave patterns embossed onto it. Also tasteful, small, and simple.

The only thing about them that matches what I pictured is the queen's lovely dark skin, beautiful like freshly melted chocolate. The queen's dress is surprisingly simple, yet queenly in the elegant cuts and lines and the rich purple matches her nicely. Her age isn't hidden either, but the lines around her eyes don't detract from her soft beauty. Her long, coiled hair is styled so long and perfect most girls with her hair would envy it for days with how long and perfect it was. Not a coil or curl out of place, and it works perfectly with her crown. Apart from that and her wedding ring, she's not wearing a single jewel, but she still looks rich and queenly.

The king is even further from what I imagined. First, he's fair-skinned. His skin tone might even be lighter than mine. I know he was a noble of the people before he married the queen, but most still are darker. He doesn't look dark or intimidating at all. His age also shows with smile lines around his eyes and a bit on his cheeks. He also has one between his brows, like he worries a lot. He has warm eyes that crinkle small when he smiles, which is often in just the few moments I've been watching them.

As I walk in, he smiles slightly in a whispered conversation with his wife. His brown hair has a slight wave or curl to it; I wonder if his staff tried to tame it by straightening it. There's a lot of grays in it too, which contrasts with the gold of his crown, which is slightly crooked. I often forget how old the king and queen are.

I shake my surprise as I dare step into the room. There is a chair across the desk from the king and queen. I bravely walk over to it as my escort closes the door behind me.

I curtsy low to the royal couple as they look up at me. It's a bit bitter to grovel for these people who steal money from my family to make their own fancy clothes while my people starve, but I have to play the game.

As I straighten up, the king beams at me. His eyes crinkle and get a hint of childlike mischief. I can't help but smile. It's warm, inviting, and safe. Like looking at an older brother who would take a dagger for you but loves you by teasing you with his every breath.

I realize he's charming me and immediately rebuke myself. This is the king who's caused the suffering of my people, the one who allowed that man to be shot in Governance Square, and here I was smiling, feeling playful and comfortable with him. How bad of a Custod can I be?

I look over at the queen to try to shake it off. Even when I do, I can still feel that warm, slightly naughty, playfulness coming off the king.

The queen smiles at me as well. Her smile is also warm, but elegant, meant to calm and soothe me. It works a little. But I also see the badly hidden anxiety in her eyes. Am I the right one for her boy?

That reminds me, and I scan the room. The invitation said the royal family. Didn't that mean the prince? I don't see anyone else but the guards. Was he pretending to be a guard? None of the guards look enough like the king or queen.

The king beams at me. "Ah, you noticed faster than most," he says, his voice upbeat and playful with a unique kind of tremor sounding both playful and unsteady. "Yes, Prince Gavril had business to attend to, sadly. I hope that isn't a disappointment. It seems someone thought it funny to say 'royal family' when it was just supposed to be my wife and I." He grins as if he secretly agrees it was a fun idea.

I try and fail to hold back the small giggle. He does have a way about him that appeals to me. What am I doing? This is the enemy. These are the tormentors, but... I just can't see it. They must be the best actors I've ever seen, and I had performed with some of the best in the world.

"Of course, having the whole royal family busy for a day would be hard. I'm sure you have more important things to do." I wish they were doing them. I have to block out those horrible whips in my mind. They could be stopping that. But, I need to impress them. Be honest, but impressive to them, right?

"Yes, getting the castle ready for fifty young ladies is much work," the queen says pleasantly. Her voice is musical. The king stifles a cough into his handkerchief.

I put the pieces together. That carriage. There are real princesses in this competition. One just arrived. The prince is greeting her.

"Yes, I would think he has duties not to offend other nations as they send their daughters to complete," I state.

The king beams again, "So you aren't upset the princesses get to see him first?"

"No. If I'm the one, it won't matter who gets a leg up on me. And if not, then I'll know we weren't right for each other. Besides, you seek a true princess. I presume born princesses get a leg up no matter how hard anyone else tries. So why fight it?" But why get so many common girls to join in the games too? How many born princesses are there? The number forty-four had seemed odd. If they want an even fifty, there are six born princesses.

"Yes, they are skipping the steps you just went through," the king says. "But there also aren't as many of them. Thank you for being patient. Would you take a seat?" The king nods at the chair.

As I do, the king turns to the queen with a smile. "I love being able to do that," he says as if it's a big new treat.

"Hush," The queen sighs, putting her hand in his. "You're the king. Behave like it."

I can't help but smile as my heart aches. I miss that. Their tender love shines in that simple movement. It radiates their love and bond. I'm jealous. I thought I had that. I want it so badly I could be sick then sob.

Thankfully, I snap back to attention as they look back at me. I realize I may have messed up some protocol.

I swallow hard, "Forgive me, Your Highnesses, if I offended you. I only know the proper behavior from my performances."

The queen has her turn to beam. "Not at all. You did perfectly. I almost forgot your profession as an actress." She looks at the paper before her, turning up the page on top. She keeps hold of her husband's hand as she uses her pen to lift the paper.

"Thank you. You know our kingdom would be gemless quickly without your skill and sacrifice," the king says, "And I know that must be hard and... well, tight."

Well, at least he knows how much he steals from us. I smile my best smile, "My honor, Your Highness." I love the job. Not how it enriches him. But I just can't bring myself to dislike him. He's polite and warm like a hearth. He is disarming. The little charmer is getting on my nerves because he's not getting on my nerves. What's wrong with me?

"Well, we better get into it and not waste time," the queen says, looking back up.

I only just hold back a laugh, covering my mouth as the king turns to her with a slight pout, making duck lips and creasing his brow as if begging permission to do something. I think he's trying to get her to relax.

How could the wicked king be this man? I knew he was, but... it just seems so out of character for a king who takes and takes from his people to now be giving his queen duck lips.

My eyes flicker to their hands. He squeezes her hand. He's so tender with her. They're so united. It pulls at my heart. I miss Jake as I look at their intertwined hands.

The king turns back to me. "You have been waiting a long time. We'll try to make sure it's worth the wait," He say as if making a declaration instead of just suggesting.

"Well, so have you. You've done dozens of these interviews," I say. "And you've looked for a princess for so long. You've been waiting."

The king and queen stare at me for a long moment. I flush. Why did I say that? I couldn't help but think of how long they'd been sitting there as well. How long they'd looked for a bride for their son. I really need to stop putting myself in people's shoes. Bad habit from trying to learn characters, I suppose.

"Yes, we have." The king smiles softly, studying me. I swallow back my feelings. I think I'd just brought him genuine comfort. "It hasn't been easy. Some of these interviews have been a nightmare."

"And we want to make sure our son is looked after," the queen says. Then her face falls just a moment. She realizes I'd disarmed them. I didn't mean to. Oh no, what had I done? I messed it all up.

"Thank you for understanding. We'll try to do the same for you." The king smiles at me to let the queen compose herself. "We will try to keep this simple for you. After the complicated tests," the king chuckles, coughing a little again, "which you did very well on by the way." The king looks down at the papers. "I was just reviewing your test. I am quite impressed."

My heart glows, "Really?"

Why am I flattered by him? He's the monster making the hell outside. I berate myself inside while keeping my face and posture completely composed. I'm such a weak Custod.

The king smiles and nods. "Shows insight I've not seen much of. But it did leave me with some questions I wanted to ask you."

I nod to him to go on.

"How do you ladies stay so beautiful with all the work you do all day? I mean, your feet must get so tired," the king says, suddenly very animated in his speech, leaning forward in pure interest.

The queen sighs and rolls her eyes, pulling the king back into a proper sitting position by the shoulder with a gentle hand. "Aster," she says warmly, but warningly.

"What? It's a legitimate question. She dances on her toes doing things that would make you or I pant like a dog, but she makes it look easy and graceful," the king insists.

"Not now, Aster." She sounds just like my mother telling off any of her actors.

The king sighs in defeat and leans back. "Alright, later," he alleges to me.

I can't help but giggle. I am falling for it. How would I survive months like this? I kick myself inside but keep it hidden under the giggle.

I'm starting to panic. What if I really can't do this? If I get close just in the interview, how could I ever get myself to do what has to be done? Honest fear makes my heart pound against my chest threatening to burst my corset. I have to remember what they caused.

"Much later," the queen says warningly, giving her husband a sideways look. The queen's next question startles me from my thoughts. "Why do you want to marry my son?"

I didn't have an answer to this. I panic, but I find myself speaking. "Honestly, my queen, I don't really know. No one knows your son, honestly. And I..." What am I saying? The truth. I swallow. "And I want to see where this takes me. What if I am the one for him? What if he is for me? I want to see where this takes both of us."

"Do you want to be princess then?" the king asks.

"Well... yes and no. I... I see how my people suffer, Your Highness. And I just want to help."

Oh my vene! What am I doing? I'm being too honest. What kind of magic is he using? But it felt so good to be honest. I really do like the king. I feel like I can tell him anything. What kind of trickery is this!?

"As princess, I can help them," I go on as my mind races. "I want to help them. I think I really can be a good princess and help them. And you. And your son. But I won't know unless I try. So, I'm trying."

The king smiles gently at me. The queen doesn't show the surprise on her face, but I can feel it. "What does it mean to you to be a princess?" she asks.

I expected that kind of question from the king, not the queen. I smile a little. This is much easier to get into.

I reply with perfect poise, "She's a servant of her people. She's a queen-in-waiting. She does her duty to her people, her king, and her queen. She assists the queen in her duties as asked. She also is a symbol of her people to her people as well as to the world. She must honor that as well as do her duty."

"What do you think the princess's duty is?" the king asks.

"That depends," I reply. I had studied for this question in the written test, "Each princess is different. A crown princess's main duty would be to prepare to be queen and in finding a good husband who would be a good king. A princess not in line for the throne would be mostly duty-bound to assist the current queen as asked as well as support her people and royal family in any other ways she can.

"But as you said 'the princess', I imagine you mean the princess you are looking for. In that case, her first duty is to her prince, the king-in-waiting. To help him with his duties and to help him and herself prepare for their royal duties as king and queen one day. And if she is someone like me, learning the more detailed duties of a princess and one day queen."

The king is beaming at me. I can't help but return it, though I try not to. I can tell he genuinely likes me. My heart glows. He likes me. Wait, that should be exciting because it means I'm winning, not because I like him.

Curse it, I was wrong. Even with a good answer, he's throwing me off again. All the Custods past forgive me. I'm such a disgrace. I blink before tears can even try to form.

I pause then get the courage to ask, "Why are you asking me this?" I'm impressed their questions are actually substantial.

"We are looking for a true princess. Not just a pretty face," the king says. "Not that it doesn't help." He winks. I smile. "You're smart and sexy."

The queen's face fills with horror, shock, and a bit of anger, and she hits the king's arm, surprisingly hard. I jump as he winces and laughs, coughing into his handkerchief again as he playful flinches away.

I'm blushing bright red, unsure what to say in response to that. I look down at my hands on my lap. I'm flattered, embarrassed, amused, and confused. How are these people the same ones sending children to be caned because they pickpocket to survive?

"But back to the point," the king tries to direct the queen's anger elsewhere. "Where were we?"

"Um..." Calling me attractive and smart.

"Asking important and substantial questions." The queen gives her husband a pointed look, the closest to what I'd imagined she'd look like before she turns back to me and smiles. Her smile is sweet, soothing, and screams "forgive my nuts husband".

She asks more questions, and I reply with perfect poise while inside I'm terrified I'm saying everything wrong. I look from the king to the queen, trying to see if my answers are still good. They glance at one another, but I can't read their silent communication fast enough before they look back at me. It's like they are competing, not me.

"Well, you show your ability and desire to handle royal life well," the queen says, brushing down her skirts as a distraction.

Am I making her nervous? What had I done? Or is the king known to lie about with younger women? Oh vene, and I thought I only had to worry about the prince getting too close. Is that why she's upset I'm doing well?

"But you didn't have much to say when I asked why you wanted to marry my son. You said something about wanting to see where it leads? Did you just mean royal life?"

I pause for a moment as I think about it. "No, not entirely." Mom's words come back to me. Her warning is to use this as a way to escape. To find my own way. I don't plan on it but knowing I could is wonderful. "I can't say I know your son. I've never even heard of him leaving the castle to see his people before. No one really knows him. And I would like the chance to. He's dealing with something not too different from me in my life. A big change. He's looking for a bride and to start taking part in ruling the kingdom. That's not easy."

"What do you mean like you?" the king asks gently.

The answer spills out before I can think about it. "My whole life was planned for me. I was alright with that. I thought I'd be about to start my own family and life then it all changed. I don't know where I'm going now. And I thought this would be a good next step to find how I can help people and move forward. I..."

My throat catches, thinking of the last time I saw Jake. I miss him. I miss knowing what life held for me. I miss feeling safe to love him. I had everything flipped upside down on me without warning. "If I can help someone who's as confused as me and help my people, why not?"

The king smiles. "Why not, indeed."

"So, you don't find my son attractive?" The queen presses.

My suddenly loose tongue gets worse. "How can I?" Some of the fear I'd held inside comes out without warning. "I can't exactly say I gush over his beautiful eyes. I don't even know what color they are. No one has ever seen him."

The king loses it. He bends over in laughter, coughing a bit as he tries to pull himself together. His laugh is warm and contagious. I chuckle but manage to hold most of my laughter in. I bite my lips, scared of my outburst. The queen watches her husband with a disapproving, yet amused look. They are the reverse of my parents. My mother would be laughing while Dad told her off.

They aren't so stiff or different from any other family I'd spent time with. My stomach knots. And my main goal is to help my friends assassinate them? That can't be right. But... they did cause all this suffering with their heavy taxes and hoarding all the money. I saw the whippings and heard their cries. The king and queen made those.

I want to save the people from them. From... a man bent over laughing at my rather rude quip to his wife. From this queen hiding her frustration with the grace of a swan. Yes, I have to save them from... these two.

I frown deeper. I'm missing something. I have to be.

"Forgive me." I flush slightly. "I didn't mean to offend. I just... I wish I could answer that question you keep asking me, but as a people, we have had little introduction to your son, Your Highnesses. That's all I meant." *Please don't realize I'm a rebel and have me whipped or hanged or worse.*

"It's quite alright. You have a fair point, Miss..." The king's eyes float down until they find my name tag. "K-Kascia?" He tries. I nod. "Good. You have a point, Miss Kascia. We are just trying to make sure we are finding girls honest of heart for our son, and not just after the crown."

I smile a bit. "I would surely hope it would be more than that. If not, then I'm alright losing." Why do I keep saying these things? True or not — and they mostly are — it's dangerous. My heart slams into my ribcage with each beat, begging me to stop before they stop it beating.

Even the queen manages a smile at that. Had I done a good job? Had I left a good impression? I have to stand out against four hundred other girls. But to do what? To then turn on these people and let my friends murder them and their son? Could I do that now I'd met them? I had to.

I need to remember why I hated them only moments ago. I need to remember why I am doing this. I lost Jake; I never really had him, though I'm bound to him still. I have to recall why I hate them, why I need to hate them, why that has to come back this instant, or I'll be in far worse danger.

"A powerful sentiment," the king says.

"I agree." The queen looks like the words are bitter on her tongue. "Thank you for your very thoughtful answers. I'm afraid that's all the time we have. We'll contact you soon if you're to come to the palace on the big day and given directions if you pass."

I bow my head in thanks and stand up. The king stands at the same time. The queen takes her husband's offered hand as she stands.

"Thank you, Miss Kascia." The king smiles that warm smile. His eyes sparkle with mischief. "I believe I'll see you soon." The queen glares at him, but he just smiles and kisses her hand as the guard sees me out.

I watch them until the door closes. My heart aches for what I see. I miss Jake being that tender. I rub the back of my own hand as I allow the guards to see me out. One asks for my name tag, and I offer it to him. He takes it back into the room with the king and queen. I keep my eyes down.

All I can think about is how I'll never have that again. I'm stuck with Jake, but the truth is Jake didn't look at me like that. He didn't have that warmth. I thought he did, but I just... wanted it to be. I long for the relationship I just saw. The warmth, the love, even the teasing and arguments appeal to me. I want it so badly. My whole body aches. I squeeze my hand shut, letting the fingers of my other hand keep teasing the skin on the back of my fingers.

Chapter 9

The next three weeks drag by. I'm sure it takes a long time to get from four hundred girls down to forty-four, but it's nerve-wracking, nonetheless. I do my shows, and Dad gives reports on what the newspapers are saying. He calls the papers a "collection of lying trash", but he still carefully monitors what they say. Most of all, he pays attention when it reports on the war, like progress on rebels taking northern cities or even flooding that happens. The papers also confirmed I was right. Six born-princesses were included in the Enthronement's Chosen ladies.

We had set the final performance for our current show for the end of the new month as the numbers weren't showing any reason to carry it on any longer than that. Plus, knowing if any of the girls who'd applied for the Enthronement in the theater could get in, and therefore, couldn't do any more shows. Mom is struggling to figure out what show to work on after the short break for the same reason. Should she keep the old plan or change it? It only added an extra layer of tension those three weeks.

My sleep is starting to be affected. Even with all the sleep tea I take, it's hard to fall asleep or stay asleep. Even though the first workday is my day off, I find myself waking up at an earlier hour many mornings. I decide I need to get some fresh air and get ready for the day.

I'm dressed and just tying off my hair when there is a knock at the door. I'm the only one up as we typically sleep in because our jobs have us up late at night. The person is lucky I'm awake.

I open the door as I finish tying off my hair. A lady stands there. She beams up at me and gives me a bob of a curtsy. "Miss Kascia?" she asks.

I nod, shaking out my hair and fussing with it a bit to ensure it's not too tight.

"Perfect!" the lady beams then offers me an official-looking letter, just like the ones that announced the next test. "This is for you. Congratulations!"

I frown as I take the letter. What is this? I'm too sleepy to take in what's happening.

The lady doesn't leave, waiting patiently with a smile, hands behind her back in a proper pose, swinging a little from side to side.

I figure she wants me to open it, and I give her a sleepy smile. I use a finger to push open the Purerahian blue seal. It snaps perfectly with a graceful pop, and the letter unfolds on its own elegantly, showing it was just folded into the envelope rather than being stuffed into one, just like the others.

Congratulations!

You are chosen for the Enthronement

Instructions on preparing for your move to the palace are enclosed.
You are assigned Chosen number 12.

We wish you the best of luck and heartfelt congratulations on getting this far.

For proving yourself worthy, you and your immediate family will be awarded a class of nobility. You and your family are now Lords and Ladies of Purerah. We welcome you to the family of nobility.

King Aster
Queen Dalilly

I almost drop the letter as numbness fills my body. I gape at the paper. A mix of emotions stirs inside me like watching different colored powders being slowly stirred into clear water. Excitement. I made it! Fear. Can I do this? Anxiety. Can I go through with it? Hope. What if Mom is right? And a strange one. Peace. I feel this is meant to be. It's like getting this letter calmed all the insanity of the last few days.

I jump as I hear a snap. I look up to see the girl had taken my impression.

"You all like surprise impressions, don't you?" I say.

"Yes, well, the first was the king and queen's idea, but this was an order from Sir Sage," the messenger says. "He said he wanted to see the faces of the girls."

I frown, "Sir Sage?"

"You'll find out," the messenger beams. "Expect the first round of your transition team to arrive this afternoon."

This afternoon! So soon?! My eyes fly wide, but I nod numbly. How soon would we be expected to move in? They don't have a solid understudy for me. Not to mention, I'm not ready to just take off at the drop of a hat.

I may have known this was coming, but numb shock is making an odd tingling sensation through my body.

My heart beats in panic. The orange-red anxiety starts to take over the colors mix inside me. I am not sure I am ready to do it all in one day. But there's no way Dad is going to help me delay it.

"Read the rest of the instructions then you should be ready for them," the girl says. "I'll see you around the palace." She bows to me then leaves, skipping in her excitement. Off to report to this Sage, whoever he is.

It's real. I made it. It's official and inescapable now. I didn't let anyone down. Not yet, but I greatly fear I'm going to. I'm going to live in the palace. I'm going to have to pretend to be the prince's girl. I was chosen for the sacrifice.

I finally manage to close the front door and collapse into my seat at the table, just staring at the invitation and reading it over and over and over.

After at least an hour, likely more, I recall she said further instructions were enclosed. I unfold the last section that didn't pop open on its own, revealing another folded bit of parchment.

The instructions don't give a lot of detail, saying today the security team will go over my protection before I enter the palace. The date I will be taken to the palace is first August. I have just about a month before the world changes. At least our final show was the day before. According to the instructions, over the next few weeks, different teams and officials would be coming from the palace to give me instructions and explain the rules and plans for when I move into the palace.

For likely another hour, I numbly read over the formal invitation and the instructions. Everything was about to change for good. I don't know if I'm excited or devastated. But deep down, from the moment I realized Jake's love wasn't true, the world had crumbled. The fear was what would I be forced to become?

"Kascia?" Mom's voice cuts into my musing. "What are you doing? Normally you're on your walk by now. Is something wr—" She stops abruptly when she sees the papers in front of me. A tiny gasp escapes her, tensely waiting for what I'm about to say. When I don't speak, she carefully goes on, "What test is next?"

I swallow hard. "I... I-I'm moving."

Mom's gasp of excitement is stronger, and she comes over to see the formal announcement I'm holding up.

Dad enters the room behind her. "Where did you get that?" he asks me, watching Mom nervously. He must not have heard our conversation.

"I went to go for a walk this morning and a messenger was waiting."

Mom hands the announcement to Dad, hardly holding in her smile. I can hardly look at them.

Dad reads it, and a smile slowly climbs his lips. "She did it! I knew you would." He beams and hugs me. Mom, still beaming, hugs me too.

When they let go, I immediately blurt out, "Papa, we need to talk." I have to tell him about how I felt in the interview. Not wanting to disappoint my parents and ashamed of how they'd tricked me, I hadn't admitted the royals charmed me, but now, I have to get it off my chest. I need help if I'm going to survive their charms for three months.

"Oh, alright." Mom frowns, a hint of disappointment in her eyes. "But please be quick." I feel guilty for making her feel left out, but she never was much for our duty as Custods. It's Dad's solid faith I need right now.

"Let's go outside." Dad puts an arm around me and leads me to the training arena. I sit on the fence. Dad paces in front of me.

My hands clench the wood on either side of me, head bowed as I fight for the words. Dad lets me sit quietly before speaking. "You know you can tell me anything."

I take a deep breath, "I'm scared. I'm scared I can't go through with it."

Dad's face falls. "Why?" His voice is full of compassion though.

"They... I've met them," I look up at my father, "and they weren't evil, Papa." I tell him about how they held hands, how they teased me and one another, how their questions were good questions looking for a true princess, not what I thought they'd want. A girl who would help their son and their people.

"How could someone like that be evil? I know they must be good to trick so many, but I just... I couldn't see it. I found myself wanting a relationship like theirs, Papa. It made me miss Jake so bad it hurt. I know they likely were putting on a show, but... but Papa. How can they be evil? What if I can change their minds? What if there is someone else tricking them? What if..." What if I'm just a horrible Custod and I can't do the job?

"Kassie." Dad puts his hands on my shoulders, so I can meet his eyes. "I know it's hard," he says slowly and carefully, "but don't worry. You'll see the truth as you're there. Just hold to the truth you know. Remember that burned district? Remember the flooded town in last week's paper? He did those. The king ordered those, Kassie. Just remember those moments. I can promise the king did them. I saw it and know others who saw even more atrocities." Dad's eyes light up. "Hold on."

He goes back to the house, leaving me anxiously swinging my legs against the fence. When he returns, he offers me an envelope. "I keep them to help me, but I think for this mission you'll need them."

I grab my second envelope of the day today and open it. I gasp in horror and look away. Inside were impressions: horrible impressions, images of burned homes, bodies, and blood-soaked battlefields. All things I'd never seen and never wanted to see.

"No, I know it's hard, Kascia, but you have to look." Dad takes my hands, so I meet his eyes. His eyes then guide me back to the impressions that he starts flipping through. I tense with each horrible one and want to throw up and send these horrible images into the sea where no one would have to see them again. Why would he make me see this?

"This is what they did. Remember that," Dad says, his eyes shining with pain and compassion. "I know it's hard, but it's the truth, and we have to stop it."

But I can't help but question if it's true. Did that sweet couple I'd met really call for this? The king would just laugh, and the queen would smack him for treating it like a joke. I feel sick and put a hand to my mouth. How can this be true? It conflicts in my mind and leaves me more confused than ever.

I wish I had something to say, but I don't want to see more, so I have to pretend it's what I needed. I force a smile, the way I do on stage even when I have had a bad day. "Thanks, Papa; this does help." It helps remind me I'm terrible at this and need to work harder to understand. I have to do this, even if I hate it.

"Good, I'm sorry it has to be like this." Dad kisses my head and hugs me tight. "I wish I didn't have to ask it of you, Kassie. I love you very much, my cygnet."

"I-I love you too, Papa." I know how it is. Duty comes first. I don't even come first to my father, no matter how much he wants to put me first. I fight tears as Dad pulls back and brushes my hair from my face.

"Well, let's get you breakfast. Then you'll be ready for your first round of orientations." Dad smiles. I laugh a watery laugh.

We go inside and have breakfast. Mom can tell I'm a bit down, so she tones down her excitement. I can tell she's holding it in. I can also tell she's worried about what Dad and I spoke about.

Dad is worried the guards may recognize him from a raid. Though he and his people always wear masks, he thinks it's safer if he's out of the house when they arrive.

I meet my first aid from the palace, my head guard, Lila. First, she covers the security details between now and when I'll move into the palace. They won't formally announce the list of Chosen girls until the end of this week, but as they don't forbid us from telling friends or family, they're sure word will spread fast on its own before it's confirmed. They fear as soon as our names are known rebels will try to launch protests or attacks on us.

To protect us, they will have two palace guards stationed outside our home. They also will have one or both of those guards escort me anywhere I need to go outside of the main city and one city guard will keep an eye on me in town. Their main worry is the theater, so, until the end of my show, one of the guards will escort me from the theater to home each night.

Once inside the palace, there are strict rules to keep us safe as rebels tried to get into the palace "often". I know they never get into the palace as Jake's friends always complained about it, and I knew Dad's men never did. And heaven knows the protestors that make up the Potentate rebellion is too disorganized to have a hope of breaking the well-guarded palace walls.

But even with that in mind, I am not allowed outside without permission and a guard with me. I am not permitted to invite anyone into the palace, and I am not allowed to leave the palace unless dismissed by the royal family for failing to pass a test. That one scares me a little. If I changed my mind, I couldn't just leave? Mom's nervous eyes reflect the same feeling.

Once Lila covered all those details, she introduces me to the two guards who'll be on my watch during the day. My night watch will switch off regularly to ensure no one is overtired from too many night shifts. The eight of them are also introduced to me so I'll know them when they come, so I'm less likely to fall for a rebel trap. Not that I wouldn't likely know a rebel on sight.

The guards officially start the next day, and Lila will come and run security on the day they pick me up to take me to the palace, but she tells me to reach out to her if I have any questions or need any changes.

Lila is warm and friendly and makes me feel a little better. Mom keeps looking at her as if wondering if she know her. She looks familiar to me as well, but I can't place it and am too nervous to ask.

The next day, the chief of staff, Lady Hydie, comes in the morning to go over the main rules of the Enthronement. She's a happy blonde woman with her hair in a sweet little ponytail. When she arrives, she's twittering in excitement like a little blue bird matching the uniform she wears a blue blazer, skirt, and pumps, all with yellow trimming, and a yellow blouse under her jacket.

She tells me the basic rules: the king and queen can only dismiss me if they can prove I failed a test: the prince can dismiss me at will. She also reviews the titles I could be awarded if I make it into the top twenty-five or top ten.

Then she covers the newer rules. If I'm caught fighting or sabotaging the other girls intentionally, I will be dismissed.

I am not to seek out one on one time with the prince or request time with him. The prince will seek out time with me when it's time to do so.

As part of the security protocol, I am only to wear the uniform which is to be a black skirt and white button-up shirt with black flats or clothing made for me by the palace. I am also not to eat anything not made by the palace staff. I am not allowed to bring any weapons or possibly dangerous possessions with me. All I may need will be provided.

I dare ask about my dance gear. Hydie asks me to give her a list and she'll check with the advance staff to see if the palace could provide it all, and if not they'd give me a list of the things I am allowed to bring from home. My pointe shoes are at the top of my list. I'd rather not have to break in several new sets.

For security reasons, I also am required to follow the guards' orders to the letter. Failure to do so may result in my being eliminated, but I do notice it is not an immediate disqualifier. As a part of that, I also will only be allowed in certain areas of the palace. As the number of girls decrease, other rooms will open up to us. When we arrive we'll be given a tour of the palace and shown those areas.

"Then of course, if you win, you will then marry Prince Gavril and become crown Princess of Purerah and take on all the duties associated therewith. And you cannot leave the palace unless dismissed for failing a test or being one of the prince's eliminations." Hydie wraps it up in a neat little bow with the happiness of a bird singing over its freshly finished nest. "All that's left to do is sign this final agreement which shows you agreed to adhere to all the rules and accept the consequences thereof, and if you win, to marry our prince and become our princess."

With a shaking hand, I take the paper Hydie offers me. I skim it over, checking for the points Hydie mentioned are there without any tricks then sign it, my hand shaking as I pull back the pen and push it across the kitchen table to Hydie.

"Excellent!" she tweets and accepts the paper, rolling it up and sealing it. "The king, queen, and prince will sign in their spots at the bottom this evening. If you ever want to review the copy, please let a member of your staff know. I have other girls to visit and a train to catch."

Hydie stands up, puts the contract away, and claps it shut with a harsh snap. "Good luck, Lady Kascia. I'll see you on the first!" And with a huge beam and wave at Mom and I, she leaves with her three guards.

The next day, I have to request they don't send any more staff as I have my afternoon and evening show that day. The palace staff accommodates me without complaint. But the following day is a long one.

I don't know what this team is officially called, but in my mind, I call them the beauty team. The first thing they do is measure every inch of me, head to toe, shoulder to shoulder, waist, leg length, bust, hips, foot size, and everything in between.

The girl who measures my feet giggles at how small they are and makes a Cinderella joke. The team laughs, and I give a half chuckle. I'd heard these jokes most of my life. They used to be funny; now they're just old. I don't mind them, but I don't think there's a foot joke I haven't heard a dozen times.

They then run a few different kinds of combs through my hair as if testing it, making notes about its texture and length. They ask me about my normal skincare routine and my skin type, also feeling it with my permission and making notes about it. They ask me a few more questions like if I'm allergic to anything, preferences I have for hair or make-up, and things like that. It takes most of the day before they wrap up.

I'm starting to feel overwhelmed and exhausted. I have these orientations then my shows each night. The shows themselves are an escape from the madness of my new world as a Chosen. My friends are over the moon for the most part. Alsmeria's only disappointment is she didn't get in too. I can hardly imagine how wonderful and horrible it would be. Fun to have a friend. Horrible to know she'd be in danger once I let my fellow rebels in.

Every morning, I have a different crew come in to prepare me. One team covers how I am to handle the press during, before, and after the Enthronement. They could have just summarized it. Before and after, not a word to the press until the whole thing is over. During, I am not to comment to the press unless I have to as part of the Enthronement process.

My guards check in with me throughout the day at regular points. Mom is starting to call them by their first names and offer them random treats when they are on break. I think she'll miss them when they're gone. Dad is nervous around them and tries to keep out of their way, but I don't think any of them have a clue who he is.

At the end of the week, the names of the Chosen girls are announced. In the following weeks, our shows are packed to capacity for the first time in years. It's not just the normal tourist crowd that makes up about fifty percent of our audience this time of year, but all the locals who saved to see the girl who might become their princess on stage, perhaps for the last time.

It makes getting home take even longer as I can't resist signing autographs and taking impressions even though the crowds get bigger by the day. It makes my guards nervous, and they increase my guard leaving the theater to five.

On rest days, I get a break from the orientation teams, but I still have my shows. Devotion day is the first truly quiet day I've had since the letter arrived. I go for a walk along the river and along the beach for as much of the day as I can, just trying to get some distance. My guards respect this and keep as far back as they can and pretend they aren't there, but I know. And it makes it all the harder.

The next week is much the same. I try to walk and be alone as much as I can on the first workday as it's my only non-devotional day off, but the press is trying to get to me. I let my guards handle them at first, but one young reporter will not let up.

I watch, blank-faced as my guard orders him away. "Come on, just one comment," the reporter begs.

"No, they are forbidden to speak to you. Now for the last time, go home." My guard's tone is fed up, tired of this type of treatment. All the press argue and try to slip past them, but none succeed.

"Alright, alright," the reporter waves the guard down and turns around as if to leave. But then he does a double-take and tries to juke around my guard on his left-hand side.

My guard is swift, catching the reporter by the front of the shirt and tossing him forcefully into a tree. The reporter hits it so hard the tree shakes enough to drop a few leaves.

"Leave now!" my guard barks, pointing the blunt end of his spear at the reporter.

The reporter looks down at the point then at the guard, waving his hands as if agreeing, but the moment the fool is on his feet he tries to dodge my guard on the right-hand side this time. My guard swiftly pulls up the butt of his spear and smacks it into the reporter's face, knocking him back.

My guard gets into a stance I know, to drive the blunted end into the reporter's stomach to drive him back.

"Stop!" I rush between them before I can think. I'm done watching the guards abuse my people. "You don't have to beat him." I glare at my guard, who'd frozen to stop himself from striking me. "I know you have to stop him, but please stop it. There's no need to pummel him." As I'd seen guards do many times when a fool pushed the limits. Our guards have very short limits.

The guard pulls back his weapon, places the end in the dirt, and bows to me like I'd seen them do to their superiors many times. "Yes, my lady."

It's such a strange feeling to have the guard bow to me like that. I have authority now. He has to listen to me. The weight of authority pushes down my shoulders, forcing me into a proper position.

I nod, trying to hide my nervous swallow. "Let's go home." I try to sound as full of authority as I am, but my voice betrays a soft nervousness.

My guard bows his head to me and nods me to lead the way, so he can remain between me and the reporter. I do, but glare back at my guard to make sure he doesn't try something while my back is turned. The guard does not move to hurt the reporter or even look at him. He bows his head to me, and we walk back to the house.

I shut myself into my room, not speaking to anyone as I struggle with the realization of what has happened to me. Before I even stepped foot in the palace, I was given power. This power protected someone, but not enough to make the needed changes. The authority makes me feel sick.

I am convenient. They haven't picked me for queen for any other reason than my bloodline, sex, and how easy it is to set me up for power. I never realized how much the power they'd make me take would make me feel. I have the ability but not the power to use it. I hate what my life has become and even more what I'm becoming.

I struggle through more orientations, one each morning. They give me a list of approved things I can bring from home, and Mom works to help me negotiate double of listed qualities, most of all pointe shoes as those will be hard to get without a good staff, and who knows what kind of staff I'll get. The idea I'll have staff makes me want to vomit.

Two weeks before I leave, my orientation is rather unique. I'm presented with a uniform I'm to wear when I arrive at the palace and several items I'm to add to it. One is a flower I'm to wear behind my right ear, enchanted to be ever-living. The other is a stunning bronze or perhaps copper necklace with an adjustable chain. The pendant has my name and Chosen number on the back. On the front is a unique symbol, an island rose nestled in a phoenix nest. I can only tell it's a phoenix nest because there are small cassia flowers in it. Phoenixes make their nests out of cinnamon plants.

"This is your Chosen mark," the lady explains. "You're to wear it at all times. You may pin it to your dress or wear it on any chain of your choice, but it must be visible around the top half of your chest, so don't turn it into a ring or bracelet or anything not easily seen."

Nametag. It's a fancy nametag. I nod as I study the craftsmanship. It's a pretty piece. Simple but well made. The chain is sturdy. I keep it safe inside its box until the day I have to wear it.

This all blurs into all too long and yet all too short of a month until it's the final day. On the morning of my last day, the final team comes to review everything with me and make sure I don't have any more questions.

The gentleman who reviews security with me asks me to see him out to make sure we have a moment alone. "If I may, ma'am," he says to me quietly. "Just some advice. If you want to win this, whatever you do, do not deny the prince anything. If he asks you out, never refuse, if he asks you to wear a certain dress, do not refuse. No matter what he asks of you, do not refuse. Do you understand?"

I do. I nod, feeling sick. My father, Jake, and now this castle attendant are all warning me to be prepared to give the prince whatever it takes to stay in. *Get by three months. It's just three months.* I repeat to myself as the official congratulates me and wishes me luck before leaving.

That night is bittersweet. It's our closing night, and the theater is full. And so is my heart but of what, I don't know. This very well could be my last moment on the stage. I give it my all and have tears in my eyes as I take the final bows and make sure our orchestra gets their due.

Then it's hugs and well wishes from my entire cast and crew. Alsmeria is teary-eyed too. "You'll be princess before I see you again," she complains, making me feel sick. I'd be queen.

Max teases me about making sure the prince doesn't get mad at him when he finds out how many times he's been allowed to kiss me. I just force a smile. I force a smile for all of them and pretend to be excited. I can't be further from excited. This, the thing I love most, is about to be stolen from me along with all my freedom of choice. I'll have to play the puppet and do whatever the palace asks me to. Then whatever Jake asks for the rest of my life.

Then I get a moment alone with my father and Mom. Dad is worried the palace guard will recognize him when they come to pick me up, so we're saying our farewell in my dressing room before I head home.

Dad beams at me, cupping my cheek in his hand, "You'll do wonderfully. I love you so much. I'm so proud." He hugs me tightly. "And no matter what, you're my princess."

That hits a deep core in me, and I smile through tears. "I'll miss you, Dad, but it won't be long, right?"

"Right," Dad promises and hugs me tightly. "See you soon, cygnet."

"See you soon." I choke out through my tears. Who knows when I'll see him again? Will I see him again? Of course, I will. But will we be the same? I feel like this is the final goodbye.

Dad doesn't though because he kisses my forehead and then leaves as if I'm just leaving for the weekend.

I stand a bit defeated. I just hope I'm just overanxious and all will be normal before long.

Mom gives me a sad smile and a quick hug before we have to face the crowd of people waiting outside to see me. This group is bigger than ever and every guard assigned to me is working hard to protect me. I sign autographs, pose for impressions, and keep the smile I always have and it's not as fake. I love meeting fans, but this will be the last time. I fight to keep that sadness from intruding on the moment.

Finally, we get through them all and get home. The moment we have privacy in the house, Mom sighs and hugs me, "You did amazing. You likely helped us fix up half the theater and more."

"Thanks, Mom," I beam. Even if the rest of this is a mess, at least we were able to make some real capital off my getting into the Enthronement.

We spend the rest of the evening finishing my packing which doesn't take long. Then I enjoy some hot chocolate with Mom. Our last night. It is nice to just sit and enjoy talking.

Mom and I review how the show went and make notes for other shows in the future. I wonder if I lose if the theater will still do as well. Then I recall either way, I won't be performing again. No matter what, I'll be queen or something else. My heart sinks.

But Mom catches on and talks of happy things to cheer me up. She tells me what I need to write home about: what the other girls are like, what the prince is like, what kind of food they serve, what I get to wear. Things like that.

I will make sure to write to her about all those things, but now comes the real test. Tomorrow, I'll no longer be just a dancer. I'll be a Chosen Daughter of Purerah. Let the games begin.

Chapter 10

I wake in the morning with an empty, painful ache in my gut. I dress in the uniform and do my make-up as I normally do: simply. I twist my hair into my favorite braid to keep the flower in my hair. I carefully pin the flower into place, studying myself in the mirror.

If not for my flower and Chosen necklace, I look like I'm about to try to apply for a job somewhere. White shirt, black skirt, and shoes, I look all business. Plain. I sort of am applying for a job, just the biggest job in the kingdom, if not the world.

I stare at my reflection for a long time, that ache nibbling at my stomach. I jump when someone knocks on the door. I turn and look to see my mother step in. She gives me a soft smile. "Perfect," she says tenderly. "You look perfect, Kascia."

I bow my head. "Mom, I look bland."

"Just because your outfit is, doesn't mean you are," Mom insists, walking over to me and bending down to hug my shoulders, making me turn to look in the mirror.

She smiles at me as I look at her reflection and she at mine. "You'll make it far, Kascia. I'm sure of it."

I wish I felt the same. But even if I did, it doesn't matter. This game may not go on long enough for there to be girls getting into top twenty-five let alone ten. I just have to get through three months. "You get to be a lady either way."

"I'm far more worried about you." Mom frowns, suddenly serious. "I want you to make your own choice." Mom turns me to face her. "To escape or—" She's cut off by a knock at the door. She sighs. It must be my guard.

I swallow hard, and my eyes go from my Mom's face to the door. This is it. My heart pounds in my chest as my stomach squirms. Everything I know is about to end and change into this new hell I've come to find. Either way, this is going to hurt. There is no happily ever after for me. No happy life. Just duty. The duty of a Custod. I'll never come back to a real home again.

I glance at my bags, packed and leaning on the wall next to the door. My eyes linger there, the last bits of home I'll ever have again. The last bits of my true heart and soul are there. And it's all I'd ever have.

I blink back the tears as Mom opens the door. I jump to attention, brushing off my skirt as I hear Lila's voice giving directions.

I pick up my bags quickly, slinging them over my shoulder, and hurry out the door.

I'm surprised when I get into the front room. I thought the team would be large, but it's just Lila and three other guards.

Lila must have seen the surprise on my face because she smiles slightly. "We want to make sure it's a small deal, so we don't draw rebel attention."

"Or more likely a fan group," another guard says grumpily. I frown at him.

"Ignore him." Lila smiles. "Are you ready?"

I swallow hard. The truth is no. And I never would be ready to step into this world where I would never get to be truly myself again. Not to my parents, not to the royal family I'm going to betray, not to Jake, not even to myself.

I grip my dance bag's strap on my shoulder tightly as if holding onto the last bits of self I have. It's sad it could all fit into one bag.

"Let him take that, dear," Lila says gently to me, nodding at another guard who steps forward to take my bags.

My grip on them tightens. I'd much rather keep them. I'm a bit scared to give up the last bits of myself. Then again, that wouldn't be ladylike. I slowly sling the bag off my shoulder and offer it to him. He takes them, tossing them over his shoulder as if they were nothing. I take a deep breath to hold in the tears.

"Well, if that's everything, we should get loaded up," Lila says. "Try not to take too long." She smiles at my mother and me. She then bows to my mother. "And as I said, I'll keep you updated, I promise." She then steps out to make sure the carriage is ready for me.

"Updated?" I frown.

Mom gives me a sad smile. "You can't write me about everything, so she said she'd fill me in, so you don't have to get in trouble for telling me things that perhaps you're not supposed to, most of all, about tests," she explains. She then lets out a long sigh. "I'm glad she's willing to keep me updated. But still, don't forget to write."

I can hear the emotion in her voice. This is the first time, apart from my Custod test, she's really had to let me go. And unlike the test, she doesn't know if I'll be back. I don't either.

I fight tears. "I will," I promise. "I'll write as often as I can."

Mom fights to smile through the tears that are forming in her eyes. She gives me a tight hug. "Stay safe," she almost begs me. "Take your shot. Don't throw it away. Be free. I wish I could tell you everything, but it's not safe yet. I will when I can, I promise."

Alarm cuts through my fear and tears. What truth? Mom always acted like she disagreed with Dad, but this feels different. Like she is revealing something last moment that I'd only seen hints of in my life.

The idea frightens me, but she's right. This is not the time or place. They are waiting. And there may never be a time or place.

"I'm scared," I confess through a fresh wave of tears, still holding my mom tightly.

"I know, and that's okay. Change is frightening, but I know this is best for you. Not for some cause, not for your Dad or Jake, or anyone but you. Don't throw it away." Her last words come out as a plea that cuts through me.

It is a plea of the pure love of a mother wanting to protect her baby. To protect me. I hadn't felt anyone wanted to protect me in so long.

"I-I love you, Ma-mama," I stammer out.

"I love you too, sweetheart." Mom sighs before finally pulling back. "Don't ruin what little makeup you have." Mom manages a sad kind of laugh as she wipes a tear from my eye. "Go make me proud." She cups my chin in her hand, "I know you will because nothing you do will not make me proud of you. As long as you make your own choice, alright?"

I swallow down my tears, slowly putting on the mask, and nod. I don't have many of my own choices I get to make anymore, but I'll try.

She manages one last smile before gently guiding me to the door. She leans on the doorpost as I walk out alone to bear my duty like all Custods do in the end.

The carriage is nicer than most but not grander than it has to be. There is a guard at the back, and two guards ride their own horses as they guard carriage sides. Lila is waiting by the door for me.

She gives me a comforting smile. "When you're ready, my lady." She opens the door and bows to me.

I nod my thanks like I had done for lady roles in the theater, hoping that is the correct way to react. I walk over to the carriage and put my foot on the lower step to get inside.

I glance back one more time, just one last look at the life I'll never have back. Mom smiles and waves at me happily, sad but also excited. Her excitement helps me smile and put my weight on the step to get into the carriage.

I sit down quickly as if getting the action over with. I jump at the snap of the door shutting. I am trapped inside. It is done. This is it. My old life is over.

I lean forward to look out the window. I thought Lila would come inside with me, but instead, she climbs up to sit with the driver at the front.

I manage a smile and give a last "I love you" wave to my mother as the carriage rolls forward. She beams and waves back. The sadness falls off her as I get further away, and the excitement she had for me gets brighter as she waves more and more until I can't see her anymore.

I sit back to try to hide the tears that want to come but freeze partway through. Hiding in the shadows of the trees, watching with a pained look on his face as if he were standing on a sore leg, is Jake.

My jaw drops open. I didn't expect to see him until this was all over. He doesn't realize I've seen him. He just watches with that pained look on his face. As we pass him, I try to keep him in view, but the trees make it hard. Did I really see him? Or did I imagine it?

Then the tears come. Had I read him wrong and deep down he didn't want to let me go? But he still had. Did it even matter what he wanted when he'd willingly handed me off to a wicked prince? Did it matter he didn't want to when in the future he may still sell me off to whatever dictator to keep the kingdom safe?

I fight to keep the tears in my eyes so I don't arrive at the palace a wash of tears. This task keeps me distracted and gets me to stop crying.

Now I just feel depressed and empty, doomed to my fate and whatever demands the palace puts upon me until I sell my soul to the devil and let the cursed rebels in to finally end the suffering. It should be an exciting, ennobling thought. It's not. It just crushes my heart and leaves me empty. No Jake to actually love me. Just the painful duty of a Custod. And nothing more.

Chapter 11

The carriage ride takes about half an hour. The guard had drawn all the curtains once I'd sat back in the carriage. I guess it's safer. We're almost to the palace when I hear the loud chatter of voices, louder than it should be for just passing through the town.

I take a peek. The empty stretch of land between the main city and the castle is filled with people. I frown as I watch, confused at exactly what is going on. Part of the crowd looks like they want to see us go by; a few hold up signs with the names of some of the girls who have been chosen.

I looked over the list a few times but decide there are too many to try to memorize. I see "Dahlia" a few times as well as "Forsythia", "Jonquil", and… I pause. Is that my name? I see at least two signs with my name. I swallow hard.

The other half of the crowd, closer to the road, are not behaving so well. They make the most noise and are trying to get to the carriages. There are a few ahead of me, likely other girls arriving. A line of guards keeps these people back from the road, forming a barricade.

One of the crowd helps another jump over the guard and, to my horror, dives, and lands on an inner guard and starts beating him as hard as he could manage. Luckily, two other guards jump down and pull the person off and shove them back into the crowd.

I flinch as a rock strikes one of the guards in the head, making her stagger and fall back. The crowd converges on the spot, but more guards come and force them back.

I pull away from the window as a shower of more rocks is thrown. I hear yells: the crowd further back with signs telling off the angry crowd.

So it's a group of rebels and non-rebels. Half just want to see the "show", the other wants to stop it or at least harm us or the palace. I wonder if Dad planned this. I doubt it. All his hopes are hung on me, and Jake isn't here. Not if I did see him by the trees. So this is either another Loyalist's work or the Potentate rebellion.

I feel helpless and defenseless inside the carriage with no weapon. I hug my knees and jump as a rain of stones hits the side of the carriage. None get in, thankfully. Insults pelt the air. I doubt they know which carriage belongs to which girl. I don't think they care. They just want to cause harm and damage to the royal family that hurt them.

I don't blame them. Part of me would love to join them. But I can't. I agree with them, but I have to pretend I don't, to stop this royal family from causing more damage. I hug my knees and bury my face in my skirt, hiding my face against my knees to try to ignore and drown out the attack outside.

It feels like a lifetime before the sounds start to fade. We'd made it through the castle gate. I dare take a look. There's a second gate. A double wall? No wonder we'd never broken in. I had no idea the castle employed a double wall. There's a line of dirt on the side against the outer wall and a moat along the inner side against the inner gate.

We pause on the bridge above it as four guards inspect the carriage from top to bottom. A lady guard comes in, apologizes for having to bother me, and checks the whole inside for any hidden rebels before she bows to me and leaves. The all-clear is given, and we're let into the main castle grounds.

Feeling it has to be safe now, I pull back the curtain to get my first look at the castle grounds. The drive we ride up is a beautiful sandstone path, making it look bright yellowish gold. It contrasts the lush grass nicely. The long drive is open, showing wide expanses of grass with decorative trees here and there. I think most are fruit trees, with decorative little fences around them, likely to prevent animals getting to them. Past this, stretching out towards the ocean side, are lush guardians of flower bushes, roses, island roses, and other plants I don't know with tasteful trellises, gates, fences twisted with flowering ivies of names I don't know, rivers and fountains, and more. It's hard to see from here, but it looks like a stunning garden paradise. I imagine it buzzing with happy bees and butterflies. I hope I can get out at least once to see them. They look amazing. I can't quite see the ocean for the beautiful plants and the way the land slowly sloped down to the private royal beaches. I wonder what's on the other side.

I slide over to the other side of the carriage and pull that curtain aside. Neatly organized orchards and vegetable gardens, a building that must be the royal stables, and a beautiful building with a steeple at the front with the phoenix, wings wide, at the top spread across my view. That must be the Royal Devotion Hall. I also think I see the road that would lead to the city's sanctuary. The sound of the ocean gets louder as we get closer to the palace gates.

I sit back in my seat as we turn right into a grand oval loop of the road that brings us up to the palace doors. I admire a stunning fountain in the center of the oval. The focal point is an island rose with water falling down its petals. A breaching dolphin is on one side, with water flowing out of its blowhole. The breaching shark is on the other side, the water running down from the top of its nose. It's Purerah's symbol.

I could spend an hour admiring it and hours sitting by it, enjoying the wonderful scent of island roses, clean greenery, and the sound of the water as I read. The palace did seem a perfect paradise, or at least the grounds did.

I look out the other window at the palace doors. They are tall, but not towering. They are painted with Purerahian blue designs to offset the yellow, almost golden color of the walls. It all contrasts nicely with cream-colored accents and even more Purerahian blue. It is a stunning work of architecture.

The door on my right is finally opened, and a footman steps aside for me. I give him a weak smile as I stand and take my first step onto the castle grounds.

Four happy women run up to me. One I recognize as Hydie beams at me. All four curtsy to me, all wearing the same Purerahian blue and cream uniforms. Hydie still has her pretty ponytail, but the others all have their hair pulled back into low, braided buns. The other thing that surprises me is one of the maids is a bit plump. I thought the king and queen — hoarders of gold that they are — wouldn't pay their staff enough to get plump.

All three of them are very pretty, pretty enough to be Chosen girls themselves. They beam at me in nervous excitement.

"Welcome Lady Kascia," Hydie beams at me. "And welcome to your new home away from home — or new home." She winks playfully. "Now." She sounds more business-like. "Let me introduce you to your lady's staff. This is Miss Vivian."

The tallest of the three bows her head and curtsies slightly. She has dark brown hair that is perfectly smoothed back into her bun, no makeup, pale skin, and bright brown eyes that study me as if sizing me up for what taking care of me will be like.

The other two curtsy as well as their names are said. Flur is daintier than Ro. She has platinum blonde hair that shows a hit of a wave even pulled back into the bun and lovely gray eyes that are accented perfectly by her makeup. It highlights her fair tones well. At least the staff get to wear makeup.

Ro is the one who is slightly plump with black hair so straight, it sits flat on her head. With all three of them being fair, I wonder if they are related, though not much else about them matches. Vivian is taller than me (easy to do), but Ro is shorter, and Flur is average and willowy.

"I'll leave you to their perfect care," Hydie beams at us before she waves us on as the next carriage rolls up.

My three maids lead me up the steps, smiling at me. Ro rushes over to get my bags. Maybe she's a bit plump because she's strong. She tosses my bags over each shoulder as if they weigh nothing.

Vivian frowns at them, "Is that all, miss?"

I nod, "I-I don't need much." But it's all that's left of me. Please be kind to it. I beg her in my mind but don't dare speak.

"Oh good," Vivian smiles as if in relief before returning to proper business manners. "Will you need anything particular that you were unable to bring, Miss?"

"Um... just the dance gear I mentioned to Hydie," I state.

"Oh." All three of my maids' eyes light up.

"You're the dancer," Ro says excitedly. I nod nervously. "Sweet," Ro beams.

Vivian clears her throat pointedly, correcting Ro's improper wording. She then makes a note in a little book she'd been holding. She tucks it into one of the pockets of her apron before she addresses me again. "That is good to know. Thank you, miss. They are all prepared for you. I will have them placed in your closet in your room. Your assigned number is twelve. Don't forget that because it won't change as the Enthronement goes on, and it will help you know where to go and be at all times. Do you require anything else, miss? Anything unique for your bedding?"

"Uh... no," I say. "Other than I struggle with a sleep disorder, but I'm sure whatever you have is fine."

"Excellent, my lady," She curtsies to me with a bow of her head. "We will bring your bags to your room and unpack them as needed."

"Please be careful." I manage to keep the rest in and out of my voice, but the compassion in Vivian's and Flur's eyes makes it obvious they understand. Ro nods as well but doesn't seem to read my mood as well as the other two.

"Of course, miss," Vivian says. "We serve you and will not do anything to make you uncomfortable. We will show you to your room later. They are having you start with the makeovers before lunch. Flur and I will show you while Ro takes your things to your room."

I swallow and nod. We step into the entrance hall. It's stunning.

The first thing I notice is the beautiful cream-colored chandelier hanging from the ceiling that makes me think of an elegant seashell. The walls are that sandy golden yellow with cream and Purerahian blue accents. Each door is lined with blue, rounded with a slight point at the top. There are many of them on our left and right. In the center of the right wall is one that is larger than the others with double doors. I wonder where it leads.

Past this main hallway is a larger room with a high domed ceiling I think goes up all the floors of the castle, which is about four or five stories. It has windows that face the front of the castle, letting natural light highlight the room. In front of us is a large, rounded cylinder with large golden doors and beautiful staircases wrapping around it on either side.

There are two grand staircases, one on either side of the room. The cylinder is the center of the large rectangular room, but it also makes up the back of it. The whole design is beautiful, light, and airy, reflecting the beautiful beaches we have.

My maids guide me to the staircase on our left. It leads to a basic hallway, with sconces that are cream and made to look like seashells, lighting the corridors when the windows along the walls failed to do so.

There are doors lining the whole wall on our left and right. The windows are spaced between these doors on our left with wide spaces between them. The pattern of yellow walls, cream, and blue decorations, and a stunning ocean theme remains. I see many ocean paintings as well as paintings of ocean life: dolphins, whales, fish, and even sharks. The palace embraces its ocean setting perfectly. I like it.

We turn right along more doors until we reach a room about midway down the long hall. Flur opens one of the double doors for me, curtsying. Vivian pauses as Ro goes on to my room.

I bow my head to them and step inside. On the right side of the room are floor-to-ceiling bookshelves, filled with books. The far wall is lined with windows that look out over the ocean stretching out as far as the eye can see. The left wall has several paintings and tables along with it as well as flanking the entrance. The room is filled with armchairs, sofas, little tables, and cushions. There's even a grand piano in the corner by the bookshelves.

A lot of girls were already here. A few are sitting in the little circles formed by the sofas and armchairs, chatting like old friends. Others are sitting at the smaller tables and glaring at the other girls. Two are standing side by side, whispering to each other as they glare at the other girls.

"You'll wait here until one of the makeover stations is ready," Vivian says to me. "You can start to get to know your fellow Chosen as you wait or pick out a book. We'll go make sure your room is ready for you." She curtsies to me.

I force a smile, "Thank you, Vivian, Flur." It takes me a moment to remember Flur's name before I bow my head to her.

She flushes in pleasure, but she doesn't speak as she and Vivian leave me alone with the other girls.

I take a deep breath to make sure my mask is fully in place. Now the game begins. It's hard to tell what each girl is like from appearance as we all wear the same uniform. But I can tell we are all very different.

Not just in appearances but in personalities. I can see quite a few dark-skinned girls, like the royals themselves, but many others range between fair and dark-skinned. It looks like the standard varying shade of the populace of Purerah. And how each girl carries herself conveys even more volume. How they sit or stand says far more.

The lightest girl I can see is also the smallest. She looks too young to even be here. She's sitting by the window, looking out over the sea, sitting with her legs tucked beside her, I presume because she's too small to have her legs reach the floor. Her black hair is pulled into a ponytail.

Well, if I have to start pretending to be excited, helping the smallest and youngest of us seems like a good place to start.

I walk over to introduce myself. "Hello," I say, hoping I don't frighten her. The way she's curled into herself reminds me of a cat who might jump and spring away at the wrong sound.

She looks up and smiles a dainty smile, her angled eyes narrowing a little as she smiles.

I return the smile, finding it cute. Jake and my father's eyes do the same, so does the king's. I seem to like that trait in people.

"I'm Kascia. What's your name?"

"I'm Lilly," she says, twisting to see me better. Her feet do not reach the floor. "I'm from Risago. Where are you from?"

"Roselpla," I admit. "I'm from here."

"Oh, how lovely to be close to home," Lilly beams. "You must love the sea then." She turns to look at it. "I've never seen it. My family runs a rice field."

I frown, "Is that doing okay?"

"They are for now, but we have had struggles in the past," she says. "I'm just excited to be here at all."

I can see why she made it so far though. She is like a dainty princess. The kind who is sensitive. She makes me smile.

"I can imagine. You would live more inland to run a rice farm, right?" I ask.

She nods, "We live along the great river. I'm used to the water, but seeing the ocean is amazing. I hope to see more of it soon. Most of all, if I don't win."

"Do you think you will?" I ask.

"Maybe. I'm the littlest." She looks around. "I'm eighteen, but I don't look it, I know."

Wow, I know royals marry young and age gaps aren't a big deal to them, but the prince is in his late twenties I think. She looks like she's fourteen.

"Do you think sharks get close to the shore?" Lilly frowns suddenly. "I wouldn't know what to do with a shark. I'd love to be in the sea, but don't know how to stay safe. You'd know, being local right?"

"Well, sharks like early morning or late night. Stay away from areas where seals like to go. They mostly want to eat seals if they are big enough to eat people. Otherwise, just be careful. If they know you see them, they are less likely to attack you. And if they try, you can push their noses away, but that takes guts."

"Oh, I don't know if I could do that." She frowns.

"Don't worry. I'll keep you safe from sharks," I promise with a slight smile.

"Oh good. Be nice to have a friend. No one is making friends, you notice?" She looks around the room. "Apart from those two." She points to the corner. "They are already 'celebrities' so they feel better than us." She scowls at them disapprovingly. Though plenty of girls are talking, I suppose they don't look like friends.

I glance over at the two in question. One has hickory skin and eyes with her coiled hair in a bun on top of her head. She has a strong-looking body, especially her legs. She has sharp eyebrows and a resting smirk face.

The other is pale-skinned, like Lilly. She has the same angled eyes, but something about the shape of her nose and eyebrows give her a snarky look. Like she's always looking down at you. The other girl is taller, but this girl is short, even shorter than me. Her darkly painted lips don't help the snotty air of superiority. Her black hair is also in a ponytail but is longer than Lilly's and straighter.

"Celebrities?" I don't know who they are.

"Yes. Don't you know them? The tall one is Dahlia Phiable, the Sparkleball player. The other is Forsythia Ghoda, the star horse jumper of the last two years. They are going to be hard to beat. Just look at them. They are beautiful." Lilly frowns.

"You are too, just in a different way," I assure her.

She flushes. "Thank you, Kascia. But still. They are already being rude. But not as bad as the mayor's daughter." Lilly nods at a blonde girl fussing with a fan in her hands.

Her mouth seems set in a frown at all times. Her eyebrows are close together as if always displeased. She is certainly displeased now, hitting her fan to try to get it to open properly. A section of it was stuck. I've had that happen many times. Maybe she isn't always so rude.

I give it a try by walking over to her. Lilly gasps in shock behind me as I go up to this girl. "Having trouble with your fan?" I ask.

Her light blue eyes narrow at me. "What would a common girl know?" she snaps at me.

"A lot." I gently take the fan, giving her a look for being rude. "Sometimes the blades get stuck." I could see where it was and carefully put my finger between where they were stuck to get them properly aligned before

I folded it up. “Happens when they are overused or cheap.” I snap the fan open properly and flutter it a bit to be sure. “There, right as rain.” I offer it back to her.

She snatches it from me. “Servant?” she guesses.

“Dancer,” I shoot back. “I do dances with fans all the time. They like to get caught when I have to snap them open and closed fast or if they are old or cheap. I just wanted to help. And by the way, the freckles are cute. Don’t hide them. The prince might like them. They make you unique.” And with that, I pivot away from her and walk back over to an aghast Lilly.

“Why would you help her?” Lilly asks, “That’s Lady Ericka. She’s the mayor’s daughter. She thinks she’s already a princess. Why did you give her advice?”

“Just because she’s a jerk, doesn’t mean I have to be,” I say. “But I also don’t have to be her buddy to bark at.” I glance back at her, fanning herself and looking grumpily out the window. Besides, being nice to the people who can’t stand you is easily the best way to annoy them back. “You could have tried to stop me.”

“I didn’t think you’d really do it,” Lilly says.

“I don’t know any of these girls. I’ll treat them well unless I have to otherwise.”

Another girl comes into the room. She has olive skin, dark eyes and brows, and beautiful thick hair in a tight braid. She smiles around at all of us.

She sees Lilly and gasps, “Do I know you? You’re from the south like me,” She races over.

“Yes. I saw your carriage.” Lilly beams.

“I’m Isla,” she says. “I was an acrobat.”

“Really?” A fellow performer.

Isla nods, “Yes, you?”

“I’m Kascia. I was a dancer and singer for the theatre.”

Isla gasps in pure delight. “I know you! Well of you; you’re a legend.” I flush. “You can stretch with me.” Isla jokes.

I laugh, “I’m sure you're more flexible than me. You’re an acrobat.”

“Maybe. I do mostly tight rope and trapeze,” she says. “I saw you in *Phantom.* You were amazing. I can’t believe you’re here. I thought you’d get snatched up by the capitol or something.”

Right, the great Armuary Theater would bother with an actress from the ghetto like me.

“Oh, you’ll be stunning at the balls,” Isla giggles and pretends to fan herself like I did in the second act of *The Phantom.* We all laugh.

“Only if the prince can dance well,” I point out.

"True. I wonder what he likes," Isla says then her eyes widen. "I'm sorry. What was your name?" she asks Lilly.

Lilly laughs, "I'm Lilly. What part of the south are you from?"

"Oh, well, officially I'm from Sadeh, which isn't really the south," Isla says. "But I grew up in Risago before I traveled with the troupe, which officially is from Sadeh. That's where I put in my application and have lived the last eight years."

"I'm from Risago," Lilly beams.

I smile, glad I won't be the only one who helps Lilly feel comfortable.

"Did you work the farms?" Isla asks.

"My father owns one," says Lilly. "I liked to work on them sometimes, but it's hard work."

"I used to dream about working the farms. Silly, I know, but it sounded romantic to me when I travel so much," Isla says. "I'd not mind the chance to stay in one place and raise land."

"I never thought of it that way," Lilly says. "You do make it sound nice."

Isla beams, "Have you met any of the others yet? Jonquil and I just met in the hall. But she's seeing to her nut allergy with her maids. She's nice. She studies bugs you know."

Wow, someone who does some non-pretty work got in. I'm impressed. Not only that, but hers was also one of the names on the signs from the crowd that came to see us. The girl in question comes in a bit later. She's a beautiful almond-skinned girl with thick brown hair and a shy expression. That is until she sees Isla and rushes over. Isla quickly introduces us to Jonquil.

"Oh, it's so romantic," Jonquil says. "Us all together to try for the prince's hand. We're his only chance. It's such fun and to be friends in it all too. I hope to be friends with all of you."

"Just not them," Lilly points out the three grumps.

"Oh, or Lantana," Jonquil says. "She's out to get the prince in bed and keep him there."

"What?" I frown.

"You'll see," Jonquil says. "She's from my district, so we came to the interviews together. It was not fun. She thinks because she's as pretty as a living Snow White, people will love her. She's paler than even Lilly with dark hair, and she wears dark lipstick. She is sure the prince will take her when he sees her beauty and cancel the whole thing. They took her into her treatment early to shut her up."

Another girl walks up to us. "Who said she's so pretty she'll just win?" she demands of Jonquil.

"Lantana," Jonquil says.

"What's your name?" I try to be friendly.

"I'm Kamala." She puts her hands on her hips, her mane of coiled hair bobbing as she did. She reminds me of the strong island fisherman who trades in the market, strong and beautiful. "And she won't win like that. This is a test. We have to push through it. I hope she's out fast, so we can see who is in it for the long hall. We are looking for the future queen, not a beauty contestant."

"Yes," Isla's eyes light up. "That's exactly it. I hope to be a good queen, but the test will tell all of us."

"And I'll win. I know how to win. I have what it takes. I hope you all do too," Kamala says. "Pick me or not, I want to prove I am worthy of it at least."

"You don't have to prove anything to anyone," I say. They'll all be dead before it's over anyway.

"Shows what you know," she shoots at me. "But I'm going to meet the others." She gives us a wave and leaves.

"Oh boy. Do you think they're all like that?" Lilly looks worried.

"No, just some will," I reply with a glare after Kamala.

"Like that girl Violet with the red hair. She's mad for the prince. Had a thing for him forever, they say," Isla says. "She is so excited. Sweet girl."

Oh no, was I the only one who wasn't either crazy for the prince or just in it to win and prove myself? Was that good or bad? I worry about that as the girls talk for a moment.

I learn about some other girls too. Marigold, who is loud and brash about her passion winning out. Hebe, who is just a loud talker all around. Candela, who apparently spends her whole time waiting with her nose in a book. Azalea, who treats all the girls like she is their mother, annoying the stubborn ones, and Bella, who had tried to make friends with Forsythia, but Forsythia didn't give her the time of day.

I listen without really taking it in when my turn is called. I leave with a flurry of whispers behind me.

They take me to a large room with a bubbling, circular water spa in one corner, a changing area in another.

Six other girls are finishing up their session, dressed in the same uniform I am, but instead of flowers in their hair, they are putting on tiaras. These must be the born princesses. They are all stunning. They start on their way out as I'm directed to sit in one of the chairs along one wall.

Most of the princesses ignore me as they pass, all but one. One with blonde hair and bottle green eyes stops and looks at me with a gentle but warm smile.

"Congratulations on getting this far." She waves at me and the other girls getting their makeovers. "I hope to meet you all later."

"Princess Zelda, come on." A darker princess with stunning coils and beautiful red lips rolls her eyes. Princess Zelda rolls her eyes back, smiles at us, and leaves with the other princesses.

Wow, one of them was nice to me. I feel sick to my stomach. She's the one who should win.

They give me a full spa makeover. They put me into a robe and polish every inch of skin on me, then they have me wash off. They ask me if I want to make any changes to my look, any haircut I'd like, change my hair color, anything like that. I have no ideas.

"Whatever you think is best," I mutter.

"Do you want to look different?" The lady in charge gives me an understanding smile.

"No."

"Then we'll just make touch-ups," she says.

They then wash and then cut my hair, more like trimming it, taking off only an inch or two at the ends, but then they cut layers into it. When they finish, they rinse my hair and put some creams and maybe even oils into it. For my curls they said. The head lady keeps looking at a book she has open, likely with notes about what they learned about me when my beauty team came.

Once my hair is done, they clip it to the top of my head and wash and polish my face, put a peel mask on then a different kind of mask, and after that put several different creams on my face, one for my eyes alone, then a few for my face.

They give me a full manicure, but don't paint my nails more than putting a protective coating on them and then do the same for my feet. It feels amazing, but I imagine some of my dancer's feet problems grosses them out.

They then put a gentle layer of makeup on, let my hair down and style it back the way I had it before. I'm impressed the braid looks so clean. I thought layers would ruin the braids.

When they show me a mirror, I don't look that different, just more polished, as they said. The layers they cut into my hair give it more shape and volume even in this braid. It also shows off the strawberry blonde streaks more easily. I like it. The makeup is simple like I would have done myself.

A few other girls come in and out, some take longer than others, but once I'm dismissed, they take me back to the room where the other Chosen are waiting.

I also notice another girl I'd seen before and frown. Or had I? Something is different. After a moment, I realize her hair is darker now. It had been blonde before, but now it's jet black. It had been straight but now it's wavy and full of volume, as if they'd tried to give her tight curls that weren't holding well. I wish I knew her name.

A few I'd heard about are there, Hebe among them. I can hear her voice above the others. "They even got all the dirt out of my nails," she's saying. "Not an easy feat."

I ignore her. Her booming voice hurts my head already, and I'm used to standing near orchestras. I walk over to try to meet some of the others I don't know. I leave the reading girl alone, guessing she's Candela.

The other two girls smile as I walk over. "Hi. I'm Azalea. You?"

"Kascia." I nod to her.

"Nice to meet you, Kascia. Glad to know I'm not the only pale brunette here." Azalea smiles as does the other girl.

I laugh. "I guess not." I look around. She's right. There aren't many of us. I touch my hair uneasily. Would that be a problem?

"But you pull it off well. And you are tanner than me," Azalea says.

"I'm still paler." The other girl smiles. "I'm Bella." She's right; she has pale skin, deep black hair, and a sweet, intelligent smile. Her hair is done up into a bun with strands pulled into it, making beautiful loops.

"Yes, you are the palest." Azalea smiles. "You're also from the south. Where is your family from, Kascia?"

"Oh." I can't tell her the whole truth. "Well, my father's nationality looks Eilimohlian or Alalusian, I'm not sure, but my mother is from here."

"Pretty." Azalea smiles.

Finally, all fifty of us are done with our makeovers just before lunch, and we get a good look at one another. I look out for the girls I'd been warned about.

I spot Lantana by her smoky makeup and confident, seductive smile. She looks so much like one of the born princesses, they could have been sisters. But I don't know if that will help her much. The flower betrays she's not — born-princess wear tiaras; common girls wear flowers.

The born princess she looks like makes me think of a dragon or an alligator. She has red hair... sort of. The top of it is dark red then lightens to a literal fiery orange at the tips, matching the makeup on her heavy-lidded eyes, contrasting her fair skin.

Hydie has us all sit in a large circle in our number order. I am between Lilly and Azalea. Hydie makes us introduce ourselves with our names, where we are from, something "fun" about us, and our favorite color. The born princesses go first as they are in the top six.

The one with the darkest skin is Princess Rose from Emilimoh, the original kingdom. Then there's Princess Amapola who is from Spearim and she looks it: fair skin, black hair, and dark, haunting eyes.

Princess Neeraja from Sedeyu. I can't quite recall how close it is. I know it's a kingdom with coasts as well, but not as many as we have or as beautiful. She bows her head a bit shyly. Her soft brown skin offsets her dark black hair that is thick and shining.

The one that looked like she could be Latana's sister is Princess Zinna of Dragia, a nation to the south known for their vicious ways. They aspire to be like the wild dragons. I made a note to avoid her if possible.

Princess Laurina is from Barug, also nicknamed the dragonlands, where the people and dragons live as one kingdom. I wonder if she has her own dragon. She bows to us. Her hair is bright red, and she looks ready to challenge us to a duel but then invite us for drinks after.

The last is Princess Zelda of Hyvil. Hyvil is across the great ocean over a month's sailing away. I'm impressed that she came to play in this game. She's the only one who gives us a real smile as she bows her head. She's the one who said hello to me. Her blonde hair is stunning gold like sunlight. Her green eyes are full of power. I like her. Something about her feels familiar, like home.

Then we got to the non-princesses. Ahead of me is Emmalina from Risago. A lot of girls seem to be from there. Bella is also from Risago. Dahlia, the sparkleball player is from Rosepla. Of course, if she plays for the national team she'd have to be. Then it is Jonquil, Lilly, me, Azalea, who is from Asteria. Lady Ericka is from Rosepla — which means she is the daughter of my local mayor. Forsythia is next to her and also from the capital. I suppose most celebrities would have to live in the capital with the most money to be made in entertainment there.

It's so hard to keep track of so many girls and where they're all from. The ones I'd already spoken to were a bit easier, but I had no hope of remembering all of them by the end of the day or even by the end of the month if I didn't spend time with them.

Hydie told us to play "I am Musical Chairs". One girl started in the middle and said something about herself in an "I am or I have" statement, and anyone else who had the same "I am" had to get up and change seats.

A girl named Bellatrix went first. She said she was an only child which made me and twelve others get up and swap places, leaving a girl named Aquila in the middle.

She said she liked to read, making me and about half a dozen others swap places. That left a girl named Larkin in the middle who said she was from Shasta. She ended up trading with a girl named Nichol who said she was blonde, making Princess Zelda, Ericka, and six others get up. It left Princess Zelda in the middle.

She grins, seemingly happy to be in the middle. "I was born a princess," she declares.

I hold in my laugh unlike others at her mean little trick. The other princesses glared at her as they all have to swap seats. Poor Princess Rose is stuck in the middle. She went with "I have royal coils". That got a lot of people up, Emmalina, Dahlia, Kamala, Hanna, Rhosan, and three more girls whose names I can't remember. Dahlia somehow got stuck in the middle. But she grins mischievously. "I have kissed a boy."

Every girl in the room gets up except for poor Lilly and Isla who sit in their seats, brick red. Hydie looked nervous at that one. That wasn't exactly a friendly question. Dahlia is fishing out the competition.

Princess Laurina gets stuck in the middle and picks on a girl named Violet when she says she has red hair. Only Princess Laurina and Violet are redheads out of the fifty of us.

We go through a few more rounds until Forsythia is in the middle. "I am willing to do whatever it takes to win." She smiles.

"Alright, that's enough," Hydie calls before anyone tries to move. "I believe lunch is ready.

That night, our staff comes to show us to our rooms. Our bedroom arrangements don't seem to have much reason to them. We take up guest rooms on several floors. I have a third-floor room in the middle corner with a girl named Pamia next to me. Past her in the next three rooms are Prisa, Larin, and Careilee.

Vivian opens the door for me, and I step into my room. Ro and Flur curtsy low to me, but I hardly see them as I take in my bedroom prison for the first time.

The room is blue, white, and gold with a lovely four-poster bed with fine gold and blue sheets and pillows. There is a white and gold desk, dresser, and a door leading into a private washroom with all I could want. I can see there are two vanities, one in the washroom and one in my bedroom.

The floor is a fine stone with beautiful Purerahian patterns colored and shaped into it. The rugs on either side of the bed, in front of the bench at the foot of my bed, below the writing desk, and balcony are a matching blue. There are two desks along the left wall where my maids can work, on the opposite side of the room from my vanity and writing desk. It's all so simple and yet put together. The molding is also painted gold. There are a few ocean paintings on the walls to help bring life to the room.

"Is all to your liking?" Vivian asks anxiously.

I smile, "Yes, I think so."

"Good," she smiles. Flur beams too.

"You sure?" Ro checks.

"If I find anything lacking as I use it, I will let you know," I promise.

"Excellent," Hydie beams. "I'm going to check on the others and let you settle in." She gently touches my shoulder before leaving.

"Do you need help getting settled?" Vivian asks me.

I frown, "I-I don't even know."

The reality of my situation is settling in. All these girls mean no harm and here I am, the plant. Just trying to murder to save my own skin.

I think my maids notice because they put on some "sleep mist". They then give me my night tea to help me sleep. I sip it as my maids entertain me with details of what's to come.

"It will be lovely," Flur says. "You'll see tomorrow."

Tomorrow. What a terrible idea.

When the services are over the next day, we are all brought back into the Lady's Chamber, where we'd first met. It's been divided up into fifty sections where our attendants are set up to meet us for the first time. My maids are there with a pale man with a shining bald head, long slim fingers, and pale eyes that are quite wrinkled, probably from squinting a lot. He looks at me with narrowed eyes.

"There you are, there you are," he says, all business. "Number twelve, correct?"

I nod anxiously.

"Hello, hello. I am Yarrow, your attendant," he says, almost bored.

He puts a hand to his chin as he looks me over. "Mmm, not too curvy, but enough," he says. I frown. "I have your sizes, so that's not a problem."

He walks around me. I don't like it. It's like being circled by a vulture. "The prince is partial to warm colors, so we'll work with that. Then you'll stand out and pop." Yarrow smiles to himself, still circling me. "Yes, yes, that will work. I have it."

He picks up a book from the table and holds it up as if he's putting it over my body. "Mmm." He flips pages then looks at my face before flipping again and again.

I glance at Vivian, silently asking what was wrong with him.

"Those are his designs," she says. "He's seeing what fits you."

By holding a picture up to me? I'd seen artists with unique ways of doing things, but this one is odd. Yarrow goes through a few, makes a few notes, then chuckles to himself. "Though of course I don't have those to work with, but I think this shall suffice." He smiles at me. "You'll be stunning in no time."

He steps closer. I step back, but he ignores my unease and starts on my hair. He takes it out of the braid in seconds.

"Mmm." He tosses my hair over my shoulder and walks around me yet again, messing with my hair. I'd never felt more like a prop or doll in my life.

"They really should have let us in on the spa process," Yarrow says. "Get a say in the hair. I don't know, I think it would be better to put up out of your face."

My maids frown. I'm a bit hurt by that. The layers they cut into my hair allow my natural curls space to breathe and make a pretty shape. I've admired it every time my maids let my hair out. I smile at my reflection. I've never liked my hair so much. I can see hints of golden blonde and red in my hair like sunlight rested in it.

"Show off those cheeks," Yarrow smiles and pats my cheeks, making me jump. "You're so beautiful. We want people, most of all His Highness, to see it. So we'll keep it up."

All that work to cut it, and he still wants it out of my face. Just my luck. But I have to let them. I have to wear the mask. Who I was is gone. I am just another Chosen Daughter of Purerah now.

"What about talents?" he asks, "The prince likes music, so really just those."

"All my talents have to do with music. I'm a prima actress. I sing, dance, act, all of it."

"Perfect, we'll have you sing him to sleep like everyone else." Yarrow rolls his eyes. "Anything that stands out?"

I frown. I have a great voice. I don't want to brag, but with all the work I put in, I'd think it's the best voice here. And he dismisses it for not being unique enough? My heart sinks. I'm not ever going to be enough for the palace.

I don't even have time to stop a tear. Yarrow is studying my face, turning it with a cold finger. "You have to have more than that, so pretty."

"I-I dance, maybe that's unique? I do ballet, all dance, clogging, river dance, you name it. But ballet is my specialty," I stammer out, feeling more worthless by the moment. But I have to let them. It was so against my nature until this moment. Something inside me is breaking. No, it's already broken. Jake broke it, but this Yarrow did the palace's work for them and finished the job.

"That is unique." Yarrow smiles. "Good, that is good. We can find some crazy ways to get his attention with that." Yarrow tries to get me excited by doing some kind of hip wiggle, but he is unable to move his hips without wiggling the rest of his body, making him look like a struggling worm.

Why did I get the idiot? I want to cry. It's finally time to let them rip me apart. I tense inside at the thought of how this is going to hurt.

As if I reminded him, Yarrow claps. "Yes, we need to test makeup styles. Sit, sit!" He pushes me into a seat, and my maids wash off the old makeup, put a full layer of creams, and then color on my face before Yarrow starts doing me up.

He pokes, pulls, scrapes, and starts over and over again. Each time he rubs my face, it hurts more. It feels like with each application and removal, he's yanking away more of who I am and giving me a different mask each time. Each rip doubles the pain.

It hurts my skin; it hurts my eyes; it hurts my soul. My eyes water and sting as he starts his fifth application. I'm letting them rip me apart. I have no choice.

The bell rings to prepare for dinner. My maids take me to my room. My face feels dry and sore. Even if I don't touch it, my face aches

Is there anything left of me? The confusion in me is churning again. I'm holding in tears as I shut my eyes to let my maids apply a final bit of color to them.

Flur in particular looks apologetic. They step into the washroom, and I hear Ro whisper to Vivian, "Her skin is so red. How can we calm it without making it worse?"

"Aloes is all I got." Vivian sounds stressed. "I just hope it doesn't hurt."

"And keep it down. Don't want her to hear." Flur sounds sorry for me.

I swallow hard and dare turn to look into the mirror. What I see startles me. I fight to keep tears in. My face is so red from all the makeup application and removal, I look like I've been crying. My eyes are sunken as if I'd not slept. He must have not gotten my eyeliner off properly. I hardly recognize myself with how red and swollen my face is. I look like a sickly mask of myself. And I am I let them change me. I let them do this.

I bite my colorless lips and turn away to try to stop myself crying. Pain and anger at Jake and my father wash over me. The anger makes it easier not to cry.

My maids return, and I pretend I haven't seen anything. I shut my eyes as they direct, and I feel a soothing cool on my skin. They gently rub whatever it is into my skin. In the rawest places, it really helps. My forehead feels moveable again.

It helps my skin feel better, so I let them put a fresh layer of makeup on. It must have been a different kind because my skin still feels better, but I don't dare look in the mirror again. I doubt I'd know the makeup-covered girl I saw any more than the ripped-up version of my face.

I try not to look at anyone at dinner. I am just holding myself together. I hate the new me. I hate my father for making me do this. I hate Jake for not loving me enough to save me from this. I hate him for making me live a life I'm scared of. I eat without even noticing what the food is like. I'm trying to contain my pain as I feel them slowly rip me apart.

Chapter 12

My maids are extra gentle in preparing me for bed and leave me alone with my sleep tea. But I don't even bother with it, leaving it on the warmer. I go right for the balcony doors, leaving the light off.

I open the doors of my small balcony to try to have the night air help me clear my head. I sit on the railing and look over the grounds. It helps a little.

Tears of anger fill my eyes anew. I hate this. I put my head down and sob. I need to breathe.

I sob hot tears. How could they do this to me? How could Dad push me into this? How could Jake think this would be fun? How can Mom expect this to free me? But most of all, I hate the royals. I hate them for charming me in the interview. I hate them for bringing me here. I hate the prince for being so picky.

I have to get out. I have to escape these walls, even if it's only a moment. I need to go for a walk.

I am only about three floors up. That's not too bad. I pick up the flower and put on my necklace.

It takes me about ten minutes to climb over the railing and down the wall. Finally, my toes brush the soft grass under them. Tears of relief spring to my eyes. Even this little freedom helps so much.

I take a deep breath of cold air. It's so good. I smell the wet grass, the ocean breeze. The cold wind, the salt in the air, the breeze teases my hair. The soft lap of the ocean on the shore and the roar of the waves soothe my ears.

I know it's silly, childish, and likely corny, but at the taste of the bit of freedom, I skip and dance across the grass for a moment — stepping, twirling, extending, and relishing the free space and fresh air zipping past my body as I dance to the sound of the ocean waves. I stop when and take a deep breath of the strong ocean scent.

Then the tears come. They flood my eyes and make my already sore skin sting even more. I sniffle and hug myself.

I don't know the grounds well, but it doesn't take long for me to find the nearest bench. I sit on it, hugging myself, and finally, really let the sobs out. They tear at my insides like claws scraping at the inside of my chest to rip all of the pain out. And it hurts to do it, but it's also healing. Each gasp pulls more and more out of me as my eyes ache. The skin of my face aches as the salty tears irritate it further.

And though the sobs hurt, they also help. It feels good to let it out. I cry for what seems like an hour.

It's time to calm down. I wipe my sore eyes and start around the castle grounds, hugging myself as if in defense. I wander through the rose bushes — their gentle scent filling my nose.

I follow the path. I watch the floor, studying the steppingstone path in front of me. My toes tickle the grass between the steps. My ears let the roar of the waves fill them to distract me from the pain and fear in my heart. It is a good exercise. It calms my mind and soothes my heart into slowing.

Too still. I'm so lost in my thoughts I don't realize someone is coming. I don't realize it until I walk smack into them.

We both stumble back. Our gasps strike the quiet air like a bow twang.

"O-oh." *This can't be good.* "For-forgive me," I stammer. "I didn't see you." With my heart pounding against my chest, I look up to see who I ran into.

His warm brown eyes like dark amber strike me first. They're wide with shock and fear just like mine. His skin is darker but how dark it's hard to tell in the dim light. His curly dark hair is brushed back out of his face as if for work. It's a bit of a mess as if he messed with it throughout the workday. A lock of it is hanging over his forehead, showing off its curl. I look at his clothes to guess who he is. It looks like normal work attire.

"No, no," he says quickly. His voice is warm and smooth like hot chocolate on a quiet evening. It makes the tension in me drop. "Forgive me, I was the one who should have been watching where I was going. I should have known better." He has a command in his voice that made me think he must be the foreman or manager of the gardeners or something like that. Maybe the stable manager. "I was so lost in thought, I forgot to watch my own footfalls. Forgive my rudeness."

He seems about my age, but with a job like a foreman, he's likely at least a little older. He brushes himself off distractedly as he speaks, but finally, he looks at me. His amber eyes meet mine with a sheepish smile.

I manage one for him too, "You too?" I say before I can think that through. A flush creeps up my cheeks, "I-I'm sorry. I was my mistake, uh..." I'm making a fool of myself. I hug myself against it. "Sorry. I just meant... I was lost in thought too. I should have been looking. Sorry..." I pause. "Sorry, who are you?"

"Oh, I... um." He rubs the back of his neck, looking to his right uneasily.

"I promise I won't tell anyone about this if you won't," I assure him. "On my word."

He gives me a slight smile, "Alright, then on my authority, I promise not to tell on you."

"So, who are you?" I ask, trying to be more pleasant.

He's still rubbing his neck, studying me, likely having a hard time seeing me in the darkness. "No one really," he finally says with a sigh as if disappointed. "I'm just..." he looks to his right and shakes his head as if exasperated, "I'm an apprentice here."

Oh, that explains it. He must be apprenticed to the groundskeeper. Why he's out here at night and not in a guard uniform. "Night watch?" I tease, though I know better.

"You... you could say that," he laughs, shaking his head with a slight smile. I like that smile. It's warm, inviting, making me feel welcome. I smile.

"Me too." I sigh tiredly. "I... I suppose you know who I am." I blush.

"Within forty-four guesses," he confirms. He notices my blush getting brighter. "Don't worry," his warm voice makes my worry vanish in an instant. "I'm not supposed to be out here either. I mean it. I won't tell a soul I found you out here. As long as you keep your end, alright?" He lifts his brows and draws them together with a slight smile as if hoping he'll get me to agree.

I smile at his cute attempt. "I already promised."

"Good." He relaxes. "Then we're both safe." He glances around uneasily, his eyes lingering on his right side for a moment. I see nothing. "If you don't mind my asking, what are *you* doing out here?"

I swallow hard, "I just... it-it's been a hard few days." I fight the tears. "A month or so I guess."

The boy's face softens. He looks down to try to see my face, encouraging me to look up at him. His golden-brown eyes sparkle warmly as if to comfort me. He's really good at it. He should be a therapist. "I bet. I can't even imagine. Has your world changed a lot? Were you pretty poor before?"

I frown at his assumption. I suppose it wasn't a great leap, but it still was judgmental of him. You don't have to be poor for this to be hard.

"No. Well, not really, not much more than anyone else out there," I snap more than I mean to. He didn't deserve my anger.

The man's face falls, and he looks down. "Sorry, I wouldn't really know. I just meant to help. Is... is it that bad out there?" he asks me uneasily.

"Don't you know?" I frown. "It's not like you've been in the castle your whole life."

"I'm supposed to learn the trade from my father." He sighs. "And he works here. I grew up here. I hear about it. Trust me, some rebels can scream really loud." That makes me laugh, winning a soft smile from him. I really, really like that smile. "I feel bad being one of you and not really knowing. It's not exactly easy here either, but... I don't know much outside these walls. My mother is scared for us to leave. Palace folk aren't treated nicely out there."

"Even though you aren't royal?" I frown.

"To the rebels, a person serving faithfully in the castle, no matter what station, is an enemy. I've seen it firsthand." The boy smiles sadly. "So, I don't get out much."

"I'm sorry. That must be hard."

"Yeah, but it could be worse. It sounds like I could be you." He raises a brow, going back to his question from before.

I laugh again. "You're good," I admit. "But there are others far worse off."

"So... you and your family are okay?"

I nod, "Yeah."

"Would... would you tell me about it?" The concern in his voice is touching. He wants to know what my struggles were like. I meet his gaze and see the honest worry and question in his eyes, as if begging to know if he can help.

I smile softly, "Well, it's not like I'm a great example."

"You're all I got, so you're the best for me." The man smiles.

I like that too. I don't know why, but his questions do help me feel better. "Well, personally, my family and I got by okay. Normally, in my job, I'd be fairly well to do, but for us, well... well-to-do is just scrapping by. I don't know what it's like to starve, but that's about as good as it gets. We can afford to run our theater and have enough for more than our needs. But I don't know many luxuries outside of what theater life brings. But I'm one of the few lucky ones."

"What if you're unlucky?" the boy asks with fear in his eyes.

"Depends," I shrug. "I just... There are a lot of beggars: old, young, fit, unfit. There just isn't enough to go around. The punishments for stealing or rebellion are high, but it doesn't stop it. Those who get caught are punished, but it's still hard for shopkeepers to get by with how many people steal. The baker likely only makes back a little over what he spends to make his wares because a good part of it is stolen. He then has to pay others for security, and even then, it's often not enough. There aren't enough city guards to keep an eye on it and even personal security only goes so far before you're broke."

"Is that what was happening to you?" he asks gently.

I shake my head, "No, I don't work in a trade that sells goods. I'm an actress."

“Ah, that isn’t much better though?”
“Not really.” I sigh heavily.
“Then why come out here?” he wonders.
“I do better outside, felt like I could breathe,” I confess.
He nods. “The castle can feel confining,” he agrees. “I know the feeling.”
I smile at him. I feel he understands. “Was that really why?”
“It’s not like I meant to meet a strange apprentice on the grounds,” I tease.
“Oh well... sorry.” His ears go red, I think. It’s hard to tell in the dark. I giggle.
“It’s alright,” I assure him again. “I’m the one who snuck out.”
“So am I,” he points out.
“Oh yeah,” I smile. “So why are you sneaking out?”
He swallows. “Couldn’t sleep. I was thinking about... well, life right now. And I was overwhelmed, and I felt trapped.”
My eyes light up. “Like the walls were trapping you in.”
“Right,” he beams too, his eyes studying me carefully. “I just had to get outside.”
“Me too.” It’s my turn to beam. It’s so refreshing to be understood. To feel a welcome friend in this world. I didn’t expect to find that here. I can’t believe how easy it is to talk to this boy.
“Yeah? I mean, I get it. Can you even imagine what this mad game is like?” Then he stops and laughs at himself. “Of course, you do. You know better than me, right?
I laugh. “I guess, but not yet. I’ve not really started. All they’ve done is train us to behave and got us all ‘pretty’.”
“Was that nice?” he asks, his brows drawing in worry again.
I shrug. “Well yeah, it wasn't all bad. My mother always cut my hair growing up, and she always said she wished she could cut layers into it. The workers gave me layers, and I like how it looks.” My face falls a bit. “Though my attendant doesn’t intend to use them much. I was worried I couldn’t braid it, but it’s not bad. Maybe a bit messier than before, but I like it. I like whatever treatment they put in it that brings out the color.”
Then I take my turn to laugh at myself. “Not that you’d care.” Not a boy. “Mom always hoped I’d grow into her strawberry blonde hair someday. She thought her daughter should look more like her, but I got this golden brown instead, a mix between my parents. But my maids made a hint of red come out in it. I really like that. I heard my grandparents were redheads. I love I got a bit of all of it.”
The boy laughs, “My mother is upset my hair isn’t more curly.”

"More?" I frown this time. "Your hair is really curly." Even when brushed to make it straight, I can see it waves trying to curl again and the strand across his head is so curly it's almost a ringlet.

"Well, at the ends," the boy agrees. "Why they can brush it back at all."

"No, I see waves. It curls above that," I tell him.

The boy laughs, "Okay, well, her hair is extremely curly. You couldn't even brush it back like this, and she hoped I'd get those cute curls too."

"You'd have coils if it was any curlier," I inform him.

"Yeah," the boy sighs dramatically, "but she still insists I should have more curls."

"Well, my mother at least got half her wish. I have a few blonde streaks here and there."

"I guess that would look nice. I can't tell in the dark. It's kind of hard to see you," he admits.

"Oh, is that why I can't see your hair is straight on top?" I tease.

He chuckles. "I think it's just been forced back so much. You're likely right," he grins. "I don't think I could brush it forward if I wanted to."

"Hm, maybe I should try. Got a brush?" I joke.

"Oh, I don't think Mom would like that," he teases back.

"She lives here too?" I can't recall if she does, or she just doesn't like him to leave.

"I told you that my family does. My father works here, so we all live here." He smiles.

"Why you're sheltered." I sigh, looking down.

He nods, watching me. "Why I don't know much of what's going on, even if I should."

"They trap you here." Just like me. I can't stop the scowl as the anger against the stupid royals comes back. It's all just about money.

"They are trying to protect us." He gives a small smile. "Rebels don't like staff any more than royals."

I never hated the people who work for the royals. Do my fellow rebels? If the royals didn't tax so much, we could break the cycle. That selfishness not only impoverished my people, but it forced me here to stop it.

Why can't they open their eyes? Why do they lock up their servants? So they can't know about it? Why can't they be open about the truth? Why did they have to trap both of us? I'm more angry for him than me. He didn't do anything wrong. Why condemn him to the palace?

Before I know what I'm saying, I glare up at him as if it's all his fault. "How can you stand it?" I demand of him.

He jumps at my sudden snap. "What?" He frowns in confusion.

"How can you stand working for them?" I ask, needing to know. He seems so warm and honest and gentle with me, yet he works for them.

"Knowing they push their people to the edge to survive? Knowing what they are hoarding? They don't even pay you well, and they lock you up in here. How can you stand it? How can you not want to snap and revolt or run away from them? How can you stand this?" I swallow. "Knowing that whatever you get paid they took from those people who hardly get by?"

I finally manage to look up and see his face. It's fallen again. He looks off into the darkness as he gathers his thoughts. There's sadness in his eyes, confusion in the crease of his brow, yet a careful calculation in how his eyes flicker as he looks off into the darkness as if he can see truth there.

Maybe the royals aren't so bad. They weren't in my interview. Maybe he knows something that the rebels and I don't. Or maybe he can help me understand how they trick so many into trusting them, including me.

"It's... not that simple," he confesses. "It's hard to afford things in a war, no matter what nation you're in. I'm not saying that makes them right," he adds quickly, "but it's not easy anywhere. And this war has gone on for over five hundred years, the longest in history and climbing. I figured they were putting it towards the war effort, you know?"

I purse my lips. I suppose that's a good cover, but I know better. They started the war by burning homes. They should have thought of that before snatching all they wanted from their people under the threat of attack. "Isn't that more reason to show they should stop it?" I ask. "Do they have to tax their already stressed people for it?"

The boy shrugs. "I guess so. I don't know. I don't know much about these things," he says. "Just an apprentice, after all." The boy watches me for a long time. "Why are you here?"

My face drops, and I pale. I should have thought that through. I spoke like a rebel, not a girl who wants to be princess. How could I explain?

Before I know it, I'm opening up to him. "It wasn't my idea. Honestly... I-I didn't want to." I swallow the pain. His careful eyes study me with warmth and compassion. I feel he really does care. "But... my family did. I had my heart set on someone else, but... but..." Tears flood my eyes, and suddenly, I'm letting out the pain like I hadn't yet. "He betrayed me. He... he was willing to... to make me do things. He was willing to all but sell me. And it was..." How could I explain?

"Well, that's not important, I guess. He never really loved me like I thought he did. It was all about his work." My lip trembles. "And I suddenly had nothing. The life I wanted was gone, and this seemed the only way out with my parents pressuring me into it, and even... even he said I should. So... I'm here. I just hope I can help someone by being here."

I flush a bit. "It's part of why I felt so trapped. I had to feel free, able-able to breathe, you know?" I meet his warm eyes again. "P-please-please, don't tell anyone. I… I can't believe I just told you. I hadn't told anyone." He is so easy to talk to. He really should be a therapist.

"Oh," the boy pauses a long time. "That's really hard. I'm sorry. I can't believe anyone wouldn't want to keep you. I-I mean…" He turns so red he's glowing in the night.

I laugh. Then catch myself. Oh my vene, what am I doing? I told him what I wouldn't even tell my parents, but I am also talking to him like he could know everything. What have I done?

Yet, I don't regret it. He understands me. He felt like a kindred spirit. He understands everything from my mother wanting me to look like her, to the pain of seeing our people suffer, to just caring about what I was going through. I'm scared of what I've done, but I don't regret it.

"I know what you mean," I assure him. "It's alright."

"Thank you for that, but no, it's not." He rubs the back of his neck, pressing his lips together in a frustrated kind of expression before he lets out a sigh and lets his head drop. "Forgive me. This isn't proper."

"Forgiven," I say instantly. "We both snuck out when we shouldn't have. It's just as much my fault."

He gives me a soft smile. "Best rule-breaking I've ever done."

I blush with pleasure. I'm about to say I agree when the man's head snaps up, and he looks behind him and to his right. I look over, but I don't see anything or hear anything.

"Oh no," he mutters more to himself than to me. He snaps around to look back at me, concern back in his eyes. "Can you get back to your room?" I nod. "Good, the guard is circling. We should go inside before they find us."

"Oh." I forgot how late it was. Yes, if the guard caught us, we'd be in huge trouble. I might be safe, but a young man like him found alone in the dead of night with one of the prince's girls? He'd be lucky if he was only hanged. "Sorry, I didn't mean to get you caught."

"Or I you." The boy smiles. "I'll see you around, right?"

I shrug. "I'm not allowed to leave. I guess so."

"Well, no one is." he shrugs back. "But I think I'll see you soon. Trust me," he grins.

I smile at his big grin. "I look forward to it," I reply. "Thank you."

He gives me a soft smile this time. "You're welcome. And thank you, M'lady." He glances around again. "I'll see you around," he promises before slipping into the bushes on my left and out of sight.

I watch the bush for a bit as he vanishes. I only wait another moment before quietly tiptoeing back to my room. It takes me about ten minutes to climb back to my balcony and into my room.

I can't believe how much better I feel!

That conversation was just what I needed, a godsend. I only meant to cry it out and clear my head. Now I feel so much better. I don't feel alone in this anymore. Even if I don't see him again, I must admit I feel better knowing I at least had a real talk with someone.

I beam and take off my over-dress and slip back into the bed. The soft sheets are welcoming. The weight is soothing now. I beam and settle into the plush pillows, really feeling their comfort for the first time. I beam and close my eyes. Perhaps the palace won't tear me apart after all. Not if I have my apprentice.

Chapter 13

The sound of curtains being pulled back mingled with the sound of general bustling around my room wakes me. Vivian spots me stirring and smiles gently. "Good morning," she says in a polite, quiet voice.

I grunt, still very sleepy from being up late and close my eyes.

"You'll want to make sure you have a good breakfast for your lessons," Flur says, hurrying to get my uniform ready.

"Lessons?"

"Yes, dance lessons for the ball tonight," Ro laughs. "How could you forget?"

"Ball?" We aren't meeting the prince until tomorrow.

"The court is welcoming you," Vivian reminds me with a slight frown.

Now she says it, I thought I heard something about that in the chatter yesterday, but I was so distracted by Yarrow ripping me apart, it hadn't really sunk in.

I push myself out of bed and let them dress me into my uniform, doing a cute low bun instead of a braid.

I notice they didn't do the kind Yarrow suggested or talked about yesterday. This one uses my layers so I have sections to the bun that give it shape and looks pretty, framing my face and the flower.

"I thought Yarrow wanted 'ballet buns'," I dare ask.

"Hm? This isn't a ballet bun?" Flur asks in mock innocence.

I smile. I'm glad I'm not the only one who hates the idea of wasting the beautiful haircut they'd given me.

Once I'm ready with hair and make-up in place, I go down to breakfast in the room beside the Ladies' Chamber. I wonder if I'll get lost, but as we're only a floor above the chamber, it isn't too bad.

The girls are all chatting happily, mostly boasting about what their attendants had planned. Even some of the girls who looked uneasy before were happily boasting now. I have to hold in my unease. Am I the only one unhappy, or did they all know how to fake it well?

After we finish eating, we are all sent up to our rooms to meet with our attendants to be fitted for our dresses, so they can do the finishing touches while we're having our dance lessons.

I'm afraid of what Yarrow has come up with, but when I see it, it doesn't look too bad. It's a floor-length tulle skirt that floats nicely with butterfly sleeves to match. The ruching style top isn't too bad either. The orange color is a unique choice. It is really… strong. But it can't be too bad. Brown and orange go well together, right? And my hair is brown.

The wrong shade it turns out. They get me into the dress with the corset and petticoats only to find this orange did not go well with my skin tone. I'm not dark enough to make a nice contrast, but I'm also not pale enough for a good contrast. In comparison, it made my skin look burned. I push my mouth to one side and look at my maids.

I see fake smiles as they look me over. I think they agree. Does the prince like lobsters?

"You look lovely," Yarrow declares as he and Vivian start looking at the fit to make sure it's all proper. I catch Ro mocking Yarrow behind his back, copying his way of speaking before fake vomiting into a nearby bin.

I smile at that. It helps me not feel so alone. At least, I know my tastes aren't terrible.

"And we will make it even better tonight when we put on the full ensemble," Yarrow says, picking up a notepad of his own and taking notes. He looks up at me now and then with a slight wince before he takes more notes. No, not even he thinks this is good. But the ball is tonight. At least I'm not meeting the prince tonight.

But what if my apprentice sees me looking like this? Maybe he won't recognize me from the dark. And the royals are elitist. They'd not let their staff join the ball. I'll be fine.

Until the other princesses saw me. I can hear them laughing. Even Princess Zelda won't be able to ignore how un-princess like I'll look.

I fight back tears as they finish making notes and finally get me out of the dress. There's half an hour before lunch, so I have time to kill. My maids suggest I get acquainted with my room or perhaps I could write home about how the Enthronement is going.

I like the latter idea. I could really use some time to vent to my mother. I am glad the desk faces away from the room where Yarrow and my maids work because it's hard to hide the tears otherwise.

I vent about how hard it is with the other girls, my fear over my dreadful attendant, and how odd it is I only saw her a few days ago. How I know the princesses are just going to laugh at me tonight and how Dad will be glad no one will take me seriously. He shouldn't worry about me being found out; he should worry about me being kicked out for not being good enough. I wipe a tear.

But… it hadn't been all bad. My mind goes back to last night and my apprentice. I smile a little. I have to share that. I pray Dad doesn't find my letter. I admit how I slipped out, being so stressed, and how I ran into him in the garden. I finish with a joke saying if she wants me to run off with some lowly servant, I had at least picked which one.

That brings a smile to my face. I seal the letter and ask Flur exactly how I should post it. She takes it, assuring me she'll make sure only my intended recipient will see it. I don't know why, but I completely trust her as I stand up and let them clean me up for lunch.

After lunch, we have dance lessons. Which is easy. I even teach some of the girls better than the teacher does. Then it's time for dinner and to prepare for the ball. Yarrow puts me into the dress with soft black dance shoes, the only nice part of the outfit. He has me wear my chosen mark as a necklace that rests right in the bend of my sweetheart neckline. He then has Flur pull my hair up into a tight bun.

At least, the bun is perfect. The shape at the back is above reproach. I like that the orange at least makes my eyes pop, but it isn't nice that the burnt look of my skin also made them pop like I've been crying.

I'm going to look like an idiot. I'm angry, frustrated, and sad. They've taken all I am and made me feel like an orange clown.

I am not supposed to look like myself when I play a role, but I'm not an actress tonight. I'm wearing my own name. And I'm going to look and feel stupid.

Yarrow gives me a glowing string of praise and kisses both my cheeks, telling me I'll be the belle of the ball. Only if that bell is rung by the royals, summoning the staff to escort me out. As soon as Yarrow lets go of me at the ballroom door, I hurry to the furthest corner I can find.

The ballroom is grand with a balustrade all across the top, apart from the west-facing side which features floor-to-ceiling windows with glass doors that lead out to the famous balcony. But it's dark, hard to see, and I'm not interested in being noticed as I open the doors to get a view for myself.

The balustrade leaves me someplace to hide under. It has sections that round out, rather like the castle walls, making a wonderful flowing pattern across the room.

Part of me is annoyed with myself for being too embarrassed to at least have a good look, but I just can't stand to let the other girls see me and make fun of me.

I glance over at the dance floor, trying to distract myself as I hold myself together.

I spot Ericka in a lovely pink ball gown that flutters as she dances the dainty steps of the dance. Princess Zelda is golden light in a white and gold dress. Princess Zinna wears a stunning red and black dress that makes even her small movements look powerful. Even Lilly looks like a perfect princess in a dark blue dress with fluttering sleeves. She picked up the dance well. I watch them in a kind of depressed stupor.

"Hello, my lady," a voice breaks into my musing. I frown and turn to see who is bothering me.

It's a gentleman dressed in a nice suit, Purerahian blue and yellow. My eyes dart over to the king and queen, holding hands and whispering to one another. They too are in those colors. I look back at the gentleman.

He is handsome, in his own way. His hair is black and smoothed back. His dark eyes help with the tall, dark, and handsome requirements. His smile is proper and a bit... I can't quite find the word. It's charming, but self-confident, trying too hard to charm and overconfident that he is.

"Hello, my...?" I question.

"Just another courtier." He brushes off my question.

I glance back at the royal family. They match. They said the prince wouldn't be here. This must be a test: see how we treat the prince. I hope he isn't the prince, but he does have dark skin, and he dresses the part. He looks a bit old to be the prince, in his late thirties maybe, but I also know the prince is older than most realize.

I manage a smile. "Then you should enjoy the party."

"So should a pretty thing like you, join me?" He offers me his hand.

"I'd really rather not," I say quickly, glancing at the other girls.

"A pretty girl like you should be part of the festivities, not hiding." He nudges me.

I really do not want to be seen, and I really don't want to dance with him. "That is very kind, but I'd really rather not." The warning from the man who'd come to my house returns, but I am too scared to be dragged out by this man.

"Did they not teach you the dance?"

"They did. In fact, I already knew it. I'm a prima actress at home. I can dance, thank you. I just rather not."

"Shy about not having it choreographed?" he asks in an attempt at being sympathetic. But the little smile comes off demeaning, the crease in his eyes almost mocking.

"No, I just don't really feel like dancing tonight."

"Oh please, just one." He actually takes my arm to pull me along.

I pull away and fold my arms tighter. "You are very kind, but I'd really rather not. I'm much happier watching."

"But your ladyship, oh..." He hits himself over the head with his palm. "Forgive me, I did not even ask your name."

"Kascia," I say quickly, hoping to divert him. "But I'm really quite happy here. It looks like some other ladies are dying to dance with you." I nod back at a group looking over at us. I'm glad he's between me and them, so they can't see how horrible I look.

The man's eyes widen and then he looks back at me. "Indeed, I will not forget though. Save one dance for me."

I roll my eyes as he leaves. I hope I can avoid him the rest of the night.

I rub my arms, my eyes sliding back to the floor. I want to go home.

"I hoped I'd see you here."

I jump, surprised someone else is bugging me, but this voice makes my heart flutter. I know that voice.

I turn slowly. My apprentice is smiling at me. That smile does make me feel so safe and welcome. It's easier to see him now, even in the shadows.

His amber eyes are deep and warm, sparkling with mischief. His hair is dark brown in the proper light. I have a harder time seeing his worker build under the waistcoat and suit jacket he wears, a proper dancing suit, though a bit worn. And it isn't a perfect fit, too small in the wrong places and too large in others. He does look good in the royal purple and white though.

"What are you doing here?" I ask. I can't believe the royal family would let servants attend.

He beams at me with a new smile. I like this one too. It radiates energy and excitement. "What? They let servants join in. They have to or these would be boring."

"Excuse me?" I frown.

"Well, think about it, would you want to attend a party that's nothing but your coworkers? Where your only dance partner is someone you've been fighting with for three hours over the national budget?" he asks me with a playful glint in his eye.

I can't help but laugh, "No, I suppose that would be miserable."

"So they have to let us in or be bored out of their minds," he smiles a softer smile. I could enjoy his various arrays of smiles all night.

"At least, they aren't that stuck up."

"Yeah, guess not," he agrees a bit more hesitantly. "I'm glad to see you here. I was hoping I would. Why are you hiding?"

I recall what I look like and turn red. I am not going to admit that to him though. At least, he's too stupidly male or kind to realize why I'm hiding.

"Just... don't feel like I fit in." I manage the truth without admitting it in full.

His face fills with understanding, and he gives me a sympathetic smile. Yes, that one from last night. It makes me feel understood and safe to tell him anything. But I am not going to tell him.

"I know how that can feel," he says. "But a girl as pretty as you should at least be dancing." He glances at the dancers. "Even if such a simple dance is beneath you."

I blush. Oh… now I really look like a lobster! "You know who I am," I guess.

"I don't know your name." He tries to meet my eyes.

"Kascia," I give it to him, so he'd stop prying. "But you know I'm a dancer?"

"I took my time guessing. I couldn't find you so figured I'd try the field," he says.

"What?" I demand. Why was he dancing with the others?

"Well, the prince only gets one. Leaves the rest open for the rest of us." His mischievous grin reminds me of someone. I can't think of who. Maybe Jake, or maybe that's just the rapid beat of my heart.

"That's gallant of you," I try to tease, attempting to pull myself out of the depressed mood.

"But it was you I was hoping to find. Took me most of the night with you hiding back here." He looks around. "I'll have to remember it."

"For what?"

"Rendezvous. I get to come to these parties all the time."

"So, I'll see you around?"

"As long as you stay." He grins again. "But come on." He offers me his hand.

"Oh no, I…"

"Come on, you have to be the best dancer here. Just one," he begs.

I force a small smile. Maybe it would make me feel better. I take his hand.

The beaming smile of triumph I get makes my heart melt a little. How does he do this to me?

He leads me onto the floor, and we join in the dance. This dance is heavily scripted, not hard to follow, but his leading is spot on. He also gets more into the dance than most people I've ever danced with.

Partway through the dance, as I pivot, I feel something soft fall down the back of my neck. I jump and reach at my neck to feel my hair. It has fallen from its bun. It felt tight. I can't believe it came undone. I flush a little. Now I look like I'm falling apart on top of looking stupid.

But it doesn't seem to hurt my appearance. It is pleasant to feel it at the back of my neck, flowing with me along with the skirt and sleeves. He may have sensed I am embarrassed because he makes me laugh by skipping with more pleasure than any of the other men and even almost doing a lift instead of an underarm turn, making me giggle.

"You're doing it wrong," I inform him.

"I'm doing it better," he replies as the song stops, and I plié and bow my head to him as he bows to me.

"You'd be far better in ballroom instead of line social dances," I say as he takes my hand and leads me back.

"Would I? Uh." He tilts his head. "Perhaps I should run away and join a theater."

"You'd have to get accepted. Can you sing at all?" I joke.

"Hm, might be a problem." He rubs his chin. "I may need a tutor."

"I may find myself with the time."

"Oh really?" He raises a brow. The way his eyes sparkle makes me laugh. "I may have to steal whatever time I can get."

"Well, as far as I know, the Enthronement doesn't dictate all my time. When you're done with your duties, perhaps we can find a music room to try it in," I suggest.

"You might get in trouble being alone with a man, not the prince." He points out.

"Bring a guard." I shrug.

"Perhaps." He bows to me again. "But this apprentice should behave better with a lady. Forgive my being rude. I just had to see you after last night."

"I'm glad you did." I smile weakly.

Even if it was just because he is the only friend I had here, I feel I need to see him too. "Just don't get in trouble on my account, alright?"

"Promise." He crosses his heart. "Shall I see you again?"

"I guess that depends on your duties and mine." I force a smile. "But even if it's just tonight, thank you. I can't tell you how badly I needed a friend the last few days."

"The girls aren't friends?" He frowns.

I shrug. "Not really. Maybe in time, but I wouldn't say that."

"Well, hopefully, that changes, and I'll see you soon." He kisses my hand. "But I should go before your attendant or someone gets annoyed I'm taking all your attention."

If only he would, but before I can comment on it, he's gone. I can't help but watch him as he goes off and starts talking to a guard or courtier or servant.

If only it was as simple as Mom said and that boy could be my escape from this madness. Oh, if only. But there is no escape, not for me. I am a Chosen daughter of Purerah now. I am in too deep. That boy can't save me.

Chapter 14

The girls were at chatting excitedly at breakfast, nudging one another and asking what they wanted to ask the prince first. I didn't join in. How could I play interested in the prince? How did I with Jake? There was no real flirting. We just realized it and were happy together.

I smile a bit as I think of our first kiss in our little place by the river. Then my heart throbs as if the memory is a razor scraping off the top of my heart. That magic would never come back. I'd never be able to get over my fear of Jake.

The little butterflies from the other night return. The soft flush of my cheeks as my apprentice stumbled over himself in the fright of running into me. Yes, that is the feeling to pretend I have with the prince. He'd fall for that.

I try to capture that feeling in my chest, so I can release it at the moment I have to play the part like I've done with a million emotions before.

We're brought back into the Ladies' Chamber after breakfast. We're waiting a long time, so long the girls stop talking, all looking anxious.

Finally, the two doors open, and the guards step in to attend them, and one man follows. He looks like a guard by his demeanor but doesn't quite act like one. He looks at all of us, his eyes lingering on me. He's not wearing a guard uniform. He's dressed all in black. Even his hair is black, parted down the middle and long, pulled into a small ponytail. His light skin and dark appearance make his green eyes stand out as they scan the room. He finally nods and steps aside.

A second man, dressed like a nobleman, steps into the room. Is this the prince? I recognize him from the ball. My apprentice had walked over and talked with him after he'd wished me good night. This man is handsome, much better than the creep last night. He has pale skin, stylishly messy brown hair, and a smattering of freckles across his nose. He gives us a slight bow.

"May I present," he says, dispelling any hope that he might be the prince. It's going to be the creep, isn't it? "His royal highness, Prince Gavril Potentate of Purerah." The gentleman steps back and in steps...

I flush and yet blanch at the same time. My stomach drops, and my heart freezes and curls in on itself for protection. I take in a quick sharp breath before I can't breathe anymore. My mouth hangs open, unable to process what's happening. It's my apprentice.

He gives us all a shy smile, one of the curls his mother wishes were a coil falls a little into his face as his dark amber eyes look us over. He's dressed splendidly in a white shirt and Purerahian blue waistcoat with Purerahian yellow designs done into the fabric, matching his cravat. My stomach tosses as I watch the light glimmer of a blue gem pin that keeps the cravat in place.

No, no, this can't be. He can't be the prince. He just... I feel like the world is falling in on itself. First the king and queen, now the prince? The prince is my only friend in this cursed castle!?

Oh, the king. That was the smile I recognized. The king's mischievous smile. I should have realized. He does have the perfect blend of his parent's skin tones, making his hue a stunning light brown, like chocolate milk.

Panic, pain, and fear fill my mind. I look away to try to take it all in and not be noticed. Again, all I know is being shattered. The one person I'd felt safe with, the one I joked to my mother I'd run off with, is the prince. What does this mean? How did the king manage to charm me like this? Do they have some crazy magic?

And what I'd said that first night... I'm lucky I am still here. Is he eliminating me today? He had to wait until we all knew who he was, but he meant this whole time to dismiss me. Dad is going to be so disappointed.

My stomach tightens. I'll have to go back having failed the job. I'd have to keep faking it, and we still wouldn't move forward. They'll be angry with me. I had never feared Jake hurting me before, but after what I learned, I'm terrified of what they'll say or do to me. I failed the mission. The thing that mattered most to him. If he has any love for me at all, failing this soon and this badly would surely take what little there is. What am I going to do? I fight tears and fear, reminding myself I still was on the stage.

The prince — no longer my apprentice but the prince — holds out his hands to invite us to stay seated. I try not to meet his eyes as every other girl in the room tries to catch it. I hear Emmalina and Violet panting in ecstasy.

I feel sicker. I would be happy to see him too if... I fight more tears. My only friend is gone, a lie. I'd all but invented him. I am not going to find him or any true friend again.

"Please, there is no need," he says, his once soothing voice making my heart ache. "It's wonderful to finally meet you all and... as myself." He looks at a few of us one at a time.

Oh, I almost forgot, he said he'd played the room. He'd danced with each one of us. He wasn't just goofing and flirting; he was testing us. If last night was a test, how am I still here? How were we all still here? Someone had to fail the first test, right? Or did we all pass? Was it just beauty? No, I'd have been kicked out so fast.

I look away to make sure he doesn't look at me while I try to keep my crumbling heart from dropping to the floor, feeling like Cinderella desperately picking up the ripped pieces of the dress her stepsisters ripped to shreds. The dress was the friend I'd invented. The real him had torn it to bits.

"May I start by apologizing for the subterfuge; it was your first test. To see how you'd treat me when I didn't bear the title of prince," he explains.

"But let's finally start to get to know one another. I'm sure you'd like to be allowed to wear the wonderful things your attendants made you. You're free to change once lunch is over. I apologize if these interviews are brief, but I have to get through all of you in one morning. I'll do my best to make them mean more than last night." He forces an uneasy smile.

"But before all that," he goes on, "I want to personally thank you all for doing this. I know it's not easy. It's not easy on any of us, I think. And I want to say thank you for your willingness, and no matter how it turns out for you, I hope you are glad you came. Even if your reasons for being here are... different." He glances at me.

I look away, turning red. How dare he use that on me! In front of everyone. Is he just a pig of a prince?

My heart breaks a little more to learn the person I felt so safe with was just... a mask. I want that boy back. I want this prince to go away and never come back. I'd rather my apprentice. No way he is going to save me now. It is certain no one could. I have to let my fiancé and Dad murder him and his parents.

"The rules bind you as well as me," the prince continues. "I will give you a rare warning. This interview is your second test. I will not tell you what I'm testing for, but please understand if you don't pass, I have no choice. I don't take pleasure in it." His brows are drawn in concern like they had been many times last night and the night before. What a good actor he is.

"So per the rules," the prince finally speaks again as if shaking himself from an unpleasant thought. "We'll start with the highest number and work our way down." He pulls a paper from his pocket, worn and well used. "Lady Emmalina, please." He looks up and spots her. He smiles warmly and nods her to follow.

Two guards stay while the man who'd announced the prince and the man clad in black follow the prince and Emmalina. She looks back at us in pure excitement, beaming and giving us two thumbs up. Violet, Jonquil, and Forsythia return it, though Forsythia looks sarcastic in her response.

As soon as they are gone, the girls buzz into talk, gushing over how handsome the prince is.

I remain sitting where I am: devastated. At least I have time to put on my face. How do I put it on when he's seen the real me under this? I have to come up with a cover story. I have to...

I jump as Lilly sits by me. "I made a fool of myself last night with him," she says, sounding terrified. "Kascia, what do I do?"

I scramble to answer her, not even sure myself, "Um... apologize?" I swallow. "I-I didn't do too well either. I... I didn't even want to dance with him."

"I openly said I was terrified of him." Lilly frowns.

I smile a little. "That's not too bad." Helping comfort her distracts me. I spend the rest of the time soothing her until she's called in.

Then I'm left to myself. I want to pace. I want to run, but I know the other girls will pick on me for that. I realize none of the other girls had returned. Did that mean they were eliminated or just that they were being told to go somewhere else once the interview is done?

I feel numb, unsure how to react. All I can think is I want my apprentice back. But that's not a choice. Just like going back to my old life before the Enthronement. How do I cover up my true self to the prince now he's seen me?

The voice of the man who'd announced the prince cuts into my thoughts, "Number twelve!" He sounds like he's called me a few times.

I get to my feet, shaking a little, and manage a weak smile as I walk over. He smiles back kindly. "Forgot your number?"

"Yeah, names are easier," I joke back half-heartedly.

"Yours is?"

"Kascia."

"Kascia, you were the one who hid."

I swallow and nod.

"Don't be afraid. He wasn't upset with you, trust me. He made sure you weren't missed. I almost miscounted." He tries to comfort me. "I'm Godwin, the prince's valet. It's like your attendant only I work for him permanently and am his right-hand man, like a butler, only cooler."

I manage a small laugh.

"See? You'll do fine," he assures me. If only he knew how badly I already messed this up.

He takes me into a side meeting room with a guard at the door. Godwin nods at him and opens the door for me with a bow. I bow my head to him in thanks. He raises his eyebrows as if in surprise as I step into the room.

The first thing I see is the man in black, standing in the back corner of the room, arms folded, leaning his shoulders into the wall, watching me with a dangerous look like he knows my treasonous intent.

I swallow and look away. I spot him. The prince is standing, hands behind his back, looking back at me over his shoulder with his head tilted down a little, making it appear he is looking up at me, with a soft smile.

My heart races in fright. I've already trusted him with so much that I can't share now. What am I going to do? What do I say to the prince who I called a torturer of his people? How did I mend my heart enough to speak to him calmly?

The moment the door closes behind us, the formal square of the prince's shoulders drops. I see my apprentice in him again. My heart aches and anger fills me. Just like Jake, just a lie. I want to throw something at him and run, but that isn't an option.

He gives me a sheepish smile. Another new smile and my heart can't help but log it with the rest. In my anger, I want to throw them all away, but I can't. I can't even stop myself from collecting them. I'm hopeless. I can't survive this.

"First," he says nervously, "let me apologize. I'd be livid if I were you."

I hate him for understanding and being open with me. That's not how the brat prince behaves! The prince and my friend can't be the same. I don't know what to do or say, so I keep on the mask.

"Please, I don't expect you to just forgive me," he goes on, "honestly... I half hope you won't."

"What?"

"I know that sounds crazy. Let me explain. Please, have a seat, my lady." He offers me the soft armchair across from the one he stood in front of.

I tell myself to just nod and take it like a lady, but I can't. "Why?" I ask, meeting his amber eyes with my angry ones. "You'll just drive me out."

His face falls as if hurt. "No, I won't," he says, a hint of offense in his voice. "Let me promise you right now, I'm not 'driving you out' today." His eyes won't leave mine to make sure I believe him. "I'm not counting that night against you. In fact, if anything, you should use it against me, but please, take a seat. I can better explain."

I swallow hard but finally take the offered chair. The prince sits down. He rests his elbows on his knees and leans forward.

"Can I start with I'm so sorry for whatever anger or hurt or pain I caused you?" he asks meekly. "I can't even imagine what you've been through in your life or whatever brought you here. I'm also sorry we didn't get to properly meet. So I'll start. I'm Prince Gavril, but when you're ready, you can call me Gavril, or just yell it at me. I'm sure you'd like to," He smiles again. He smiles a lot. "I am sure you're quite angry. I know how that feels, so feel free to yell at me. Just don't expect me to not be hurt. I'll try, but I'm only human."

"You don't want me to yell at you?"

"Well no, but yes." He shrugs one shoulder. "Miss Kascia, you have to understand. As you said, I don't know my people. I want to, though. I want to so badly it hurts. I want to help them, but I don't know how. I can't understand them locked behind these walls. You... you let me see into that world is like even just a little. You have no idea how badly I need and want that.

"For that alone, I want you here as long as I can keep you, win or not. So don't stop yelling at me. Don't stop letting it out. I want to know. Even if it hurts. No, I don't like being yelled at. But having needed to yell it out myself many, many times, I know you may need the healing, and I need to know what pains you've faced. So please, if you need to, get it out. Why do you hate me?"

I don't. I hate the prince, but I don't hate the man sitting across from me. "You lied to me." I wish I sounded angrier, but it comes out in a low, hurt voice. "You're no apprentice."

"I am so," the prince defends. "Am I not learning the family trade from my father?" the man in black huffs derisively. The prince turns to give him a telling-off look.

I frown deeper. "You stole that from a play."

The prince's brows draw together in an offended frown. "I did not."

"Did too. It's from Cinderella."

"Oh, is it?" He looks back at his guard. "It was his idea."

"He wasn't there."

"Oh, he was," the prince assures me. "He's my Custod guard. Always assume he's around, even when you can't see him, unless I say he isn't."

My face drains of color, and I look at the Custod guard. Does he know me? Is he one of the few Custods in on the secret, or was he not told, so he could play the guard? I'm surprised the Head Custod sent a Custod guard. That doesn't make sense.

The pained clash in my chest grinds together, making my chest and heart hurt all the more.

"This is Sage." The prince introduces him. "I will say from the start he's not a fan. He was mad I hung out so long that night." He was the one who had the messenger take the surprise impressions. He must have memorized our faces.

"That makes him a good guard. You weren't supposed to be there, and I must look like a huge security threat." I hold back tears. I don't mean to be a threat. Well, perhaps I do; I still don't know.

"It's okay." The prince smiles. "I think he's wrong."

I meet the prince's eyes in shame. "How can you know?" I ask. "I-I didn't mean to be rude. And I didn't lie to you. I may wish to hide some of those feelings, but really, I..."

"And so was I," the prince says firmly, "So let's just log that conversation as if it were part of this one, alright?" He studies my face.

"You aren't throwing me out?" I ask.

The prince shakes his head. "No. You haven't failed any parts of the test yet. And until you do, I don't plan to throw you out." He smiles once more. "I need your help to know my people, Lady Kascia. Don't deny me that."

"Why? So you can toy with me?" I demand, the pain rising inside me. "Like you've been playing with it since this started? Throwing the oddest tests at us and asking more. What even is this? Can you not find a girl any other way?" I stop myself in horror. "I-I'm so sorry. I rarely yell like that. Forgive me. You sh-should dismiss me. I can't believe I..." I bite my lip to stop it from shaking. Why am I volunteering to be sent home? What's wrong with me?

But the prince just smiles more. "No, I'm glad you did. I want to hear it." The honesty in his voice gets me to look at him.

He leans forward once more. "Kascia, I admire your honesty. To tell you the truth, I think you've been more honest with me than anyone in my life, and I long for that." His guard huffs, but the prince ignores it. "You catch my eye for reasons everyone else worries about. But I want to know the truth. So let's just understand that you will only be sent back if I find your actions not in line with a true princess or you fail one of the tests. And so far, I see nothing that isn't in line with a true princess.

"You're honest. You're standing up for yourself, and as I saw it, our people. You know our people and care for them the way I want to. So please, keep defending them to me and them."

Could there be hope that he might actually turn everything around? That if he knew the truth that he'd end the tax and lift the burden from his people? I had never, not even once, thought that was possible. But this isn't the prince my father and other rebels hated. As he looked at me, I saw my apprentice. As I look at him, I see my apprentice and the prince. Do I really see hope?

The images my father gave me flash to mind. The prince helped them do it. He was part of it. Or was he? I have to know. I have to calm the storm and fear in my chest. I have to stay and play the game. It is the only way I'll find the truth. I have to pretend to want him. But don't I? I want my apprentice, but can I let my apprentice and the prince be the same?

"Can you do that?" he asks me.

I take a deep breath, using the air to quiet the storms inside of me and nod like the queen I have to pretend to be. "Yes, Your Highness, I will do my best."

"That's all I ask." He smiles and sits back, looking me over. I see a question in his eyes, but he doesn't ask it. Instead, he looks into my eyes. "So, can you forgive me for all the pain I've caused you?"

I nod before I get my mind around it. "If you can forgive me."

The prince smiles once more. "Forgiven." And his tone makes me think he added: "now and always" in his head.

My heart skips a beat in its flutter, and I swallow. What is he doing to me? I have to get my head back. I need to breathe. But I don't want to leave that warm circle either.

"So, as this is supposed to be the moment we meet." The prince leans back. "Tell me more about you. You danced for a living?"

"I was a performer," I say. "A triple threat as we say in my business. I sing, dance, and act. But dance is likely my favorite, and ballet is my passion."

"Ah, how you knew Sage's Cinderella reference when I did not." The prince smiles at his guard. The guard glares back.

I force a smile and a small nod, "Yes, my lord, that is how I know. I performed as her in the musical. We blended in ballet for the dances as Mom knows I love it."

"The one who wants you blonde?" he asks.

I can't help but smile at the fact he remembered. "Yes," then I put the pieces from our conversation together with what I know about him, "Your mother hoped you'd have the royal coils."

"Indeed." The prince smiles. "She did and still says I will grow into them one day. She's wrong of course. I'm far too old to grow into anything, other than infirmity. But Mom still tries to get coils out of my hair. Never happening. My servants or I have to fix it after she tries."

"You do your own hair?" I assumed a pampered prince would have servants do that.

"I like to do things for myself when allowed."

I frown. "Is it that rare?"

"Yes, for larger things most of all," he says. "Why I know so little. My parents are very protective of me. Would they run such a contest if not? Why couldn't I just choose for myself otherwise?"

"Oh." Everyone knew they were protective but this protective? "Are you happy with it?"

"Happy to find a way to finally marry and do my duty, yes." The prince nods. "I hope to find true love here." But his tone doesn't sound hopeful.

I smile a little, "I hope you do too."

The prince grins widely. "And I hope you at least get your heart healed after what your former lover did to you."

My heart falters. I wish he didn't know that. I don't want him to have that against me, but he isn't using it against me. He is trying to comfort me. I stop my lip shaking.

"Is it really over with him?" the prince asks, sympathy and pain for my ache in his eyes as he studies me. I hate how he does that because... I love it so much. I feel Sage's eyes boring into me.

I turn away from him before I squeak out my answer, "yes." My heart can't trust him again. To try to get Sage off me, I go on, "I promised to give the Enthronement my all. So I will."

The prince beams. I can see even his Custod guard is impressed, but he still seems displeased.

"Good. Because if you wanted to go back, I'd release you now and tell them you didn't pass," the prince says, "Even though it would hurt to lose the most honest friend I've ever had."

"You've known me one night," I protest.

"Two." The prince holds up two fingers. "And that is the sad fact of it, Miss Kascia. That still is completely true. You're the most honest friend I've had."

I frown in disappointment for him. Then I glance at Sage. "Not your guard?"

"Well, true point, he is really honest with me," the prince agrees. "But as he says we aren't friends."

I glance back at Godwin who's been beaming from ear to ear as if delighted he was caught in mischief. Palace servants are odd, aren't they?

I turn back to meet Sage's green eyes. He is still watching me. He scares me. He's the one person who might guess why I came here and the game I am playing. But I'll stick to my current plan. He can't know then.

"Though he's lasted longer than most Custod guards do. I go through Custods quickly. They don't like to stay. It's confusing, and my parents are demanding. Sage is one of the longest-lasting and my favorite. He's my ally. So more than a friend, I guess."

"I suppose it's better than nothing."

"I agree." The prince nods. "So tell me—"

"Your Highness," Godwin cuts in. "You have thirty-nine more to go." He looks at the clock.

"Oh yes, sorry." The prince also looks at the clock. I do too. Oh no! We've taken more time than the other interviews already.

"I will not take up more time." I stand and curtsy to the prince. "I will see you around."

The words strike me like a blow to the chest. It isn't a question like the other times we said it. But it wasn't as hopeful either. I have to share him with the other girls. I also am not sure I'll get to keep him. I may have to let him die to save myself. My throat tightens.

"At lunch." The prince nods as he stands with me. "Enjoy the rest of your morning, Miss. Kascia." He bows to me. "I believe we have a grand adventure ahead."

Chapter 15

I hug myself tightly as Godwin sees me out. He gives me a gentle smile. "You did perfect," he says. "And I'll be asking about that other night for sure." I flush, forgetting he heard all of that and didn't know about our first meeting.

He doesn't press as he brings me into a different sitting room. The other girls who went ahead of me are frittering about. I look at them all, then frown. Something is wrong.

There should be five girls. I only count four. I think it through and realize the one I didn't know well, the first on the list after the princesses, was gone. I see Bella, Dahlia, Jonquil, and Lilly, but Emmalina is gone. Why isn't she here? The prince told me I wasn't going yet so...

"Oh, she made it." Dahlia sighs as if disappointed. Lilly on the other hand beams.

By the time all is said and done, ten girls have been eliminated. At least the prince seems to know what he wants. Though it makes me nervous. What if it's over before the Harvest Ball?

We're taken into the main dining hall for lunch which is on the north side of the entrance hall. The head table is at the top of the room with a seat for each member of the royal family. Long windows line the right side of the room, opening to the front gardens.

There are two long tables in the center of the room with room for ten people on either side of it, two tables, twenty girls each. They are perfectly set for how many girls are left.

We all filter in, trying to be proper and princess-like. The born princesses don't bother though, chatting as normal.

I'm sitting across from Princess Rose with Azalea next to me.

Azalea is beaming and looking around in delight. She takes her seat and a servant pushes her chair in as another does for me. I turn and nod thanks to my servant.

I hear a slight whisper to my right and look over to see how close I'm seated to the high table. I don't hear what the prince whispers to the king, but the king's chuckle I couldn't miss. He sits at the center of the table with his son on his right and queen on his left, making the queen the next closest person to me apart from Azalea.

As the other girls settle in, I notice the royal family may have been open to chuckles, but I can tell from the crease on the king's and queen's brows they're a little concerned, whispering in low voices, so the girls can't hear. I notice the queen glancing over us in worry and catch the king doing the same under the pretense of coughing into his handkerchief. From the tone of the whispers, the king is grilling his son with questions. They must be surprised by the quick drop off too. The prince is smiling as if amused as he replies casually.

I look a bit behind the prince and jump to see his guard, Sage, looking right at me as if trying to catch me. I give him a smile, unsure what else to do. I distract myself by looking down at the table. Bella is now sitting beside Princess Zelda. The former number one common girl is already gone.

I wonder if that's what the king and queen are worried about. If she was their top pick for a non-born royal, they must have thought highly of her. I wonder what she lacked that made the prince dismiss her. Didn't yell at him enough? I fight to stop myself from flushing at the thought.

We finally are all seated, and the king welcomes us. "It will be nice to have a home full of happy voices for a while," he beams widely. "Princess Zelda would agree." He winks at her. She smiles and nods. "We can finally pretend to have a big family." I and a few others laugh.

The king takes the chance to stifle a cough and sit. Few girls look at each other with narrow eyes. They just see competition. Others, though, look like friends already, like Azalea and Bella who are chatting every time they are together.

I look at the princesses. They are eating properly, and none are talking to each other. Princess Zinna is trying to catch the prince's eye, but he's still talking with his parents.

After the king offers devotion, the meal starts. I glance at the royal table. The prince is sitting up, no longer turned to his parents and is looking at us.

Oh flames, he's judging still. He's looking at table manners. He spots me looking at him, and he smiles. I return it and go back to my meal.

I look down at the table at Lilly as a distraction. She's shrinking in her seat. The poor thing is perhaps too young for this. It doesn't help Jonquil, who sits on her other side, is a bit loud, chatting away with anyone and everyone who'll talk to her. She's talking about her twin brother and how odd it is not to have him here.

The other girls eventually relax as the meal goes on and start chatting. Azalea starts asking me about the interview, well more like telling me about her interview.

"Isn't he just the gentleman?" she asks me. "And the way he looks at you..." she stares off into space.

"I suppose he has a way about him." I admit, trying to hide the storm inside my chest. I am glad it's just soup today. Not sure I could stomach more.

I glance at the prince. He's still looking at us. I wonder if he's trying to remember names or is looking to see who doesn't eat enough like a princess. Perhaps he is as shallow as I thought. My stomach knots, and I take another bite of soup.

After lunch, the guards take us back to the Ladies' Chamber. We are free to do as we like the rest of the day, even to change out of the uniform. Many girls do, but I decide I'm alright in this for now. I take the chance to observe the girls in a more relaxed state.

"Kascia!" Azalea's call makes me jump. "Come, join us," she laughs at my jump.

I hesitate. Do I dare get close? Then again, wouldn't I stand out more if I didn't? I glance around the room. Not a single girl is sitting on her own. I get up and join the group.

"Jonquil was just showing us her sketches," Bella beams at me. "They're really neat."

I look down and see the drawing book Jonquil is holding. There are beautiful sketches of butterflies, moths, dragonflies, beetles, and more. Normally, I don't care much for bugs. I've never seen them as beautiful. Not until seeing how Jonquil sees them. Even a creepy crawler looks beautiful in her artwork.

"These are all the same species, but depending on where they live, their color and power changes," she explains. "And this one even changes with the weather. If there's lightning in the air, they get yellow along these lines. And if you freeze them in that state and you make the potion, it will help you resist electrical magic. Though having to kill them is a bit of a bummer."

"That's amazing," Bella says. "That's amazing detail."

"It's for my reference. I never thought of it as pretty." Jonquil shrugs.

Bella smiles. "I like it. It would be a good decoration in an office or in your family shop."

Jonquil tilts her head. "I'd never thought of that. My brother would laugh me silly."

"Elder brother?" I guess.

"Only by about seven minutes." She smiles. "He's my twin. No one realizes as he doesn't look much like me, but he and I would hunt bugs together. It's actually really weird to be away from him so long." She frowns. But after a minute, her face lights up again. "But... if I get to marry the prince, it's worth it. It will be amazing to get further. If I don't make it, at least, it hopefully will help me move on. I've never managed to like other boys. Isn't that horrible?" She flushes.

I laugh. "I can't imagine."

"So why did you try out?" Jonquil asks me.

My face falls. Why does everyone ask that? I try to be honest, but I also don't want to talk about my Jake problems or daddy issues. "Honestly, my mother thought I needed a life change. I was with one guy for a long time, but then he did something that proved he didn't mind losing me. And I'd like to help my people. So I thought, why not try?"

"Wow. Now that's sad and amazing." Jonquil smiles. "A real princess reason." She nudges me playfully. I roll my eyes.

Azalea tactfully changes the subject. "I heard you're a world-famous performer," she says with a smile.

I force a smile and nod. I don't like to say I'm that famous, but it's true.

"You do ballet, right?"

"Yeah."

Azalea beamed wider. "I wonder if you'd like to let me do something I've always dreamed of."

My brows draw together. "What?"

"Well, I play the flute," she says. "And I always wanted to play for a dancer to dance to. It was something I wanted to do when I was little. I don't know why. But maybe we can try it sometime."

I smile. "I'd like that."

"Do you need certain songs you know the set steps to?" Azalea asks.

"I don't need it. I can improv." I chuckle. It is one of my favorite games to play.

"Can I watch?" Lilly asks.

"Sure," Azalea beams.

"Can I join?" Jonquil proffers timidly.

"The more the merrier," Azalea laughs. "If you don't mind," she adds to me. I smile and nod. "We'll make a party of it!" Azalea beams.

"I love a good party," Bella adds. They all giggle. I wish I felt as giggly about anything.

We decide we can try it out tomorrow morning, and we chat for a while, watching the other girls and trying to get to know them. Bella and Azalea are social butterflies, or they're flowers that attract the social butterflies. Soon Isla, Florence, Violet, and Bellatrix have joined us.

The days pass by without much happening. The prince starts asking girls out one on one pretty much right away, but he doesn't ask me, adding to my nervousness. And what Yarrow makes for me is even worse than the other dress. I wince as I look at another "Burn me orange" piece he's made.

"Are there any other options?" I ask timidly.

"Um... not really," Vivian says and nods to Flur to show me the other five dresses I have to choose from. Alright, one of them is a softer orange. The lighter orange is much better. I opt for that dress instead.

The bad color might have been more tolerable if it was better designed. All the dresses are one fabric all the way through with no variation, not even a lighter or darker color for contrast. They all tie around my middle and the only unique features apart from varying shades of orange between dresses are the sleeves and collar.

At least I'm not the only girl with bad designs. Some girls are clearly not well matched. Perhaps it's just that there are only so many good designers who will work for this contest and bad pay.

The Ladies' Chamber is always interesting. The three self-named celebrities have formed a clique and like to bully anyone they can. The princesses sit to themselves. Though, Princess Zelda is mostly playing with that odd tablet of hers. I've never seen anything like it. I thought it was a gaming system at first, but it's clear hers does more than that. She writes on it like paper, takes impressions, and reads off of it. But I don't dare try to ask more about it.

On the Service Day of rest, my maids slip me into a nice white dress that's better than anything I've been given yet. I doubt my attendant approved the dress. There's no orange. I notice Vivian, Ro, and Flur are trying to make sure no one sees me in them. I suspect they picked out this dress without Yarrow's permission.

The group devotion is small. It's just the royal family, a handful or two of servants, and the Chosen. I try to see if they're all here, but I can't quite tell. I mean, for a rest day, it's a bit early at nine in the morning, but it's not that bad.

To my surprise, the prince runs the service. It must be something they do to help him prepare to be king. Sage is there as well, helping with the proceedings. I thought a royal meeting would be different, but it's not that different from what I'm used to.

My maids accepted my offer to sit on my left, and soon after, Lilly, Jonquil, Isla, Bella, and Azalea sit with me. I notice the rest of the cliques sit together too.

We then go to lunch with the royal family. When we get there, I frown. The other table isn't full, but there are no extra place settings. Two girls are missing. That makes only thirty-eight left. Apparently, true princesses attend services. I swallow, glad I was brought up religious.

But another week goes by, and the prince still hasn't asked me out. Two more girls are eliminated, none I know. Some girls are boasting two dates now. I'm the only one not to have had a date yet. Why hasn't he just eliminated me?

On top of that, I fear what happens to the girls if I let the rebels in. Jake's friends might hurt them. That fear creeps into my dreams and wakes me up, and I hug my knees until my maids come in to get me ready for the day. I can't let them get hurt, but what else can I do?

I write Mom at the end of each week, but don't mention the prince being the apprentice and pretend the evening meeting never happened. I write Dad too, but much more general updates at first, pretending all is well while fearing I'll be eliminated any moment. But in my last letter, I decide to ask him to promise not to hurt any of the Chosen girls still here. They are victims too after all. Once I get that message back, I'll feel much better.

I try to pretend all is normal, using the day to play games. I am distracted as Azalea shows us her talent today, explaining how her flute works.

We'd taken it in turns after I showed them my pointe shoes to teach other about our old jobs. It's Lilly who notices my mood first.

"What's wrong?" she asks.

"Nothing," I promise with a small smile. "I haven't slept well."

"Is this about the prince not asking you out yet?" Jonquil asks.

"He will," Azalea says confidently, "He's just getting the others out of the way. I'm sure he is looking forward to it."

"Best for last, like I said," Jonquil reminds me with sympathy in her eyes.

"Yeah, and maybe he thinks you'll have the most fun," Lilly says. "We had fun. I think he likes fun. And as we know, you're always fun. He even calls you pigeon too."

I had noticed he addresses many of the Chosen girls as "pigeon". None of us know what it means, but we all presume it was a good thing as it sounds like a sweet pet name.

I flush as the girls agree it's sweet name.

Isla puts her hand on top of mine. Her eyes meet mine. "Sometimes, those with the greatest blessings coming have to wait the longest," she says. "Think of the old writ. How long the Merlin waited for a child. How long the people waited for him. The greatest blessings take patience. You'll have your time."

"Thanks, Isla." She is quiet but so full of faith. I admire that faith. I wish I was more like her.

"You're welcome." Isla smiles. "Don't forget it. I think you will make it almost all the way. Just watch."

Chapter 16

I go to my room as soon as I can get away. I thought I knew the way by heart, but in my depression, I get lost. I frown, hugging myself and looking left and right. I spot a window and walk over, hoping to see where I am.

A voice stops me short. "No, I told you, just because I'm here, doesn't mean you get a quote," the voice says. It seems familiar; I can't place it. It's a man's voice, that is certain.

I rush over to a door and slip inside the room, cracking the door so there isn't a sound of me closing it, but I'm also hidden behind it. The voices are getting closer. I glance out the gap and spot two shadows.

"Aw, come on, cuz." A second voice, also male, begs. "I'm heading up there now. Just one comment on the events, just one small comment from the royal family."

"I don't give comments. I told you that before I even came here," the first insists. "How did you even get in?"

"I'm nobility like you, remember?" The second voice sounds amused.

"Lovely." The first sounds annoyed but amused. "So no tossing you out then?"

"Oh, come on, cuz, a small bite."

"Honestly, I don't even know what event you're talking about."

I glance out the crack to see if I can see them, but all I can see are shadows, two men for sure about the same size.

"Oh, so the prince is clueless." The second man sounds excited.

"I didn't say that. I thought we had an agreement it's off the books unless I say otherwise." The first voice still is a bit playful, but I hear a serious note of warning in it too.

"Ah, come on, I need something."

The first person sighs tiredly, "So what even is it? Just because I don't know about it, doesn't mean he doesn't. I told you, he's still warming up to me. He doesn't like me around all the time. How do you think I have time for this?"

"Alright, alright," the second dismisses his worry, "but you aren't even in on their meetings?"

"No. What do you want a quote for?"

"Oh, just the thousand plus refugees evacuating over the latest rebel attack on Nerine," the second man says as if it's nothing.

I freeze in horror.

"E-excuse me?" the first finally says while I'm still reeling.

"Yeah, and that's the lower estimate." The second voice is now business-like. "I'm just about to cover it. Just one little bite before I go. The royal family can't keep quiet."

"There's a reason you aren't allowed to go to them to get it. They don't give quotes for the begging."

"Alright, fine, but the prince has to have a reaction, something, anything. They can't keep quiet."

"You have the press representative. Ask him. I'm not your personal information booth."

"You're saying the royal family has nothing to say to these people driven from their homes when the camps are already full?"

"They don't share their thinking with me," the first sounds tired of repeating himself.

"Not even the prince?"

"He's not that fond of me. No. I can't give you a quote."

"So, they say nothing to those people?"

"Don't you dare write that."

"I need something. Come on."

There's a long pause in which my heart thunders in my chest, terrified they'll find me here. I feel like anyone could hear my heartbeat with how it's thundering in my ears.

"You can't quote it," the first finally says.

"But..."

"But," the first cuts him off, "to the refugees, you can say this, and you can quote whatever *they* say, but you can't use what I say as if it comes from the royal family. It doesn't."

"So, they'll be silent?"

"You're acting like I can make up a quote for you."

"You can get one."

"That is not a good idea."

"Why not?"

"I told you he's not fond of me. He will not give me a quote. I'll be lucky if he doesn't throw something at me."

"Your people skills are getting worse," the second says with a taunting drawl to his voice.

"Oh, shut up," the first pushes the second playfully, at least the shadows look like it. "It's not that easy. You know he's busy."

"Yeah, yeah, I know. The whole world thinks it's so fun," the second says sarcastically. "The beauty pageant got dull the moment all the girls were picked. The royal family is too tight-lipped. No one cares when there's an actual war up north."

"This is a game to you, but this is his life, alright? So understand that giving you—of all people—a quote might annoy him," the first chuckles. "This is why I don't invite you to things."

"I know, you got the job and didn't even tell me," the second pouts like a little brother.

"And this is why," the first laughs. "But you can tell the refugees that the prince is sorry for what they're going through and wants to do all he can to right it. Don't quote it in your paper," the first man says this with deadly seriousness.

"Okay, okay, off the books, but I can say that to the refugees and quote whatever they say?"

"If you want to."

"Deal!" The second voice is utterly delighted.

The first sighs tiredly. "This was much more fun when we were kids."

"The war gets real when you grow up." The second shadow dons a cap. "I'm off to record history."

"No, you're off to make trouble with what you write about history," the first laughs.

"Just making sure history isn't boring."

"Get out of here before I have the Custod guard have at you," the first chuckles. "And... write me what you find."

"Now you care?"

"I always cared, just... mark it private for me, alright?"

"Fine, not that anyone will read the prince's mail."

"That's who I don't want seeing it. Mark it for me," the first says seriously.

"Alright, does that mean I get more quotes?"

"I didn't give you a quote," the first laughs, "and you won't get any until his highness wants to."

"So I can ask?"

"You're going to ask even if I say no."

"Eh, true," the second man chuckles, "but will I get them?"

"Never," but the tone of the first voice sounds too playful to be serious, though his voice is more serious as he speaks again, "Is it really that bad?"

"So my correspondent says." The second sounds grim. "That's the fifth attempt they made on the city, but they were holding back well. Half the people left for the damage the rebels did and the other left before it was them."

"And they're all going to the camps?"

"So I heard, but I'll find out. You'll get to read the early edition."

"Oh Merlin, don't send me your stupid paper, actually write me," the first laughs.

"Why?"

"I don't trust your rag of a paper."

The mock gasp of horror is so sharp and out of place I almost laugh, covering my mouth to stop myself. "You take that back, cuz." The second voice is trying hard not to laugh.

"The only honest person I trust there is your editor, and he lets you do whatever you want to make things sound scandalous, so write me real news, then I'll buy a paper."

"Done! I'll see you whenever I get back then?"

"Just don't beg for more quotes and... do come back." The tone of voice makes me shudder.

It had never really occurred to me that everyday people, not rebels or guards, would fear for their lives going up north, but the tone of the first voice makes it suddenly very real. He honestly fears he'll not see the second man again.

"I always do. I can charm myself out of anything with a quote to boot." The second voice sounds cocky.

"That 'charm' is going to get you on the wrong end of a rebel one of these days." The first man sighs. "Phoenix speed, and for Merlin's sake, stay safe."

"Always," the second sounds too upbeat, "insider of the palace."

"Hey!" The first voice protests, but the second man's shadow is gone, indicating he's left. "That is not going in your paper!"

Chapter 17

"Oh, we were just about to send someone for you," Vivian says as I step into my room and quickly shut the door.

I frown. "Why?" Did someone know what I heard? My heart beats rapidly in my chest. They'll figure out I'm a rebel. I'll be executed or worse.

"They had some staffing changes." Vivian is watching me with a slight frown. "You have a new attendant."

"What?" I knew a lot of girls have left, but that still seems odd.

"They just said they had to move some things around, so a few girls are getting new attendants." Vivian shrugs with an air of "good riddance". But what if this new guy is worse? I bite my lips.

"Any change is good," Ro tries to encourage me. "And just in time too."

"In time for what?" I frown.

Vivian nudges Ro with a bit of a look. She frowns and mouths "sorry".

Flur comes over to try to make sure my hair is still perfect. Her eyes long to yank the bun out, but she doesn't. I try to be still and be the good lady they all want me to be while holding in the turmoil inside.

Not only am I hiding my reactions, or really deciding my reactions to that conversation, but now I am meeting my new tormentor.

Thankfully, I don't have to wait long before Vivian shows him in. He's younger and better looking than Yarrow: dark haired, well built, with pale skin and deep green eyes. The lavender waistcoat and cravat he's wearing make those eyes stand out. The rest of his suit, including his jacket and slacks, are a dark grey with black boots. His black hair is tied back with a ribbon that matches his waistcoat.

He's a head taller than me and looks like he may be close to my age, maybe even slightly younger. He holds his hands clasped behind him at first, but as he enters the room, he brings them forward, twirling the black cane he holds. His steps are smooth and precise, as if sure of himself even in a strange, new place. His eyes dance around the room as if taking everything in instantly before landing on me. His eyes widen slightly as they dance down to my feet and back up to my face.

I resist the urge to swallow. I feel like he can see right through me or at least tell everything about me just with his sweeping look. I look down as Flur keeps at my hair.

I'll let him use me as his doll as I have the others. I just can't be happy about it. Can I be about anything anymore? I do at least put on a smile for him.

A charming smile spreads across his lips, tucking his arm in front of him and bows deeply. "Damian Lexus, at your service, my lady," he says then straightens up. "I am to be your new attendant." He sounds Englarish.

I hope he doesn't see right through me. At least Yarrow was too blind to see how I felt. I have a bad feeling this one wouldn't be. What if he found me out?

"May I ask your name?" he asks.

I blink in surprise. "Kascia."

"Beautiful," he smiles. "Like the flower?" I smile and nod. I fiddle with my chosen mark.

He gives me a nod then glances down at my dress. "And do you, Kascia, have a fondness for the colour orange?" He looks up at me with just his eyes.

"No," I say instantly and quietly, afraid to offend, but I can't even pretend I liked the color.

"Oh, thank goodness for that." He smiles, relieved. "Because it's hurting my eyes," he jokes.

I force a small chuckle, honestly relieved but still unsure.

He tilts his head slightly as he searches my face, smiling gently to assure me. "It's alright, Kascia. I'm not going to hurt you."

"I know," I say quickly. None of them mean to harm me. I can't help but notice my maids are nervous in hopeful anticipation.

He nods slowly. "Well." He takes in a breath as if to relieve the tension. "I suppose we can work and get to know each other at the same time." He turns to Ro. "What is your name, miss?"

Ro blinks in surprise and looks from me to him. "What?" I almost laugh at her surprise.

"Your name. Do you not have one?" Damian smiles at his jest.

"Oh," she laughs, "sorry, I'm Ro."

"Just Ro?" He arches a brow in curiosity.

"Yes, I go by Ro."

"Very well then." He collects himself. "Ro, would you be a dear and fetch Lady Kascia something more suitable to wear?"

She beams, "With pleasure, sir." She gives Damian a bob of a curtsy before she comes over to me. She pulls out a screen, so I can change into the white dress. I notice Flur glancing at my hair as if it is the one thing still wrong with me.

"Now then." Damian claps his hands and smiles at Flur. "What next? And yes, you can take that out, Miss...?" He looks at her as if searching for her name.

"Flur." She blushes a little, but gets up and quickly takes my bun out. She lets it all down, and I feel my shoulders relax. I hadn't realized they'd been tense.

I try not to look at Damian as he must be studying me, deciding what I should look like next.

"Kascia." Damian turns to me, "Or would you prefer 'my lady'?"

"Kascia is fine," I say, managing a small smile as I dare look at him.

Damian smiles and nods. "Very well. Kascia, what is your favorite colour?"

"Oh, ah," I try to remind myself it's alright to be honest about my favorite color, "blue, I like ocean blue."

"Lovely." His eyes shine. "Then blue it shall be. Unless you have another preference?"

"Not orange." I manage to get out.

They all laugh. "True. Not orange." Damian nods then turns to see the pile of dresses. "Good lord!" His eyes widen. "What on earth is all this?" he asks rhetorically as he starts filtering through the dresses. Ro laughs loudly. Vivian gives her a scolding look.

I manage a half-smile and look at the dresses. "These are all the designs made so far," Vivian says. "Just causal. He didn't have us work on anything for a date as she hasn't been asked yet."

I bow my head. Well, he should know he's working for the losing girl.

"Well, at least, we have that working in our favour," Damian says.

At least someone thinks the fact I'm the only dateless girl is a good thing. "You never want to be an early contestant," he says more to himself then gives the ball dress to Flur. "Tear that into thick stripes, will you please? Anything greater than five inches would be lovely." Flur's smile is delighted to be shredding it.

I sit by my vanity. Odds are Damian is going to try out makeup on me. I'll be raw by dinner. I fight the sick feeling in my stomach.

Damian still has the last couple of dresses to look through. He would have been done already except he stops once or twice and looks at me, tilting his head a little. His eyes narrow ever so slightly as he focuses on me.

I try to keep still as he examines me. It's like what Yarrow did that first day. At least he's not holding up pictures to compare me to. I look away, looking out at the sun shining on the ocean.

Vivian decides to cheer me up by giving suggestions on other things we can do with my hair, using the curls this time instead of hiding them. I try to smile.

Suddenly, Damian lets out a shriek. "Egad, what is that!?" He finds the dress at the bottom of the pile.

It's mostly orange with a long slit on one side. Well, really all sides of the skirt, forming square shapes, like the bodice. It looked like someone had orange squares and tried to make a dress shape out of them. I had vowed never to wear that thing.

"It's as if someone tried to sew hand towels together." Damian frowns deeply. "What was he thinking?" Ro is beaming like Christmas came early. "Oh, that is so cursed. Take it away." Damian hands it to Vivian. "I never want to see it again."

He then pauses, clasps his hands together, then points at the dress. "Burn it."

I laugh the first real laugh I'd managed in at least two weeks. My maids laugh too.

Vivian takes the dress, and Ro jumps up to help her. Damian chuckles.

Vivian and Ro almost skip over to the fireplace. Ro is giddy with delight. Vivian rolls her eyes but is smiling too. They're having fun. The most fun they likely have ever had, at least working with me.

"So..." Damian says as he places two other dresses in the pile for Flur to rip up and tosses the rest. "Kascia." He looks at me. "Does that come with a last name?"

"Thorapple."

Damian's brows lift in curiosity as he smiles slightly. "Interesting name."

"It is." I force another smile. "I'm not sure where it's from. My mother is native as am I."

"I see," Damian says as he picks up a black cane with gems or rhinestones studded down the silver top. He gives it a short twirl as he slowly walks over to a chair but doesn't sit down.

"And what does your family do for a living?" he asks then, in one fluid movement, he turns to face me, sits in the chair, and crosses one leg over the other. He commands the room like it's his stage.

"My mother runs the royal theatre. I worked for her."

"Really?" he smiles wide, and his eyes light up. "So you helped her run the theatre?"

"I perform like she used to."

"Is that so?" His smile grows, and a twinkle of excitement sparkles in his eyes. "What productions have you done?"

I review my last show, the ones I'd done most, and tell him I'm most famous for *The Phantom*.

"Brilliant," he beams. "Those are some of my favourites. I worry sometimes with money so scarce, who has time for the theatre?" Damian sighs, "But I'm glad to hear it's still going here."

"As much as it can."

There's a pause before Damian leans forward. "So that's your talent then?"

"I suppose," I frown, "I am a triple threat. I sing, dance, and act." I glance at the pointe shoes my maids like to put as decoration on my desk when I'm not using them.

Damian glances at them then looks at me. "That could prove useful. After all, there is a talent show coming up." He smiles softly while resting his chin on the knuckles of his left hand.

"What?" An easy part of the Enthronement? Can I be that lucky? Then again, without winning one date yet, does it matter?

"You heard right." His smile grows. "In little more than a week, you'll be able to show off a little."

His way of phrasing it makes me smile. He's not trying to make sure I'm something different that the prince will like. No more scrubbing my face off. But... that's how the game is played. "So, what will we do?" I am sure he has a plan. The attendants always do.

Damian chuckles and sits back, "That, my dear, is entirely up to you. I'm just here to help."

"What?" I've been told how to do everything. I'm being groomed to win so my team doesn't lose their jobs. Now suddenly I'm in charge? "But you've... well, people in your role have not given me a choice."

"Well, I'm not like them," Damian smiles, amused by the assumption. "Kascia, you are in the running to be a queen. That alone makes you someone people should honour and respect. And as such, I respect you. You are the star here. I'm merely here to make you look good."

That's not what I've seen from my last attendant or even the other lady's attendants. They helped guide our strategy to win. I want control again. I'm tired of being used and heartbroken. I don't know how to fix it. I don't know how to make a choice anymore.

"Alright, well, what would you suggest?" They all know the prince better. If I'm to stay in or try to win, either way, I need to do my best to impress them.

"Let's look at what we have, shall we?" Damian leans forward again, placing his hand over his mouth before dropping it and knitting it with the other with his elbows braced against his knees. "In exactly ten days, you'll have to be on stage, so it may be best to do something you already know. It would save you time and stress from having to learn something entirely new."

"Well... I know a lot of songs," I say. "What could we do that would help me stand out?"

"I can work with that. I would assume they're all from plays?" Damian asks.

"Most."

"Do you have a favorite or a favorite role?" he asks.

That is easy. *The Phantom*'s lead singer is my favorite role. "What kind of things does the prince like?"

"Does it matter?" Damian asks, sitting back against the chair. "This isn't about him. It's about you. If he likes swimming, would you try doing that on stage?" He arches a brow with a bemused smile.

I laugh and shake my head, "No, but perhaps he'd like something that is about the ocean or water." Perhaps something from *The Island Princess* would be better.

Damian rolls his eyes, still smiling. "Perhaps, but there may be time for that later. It's your night. Don't spoil it with frugalities. No one wants someone who merely mimics what they like. So be you. Dynamic and long-lasting relationships thrive on diversity because they can build on one another. Now if you, in truth, share many common interests then, by all means, build on them because relationships need those as well.

"Of course, this may be irrelevant for now, seeing you don't know the prince, and he doesn't know you, but that's why it is all the more important to play to your strengths. Don't cheapen your experience just to please someone else."

Don't cheapen the experience to please someone else. That's what my mother would say, but what experience? The heartbreak of losing Jake, of learning the friend I'd like most here is the prince? Of having my face ripped away? At least if I did as asked someone else would be happy. I ache to be happy again, but I don't know how.

"Perhaps we can play to my more recent experience."

"You mean from your last performance?" Damian arches a brow.

"I think something from that would be good."

"Your role was Esmeralda, was it not?" Damian asks. I nod. "Hmm." He places his hand over his mouth and tilts his head at me. "Well, there are a few songs she sings in the play, but the first is a bit too promiscuous for what we are going for," he says. I'm not sure if he is talking to me or himself. "But..." He drops his hand, rubbing them together as he looks to the ceiling. "The second would be perfect." He then smiles at me. "If that's what you want to."

I bow my head to him, "I think it's perfect for the occasion and makes it easier on you."

"Wonderful. Then I should start work on your dress." he beams. "Though I should also ask, would you rather do this acapella or have an accompaniment?"

I wince. "Well... if we can get good accompaniment, be nice, but..." I've seen the quality of what they give me.

Damian smiles and stands, straightening his jacket, though it was hardly less than perfect. "Worry not. I know just where to go."

I smile weakly. I like Damian. A lot more than the last guy. Something is caring about him. He also is the first person who doesn't bow to be my servant yet doesn't try to control me. First since my apprentice. I frown. Why do I think of them separately? My apprentice is still the prince.

"Thank you," I say to Damian, trying to divert my thoughts. "You've been most helpful."

"Of course, my lady." Damian bows to me. "Need anything else of me?"

Save me. My heart squeaks, but instead, I say, "I don't think so."

"Oh!" Flur jumps up, "I almost forgot."

Vivian's eyes widen in terror. Ro has an amused smile. "This came for you just before we were introduced to Mr. Lexus." Flur offers me an official envelope.

Oh no, are they finally dismissing me? But then why did they assign a new attendant to me? My heart thuds in a panic as I open the letter, my hands shaking. But it's not a dismissal. I let out a huge sigh of relief.

"I knew it!" Ro cries. "When?"

"Day after tomorrow, after dinner."

"I knew it. He didn't forget," Flur smiles reassuringly at me.

I keep reading it. I don't like this. An invitation to be in the prince's private chambers after dinner.

The horrible image of having to let him have his way flashes through my mind.

I shudder. He invited me, but I can't... I can't do that. I can't give up that part of me. I'm not strong enough for that yet. *Jake, forgive me.*

What can I do? I finally get a date then turn him down? I'll be dismissed and then what will my life be? What will my life be if I let him have his way? I bite my lip to stop it from shaking.

"Is there a problem?" Damian asks coolly while my maids are dancing about.

I don't know why, but something about Damian makes it come out. "I-I don't know if I'm ready for this."

"It's just the first date." He tilts his head a bit. "Weren't you waiting for it?"

"Yes, and I want it, but..." I take a deep breath, "I'm not ready to... to be in his chambers."

"Ah, yes, that would be a problem," he agrees, studying me with interest. "So, what will you do?"

I swallow hard. I don't know. I just don't want to feel like this anymore. Would he really force himself on me? Oh Merlin, did he do this on everyone's first date? Did everyone else let him? That only makes me feel sicker.

"I c-can't do it," I manage to say.

Suddenly, confidence fills me. The tears that were at the edge of my eyes retreat as I take a deep breath. I could make a compromise like I had entering the Enthronement. Yes, I want the date, but I'm not ready to go to his chambers.

I take the paper meant for a reply and sit at my desk. I miss the small smile that crosses Damian's face.

I write my proposal and put it into the designated envelope. "Flur, would you send this back?" Flur takes it in pure delight and leaves.

"Well?" Damian asks, arching a brow.

"I said yes, but only if we arrange a better location," I say honestly, trying to sound like a queen when a part of me is trembling inside. Had I just sealed my doom?

"Perfect," Damian says with a smile that makes me feel like he knows something, reminding me of Mom's proud smile. Why would he be proud of me for throwing it all away?

"Perfect?" I frown.

"Why wouldn't it be?"

"Well..." I play with my fingers. "I could be dismissed."

"Ah, I see how that can be a bit unnerving," Damian nods nonchalantly.

"A bit? I can't just let him take advantage of me like that, prince or not. There's no other reason to meet in his bedroom."

Damian smiles at me, "You think so?"

"Think so?" What is that supposed to mean?

"Well, there could be another reason," Damian shrugs.

"Like what?" I challenge.

"Well, to be blunt, it could have been a test," Damian says with another shrug.

I frown. "So, I'm supposed to let the spoiled prince take advantage of me?" The anger I felt towards Jake and my father for making me do this returns, making my cheeks flush.

Damian chuckles, "No, dear girl. You're supposed to say no."

I freeze. No... that didn't.?. make sense. Then again, if my apprentice was really the prince, and not a mask the prince had worn... If the king and queen were how I'd seen them instead of how I thought of them... That made a lot of sense.

Would a true princess sell herself? I don't think so. Did they agree? My stomach tightens.

"Maybe. We'll just have to wait on his reply," I manage.

"Indeed. Meanwhile, I'll get to work," Damian smiles as he goes to the work desk. "Though Vivian, would you mind fetching me some tea, please?"

"Sure, if you don't mind, miss." She bows her head to me.

I shake my head that I don't mind, and she goes to get tea. Perhaps I could use some at this point. I'm so nervous.

Damian sits back in his chair, leaning away from me, then gives me that close look again, the one that makes me uneasy. His eyes narrow just a little as he studies me, then he pulls a small black notebook from inside his jacket and starts drawing.

Flur returns before Vivian. She has the envelope for me. That was fast. My hands are shaking as I take it. I take a deep breath and open it.

Once again, my whole body relaxes as I let out a sigh of relief. It says we'll meet at the same time, but he'll fetch me from my room. As long as we're not going in it, we'll be fine. Of course, it was a test. I should have known. But just because he's picking me up from my room doesn't mean he doesn't have other plans. I swallow.

He's also your apprentice. He'd not do that; just trust him. Let him try, I tell myself.

Then I have an odd thought. Damian wouldn't let him. I glance at Damian, still working and looking at his sketches. Something inside me tells me that's true. Like he has some power or authority that would protect me. How odd. I'd... never felt that before. Other than with the king and my apprentice.

Chapter 18

The next day, I try to walk new paths to meals and to the Ladies' Chamber to try to find the voice I'd heard yesterday. If I found them, maybe I could get some answers on what is going on. The idea the rebels, my people, drove innocents from their homes shakes me. I thought we were defending the people. What if it's not true up north? It leaves open the idea that the entire cause is not true at all.

But even with all of that effort, trying to say hello to every male guard I see, stopping every male servant to ask a question, and going to as many areas as I felt I can get away with, not one voice matched the voice I'd heard in the hallway.

How could I find out more of the real truth if I can't find out who knew what was happening? I couldn't trust the paper, even if Jonquil did. She's obsessed with it, eager to get her hands on it every morning. She refuses to talk to anyone until she's read it cover to cover.

I feel rather dejected at having nothing but more dead ends as I go up to my room.

But I have a lovely surprise waiting: letters from home have arrived. I'd get Dad's promise! I know he'd promise to protect them, but I have to see it in writing to feel comforted.

I am a bit dismayed though. Dad had taught me coding, so he could send me coded messages if needed while I was here. I hated it. And so far, we'd not needed it. I'd used a simple one to ask him to make sure the girls are safe, but Dad's reply is all in code.

I glance to make sure my maids aren't watching. They are facing the wrong way. I turn back and take the side of the ruler and scratch off the coating that hides Dad's numbered system on the back. I jot it down and flip the letter over to the front again.

I have quite a headache after ten minutes of decoding before I finally write down his reply to my request.

As much as I'd like to make such a promise, I can't control the Loyalist's men. You know that. I can't make such a silly promise. Why would you even ask? I can say I'll do my best, but this is war, my love. I look forward to seeing you again at the Harvest.

I'm so shocked by his answer I just gape at the paper for a moment. He said no? *Silly?* He called it silly?

I don't think my request is silly. I'm only asking for protection for the innocent. That doesn't seem crazy, right? How hard was it to just tell them not to touch the Chosen?

Annoyance and anger surge like a wave in my chest. He shoved me into this, and he can't do this one thing for me? I can't imagine allowing the attack to happen knowing my friends could be hurt. I'd have to warn them or something, and the royal family would catch on to that. If he can't promise, what will I do? I can't stand back and let them hurt my friends, but...

I decide to move on to Mom's letter to see if that put me in a better mood. She talks about her plans for the theater and says she's glad things are going well so far. She also reminds me I can do whatever and she'll be proud as long as it's my choice.

I smile at her words, running a hand over the page. I put her letter into my pocket. I take Dad's and slowly rip them into as many pieces as I can before letting the wind carry them away.

I look over at my maids to include them, "I know it might be hard, but is there any way I can get an impressionor? Mom is begging for impressions."

Vivian pauses to think. "Maybe." She smiles at Damian, "I might be able to do that." I frown and look at Damian, wondering what the smile is about.

"I think we have the budget for a camera," Damian says with a smile.

Camera? I'm sure he means impressinor; I'd never heard it called a camera before.

I smile a little. "Thank you. I'm sure Mom would thank you too."

"Well, you're welcome to the both of you." He smiles with a slight bow.

Vivian put down her sewing, a pretty lavender thing. Well, it will be, I'm sure. She leaves to see what she can find. Flur smiles and goes back to working on the dress Damian gave her.

I go back to my writing desk to work on my letter to Mom. As I do, Damian goes back to the workbench. A moment later, Damian makes a noise of disgust.

"Ugh!" Damian frowns as he sets down his teacup. "Flur, would you be so kind as to take that away and steep more tea? This one has gone cold."

Flur giggles and nods, “Sure, Damian.”

I watch Damian for a moment, realizing he always seems to have tea. “You like tea. Does it help you think?”

He nods. “And it calms me down and allows me to step back and focus.”

I’m debating what to say next when Vivian returns with an impressinor. I smile. It’s one of the nicest I’ve ever seen. “It will print out the image right here.” She shows me. Those are fun.

Flur returns with fresh tea as I take impressions of the room for my mother then settle down to write her back. Then I realize I should do Dad’s first so I can get it out of the way.

I remind him I’d given up everything for him and what I’m asking is not just simple but how our family should do this.

I finish Mom’s letter next. Venting so many of my fears helps. I even told her about the news I’d heard, but vaguely to make sure no one else knows exactly what I am talking about and ask her help to know where to get accurate news now I don’t have Dad’s sources.

That’s when it hits me: Damian. He has given me every reason to trust him. He may not know what’s happening out there, but I have the strong impression that if anyone could find out the truth for me, he could. I don’t know why I believe he can find the answers, but I know he can.

I bite my lip and look over at him. But now it’s time for dinner and afterwards, the date. I try to hide the anxiety in my stomach at the most exciting and terrifying event I can remember.

When I return from dinner, Damian displays what he’s made for me. It takes my breath away. It’s not the prettiest thing I’ve ever seen, but it is high up there. It's much better than anything Yarrow made for me. It’s beautiful: white with a flowing skirt and top. The sleeves are made from the orange strips, like orange flowers flowing down.

I can’t even find words. I can’t believe it’s real. Part of me is waiting for the trap, the trick. I have to agree to sleep with the prince or ask him for some favor for Damian or something before it’s mine. But there’s no stipulation, no manipulation, just the gift. I am touched and overwhelmed as I try to force the truth into my trembling heart, so scared to believe and be hurt again.

Damian smiles, “Do you like it?”

I swallow and nod, “It’s amazing.”

Damian beams, “Glad to hear it. Well, go ahead and try it on. Then we can add the final touches.”

I nod, still in awe of it. My maids come over and help me change. It’s comfortable as a nightgown as well as beautiful. The skirt swishes against my legs. It’s so soft against my smooth skin.

They secure the belt around it and make sure the dress is tucked and the sides pulled in the right places. When they're done, they have me walk out for Damian to see it. I'm in awe of how it feels.

Damian beams as he turns to look at me. "Simply exquisite," he grins. He then places his hand over his mouth as his other hand braces his elbow. "Give us a turn."

I give him a full turn. He smiles and nods. "Lovely." He brings out a pair of ankle-high sandals. "Vivian, could you help her put these on?"

The sandals fit amazingly well. Not easy to do with my small feet. I wonder if he went to town to find out my size. I'm pretty sure Jashon has molds on my feet by now. They feel like they're hardly there, yet I don't feel barefoot.

Damian watches with that careful look he seems to have when he's studying me then meets my eye. "How do they feel?"

"Amazing," I breathe.

"Brilliant," Damian smiles. "Now, if you sit down at the vanity, we can start talking about your hair and makeup."

Damian stands behind me and starts combing back the sides of my head and gathering the hair at the back. He's so gentle. Not like Yarrow had been. His touch is almost softer than my maids. "I'm thinking... something like a high ponytail or updo, so her curls can cascade down the back," he says to my maids.

It makes my heart glow. Someone who wants to let me be me, and use the good work the stylists did on my first day. It's like Damian is slowly putting my face back together, but better, without taking away who I am, only drawing attention to the beauty I have. Then again, what new good had I found since being here?

My maids rub me down with lotions and spray perfume on me that helps my skin look just as perfect as the dress itself. They are miracle workers!

Damian plays with the curls of my fringe as if he can make them twist a certain way. He brushes it gently into place then steps back, beaming. "There. You're ready."

I swallow and stand up to take a look. I take my own breath away. My mouth pops open, unable to believe what I see is me. The gold makeup Damian has chosen is a perfect touch, highlighting my face and blending me seamlessly with the white, gold, and orange of the dress. I finally don't look sunburned or washed out. The slightly darker makeup contours my face perfectly.

No, that isn't me. I'd never seen myself look like this, but I look... more myself than ever. I'd looked pretty as plenty of characters but... seeing myself like this. That isn't me done to look like the beautiful so-and-so. This is me.

I swallow, looking back at my own wide blue eyes, shining beautifully against the white of my dress and the makeup they've done. I turn my head, admiring how my brown hair looks with the natural curls and flows. I love the feel of it on my neck and how it gently teases my cheek as I turn.

I manage a smile, trying to hide the power of this moment. I don't want them to see my tears of relief. There is hope, no matter what else happens at least I'll get to be myself not Jake's tool or my Dad's tool, or my mother's actress. I'll get to choose or accept my given fate as me, not the Chosen girl thrown into this fray.

"It's amazing." I put on the show, looking up and letting my beam shine through. "What can't you do?" I tease Damian as a deflection.

He turns his eyes to the ceiling for a moment. "Emmm..." Then he looks at me with a smile, "Cook. At least, not well."

"You're a miracle worker," I declare.

"My dear girl, you are a true beauty. I'm merely helping you show what you already have." Damian smiles gently.

Ro smiles and holds up my impressinor. I shut my mouth quickly and smile. I try to pose cutely for my mother.

The nervousness settles back into my stomach. I wish they were more like stage jitters. Instead, it's worse, like when I thought I was meeting the prince at the interview. I try to let my shoulders relax and take a deep breath. I can do this. I'm not failing tonight.

"Break a leg." Damian smiles at his joke. I laugh.

Chapter 19

Finally, there is a knock at the door. Damian and the others finish their touches on the room to make it presentable before Flur goes to answer the door. She takes a steadying breath before she puts her hand on the handle and opens it.

"Good evening." I hear the prince's warm voice. "Is Lady Kascia ready?"

Flur bows to the prince and nods, "Of course, Your Highness." She smiles at me to say it's time.

I take a last deep breath and walk over as Flur opens the door and steps out of the way to present me.

The first thing I see is the light and hint of nerves in the prince's golden brown eyes, trying to hide behind a smile. Then he looks me over.

I look him over as well. Is he wearing an orange waistcoat? I blush. He doesn't seem to notice though. He's just smiling wider and wider as he looks me over.

"You look perfect tonight," he says. "I've been looking forward to this. May I?" He offers me his arm. I can't help but notice he seems unsure too.

I fight not to swallow and smile graciously before taking it. I'm distracted by what I feel and look down for a moment. In dance, I took a lot of arms. I'd felt everything from wimpy arms, flabby arms, and the most toned of dancers. But the prince's feels stronger than even that, firmer, rounder. That makes no sense. Why would the prince, the spoiled boy not allowed outside his own castle, have one of the strongest arms I'd ever felt? Is it padded? I can't help but like it and want to feel more, but I'm not dumb enough to try.

"Where are we going?"

"Just sharing my thinking spot," the prince says with that warm smile that made me feel so welcome when we first met. "Makes me less nervous. I've dated a lot in the last few weeks, but before that, I never had. So, it helps me relax for a first date. Hope you don't mind."

I shake my head that I don't mind. We're silent for a moment. I try to think of something to say, but thankfully, the prince speaks first. "So, you like orange?" He guesses, his eyes going over the flower-like sleeves.

I flush a bit. "Not especially."

The prince frowns, "So why do you wear so much of it?"

"My last attendant liked it, I guess," I shrug.

"Well, it's not like you looked bad."

"I looked sunburned."

"Oh." The prince's face fills with understanding. "That explains it. I wondered why you were letting yourself get burned over and over. I hear some girls are trying to look as 'royal' as possible. I thought your attendant thought you should look darker so had you try to get more tan."

I'd not put that past Yarrow. "Oh." I don't know if I feel better or more embarrassed he hadn't realized it was the stupid color.

"So then why so much orange?" he asks.

"I wasn't given many options," I admit. "I guess I could have pushed, but..." How do I explain to him why I have to let them rip me apart?

But the frown that crosses his face tells me he sees there's more to it. "Are all the girls so commanded?"

"I doubt they all allow it," I confess. I'm the only one who has to hide. I'm the only one whose survival depends on making it at least until the end of October. Just until the harvest. I tense at the thought.

The prince glances at my arm. Oh no, he felt that. Where was the acting cloak I'd been wearing? Why did he make me take it off without realizing it?

"Well, I didn't think you looked that bad," he bluntly lies. I give him a look, making him laugh. "You could have looked worse." The prince defends. "Why I thought it must be a favorite of yours," he grins mischievously. "But I don't think it's your color." He looks at my dress again. "But it makes a good highlight."

"Thanks." I hope we can find more to talk about than how I look. But what would I expect of a brat of a prince? That might be all that matters to him.

But that didn't matter to my apprentice who liked me with my face burned, hair a mess from tossing and turning, and my eyes red and swollen from tears. Confusion starts to stir in my heart again like a slowly spiraling ocean storm.

"So you said old attendant?" he questions. "I heard they move around with so many girls gone. So, you got a better one, one who knows better than pure orange."

"Yes, he's been a godsend."

"Good, you needed something." He smiles.

I feel defensive. I know he knows I've been struggling, but the idea the prince knows makes me feel exposed like I'm one wrong word or one wrong move away from being uncovered.

I try to distract myself with a different thought. I wonder who had Damian before. Which girl who'd left had him? "Do you miss any of them?"

"Them?" The prince frowns.

I try not to flush. "The girls who left."

"Oh." The prince takes his turn to flush. "I don't know, really. I only spoke to them on dates or when we first met. I don't know what I'd miss." He looks around the hall we're walking down. "And between you and me, you have to be pretty bad to fail this date." He winks.

"Oh vene, what did they do?" I demand. Then I flush too. "Sorry, I don't think you're allowed to tell me."

"Let's just say you have to be really dumb." He smiles. "Or desperate."

We reach a set of glass doors. Two guards open them, and the prince leads me into a large conservatory. It's beautiful with stunning trees, greenery, and it smells so clean and pure. I hear running water, and I smell it in the air too. It's peaceful, and yet, exciting at once.

When we step inside, tension enters the prince's body. I thought he said this was his favorite spot to think.

"This is the only outdoor place I can walk as I like... mostly because it's indoors." The prince smiles as he starts our walk around the large room. "I'm here a lot. Most of all at night."

"For socializing?"

"Well lately, but normally, just to relax. I'd rather be outside, but as you know that's a big no, not without a guard. And that ruins the fun."

"What about Sage?"

"Oh, he's around," the prince shrugs. "Hanging like a bat somewhere."

I amuse myself picturing Sage hanging upside down, wrapping himself in his black cloak like a bat. I giggle. Then my face falls slightly. "He's not a fan of me, is he?"

"He doesn't like most girls," the prince says quickly. "But tell me more about you. We didn't get much time in the interview."

"I'm supposed to get to know you too," I retort.

"Oh, trying to be attractive by being mysterious," he teases, but something about it feels... deflecting. Like he's trying to hide something. Why?

"But the other girls mention you now and then. You are popular," he states as if it's a grand fact I hide.

"No, I'm not." I quickly look away to hide my embarrassment.

"Jonquil mentioned you are a stunning ballerina," the prince says, still stating a fact. "Which you kind of mentioned, but seem to want to hide too."

"I'm not hiding." I just don't know what to say about it. "Besides, you knew I was a professional dancer at the ball."

"True." The prince nods, looking up as he thought. "And you said you can sing and act too. So that talent show portion will be cake for you." He grins. He's trying to help me feel confident. Why?

"I hope so."

The prince nods. "I look forward to seeing what you pick."

I want to ask if there will be more than one, but I think better of it. "It will be a long show, I'd think."

"Dad has a whole night planned. He's more excited than me or anyone else." The prince smiles.

I laugh. "Not as much as my attendant."

The prince gives me a challenging, sideways look. "Oh yeah?"

"He went right into it when I met him. He has been planning every bit of it when he's not fixing all my orange messes."

"My father is counting down the days and teasing me about it every chance he gets," the prince says with a roll of his eyes. "But not around Mom. I guess the idea of him leering at you girls isn't her favorite topic." We both laugh.

"Though she seems to let him. Or we'd not even have the show," the prince shrugs. "Or maybe yet another compromise," he says the last word with a lot of emphases.

"Compromise?"

"Well, not everyone has the same idea of what a true princess is, so sometimes to make the tests we had to trade or compromise on things," the prince explains.

"Are you even allowed to tell me that?"

"They didn't tell me that, so I assume it's fine. I have a lot fewer rules than you girls do," the prince says.

"Really?"

"I'm not allowed to just help one of you win or give anything away, but what that means is a lot more loss for me versus all of you," the prince explains. "For example, I can't tell you why the other girls failed until after you pass the same test. So next date, remind me, and I'll tell you."

He seems so sure I'll have another date. I'm not so sure. I've already nearly slipped and tipped him off so many times. I try to think of a lighter topic to change it to. "Well, I at least think I have the best attendant," I joke. "If I win, it's thanks to him, not me."

The prince's mouth flattens to a line; his brows draw together, and his face scrunches with it. The expression makes me laugh. "What does that mean?" I can't answer for laughing. "Seriously, you think you'll win just because he does good makeup or something?"

I manage to stop laughing when he gives me a sideways look. I see the warm smile, but I also see a concerned question in there. *Do you really think I'm that shallow?*

I see my apprentice in that question, and it makes my heart flood with comfort, and yet, questions. No, the man who'd melted my heart was not that shallow. But was the prince?

"No." We start to walk again. "I mean he's good at helping me through it. How the lowly number twelve got him I don't know."

"It was randomly drawn," the prince shrugs. "I wonder who he was with before. I didn't pay attention."

"You don't seem to pay attention to us unless it's a date."

The prince pauses a moment, though we keep walking. "Does that bother you all?" he asks after a moment.

"What do you mean?"

"I know Princess Zelda gave me a good telling off for it," the prince explains. "But does it bother the rest of you?"

I shrug. "You waited so long, I thought I'd be out before I even got a date. But other than that, I haven't thought about it." I swallow. Dare I ask? He was open that night in the garden. "Why don't you talk to us then? You could at meals."

"At meals, only so many are close, which might be an unfair advantage. Or some might say." A small hint of a smile plays at the prince's lips, making me think he had a name to go with that complaint in his mind.

"And outside of it?"

The prince pushes his lips to one side. "I know this likely looks like a blast to you." I hear the hint of sarcasm in his voice. "But this is my life. And whoever wins, no matter what, is who I marry. What if I get attached to someone who fails? What happens to me then? So, I guess I'm scared of getting too attached until it's closer, and even then, I'm nervous. I don't know what it will do to me," he sighs tiredly. "So at least until the numbers are down, I'm being careful. And fair. I don't want in-fighting over girls feeling I'm not being fair."

I frown a little. "Do you not get that much say in who wins? Isn't it just who you like?"

"Not really. It's who wins. I must marry a true princess. Doesn't matter if I like her." Then he puts on a smile. I spot the acting. "But that's fine. I can love who wins. That's the easy part. I fear getting attached to someone who doesn't win. I don't know how I'll take it."

"You have always had anything you want."

The prince stops with how hard he's laughing. I frown. "Oh, let's just say I don't always get what I want," the prince smiles at my confusion. "I'll explain another time."

He's said that twice now. The reason hits me. We're not alone. I knew the guards were around, but his behavior could mean "testers" are watching.

"But I failed my question from before." The prince starts walking again. I feel his arm flex a little as he moves. Wow. He feels so solid under my grip. "I asked about you, and we've not really talked about it. You're a dancer, singer, actress by trade. Any siblings?"

"No, just me."

"Oh," the prince pauses. "Isn't that odd?"

"You're an only child."

"Yes, but I just thought out there it was more normal to have many."

Out there? He says it like he is talking about another world. He really is sheltered. I'd talk more about it, but if his parents are watching I'd rather not. "It is. My mother just never had more. We don't talk about it, so I don't know why. Guess the Maker had other plans."

The prince smiles, "I guess that makes sense. Life chooses, not us." He pauses a moment. Then he beams, "Is that why she wanted you blonde?"

I laugh at the reference to our forbidden meeting without letting it slip, "You still owe your mother coils."

"She tells me every day." The prince rolls his eyes, beaming to himself. He looks up to the sky for a moment before turning back to me. "How about yours?"

"Not daily," I smile. "Though she did ask for impressions in her last letter. I was able to get a few."

"Hm. I may need to think of excuses to make more then." The prince smiles. "I like impressions. Lets me see things in places I can't go to. I have a lot of books about other places."

"Like?"

"Oh, anywhere in the royal library. Do they let you in there yet?"

"No."

"I can let you in." The prince winks.

"But then you're talking to me on a non-date. What if you get attached?" I tease.

"Hm, true. Maybe I can wear an anti-stick powder." The prince muses.

I laugh. "Not that kind of attached."

The prince smiles to himself. "How about your father?"

"What about him?"

"What does he do?"

Plan your death. I can't tell him that. What can I tell him? "Manages the theater finances."

"So, Mama is in charge." The prince grins.

I shrug. "I guess so."

The prince nods again, and we're quiet for a moment. The prince's grip on my arm tightens a little. I try not to smile. I like it. Without the formal talk and avoiding certain topics, I feel safer, like it is just my apprentice and not the prince I'm walking with.

That thought makes a smile slip out. Why does this have to be so complicated? What would this be like if he wasn't the prince, but just... that boy who helped me feel at home that night?

Then something odd happens. Sprinklers go off on our left. I jump as it gets us wet. We both laugh.

"Sorry about that." The prince tries to shield me from the water. "I guess they forgot to turn them off."

"Sorry?" The water feels good in the humid room.

The prince grins and looks back at me. "What? It's not a bad thing?"

I feel bad getting all their hard work soaked, but...

I smile wide and push my apprentice into it. He cries out in surprise as he falls. I laugh as he does.

He gets to his feet in an impressive fluid movement. On his way up, he hits the sprinkler, and it starts shooting into the air, making a light kind of rain around us.

I laugh and twirl in it. The prince laughs at me, "What are you doing?"

"Dancing in the rain."

"Uh." He looks up into the softly falling water, almost a mist. "Isn't rain heavier?"

I stop and look at him in a new light. Has he not been out in the rain?

"Sometimes," I say slowly, watching him. "You really don't know?"

He shakes his head thoughtfully, watching the water fall around us. "Hmm." His face tilts a little in thought. Then a smile slowly climbs his face, and he tries to copy me.

"Careful." I laugh.

"I'm not exactly a ballerina," he retorts. "I do better with a partner." He grabs my hand and leads me into a twirl. I laugh. He does it flawlessly.

He easily leads me into a proper twirl as if it were choreographed that way. I laugh more as he helps me up to my feet to twirl back out.

"What are you doing?" I ask, still laughing as he keeps leading me into more twists and turns around each other.

"Dancing in the rain," he quotes me with a smile.

"I thought you weren't exactly a ballerina," I tease.

"I'm not. This is ballroom," he corrects me. "Don't you know?"

"Of course, I do. You just don't want to be the one spinning," I accuse.

"Yeah, I don't worry about getting dizzy and falling again," he agrees. "Unless you cheat again."

"Cheat?"

"Like this." He pulls me closer to him in the spin. I pause, realizing how dangerously close we are. A wicked little grin splits his face, and he takes his turn shoving me into the flowers.

It doesn't hurt at all, making me laugh. Maybe white was a bad idea.

He gently helps pull me out, more easily than anyone ever has. His arms aren't just for show. He must be one of the strongest men I've ever met. It's so easy, he pulls me up too fast, so I stumble into him. He catches me effortlessly. I pause. That's really close. Worse than the moment before he pushed me.

Jake laughing and catching me like this flashes to my mind. I swallow and pull back. My heart aches, and I fight not to tear up. I miss that. I miss him. I miss what we had. I hug myself protectively.

The prince lets me with a sheepish smile. "Sorry. We can get out of the line of fire." He takes my hand, and we walk away from the waterworks, making me unfold my arms to follow him.

"Your attendant is really good. I can't even tell you were in the rain." The prince looks me over. "I bet I'm a right mess."

"I pushed you into the jet of water." He doesn't look that wet. The water had been pretty light once he mistakenly kicked it.

The prince shrugs and looks up towards the rafters. I'm guessing that's where we're being watched. I wish we weren't. He's guarded. I can feel it. But he's trying not to be. He did instigate the play once the sprinklers went off. I think he wants me to impress them. But do I want him to want it? The flash of Jake in my mind makes me uneasy.

"Well," the prince looks back at me, "now we got the servants right mad at us, what shall we see?"

"There's nothing but plants in here."

"Yes, but there are lots of kinds," he says. "There's fruits and veggies and flowers. We were rolling around in the spices. See?" He holds out his sleeve for me to smell. It smells of rosemary. I laugh.

The prince smiles. "And you were rolling in mint."

Oh boy. I'll be minty fresh all day tomorrow.

"But there's one part you may like." The prince smiles wide. "Do you have your impressinor?" I shake my head.

The prince calls a guard to get it and offers me his arm. I take it, and he shows me to an area towards the back. There are a few ponds and rivers here with statues dressed in different styles.

"You match." The prince grins.

The servant returns with the impressinor. The prince takes it with a nod of thanks. "Let's see if they can tell which are you and which are statues. Pose with that one." The prince grins.

"What?"

"Come on, it will be fun. Here, I'll show you." He hands me the impressinor and goes over to the first one, the one of a large man, and mockingly mirrors the pose the best he can manage. I laugh and so does the prince. "Give it a try," he encourages.

Well, at least the girls weren't in as funny of poses. I dare go over to the one pouring out a vase that makes the start of a river and pretend to help her pour it out.

The prince beams and snaps an impression. He guides me into doing a few more then swaps me for a few, so I'll have some of him. Too bad we couldn't get some with both of us.

"I'll get copies to send your mother," he beams as he shakes out one of the impressions, so I can see.

"I thought this would be below a prince," I smile at him.

"I live in a cage. Being a show bird keeps it more fun," he says. "Who's to judge in here?"

He has a point. Not like his parents could care or stop him. I'd never realized he was kept so tight against his will. Even the spoiled want more.

"What do you think?" He shows me the impression. I laugh at how silly he looks in the picture, even more than in person. "Perfect! I'll have the copies brought to your room tomorrow." He pockets the impressions.

The prince and I both notice the late hour, but the prince doesn't seem ready to end the night and asks if I'm hungry. I have to admit I'm not. I'm wondering if my maids should start on tea.

"I guess it is late for that," the prince admits. "I should let the servants fix the water." He glances at the sprinklers we'd left behind. "I can take you to your room." A hint of disappointment hangs in his voice. I'm not sure I want to be done either, but I will be glad to not be watched.

We go around the waterworks on our way out. The prince nods at the guards as we pass them.

Once outside, the prince relaxes. I'm guessing his parents are spying from in there. "I hope that wasn't too silly for you." Nervousness hangs in his tone.

"Not at all." I actually had a good time.

"Good." Relief fills his face. "And you passed. That's important."

I sigh in relief. I was worried I'd been too forward. After all, I pushed him into a rosemary bush.

"All you had to do was not jump me or be really sleazy," the prince laughs.

"The others were?"

"A few, but a lot failed other tests that are still coming up for you." The prince smiles. "Which reminds me, you free this rest day?"

"Am I ever busy?"

"Hey, you have girl pals here, right? Jonquil likes you," the prince says. "You may have plans with them."

I shake my head. "No, no plans."

"Perfect." The prince grins. "How about our second date then?"

I smile and nod. It makes this feel like tonight doesn't have to end. "What shall we do?"

"I picked tonight. How about you pick?" The prince suggests.

My face falls. I have no idea. My idea of planning a date was Jake and I sitting out on the river. Not exactly a proper date. We mostly just talked and... well, we didn't exactly engage in princess behavior.

"You can let me know tomorrow," he says as we reach my room. He bows and kisses my hand. "Thank you." He looks up at me. "I really wanted to make sure you got through."

I frown. "Why?"

"Miss, or sorry, Lady Kascia," he corrects himself. "I stand by what I said. You've still been the most honest with me, and you know my people. Something I still long for. When we're not so watched, I hope, at the least, we can still be friends like we were that night." I see nothing but my apprentice as he stands and looks into my eyes with a longing I've never seen before. It makes me feel like I long for whatever he is too. "I did have a good time. I look forward to your message tomorrow."

I smile and play the role. "I did too. Thank you for a lovely evening. I'll see you soon." Normally, at this point in dates past, I'd kiss Jake on the cheek because we were trying to be close. But I don't think that's a good idea here, so I curtsy before going inside.

I close the door, pressing my back to it. I have to plan the next date? What am I going to do? I still don't know where I want this to go. But he at least knows. He wants us to at least be friends.

He feels I'm his link to his people, the people he wants to know. Can I let my people hurt him when he seems like he wants to help? What if we didn't have to keep fighting each other to save our kingdom? What if it's just getting the prince to see the truth he's blind to? What if... what if.

I suddenly am engulfed in the memory of how I'd felt being that close to him when he'd pulled me up from the garden floor. The boy I'd joked I'd run away with. What if?

Chapter 20

The second date must be a test. I have to choose carefully. I could set up a walk on the grounds, but the king and queen might think that reckless and kick me out. All my ideas would. And then he needs to like it. I wish I could get him on his own to talk freely. He seems to want to.

"Is something the matter, my lady?" Damian asks the next morning, looking up from his work with kind eyes.

I sigh and sit on the bench at the end of my bed. "I have to plan the next date. I'm sure it's a test. And I have until the end of the day to tell him my idea. And I can't even think of a place that won't have the king and queen ready to throw me out and still be somewhat private," I say honestly. "I'll be out of here before I can blink."

Damian frowns, then tilts his head, "What about the library?"

I pause, "I don't know. I've never been there." I glance at Damian's normal serving of tea. "Have you been in there?"

Damian chuckles, "Yes. I have. I feel like I've lived in a library. It's a place no matter where I am that I feel at home."

"And there isn't anywhere someone could just spy in on us?"

Damian thinks a moment then shakes his head. "No, I don't believe there is. There is a second level, but if anyone were there, you'd be able to spot them."

I beam and kiss Damian's cheek in thanks without thinking, like I would my dad. "Perfect. Thank you, Damian."

I go over to the writing table to send the formal invitation. There is no way the king and queen would disapprove.

Damian chuckles, "You're welcome. Glad it makes you happy. I'll even serve tea for you both if you like."

And I trust Damian to be quiet. I beam, "Thank you; that would be perfect. It will be this rest day."

"Excellent. I'll be sure we are both ready," he promises.

Now I'm overflowing with excitement. It's only three days away. But then, as it always does these days, a darker thought crosses my mind. Better now than never.

"Damian, do you... know how to get information?" I ask awkwardly.

Damian pauses and raises a perfectly arched brow at me, "What kind of information?"

"Like... verifying something." I bite my lip nervously.

"Depends, like what?" He's studying me with interest.

I take a deep breath to get my nerves, "I... I overheard something that's shaken me. Learning what's going on outside these walls is near impossible, and I don't know how true this is. Could you help me find out if it's true?"

"What did you overhear?" He leans closer to me to give me his full attention.

"That a rebel attack on Nerine forced over one thousand people to have to flee their homes and they're trying to find refuge in already overloaded refugee camp."

"And you find that hard to believe?"

I nod. "I've never heard anything like it. I just... is it true?"

"I can certainly check my sources. I have very reliable contacts," he smirks confidently as he leans back in his chair. "I'll most certainly have an answer for you shortly, just give me a day or so. There is much to do with all that's happening." He smiles at me. I see a sparkle of something in his eye, pride? Is he impressed with me?

Meanwhile, I also have work to do. I write up and send the invitation to the prince. I get a formal reply accepting the offer. I wonder if the prince himself wrote it or if his attendant wrote it. The handwriting is impressively perfect, looking almost printed.

I can't even explain to myself why I'm so excited. It should stress me out like the last one, but my good mood lasts until the night before when I get a post from home.

I take the letters eagerly from Flur and rush over to my soft reading chair to enjoy them. I pause. It's not letters, it's *a* letter with Mom's handwriting. I open the envelope as quickly as I can. I check the envelope twice, but it is just Mom's.

I sit back, feeling my heart sink. Maybe father's message uses Mom's as the base code. He hasn't done that before, but maybe.

My heart picks up, and I scrape the back to see the code, but it's not there. I try until I'm about to rip the paper. I look at the envelope and everything else that might hold a hidden clue, but there's nothing.

My heart drops to my toes as I fall back, fighting frustration and tears. He can't be ignoring me. Right?

I pick up Mom's letter to read it, hoping that will cheer me up. She tells me Dad is out of town but didn't go far. She forwarded my letter to him. She also tells me about the show they picked.

I smile a little. With Dad gone, it will take a bit longer to receive his letters. Perhaps that's why I didn't get one from him, but at the same time, I feel like he should have written to me by now. He's stalling.

I frown in hurt, anger, and frustration. I turned my life upside down for him and his cause! And he can't make me a simple promise. I curl up in my chair, trying to read Mom's letter to cheer me up, but it doesn't fill the hole inside me or soothe my anger.

I open a drawer to pull out the pictures Damian and my maids took. Writing my mother back should help, right?

I start flipping through the impressions. Now this cheers me up. I look like I'm having fun in the impressions. Copies of the impressions the prince took are also there. I laugh as I flip through them. I can't recall smiling this widely in a long time.

I notice an extra one. I don't recall taking this one. The prince and I are laughing under the sprinkler rain. It captured us mid-spin around each other, both of us smiling, facing each other. It's beautiful.

I frown and tilt my head. The guard must have taken it. I've never seen a smile like that on my face. I take a deep breath. I feel like I should add it to my mother's letter. But I can't bring myself to do it.

I tell my mother all about Damian, the stunning dresses, about my date and the sprinkler going off and dancing in the "rain". I express my confusion about how sheltered the prince is and how he isn't at all what I expected and now I'm unsure. I also beg her to have Dad give me an answer right away. When I finish, I add a few impressions and feel better.

I stare at the impression of the prince and me in the rain, debating if I should send her one of the copies.

I bite my lips. I make a choice I may regret. I write on the back "my apprentice".

I smile and seal the letter. But I still feel a bit empty with nothing to write to Dad. What will I do if I don't hear back soon? This first rest day marks four weeks, pretty much a month since I arrived. There are only two months left, and I'm still not set on a course of action. I need his promise.

I spot the impressions Dad gave me. I hesitate. Should I review them? My heart trembles. I don't want to see them, but I have to remember why I came here. Even if going back to Jake sounds horrible. I need to recall why I let them rip me apart.

With a shaking hand, I take out the images, hidden in an envelope under the protective bottom of the drawer, tucked so far back I have to dig them out. I was hoping I'd get to hide them there forever and not need them. I was wrong.

Each one makes my heart ache as I see the destruction, pain, and smoke. All of these impressions are black and white, showing they didn't have the money for a full-color impressionnor, but they did the job: the dead, the wounded, the starving, the lost, the tears.

I am tempted to toss them out, but with how things are going, I'll need them. I take them and all my letters and put them under the flap in the drawer to stop them sliding around and to keep those impressions out of sight.

I pause, sitting still to evaluate how I feel. My face falls. I feel more confused. Anger doesn't fill me as expected. I'm not determined to do anything to bring down the royals. Instead, I think about how the king teases his son about the talent show and how he teased Zelda at lunch on the first day.

How could the proper queen stand to know this is happening? And the prince?

Should I show him these impressions? He wants to know what is happening. He said he wants to be friends, so he could understand. If that's all it would take to have his rule be the end of it, why not? Should I show him? But then I'll have to explain where I got them. Would I be executed? Maybe if I was alone with him, but not before.

I wish I could talk to Dad, but I know the rule. I cannot invite anyone to the palace.

I can't shake the depressed feeling. I pace a bit, but I don't feel like sitting with the other girls. I prefer it in my room.

Damian can't help but notice my mood. "Bad news from home?"

I shake my head, surprised he spoke. "Not bad, more... confusing."

"New circumstances can do that. But if being here caused confusion, and I imagine you were not so confused at home, but will going back grant you answers?" Damian asks as his eyes lift and meet mine intently. I can feel his concern.

"I just... There are people I want to talk to. I don't know if I want to 'go back'. I just—" I sigh heavily. "I don't know where I'm going anymore." I watch the waves for a moment.

Damian sets down his work and comes over to me. "And you think these people can help you figure it out?"

I nod a little. "I think so." I start to play with the ring on my right hand, my secret bond to Jake.

After a moment of quiet, Damian reaches out and rubs my shoulder then my back. I smile back. "Would an update on your question help?"

My eyes light up, and I nod eagerly.

"What you heard is correct. My contact didn't have exact numbers, but the rebels took part of Nerine. Half the people fled because their homes were caught in the crossfire. The other half left because they knew their lives would be next, so they took whatever they could and fled. The camps are overflooded and struggling to keep up with the need. The royal family is doing their best, but with numbers growing and rumors of rebels sending in spies to take resources and trying to talk refugees into joining their cause, it's not easy."

My face falls. "Why are they attacking cities?"

"It's an age-old tactic. The same one the Merlin's rebel forces used to take over Heklis's regime," Damian explains. "The different rebel factions have been trying to use them in this civil war since the beginning."

"I see." I look down. It's far worse than I knew. I'd ignored it.

"I take it you're only more confused," Damian correctly guesses. I nod. "Were you awaiting news that you didn't receive?" Damian glances at my stationary.

"I was expecting to hear back from my father. He's not normally slow to respond to me. He was the main person who wanted me to do this. And now I'm not as sure."

"Because he didn't answer you?" I nod. "Did your mother say anything about it?"

"He should reply; he's away for work. I can't shake the feeling he doesn't want to answer."

"Why is that?"

"I asked a favor of him, and I don't think he is willing to agree," I say as honestly as I can.

"I'm guessing it's a big favor." He smiles a little.

"Honestly, with what I agreed to do for him, it's not that big." I look away, still holding myself.

"So, if it isn't a big favor, why wouldn't he agree?" Damian asks then adds, "You don't have to answer if you don't want to."

I sigh angrily. "I don't know. He thinks it's silly."

"But you don't think it is," Damian guesses.

"No. It's really not." After all, isn't this mission all about protecting people? I'm just trying to protect the people who have suffered and gotten into the Enthronement to try to escape.

"Then fight for it. If he doesn't listen, then that is his loss. You are an intelligent young woman, Kascia. And while he may be your father, sometimes it is our children that teach us what is most important," he says with a gentle smile in his eyes.

I look up. Me? Smarter than my father? That feels impossible. He had experience I'd never have. He is the purest Custod I know. And I know they're right. "With him so far, I'm not sure how."

Damian smiles softly, "You're a smart girl. I'm sure you'll figure it out."

I sigh, "I hope so." Perhaps a more private conversation with the prince will help. What if it doesn't? What happens to me then? If I don't let them in, then what? I'd still be here, but for how long? I'm not a true princess. I can't win. Or could I? What if I tried. Curse the what-ifs!

"Well, everything is ready for tomorrow if you want to take a look," Damian smiles.

I smile and nod. Damian pulls out the mannequin, which is wearing a white and light blue dress. It's a nice dress as before. Perhaps more pretty than the last. It has a high collar around my neck and white cap sleeves for the bottom layer. This "undershirt" is mostly lace with a transparent underside to give it more color. The vest on top has a squarish shape but dips a little into a V at the bottom and comes in closer around the necklace collar. It's mostly periwinkle but has intricate light gray detailing and a dark sash holding it all together with a matching periwinkle skirt that's just a shade darker than the vest.

"Wow, it's amazing."

Damian beams, "Thank you. It did come out rather lovely, didn't it?" He places his hand on his chin as he admires it.

I beam and feel the soft skirt, "It did. I don't know how you do it or why I deserve it."

If I was trying and want to be queen one day, maybe. But that raises the question. Why not? I did agree to take the throne with Jake. Why not with Gavril?

That thought makes electricity zoom through my veins. Could I? What if? But I'm not what they think a true princess is. Does that matter? Could I sneak my way to a win? Do I want to? If I don't have to rule with Jake... did I have to at all? Could I go home and dance?

But... my apprentice. My heart begs.

"I don't see why you don't deserve it." Damian smiles then pulls out a golden pocket watch and checks the time. It's one of the nicest watches I've ever seen with the phoenix crest on the front.

"I don't know. I'm starting to wonder if I'm here for the right reason."

"And what makes you think that?" Damian asks as he puts his watch away and looks at me.

"I didn't really want to come."

"Don't like royalty?" Damian says in a half tease.

"Not these ones. I know you're not from here, but you must have seen it," I say, looking at him as if for answers. "What it's like for people here." Maybe his outside view would help me see the truth, like how the man in the boat sees the danger in the waters better than those swimming in it.

Damian thinks a moment then nods. "Not all of it, but some, yes. It really isn't my place to judge. I am a foreigner, raised in a different setting with different struggles and ways of life. How can I cast blame on either side when I don't know the full story?"

I sigh. “Sometimes, seeing from the outside is better. You’re not biased, but I hate what I see. I had a different idea of what things should be like. And now, I… I don’t know what I want anymore.”

Damian watches me for a long moment. “I hate to overstep my boundaries, but I feel like you need this,” he says, then takes me in his arms and holds me.

I really need it. The tears rise to my eyes. When was the last time I was hugged? “I don’t know what any of us should do anymore.”

“Sometimes, when you don't know what to do, all you can do is take each step as it comes and do what is right,” he says.

“I suppose so.” I smile at Damian. “Thank you. You’ve made all of this a lot easier.”

He smiles back. “I do what I can.”

“So, what’s the plan for tomorrow?” I ask. I go back to the distraction Damian tried to give me before.

He walks me through how he will set up the library and how he and my maids will serve us tea and treats, then step away to give the prince and me privacy. I sigh and lean back as he finishes.

“Just to get through tomorrow morning then.”

“True. Do you not enjoy devotional?” Damian asks.

“No, it’s just the anxiety of waiting, knowing I have a big test right after.” I laugh.

“I see.” Damian smiles. “I’ll try to make the test as enjoyable as possible then.” He whips out his notebook and pretends to jot down, “Extra cookies.” I laugh.

Chapter 21

Devotional the following day is calming. The prince really knows how to run a proper service. I notice Damian attending, sitting towards the back. *At least he won't be kicked out,* I joke to myself.

As soon as it's over, Damian sees to the arrangement while my maids get me ready.

They put my hair into a stylized, messy bun with a headband to match the skirt. They only touch up my make-up, adding a little matching periwinkle to my eyes.

The knock strikes the door just as we finish. Flur answers the door. "I'm sorry, what was your name?" The prince greets her. Flur blinks like caught in a spotlight. The prince laughs.

"It's Flur, your highness." She bows.

"Flur, thank you. May I come in?"

"She's ready for you." Flur nods at me.

The prince had changed. He has left his service jacket behind and wares a casual waistcoat. His white shirt looks a little finer than he's worn before, and his servants have tried to get his hair to behave.

"Are you ready, pigeon?"

I smile and nod. He offers me his arm, and I can't help but admire how strong it feels as we make our way down the hall.

"Hopefully, you'll be allowed free reign of the library soon. It's a decent library as far as I can tell. You'll be free to read any books you like. Though you likely will run into Princess Zelda. She likes to explore our books," the prince says.

"Hopefully, it's more private today," I hint.

"Yes, much more." The prince smiles. "So why the library?"

"You wanted to tell me something 'later'. I hoped the library allowed later," I explain.

"It does." The prince grins.

The prince opens the door. The library is a unique shape. On my left is a large fireplace with beautiful wave carvings. On my right is a large window open to the gardens. The rest of the walls are bookshelves. To the right of the windows, bookshelves run off into dark halls. The second floor is more like a balustrade that wraps around the room and over to an open reading area in front of the windows.

On the lower level, Damian set a table with saucers, cups, and spoons. To the left, is a rolling tray with several covered plates and a teapot.

He turns to us as we come in. His jacket is missing. Instead, he's wearing a dark blue waistcoat with a towel draped over his arm. I give him a big smile.

He smiles and bows. "My lady. Your Highness." He gestures and welcomes us to the table.

"Thank you," I nod to him. The prince smiles and pulls the chair out for me. I nod my thanks to him. He returns the nod as he pushes me in.

He turns and thanks Damian as well. Damian nods to him and pulls out the chair for the prince, "Your Highness." The prince nods him another thanks as he sits down. Damian impresses me. He's a servant, but I know him. He's no mere servant.

Damian nods then gives a sharp snap. Flur, Vivian, and Ro appear to assist him. They have the tray of fresh tea and start laying it out as Damian uncovers the cream and sugar bowls. He's efficient. Vivian places a tray of little sandwiches, and Flur sets down plates of dumplings decorated with tiger stripes or pure black as is traditional. Ro places down stunning napkins.

"Thank you, Flur, and... goodness, how many maids do you have?" the prince teases me. "And your names?"

"Ro." Ro bobs a quick curtsy.

"Vivian." Vivian bows her head as she curtsies.

"Vivian." The prince tastes the name like it's familiar, but he doesn't say anything. Relief shows on Vivian's face. "Thank you," the prince smiles at them.

Vivian beams as she serves the prince tea, adding the right amount of cream and sugar without asking. Do all the servants have the royal family's preferences memorized?

Once we're set, they step back to await orders. They smile at each other then at Damian. Damian smiles at me then nods to the others. They bow to him and slip out of sight.

The prince is watching me. "You got the best servants for today," he says, getting my attention back on him. "At least, I can tell you think so."

"You'll see," I tease as I take my first sip of the perfectly brewed tea.

The prince grins, "Oh, will I?"

"Yes," I say confidently and give Damian a small wink. He smiles back as he sits down with a book nearby.

"I'll take that challenge." The prince sighs and puts down his cup, "But you picked a quiet setting. I'm guessing you are hoping to get some answers."

I smile slyly. "You are observant, my lord."

"Hopeful. I was hoping you'd want more answers in a quieter spot. I didn't think you'd set the date up around it," the prince says as he samples some of the sandwiches. "Was there something you wanted to talk about first?"

A million thoughts run through my head. What did he really think of me before I knew who he was? Does he feel the same as me? Does he really not know what was going on out there? Was he really the prince I'd thought he was?

"Are you alright?" He bends to try to see my face.

"I don't even know where to begin."

"Alright, then I can start. You came, even though you dislike us, to avoid a bad breakup. Mind if I ask how bad?"

That's where he starts? Does that mean he likes me? I try to ignore my heart thudding faster. "It's... worse than he likely thought it was."

"Mind explaining?" He frowns. "Don't get me wrong, I'm happy you're here. I just don't know how anyone could be so stupid. And it hurts you. Not one conversation we've had hasn't shown its influence you. I wish to never cause that pain again."

"I don't know if there is much else to say," I explain as much as I can without giving dangerous details. "I was with someone else, and he turned out not be as invested as I thought. It changed... everything about my life." I deflect tears by stirring my tea. "If life was about to get thrown on its head, why not do it at the palace?"

"Are you alright?" The prince studies me in concern. Those brown eyes are like magic keys unlocking all my heart's secrets.

"You want to talk about old flames on a first date?" I challenge as a deflection.

"Second," the prince corrects me. "I guess it might be rude. I want to solve the riddle that is you. I don't want to make you stay if you don't want to be here."

"Would you really let me go?"

"As much as it would hurt, yes." He looks me dead in the eye. "I do want that friendship. Perhaps you could write and send impressions to tell me of my people. Assuming my guards wouldn't confiscate them." He rolls his eyes.

My heart aches for him. Maybe I should have brought the impressions. "Is... that even safe to discuss here?"

"Why wouldn't it be?" he asks me with a slight crease to his brow. "You mean your ex? Do you still care about him?"

"I don't know," I say too fast. The tears come faster than I can control them. Part of me still loves him. A part of me hates him. "But right now, he's not an option, so I try not to think about it."

"Would he be if you went home?"

"No." The word comes instantly and so forcefully I surprise myself.

The prince is equally surprised. "I guess I should be glad for it." He manages.

That makes me laugh slightly. "Only if I win."

"Guess sucks for you if you don't then."

I don't know. I take a sip to help me get my nerves back. It works, and I take a bite of a sandwich.

"Okay, I won't press." The prince takes a sip, "But I think I owe you some explanations too. Don't let this be one-sided."

I nod, but I don't know where to start.

"Alright, I'll keep going then." He frowns in confusion. "But the big thing I want to ask is why you were so angry. You asked if I knew what it's like out there." The prince pauses. "I don't. But I want to. You seem to hate my family for making the mess. I want to know why it's our fault. I want to fix it, but how do I fix what I'm not allowed to see?"

"You're the prince. You can have anything you want."

The prince laughs and takes another bite, "No, I don't. It might look like it to you, but it's sadly untrue. If I had what I wanted, I'd know the city like the back of my hand. If I had what I wanted, this contest wouldn't be happening. If I had what I wanted, we'd be keeping a dog off the food." I laugh.

The prince smiles. "I want to walk around my own garden without begging. I got lost the one time I got out there. My parents guard me like I'm made of glass. I don't get what I want. It's really rare I get what I want." He takes a breath. I see a question in his eyes. Like he wants to tell me something.

"Why? I thought it was just security."

"Well, I'm a miracle," the prince shrugs. "I'm the fifth baby my mother had. So, she's really protective. So is my father. They behave like I'm still a child. I have a Custod guard who is not allowed to leave me. Custods have been dismissed for giving me too much freedom. I don't get freedom. I don't get to know how bad the world is. I'm too precious for that," he gruffs bitterly.

"It's not because you're the heir?"

"It's that too, but mostly... it's my mother. I don't understand it, but I try. I guess when we lose a loved one or a hope of having a family, we'll know. Can you imagine what it's like losing four babies then finally having your wish? They tried after me too. Imagine how that increased my worth. I don't understand it, but... I can try." He gives me a sad smile. I frown in confusion, making him chuckle. "Any questions?"

"Not really. I can't even imagine. I thought my parents were guarded."

"Doesn't help three groups of crazy people want to kill me," the prince smirks slightly. "And it sounds like you may know them pretty well. You might not even call them crazy, would you?"

"What?"

"Your challenge to the royal family read right out of a rebel pamphlet." The prince takes a fresh sandwich. "I know it when I hear it."

"Well, maybe I have some friends who sympathize with them."

The prince nods. "Am I to gather that's most people?"

"I don't know, just people I've spoken to about it."

"So why come? Do you not plan on winning or even trying?"

I wish I had an answer for him. "Of course, I'll try. I'm here."

"But you agree we shouldn't rule anymore?"

I bow my head. "I-I don't know. I agree things aren't great. I want to help fix them. I don't know who should rule. I just know this has to stop."

"Mind telling me what 'this' is?" The prince tilts his head to see my face.

"The suffering," I say the obvious.

The prince lets out a heavy sigh through his lips, making me look up. He looks frustrated, angry, hurt, perhaps a mix? He looks off into nothing, jaw tense. I tense too.

"That's descriptive for a guy who looks into town and only sees pretty lights. I don't know what 'suffering' is happening." He gives me a sharp sideways look that would be great at getting confessions out of criminals. "I get to hear it's 'bad', it's 'terrible', but what does that mean? To someone who knows nothing outside the bubble his mother has built, that means quite literally nothing. I don't need more vague ideas, Lady Kascia. What pain have we forced them through? You through?"

I look away. Oh wow, he is going to scare the daylights out of a lot of my rebel friends. I am not sure even Jake would have kept quiet with that dangerous tone and look.

It should scare me. I am the enemy. I came here to kill him.

But I don't. I sense his power and desperation. I feel the same passion and desire I'd felt from Jake to stop the kids from starving and dying. If anything, it's stronger, purer, than Jake's passion.

What did his family put me through? Nothing. What they'd done to ruin the kingdom hadn't ever hurt me personally. All my pains came from the rebels, my father, Jake's fake love. The Enthronement wasn't designed to hurt me or anyone. They didn't make it hurt me. Those I love did.

"It varies by how badly the poverty hits you, I suppose." I try to think of something the prince could understand. "You don't see children coming to beg for food at the castle gate? You don't hear them in the streets?"

The prince shakes his head. "My lady, I'm lucky if I can even see the castle gate from the front doors."

I gape in stunned silence. I can't believe that's true. He's the prince. He's next in line. "No reports cross your desk?"

The prince laughs bitterly, "Nothing crosses my desk. I don't have a work desk. I don't attend meetings. It's lessons in the morning, and since this started, date after date. That's it. I have lessons mocking what it will be like to run battles and plan resistance defenses and rulings, but not once have I done anything real. They never catch me up to speed. I know there are three groups out to get me because each wants a different king or queen or whatever. But I want to know. I want to help, but I'm powerless when I don't know what is happening. So please, what suffering?" He's slowly losing his patience. Why is that attractive?

"The things I see most are those starving. So many can't afford three meals a day, let alone one. I never could go out alone at night for fear of one of those beggars trying to mug me. There are not enough jobs to go around. There are more children on the streets begging than in schools. There are more people out of homes than in them. They try to grab even a bit by stealing but are caught and whipped. The lines for beatings are so long they stretch down alleyways. Crime is rampant."

The prince nods a little, his eyes intent on me as he tries to understand. "So, what do you, or your rebel friends, think to do about it?"

I sigh. I don't know anymore. If I did, this conversation wouldn't be happening. "All they say get someone on the throne who will give the money back."

"So... money solves the endless crime?" The amused disbelief is clear in his tone.

"Why not? They're stealing, so they can eat."

"So, say the money just suddenly came back, then what?" He raises a brow.

"Um..."

"I'm not trying to mock you. I mean it. Say that somehow happened. How does that get the starving children into a home if they're on the streets, for example?" He's studying me as if I had actual answers. I don't. He smiles a little, "So... your friends don't have an answer for that?"

I laugh. "Not that they've told me. I guess I've been naïve."

"Hey, you know what's happening. You're one up from me. So, if I'm five, you're eight. At least you're accountable," he jokes.

I roll my eyes. "Very funny."

"So... are you saying the rebellions just want their money back? Say we pay them off, they just... go away?" He takes a bite.

"Yeah, that's what they say." I shrug, taking a sip of tea, suddenly relaxed.

"Crime sounds like a problem. And we just... pay them to stop being criminals? Sounds like being held hostage to me."

I sigh, annoyed at how hard he is about it. "You have no idea what it's like to suffer or starve. How can you judge them? Do you even know what it's like to be hungry, like really hungry? Not just hungry, but actually hungry, sick for the need of food or dizzy or desperate at the sight or smell of food you can't have?"

"I'm religious, my lady. I may not have ever been starving, but I've done fasts. So... maybe a little bit."

His answer surprises me. He doesn't snap that of course he doesn't and he didn't pretend he doesn't have a clue. He just states he has a small idea. That felt out of character for the prince. But it certainly is my apprentice.

He lets out a heavy sigh. "Maybe that's why, but I have a hard time believing money alone fixes anything. Money is a tool, not a power in itself. It doesn't make someone who likes to get something for nothing suddenly decide a job is better than picking pockets."

"No one wants to pickpockets."

"Do they?"

"Of course not!"

Prince Gavril pauses, running his finger over the rim of his teacup as he thinks. "So, you're telling me none of the people stealing aren't just people who like getting something for little effort. That all rebels would behave if their political aims were met and aren't the kind of people who like causing trouble?"

"Well, I suppose not all of them."

"What about them?"

"It's a smaller amount," I argue.

"You really think paying them off will work?" He raises a brow, reminding me of Damian.

"Well, why not?"

"Alright." He nods. "Let's pretend we agree that works. What kind of money would that take?"

Oh, I have no idea. They just say "give it back". But what did they even take? "Well, what do you get in taxes on average?"

The prince bursts into laughter, bending over the table to try to control it.

I frown. "You don't need to mock me."

"No, no, it's not you." The prince sighs, "It's that they don't tell me. I learned to count money with play gems. I've never seen a real gemlet. You see, you're not wrong to say I'm doing nothing. But it's because I can't. Until I'm married to whom they deem worthy, I am still a little boy. A precious pet you don't let outside for fear of a hawk eating it. Does that make sense?"

"No." That sounds like insanity to me. A future king is not a pet.

The prince sighs. "It's like..."

"No, no, I know what you mean. I just don't think it makes sense. You don't set up your future ruler like that."

"I told you; you ask my parents, I'm five." The prince gives me a sad smile.

I really should have brought the impressions. That would be better than the stupid things I'm saying.

My team rescues me. They change out the sandwiches and what few dumplings are left and exchange them for dried fruits, tarts, and scones with various jams. Damian makes up our next cup of tea.

"Thanks." The prince smiles at Damian. I realize the king and queen don't normally speak to the servants, but the prince and Princess Zelda always do.

"My pleasure, Prince Gavril," Damian gives the prince a slight bow.

I nod at Damian before he goes. "Well, sweeter things should lighten the mood," the prince jokes. "Sorry if this is dull or frustrating or more likely offensive to you. I'm still learning."

"I'm impressed you're not offended or angry with me."

"It's not your fault. I'm sorry if I have been rude. I get... angry. My father never takes my attempts to learn seriously, telling me it takes experience. And my mother still thinks I'm five. After all, she still thinks I'll 'grow into coils'. I passed that mark a long time ago. I sometimes wonder if she knows that." The prince shakes his head and takes a bite of a tart. "You'd be surprised about the things I should know how to do, but I don't."

"You can ride a horse."

"Nope, what if I fell off wrong?" The prince smiles, a challenge in his eyes.

"I'm sure you can swim."

"But then I have to get in deep water." The prince smiles wider.

My face falls. "You live on a beach!"

"Yup, I can get my feet wet, but no going in because I can't swim."

"And you can't learn... unless you get in."

"I know in theory. I've read books on horses, swimming, and fencing. I am surprised they let me handle butter knives. Oh wait, they don't. Servants do that. Ever noticed?"

I shake my head.

"But I know how." He butters a scone, smiling. "Unlike a horse."

"Not even pony rides?"

"I've never seen a pony," the prince says as if calling "check" in a chess match. "I told you I don't get what I want."

"I'd think, not even as a child, you'd want a pony." I laugh.

The prince shakes his head. "No, as a kid, what I wanted most was a friend or a pet. You'd make my day with a trip into town to play tag with a child my age. Servant children were scared of me. If they were playing with me and I scraped my knee, they'd be beheaded. Or so their parents told them to make sure they didn't get into trouble. And no Custod guard stuck around long enough to be a friend."

"Not even your guard," I recall what he said before.

The prince nods. "What about you? Lots of friends?"

I smile and tell him about some of my castmates, that many signed up but didn't make it to the interviews. He jokes he should look up why.

"Can you do that?"

"Yup, if it's in the past, I can share anything. Two tried to get too close during their first date. Well, one did, the other dressed so scantily it was about the same. One made me very uncomfortable with a matching game she made that showed how alike we were that had hardly a truth about what I actually like in it." He clears his throat uneasily as if wanting to forget. "Some girls were chatty, frankly slutty, or their fangirling creeped me out so that I had to say no. One of them went on so long I lost track. As I said, you have to be dumb to be kicked out this early."

"Then why wait so long on mine?"

With how his face falls I wish I hadn't asked. I take a sip to give him a moment. He looks ill. I'd forgiven him for it, but it clearly is deeper than I realized. I don't know if I should apologize or if that would be worse.

"Well, I technically have had more time with you than the others," He finally gets out.

"Sorry I asked," I manage.

"It's not you," he says quickly.

Was there someone who'd left he hadn't wanted to let go? Had that made him worry I'd go soon too? "Sorry to remind you. I know how it can hurt—"

His laugh surprises me so much I freeze mid-sentence.

"No, no, it's not that." The stiffness melts away. "Sorry, I... I'm not sure we're at a point that I can tell you why. I'll tell you if you last long enough, that fair?"

"Oh come on, I got this far," I try to keep the joking up to make sure I don't get into more trouble. "Or is it the 'politics'?"

He studies me a moment. "Let's just say, for now, I wasn't ready for your reaction if you failed."

That raises far more questions than it answers. But he crosses me with a new question. "I've been wanting to ask: how did you get out that night?"

I flush. "Climbed."

"And you were just stressed? I know those are easy to climb, but that took guts," he smiles.

"You've done it?"

The prince's face falls. I think I hear Sage curse. "No, well, yes, sort of. It was a long time ago."

"Was that when you got lost on the grounds?"

"Yes," the prince says quickly. "Yes, yes, it was. And... Well, recall Sage is here, and he wasn't the guard at the time."

"Oh, sorry," I flush, "I didn't mean to get you into trouble."

He shrugs, "Well, he's an assassin. He'd have figured it out."

"Right..." I try to think of a change of subject. It's hard when the terror of what the prince says lingers. Sage is an assassin Custod. That is the most elite class. He'll figure out who I am in a heartbeat, and Dad said only our team was told the true mission to keep the secret. "Well, I climbed down and walked the rest of the way. I just wanted to be outside and cry."

"Apart from the crying, I know the feeling. Sage is more willing to let me out," the prince says. "This place does that. Makes you feel trapped. You are limited to so many rooms, so am I. I have never seen the kitchens, armory, gym, tool shed, and... maybe one or two other places. Look at all the dangers," the prince laughs then mocks terror. "Hot ovens with closed doors, stoves I could touch. And the army of knives." I laugh, and he chuckles. "I get feeling trapped here. It is like a fancy cage. Dad gets nervous when I lean over a balcony. Can you imagine that?"

No, my father was happy to let me do dangerous things. "Thinks you'll fall?"

"Thinks I'm going to get shot."

"Oh, wait, how? The rebels can't even get on the grounds."

The prince pauses. "They didn't warn you?"

"About what?"

"They do get on the grounds. They set off alarms, so we go on lockdown. They didn't tell you? Do you even know where your safe room is?" The prince frowns.

"What? No," I frown too.

The prince huffs, "Well, guess the only thing they really need to guard is me." His tone is so sad and bitter it makes my heartache. "Well, for the Ladies' Chamber, it's under the painting by the window on the left side, press into the wood under it, and it opens. If the alarm goes off, the guards will push you all in. I think the ones for the bedrooms are under the bed. I know mine is."

"I'll check for it." Though if they got in, I doubt they'd hurt me, but what about my friends? I think about the letter I'm due to receive any day now. "How fast is mail normally?"

"You'd know better than me. I have no one to write to," the prince says.

"Oh, that's so sad." It comes out before I can think.

The prince shrugs. "No friends, no family alive, and even when my parents were talking to prospective brides, they did it for me. So no, not even a performer to write fan mail to. I've not seen a live performance."

My jaw drops. "Not one?"

"Not one."

"No one comes for Christmas or anything?"

The prince shakes his head. "Security is a nightmare."

I can't imagine it. "So just impressed music?"

"I taught myself piano. That's the best I get," the prince says.

"Really?"

"Yeah, started with books in the library. I self-taught a lot of things."

I frown. "Like what?"

"Well piano, how to read music. I learned how to navigate by the stars too," the prince says. "And all the 'theory' about riding a horse and swimming."

"What would happen if you got on a real horse?"

The prince laughs, "I'm sure I'd try to do what I read and end up flat on my face," he smiles, "In the dirt, because I fell off wrong. Because I read in a book you grip with your knees and so I do it too hard or pull on the reins wrong or... something."

"So if you had to leave the castle?"

The prince sighs and pulls up a napkin. "I, Prince Gavril," he says what he's "writing" out loud, "start my last will and testament." I laugh. "Yeah, I'd be screwed," the prince chuckles. "I know a map, but that doesn't really tell me how to get anywhere."

"So why didn't you kick me out after I said you were a monster hiding in this castle?"

"Because you did and do what no one else does," the prince smiles. "Take me seriously and tell me how it is. Again, I don't know what it's like out there. I heard bad, but for all I know, the war is a big plot made by my parents to keep me inside all the time." The prince frowns. "It's not, right?"

I laugh, "No, it's not."

"Good, because that would mean the Custods are jerks for playing along." The prince smiles. I chuckle. "I wonder what it's like and how I could ever dream to fix it when it's... it's my turn."

"Well, I guess you'll get to know more once you're married," I try to cheer him up.

"So they say. I can only hope." The prince gives me a weak smile. "But I guess it's not your problem."

"Well, wouldn't it be if I win?"

The prince beams, "So you're trying and not pining over your ex?"

"Either way, if I'm in the game, I should be in it. I don't mind you talking about it."

"What if you lost? What will you do?" the prince asks with honest curiosity in his voice. "Go back to the stage?"

Is that going to be an option? "I have no idea. I hate to think about it."

"Worried about your family?" the prince says. "Oh, and I ask everyone that question. Don't worry."

That does make me feel better. It isn't a sign I am about to be thrown out. "I know my mother won't mind. My father may get upset. I don't know. I'm scared to find out."

The prince nods, "Well, guess we'll all find out. I have to try not to get too attached to anyone, but I also need to have a relationship with the one I end up with. It's kind of terrifying."

I shake my head, "I can't imagine."

"I try not to. I end up with nightmares about random things like the one who wins is terrible," The prince smiles.

"Do you have any you don't like?"

"Hey, don't get me in trouble. What if they hear? Or worse, you tell them." The prince gives me a stink eye.

I shake my head, "I'm not that petty."

"I bet," the prince chuckles and shakes his head. "I am not laying my cards out like that. I try not to have favorites. And I try not to hate any of them."

"Ah, try?"

"Nope, not telling," the prince smiles. "You're only on test four."

Only? Great, that means there are a lot more. "Are all the tests dates? Or are all dates tests?"

"I can't tell you that."

"What happened to not as many rules?"

The prince laughs, "You're asking questions about my only rule."

I pout, "Not fair."

"Says the girl who is trying to cheat the others," the prince smiles. "I thought backstabbing was for later in the game."

"Is that a test?"

The prince groans, "See, if you ask it like that, I can't tell you."

"You're no fun."

"You need to stop trying to cheat."

"No one else asks these questions?"

The prince laughs, "Well, most try to get me to talk. Or they talk on and on and on."

"I'm not doing that?"

"No, you're eating and drinking tea," the prince smiles. "And you brought friends. Others have tried to be more alone."

I frown, "You can get rid of Sage?"

"No!" I hear Sage's voice.

The prince doubles over laughing. "Oh, I wish," the prince says. I can almost hear Sage having a fit, even if it's only in my imagination.

I chuckle too, "Do you ever spend time alone?"

The prince shakes his head. "Sage guards my door, so I guess I'm alone in my room, but there are guards everywhere."

"Must be hard not having time alone."

"What do you do when you're alone?" The prince picks up some dried fruit.

I smile a little. "Well, depends. I like to walk along the river. I'll dance in the studio or read a book. I like time alone to think. I don't know what I'd do without that quiet time."

"I'm only alone when— ow!" The prince rubs his head. A book had thwacked him in the back of the head.

I realize why and laugh hysterically. Sage just stopped him telling me the one time he is alone.

"What was that?" the prince demands.

"Um.... a book," I say.

"Sage!?" The prince looks up. "You get down here!" I can't breathe for laughing.

"No," Sage replies.

Vivian and Flur are fighting their laughter. Ro is laughing along with me.

"Perhaps the library wasn't the best idea after all." Damian tries not to smile as he brings over fresh tea.

"Where else would we talk without unexpected spies?" I ask Damian as the prince keeps rubbing the back of his head.

"True." Damian sighs. "Then I suppose I should have 'disarmed' the library before you entered. Didn't think it would be dangerous." He looks up to a corner of the room. "Though if he gets a bump on his head, you'll have to account for that."

"Oh please, I hit him with 'One Fish, Two Fish, Red Fish, Blue Fish'!" Sage calls back.

Flur picks up the offending book. He's right. That's what hit the prince over the head.

"Maybe we should find another topic." I tease the prince.

"Alright, alright. I'll leave you a note about alone time later." The prince smirks. I picture Sage getting a new book in my mind's eye.

I roll my eyes. "Well, what should I know about you?"

"Um.... well, I think I can dance. I had dance lessons."

I gasp mockingly. "What? But what if you broke a leg?"

"Can you really do that dancing?"

"Yeah, I know dancers who broke legs or had other injuries."

The prince nods slowly. "Don't tell my mother." I laugh. "But really, I got a safe education. I can dance, know world history and geography and all that. Just no experience in anything, you know, important," He smiles.

"If you weren't a prince, what would you want to be?"

The prince pauses. I don't think he'd thought of that before. "A sailor or something like that. I'd like to explore the ocean and the animals there. I like the water, even if I'm not allowed in it."

"I used to sit on the beach often, but I don't know much about it. I know a neat spot to see a lot of animals hunting together."

"Maybe one day you can show me."

"What will you show me in return?"

The prince doesn't miss a beat. "The stars. I'll show you the patterns in the night sky. I like the phoenix and the dolphin best, but this time of year, we may see a Christmas star or harvest moon, or maybe a harvest comet."

"Can you really see all that?"

"In the right places if you wait for your eyes to adjust." The prince nods. "If you get far enough, I'll show you."

I smile. "I'd like that."

A moment later, Damian and the others change the dishes out for a fresh course. Flur puts down a plate of éclairs next to me. The prince is smiling at them. Then he looks back at me. "You really went all out."

"Damian went all out." I nod at him. "He's the best." Damian only smiles and bows to us humbly.

"You seem good at that. Getting the best out of people." He smiles at me. I blush furiously. "You get people to like you. Oh, reminds me." The prince reaches into his pocket. "You got fan mail. One of the boys we hired to help us with the tests wrote you a note saying thanks again for not asking for more impressions."

The prince hands me an impression. I take it, and my mouth falls open. I see the boy who took my impression, Jashon, Alsmeria, a few other girls from my troupe, and even Jake.

"Flip it over." The prince smiles.

All of their signatures with a good luck note are written there. I bite my lips. I can't believe they are polling for me.

"And I'm guessing it's because they know what I saw that first night. You care about them." The prince smiles.

Yeah, I often was lip-locked with one of them. Jake does look happy in his impression. Is he doing alright without me? Part of me is happy about that; the other half of me is furious he's not broken like me.

The prince frowns, "Are you alright? Sorry, I thought it would help. Did I make you homesick?"

"No." He made me Jake-sick. Which is worse.

"Then what's wrong?" The prince puts his hand on mine. It sends a warm sensation through my body. I want to retreat from it, but that would be a bad sign. I have to pretend to want this. But what am I pretending to want?

"Just... conflicted, I guess. This is much more real when I'm here. It's hard to merge the two in my mind," I try to explain. The prince and my apprentice, the same? Or is one made up in my head?

The prince nods. "I know what you mean. I'm in the same place, but having you all here flipped my world upside down. I felt caught in the tide, like a bit of kelp. Everyone had their opinion of what I should do, but I just want to have things... I don't know... I guess, how I expected. Honestly, it was supposed to be six, and that was it. Then it was fifty.

"I won't lie, I almost fainted when I saw all those applications," the prince laughs. "I can't imagine how hard it is for you. So... I guess, thanks. For throwing your world upside down to give me even a chance."

The thank you is nice, but what really touches me is what he said. That's how I'd felt about it all. Everything was flipped over. Everyone had their plan for me, and I was caught in it all. I wish I knew which way I want to swim for safety.

"Well, you're welcome. I hope it gets solved for you too." I smile.

"And it will for you. I promise." My apprentice smiles.

That's all I can see in that warmth; all I can feel in his touch. Did I make him up or the prince? The prince can't understand that. I cannot let that... this, happen. Can I?

Chapter 22

A servant had to come in and remind the prince we had dinner to attend. My maids quickly take me up to my room to help me clean up. But they left Damian on his own to take care of the library, so I assure them I can touch up my make-up.

I finish touching up and stand to go when a shadow blocks my way. I jump a mile and pull back. Sage is glaring down at me with his startling green eyes, narrow in suspicion.

I almost trip over the vanity bench. He towers over me. What is he doing in my room? He has no right to be in here, most of all, with my maids and attendant gone. Part of me wants to slap him, but even as my hand twitches to do it, I don't dare.

"What are you doing here?" Sage demands of me, jaw tense as he glares at me.

"It is my room," I retort. I have to be careful, or he could be the death of me or worse.

"Not that. I mean here, in the Enthronement." He steps closer, pushing the bench aside. I back up. The fact he's an assassin Custod rings hundreds of alarm bells in my mind.

"You don't want the throne at all. You seem intent on overthrowing it. I know that rhetoric. I know the arguments they use. You speak like one of their little missionaries. So, what are you really doing here?" But the tension in his voice isn't what I'd expect for someone accusing me of treason. It sounds more personal.

"I told him and you the truth." I stand firm, but inside, I'm trembling. The truth is, I don't know what I'm doing here.

Sage huffs and begins to pace. "Right, to avoid some boyfriend. That's another thing. Who is this boy? Hmm? More rebel lies?" He gives me a glare meant to scare me into an answer.

I lose my temper. "Yes!"

Sage blinks in surprise. His shoulders relax as he watches me.

"He lied to me! His stupid causes meant more to him than I did." My heart falters. Which 'he' did I mean, Jake or my father?

I don't fight the tears this time because they're hot, and I want Sage to see them. I want him to know how much I hate what they did to me. How everything I knew was thrown to the winds. I hate all of them for making me do it.

"And I don't even know what causes he meant." I hug myself, trying to gain some control. Sage is not the person to scream at about this.

"Are you saying he was a rebel?"

"A sympathizer, at least." I shrug. "I never saw him doing anything."

Sage studies me. "Did you?"

I groan in frustration and glare up at him. "Look," I state boldly. "If you're looking for guilt on my face, it's going to be there. Of course, it is. Alright? I'm not proud of having friends like that now I'm here. Most people think that way out there, okay? It's just awkward to have friends say one thing, then have this."

"So why did you come if your friends didn't like it?"

"Because not all of them did. These are some of my best friends." I pull the picture out of my pocket and shove it into his chest forcefully, making him take it. "None of them are rebels, and they told me to do this. Jashon was the first person to tell me I should join and just because he thought I'd be good at it. Not all my friends are like that. My parents thought I should do it too. I didn't want to, but they talked me into it. I wasn't sure how I felt about the throne, alright? I'm still figuring it out. I can't be the only one unsure now they've walked into this palace."

"No one is voicing it so much," Sage says.

Oh, if only he knew how little I was voicing. "Wouldn't a spy keep their mouth shut?"

"You lost that chance when you told the prince who you didn't think was a prince." Sage is studying me with that hard expression, but that expression is fading. I see confusion reflected in his eyes and concern, but for what, I have no idea. "You were stressed and that made it easy to slip. No one else was so freaked out that night."

"As far as you know, and I told you why," I snap back. I feel exposed, and I hate that. "I didn't want to come. I don't know what I want anymore. It was my only choice left. But that's not what you care about." I latch onto the only change of topic I can find. "You just don't like I got a meeting out of your silly rules."

"I couldn't care less about those stupid rules," Sage snarls back. "I don't like the threat you pose," he hisses, narrowing his eyes and stepping closer, almost getting into my face. "There is something off about you. And I will figure it out. And you'll regret coming when I do."

I shove him away with my eyes sparkling. "I already do," I snap at him.

Sage's glare changes to a frown; his narrowed eyes stay the same, but the confusion and concern are back in greater measure. "Really?"

His tone scares me. Was that pity in his tone? "Of course not. You must be blind not to see I did at least have a good time with him."

"Doesn't mean you don't regret what this has done to you." Sage steps closer to me, studying me but with a much softer expression like I'm a puzzle he's desperate to solve rather than a threat he's desperate to swat.

I step back, afraid of him understanding. He'll realize I am a threat to be disposed of. I wish I could force him away. I miss being armed. I miss feeling able and strong enough to push these people off me.

"It doesn't matter," I try to spit with all the venom I can manage. "I'm not here to hurt anyone. My being here has nothing to do with my rebel friends. I don't take part in it. Yes, I want what's wrong with my people fixed. But not everyone thinks it has to be done with a new ruling class. I am finding out for myself. You have a problem with that?" My acting impresses even me. I feel rather proud of myself.

"It does if your fallback plan intends any harm to the boy I protect," Sage hisses at me. My acting snapped him back into threat mode. But hadn't I wanted that? It worked. He fell for it. Maybe that was dumb. "I don't trust you," Sage's tone is low and threatening, "and you charm him differently than the others. I don't know how you do it. And it isn't safe for him or you."

"Then tell the king and queen, and I fail instantly." Inside, my heart begs him not to. I can't go back to my family yet. I don't know if I ever can, but I have no means of escape if I leave now.

Sage's mouth twitches. Why? Perhaps he doesn't have enough evidence to have me thrown out yet. I think the prince likes me well enough, and the king enjoyed our meeting. He'd need enough to get them over that. Sage doesn't have what he needs. He is hoping to scare it out of me.

Though I don't feel it, I put on a smirk. "You can't," I gloat. "And you won't get enough. Because I'm not what you think I am."

Sage falls for it still. "Oh," he says in a low voice, "I'm pretty sure you are. And when I prove it, you'll regret it."

"Well, best of luck finding evidence that isn't there." I tilt my shoulders in a kind of cocky shrug.

A shadow of doubt crosses Sage's face. Was that too much? *Please, don't see through me.*

"I'm a Custod. I don't always need their approval," he says, looking from one of my eyes to the other. He's testing. I shiver at his gaze. He is terrifying when he wants to be. My heart quivers.

Thankfully, the door opens. Damian strides in, and immediately, looks Sage down and up with a brow ached at a sharp angle. "Well, well, what do we have here? This isn't the room you should be guarding."

"Maybe it is." Sage gives me a last searching look. "I will remind you none of you are allowed to be alone with him."

"I know." I make the promise he's asking for in hardly more than a whisper.

"You'll have no trouble from her. I assure you." Damian gives him a slight bow, pressing his cane into his chest. "But you should go cool down. You work yourself too hard." He smiles gently at Sage, but there's something more to his smile as if communicating something with his eyes.

"You should," Sage replies, confusing me. Sage bows his head to Damian, gives me another searching glare, and with little more than a whip of his cloak, he's gone.

"Pleasant sort of fellow, isn't he?" Damian looks after him with a sort of amused sarcasm in his voice. He then turns to me. "Are you alright?"

"Yes, he didn't touch me."

Damian nods with an empathetic smile. "True, but that doesn't cover the question. He can do other things without touching you."

I put on a sweet smile of gratitude. "I suppose you're right, but I'm fine. He didn't hurt me." I assure him with a sweet, comforting voice.

That doesn't get past Damian though. He tilts his head, watching me carefully before bowing his head to me. "You don't have to tell me if you don't wish to, but please, accept my apologies on Sage's behalf. This room is your safe space. He should not have invaded it the way he did."

"Well, we know he won't apologize." I try to brush it off.

"That's why I am doing it for him."

I swallow and nod, trying to calm down. But Damian's searching gaze is similar to Sage's in getting me to want to spit it out.

His eyes fill with kindness as he considers me. "Kascia... are you sure you're alright?" His brows are pinched in concern.

"I..." I take a deep breath, "have to be."

"Not in here, you don't," Damian reminds me. "If you wish me to leave, say the word and I will."

"It's not like I can hide in here forever," I try to joke.

"Perhaps not." Damian nods with a sigh. "Then I would suggest touching up beneath your eyes before you head down to dinner."

"Oh," I flush. "Not that good of an actress, uh?"

Damian smiles gently. "Not at all. But even the best of actresses let a tear slip once in a while. And Kascia, just remember, no one can make you feel inferior without your consent." That same gentle smile and look of compassion feel like they are trying to reach into my heart.

I look down and try to swallow more tears. What happens if you accidentally gave the person whose opinion matters most consent before you knew what was done?

Damian sighs and steps closer. He puts his arms around me in a comforting embrace.

I accept it. I'm still so unsure about everything. I want to admit he's right. Does it matter if I let him make me feel inferior if he is right? I hide my face in Damian's shoulder.

Damian holds me tight for about a minute, maybe longer, before he pulls back to meet my eye. "That help?"

I sniff and nod, wiping my eyes. "I just don't know anymore."

"Don't rush yourself. These things do take time. Sometimes, the answers come quickly. Other times, the pace is more like that of a dying turtle," he says with a hint of jest.

I laugh a little then sigh. I will have to cover this up. I try to dry my eyes before daring to face the mirror.

Once I'm ready, Damian checks me over one more time. "And you are sure you're alright? I know you said Sage didn't hurt you, but you seemed shaken when he left. He may be the prince's guard and as such may have a right to question things as needed, but you are my charge, and I want to make sure you are cared for."

I don't know why, but that does help me feel better. I nod. "For now, I'm as alright as I can be. You've fixed more than you can know already."

He smiles a little. "Alright then. With that said, I believe you are ready." He offers me his arm.

I smile and accept it. "I don't deserve your help."

"I highly doubt that." He returns the smile and opens the door for me before leading me down to the dining hall.

At dinner, the girls giggle and tell me Prince Gavril is trying to catch my eyes. Sure they're just teasing me, I resist for a long time, but finally, I look. I struggle to hold back a laugh at the pout the prince is giving me.

He nods at his plate with raised brows, clearly asking me if I am full too. I smile and nod. Then he nods at his mother and mouths "watch". He puts down his utensils.

"Gavril, are you feeling alright? You hardly touched your food." She frowns instantly.

The prince fights a smile as he replies, "I'm fine."

"You didn't even finish the potato; you love those. Just a few more bites," she even pokes at it with her folk like one would a toddler.

"Don't worry, I'm just full. I ate my veggies."

The queen frowns. "But..."

"Dalilly," the king turns to look at her, "he's fine. You wouldn't freak out if I chose not to eat."

"Yes, but he's not..."

If she says "an adult", I think the whole table is going to lose it in laughter. Even Princess Rose is fighting not to smile so much, she's biting her lips.

"King," the queen finally says.

We all slowly relax, no longer afraid of losing our dignity by laughing like hyenas at the royal table.

The king decides to change the topic to help Prince Gavril escape. "Well, the talent show isn't far, who are you looking forward to seeing most?"

I look away but not fast enough. The prince meets eyes with me and smiles a little before turning back to his dad. "I don't know. They don't tell us what they're doing until the day of."

I'd almost forgotten. Now the dates are over, Damian is hot on preparing for the show.

When I meet with him in a spare room the following day, beautiful music is pouring from the piano inside. Damian is playing.

He's lost in the music, eyes closed as his fingers danced across the ivory keys as carefully as my toes ever did.

The song gently wraps up to a close, and Damian takes a breath and opens his eyes then blinks as if returning to reality. He turns and smiles at me, "Oh good. Did you find the place alright?"

I nod. "Yes, thank you. You play amazingly." I've never heard such talented playing before.

"Why, thank you," Damian smiles graciously. "I do quite enjoy it. Now then, are you ready to rehearse? I, of course, am the accompaniment I spoke of, so we're all set."

We get started, making adjustments in the song as it's now a full solo rather than having sections where the ensemble joins me. Working with Damian isn't like working with anyone I've ever worked with before. He is as stern as my mother, but also more joking. Damian's only flaw is he has a tendency to get lost in the music.

But after a couple of run-throughs, he decides we can use the extra musical sections to help me stand out by taking advantage of my unique ballet background. Damian's ability to put it together impresses me. I ask him if he's done this before. He just chuckles and says he had "close friends" who taught him the lingo. It seems more than that, but as he doesn't press me, I don't press him.

The next day he asks me an odd question, asking if he can see my foot. I'm not sure why, but I slip off my shoe and let him. He starts comparing various fabrics to the skin tone of my foot, trying several before choosing one, thanking me, then walking off to make notes.

I glance at my maids, but they seem to think it is perfectly normal as they chat happily with each other. They never did that with Yarrow around. I suppose Damian helps us all relax.

A few days later, he gives me a pair of brand new pointe shoes that perfectly match my skin tone. I can hardly tell where they end and my skin begins. My eyes bug out in delight. I've never had such a perfect match. I waste no time trying them on and breaking them in. Damian chuckles in amusement.

When I am not working on the music and dance portions with Damian, he and my maids are hard at work on the costume. I prefer hiding in my room watching them, but I can't hide forever so I join Lilly, Bella, Jonquil, Azalea, and Isla in the Ladies' Chamber.

I suppose with fifty girls in one palace, it was only a matter of time before one of them had a birthday. Lantana's is at the first of the new month, and she is excitedly telling anyone who'll listen that the prince asked her out for a special birthday dinner. Not that it proves anything. The prince acts the same towards most of us, calling us all his "pigeons" each morning and evening.

We're two days away from the talent show when something changes in the dining hall. I notice Marigold is talking loudly with Hawi at the same table. Poor Hanna and Nichol don't seem too happy to be sitting between them. Lantana used to sit between them as well. But her seat is missing.

"What did the silly girl do to get thrown out?" Princess Amapola wonders, watching the insanity at the other end of the table.

"More like what did we do? Can they not be so loud?" Princess Neeraja frowns. I suppose it is punishment to us to hear them talking so loud.

"Just ignore them. Some etiquette teacher will teach them, or maybe we'll get lucky, and that will disqualify them," Princess Rose says patiently.

"I could speed it up," Princess Laurina mutters.

Azalea looks sad. "Must have been one awkward birthday date," she says.

"What?" I frown.

"Maybe she wanted to go. Would be fair." Azalea tries to sound hopeful. I doubt that, but that does mean the tests are still going on even as we prepare for this next one.

The morning of the show, Damian and my maids help me get into the costume. It's perfect, better than the one I used on stage for the professional performance.

We rehearse most of the day before the show begins. I've never had to watch a show. It's a strange feeling. And I wish I didn't have to.

When we start the actual show, a few girls are so dull I think the king fell asleep. Then one girl says she is singing, but she is actually demonstrating the mating call of some kind of animal. It's a terrible caterwauling.

"Someone, please, get her off the stage," Damian moans, covering his ears. "My ears are bleeding."

I hide my chuckle and try to give her a break. "Well, maybe it's her people's way."

"Well, then she and her people should be banned from the stage," Damian groans.

I cover my mouth to hide my laughter. I've ever heard Damian speak like that. It's funny and amusing to hear him be so rude.

Finally, the girl finishes and leaves the stage. Damian folds his arms, "Ugh, finally. I've said it before, and I'll say it again. There is but one sin that has no forgiveness in this life or the next: a bad performance."

I laugh. "Do you just memorize the quote book?" I ask. Mom likes that one. It is her main poster.

Damian looks at me and smiles, "I have a good memory."

"Guess having the same name as the posters helps."

"True," he smiles. "I suppose you could say we are a lot alike."

"Your parents named you well," I smile back.

"Indeed. Come on, we should head backstage," Damian tells me.

My excitement mixes with nervousness at last. Will I be good enough to stay? The prince likes me enough he isn't looking for an excuse, right?

Damian rubs my shoulder. "You'll be great. Don't worry about the others and try not to compare. Remember, the stage is your world. Own it."

I accept it and get into position. I let the butterflies excite me. I close my eyes to make sure to get my head in the right place until I hear the first note and let it transform me into the me I get to be in this moment.

This is my place to think. I feel and think about the words, the music, the movement, the emotion that drives it all. The world slows and becomes mine. It's as natural as breathing. Damian's playing works with me as a musical guide for my train of thought, letting the hours of practice guide actions that can be subconscious. It flows perfectly, easily. I sing her questions as my own.

I keep this train of thought until the song ends. I am snapped back to the world I really am in by the applause. I look down and the first thing I see is the king beaming. It all rushes back as if I'd forgotten it.

I can't stop beaming. I try not to look at the prince's reaction to try to enjoy the moment, but I can't help it. He's beaming, but even more, he's thinking. He may have never heard that song before. I'd not thought of that.

I smile wider as I take my reverence, bowing my head a little and looking up only to meet Sage's glare. I hide my reaction as I do not want him taking my moment. I give a second curtsy before I try to step away, but the clapping isn't stopping, so I take one more, feeling a bit smug to be able to enjoy the moment no matter what Sage thinks.

Damian follows me off stage and takes my arms, grinning from ear to ear. "Simply wonderful. There isn't a woman here or anywhere that could have done better. Well done. You were stunning."

"You made me stunning," I say with a smile of gratitude.

He smiles. "I played my part, but the voice and dance were all yours. Your heart was in it, and that made it all the more special. Once again, well done."

"Thank you." Though I still feel he's the one who made it truly magical.

When it's over the king stands up and thanks all of us for our efforts and says he greatly enjoyed watching us. I hold in a smile. The old man may have enjoyed it a bit too much.

Prince Gavril looks embarrassed by his father's joke and mischievous little smile. He's trying to sink into his seat as if he's not there. I have a strong feeling the king wants this test more than anyone else so he could watch a show.

We are all dismissed to go back to our rooms. I thank Damian once again before letting my maids help me change and settle in for the night. I wonder how many of us will be leaving tomorrow. The king didn't say. I am assured of one thing, I'm not going anywhere yet.

Chapter 23

Sadly, though several are missing at breakfast, none of the girls I dislike are gone, but they have other topics to gossip about.

We're heading into September now, and two more girls have their birthdays, both of them born princesses, and get special dates with the prince this month.

But the birthday girls aren't the only ones getting dates. The born princesses seem to go out with him at least once a week. But even for all of those dates, we remain stubbornly at thirty-one girls.

That only makes my anxiety over no reply from my father worse. I try sending him another letter with all the ones I write to Mom, but after a week, I know it's pointless. I am starting to wonder if I'll ever hear from Dad again if I don't go through with this. I'll throw away the man who meant everything to me. But with how he seemed to have dropped me, do I care? Might be nice to get back at someone for the pain I'm in.

The anger builds inside of me, making me miss fencing. I love dance best, but sometimes, its coordinated movements aren't as good at letting out frustration like a good fight.

But finally, something changes, and though it is nice to feel like we aren't in limbo, it adds heightened tension to the castle. There is a failure. And it's one of the born princesses.

The first clue is I've moved. I am now on the right side of the table on the opposite end of the royal family, sitting next to Lilly with Ayesha across from me.

I frown and look at Lilly, who nervously scans the table. It is a big deal for someone in the top ten to be gone. I am worried by Lilly's expression that it is Bella, but she is there, talking quietly to Princess Zelda. Sadly, Dahlia is still there, smirking as she looks up at the table.

When I catch on it is a royal, my stomach drops. I look and see why Princess Zelda is finally free to talk to Bella. Her other neighbor, Princess Zinna, is gone.

I lean over to look at the royal family. They are deep in whispered conversation.

My jaw drops. "She's gone," I mutter to myself.

The royal family appears stressed. They now have to answer to the princess's country as to why she didn't pass their true princess test, and not only that she failed, but that she didn't even make it to the top ten or even the top twenty-five.

"No way, it's too soon," Jonquil frowns.

"It's the only reason they'd move me here," I point out.

"Oh, she's gone," Princess Zelda beams. "And I don't mind. She always forced me to talk to her and never had anything nice to say."

"And we don't even get to know why," Jonquil pouts.

"Oh, I think I know why," Princess Zelda huffs. "But it's only a guess."

"What?" Lilly and Jonquil ask: Lilly in fear, Jonquil in delight.

Princess Zelda makes sure the royal family isn't looking. "I heard she got a bit too fresh with Prince Gavril."

"Someone told you that?" Jonquil asks.

Princess Zelda shakes her head. "No, I mean I heard it. He must have been taking her back to her room after a date. I heard something hit my wall. I went to take a look, and Sage was holding Princess Zinna back while poor Gavril looked as confused as could be. He had lipstick all over his cheek and around but not on his lips. I think she pinned him to the wall to get some 'action'."

Jonquil laughs in pure delight and amusement, "Seriously?"

"Looked like it," Princess Zelda says.

"A princess did that?" I frown. I thought they were taught better.

Princess Zelda shrugs again. "I don't know. I can only guess from what I saw, but it happened last night. They would have sent her back right away."

I sit there, stunned. I glance down both sides of the table to see everyone else gossiping about it too, looking worried. They all are likely afraid of what a princess had done to get kicked out and wanted to be sure it wasn't them next.

I can't believe a princess was so foolish. It is against the Potentate laws. It prevents a lot of political strife with illegitimate children or broken relationships. If she was trying to start something like that, in front of Sage, there was no way she was going to stay.

I wonder about it the rest of the day. I've been so distracted by the eliminations, the talent show, and the lack of answer from my father, I haven't even realized I'd not had a date in over a week.

I'm sharply reminded when, after dinner, the prince asks if I'd like to join him. I don't dare say no.

He offers me his arm, and I take it. I can't help but marvel at how strong he feels every time. What do they have him do to feel so strong? Is it his suits?

The prince doesn't speak until we're away from the other girls, apparently alone.

"I realized I was so busy trying to keep track of everyone that I almost forgot you'd not had your turn in a while," Prince Gavril finally speaks.

"Sage didn't say you can't ask me?" I try to tease, but I also want to see how bad Sage's distrust is for me.

"Well, he doesn't mind the long gaps," Prince Gavril shrugs. "But if you aren't busy, would you mind a walk? I can show you parts of the castle you've never seen before."

I like that idea, so I let him lead me around. I do recognize one passage. It's one I got lost down.

"Where does this lead?" I ask.

"Entertainment rooms mostly." The prince shrugs. "The Ladies' Chamber used to be the smaller party room and the one next door for smaller dances. My mother talks about having her sister's birthday party in there."

"That explains the dance floor and mirrors."

"Yes, they cover the mirrors up for parties and use it as a room to teach dance at other times. It's where I learned," says the prince.

I hear a sound and turn to see the prince's valet coming out of a double-doored room. He spots the prince and smiles. "It's all clear."

My stomach drops. That's him! That's the voice I'd heard talking to the man wanting a quote. That's why the man thought he could get a quote from the prince. It makes so much sense I can't believe I didn't figure it out.

It stuns me to silence as he walks over to us. "Glad she agreed." he smiles at me.

"Yes, Godwin here is the 'adult supervision'." Prince Gavril rolls his eyes.

I frown in confusion. "Sage isn't enough?"

"He's the one I'm watching." Godwin gives Sage a look.

"He saw the mark on my head from the book," Prince Gavril explains.

Godwin looks royally annoyed with Sage. "So I told him I had to protect him from his guard next time you go out," Godwin explains, still glaring at Sage.

"I can't blame you." I shrug, unsure what else to say. I can't ask Godwin in front of the prince, let alone Sage.

"And sadly, I can't seem to bribe him into letting me guard for a date," Godwin jokes.

"What would you bribe him with?" I frown as Sage decides to remind us he is there by popping out of the shadows.

"Um... food?" The prince guesses. "Some Custods are suckers for good food."

I give Sage a once over. I don't think he's one of them.

Godwin mouths "he is" to me. I hold in the giggles.

"Maybe... games. Some of them fall for that," Prince Gavril suggests, looking up in thought, making him miss Godwin's mockery of Sage.

"Good guard," I comment.

"Most of the time," Godwin mutters. I smile.

"Those talents come from his other job," Prince Gavril says, ignoring Godwin again.

We walk into the room Godwin walked out of. It's a large gallery of various kinds of art. I can't help but go over to one amazing piece of a model sailing ship. It looks so alive like it's really moving across a huge wave in a storm. The shape of the sails makes me believe the wind really is pushing it.

"Well, you found my favorite fast," the prince laughs.

"Is it? It's so alive," I say, admiring it.

"Have you been on a ship like that?"

I shake my head, still examining the stunning art piece. I've wanted to. I'd gone diving once on the cold reef, but that is it.

Gavril looks around then leans in close, "Would you like to?"

"Fat chance here." I laugh. But I'd love to see one up close. They look so beautiful on the water.

The prince looks at his two servants. Sage gives a quick nod as Godwin nods so excitedly I think his head may pop off.

"Alright, we don't have long." The prince takes my hand and guides me out of the room. I'm so surprised and intrigued I don't object.

We move quietly, as if sneaking, to the entrance hall and then over to another area I've never been to before.

The prince pauses to let Sage unlock the door. We step inside a gym with a training pool off to the left. There is a four-story climbing wall and an open fencing area near the pool. Weights, other training spaces, and pull-up bars bespeak the room. It's empty now, but I can smell it's used often.

"Sorry for the smell, but the gym has a direct path to the royal dock," Prince Gavril explains. "Few people use it. At the change of guard, no one is in here."

I frown, "You're allowed in here?"

"Not officially," Prince Gavril admits, a bit embarrassed.

"Sage lets you get away with things, doesn't he?" That's why he doesn't care about the king and queen's rules. He is an assassin. They play by their own rules.

"Not him alone," Godwin states with a hint of offense.

"Not officially," Prince Gavril shrugs. "Like this outing."

"Outing?" I repeat as Sage unlocks another door that leads us outside. Gavril quickly leads me out with Sage and Godwin following. Sage locks the door behind us.

"Will we see our dolphin friends?" Godwin asks with a smile.

"What?"

"Well, many dolphins, though wild, are trained here. Their families bring them because they know they are rewarded," Prince Gavril explains. "With things they can't get themselves, rarer fish, but mostly, they like ice cubes. They like to play with them or chew on them. The palace doesn't 'own' any dolphins, but we have seals."

I had heard the navy has sea creatures trained, but I didn't know it was that extensive. "Have you trained them?"

"No," Prince Gavril says defensively.

"Yes." Sage rolls his eyes.

"Jealous," Godwin pipes in.

I laugh. They are like siblings, including Godwin. The three oddball brothers: the Potentate, the Custod, and the common boy.

"Officially," Sage corrects himself.

"I don't train them. I just... know how to get their attention when I'm out there." The prince defends himself.

"Do you have favorites?"

"Of course not, that's rude to them," Prince Gavril jokes.

"Just like you don't have favorites among the Chosen?" I raise a brow.

"Yeah, like that." The prince smiles.

We make it out to a dock, oddly worn looking, and I spot what Gavril wants to show me.

It's a stunning ship. I can't quite tell the colors in the dark, but she bares the Purerahian flag. The ship itself is easily at least two hundred feet long. I've never seen anything so big able to stay afloat, but it is bobbing gently in the water, showing her seaworthiness.

"This is the royal flagship." Prince Gavril smiles.

"And the guard on board will keep quiet," Sage assures the prince.

"They let me up here all the time, if the right Custod is along." The prince winks at me.

I'm still staring at the ship in awe. She is lined with ports for the cannons and the back is lined with glass windows. Through the windows are three short floors below the main deck. It's a stunning view I've never seen the like of. I've seen merchant ships before, but nothing like this spectacular piece of craftsmanship.

"Want a closer look?" Prince Gavril asks me.

"How close?"

"Board her?"

I nod, unable to help it. There are so many rope systems it makes my head spin. How could they ever steer it?

The prince's smile is as wide as the river bend as he guides me onboard. I'm a bit unsteady and pause the moment I put weight onto the plank, feeling off-balance. There's a slight sway as the ship rode the soft waves.

The prince pauses and turns back to me, feet firmly on the plank with my hand still in his.

I feel the rocking under my shoes and want to pull back. I'm used to solid ground. I have good balance as a dancer and places where that confidence is taken causes me to flinch and get anxious.

"Hey, I got you." Prince Gavril smiles a little. "I've never seen you flinch at anything."

"I just... I'm used to knowing my balance better than my name," I state. "This is not how balance works."

"Well, we'll just learn a new balance. It feels worse when you're half on land half off," the prince assures me. He still hasn't let go of my hand. "Come on." He gently pulls my hand, and I step on.

I don't like it and tense. But the only thing to hold on to is him. I grab on with both hands. The second I do, I flush red.

Prince Gavril laughs at my embarrassment. As he laughs, I again feel the muscle in his arms. I guess I know where he got them now, but I still don't know why when he doesn't even need them to cut food. And no one sees them. A prince's attire covers his arms. Besides, no one knows what Prince Gavril looks like, so why does he care? I picture him flexing for himself in front of a mirror to try to get my anxieties in check.

"Sorry, I shouldn't laugh at you. I'm sure I'd be as nervous doing something normal to you like..." He tries to think, looking up at the sky for a moment. "...buying things. I would be terrified to speak to a teller to buy something, anything." The prince looks back at me. "Like, what do you say? 'Hi, I'm Prince Gavril, your finest long socks, please?'"

That gets me to laugh. The prince uses that moment to help me up onto the ship. The rocking is worse here. I take a deep breath as I adjust.

Then I take in the view. It's amazing. I see the guns lining the side of the ship, several openings to the lower decks, the hundreds of ropes like webs holding everything together. It's so simple, and yet, elegant.

"Stunning, isn't she?" Gavril asks. "She's called the Great White."

"Great white? Like the shark?"

The prince nods. "Like the one on our emblem. She's our fastest and most powerful. Hasn't seen much action lately as we handle the pirates with similar ships."

"How can she be so fast? She's huge. What if the wind faced the wrong way?"

"Let me show you." The prince smiles and brings me to the wheel thing used to steer.

He shows me the helm and shows me how it works. He has me take the wheel and stands behind me. I try to turn it, but it's a lot heavier than I thought it would be. I can hardly move it.

The prince puts his hands on mine and helps me adjust it. "Right to go starboard and left for port."

A strange warmth yet cold runs through me at his hands on mine, making the tips of my fingers tingle. I force myself to focus.

"Isn't it backwards?"

He shakes his head. "No, because of the pressure of the water." He points at them. "When you turn it left, the pressure is on the right which turns your port side."

"How?" I ask, not because I wonder but because I am trying to distract myself from how close he is.

The smile that crosses his face makes my heart light a little. An excited smile to tuck away in my memory to enjoy. He takes my hand and leads me below deck and explains how the rope goes down to the rudder.

The prince takes my hand and runs it along the rope until I feel the place where it leads out. He's completely unabashed about touching me. But it has little to do with any kind of attraction. There's an innocent excitement in how he explains how the ship works. I'm too focused on how firm his touch is to really listen.

He says something about the rudder being key to steering the whole ship. "How does something so small change the direction?" I ask, desperate to keep my mind on what he's saying. "It's not the sails the wheel turns?"

"They work together."

I give him a blank look. The prince frowns. Then his eyes light up once more. "Let me show you."

The prince takes my hand once more and brings me back on deck. He takes me to a cleaning station where water is pumped to a table. He steps on a press, and the water runs through like a river.

"Think of your hand like the rudder." He takes my hand and put it into the cold water so it's parallel with the stream. "Feel the water rushing past?"

I nod, keenly aware that he's even closer than ever. His hand is warm against mine even in the cold water. I worry he'll feel my heart flutter with how close he's standing to me.

He angles my hand, so I feel the water pressing more strongly on the front and less on the back. "Feel the pressure change?" he asks. I nod, but I'm not listening. "That pressure would push your hand the opposite way, like this." He guides my hand into moving with the pressure. "And that is strong enough to steer the whole ship."

"Then why do you need the sails?" I ask.

"The sails catch the wind and provides an opposing force and, more importantly, lift. It's hard to explain without a model, but if we want to sail into the wind, we need two forces to balance each other. The pressure of the water," he taps my hand, "and the pressure of the wind." He uses his hand to press the top of mine.

My heart pounds. In putting his other hand on my arm, he has wrapped his other arm around mine. He's so close. His warmth contradicts the cold water and chill of the night. I lose all track of what he was saying.

The prince laughs, "It's only half making sense, isn't it?"

I yank my mind back on track. "I think I get it. It's like how I push down to rise off the floor."

"Exactly." The prince smiles, our eyes meeting.

I smile a bit. "For a boy locked in a castle, you know how to explain it well."

I'm enchanted by how he showed me. He didn't tell me. He wanted me to experience it. I learn better that way. It's the dancer in me.

Prince Gavril smiles and starts explaining how the two pressures provide direction and lift. I hardly hear him, smiling at the passionate light in his eyes as he explains, taping and putting pressure on my hand to illustrate the forces.

All I want is to call him mine. But he's not just the boy I'd met on the night I needed him most. He's far more. He's complicated: the enemy I came here to eradicate. My heart sinks as it battles that knowledge and my desire to pull him close and claim him. I want him the way... no, it isn't how I'd wanted Jake. I want him to be mine, but in a different way than Jake. I can't explain it. Is that a good thing?

"That help?" He looks up at me, snapping me from my moment.

"You know so much."

"I read a lot." The prince lets go of my hand and leans back.

"You learn about stars," I tease.

The prince nods. "Sure, stars, piano, ships, and the sea, and when I can get away with it, I used to game a lot."

"You have a game system or board games?" I ask.

"I have an Imajoel, you know, those enchanted devices for playing games."

Of course, he does. Those devices are rare, expensive, and highly sought after. The spoiled prince of course has one. I wonder if his is like the one Princess Zelda is always reading and writing on.

"Maybe we can try it out sometime." I never thought I'd play Imajoel games with the prince of anywhere, let alone the prince of my home country. "The games take me to other worlds as much as a book, though in a different way. Sometimes I want to go there in my mind, and I read a book. Sometimes, I want to interact with it, so I play a game. Helps you feel in control when there is nothing to control."

I frown a little, resting my forearms on the side of the boat. "I can't imagine it being that bad," I say, looking out over the moonlit water.

The prince smiles a little. "I hope you never do. It's the one reason I feel bad for whoever wins." He looks over the water. "Unless I'm lucky, for a while, she'll just join me in the cage. Unless my mother sees my marriage as a sign I'm finally grown up," he laughs. "Which is almost worse."

"Why?"

"Then she wants me to get busy. She'll want grandkids." The prince gives me a look as if confessing something gross. I laugh. "How demanding, right?"

"Well, she did want more children. I guess she can have yours."

"Oh boy, heaven save them." The prince looks to the sky. I laugh. "Have to make sure she doesn't control their worlds too," he chuckles. "How about your mother? She chomping at the bit? You're an only child too, right?"

"She's never mentioned it. Dad either."

"Uh, thought all adult children did. My mother just sees me as too little to think about it." The prince sighs. "It's getting cold, should get you inside."

"Not you?"

"Nah, we let him do whatever he wants," Godwin jokes, making me jump. I forgot they were there.

"I wish, how can I get that to always work?" the prince asks as we walk.

We're about halfway to the plank when I misstep in the dark. I try to catch my balance but misjudge what made me stumble. I hadn't kicked something. I had stepped into it. My heart leaps into my throat as the horrible falling sensation rushes over me.

In the blink of an eye, something catches me and lifts me as if I weigh nothing, swooping me back onto the deck.

I have to blink a few times to take in what happened. I'm standing directly in front of the prince, his hands on my arms to ensure my balance. Inches from my face is his chest, his steady breathing catches my eyes as my heart races.

He just pulled me up out of a hole single-handedly as if I were as light as a handkerchief! It isn't even like he pulled me out of the water. He'd just grabbed me and pulled me up as if I were no more than a pixie.

"Woah, careful! I got you," the prince says. "Are you alright?"

He's really got me. I nod, unable to say a word. I take a sharp breath. He's really close. I don't think I've been this close to a person who's not in character or I'm not related to. Well, Jake when we're alone. The prince's strong hands are still on my arms.

In my attempt to keep my balance, I put my hand against his shirt. I stiffen. I'm suddenly very aware of how his coarse shirt feels against my hands, how his breathing presses into my hands, and how firm his chest feels.

I feel the huff of air from his chest, amused by my reaction. "You're fine. Here." He helps me sit down. "Are you sure you're alright?"

I nod as he takes my foot to make sure I didn't hurt my ankle. I bite my lower lip, feeling tense at how close he is.

He clearly doesn't notice as he lets go and smiles gently. "See, right as rain. Sorry, it can be tricky in the dark." He stands up and takes my hands to help me too. "There, see? You have your balance."

He knows I don't like not having my feet. He made sure I knew I had them. Not that he fixed my problem for me, but reassured me that I could handle it. Like I'm sure he wants someone to do for him. The only trouble now is we are really close. I force a smile, scared to look up into his face.

"Thanks," It's more air than voice.

"No problem." The prince steps back. I take a deep breath. Why didn't that feel wrong?

Godwin is giving the prince a look. Prince Gavril frowns back in confusion. Goodwin rolls his eyes. The prince looks back at me. "Sure you're okay?"

Right, I'm still standing frozen. "Yes, sorry. I just... I-I didn't think anyone could pull me up like that."

"I'm just glad you aren't hurt," says the prince. "Let's get you on solid land."

He takes my arm to help me down the gangplank. But my mind is elsewhere, on how strong his grip on me is. How solid he feels next to me. How close he is. I'm hyper-aware of his breath near me. And how much I want to be closer.

"Sorry it was short. We don't want to get caught," the prince says.

"Short?" That hadn't felt short. It was wonderful. I try to beat my mind into remembering why it's bad. But I'd loved it.

"Glad you enjoyed it that much," the prince chuckles.

I am so ready for him to drop me off at my room, and yet, I don't want it to end. His sudden closeness, the passion and intelligence he showed in his knowledge and passion for the nautical, the light in his eyes, and how he forgot the rest of the world in what he loved is making me forget who he is. He's the prince. He's not my apprentice. I have to remember that.

"I really did." And not just the amazing place I got to see.

"Good." The prince nods.

Once we're in the entrance hall, the prince checks the time. “I should see you to bed.” He sighs.

He leads me up the left-hand staircase to my room. He says goodnight quickly with Godwin making faces as if disappointed he didn’t try to kiss me.

Thank heavens he didn’t because I’m not sure I’m ready for that. Yet, I’m not sure I would have had the power to say no.

Chapter 24

There's an odd tension in the Ladies' Chamber the next morning. But no one is missing, so I pretend not to notice. Bella suggests we play a game. I join in half-heartedly. I'm not much for games, but I want to be a good sport.

Jonquil reads her paper. Azalea invites her to join us for the next round. She agrees but wants to get her deck from her room.

We continue the round we'd started, hoping to finish before Jonquil gets back.

"Then she can't back out if she changes her mind," Azalea jokes as Lilly finishes her turn. "Lilly, you're good at this."

"It's all luck in which cards you draw," Lilly laughs.

"It's more than that," I assure her. "I've not played much, but I notice you're good. You get in the top ranks anyway." She flushes in pleasure.

A loud gonging bong strikes the air, making most of us jump. But it doesn't ring once; it goes off once every second. I frown and look for the source.

All the girls are looking around in confusion. I look to see who's missing, maybe it was someone in the practice room next door.

Hawi, Nichol, Ayesha, Jonquil, Florence, and one other girl are missing. I can't recall who the fifth one is. I do a quick headcount of twenty-five and try to see whose faces I know. Is it Larin who's missing?

All this passes through my mind in about a second before a sick feeling enters my stomach. The gong goes off a third time. That isn't some game. It's an alarm. Oh no, no, no. The prince warned me about this. The other girls are clueless.

I shoot to my feet in one quick movement. "We have to move," I snap at the girls.

"What?" Bella frowns.

"It's an alarm. We have to go," I state firmly.

Just as I speak, a group of guards enter the room, more than just the Custods who normally guard the door. "There's been a breach in security. We need you all in the safe room now." The lead guard orders us gently.

As he speaks, the rest go to the left side of the room and open a safe room, just like the prince told me.

Most of the girls freeze in fear. I grab Lilly's arm and guide her to the safe room. When no one else moves, I push Lilly on and pull Azalea to her feet. Bella blinks a few times and starts getting up as I go over to pull her up.

"What about the girls who aren't here?" I ask the head guard as Ericka's little dog barks at him while they pull a shocked Ericka to her feet. She picks him up to keep him quiet.

"My lady, we have this," the lead guard says to me. "You too."

I walk with him to the safe room. "What about the other girls? I think about five are missing. Jonquil went to her room to get something."

"The guards are checking every room," he assures me. "They'll get her into the nearest safe room. Meantime, your duty is to get into your safe room and stay there."

"W-why? They don't get inside the grounds, do they?" Bella asks.

"Yet. Better safe than sorry," the guard replies. "In." He pushes me inside.

I resist. "I will not be bossed around. My friend might be in danger."

"Trust us." The guard smiles slightly. "We will handle it." His smile is almost proud. I glare.

"Kascia, please," Lilly begs.

"And our maids?"

"We have it," the guard chuckles. "All will be looked after."

"You sure?"

"Yes," the guard smiles. "Let us handle it."

Damian, Damian might be there. Damian would look after them.

"You'll answer to me if anything happens," I say.

The guard laughs, "Alright, I will make sure you know if anything happens. Now please, get inside."

I don't want to budge, not because I mind going into the safe room, but I don't want to be treated as incapable. I'm likely the best fighter of the girls.

Lilly grabs my arm to pull me in. I turn to her and smile. I step in with her, and the guards close us in, leaving one behind to protect us. Lilly is shivering against me. I frown and turn my full attention to her.

"They got in?" she asks in a squeak.

"Just on the grounds. Prince Gavril told me that happens, and they put us on lockdown when they do just in case. We're safe, don't worry."

"Then why lock us up?" Lilly asks.

"How do you know?" Dahlia demands, stepping over from her circle with the other "elite".

I sigh. "Know what?" I turn to her.

"About the alarm and the secret room?" She puts her hands on her hips.

"As I told Lilly, the prince told me. Ask him about it. He'll tell you."

"When did he tell you?" Dahlia steps closer.

I stand straight. "On our date, just like you. He doesn't talk to me outside of them any more than he does you."

"Sure? He seems awfully chummy with you," Dahlia accuses.

Was that why I felt tension this morning? Bella and Azalea were quick to get me busy. Is this why? Did someone see us last night?

A bang makes us all jump. Lilly squeals and grabs my arm. A few other girls squeal.

"They're getting in," someone cries, but I can't tell who for all the screaming voices.

"It's okay. They can't get in," I try to assure Lilly.

Muffled voices come through the wall. I know that sound: men fighting, blurred orders, and arms clashing. They got inside! How? That shouldn't be possible without help.

"Get back," I direct Lilly deeper into the room.

"They got in. You are just trying to get us to run out there and get killed," Dahlia accuses me.

I groan, "If any of you try to leave this room, I'll knock you out and drag you back myself. Alright? Besides, I just said get deeper. That will make it harder for them to hear us, not easier."

"So, you're the boss now?"

I set my teeth. "There's no need for this."

Jaine steps up to me. "What if the prince knew you were bossing us around?"

I frown. What does that have to do with anything?

"Go ahead and tell him on your next date. I really couldn't care less, but please, they might hear us. Keep it down," I warn.

"Why don't you make me?" Jaine gets into my face.

"I don't want to force anyone." I pull back.

"Then why threaten us?" she retorts, "Just because you got the longest date doesn't make you the boss."

"I'm not saying I have more power than any of you," I snap back. "This is about keeping safe. I'm used to these things where I'm from. I want you to be safe."

"Do you? Or are you just trying to use the fact he likes you to get us all kicked out?" Jaine shoves me.

I glare at her. I don't know much about her, only that she hangs around the elite a lot.

Is she trying to get me thrown out to show she belongs in their group?

"There's no need to be rude. I am only trying to keep us safe," I insist.

"Are you?" Jaine steps up to my face again.

"Stop!" Lilly screams.

Jaine takes pride in scaring her and gets closer to me. I grab her arm before she can grab me. "Please stop," I beg. "This is stupid. I'm used to things like this. If they are inside, we need to be quiet."

Jaine smirks, "You have no right to touch me." She pulls back. "I'm telling the prince about how you've behaved. You'll get thrown out."

"Go ahead." I doubt the prince will believe it. Besides, he admitted many times he doesn't have the power to eliminate us.

A bang shakes the room. Jaine screams worse than anyone. I push her back to the far wall. I put a finger to my lips to insist they keep quiet, looking around at the others too. The rebels might be hitting around to find the room we're in. Why are they after us?

If rebels got in... how? Dad said we needed an insider to get us in. So how did they do it? And why are they after us?

I keep by the door while the other girls stay quiet. Lilly whimpers in fear. I don't know what would help her feel better, me at the door on guard or giving her a hug. I decide to go for a hug when the banging stops.

I'm holding her for a while when there's another bang. Lilly and the others scream. Lilly presses tighter into me.

I smile a little and hum "a little lullaby", the same one Mom hummed to me, to soothe her. I think it calms down the others too.

I don't know how long we're in there before the guards finally come to let us out.

The girls are nervous to leave. I decide I'll have to step out first to assure them it's safe. Lilly latches on to my arm to stop me.

I smile a little. "It's fine. The guards wouldn't let us out if it wasn't."

I gently pull myself away and step out. My mouth pops open.

The room is a mess. Tables have been knocked over, even sofas and chairs are upended, and some chairs are on the opposite side of the room from where they started. Cards, game pieces, even stuffing from a few cushions and pillows litter the floor along with some wood splinters from broken furniture. It looks like the rebels had thrown the items at the walls to try to find the safe room.

The other girls slowly follow, all as stunned as me. Ericka lets out an offended gasp. Her dog snarls. Others are quiet, staring wide-eyed. Lilly grabs onto my arm. I slowly walk through the room with her walking carefully next to me.

There are cut marks and slashes in some pieces of furniture and a curtain is slashed. Two have been pulled down. The paintings on the walls have been thrown onto the floor. One is missing until I spot it out on the balcony where the door swings in the breeze, making the stuffing on the floor flutter.

I slowly walk towards the door. Lilly lets out a squeak of fright and lets go as I peek into the hallway. A sick feeling, like acid longing to be thrown out, churns in my stomach.

The hallway is worse. Paintings have been knocked over and scattered. Bits of broken furniture litter the floor. I see marks on the wall where something heavy had been shoved into it, likely the first loud bang that made the girls scream. But far worse, I see blood. It's stained on the scuffed wall, splotched on the floor, and smeared splinters. I see a dark mass of it on the end of a broken chair or table leg.

At first, I'm filled with stunned horror. I can't believe rebels, my people, did this. They had to fight the guards, sure, but they'd done far more damage than needed. And why go for the Chosen girls?

Anger fills me. How dare they? How dare they come after us? I agreed to help them. I was one of them, and they went right for my friends. Why ruin the palace they soon hoped to own? They'd attacked everything in sight.

"The procedure is to get you all back to your rooms." The lead guard's voice cuts into my anger. "They didn't get far, and it helps us keep account that we have found everyone. Let me escort you," he asks with a bow.

"What? No." Lilly steps out.

I quickly back her into the room before she can see anything else.

"Miss, it's to protect you." The guard assigned to escort her frowns.

I bend to Lilly's eye level, "Lilly, it's alright. It is going to be fine. The guard will protect you. No need to worry. They wouldn't let us out if they weren't gone." I promise. "I'll see you later, okay?"

Lilly swallows and nods. She's trembling and looks around as if for help. She's not the only one though. Ericka, Princess Amapola, and Princess Neeraja look shaken, eyes wide as if unable to believe it's real. Princess Rose looks angrier, her lips in a flat line. Princess Laruina and Princess Zelda look shocked too and keep glancing at each other as if communicating this is worse than they thought.

Hanna, Rachel, Lark, Nichol, Ayesha, and Jaine all wear similar frowns as if sad to see something they've seen before. These must be the girls from the north. Were any of them from Nerine?

The rest of the girls look scared, unable to believe this reached the castle. I wonder how many came hoping to be safe from this kind of thing. Would they wish they didn't come?

Slowly, one by one, the group of guards escorts us to our rooms. I notice the guard who'd been in the room with us talking to another officer in a low voice.

"Come, M'lady," the lead guard says to me. "I need to escort you and report."

"Alright." I pray my team is there and safe. I give Lilly a reassuring smile before I go. The guard who'd been with her immediately uses the opening to escort her back.

Once we reach the third floor, the carnage stops. Ayesha is being escorted to her room. She and I are the only ones left on this floor. She's hugging herself and looks forlorn, perhaps disappointed. She notices me looking; I give her a comforting smile. She returns it weakly. We've mostly ignored each other, but in this moment, I can tell she needs it. I think she's one of the girls from up north.

The guard opens the door for me, thanks me for my cooperation, and nods at Lila. I give her a small smile of gratitude as Lila nods back. Lila reminds me of someone, but I'm never sure who.

Relief floods me once I enter the room and see all three of my maids. They seem hardly bothered. Vivian is giving Flur and Ro directions on getting ready for me. "We'll need to make sure we have her night tea handy, and perhaps..." She stops short when she sees me.

"Glad to see you well, miss." Flur curtsies timidly.

I'm so glad they're unhurt I rush forward and pull them all into a group hug. If something happened to any of them... The fear and anger I'd felt when I saw the mess returns.

"I'm so glad you're safe. Was Damian with you?" I pull back to look at them.

"Yes, Miss. He told us to get into the secure room under the bed." Vivian points. "Then said he was going to help."

I frown, "To help? Have you seen him since?"

"No miss, but I imagine he'll be along," Vivian says. "I'm sure he could handle it if he said he could."

"Besides, it's nothing. They do this all the time," Ro says. By her smirk, I think she's amused by how happy I am to see them. "Hiding is just a precaution. They've never...'

"Hush, you know that's not true," Vivian scolds her. "We all know what they can do."

"Only to those caught on the grounds. Why our ladies aren't allowed out there," Ro reminds her.

"Please, I get nervous enough," Flur begs.

"But you didn't see anything?" I ask.

"What is there to see?" Ro huffs. "They never get in."

"You don't know?" I frown.

"Know what, miss?" Vivian frowns in worry.

"They did get in."

They all freeze, staring at me.

"You're sure?" Vivian demands.

I nod, "They made a mess of the second-floor passage and the Ladies' Chamber, but they didn't find us."

Flur gapes in horror and covers her mouth. Ro is wide-eyed. Vivian's brow is drawn in anger. I watch her fists tighten and a determined line come to her shoulders.

"How?" Flur finally whispers.

"I-I don't know." I'd wondered the same. Dad said they'd need help. Did that mean someone helped them? A servant, a new hire for the Enthronement, or one of the Chosen? Was I not the only spy to get in?

Chapter 25

To calm my maids, most of all poor Flur, who is extra anxious, we wet tea and try to have a normal chat, trying to keep cool heads when there is a knock at the door.

My maids jump, but I turn as the door is opened. Prince Gavril steps in, Sage right behind him. My maids immediately stand.

The prince's eyes land on me. He sighs in relief, a small smile crossing his face. "Why hello, my pigeon. I guess I can just leave. You look like nothing happened."

My brows draw together as I curtsy to him. "What do you mean?"

"I checked on all the other girls, and they're all nervous or mocking," the prince says as he steps closer. Sage closes the door behind them. "You are relaxing with a cup of tea and your maids." He smiles at them. Flur flushes.

"Oh, well, guess I'm just calmer."

"Even Princess Zelda was shaken up. Not you." The prince is still smiling. "You're really okay?"

I nod. "Yes, just fine."

"Good. You'll have to spend the rest of the day in your room while the staff cleans and secures the area." The prince sighs. "But if you're alright, as much as I'd like to stay, I still haven't seen my parents."

My jaw drops. My maids are white as sheets, eyes wide.

"You checked in on all the girls first?" Vivian dares ask. Flur hits her arm as if horrified.

The prince smiles and nods. "Yes, I did, but I should check in with them if you're alright. Sure you don't need anything?"

I shake my head then realize. "Is Jonquil okay? She wasn't in the Ladies' Chamber."

"Yes, she was in her room on lockdown like everyone else. I saw her a bit ago. She's shaken up, but they all are."

"I hope Lilly felt better." I recall how scared she was.

"Well, honestly, she was the worst, shaking and babbling, but she calmed down. I hope she gets used to it." I can hear the "or she won't make it here" in his tone.

"Are you going to send her home?"

The Prince shakes his head. "We aren't deciding until later. A few asked to go home, but everyone is frightened. They've never gotten inside before. Not in my lifetime. So we're not making any choices today or maybe not even tomorrow. I don't get a choice, remember?"

"Was anyone hurt?"

"I don't know. I checked on the girls first." The prince frowns. "And they may not tell me, but I'll find out what I can and let you know after dinner, alright?"

I smile a little. "You don't have to do that."

"I'm checking on everyone." He smiles. "But be prepared for that to change."

I swallow. So it will change. When, I don't know. I nod to the prince and curtsy again. "I understand. I'll expect you tonight."

The prince bows his head to me, "Until then, my pigeon." He takes my hand, surprising me, and kisses it briefly before leaving.

I look up to watch him go, my hand still floating where the prince left it. I meet Sage's eyes. He smiles slightly before following his prince.

But the door doesn't close right away, Sage looks grumpy as he holds it open. I hear Prince Gavril laughing.

Damian steps into the room, cane in hand. His eyes glance around the room before landing on us. "Are you all alright?"

I nod and look at my maids. They bow to Damian and nod as well. "Are you alright? Where did you go?" I ask.

"I wanted to see if I could help, and if I could find out anything. Then I had to check on my brother to make sure all was right with him," Damian replies.

Brother? Did he mention a brother before? Even more, did he mention a brother being here? I can't remember, but the idea he has family here is a bit of a surprise. I guess it makes it easier to hire people who you know you can trust through family ties.

"Did you find out what's going on?" My maids sit at attention to listen too, anxious as I am. I wonder if they have friends or family they're worried about.

"Only that it was a fairly violent attack and they managed to kill a few servants before the guards could push them back." Damian sighs and sets his cane down by the workbench and sits down. My maids stiffen.

"No idea how they got in?" I frown.

"No, not from what I could find out," Damian says with a sigh.

"I can't believe anyone got in. They kept them out so well." Someone had to let them in. Especially if no one knows how they got in. But which of the five missing girls had done it? Was it even one of them?

Does it matter? I am no different than they are. I was sent here with the same plan. Was this my father's backup plan, or had another rebellion managed to get someone in?

Damian smiles at me weakly as if to admit he can't believe it either but isn't sure what to say. In the silence, he drifts off in his own little corner, running his finger around the lip of the teacup at his table, humming to himself. My maids go back to work. I sit there, anxious. I'm a Custod, after all; I should be doing something. But all I can do is wonder who helped them and if my father knew.

I start singing a bit of a song to myself. I fiddle about my room, singing to myself and not noticing the others not only listening, but Damian subconsciously singing the other part along with me.

I could try to ask Dad. Maybe he won't reply to my insistent request, but he can't ignore this. I write it the best I can, in code to be sure no one else knows what I'm demanding.

Dinner arrives shortly after. My maids have a quick conversation with the servant who brought it that calms them. Damian plays server as always. My maids make sure I'm looked after first.

"It's fine. It's just me," I object.

"No trouble, miss," Flur says, still fussing about my plate.

"Really, I can get my own."

"Miss, you'll either be a lady, a princess, or a queen before this is over," Vivian says. "Get used to it. It's what we're paid for." Her impassioned scolding shuts me up.

Damian has a smile on his face he's trying to smother. He looks at me. "It's really alright. It helps it feel more normal and settle some nerves."

"And it's our way of helping," Ro jokes. "Making sure the future queen is alright." I blush even more.

"I guess that's true." I fiddle with Jake's ring on my finger.

It feels so strange to be treated like royalty when it's just me. But no matter what, she's right. I will make it to the top twenty-five no problem now. And that gives me a right to take any job as a lady. And maybe more in time if things get down to even smaller numbers before the harvest.

If I even end this at the harvest. If I can do it. I shudder to think of letting this happen again. I think of Lilly's terror and the northern girls' pain.

"Is there anything more we can do for you?" Damian asks, the concern vivid in his eyes.

I smile weakly and shake my head. "No, thank you, Damian. It's just... odd to think that way."

The moment I finish my sentence, my three maids react like it is a cue. They take their share and sit over in their corner, though there is plenty of space. I frown. They've never done that before.

Damian watches me a moment longer. "Are you sure there isn't anything? Even if it's just talking, I'm an excellent listener."

I smile a little. "I don't even know." I couldn't find a way to tell him last time, even when I tried. "It's a strange way to think about things. The world really. I heard rebels attacked, but this..." I frown deeper. "I saw the mess. I saw blood. They didn't just try to go for their target. They targeted everything."

Damian thinks a moment then nods to the side before meeting my eyes again. "Some might consider it the casualties of war, where all is fair."

"But why come after us? What did we do? They clearly were trying to get into that safe room. They tore up the room for a reason. Guards maybe, but random servants?" Aren't those the people we're trying to protect?

"I know, and I agree. It isn't right. You girls did nothing wrong. And no one is justified in attacking you, but that rule is determined by a just and moral society. But not everyone is governed by the same moral compass we are. Some men have none at all. And clearly, the men who attacked today have fewer morals than we do. To them, anyone in the castle is in league with their enemy, and therefore, is their enemy by association. They don't care about the people that get in their way, like the servants whose lives were taken today," he says sadly. "And I'm afraid when it comes to you women, to a group of rowdy, violent men, you are free game. It's possible they didn't even have a target, just the simple goal of breeding chaos and getting what they could."

"So the leader of that raid was just a schmuck?" I ask.

Damian smiles a little. "I suppose you could say that. If they had a leader."

That is a scary thought. "Wouldn't they need a leader to manage to break in?" If not, the security here is in real trouble.

"Not always," Damian says, "But it depends on what you define as a leader. A leader can be a point man. Or he can be the one that is solely in charge of everything. Or he can be a man who takes responsibility for the actions of his group and directs their actions. A true leader takes responsibility for all in his group, the good and the bad. And not every group has one. In fact, a group of wicked men never, if ever, have such a leader because it would mean he would have to deal out punishment for their evil deeds.

"For instance, Heklis was in charge and led his men against the Custods in the great war, but he was not a true leader, and neither was anyone underneath him. In lesser ranks, it was even worse. Cedrick and Roxorim Custod led their forces at the battle of the Vanishing Mountain against an army that was supposedly greater than their own, but the opposing force had five leaders that squabbled among themselves."

"So then, what does that mean for the masses just fighting for the freedom to live their lives?" I frown. "It's not like what they're asking for is outrageous. I mean, they have leaders. So then why aren't they involved in attacks?"

"Maybe they don't care," Damian shrugs. "Or if they do, they don't get directly involved. After all, if your leader dies in an attack, who do you turn to for leadership? Without the leader directing them what to and not to do, the men are left to their own morals."

"So, is it ridiculous to expect a leader to keep his men in line in an attack?"

"No, I'm not saying that. That's why the army has captains and commanders. They follow the chain of command up to the leader. Look at General Mercutio's men during the war with Heklis. Every group had a commander who would hold them accountable. But it requires a good deal of organization and order that must be constantly maintained at all times. Because if you can't have order during times of calm, it will be impossible during times of commotion. A man who cannot control his men is not a leader. He may be the one who calls the shots, but he has not earned the respect of those who follow him. In the midst of chaos, he is as important to them as the ants in the dust."

I smile a little. "So it is silly to think a leader could just say he's not really responsible for his men."

"Absolutely preposterous." Damian grins.

I sigh. "It seems so much has changed so quickly."

"Does it still bother you?"

"Well, when you live out there, the rebels don't seem so crazy. You can see where they're coming from. But this... makes me question what I knew. This is not what they seemed to us."

"'They' being the royals?" Damian checks.

"I mean the rebels. They act and seem like they are protecting, but that's not what I saw today." Or heard from the paper. I'm so unsure of all the truths I once held.

"Sometimes, people put up a front to gain your support, but their true colours show when they think your back is turned," Damian says with a bit of sadness.

I shake my head a little, "I don't know anymore. What would you do?"

Damian blinks, surprised. "Me? What makes you think I have a say in anything?" He smiles as if amused, but his eyes hold a question.

"I didn't say you did. Just... if it were up to you, what would you do?"

"Ah, hypothetically," Damian smiles and nods. Then he pauses a moment before looking at me. "Now that may be difficult to decide. But I would want to do what is best for everyone. What that is, I can't say. So I would ask The Father what He would have me do."

I sigh heavily. "Bit of a cop-out, isn't it?"

"It's not a cop-out. It's the truth," Damian says in mock offense, but I can see his smile teasing me back.

"Yes, but it doesn't tell me what you think. It's avoiding the question," I smile and tuck some free hair behind my ear.

"But it isn't a false answer," Damian smiles. "However, before asking Him, The Father asks us to study it out in our minds. So, to know which is right, I would go to each leader and ask what they would do to end this war and who they would elect to rule. Then I would learn about the man or woman each leader chose, then I would make my decision and take it to The Father to know if it is right."

"Why bother with the leaders then? Why not just speak to who they'd have rule?" I frown.

"Because each leader elects a person for a reason, and it is usually because they have a direct or indirect influence on that person," Damian explains. "For instance, it is easy to know who the royals would elect. That would be their son, Prince Gavril. They have shaped the way he thinks since he was a boy. And now, his guard and all the women here have an influence on him, for good or bad. That will impact his judgments when he goes to rule. So, by learning about the people in his sphere of influence, I can have a rough prediction of how he will govern. And if I were to go to a leader and they have chosen no man, that group I would fear above all others if they should succeed."

"Why that one most?" I frown. "Wouldn't it be good to let the people decide?"

Damian shakes his head gravely. "No, my lady. From such an ending, there can be no peace. There would only be chaos and death."

"How so?" I frown deeper.

Damian gives me a tight smile. "Let me tell you a story. You know the play 'The Miserables', correct?"

I smile and nod. "Of course. Played various roles in it in my time."

"Glad to hear it." Damian smiles then lets out a sigh, "Well, while the story is a work of fiction, the events are historically based. The play reflects the state of a county after suffering for nearly one hundred years with civil unrest. That all started with a rebellion that has a striking resemblance to the ones we are seeing today.

"You see, they had a king and queen too. The king taxed the people heavily, so he and his noblemen could build spacious mansions filled with the finest works of art. Meanwhile, two decades of drought and cattle disease, coupled with the heavy tax, meant people could not afford to buy bread. Two rebel groups sprang out of it rather like the Potentate and Loyalist rebels here.

"The more moderate group petitioned the king to give the people a fair say, but the king continued to negate them. Angered by the king's responses, the group of extremists rose up and laid siege to the castle, arrested the king and queen, charged them with high treason, then beheaded them both. They were free from the king's rule, but their troubles were far from over.

"The leaders of both rebellions tried to establish a new republic, but the leaders didn't agree. They fought among themselves until extremists seized control and put to death anyone who was suspected of being an enemy of their revolution. The following hundred years was a bloodbath. The nation struggled as one king or rebellion replaced another until the time in which the play is set. And that nation is not alone. Many other nations have suffered similar fates."

"Because they didn't already have a plan in place?"

"In part. It's also a matter of the kind of men who took over. They were violent and did anything to get what they wanted which led to more violence," Damian says soberly. "And that is what scares me in this situation. There are three parties in rebellion. If a party cannot decide among themselves who will rule, then it is doubtful they will be satisfied with any one person of another's choosing, and if there is to be peace, the next ruler must be able to appease or control all parties."

"So saying 'let the people decide' isn't being noble. It's just another cop-out."

"Exactly. They don't want to decide, so they choose not to decide anything," Damian says with a nod. "And their lack of a decision makes them much harder to please once a new candidate is put forth by another party."

"It's just... I thought they might be right, you know?" I look up at Damian before I get lost in thought again. "At least they were trying to do something for the starving droves."

"And you don't think anyone else is?" Damian arches a brow.

"Not that we've ever seen," I admit.

"Well then, perhaps it is time we take a closer look," he smiles.

I nod thoughtfully. "Being royalty isn't much like the stories try to tell you, is it?" I knew that, but it is hitting me more and more.

Damian chuckles, "No, it isn't. It's much harder than most realize. You know for the first twelve years of his reign, King Roxorim never took a day off for himself?"

I laugh, "How can you survive that?"

Damian smiles and tilts his head. "I don't know. The only days he'd take off were his children's birthdays and Christmas. He was afraid if he 'abused' his power 'like that' the people would get offended."

"Wish we had him now." I hug myself. "Just hard to know. Locked up in here, we can only see so much."

"You mean about the other leaders?" Damian checks.

I nod, "Or anything. It's like the castle has rose-colored glasses, and home has blue ones."

"That's why it is important to get a look at both sides."

"It's just impossible in here," I admit.

"Perhaps I can help with that."

I laugh. "What can't you do?"

"I think we already answered this question." He grins.

"It's rhetorical," I grin back, feeling a bit silly attempting the grin.

"I understand. Though honestly, I do think I could get you out and back in without anyone noticing. Though I don't know how to find the rebel groups," Damian says.

I frown. "That's against the rules. Why would you help me do that?"

"Because you are a contestant to be queen. And if you want to know what is right for the people, this is more important than following the rules to the letter," he says matter-of-factly.

I frown deeper, "Are other girls doing this?"

"Not that I'm aware of. I won't push you to do it. I only thought if you wanted answers, I could help," Damian says.

"So... not a test?" Not that he is allowed to tell me directly, but I feel like Damian would give me a hint if it was in how he said no.

"No, it isn't a test. I swear I'll not tell anyone, except maybe my brother, but only because I confide everything in him."

"Who is this brother?"

"Oh, I thought I mentioned him before. His name is Cedrick. He's my best friend, really. He has been through a lot, more than most, and sometimes, he has trouble trusting people, so I try not to hide anything from him. If you don't want me to tell him, I won't. I'll just have to explain it to him," he says.

I smile a little. "I don't mind if you trust him. What does he do?" Maybe I can get answers on the mystery that is Damian.

"He works with the guard and advises the court on certain matters," Damian says.

I frown. "And you feel telling him is safe?"

"Oh, most definitely." Damian smiles. "As I said, he works with the guard. He isn't on the guard, but they respect him. He's seen more than his share of battle, so when he has advice to give, they take it."

I want to ask, but I also am not sure I want to know. I nod. "I'd not mind." I swallow. "Can I be honest with you?"

"I'd certainly appreciate it. Anything you wish to confide in me, I will keep with confidence as I have outlined." His smile makes me feel safe.

I admit small things, testing the waters. I tell him about Jake, but just as much as I'd told the prince, and how my father talked me into this to help people. "I just wish I knew how to help people when... most people I know thought taking over for the prince was best."

"That can be difficult, but if anyone can figure it out, it's you, my lady." Damian gives me a warm smile and a slight bow of his head. My heart glows. Perhaps I really can do this.

Chapter 26

The prince comes just after I finish talking to Damian. When Damian answers the door, the prince smiles at him. "You have to be the most involved and attentive attendant of the lot."

Sage follows, repressing a smile from the prince. He nods at Damian.

Damian nods back. "Just trying to do what I can, Your Highness." He bows and moves to help clear away the dishes.

The prince shakes his head a little. "He is the oddest attendant. I only have met the others briefly. Yours seems to like to be in everything. Even cleaning." He's watching Damian with an amused smile before turning to me. "I guess a bit like you." I flush, making the prince laugh. Prince Gavril looks around the room. "Mind if I sit down?"

"You both can."

The prince laughs, "I'd have to tie Sage down." I laugh too.

The prince takes a seat across from me. Sage blends into the shadows like he's one of them.

Once Damian and my maids are done cleaning up the dinner dishes, he leaves with them to take the dishes to the kitchen. I watch them go then look at the prince. He's watching them too.

Finally, he turns to me. "Are you okay?"

I smile. "Yes, I told you I'm fine. No need to worry." It's cute how he keeps checking.

"It's just that most girls are freaked out. Even the born princesses find it awkward. Most don't deal with attacks like that," he explains. "I feel like you're hiding it all behind a smile."

I shake my head. "I'm fine, really. I'm more anxious to hear exactly what happened. How did they get in?"

"That's the funny thing. No one seems to know. Nothing was broken. It's like they had a key and knowledge of the door." Prince Gavril sighs heavily.

"Could..." I can't help but think about it, but if I voice it... I glance towards Sage. He had vanished from his spot. Who knows where he is lurking?

"Could someone have let them in?" The prince smiles. "I wondered that too. But I... I don't like to think about it. No one has before. And the staff hasn't changed. Apart from all the new hands for the Enthronement, but even then, they were all vetted and all have been here at least a month. They'd have acted sooner, wouldn't you think? Or wait until there was more distraction."

Like Dad wants to. I let my foot tap under my skirt to let out the anxiety.

"But until recently, the girls were more limited," the prince swallows hard. "So I wonder it. I know Sage does." Prince Gavril rolls his eyes. "But he always thinks you're all up to no good."

"Not just me?" I play pout.

Prince Gavril laughs warmly, "Not just you, but mostly you." He winks. "You're trouble."

"Yeah, I'm a drama queen already." That got a real big laugh out of Prince Gavril. I like his big laugh, strong and warm, coming with power from his chest.

"Yeah, 'drama' is the word," he grins. "But the kind on the stage. Ericka has you beat on day to day."

"She does hide up in her room a lot," I agree.

"Yeah, with that dog of hers," the prince sighs. "But I'm sure she's nice when she's not doting on her dog."

"Have you not seen it?"

"I'm keeping an open mind." he smiles back. "But we didn't come here to talk about my dating nightmares."

"No? I thought that's why we do this."

The prince rolls his eyes. "Alright, but you know what I mean. You asked for information. I said I'd give it when I check-in."

"Did you really check on everyone else first?" I frown.

The prince nods. "Most wanted to go to bed and sleep it off. They gave Lilly a lot of calming tea to get her to wind down. I made sure she was safe and asleep, but each one only took a few minutes. Most of it was getting to your room. You are the furthest out."

"Luck of the draw, I guess," I shrug.

"Well, I'm sure Sage likes it," the prince sighs. "Unlike what we found." He gets right into it. "There was a lot of damage. I think they got word of the safe rooms. They scraped at a lot of walls, tore down paintings, and turned over furniture looking for them. Or that's what I think. Parents think they were making a big mess just because." The prince shrugs. "And what would I know? I have no experience."

"Hey, at least they told you," I try to cheer him up.

"No, the guard told me." He smiles at me. "He also told me what happened when they made you go into the safe room. Take charge much?"

He teases me. I flush. "Impressive show of command from what he said. He joked if you lost, he'd have to hire you to keep the girls in line. The guard in the room also told us what happened inside. Actually, inside all of the rooms girls were in."

"So even Jonquil and the others?" I ask.

"Jonquil was one. She was on her way to meet with you. Ayesha was the other. She said she was heading to her room," the prince says.

Ayesha? She is quite unassuming. I sit across from her now, but I don't speak to her much. She is quiet, but she does ask a lot of the servants. As I recall, she used to be a maid. Where did she work as a maid? Did she used to use that to spy too?

"But they all were kept safe. The guards reacted quickly. If we didn't have that policy, it would have been much worse." The prince shakes his head. "I just hope we can stop them faster next time."

"Next time?"

"There always is a next time," the prince says firmly. "They never stop."

I swallow. "Do you know which rebellion it was?"

"My guess from the mess, Loyalists." Prince Gavril gives me a bitter smile, "It's how we tell most of the time. Potentates run violent rallies. They yell and maybe hit guards. They throw themselves at the gates to try to get in only to deface things, beat up guards, maybe scream at servants, but they are just angry and oddly violent protestors. At worst, they knock over a carriage and try beating up the people inside. They only target staff and are reacting out of anger.

"Custods, you know it's them because they are precise and only attack what they are after. Making them the most dangerous.

"But Loyalists, they are a mix. They are easily the most violent. They attack, break, and maim; they are after people, not things. Their anger drives them to hurt. Potentate rebels don't care if they break a nose or a nose off a statue. Loyalists, on the other hand, want to not only break the nose but behead the person. So, judging by the drive for people and attempts to find those locked away, Loyalists."

"Your guards are really observant." I admire their attention to detail.

Prince Gavril bursts into that warm, heartfelt laughter again, this time coming deep from his stomach as he was unable to hold in the laughter. "No, no, guards don't tell me that. No one does. I grew up watching these attacks, and I normally found out who it was later. When I got older, I figured it out.

"I can spot the kind of rebel from watching the carnage they leave any day. Potentates leave a mess with paper, broken glass, and sometimes, even broken weapons. It looks like someone got drunk and partied too hard. Custods leave only the marks they want to or ones needed to get what they want as, of course, they never have gotten what they wanted. I'm still breathing." He smiles. "And so are my parents, but they get close, leaving hardly a trace. Loyalists leave a blood bath."

I gape at the prince. That is really observant of a boy who was told nothing about the wars and attacks. He's right though. I had noticed those hints of traits in the rebellions when I dealt with them.

"But there was an impressive mess." Perhaps it was Potentates.

The prince gives me a sad smile. "We have three or so maids missing. We lost a few guards, a few more are badly injured, and many have some injury of some kind. Four servants are dead; two more wounded and unsure if they'll make it. And a few were beaten. If the rebels found you, you'd at least get a bruise if not worse. Loyalists do that, not Potentates."

I shake my head, "How can they do this when they claim to be trying to help the people?"

"I don't know what they need help from," the prince shrugs. His face is trying to be blank, but there's bitterness in his eyes. "I just know they say taxes are too high. Which, from a paying for room-and-board perspective, is a real problem, but I can't say I really understand. I haven't seen the pain. And I hardly hear about it either. Not good for 'little ears'." He sighs bitterly, "So I can only judge by what I see and the reports I can sneak in."

"Does Sage steal them for you?" I ask.

The prince smiles slightly. "No, actually. Most happened when I was little. I'd take the papers from my father's desk at mealtimes, take them to my school desk and 'play daddy'. I didn't understand them when I was young, but I remember a lot of them."

I smile at the idea of a miniature version of the prince running around with important papers and scribbling on them, pretending to be king. I wish they wouldn't treat him like he is still that little boy just "playing" at being king.

I frown slightly. "Hey, you said they'll give your more information once married, right?"

"I never said that. I think it sometimes, but then I question it more." Prince Gavril sighs. "But I also feel like they expect me to just magically be the savior they need."

My eyebrows draw together. "What do you mean?"

"Nothing. Just me being paranoid." The prince smiles. But I hear the tone. He can't say more.

What are the king and queen expecting from him once he's married?

"But that's sadly all I know. I hope that soothes you." He studies my face carefully.

He's so careful, observant, and able to understand what he sees. I'd say highly intelligent, if not wise in how he can read what he sees so accurately. He definitely cares for his people. What do his parents think he lacked?

"On what happened, yes," I say, but I'm more worried about this fallen prince. He wants to help but has no idea how.

Can I use that? Is it possible to prove to my father that he is worth working with? Maybe Dad can help him like Sage does. Dad can convince the other Custods, right?

Concern fills the prince's eyes. "Then what is it you aren't satisfied with?"

"Oh." I flush. "I... I just meant you still seem down. You know a lot. More than you give yourself credit for."

The prince huffs angrily, "You don't have to patronize me."

I put my hand on his without thinking and look right into his amazing brown eyes. "I'm not. You have sharp eyes. You know a lot, and you only know it by observing. Don't sell yourself short, Your Highness. You will handle the role of king well." If he ever gets it.

I can't believe I just said that, but I know I mean it. How did I become so confident in him?

Prince Gavril smiles softly at me. "You're just flirting."

I tense. He took my attempt to help him and slapped me with it. I am likely going to sell my life, heart, and soul for that conviction, and he treated it like I was just trying to win points. I'm wounded by the comment. I'm angry that he can't believe it, angry no one has put enough hope in him for him to understand I meant it. If I wasn't afraid of Sage, I may have slapped him.

Gavril frowns, "I'm sorry?"

"You should be," I snap harder than I mean to. "I mean it. It's possible for a girl to say something nice to you and mean it without flirting, you know. Who is there to impress here?"

"No one... takes me seriously," Gavril says with a firm grimness.

"Doesn't Sage?"

"He likes to smash me when I'm feeling down on myself. Is that serious?" Prince Gavril asks.

Sage makes a noise as I burst into laughter. "What?" Smashed him?

"Yeah, I'll be sitting in bed, venting, and he'll just collapse on top of me, he'll fall backwards, on top of me, to try to smash some sense into me, I guess. I'm not sure. He talks like nothing's happening. As if he's just standing by the door still." Prince Gavril smiles. "It's really silly. I don't get it. He is serious but then he's not sometimes."

I can't imagine Sage being that playful. I wonder if that's what it would be like to have a sibling. Someone to tease you, be different, and yet, get along so well. It reminds me of how I saw Godwin tease the prince. I had often wanted siblings, but it never happened.

"Which is why I never know if he really distrusts you girls or is just trying to make what I'm dealing with harder." Prince Gavril smiles.

"So it really isn't just me?" I want to be sure.

"He particularly worries about you, but no, he worries about others too," Prince Gavril promises. "I'd give a list, but I might be struck with a book again."

I laugh. The prince smiles, watching me with a look that makes color rise to my cheeks, but I can't say I dislike it.

My poor aching heart longs to return the look, to give him a chance, to sit near him, test the waters, heal the wound Jake left in my heart with him. But I can't. He's my target. I'm here to see the end of him. My heart quivers. *But... he is my apprentice.*

"You sure you're alright?" The prince leans towards me as if making sure.

I manage a smile and nod. "I just... wish things were different."

"Me too," he sighs. "What do you want to be different, my pigeon?"

"How complicated this all is," I confess before I can stop it. I wish he was just the apprentice I'd met that night. Then we could try this. I could be off with the prince and let the kingdom solve its own problems.

Gavril gives me a small smile. "Me too."

I can't look away from how he looks back at me so directly. Does he feel the same? No, no, the prince can't feel that way. I have to forget all about that boy, but it was so hard. He's right here. I see him in his face. His clothes tell me he's the prince, but the look he gives me, that hint of a smile playing at his lips, his stubbornly curly, not coiled, hair; he's my apprentice. And he's the prince. And his care for his people made me want him more.

"Your Highness," Sage's voice makes us both jump, "it's getting late."

"Yes, and being with her this late will not look good," the prince says quickly, standing and bowing to me. I quickly rise too. "Until next time, which I hope will be soon. They will keep you on lockdown for your safety and..."

"To see if it was one of us. It's alright, your highness." I curtsy and bow my head.

"I will call on you soon. If I get more news, I shall inform you or send Godwin with a message," he promises, taking my hand and bowing to kiss it. His grip tightens a slight moment before he lets go.

"Good night, Lady Kascia."

"Good night, Prince Gavril."

Chapter 27

Two days later things are back to normal other than a few eliminations. Rumor has it some girls asked to leave and were permitted to do so, but in Jaine's case, I'm sure it was not by choice. Ayesha may have gone by choice, but it's impossible to tell.

I avoid the others to hide my mixed feelings. After what I had confirmed by Damian and what I saw, I can't imagine letting the rebels in. How could I let them do that to so many innocent people here? How could I let them hurt my apprentice?

I hide out on my balcony when I struggle to hide tears. It's getting colder as fall sets in, but still warm enough to sit on the railing and watch the waves, hoping no one saw the tears or hears the little sobs that escape.

Dad hasn't replied to either of my letters. What will I do if he says no or worse but more likely never writes me again? How can I know who's right, and therefore, the right next step to take?

I hug my knees tighter, looking out over the bit of ocean I can see. What happens when the Custods disown you? I could ask Sage, but he'd be suspicious. I be executed or worse: rescued by and trapped with Jake. That's the last place I want to be. But I'm not getting what I want, am I?

I wipe my eyes again as more tears and sobs escape. What is left to me? My old life is dead. There's no going back. But how do I stop my new world from being worse than it is even now?

After several minutes of crying, I feel arms wrap around me and hold me tight. I take the arms without even thinking about it.

I need to not feel alone, but the truth is I have been alone. I can't talk to anyone. I can't use code to Mom; Dad won't write back; Jake is forbidden, and it's too dangerous to tell anyone here. What have I gotten myself into? I finally blink away enough tears to look at who it is.

He feels me pull back and loosens his grip so I can see his face. Damian smiles down at me with concern and compassion. He uses his thumb to gently wipe away some of the tears on my cheek and softly brushes away the loose strains of my hair then meets my eye again with that same mingled compassion. "I apologize if I once again overstepped my bounds, but I felt you needed that."

I nod. I really did. "Just have to take it one step at a time."

"I understand. Sometimes, that is all you can do," Damian says with a small nod. "But if you want to talk about it, I'm here for you. Getting it off your chest can relieve some of the burdens, even if no immediate solution appears."

I swallow. "I just... I can't." He'll be in as much trouble as me if he knows.

"You think I'll judge you, or afraid I'll have to tell someone?" Damian asks with a tilt of his head.

"I don't want to get you in trouble."

Damian smiles slightly. "I see. Though, it sounds like you are in trouble." His eyes search mine.

I bite my lips and finally nod, "Yeah, that wouldn't be too far from wrong."

"Is there anything I can do to help?" he asks, still searching my face.

I pause a moment. There is one thing. I look out over the water again. "Can you really arrange it?" I ask quietly.

"I can." Damian nods firmly, understanding immediately. "Say the word, and I will."

I nod shortly. "Let's do it."

"Alright, give me two days to prepare," Damian says.

Then I realize I am unsure I want him hunting Dad down. I'm dying to speak with him, but if he arranges it, Damian would know. He would have to report it to at least his brother.

Damian claps my arm. "Lady Kascia, it will be alright. No matter what, I will let no harm come to you."

I force a smile. "It's more if we're found out."

"We won't be. I promise." Damian smiles. There's a look in his eye I'd seen in others but never yet in his. It was a kind of confidence that is almost cocky.

I smile. How does a guy like him not feel cocky more often? "Hope so." Or I'd rather have any other of my options.

"Count on it." He smiles and as he smiles it turns into more of a cocky grin before he twists his head and smudges the grin off his face. "In the meantime, is there anything else I can do for you?"

I shake my head. "All I truly need are answers."

Over the next few days, I'm anxious, bouncing between excited to try to get answers and scared of what I'll find. My maids notice and try to help me relax. Vivian is the one who notices the most and calls me "princess material" and "queenly" at every chance to help me feel ready for the job.

But what they do the day of my outing is planned takes it to a new level. They see my tension and are extra kind as they get me ready for dinner. I should have known then and there something was up.

They put my hair into the relaxed, stylized bun, letting parts of my layered, curly hair fall in my face and shoulders in just the right places before they wrap my hair around a headband made out of silver flowers. That's different.

"Oh, that is so pretty," Ro declares. Vivian beams and nods her agreement.

The high collared dinner dress they put me in is a bit nicer than normal. It is a deep blue, like the ocean at night, with hints of lights on it, like stars or light reflecting on the water. A beautiful, floaty, lightweight material over the long skirt makes up a hint of a train. A lovely gathering around the waist clips at the front with a beautiful silvery, star-like broach. The sleeves are long, coming to a point at the back of my hand.

I love the dress, most of all the floaty designs contrasting the tight top, like a dance dress, but as I look at it and think about how they did my hair, I realize this is much nicer than normal for dinner.

Dinner dresses are always a step up, but this is different. Why? The prince hasn't asked me to dinner, and as far as they knew, tonight is a normal night.

I open my mouth to ask, but Vivian speaks first. "You got a letter today. You have some time before dinner to read it if you like. Ro would you bring the letter. Flur would you mind fetching her shoes?"

"Girls, what..."

Ro cuts me off by handing me the letter. "Your post, m'lady."

Her distraction works. It's not my mother's handwriting. It's Dad's. I immediately tear into the letter to read it.

My dear cygnet,

My apologies for not writing sooner. I've been away on business, handling all the accounts and tour arrangements and all that, which reminded me I needed to write you back. Your mother is hard at work on the designs for the costumes for the upcoming harvest play. I remember how we'd reuse them for the harvest celebrations. It made me wonder what you'll all be for the harvest ball. Make it easier for us to spot you.

Do you yet know what the prince will go as? Will you and the Chosen match? Will the guards dress up? That could be fun. I know you like to get all cute as different characters. Being able to pick your own unique harvest costume could be fun for you, unless the palace decides for you. In that case, it will just be a normal harvest.

You should ask the kitchens if they'll make some of our traditional treats. Perhaps you can introduce the prince to a new favorite. Will his and her majesties be dressing up? I wonder if that's what decides the most popular get-up of that harvest. There always is a pattern. Will you get to hold it in the ballroom? I hear it's one of the most beautiful in the world. Have you seen it yet? Well, I'm sure your mother keeps you up to date. Jake says hello as do all the other performers as always. Stay the course.

Your loving father.

I tense as I read it over. There's no code this time. I know what he's asking without it. He's asking for the information he'll need when he gets in. The palace traditionally has the harvest ball be a masquerade to encourage wearing costumes per Harvest tradition. To find the royals, to find me, and others, they'll need to know what they are wearing. He wants to know if I know the layout of the ballroom and how to get in. Not one mention of my request. He didn't even ask what the girls will be dressed up as so they can give orders not to hurt them.

I crumple the letter in a fist. How can he keep ignoring me? I sold everything to do what he wants and he won't even respond to my repeated requests. He ignores it and asks for reconnaissance.

I miss him so badly. I need his help, and this is what I get? I have never wanted to go home and have things normal so much in my life. I want my papa back. I want to pretend this version of him never happened. I wish it was cold enough for a fire, but it's not. I want to burn the letter and forget about it, but I can't. Anyone else reading this might think he is curious about my holidays. Instead, he's set on the mission. I used to admire that in him and Jake.

Now I wonder why I had. It leaves me with nothing. I toss the letter into the bin and sigh angrily.

My maids, always respectful of my privacy, don't ask, but are gentle with me. Vivian brings over a silver necklace, simple, but it shines in the light like the specks on the dress. Flur bedecks my ears with matching earrings. I let her put them on, just looking at my blank face in the reflection.

I don't quite recognize her. She's not the actress who played the role perfectly without question. This girl is more sure. I am not as certain, but I am not as naïve either. I am wiser and perhaps stronger, but also nervous, walking along the edge of a blade. But it seems to suit me. I look powerful.

I think of all the countless roles I'd played: princesses took thrones; princesses who grew into queens, or the women who failed. Their people demanded everything. And they gave it, or they failed to save them. I am not playing that role anymore. This is real. I've never thought of how much they gave up, the things that the failures would not sacrifice. And it was their downfall. If I gave it up, what would become of who I was inside? I could play the queen, but who would I really be?

"Oh wow." Ro startles me out of my thoughts, and I turn to them.

"That is just stunning," Flur breathes through her hand.

"What?" I get up and take in a breath.

This dress makes me feel as beautiful as they say. Its soft fabric flows around me, like comforting warm water across my skin. I can't believe it's me I'm looking at.

"Wait," Vivian comes over and adjusts some strings on the back. "Perfect."

Ro is beaming like the moon in its fullest. "You look perfect, I knew this design would be perfect." She adjusts the skirt and helps my hair frame my face.

She was right, the hairstyle, the silver headband — almost a tiara — and the high collar, long sleeves, and flowing skirt makes me look like a queen. Not that I'm playing a queen, but I am a queen.

The taunting thought returns. Can I actually try and win this? Can I win?

My mouth hangs open slightly as I admire myself. I look like the goddess of the night sky over the ocean winking the lights back at me.

"Why are we doing this?"

"Come on. You'll be late." Vivian doesn't answer my question as she sends me out the door.

Walking down to dinner, wondering what my maids are thinking, I stop at the door into the dining hall. But my days of hiding are over. I have to decide who I want to be.

That's what tonight is all about. I have to make a choice and stick to it. I can't rely on my father to make it or my mother or my servants. I have to decide. And if I am going to even think of becoming the girl I saw in the mirror, I have to try it on.

I take a deep breath, square my shoulders and step into the hall.

The reactions aren't instantaneous. I try not to hurry and draw attention. But attention is unavoidable. I hear a jealous huff from Ericka. Dahlia and Forsythia are muttering angrily to one another. Most girls gape at me. Their dresses aren't that different, but the theming, makeup, and jewelry in mine made it seem so much fancier. I look like midnight and starlight.

Lilly is beaming at me in happiness. Azalea's and Bella's mouths are open in awe. Jonquil's face matches Bella's until it falls. I'm not sure why: concern, confusion, fear?

I take my seat. As always, a servant pushes my chair in. I wait for the servant to put down my plate and glance over the table to make sure we're ready to eat.

Each girl is looking at me, many in envy, others in confusion. Most of the princesses look slightly offended. Princess Zelda, though, looks at me in a way that almost brings tears to my eyes, like she's proud. I don't know what she's proud of.

The meal formally begins, getting all eyes off of me. I try to focus on my meal. If I didn't have a wild night planned, I'd be having a few words with my maids tonight. What were they thinking?

"Did you see his face?" Lilly whispers to me after a few minutes.

"What?"

Lilly smiles, "Did you see his face?"

"I don't know what you're talking about."

Lilly giggles, "There are only two 'he's' in the room."

"Not all the guards are girls," I point out.

"You know what I mean. Did you see Prince Gavril's face?"

I shake my head. I honestly hadn't even thought of that. I was thinking of the girl's reactions.

"How could you miss it?" Lilly complains. I glance up at the prince, but he seems to be copying me, trying not to look at anyone. "It was like no one else was in the room."

"Everyone was staring," I point out.

"Not like that," Lilly smiles. "The king didn't look too displeased either."

"He's married." I don't like where this is going. Why did I get the best maids and best attendant when I don't know if I want to win?

Lilly laughs, "You know what I mean. And even the queen couldn't help but admire it. She didn't look happy about it though, but rumor has it she has her favorite already."

"The king and queen do; she's numbered one," I remind her.

"Maybe that's not the king's pick," Lilly states, "or there would be no contest."

She has a point. Prince Gavril said something about that. This contest is all about compromise. Who is the king's favorite? Me? Another princess? Was it the number one who left the first day?

"What are you playing at?" Jonquil leans over. "Trying to do something, or do you have a date with him after dinner?"

I flush, "No. I don't." Not with him anyway.

"Then what are you thinking?" Jonquil demands.

"M-my maids just dressed me like this. By the time I realized... I didn't have time to make them change it," I admit. They did that on purpose. They distracted me with the letter. Yet they distracted me from the letter with the dress. They are devious.

"They are brilliant," Lilly sighs. "You should have seen Prince Gavril's face. That was good planning. You passed up looking like a true princess and went right to queen."

"I wish I'd thought of it," Jonquil gripes.

Bella surprisingly calls down the table, speaking around several other girls to address me, "I need to get the pattern for that dress. I don't care what anyone else says; it's perfect." I flush in pleasure. As a former seamstress herself, she'd know.

"Damian is really good," I agree. "It's he and my maids that got me this far, not me."

"Maybe," Bella says, "but if it was up to the prince, I think we'd all have just gone home."

I turn red. "I don't think so."

"I do," Lilly and Bella say together.

"Dream on," Dahlia snarls. "Looking the part isn't enough. We all know that."

"Well, she did it first. If anyone else goes and tries it won't get them far," Lilly points out. "Even if it wasn't enough for Gavril, I think the king and queen finally took note of her."

I can't help but picture myself for a moment, looking like this and accepting the crown with Prince Gavril. For once, it doesn't seem so insane.

"You'll at least get into the top twenty-five," Bella says.

"Not if I have anything to say about it," Dahlia says.

Oh no, now the elite are on me. I glance up to the other side of the table and see Ericka and Forsythia giving me the same kind of glare Dahlia was. I flush deeper.

"What would you even do?" Jonquil challenges.

Dahlia smiles wickedly. "Oh, you'll see. You're not getting to the top. None of you have what it takes, even if your staff does." She looks me over in contempt.

"You can't all make it to the top either," I point out. "How long before you're turning on each other?"

"Long after you're gone," Dahlia retorts.

I feel new eyes on me. I look over; the prince is looking over at us, frowning. Oh no, bickering can't be good for any of us. I give him an apologetic smile, trying to say I didn't mean to start or get in a fight. But he doesn't notice as he's looking over the situation. His brows were drawn in concern. I guess he's not used to girls fighting over him.

"Not if he notices," Jonquil warns. The three girls back down and go back to talk among themselves. I swallow. Who knew standing out would cause that much drama?

"He's going to ask us about that," Bella says.

"Good," Lilly says. "Be honest, maybe he'll kick them out."

"He doesn't get to pick," I remind them.

"Still, he can tell the king and queen," Lilly says hopefully.

"Like they'll do anything," Jonquil huffs. "That's how stuck-up princesses behave."

We finish up our dinner, and I wait until most of the others have left before I go to avoid more fights. I'm almost to my room when someone calls my name.

I turn and see Prince Gavril jogging up to me. "Glad I caught you. Sage would be mad if I went into your room alone." He winks. I look around. Sage isn't there? "Anyway, what were those girls saying to you?" The look of concern is back on his face. "They didn't look too happy. You steal their dress or something?"

I frown. "It is mine," I defend.

"I don't mean that one," he beams, looking me over. "I meant a dress, I don't know, something."

"No, they just didn't like I wouldn't share tips." I want the girls gone, but I don't want to have others on me for being a snitch.

The prince frowns, "Tips?"

"Well, this was really..." But did I want to admit this wasn't my idea? I hate this game. I want to be honest.

"I'm guessing your attendant came up with the look. So you couldn't give tips anyway." Prince Gavril is studying me. "But it was Ericka, Dahlia, and Forsythia, right?" I nod. "I know they give other girls a hard time. I'm not blind."

"You don't see us outside meals," I accuse, feeling defensive.

Prince Gavril frowns. "Maybe not, but I'm not blind. I can see how they behave, how they talk about others. I expected at least some girls would be competitive. And I can give some leeway for that, but that didn't look friendly or gentle. What did they say?"

“Just the normal stuff.” I don’t want them thinking I’m such a favorite people get kicked out just for crossing me.

“What do they normally say?” Anger is now in the prince’s voice. I’d never heard it before. Which is odd. I’d heard that he had a bit of a temper with his servants. But his anger isn’t just hot, it has power to it. A power I’d seen hints of.

When I don’t answer fast enough, he presses on. “If this is normal, I want to know about it.”

I stiffen my resolve not to be pushed around. “Well, maybe not normal as in they always do it, but it’s what competing girls say all the time. I’m used to it. I grew up in a theatre of actresses, after all.”

The prince shakes his head. “That’s not the point. I want to know what they said.”

“Just dumb stuff,” I insist.

“I want to know the dumb stuff,” the prince also insists.

“You really don’t.”

“I do.” The prince steps closer to me. I step back. He moves as if to stop me from backing away, but he stops himself.

I pause. I didn’t think he’d dare touch me or even try to. I gape at him, shocked. He does have a temper. That scares me slightly. Maybe he never had to control it before. “Kascia, I’m not going to hurt you,” he says firmly. “But if they said that to you, then they are saying worse to others. What did they say?”

“Just arguments, you know,” I hedge.

“Like what?” he snaps in frustration. “Why are you being so stubborn about this?” His jaw is tense in his anger.

I huff, “I am not going to be known as the girl you have to rescue.”

“What?” He frowns.

“If I tell you and you get them kicked out, they’ll say you did it to defend me,” I state. “I’m not going to get pushed around.”

“You do a fine job letting yourself be pushed around on your own," Prince Gavril points out.

“Excuse me?”

“You could have put them in their place. You do it to me. But you don’t to them. And besides, it’s not just you I’m defending. I know they pick on Lilly endlessly. They tried with Princess Zelda, and she neatly put them in their place. And frankly, I couldn’t get them kicked out if I wanted to, but I still want to know what they’re doing. If you won’t stand up to them, I will find a way to.”

“I can handle it.”

He smiles a little. “Hm, perhaps a challenge then?”

“What?”

"How would you handle it? If I let this go, then what? You just ignore it?"

"Of course not."

"Then what?"

Then what? He's right. I have to do something. Do I pit them against each other? No, that won't help. I'm not good with girl drama. I guess rebel warriors are easier. I don't know how to stand up to them other than not let them get to me. That part is easy.

"Sounds like ignoring it." When I don't reply for a long time, the prince goes on. "Not really a solution, Lady Kascia. If it's nothing, why not tell me?"

I sigh. "Just the normal banter, you know, 'you don't stand a chance' kind of thing."

"And they do that a lot?"

"I thought you said you weren't blind," I challenge him.

"I'm not. But to my parents, I'm a toddler, remember? 'Adult' witnesses help." He folds his arms bitterly. Yeah, if I was a favorite, I think I just ruined that. But I guess that's a good thing, right?

"Witnesses?" I realize he used the plural.

"Princess Zelda told me about them almost right away, and Lilly does though she won't name names. She's scared of them. And if you must know, Jonquil is quite happy to complain about them too. So why won't you?"

"I don't want to be picked on as the favorite you save." But if others were complaining, I am being silly.

"I admire you don't want to be a tattler, but I asked you a direct question, and you wouldn't let it go. Don't worry, they aren't likely to get kicked out over that one fight, but at least if they keep at it, I can do something."

"To defend me?"

"To defend me!"

I jump as his temper gets the better of him. It shuts me up.

"You think I want to be stuck with one of them for the rest of my life if one of them gets away with this long enough to win?" he demands. "It's not a game, Lady Kascia. Even if it is to all of you. It's my life and my one shot. If I can stop it from turning into a living hell, then you bet I'm going to.

"I try not to have favorites, but I have to admit I have ones I don't like. I don't want someone who bullies and tries to manipulate their way into what they want. Then they turn that on me next when I'm not the prize but a means.

"How can you all be so blind about what it's like for me? There is no losing and going home for me. It's one of you or nothing. Can't you see that? There is no escaping this damned cage. It's one of you or the rebels get me. I don't want the brats to win even more than you do. You have an escape. You all do, but I have nothing.

"So please remember, if you all can, that this isn't a game. It's why they avoided terms like contest when they could, because it's not a game. It's a throne. It's a life. It's a job. It's all of my stupid little world in this cage. So, forget the stupid catfights and recognize that there's more than just the squabbling and backbiting of a girls' pageant. Give me some help here."

I swallow hard. No, I hadn't thought of that. Frankly, the way the girls talk, none of us have or do. Not the elite girls, not the princesses, not my friends. At no point have any of us stopped to see it like that. To me, it's been similar. It's my life on the line, but not like him.

"I'm sorry," I say. "You're right. I didn't think of that."

"Thank you." The prince still sounds angry. "So, they're just trying to intimidate you?" I nod. "Alright, thank you." The prince sighs and runs his fingers through his hair. "Well..." He pauses. "I'll talk to you tomorrow. Alright?"

I can let him put it off. I nod. I'm sure Damian is waiting for me, so we can plan our slip out anyway. If anything was going to remind me how real this is for him, tonight would.

"Good." The prince nods and takes a deep breath. "Sorry for snapping at you. I'm... I don't mean to excuse it, but this isn't easy for me. And frankly, I'm not used to people." He smiles a little. "Most of all girls."

"Yeah," I smile and huff a little, "It's not hard to tell."

He smiles too, but his eyes are far away. "Good night, Miss Kascia."

I swallow and curtsy. "Good night, Prince Gavril."

Chapter 28

I walk up to my room, wondering if I could make today even worse. I catch a glimpse of myself in the mirror. The prince was right. I could have and should have put them in their place. Why do I struggle in girl drama?

The door opens, and someone touches my shoulder. I hear Damian's voice as his head tilts into view. "My lady?"

I turn from my reflection and smile at him. "Hello Damian." How does he feel about me in some of his best work? I'd likely tarnished it with my actions.

Ro, on the other hand, is beaming, trying to see if Damian approves of their idea. Vivian is watching too, pretending to be cleaning. I'm sure they cooked this up with Flur's help, but she's pretending not to listen too.

Damian smiles back at me. There is something in his eyes he quickly hides as he beams. "You look gorgeous."

I smile shyly. "Thank you."

"She looks like a queen," Ro gushes.

Vivian smiles. "I hope the prince noticed."

Oh, he noticed. He likely wanted to say something about it. I shouldn't have yelled at him.

"He did," Damian assures them. "You ladies did well. I couldn't have done better myself. What do you need me here for?" He grins in a tease.

They all giggle. "They don't have time to design," I tease.

"What did you even make the dress for? It was just in the closet," Flur wonders. She seems most comfortable talking to Damian.

"It was meant to be a ball gown." Damian looks it over. "I thought the starlight crystals would help her stand out in a crowd. I guess it worked," he smiles to himself.

I brush my hair back. "Yes, it did."

Ro beams, "I'm so excited it worked. You're going to pass them all. I just know it."

It should have worked and been perfect. Instead, I made the prince angry at me and messed it up, royally. "It's going to take more than looking like a queen, but your work is spectacular."

"My dear lady, I can make you look the part, but that will only take you so far. You have to make it yours," Damian says, making sure to meet my eye. "You have something truly special inside of you. Don't hide from it. You are more powerful than you realize. None of the dresses I have made were meant for the prince. They were all made for you."

This design wasn't made to get his attention? Damian designed it for me. There are still twenty-eight girls. My maids want me to win. Does Damian?

"Can I do this?" I ask timidly; I don't know if anyone could hear me.

Damian smiles warmly, tilting my chin up slightly. "There isn't the faintest doubt in my mind that you can."

I swallow and force a smile. I guess tonight we'll test it more. I have to prove it to myself as much as them.

"Think we'll tone it down for a bit then, be powerful but humble, meek is the word," Ro rambles in excitement. "If you're not at least at the top of his list, I don't know what will put you there." Ro is excited: she's always excited. "But now let's make you as comfortable as a queen," she jokes.

I go through the normal routine, getting cleaned up and ready for bed. I dismiss them early, saying I'll send Damian for the tea.

"It has been a long day," Flur says understandingly. "We'll see you in the morning, M'lady." She and the others curtsy and leave me for the evening.

As soon as they are gone, Damian turns to me. "I heard your argument with the prince. Are you alright?" he asks in genuine concern.

I blink. "Oh, Yes, he didn't touch me."

"If he had touched you, I'd have stepped in. I meant more than that," Damian says, searching my eyes.

I swallow. "I don't know. I just..." He was right. I shouldn't have worried. I got caught up in the drama as much as them. "Maybe I can't do this." Dad was wrong. I could play a princess, but I am not one.

"And what makes you say that?" Damian arches a brow.

"He was right. It was all working, and I'm the one who backed down."

"Well, that may be. But that doesn't mean you were completely wrong either. And a true princess knows when to act and when to hold her tongue. I am proud of you for standing up to him. He needs that if he is going to be a leader, and he should have explained without losing his temper. I feel he fears this competition more than necessity calls for. But I can also understand why. He has never had control of his life, and he fears the end result may be unfavorable. But I, for one, do not believe that will happen. And he needs people like you to show him that he need not be afraid."

"Well, he did apologize." But did I?

"True, he did that." Damian nods and smiles at me then lifts my chin. "And don't worry. All healthy relationships have their fights. If they didn't, it would have to mean that either: A: They are perfect people, which is not true of anyone. Or B: One side of the relationship is domineering, which isn't good for anyone."

I still don't know if I want him. I think of Jake. Will I see him tonight? What will happen if I do? I honestly would rather never see him again. But do I want Prince Gavril instead?

Damian seems to see my thoughts because the mood immediately shifts. "Are you still up for tonight? Should we reschedule?"

I shake my head. "No, let's do it tonight."

"Alright." Damian nods then goes into the closet and pulls out something from the back. "Then you'll want to put this on." He offers me a dark brown dress and a long, black cloak with a hood. I change into them as Damian puts on a black cloak.

I wish I had my sword. This is going to be dangerous, wandering the city at night. Damian nods and takes his cane in his hand. "Put your hood up. If they do spot us, I don't want them seeing your face. I'll go make sure your guard is distracted, so you can sneak out then I'll meet up with you around the corner."

Damian turns the handle ever so carefully as to not make a sound then turns to me. "Count to ten then go," he whispers then slips out, leaving the door open a crack.

I swallow one last time and slowly count to ten. Once I finish, I step out quickly and go to the end of the corridor as Damian instructed. I try to keep to the shadows, but the castle halls are surprisingly dark. The guards have lights on them, but the hall lights are off or dim.

Damian arrives then smiles. "Sorry to the poor maid whose dishes I tipped over. But I made sure the door was closed, so he won't know we were gone. You alright?"

I nod. "Let's go."

Damian takes my hand and leads me down the darkened corridor, edging corners to the wall as we come to a cross-section then picking a direction and quickly slipping down the next hallway. The third time he does this, he stops at the corner and pulls me flat against the wall. A light glows around the corner more brightly than the previous ones, and we can hear guards talking and walking closer to us.

My breath snags. Damian edges closer but doesn't lean around the corner. He flicks his wrist, but it doesn't seem like he throws anything. The guards' voices rise in alarm. "Who's there?" I can hear their feet break into a run. I tense, ready to move at Damian's cue.

But the footsteps start to fade, and the light goes with them. Damian double checks around the corner then squeezes my hand. "Come on." He pulls me down the hall and goes down through what must be a servant's passage until we go right into the gym.

We have a few near run-ins, but they all go much the same. Damian must be the luckiest man alive.

Getting across the grounds is easier with the decorative walls, pots, plants, and other decorations to hide us. The hard part is the wall. I don't think I can climb that. It's made of smooth stone, and there are two walls wrapped around each other.

Damian looks up the wall. "How good is your grip?" he says as he slips his cane through a loop on his belt.

"On what?"

Damian glances at me with a small smile. "Climb on my back."

"Oh." I swallow and jump up in a smooth leap, locking my arms around his shoulders and my legs around his middle. He turns to the wall and starts the steady climb.

His fingers manage to find the finest grooves, which allow him enough grip to pull us up. He takes some risks when a groove is too far and leaps up, catching the groove and resuming his climb. I hold on tighter each time. For how high the wall is, he gets up pretty easily. But now he has to get down and do the second wall unless he conjures up another idea.

"Don't get scared," he says, a bit breathy from his climb.

"Um, okay."

Damian takes a deep breath, breaks into a sprint, and leaps into the air. I gasp and hold tight. That gap is way too big, but he makes it.

He grabs the ledge and hoists himself up, taking a moment to shake out his hands.

I gape. That's all that's irritated? That jump was superhuman. Where is he from? The moon?

"Now the fun part." He drops over to the other side and starts the climb down. I tense and try not to hold too tightly. I press my face into his back to stop myself from looking down. I was fine, but now I'm painfully aware of how high up we are. When he nears the bottom, he drops to the ground, landing in a crouch. I let out a breath of relief. At least for now, we're done.

Damian looks back at me with a smile. "You can let go now."

My legs feel funny after holding on to him for so long, but after a few off steps, I get my balance.

"I'd make a decent hunchback, don't you think?" Damian jokes, looking down at me as he stands up.

I laugh as feeling returns.

Damian straightens out his waistcoat and sleeves then picks up his cane. "I believe it is your turn to lead, unless you need me to take you into town first."

I lead the way. I have to rely on Damian to check for muggers or guards around the corners but getting to the capital is easy enough.

It's a surreal feeling to see places I knew, the main square, the cobbler's shop, the street I'd trod a dozen times: places I've known from birth, but they feel like shadows of their old selves.

The forest is almost worse. The darkness in here would hide us if we stood still in our cloaks. I look at Damian to see if he's noticed anything. His eyes glance around, their green color black in the dark. He would blend in perfectly, saving for the paleness of his skin. He shakes his head.

I go up to the tree and knock. The covering at the base of the tree slides away. "What do you want?"

"My name is Kascia. I'm here to meet with your leader."

The opening opens completely. "Know the way?" His leering smile glows in the dark.

I nod. The man steps aside, still leering at me as we pass. I ignore him. Damian stops just inside the passageway, his eyes bore into the guard with a fierce, harsh glare as if daring him to look at me that way again. I hide my smile as we go down the passage. It's dark, but tall enough for even Damian to stand in. We walk along the padded earth until the passage evens out.

We come up into the clearing. The ocean roars on the cliffs below to our right. The air is colder. There are a lot of people, counting gems, sharpening weapons; a few are drinking.

"What you want?" a young man barks at us, trying to look in charge, but he can't be more than sixteen.

"I'm here to meet with your leader. He should be expecting me," I state firmly.

The boy gives me a once over I'd slap him for if I wasn't on a mission. "Oh right, he's up top." He jerks a thumb up the hill towards the highest point. "Think he is expecting you. Hoping for the insiders." He winks at me. "I might hope for some me'self."

I ignore him to make my way up the cliffside.

"Keep to yourself, boy," Damian says then puts his hand on my shoulder and ushers me on. I give Damian a small smile as we go on.

The leader is waiting for us. I've not seen him in years. He looks like his son, only messier and larger, but not in a good way. He has the same dark skin and hair. His stubble is more a beard too short for him to maintain. He doesn't have his son's eyes though. His are black and larger. On his right rests a hawk I've seen many times, bringing messages to my Dad.

The leader looks up from sharpening his blade as we enter. His two personal guards are looking at us. One of them comes closer, a hungry look in his eye. I tense. I don't recall their forces being this rude.

Damian steps around me as smoothly and quickly as a breeze rushing past. In the same fluid motion, he produces a sword and angles it at the man's throat.

"Dare another step or look at her that way again, and I shall remove your ability to reproduce. Am I clear?" Damian says as calmly as asking about the weather while looking down his sword at him. "Or do you need a demonstration?"

The man's eyes are wide, but he clearly doesn't plan on getting any closer. I smile a little. *Wait, where did he get the sword?* I check Damian's belt. There's nothing. Damian got that from his cane. Has he had that this whole time?

"Impressive," the leader chuckles as he puts his sword away. He strokes his hawk. "You keep good company." He appraises Damian carefully.

Damian lowers his sword and relaxes his stance but doesn't put the sword away just yet.

"Well, that's how you win anything, is it not? With good help?" Damian states, stepping aside and giving me the floor.

The hawk must recognize me because he flies over. The leader frowns. I laugh. I always give Marlon a treat when he comes by. He nibbles at my ear affectionately.

"Sorry, I don't have any treats for you, maybe next time." I stroke him.

"Hm, you made friends with my bird no trouble." The leader observes.

"Well, princesses are known to have animal friends," I reply. Marlon makes a little sound then settles on my shoulder. I guess he wants to stay even without treats.

"Hm, making plenty of them at the palace, I hope." He leans back.

I shrug. "The ones I need."

"So, what did you want to ask me?" The leader opens his hands invitingly. It reminds me of Jake. I glance around to see if he's there, but there is no sign of him.

"Well, about your plans." I look back at him. "If you got what you wanted, what then?"

"Ah, want to bargain, I see." The leader nods, "Smart girl. What is it you ask?"

"Tell me, if you got your man on the throne, what then?"

"Ah, my man?" he chuckles.

Yes, yours, he's not mine after the stunts you pulled.

"I see your meaning," the leader goes on. "Well, first, get the people their wealth back. Get money back in the right pockets."

"Then?"

"Then keep the peace."

"How?"

"Like other kingdoms do."

"With this guard?" I nod at them.

The leader laughs, "I see your point. But peace often brings agreements that wouldn't happen otherwise."

That is what Damian's stories warned against. Nothing is as simple as they'd made me believe. I'm so naïve. No wonder Dad didn't like me meeting him. Dad must use him to get what he wants. Letting the Loyalists win was letting my father win.

"Really? How do you intend to ensure that? There will be two unhappy factions if you win. Let alone what the Custods might do," I point out.

He laughs at me. "Oh yes, Custods." He rolls his eyes, "Who do nothing in this war but birth their own faction. They don't care about Purerah, lass. Never have."

That was rude. He knows who I am. I ignore it though for diplomacy's sake. "So, you don't fear what they'll do?"

"No, they let us sort out our own mess. Have since the king enforced his mad tax," the leader shakes his head. "The people don't have a plan. Potentates riot when they get annoyed. No one does the work for Purerah. Not like we do."

"So, when you win, what work will you do?" I challenge. "Winning isn't enough for Purerah or her people. What will you do to preserve it?"

"To ensure peace? When the people get what they need, the griping stops. How many bandits do you know who steal only for lack of work? How many for lack of other means to simply eat a decent meal? What happens when you give them what they really want?"

"Fair, so how will you give it to them?"

The leader chuckles and sits back. "How would you do it, Miss?" He throws the title at me mockingly.

"I came here to learn about you. I didn't say I had any plans."

"And you demand them of me?"

"You have sat there since before I was born saying you want to right the wrongs of Purerah. You've had time to think on it long enough," I reply.

The leader nods. "I see." He puts the tips of his fingers together. "The palace taught you well." He glances at Damian.

That does it! "I come speaking for myself, thank you. You want him to leave?" I'm getting tired of these "boys" controlling my life. "I'm not just a part in your machine. I can speak my mind."

"And loudly," the leader chuckles to himself.

I've heard enough. I am not letting that rabble in. "I see. Then I suppose we have nothing more to discuss," I state coolly.

"You impress me," the leader says. "I look forward to meeting again."

I bow my head, but no more than that. I am not curtsying to him. I look at Damian to lead the way out.

Damian doesn't move just yet. He eyes the leader. "This man you wish to establish as the next ruler. Where is he?"

Oh, why hadn't I thought of that? Damian suggested that.

"Ah, he is about. He likes to wander the night; he's not the most obedient little boy. He doesn't like to come when called." The leader glowers at that.

"You call him a boy, yet you expect him to rule?" Damian arches a brow, "Intriguing. Though I'm sure one of your men might be able to persuade him to present himself."

"Do you not ever call your son your boy?" the leader asks, "Most of all when he's being stubborn about a foolish point. Like appearing for an important meeting."

"My son doesn't need to be called a boy," Damian says coyly, "because he understands the depth and breadth of meetings and their importance. But if such discipline has gone amiss among your ranks, how can you expect discipline in your new order when you seek to command not just your people but all others?"

"Because people unite under a common desire. When the divisors between them are gone, people corporate."

"Oh, like they did on Restoration Day?" Damian arches a brow. "I doubt that very much. But... for argument's sake, let's say you're right. You storm the castle and kill the ruling family, then what? You claim you will give the money back. But to whom? And how? And that's under the notion that the money is actually in the castle."

I frown as the leader laughs. That is a good question. I'm sure I'd never be allowed near it. And I have no idea where the royal treasury is. "Where else would it be?" The leader is still chuckling to himself.

Damian sneers and shakes his head. "You haven't a clue, do you? You think five hundred years of gems are just sitting there, ready to take? But taxes don't just go to the royal family. They pay for the city guard and everything official you meet. You think you can just take that from them? That's their living too, isn't it? They still have to eat, drink and keep a roof over their heads. But why should that matter? No, instead, you'll steal what you think you've been robbed of. Trying to get it back into the 'right pockets', right? But whose are they? By the state of your living quarters, I doubt you even pay taxes. I very much doubt your men do either. Yet, I'm sure you'll still want a 'cut' for your work. And who determines that? How much is your share? Do the people get a say on what you decide to do with their hard-earned money? Or will you take what you think you've earned before giving it back to those who actually pay the tax? Can you call that fair? Can you be satisfied with what the people say you earned, or will you become as those you hate by simply taking however much you want and expect the people to be happy?"

I'd not thought of that either. I have no idea what kind of money they take from the raids just that it is never "enough". I know a lot of it goes to helping the children in need. That's why Jake was always annoyed when they didn't have enough for them. But you have to keep this operation going somehow. The Custod rebels don't take a cut. But do Loyalists?

"And you think you know better?" the leader challenges Damian. "That you know what it's like to be those cut off from even making a living by this overburden?"

Damian chuckles. "My dear boy, you have no idea. My father cut me off when I was a youth. I am what I am by what I did on my own merit. And I have traveled nations. Kingdoms and empires collapse on the back of greedy men with 'good intentions'. You are a fool to think that blood and money will satisfy you or the masses. And if you do succeed in your plan, it will be your blood the people demand next." He meets the leader's eyes with a narrow intense gaze as if daring him to deny it.

The leader just shakes his head. "So, this is why the change of heart." He glances at me. Of course, I can't have an opinion of my own. But I keep my mouth shut. No one will listen anyway.

"The lady speaks for herself, and I for myself," Damian says firmly. "But if you will not heed the warning and cannot provide your man, then I believe the lady is right, and we have nothing further to discuss." He slips his sword back in the cane and twists the head until it locks. I like the satisfying click it makes.

Damian guides me out of the Loyalist's den as if he'd walked the path many times, keeping his hand on my shoulder to ward off any who might try to affront me. I'm thankful for that, so I can think.

Once we're out, I turn to him. "The Potentates are more in town. Do you know the burned district?"

"I've seen it before, but only briefly," Damian replies.

"That's where we're meeting them."

Damian nods to me. "Then let's be off."

He leads me through town, keeping a protective hold on me until we arrive. Soon, we're surrounded by the Potentate rebels.

It's a strange mix. Some are jeering at me, mocking me for being part of the problem. But unlike the Loyalists, they keep a respectful distance, for the most part. A few younger men try to get into my face.

Each time, Damian moves just as he did in the leader's presence, getting between them and me faster than they can blink. "I'd keep my distance if I were you." He glares at each of them with a frightening glance as his sword slides out of his cane again and becomes a yardstick between them and him as he guards me from all sides.

I smile my thanks at Damian as we press on. We pass through ruined buildings, large meeting areas, but none of them take us to a leader. I try to ask, but it's hard over all the yelling.

"I said I'd come to meet with your leader!" I try. "Where is he or she?"

"That's me." A shockingly young man steps up.

"Uh no, that's me." A girl only a little older stumbles forward drunkenly.

Damian glances at me with an arched brow then turns back to the people. "Whom do you follow?"

The replies are loud, almost violent, and none match, making it impossible for me to know who they are cheering for.

"Seems they cannot agree among themselves," Damian says to me.

"No." This is the worst sign yet. "I guess I got my answer." My heart is sinking.

All I'd known was a lie. And I had to sell my soul for it. I only just stop my tears, though I think I feel one slipping away down my cheek.

I jump back as a splat lands at my feet. Some laugh, others tell off the person who'd done it.

I look at Damian. This is out of hand. I can see why their trademark, according to the prince, is a mess like a drunk party. I worry that's what I smell.

"SILENCE!" Damian calls out over all their voices.

That shuts them all up apart from a few drunk giggles.

"If you cannot talk civilly and appoint a few to be spokesmen, then no further good can come of this meeting," Damian snarls, looking ten times more dangerous than I've ever seen him. "Speak with us or depart," he commands.

"And who is going to make us?" The speaker looks drunk, swaying and trying to look big and strong, but not succeeding.

Damian meets his eye. His presence is commanding, dark, and almost foreboding. "I will," he says darkly. "And you'll be the first to fall. I can promise you that."

The man stumbles back.

"Let's just go." We don't need to make a scene. They can make a mess and yell at each other all they want.

"Very well. This meeting has ended. Go now and be gone. Any who tarry will answer to me," Damian says commandingly.

The crowd doesn't listen at first. I'd rather just go, but I can't stop Damian. It takes a long time for them to start filtering out, seeming annoyed and disappointed.

Once most are gone, Damian takes my arm and leads me away, still very watchful of our surroundings. I let him, trying to stay close to him and keep an eye out. After all, I am not helpless.

Once he is sure they are all gone, he relaxes and puts away his sword. I let out a breath and shut my eyes.

Well, this was helpful. I wish it had been more soothing and comforting, instead, I only affirmed what I feared.

Damian watches me a moment before offering his hand. "Shall we press on?"

I nod. "How do we get in?"

"In what?" Damian asks.

"Oh, I was only able to arrange for the two of them tonight."

Damian tilts his head and gives me that searching look. "Kascia, if we go back now, I can't guarantee we can do this again."

I swallow. "I know. I wouldn't ask you to try again."

I know I can't meet with my father in front of Damian, no matter how badly I want to. I want nothing more than to feel his hug, to beg him for answers, to sort out the pain in my heart. Yes, I'm angry with him for making me do this, but I still love him. He's my papa, my truth and guide. I'm sure he can help me figure this out if I just share it all with him.

But it's too dangerous for Damian to see that. I can't ask it of him. He's been too good to me already.

"Can you be satisfied without finding out those answers?" Damian asks.

I nod. "Yes, I am." I give him a smile and fold my arms. "I got my answers." All that I can get anyway.

Damian's brow arches more sharply, and he tilts his head the other way. "You're sure? You seemed pretty upset and conflicted before."

I bite my lips. I'm tempted. He could pin Dad down, I'm sure, but... "Let's just... I know them pretty well. I don't need to see them."

Damian pauses a moment, his face almost blank, except for his eyes searching mine. "He's your father, isn't he?"

Tears rush to my eyes as the huge weight of having no one understand or know my secret lifts in a moment.

I nod. I didn't tell, Papa.

Damian relaxes and pulls me into a hug, stroking the back of my head. "You poor girl."

I accept the hug and hide my face in Damian's shoulder. He holds me for a long time before pulling back with a gentle smile. "Don't worry. I won't tell."

I nod my thanks and wipe my eyes. "I didn't want to do this. I want it to go back to normal, but it's far too late for that."

"Sadly, things always seem to happen that way," Damian says sympathetically. "Come on. It's late, and you need your rest. You can tell me the rest another time. Perhaps tomorrow if it suits you."

I nod. Part of me is begging me to ask Damian if he can help me see my father, but the other part feels Damian is right and we should head back.

"I miss him, but I'm so scared," I confess.

Damian studies me for a moment. "Would it help to see him?"

I swallow hard. "I don't know if it's safe." I pause. "But... I do want to."

Damian nods and thinks for a moment. "I will protect you. No matter what," he promises. "It is your decision, my lady." He bows his head to me.

"Is it really safe? If anyone sees..."

"That's what hoods are for." He smiles and puts his hood up.

I manage a smile and wipe my eyes. I debate for a moment.

"He should be home. I know the way, but not sure how to avoid the dangers in between."

"Point the way, and I'll get you there safely," he promises.

I guide with Damian making small corrections and pausing to let unseen people pass. Damian must have eyes like a cat and ears like a fox to know they are there because I'm clueless.

We finally reached my old home. It's so odd to see it dark from the outside. A candle in the window shows my father working in the front room.

I swallow and move towards the window. I glance at Damian, who stays back and nods me on. I tap lightly on the window with my nail the way the messenger birds do.

Dad looks up and sees me. His face fills with shock then worry. He's up and at the door in moments.

The second he opens the door, I rush to him and hug him tightly.

"Kascia, what are you doing here?" He sounds tender but also worried as he hugs me back just as tightly but pushes me back just enough to see my face. "You weren't found out, were you?"

"No," I admit. "I just... I had to see you. I need answers. Papa, you have..."

Dad sighs. It's a mixed sound. He sounds annoyed and angry but also sad and hurt.

He pulls me close again. "I know. I know it's hard. Our biggest missions always are. I'm sorry. I should have prepared you better." His next sigh told me what he is about to say. "But you have to go back. If you're found gone..."

"I had to talk to you, please. I hardly hear from you, and your last letter ignored everything, and I know it's dangerous to write so..."

"Oh, my sweet cygnet." He hugs me again, holding my head to his chest. "I understand, but there's no time. If your mother or... others..." he glances around.

"I'm sorry, papa, but I just..."

"I understand. Really, I do, but we have to do this. You have to go back before anyone sees you." Dad's dark eyes dart around. I realize he may be expecting company.

I nod sadly, "I love you, Papa." And I might have to betray him.

"I love you too, cygnet, but you have to go." He gives me another tight hug. "I'll see you soon."

Right, in a month in his mind. But I'm not going to be able to do it. Would he ever see me and love me again?

He kisses my head and tells me to run before he ducks back inside.

Just as the door closes, Damian drops down from the roof. I jump. He's as tricky as Sage. Thank heavens Dad didn't spot him.

I hug myself and nod at Damian to lead the way back, holding back my crushed heart for the moment. I understand my Dad's reaction, but I just wanted to talk to him. Really understand.

Damian gives me a sad smile then ushers me into the next street then down a darkened alley before turning to me and pulling me into a hug.

I hug him back tightly, needing the moment as tears flood my eyes. That moment helped so much and yet hurt so much. It was the last time I would see him before... I had to do whatever I had to do. And I'm sure it won't make him happy. I want to break down and cry, but it's not safe here. Would it ever be?

Now I'm truly scared. I see the truth of what I have to do. I have to say no. I can't let them in. I can't let them win. I'll have to betray my family, my duty, the oath I swore. What is to become of me? My life is over. Dad won't let me home if I don't let him in, and Mom will try and fail to help me. I'll have nowhere to go.

But can I win? Can I still do what Dad wants just in a different way? The image I'd pictured at dinner flashes to mind. I don't shove it away. I try to believe in it, but I can't. I came here on a lie. I'm no true princess. I'm not even a true Custod.

I fight to stop myself from crying, hiccupping a bit in my attempt.

Damian gives me a long moment before pulling back and putting up my hood. "Come on. Let's get you back to the palace."

Chapter 29

The next two days are a daze as I try to take in the reality of what I know I have to do. I know what I have to do, but do I have the strength to do it? What will happen to me when I do? What scares me most is what my father and what the Custod Council will do to me.

I get a letter from Mom the next day, but it mentions nothing of last night. She doesn't know. It likely should stay that way. She'd be worried.

On the second rest day, my maids take more time to themselves to rest, per tradition. I don't mind the space. Damian comes in to check on me and asks me if I'm alright.

I admit I'm not, but ask if he has questions now he knows my secret.

"Are you really a Custod?" he asks.

I nod and tell him about how Dad would spend hours training me to use my blade, hand to hand, and other needed Custod skills after rehearsals while Mom made dinner.

He then asks if it's true all Custods have to go on a quest on their own.

"It's actually called the Test," I explain. "It's normally done in your teens; I went when I was fifteen. The first time I'd been outside of Purerah. I followed an enchanted map to the capitol in Emilimoh to take the full oath and authority of a Custod. Though, mine seemed easier than for others, or so I've heard," I admit. "They said it tests your biggest flaws as a Custod and has you overcome them." I suppose that was because the Enthronement is supposed to be my real big test. Am I passing or failing?

"Then why are you afraid of Sage if you're a Custod?" asks Damian.

I sigh and explain how the Head Custod gave us this assignment and warned us it had to be kept top secret even from other Custods to ensure the secret is kept. They didn't need the Potentates of the world turning on them.

I pause for a long time after I explain. "What happens to disowned Custods?"

"Why do you ask?" Damian frowns.

I swallow painfully. "Because... if I do what I think I have to do, it will be me." I fight more tears, the tears I'd been fighting all day.

Damian gives me a sad but understanding smile and nods slowly. "I see. Well, I have done research on the Custods in the past, and there are a few who were disinherited. From what I've read, they..." He winces as he looks at me. "They lose their magic. The magic that gives them the talent to fight as well as they do. Those who have been cast off had to retrain themselves if they wanted to fight again. And when they are disinherited, their children suffer the same."

I nod. I suppose that isn't too bad. I never wanted this life, right? But then there is the rest. I'd lose my family, position, all I'd ever had. For what? When this is over, when I leave, what is left to me?

"What will I do?" I ask in a frightened squeak.

"Honestly, that is up to you to decide. This contest offers the possible potential to be an influence among your people. Even if you aren't princess, there are ways and offices that will still allow you to help end this war, if that is what you sincerely wish to do.

"But that doesn't mean you should settle for anything less. I understand that this has placed you in a difficult spot, but after the other night, I know I'd definitely not choose the Potentates or the Loyalists as my winner for this war." He smiles a little. "And honestly, I have my doubts about your father as well. But..." He pauses and gives me a gentle smile. "Those doubts do not extend toward you. I still have every confidence in you."

I blink and look up at him. "Really?"

Damian's smile grows. "Absolutely. So far you have shown yourself to be kind, bold, and forward-thinking. You haven't simply sat back and let others do your thinking for you. You have sought counsel to make sure of the right decision, and you have a genuine care for your people and even those who stand against you that others sorely lack. You seek understanding and consider the feelings of others. And... your mind and your heart are open to new thoughts and new possibilities. And something tells me that those qualities are exactly what this kingdom needs."

I swallow. "When you say it like that." I pause. "But... I'm a fake. I came here on a lie. I can't pass for a true princess. A true princess is honest."

"Your father may have lied and forced you to lie, but it is not our thoughts that condemn us, but our choices, and you, my dear Kascia, have done nothing wrong," Damian says simply as if it is really that simple.

"I just snuck out to meet with the enemy," I point out with a sad smile.

"It was a diplomatic meeting between opposing sides to see if a truce could be made. Kings and queens have held such meetings in countless ages past." He smiles smartly. "But if you feel that bad about it, you can put the blame on me. I did talk you into it."

That does make me laugh for real. "I suppose if you put it like that, but I'm not a princess or queen yet." I sigh. "I'm not even really Lady Thorapple."

"Well, thank heavens for that because it's a terrible disguise anyway." Damian smiles. "I have to say, your father could have picked a better last name for you."

"What?" I frown.

"Thorapple?" Damian chuckles. "I assume it comes from the thorn apple flower. It literally means disguise."

I chuckle. "I didn't know that. I never thought about it."

"Yes, well. From the moment I heard your name, I started having my suspicions," says Damian. "What is your father's name?"

"Peodrick. I forgot what it means other than it's connected to the name Cedrick. Original, I know." I smile a little. It's popular to name your son after the Merlin.

Damian chuckles. "Right. You know, my brother's name is Cedrick," he smiles.

I giggle, "Only non-Custods can get away with that."

"Oh?" Damian tilts his head with an arched brow.

"Well, I heard there's a rule about that, but maybe it's just a story. Custods can't name brothers that, or it gets confusing for when the Merlin actually shows up. It's said he does," I explain.

"Really?" Damian seems intrigued. "I thought he died thousands of years ago."

"Well, he is a phoenix," I say. "So they say he appears when he's needed."

"Well, I let you know if I ever see another Cedrick and Damian walking around claiming to be Custods," he smiles. I laugh. After a moment, he looks at me. "That does mean that you were a noble lady long before entering this contest."

"Technically yes," I nod. "Like other Custods, nothing special."

"I disagree," Damian shakes his head. "You just can't see it yet."

I sigh heavily. "So you're saying I should accept this and try to win?" Part of my heart dances for joy while the other part cowards back. One part still sees only my apprentice in the prince. The other remembers what Jake had done to me all too well.

"I'm saying, if you did win, your country would be all the better for it," he says with a mixed emotion in his eyes. It is somewhere between proud and a dare.

"I don't know how I can handle this game," I admit. "They already broke me once." Jake broke me once.

Damian takes in a sigh. "I understand. And I won't say it'll be easy. But if you want it, it will be worth every struggle along the way."

"I… I don't know if I told you how I actually met the prince, did I?" I ask.

"I don't believe so, only what I overheard during your second date with him," Damian admits.

I chuckle and explain what happened and how it's left me confused about who or what the prince really is. I admit the truth about my arranged engagement with Jake in more detail than I'd told anyone. I take a deep breath to stop the tears. I'd not talked to anyone openly about this. "I thought he'd… I thought it was real. That I mattered to him. It took years for us to even like each other. But… I-I love him. And I thought he loved me, but… but it was the mission. It always was. A-always will be, no matter how much I want to change it." I take a shaking breath to stop myself from sobbing. "I'm not first to anyone."

And I won't ever be.

Damian gives me another sad and understanding smile as he leads forward and gently touches my hand. "I know how that feels," he says compassionately. "Perhaps in a different way, but I understand the feeling. I've been there. And I'm happy to say it does not last forever. In time, that wound will heal. I know that seems impossible right now, and it may not even help to know right now. But it will come. It's just difficult when you put so much of your soul into it, into him. How long were you two together?"

"We were engaged when I was young. Not even old enough to like boys yet. He seemed so old then. We were expecting to be married all that time," I wipe my eyes, "but we didn't realize that we might like each other until I was about sixteen."

Damian nods quietly. "And when your father told you about the Enthronement, what happened then?"

I explain the hurt and fear. I confess the anger that filled my heart and how the powerlessness broke me. What Jake said when I tried to talk to him. "I couldn't take it, and I knew the only way to get distance was to agree and then… I was caught in the tide. I let him shove me off the ship, and I've been dragged up and down and left and right by the currents ever since, hating him for what he made me do."

I wipe my eyes to try to stop crying, "Yet I still… Part of me still loves him, but I can't go back to that. I-I can't. I don't trust him anymore. The love was all in my head. And I hate them for it!"

Damian comes around and sits by me, wrapping his arm around me. "I am so sorry, Kascia. I don't even know what else I can say to that, except that I am sorry he didn't care the way he should. No one — and I mean no one — gets to ask that of you. I don't care what rank or title he has. Custod or not, royal or not. Nothing is more important. If any man dares, you get out as quickly as you can, any way you can, and you come find me. Understand?" He tries to meet my eye.

I swallow and nod. "Alright." I doubt the prince would do that now I know him, but it was possible. "I don't know how to do what I must do."

"I wish I had the answers." His eyes fill with sympathy. "But know that no matter what you choose, I will protect you. And if you want to win this, I will help you get there. Just say the word, and I'll be there."

"I'm scared of being ripped apart again. Part of me wants him to suddenly not be a royal again and make this all easier."

Damian's smile grows a little as he chuckles with warmth. "Royalty certainly has a way of complicating some things, doesn't it? Just think of Aladdin's reaction when he learned Jasmine was the princess."

That makes me laugh. "I had to play her part. It's just odd to make it... real," I frown. "Can I really do this?"

"I already said you could," he chuckles. "And remember, Jasmine was the same person before Aladdin learned who she was. Sometimes, royalty is just a title," he says with a hint in his eyes.

I force a smile. "So, I just try to get as far as possible?"

"I would say, aim higher than that. And the first place to start is believing you can get there." He smiles gently.

That gives me something to work on. Even if I change my mind. "I guess that's where I can start." I manage a smile. "Though after that fight," I sigh, "I may no longer be the favorite they think I am."

"Oh, I doubt that. Good working relationships endure many arguments. I doubt even the king hasn't spent two or three nights alone after disagreeing with his wife." Damian smiles a little. "Remember what I said before: healthy relationships have fights. It's inevitable. Don't fear them. I doubt his affections are so easily swayed."

I fight tears. "I just wish I could go back, and yet, I hate to go back."

"Well, as sad and rude as this might sound, you are here, and wishing you weren't isn't going to change anything. So, you might as well learn to be okay with it and move on. The sooner you do, the happier you'll be. It took me a long time to learn that." He smiles sadly.

I shut my eyes and keep trying to hold tears in. The problem is it's not just that I don't want to be here. I don't want to be anywhere anymore. I don't want to do any of this anymore. I don't want to breathe anymore. There's no point anymore. I can't do it. The one thing I'm for, and I can't do it. I can't let them in. I can't win this. I'm a spy and a liar. I can't do any of it, and I don't want to try.

But once more, I have no choice, I never do. I have to keep holding it in with no reward at the end. I fight to keep in the sobs that shake my body. I'm trapped.

I accept the hug and just sob. The trip did what it should, but I was hoping for a different outcome. Instead, I have to give it all up again for what? A hope I struggle to trust?

"I just don't want to be anymore."

"I understand. More than you know," Damian says sadly. "But I'm here to tell you that it does get better. It may not be the same, but that doesn't have to be a bad thing. You'll be stronger and better for it in the end. Sadly, sometimes those we love most can be so blinded by their own obsessions and ambitions, they can see nothing else. Doesn't mean that we love them any less, but if you do what is right, you will be blessed, and those you love may be blessed through you. But you have to take the first step."

"What step?" I ask desperately. I don't see any path forward. Any step in any direction will cause me to fall.

"By being an example," he says. "As a lady, people are watching you. They watch and listen to the things you say or don't say, do, and don't do. Even by abstaining from something, you send an example for all those watching you."

"This castle is under lock and key. No one sees us."

"Perhaps, but that can't be completely true. The prince observed how each rebel group acted, and they didn't even know he was watching," Damian says. "People are always watching and learning from you, whether for bad or good."

Great, so I can make more messes like the other day. I wipe my eyes again. "How can I manage that far when I don't know how I'm getting through the next hour?" The idea of dinner makes me feel sick. The idea of going home makes me sick. All options feel worse than the last.

"Take it a moment at a time. And maybe try to focus on what you enjoy right now, instead of wallowing in worry, doubt, and stress. And for starters, stop telling yourself that you can't do this. Because you can, and you will. You only make it true by telling yourself that you can't. What happened to the girl who wasn't going to be pushed around anymore?

"You put the leader the other night in his place, and you didn't take any flak from him, did you? No. You took charge, and you made a decision. Yes, it is going to be hard. Accept that. Yes, in many ways, it is going to hurt. But make a decision and own it. It might be the right one; it might be the wrong one, but we have this life to make mistakes and learn and grow from them. You are a lady, and you are going to have to make some tough calls. They are not all going to be sunshine and rainbows, but you can make it work. But you won't do any of that if you remain here, wallowing, letting your father and you beat yourself down and push yourself around."

Easier said than done when even that choice feels like it's dropping me into the abyss. I am damned no matter what I do. So, I have to choose a path that damned as few people with me.

Damian watches me. "I'm sorry if I came off harsh. That wasn't my intent. And I don't mean to shut you up or shut you down. But the way I see it, you are trapping yourself in a cage by repeating a vicious and depressing cycle. I just want to see you free yourself and be happy.

"You have a spark inside you that people need, but don't force suffering upon yourself to satisfy others. That never ends well." He smiles a little. "I'm sorry. I just hate seeing you so upset and not being able to do anything to make you happy."

"I-I'll get there. I think," I lie, forcing my shoulders to unclench, forcing myself to decide I am alright even if it is a lie.

"Pray very hard." Damian smiles, but I can tell he's serious. "Though, one thing you should consider in all of this: the world may not listen because they have their own wants and desires they want to force on you. So ignore them. Instead, turn your attention to the one person who has been listening. Prince Gavril was eager to learn what you had to say about the people's troubles. And while his parents may be ditsy at times, they are good people at heart. And perhaps this contest is more about the people than the people realize.

"You asked me once, if it were up to me, who would I choose to rule and end the war. And after all I have learned, I would choose Prince Gavril, without question. He is a good man, even if he is still learning and has a temper problem. He has a good heart, and he wants to do what is right. He just needs someone to help him and guide him to unite the people once more."

He said exactly what I needed to hear. I'd thought the same. Win or not, at least I can do my best to prepare him to do what I used to believe the rebels could and would do.

"Thanks Damian." I manage a watery smile.

"Of course." He smiles. "What are friends for?"

"Sneaking out at night?" I joke back. But my heart isn't in it. I am unsure I'll be getting it back.

He smiles. "True." Then pauses then asks, "Do you regret it?"

"No." I want the truth more than a lie. At least then I know what endless hole I am stepping into.

Damian takes out his stunning pocket watch and glances at the time. "It's about time for the girls to prepare you for dinner. Did you have any questions for me?" I shake my head. "I shall leave you alone for a while then. I should check on my brother. If he gets bored, it will not end well," Damian says with a shake of his head. I manage a bit of a laugh.

Chapter 30

With the time to myself, I am able to get myself to cry out some of the pain. I try reading Mom's latest letter to soothe the ache, but it only makes me miss what I'll never have again. In many ways it helps, but an emptiness takes place of the pain. I am resigned to my fate once again.

But at least I can cover emptiness with acting. I manage to look normal at dinner. I'm happy it's over when I get back to my room where I can just let the emptiness be, even if I normally would rather have music or dance.

I ask to get ready for bed as soon as I'm in my room. My maids have hardly started when there's a knock on the door. Who'd be knocking at this time?

Flur opens the door and bows instantly. I turn pink and look away as Prince Gavril steps in.

"Are you alright?" the words pop from his lips as he steps in without invitation for the first time.

To my shock, he kneels down to get a better look at me as I sit on the vanity bench and cups my chin in one of his strong hands. He's not harsh or forceful. His deep brown eyes carefully study my face as if looking for injury.

"What's wrong?" He pulls his hand back, but his concerned eyes are still on my face, darting desperately seeking the hurt.

"I don't know what you mean," I confess.

"You've been upset. You look worn, and I think your eyes are red," the prince says. I flush. I thought we hid it. No one noticed at dinner. Well, no one else.

"Did you not sleep well? Are you simply exhausted? You take that sleep tea, but... it's more than that. What's wrong?" The prince is determined. For him to follow me into my room so quickly, he had to dodge his parents and race here. Did he really sprint for me? Even more impressive, he's not even winded from that sprint up the stairs.

"I was up a bit late, but I'm fine." I feel I should pull back, but it might throw the bench off balance. He pulls back to give me space. "You-you have no need to worry." I swing my legs around to stand and step away.

The prince doesn't let me. He is up to his feet in a moment and gently takes my arm, but it is softer than any other grip I've ever felt. When Jake stopped me, it was harder, just like Dad. But I could easily break the prince's grip. He is asking, not forcing me to stay.

"No, it's more than that. I am sorry if it is what I said." Heartfelt remorse reflects in his eyes, brows creased in concern and regret. "I tried to apologize. I didn't mean to yell at you. I had no right to, I know that. I rarely get to let my feelings out. So when I do, I can be harsher than I mean to. I'm so sorry."

I manage a weak smile. I pull my arm free, but I don't step away. "It wasn't you," I assure him, but I fear a tremor of my inner turmoil has slipped out.

"Then what?" The prince sounds desperate. "Your eyes are empty. What happened?"

I glance at my maids, hoping for help, but their frowns agree with him. They missed what Gavril spotted. How? They know me better.

"Kascia," his voice is soft, "please."

His use of my first name alone makes my heart melt. His tone is so gentle, yet so scared, tears breakthrough. "It's nothing."

It's that I'm lying to you. It's that I lost my world.

"It's not nothing. If it hurts you, it's something," Prince Gavril says firmly. "You've been like this all day. Did I offend you? Why are you locking up?" The prince frowns, still studying me as if trying to see what made me sick. "What is it?" The desperation to understand in his voice is another prick in my already aching heart.

"Nothing you can fix."

"Do I have to fix it to know what it is?" he asks, "I just... I want to help."

"Why? You're angry with me too," I ask timidly.

"Angry?" The prince frowns. "No, I'm not angry. I wasn't ever angry at you. That's why I apologized. I didn't mean to. I get worked up about this... odd dating situation. My parents' tests and demands are nuts. I just... I'm so sorry, Lady Kascia. I didn't mean to hurt you."

"Really, it wasn't you," I promise him, sitting on the bench at the end of my bed.

"Then what—" he stops mid-word, a light of realization coming to his eyes before his face fell into a sadness I can't understand. "Was it the letter?" He frowns in hurt. "Of course, I'm sorry. I shouldn't have assumed it was me. And I understand why you don't want to tell me."

He's confused me again. What did he think the letter was about? He glances at my writing desk.

"At least he wrote to you. I know you miss him." The prince swallows. "Say the word, I'll help you fail the next test."

"What?" My brows draw even closer and lower. "Why?"

"If he really wants you back—" He glances at my desk again.

Now it's my turn to have my eyes light with understanding. He thinks the letter is from Jake begging me to come back, and I've been down since because that's not possible. "No, it's not really that," I state.

"Then what is it? Is it him?" The prince is poised to back away if I ask him to.

How do I safely explain this? "In part, I… it's most of… home."

"What do you miss? The stage?" he guesses, daring to get closer.

"That, and how my family was. They… things will change when I go back."

"If," the prince says firmly, kneeling to see my face again. "Unless… that's what you wish."

"You don't get a say."

"No, but it's still if, not when, unless you give me the word."

"That's fair." I force a smile.

"Hey," the prince pauses until I meet his gaze, "you know the one thing I like most about you? You have been honest with me. You let it out that first day, and it took down the walls. But now they're thicker than ever. I won't tell. Sage is outside. I had to fight him over it, but that's how it is. He's not here to judge you. You can say it."

Oh, I want to. I want to tell him everything. That inviting, warm smile, those stunning brown eyes flecked with gold encircle me with a safe warm circle like a fire. He has that effect on me. He did that night. Would I ever not want to spill the world to him?

But I can't do it. I'll be tried for treason. I'd be locked up for life, or executed, or worse: rescued by the Custod rebels to be trapped in their world never to escape.

"It's not your problem."

"It is now Sage is waiting for a report. One I won't give if you ask me to. You can say it."

"Say what?" I demand. "What do you want to hear? That I'm scared I'm losing my whole world? That I can't stop—" I only just stop myself.

"Stop what? Are you in trouble at home?" Prince Gavril's brows draw together. There's a hint of anger in that expression.

He's angry for me. He's ready to spring up and defend me. My heart quavers, wanting to let him, wanting someone to take that spot in my heart, while the other half desperately fights to drag that door shut like trying to pull a hatch closed with water flooding out.

"No." *Not yet*. "It's just the home I knew is gone for good. I miss them."

"It's not just that. Unless there's something else in that letter," Prince Gavril guesses right.

"What do you want me to say?" I demand. "To say I miss him? That I stand no chance here? What do you want?"

"The truth," the prince says gently. "But I think I just got it. What made you feel this way?" His face hardens a little. "Did they say something to you?"

There he goes, wanting to defend me again.

Just drop the royalty, and I'll follow, the irrational part of my heart begs.

"No," I swallow, "it wasn't the girls. I just..." How do I walk this tightrope? More like a knife-edge. "This didn't feel real before. I never thought I could win."

The prince's magical eyes have not left my face. "Or wanted to?"

I take a sharp breath. "Or wanted to."

"I'm guessing the rebound wasn't as smooth as you hoped?" He gives me a sad smile, clearly trying to joke to cheer me up, even if it was at his painful expense.

"No," I say instantly. "I am not... I won't deny that part of me still misses him. But that's over. It's never going to be real again."

My past self falls into a wash of tears with how devoted I'd been to him. The idea that we would never marry would be a blow my past self couldn't ever take. But I have no choice. Even if he asked, the answer is no. Jake had broken and betrayed me. It's over.

"Mourning what would have been better?" He keeps trying to get me to laugh.

"Don't be so rude."

"Rude?" Prince Gavril frowns. "What do you mean? I only insult myself."

"That's what I mean."

"Oh, no worries, I am sure I'm a horrible rebound with lots of rules and stuff," the prince shrugs. "No offense taken."

"Why?" The question comes out with more desperation and heartbreak than I expect.

We both stop, looking at each other.

After a breath, Prince Gavril gives me a little smile. "Because I want to help."

"Why? Do your duty with Lilly then. She's easy to comfort." I can't let him be that for me. I can't be broken again when I lose. Why is he so focused on me?

The prince's face falls. "I-I meant I want to help you."

"I'm one of dozens, Your Highness."

"So is the possible winner. I can't treat you all like that?"

"That's not why," I argue. "Or do you run at full speed up two long flights of stairs for any girl?"

Prince Gavril pauses a long moment before replying. "Only one," he says, "knows me as nothing more than an apprentice."

I barely stop myself from letting out an "oh" of pain and delight. Does he know how that would hit me, cut me? How much I just want him to throw off the new version of him I know and show he really is just my apprentice underneath.

She was the same person before he learned who she was. Damian's words return to me. But was he?

"I know I'm not good at this. I have no experience, no social skills, and I'm likely dripping with the stupidity men have about women and their feelings. I want to help you because you're you. Don't discount that I want to just because I'm absolutely hopeless at it," the prince begs.

"It's not that." Tears return.

"Like I have no idea how to handle crying," he admits with a nervous smile, "and doing what my mother does certainly won't help." I manage a laugh.

The prince pulls a handkerchief from his breast pocket, getting up and sitting next to me. "Tell me if I'm crossing a line or something." He offers it to me.

"That is the right line," I accept it.

The sudden drop in the prince's face makes me realize I wiped off the makeup that hides how red my eyes are. "You sure the girls didn't say something?" He checks again, eyes creased in concern.

"It wasn't them," I promise. "It's nothing you need to worry about, Your Highness. I assure you."

"Need and want are quite different."

I pause, swallowing hard. "Thanks."

"Oh, um... welcome." Prince Gavril frowns in nervousness.

I laugh. He gives me a crooked smile. "But that still leaves only one other answer on what is wrong."

"Which is?"

"You miss home for... other reasons," Prince Gavril looks away as he says it. "He finally came to his senses."

"I only wish," I huff.

"Oh," the prince blinks, "so then why is he writing to you?"

"I never said he was," I defend.

"Did someone else tell you about him moving on?" Prince Gavril guesses.

Worse, so much worse. I am going to break his heart like he had mine, and he won't understand why. I still am angry with him for betraying all I thought we had. But I am not sure I want to hurt him back. What if he stormed in here trying to get me? Then again, he was willing to sell me off to the man he hates. He can't be that desperate to have me. I blink back fresh tears.

The prince's face falls further. He straightens his shoulders then does something I know is hard for him to do. He doesn't force me to look at him, but he gives me a comforting hug. "I'm sorry whatever he said hurt. I'm sorry you had to come here like this. I hate this as much as you, if not more. I'm sorry for the pageantry, the drama, the rules keeping you from your family, all of it. I'm sorry you got sucked into my hell." His voice grows more angry and impassioned as he speaks. But then he pauses. "And I'm infinitely sorry if I'm doing this wrong. I-I've only ever hugged my parents."

I laugh a watery laugh. He's so innocently cute and stupid, and yet, so capable at the same time.

When I don't pull away, the prince swallows. "And if you really hate it all that much, I really will help you 'lose' and go home if you want." His grip tightens a moment.

I pause before I look up at him. He doesn't want me to go, but he'll still let me.

"I can't go home."

"To stay away from him?" The prince guesses, pulling back at my movement.

"You're fine." I manage another sad smile. "That hug was proper." Prince Gavril's sigh of relief makes me laugh. "Besides, the one you really want to stay around is Damian. He has the good ideas. I just agree to them."

"I wasn't going out with Damian." I hear the hint of a laugh in the prince's voice. "You always had the leg up. The girl who yelled at me for answers in the garden was always making me curious."

"Great way to start a relationship. The others are more attractive and mysterious."

"Really? You openly admitted you didn't want to join the Enthronement over a guy you hardly talk about, and that still doesn't seem to be the whole story. I think you're winning in the mysterious department." The prince raises a brow at me which makes me laugh.

I sigh tiredly. "I'm sorry. I'm here on a lie. I told you I didn't want to come. I—" I stop suddenly when I realize how close he is to me. But I don't try to get him to move. "I only came to mend a broken heart. I think I just made it worse."

"I really will help you go home." He frowns at me.

"I didn't mean for me," I dare look up at him.

"So? Most girls didn't come here for their people or because they love me. Some came to learn, or escape, others for fame, others for power. They all have other reasons. I never was the attraction," says the prince.

He's right. The princesses came out of duty. Others for love of the position of princess or fantasies about prince charming or riches. None came to be his.

"You didn't lie. We all knew you all had secrets," he goes on, "and I expect no more or less. If you really want to go back, the next—"

"Don't you dare!" I snap at him.

He pauses, so stunned he's completely frozen in shock, looking down at me with those stunning amber eyes.

"I said I didn't want to go," I state. "Don't, *don't* get in trouble for me."

"If that's what you want, I'll give it to you, trouble or not." We lock eyes for what feels like a long moment. He isn't backing down; he means it.

"Why?" I ask, getting closer to him, desperate to know.

"Because I..." The prince's eyes flicker to my lips then to my eyes. "I want to give you a chance. I shouldn't have favorites, and I don't really... I just... I want to take you seriously. I..."

We're too close. I can feel his uncertain breath on my cheek. The steadiness of his presence is intoxicating to someone caught in a moving tide.

The prince's mouth moves closer to mine. Just before lips touch, he pulls back, panting. He runs his fingers through his hair, eyes darting about. "I-I'm so sorry. That was not appropriate. Forgive me, m'lady." He stands up. "I didn't mean to affront you, I just..."

I think my heart breaks all over again. I'd forgotten his title. I remembered the stupid game, but forgot who the prize at the end really is. For a moment, I let the softer part of my heart run away with it.

When the prince pulled back, I remembered he is the prince. We aren't going to just suddenly make this work. I am one of twenty-eight. He's far more than my apprentice.

"I like you, okay?" the prince says. "And I really want you to be in the running when things get more serious. But I understand you love someone else. I'll let you go, just say the word."

"Why do you keep offering? Do you want me to go?" Tears are back in my eyes. I suddenly feel completely alone and that he is my only hope to escape it. "I don't know how to keep going in this."

"I don't want you to go. I just hate seeing you so upset," he admits.

"I thought you didn't like crying girls."

"I don't see many, that's all. I..." The prince takes a deep breath. "I want to try, alright. I want you to get further."

"To win?"

"I can't say that yet."

"Don't send me home," I beg.

"I won't."

"I wish this was simpler." I look up at him.

"Me too," the prince sighs. "Hard when you do it alone. No one listens. No one is really taking it in. They try to fix it."

"Yeah, I guess so."

"Just... this is a nightmare. I understand the Enthronement isn't fun. I hate it," the prince huffs in frustration and starts to pace. "But I'm enduring it with you. If that helps at all." He studies my face. "I know what it's like to feel alone in a room full of girls. To feel like you have no one to turn to. To be trapped in this game. But if you want to be free, I'll help you. But know, if you stay, I'm struggling right along with you."

My lip shakes. "I-I don't know if I can win. I-I came here on a lie."

"You aren't alone. I think that's enough," Prince Gavril says. "So what will it be?"

"I want to try," I state firmly.

Prince Gavril takes my hand and kisses it. "Me too." He squeezes my hand, "Me too."

He turns and leaves without another glance or word. I don't lower my hand as if reaching out for him to come back.

This only leaves me with one choice. I have to brave the world I fear ahead. I have to play to win.

Chapter 31

Mid-week, I get an invitation for another date set for the day before the rest day. I latch onto the invitation with the hope it might help me settle into this new world. The night of the date, my maids clean my room, making sure the bed is extra nice.

Damian has the outfit for tonight on a mannequin for me to approve. He makes a few adjustments then sits back, his arm crosses his body, bracing the elbow of his opposite arm as he holds his hand to his mouth as he normally does. He tilts his head then looks at me as he steps back. "I'm trying something new. What do you think?"

I frown. This is not Damian's normal style. He's right about it being new. It's brown, but that isn't the problem. The corset is the main part of the dress; it's sheer, except for the cups for the breasts and the ribs of the corset. It would sit low on my chest, lining my breasts, and makes a sharp dive down between them. The skirt is gathered in the front so it's hiked up almost to where my hip would be, while the back floated down to the floor. And people thought my Esmeralda outfit was borderline.

I know Damian said he wants to help me win, but with him telling me I had every right to defend myself, what message did this send? I try to imagine wearing it. I'd feel more naked than clothed.

I swallow hard. "Um... it is different."

How am I supposed to look the prince in the eye wearing that? I don't understand why Damian would design this for me. Does wanting to win mean I agreed to give myself up?

"Yes, yes, it is." Damian nods, looking at the dress then back at me. "But do you like it?"

"Um..." I can be honest, right? Unless he explodes when I'm unpleasant like the last boy I dealt with. "I'm not sure I'm comfortable showing... that much."

Damian rests his finger against his cheek then gives a kind of half-shrug. "Well, the main parts are covered."

"Damian," The nervousness and sick anxiety bubbling in my stomach rises to my throat, making it hard to say what I want to. "I-I..." I can't play this game. If this is how I have to win, I can't do it. I take a deep breath. "I don't think I can do this."

I turn away and pace, biting my lip, running my fingers through my hair, then biting down on my thumbnail before doing it all again. "I-I don't know if I can do this."

Damian watches me, his eyes following my movements. "So I take it you hate it."

"I..." I sigh. "It's not that. I just... I-I can't do this. I don't know why I thought I could. I can't play this part."

"I'm not asking you to. If you really hate it that much, I did design one more dress than may work for this occasion," Damian says, still watching for my reaction.

I bite my lip and look at Damian, still pacing. My maids are watching me anxiously. I don't want to let them down, but... "We can look at that."

Damian bows his head then gives a sharp nod to my maids. They set to work to lay out the backup. The way Damian said it makes me wonder if he's questioning if my choice is wavering. It's as if that is how I have to win this.

It doesn't take them long to display the new dress. This one is better, but still more showy than Damian's normal style.

The off-the-shoulder sleeve is a stunning bright wine red with the black stones reflecting the light like stars. The same pattern shows up in the floating material of the skirt that has a slit rather than a gathered skirt. The bodice is black and as is much of the skirt but for the edges where the floating wine-red material with the black gems reappears.

I see the theme. I take a few deep breaths, debating running out the door and begging the prince to get me out of this. But I can't do that. I have no life if I return home now.

I try to swallow the sick feeling in my stomach. "I... I need a minute." I push open my balcony door to take a deep breath of the chilling autumn air.

I can't do this, but I have to do this. I can do it this one night. If it goes too far... I can call for help, right? Damian said he would, right? But he also designed the dress.

I hug myself against the cold and take deep breaths of it to try to get my head in the game. What a twisted game.

After a few quiet moments, a gentle knock on the doorpost behind me asks for my attention, but letting me know they would go away if I choose to ignore them.

I suck in a breath then nod and turn. Damian stands in the doorway with concern on his face. "Are you alright?"

I nod and straighten my shoulders, "Yes, sorry. I-I can do this. I'll do this. Just need to take a breath, but I got this."

His eyes sparkle with compassion. "Oh, dear one." He takes a step forward and takes my hands. "I'm sorry I made you uncomfortable with my designs. If you like, you don't have to choose the second one either." He smiles warmly. "Don't ever let anyone force you to change or lower your standard, not even me. I am proud of you, Kascia." His smile grows as a warmth shines in his eyes.

My face falls into a confused frown. "What?"

Damian pauses. "If you would like, we can modify the second dress to make it more appropriate to your liking. Or... I'm not a fan of it, but... given the circumstances, you can even select another dress you've already worn, if you would like."

I shake my head. "I understand. It's alright. I... I can wear something under the skirt, right?"

"If that will make you more comfortable, then yes." Damian nods.

"Alright. I can do that. I can do this." I manage a smile. "I'm playing this game."

"Alright, shall we get you dressed for your date?" He smiles.

"Yes, I'm ready," I smile, "thanks."

"Anytime." Damian returns my smile then leads me back into the room.

I let him lead me back and my maids smile at me with delight.

They work extra hard to be efficient and make me comfortable. I kind of like the way the dress makes me feel. I look powerful, different, but still like me. I smile as I let my hair flow across my face. They'd left it down but made the curls perfectly smooth, almost fiery. It's kind of fun.

I look up at Damian, biting my lip. "He'll like this, right?" Help me win?

"Darling, he'll love it, but that shouldn't matter." Damian meets my eye with an inquisitive smile. "How does it make you feel?"

I smile. "Beautiful." *Strong.*

"Then that is what is important." Damian beams. "Knock 'em dead." He gives me a little wink.

I do stage breathing. "I hope not."

Damian smiles. "Well, not literally. But you'll do wonderfully. I'm sure of it."

I'm wondering how when there's a knock on the door.

Flur answers it. "Hello Flur," the prince addresses her as he comes in.

He's dressed finer than I've ever seen. He's wearing a well-fitting black suit, a deep red waistcoat, and a loose-fitting neckerchief. His dark hair is brushed to one side, giving his face more shape. He looks darker, sharper, like I do. I like it.

The prince pauses as he looks me over. "Wow." I can hear the 'I could get used to this' in his tone. I smile and try not to flush. "This is different."

"Yeah. Like it?"

"Perfect," he says. He tries not to linger on certain parts of the dress too long. He better not be doing what I fear. "Well, I'm sure you're hungry," He holds out his arm. I take it.

This is it. I am officially starting to play the game. I have to keep focused. And with how his arm feels under my hand, it's not going to be easy.

Damian smiles and nods me onward with confidence in his eyes. That helps me feel confident as I nod back and let Gavril take me away.

"Well, you seem to feel better," he says.

"Maybe." It's mostly a distraction.

"Do you help plan the outfits at all?"

I shake my head. "I'm used to being dictated to."

"Makes two of us." He smiles. I laugh. That's true. For people from different worlds, we really do understand the bigger struggles the other has. Only he doesn't know what my father wants. I tighten my grip on his arm as if that would protect him.

"You okay?" He must have felt my pressure.

"Fine, sorry. Am I holding too tight?"

Gavril shakes his head. "No, I just thought it might show you're nervous." He smiles. "Not that you look it." He looks me over and stops himself from looking at some places he normally wouldn't.

I smile a bit. It's kind of fun to know I do that to him. "I have to give Damian all the credit. And my maids. The other night was their idea." I flush.

The prince manages a sad smile. "Well, it was a good choice. I'm sorry the other girls were rude to you. That... conversation did not go the way I planned at all. I thought you'd brush off what I asked and move on. I..." he swallows, "...It felt like the first time I saw the real you."

I turn pink. He thought that starry girl is the real me?

"And though I'd take the chance to tell you so, but... I am not good at being social. Hard with no practice." He gives me an apologetic smile.

"You're not too bad. I've dealt with worse. And they had plenty of experience."

"Thanks. Not sure if that's comforting or not," he shrugs.

We go down to the main hall that leads to the ballroom then take one of the side doors, up a set of stairs that turn around the core of the building. Many doors branch off on our left-hand side.

"I was thinking this would be quieter. I know you don't like to be overheard," Prince Gavril explains. "But most of the others are at the main dinner, so not too much to worry about."

It takes my breath away. It's a small room with windows and a balcony overlooking the best view of the ocean I'd seen yet. Two servants are waiting along opposing walls. There is a table for two in the middle with seats facing one another yet slightly angled toward the view.

The night stars and the moon set the scene off perfectly. The lights shimmer as the waves press towards the shore. The vastness fills me with wonder.

"If it gets cold let me know, and we can close the glass," Prince Gavril says as he takes me to my seat and pulls it out for me.

I smile a thanks and sit down. Prince Gavril pushes my chair in before sitting himself. A servant assists him with his seat before fading into the background. They present the first course, cool cube salad, and cheese fried dumplings.

"Trying to outdo me?" I ask.

The prince chuckles and shakes his head. "No, just trying to set up a good date. I can't pull off what you can, or I'd actually, you know, get out more." He smiles. I smile too.

The prince's amber eyes settle on me for a long time before he smiles wider and pulls his gaze away. I'm not used to that outside a stage. Jake rarely looked at me like that, like just looking at me was more than enough. I quickly pop a dumpling in my mouth to distract my mind.

The prince takes that as a cue to start eating. We're both using it as a distraction. It helps me relax. That is a good sign, right?

"So really, how are you doing?" he asks, looking up at me after we'd enjoyed the food for a while.

I sigh. "I'm alright. It's just... hard to have it all vanish. It hit me that I'm never really going back."

The prince nods. "I can understand that. The world changes on you, and you can't control it. You mentioned you didn't want to do this, right?"

"Not at first."

"Fair to say you were pretty much forced into it?" Prince Gavril tries to see my face though I won't look directly at him, pretending to enjoy the view.

He'll be hurt to hear it, but I nod. "Yeah. I didn't really want to come. Mom helped me be excited, but... it was all just a band-aid."

The prince frowns, "You know, that's not a bad thing." I look at him in surprise. "I was forced into it too," he points out. I have to think about that before I laugh.

"Where would you go?" Prince Gavril asks. "If you could go anywhere you wanted after this, where would you go?"

"You mean when I lose?"

"If," he states again.

"Okay, if." I think hard. "I don't know. I don't want to leave here." I turn my gaze to the starry sea. "I want to help my people." Even if they aren't quite mine by Custod laws. "And I'd like to keep singing, dancing, and acting. I love it. I've learned so much from those I've played, and I love how the movement makes me feel."

"So you'd do exactly what you're doing," the prince teases me.

I smile back, "Yeah, only not helping people much."

His face falls a little. "You help me," he tries to cheer me up.

"One of dozens," I state.

"Two dozen, or thereabouts," the prince jokes, "But no. They don't... talk to me like you do."

"I doubt that." I force a smile.

"Well, they don't. I'm used to it," the prince shrugs.

"Not that you don't work around it," I smile, "with official and unofficial things."

The prince puts a finger to his lips. "After they bring out the main course, we can send them off." I giggle at his manner. Like he is the rebel breaking in.

"Well, officially you can play an instrument, right?"

"Piano, self-taught. I try to sing along, but no one can tell me if I'm good. And no way." He sees the question in my eyes. "I'm not learning I'm terrible from a woman who sings *Phantom* for a living." I laugh at that. "I've heard you. I know what I'm being judged against."

"Come on. I'll be nice," I promise.

"No way in vell," he insists.

"Fine. Ask Damian."

"Oh, that's better."

We both laugh.

The next course is served: a soup to cleanse the palate. It keeps me warm from the October air. So long since the summer when this all started.

"It must be good. You went quiet," Gavril jokes after we're most of the way through the soup.

"Oh, sorry, I got lost in thought," I admit, putting another spoonful in my mouth.

"About?"

"How long it's been." I take my last bite of soup and put the spoon at the right angle to say I'm finished. "I first heard about this in the spring and now, just feel how cold it's gotten. It feels like a lifetime ago."

The prince huffs and nods his amused agreement. "Yeah, it was spring when they started to arrange this. This has been a new life, hasn't it? I've never had so many people around the castle. I've rarely, if ever, seen a crowd of fifty before you all. It's almost like I was a different boy back then."

"A better one?"

The prince frowns, brows pressing together. "I don't know. I hadn't thought about it. I've learned a lot, but I still know so little about the real world." I frown deeper. He finishes his soup and sits back a little. "I can say you've helped me learn a lot more for sure, but it's hard to explain. I don't comprehend it the same. I just wish I understood. Then maybe I could fix it."

I study his face; his eyes show the pain and frustration. "I think you understand better than you know."

"Then why don't I have the answers?" he asks dejectedly.

"Don't be so hard on yourself. No one has had the answers in over five hundred years. You're supposed to just know?" I tease.

What I don't expect is for him to tense. His jaw locks as he takes a sharp breath through his nose. I study his face with a frown. I meant it as a joke. He acts like I insulted him.

"I'm sorry, I was just joking to point out you don't need to know now. You'll figure it out."

"How?" he demands harshly, more than he means to.

"Guess you pray and learn." I shrug.

"How? When no one will let you see or teach you?"

"Unofficially?"

Gavril laughs pretty hard as the servant presents the main course.

It's a nice noodle dish with vegetables and scallops cut into it with a watery red sauce. They also offer more of the cheese dumplings, making the whole thing come together wonderfully. I let out a sigh. I may have a new favorite.

The prince laughs. "You like it," he observes.

I nod. "Impressive."

"Good. Not easy to pull together an upscale dinner when your dinners are from a palace," he jokes, making me laugh.

"Have you ever had a bad meal?"

"Well, things I don't like, sure." He looks around as if to be sure he doesn't get caught. "Not a fan of some veggies." He nods at the plate. I'm guessing he doesn't like the purple ones. I laugh. "Or maybe I do. Who knows." He starts on his food again.

It's amazing how this time almost makes me forget my troubles. He's part of them, but he somehow makes me forget and enjoy myself. I sit up, suddenly feeling the need to ensure my dress isn't too low.

I pop a dumpling into my mouth as I think. I want to go back to forgetting, but now I let it in, it's all I can think of. "Can I ask how long before a winner is declared?"

"When all the tests are done, there will be a last girl standing," Prince Gavril clarifies. "But I know my parents would like to have fewer girls for the Harvest Ball. Makes attendance easier when they are so careful with guests. And of course, dealing with having so many masks and costumes made."

"What will you be?" I wonder. "Are the girls supposed to match?"

"No, they can be whatever they want," the prince shrugs. "No rules on that."

"Just don't be a slut," I joke.

"Yeah, bad idea," he smiles at me. "What about you?"

"No idea. I'm sure Damian has something."

"The most stunning of all, I'm sure," Prince Gavril grins.

"Stop it," I laugh.

"What? He's really good." Prince Gavril smiles wider.

"What will you be?" I ask, recalling he deflected my question.

Gavril clicks his tongue. "Almost got away," he jokes. "But I have no idea. I haven't thought much about it. Been busy."

"Don't deflect my question again."

He laughs, "I didn't. I have no idea."

I think it over. "Be what you want to be," I grin. "Be a sailor."

Gavril laughs, "Ah, I see what you mean. Not a horrible idea."

"Unless other girls give you better ones."

Gavril shakes his head. "They haven't mentioned it. And again, I've not thought about it. Been busy."

"With dates?"

"Yeah, that and lessons."

"What do you most like to study?" I lean forward, honestly curious.

"Not sure. I have been so overeducated that I'm not sure what I enjoy anymore. These days, I focus mostly on the ones that seem most important, but it's hard to know which ones those are. I used to study a lot of history. I know it backwards and forwards. And can do more advanced math than most from having to do it over and over and over," Prince Gavril rattles off. I laugh. "But I like my science lessons. Most of all biology when it's marine life. And at night, I go out and track star movements. I find that fun. Then when I get to work on the piano."

"You aren't much of a reader?"

"I enjoy Shakespeare and classical plays," Gavril says. "But I've only ever read them. Accounts of the Merlin, older legends, the dragon hunters, the explorers, those classics. I mean, I have literature lessons too." He smiles. "But I guess I am more of a science-minded person than art if I have to compare."

I smile, liking that we're not exactly the same. He has interests in things I struggle with. I realize I'm letting the giddy side of my heart drive; I quickly reign her back in, sitting upright. I wish I hadn't finished my food.

The prince finishes his while I cope with the odd feeling inside me, and the servants clear it away. I brush out my skirt as if it needs it. I also make sure my sleeves are in place. Of course, they are. Damian's work is never less than perfect.

The servants set down dessert. My eyes go wide. It's a chocolate souffle with a thick vanilla and chocolate cream inside and fried bananas. I'd never seen or had such a fancy dessert before.

The prince again nods his thanks to the servants. A hint of nervousness comes into his eyes as he gives them a special nod. They don't do anything different though. They still fade into the background.

I want to ask, but then the prince picks up the dessert fork and gives me a smile. He's daring me to try it.

I am really looking forward to the chocolate, so I take a careful bite, making sure to get the cream inside. I shut my eyes in delight. This is so good.

The prince laughs in joy, "It is pretty good, isn't it?"

I nod. "The best."

"Try the fruit." He smiles wider.

I do. It surprises me with a slightly spicy taste, but it contrasts the chocolate's bittersweet perfectly. I smile as I swallow. The prince laughs again.

I watch him and pause. He's enjoying my reactions more than his food. He's enjoying treating me to something special. I swallow though I don't have anything in my mouth. He's enjoying spoiling me.

"I thought you'd like that." He takes his own bite. "It is unique."

"Really is." I take another bite to hide my unease. I want to win, right? I should be glad. I guess it reminds me of the things Jake did that made me fall for his lies.

"What is normally your favorite?"

"I'm never really supposed to have desserts. Not good for a dancer's figure," I say. "But..." I recall all the times Jake tried to treat me. "My friends knew to treat me with a chocolate cake now and then. I like the cream inside the chocolate most."

"Ah, so lucky again. Souffle isn't that different," the prince smiles. I nod again. He frowns. "You okay? Oh," the light goes out in his eyes, "that friend. Sorry, I won't bring it up."

If only he knew, but thank the heavens, he didn't. "Thanks." Did he do that with the other girls? He must. He doesn't know girls. He must find it fun to see how they all react differently. He said he was more science-minded. He is curious and enjoys seeing the girls' reactions. I take another bite.

"You're welcome. I'll remember you like chocolate." he smiles. "Darker or milk?"

"Dark." Always.

The prince smiles. "Healthier, I should have guessed."

I laugh too. "You?"

"I don't care. Never thought about it," he shrugs. "I like sweet, I guess. The semi-sweet is what I would sneak when I could as the baking chips around here always are. I'd beg the older cooks to slip me some as a child. So, it's what I'm used to."

I try to picture him doing that. The little prince who stole his father's paperwork to play king and eat stolen chocolate baking chips from sweet old ladies who thought him too cute to say no. I can picture the chocolate smudges on the paperwork as he played his games.

I smile a little. I can't help but love that sweet little boy. Is it only a matter of time before the adult version has me as ensnared as Jake once did? Would he betray me too?

I try to distract from that thought. "So, earlier I asked about your skills, the 'unofficial ones'," I hint.

"Well, I had to lie about not being able to swim. I can do that. Sage and the other Custods thought it too much of a liability I couldn't fight, so I can use real swords," says the prince.

"You'll have to try me some time." Oh no, did I just admit I fence?

"Maybe Sage will let me show you," the prince smiles.

We're quiet as we finish dessert. The prince gets nervous and finishes before I do.

I take my last bite, and the servants clear it away. I wonder if he's nervous about the end of the date. Maybe he's not ready to be done. It's not that late.

"Well, if you're done, we could enjoy the view," Gavril suggests, nodding at the balcony.

I like that idea and nod with a smile.

He grins and pulls my chair out before offering me his hand. I take it with a smile. I think he wants to keep holding my hand but offers his arm instead.

It's colder out here. I wish Damian had given me something to keep warm. The prince lets me lean over the railing to see the view. "In a few months, you might be able to see migrating whales. The Great Whale likes to come through here," the prince points out a spot on the water. "They are so far out you can only see them up here. I bring a scope to get a good view."

"That's amazing. You really know the timing," I say.

"They do it every year as annually as Christmas or birthdays," he smiles as he leans over with me.

He crosses one ankle over the other. It looks nice. He looks nice. His suit shows his strength better than his day-to-day suits. I look at his arms, wondering if the rest of him is just as toned.

"And sometimes there are blooms of squid or jellyfish. You can see dolphins gather for mating season. These views allow us to see things we'd not normally get to." He glances at me.

"Your lessons pay off to let you see more of the world than you normally would get to," I agree and shiver a bit. It is cold in the breeze.

"You okay?" The prince frowns.

"Fine."

The prince frowns deeper. Then he guesses. "Cold?"

I smile sheepishly and nod.

The prince takes off his jacket and puts it over my shoulders. His hand runs along my exposed shoulder. Once the jacket is on, he runs his hand down my right arm, pulling me into his side." I shudder again at how close he is.

A million stolen nights with Jake run through my mind. Nights where we had to pull away to stop ourselves breaking my Custod oath. I remember how I loved his breath on my skin, the warmth of his hands on me. Suddenly, all I want is for Gavril to do the same. I feel so empty, lonely. I want that void full once again. I don't know if I've gone this long without it since I first kissed Jake.

Fear fills me. No, I can't do that. The prince won't show the same respect as Jake, will he? I'm too scared to find out. I should have said no. This night was lovely until now. I know this was the point. I knew it from the moment I saw the dresses. How could I forget? I should have said no.

"Better?" Gavril asks, his other hand takes my left hand, running it over the back of my hand. I like that too.

"Yeah." It's a lot warmer. The heat is in my face. I want to push him away, but I'm scared to.

"Good." He runs his hand down my exposed skin one more time before quickly pulling back. "Would..." He clears his throat. "Would you be warmer if we sat?"

"Maybe."

The prince watches carefully. "Well, there is a raised bench, so we can see."

"No. I think it's fine."

He nods and looks around. He's battling with himself. Why? Is he trying to figure out how to get more out of me? Can I give him anything safely?

Do I want to if that's all he wants? Am I wrong and he is only the prince, not my apprentice?

"When it gets late, sometimes I see lights out there. When there is no moon." The prince points to an area to our left. "I wonder if it's merfolk, but it's more likely a deep-sea fish coming up. Seafolk say fish of the deep have their own glow. I'd love to see that one day. Princess Zelda says she's seen some examples her Sirea people fish up out of the ocean."

"What is that?"

"It's a race of her people that are merfolk mixed with humans or Hyvians as they call them," the prince explains. "She said the fish they catch glow in the dark. They have tanks in dark caves to try to breed and study them."

"Wow."

The prince looks down and frowns. "You're a bit pale. Sure you aren't still cold?"

I flush. "Well, a jacket can only do so much," I defend.

The prince puts an arm around me. "We can go inside."

I want to, and yet, don't. I'm scared of what he wants, but part of me wants to know that's not what he wants. "It's alright, just a bit longer."

We're silent for a moment, standing close together, leaning on the balcony. I can see his waistcoat better now he's given me his jacket. It looks darker red out here. The lighter wave-like patterns shine in the low light of the stars. It makes his skin darker. His white shirt stands out against it. I look at the neckerchief he's wearing which almost blends into the darkness.

I can't help but notice it's easier to see his well-built form with just his shirt and waistcoat. It fits perfectly, showing his strong arms, shoulders, chest. How does he get so strong? Is it a trick of the clothing? Part of me longs to reach out and feel for myself.

"Sorry, it's just..." the prince suddenly speaks, looking over at me. "He does a good job." The prince looks me over, over my dress, lingering on my exposed leg. I adjust it. What was Damian thinking? What am I thinking? I shouldn't be doing this. "You're easily one of the most beautiful."

I try to break the mood. "Who is the most beautiful?"

"I always feel like it's the one I'm currently looking at."

So is he saying me, or that it changes depending on who he's looking at? "You're a good politician." I have to admire the tact of that reply.

"What?"

I laugh, "Are you that blind to yourself?"

"I'm too busy with you." He blushes instantly.

I laugh so hard I have to cover my mouth. His jacket falls off my shoulder.

The prince catches it to put it back over my shoulder, running a hand along my arm again. I wish he wouldn't, but I like it too. I'm not sure we should be this close.

As he does, his leg brushes against my exposed leg. I'm thankful for the tights protecting my skin. But as I glance down, he quickly pulls away. "Sorry," he mutters. He tenses as if to pull his arms away from around me, but I don't think he wants to.

"Stop," I whisper, unable to handle it anymore.

"What?"

I back away, letting his jacket stay in his grip. "Please stop," I say, hardly louder than before.

"Stop what?"

Maybe he is too innocent to know what he's doing. He has no experience with women. He's lucky if his parents even talked to him about girls.

"Sorry, I just... get nervous," I admit. I don't get as close this time though part of me wants to. The feel of his warmth, the sound of his breath. It's enchanting. My mind keeps going back to those nights with Jake and imagining what it would be like... enwrapped in those oddly strong arms. My eyes flit to his lips.

"I guess it is the most alone we've been," the prince agrees.

I look the prince over again, fishing for what to say. His neckerchief has come a bit loose, showing a bit of his neck. I look away quickly.

"I thought this would be a good spot. One of my favorites," he says.

His eyes look over my dark lipstick and then down at my stunning dress again. I see the temptation in his eyes. He's struggling just like me. That makes it worse.

"Please don't," I whisper again.

"Sorry, sorry," Gavril pulls his eye away and looks out at the stars.

It makes me laugh. He really is trying. "You... wouldn't ask that of me, would you?" Why did I ask?!

Gavril quickly turns and looks at me. "What?"

"I just..." I am surprised tears don't come. "What they all said. That sooner or later... don't ask that of me, please," I beg a little.

His eyes fill with pity and horror. He reaches out and takes my hand. A flood of warmth fills me, making me feel safe. But Jake felt safe too.

Gavril squeezes my hand gently. "Hey," his soft voice gets me to look up at his face, "I'm not going to hurt you."

"What if you don't think it hurts?" I ask.

"Then tell me, and I'll stop," he promises.

I shut my eyes and look away because the temptation floods me. I am so relieved I want to kiss him in thanks. I don't. But I want to. His willingness to let me say no makes me want to give myself to him.

He frowns at my reaction, unsure. "Hey, it's alright."

I nod. I squeeze his hand back. It helps soothe the desire that rises inside of me. A shudder that has nothing to do with the cold rushes through me, like that night when he came to check on me. I feel the electricity in the air. The tingle on my skin excites me.

I'm too warm. I use my free hand to pull the jacket off and put it on the rail next to me. The cold air wakes me slightly.

"Hey, careful it's still cold." Prince Gavril puts an arm around me again. "You alright?"

His warm hand on my exposed arm is far warmer than the jacket was. His body is turned to me, unlike last time, making an even warmer circle around me. He's so close. I remember the ship, his face only a few inches from mine. Is he that close this time? I don't dare look.

Subconsciously, I move closer to him and shudder.

"Hey." He pulls me closer as if to keep me warm. I think that's really what he meant to do. He freezes as the arm he'd slung around me grazes my back.. I think it surprised him too. I'm facing his chest. He's so close, so still.

I shut my eyes and take a deep breath. His hand is frozen on the small of my back. I think we're both scared to move, scared of where we'll go next. We hold it. It feels like a lifetime.

Please, don't take advantage of me.

This is better than even the times I made out with Jake. But I'm so scared. I am terrified. What if he... will he?

I dare step back. The prince lets go without any resistance. He relaxes as I step away. I catch him sigh in relief and close his eyes.

"Sorry, I didn't mean that to get uncomfortable," he apologizes. "And I just promised."

"It was just as much my fault." I hug myself.

Gavril smiles again, surprisingly happy. He takes my hand and kisses it. "Let's get you warm." He picks up his jacket and tosses it on almost lazily. I like how he moves. My eyes go to his waistcoat buttons. Does he look so slim with it off? I shake myself and hug my arms tightly, a barrier between me and what I want.

The prince puts an arm around me, and we go inside. I think tonight is over. I want to be in my room before things get worse. We feel alone here. The servants are gone. The plates are too.

That scares me. Is this when he'll make the move?

Gavril's eyes rake over the same places mine do and he tightens his arm around me, the same way Damian did when trying to protect me.

"It's late. We still have things to do tomorrow," the prince says. I can hear it in his voice too, a protective edge. He's worried. He is defending me.

Comfort floods me, which is annoying because the desire to kiss him in thanks returns. I want to get back to my room where this mess isn't a problem.

We're both quiet as he takes me back to my room. He only lets go in front of the door. He's tense in fear. Is he thinking I may try more? This is my bedroom after all.

I give him a comforting smile. "Thank you." And I mean it. He put up with a lot from this awkward encounter. "It was a wonderful night. I really enjoyed it."

The prince smiles, "Me too." He takes my hand and kisses it respectfully, ignoring the shudder that goes through him. It makes my skin tingle.

"Good night, your highness," I smile, fighting the desire to give him more.

"Good night, Kascia." I like how he says my name. He squeezes my hand one more time before backing away.

I smile, not wanting to go. I'm scared of it, but I don't want to be away from him.

That does it. I open the door as if in a fright and slip inside, willing myself not to look at him.

I shut the door behind me and press my back to it. I did it. I got away. I take a deep breath. All I can smell is him, and I like and hate it.

Damian stands from his workbench when he sees me enter and comes over to me. "How did it go?"

I force a smile. "Lovely." And terrible.

Damian beams, "Glad to hear it. You passed."

"What?" I pull away from the door and go to brush out my hair as a distraction.

"What? You think I actually enjoyed making that scanty dress? Well, the first one. This one was a bit more fun." Damian smiles as he casually walks the room.

I blink as he paces. "What?" That was a test?

Of course! That's why it was so different for Damian. That's why he let me cover as much as I wanted. That's why the prince behaved the way he did.

I thought I'd be hurt that he'd try to seduce me. Finding out he did only hoping I'd reject him feels so much worse. Not only that, he'd done that exact thing with the other girls. He was acting the whole time. It was to see if I could pull away. I start braiding my hair, shoving down those feelings.

"Oh, of course. Explains it." I am the only one who felt any real attraction. I feel so stupid and hurt.

This was why I didn't want to play this game. Can I take more of this after Jake ripped my heart apart? I was only just getting it back together.

"Well, to an extent, yes. But I saw the prince in the hall. I think it is fair to say you turned his head," Damian smiles softly.

"Well, wouldn't that..." How did he see him in the hall just now?

"He was struggling. I could tell. He likes you, Kascia."

"You do a good job." I force a smile. How could I think it's what he wanted to do?

But what scares me more is how much I wish it was genuine for both of us. I want to cry to Damian as I had once cried to my mother. I'm so scared to love him, yet I'm sick with how badly I like him.

"My lady, I have said it before. I only bring out what you already have. I never add anything. He likes you, just for being you," Damian says, straight-faced. "I'm sorry my mentioning it was a test made you think otherwise. Honestly, I thought you'd find it comforting."

I pause, wouldn't I? I am scared of him pushing himself onto me. "I should... shouldn't I?" I frown.

I try to keep my heart together before I can even think about how silly my feelings might be.

"That is entirely up to you. But with your experience, I thought I should assure you that the prince had no intention of crossing that line. First off, his mother would lose her over-worried mind." Damian rolls his eyes. "And secondly, and more importantly, because he was simply not raised to behave that way. I have no doubt, however, that his reactions to you were entirely real."

"I know, it's silly." Damian is right; that should be comforting.

But all I can think is he did it because he had to. He must have struggled with the others. I try not to picture him being that close to Ericka or the others. I'm in such trouble. I'm jealous.

"I didn't say that." Damian smiles softly. "Just... surprising. Still, I am sorry my words of assurance brought you grief."

"Don't worry; it wasn't you." I already was struggling enough.

I bite my lip. He's right. I really should be comforted. What's wrong with me? I guess it's the hurt that I was the only one tempted. I might have slapped him if I realized it in the moment. Now... I hate myself for falling for it again. I'd just warned myself not to.

Damian lets out a breath. "Did you at least enjoy the evening?"

I smile a little and nod, still hugging myself. "I did, mostly. Until it got, I suppose, to the real test part." I look down. "I'm going to break myself all over again, aren't I?" My heart cracks just a little.

"Not necessarily. Kascia, please remember, that while these are tests, it is all extremely real for him. I may not have seen what he did, but I know the prince's character, and I've seen the way he looks at you. No one asks him to do that," Damian says plainly.

"But he doesn't choose either," I remind both of us.

"But his heart doesn't know that." Damian's face softens to a smile. "Love is illogical. The mind may require strict obedience and discipline, but that doesn't mean the heart will listen. Sometimes, our heart makes a decision before we ever realize one was made."

"So what's better? Winning his heart only to risk ripping it away or trying not to trap him and trying to win?" I frown. I don't want him to feel the pain I'd felt. This isn't fair to him or any of us. We were mad to sign up for this.

"Well... his father does consider his feelings, so there is hope for him," Damian replies.

I nod. "This is only going to get harder, isn't it?" It was easier when I didn't want to win.

"Sadly, I can't deny it." Damian gives me a sympathetic smile. "But the best things in life don't come easy. They require patience and hard work. And honestly, I expect no less from this contest."

I nod tiredly. I realize I should change and step behind the changing screen. "You know, you don't have to wait up for me," I tell him.

"I do if I'm to help you with the night routine," He smiles.

"My maids can do that," I say and start looking to see if my dress slips off or has a zipper.

"They looked tired, so I dismissed them for the night," he says.

I smile a bit. "Still, you don't have to be the one checking on me. You have a life, I'm sure." He shouldn't always have to stress about mine.

"I suppose you could say I'm married to my work."

"You have a ring and all," I tease as I step out and start to work on washing off my makeup.

"Yes, well. She is always watching over me," Damian says, fiddling with his ring.

"Oh," I frown, "sorry." I wish I hadn't teased him about it now.

Damian meets my eyes and smiles gently. "It's quite alright. It was a long time ago."

I nod a little. "You don't look that old."

"I get that a lot," Damian smiles. "But I am older than I look."

"What aren't you good at?" I keep it up as I wash my face. If he is older, it explains why I feels so safe with him, like a parent.

He smiles a little more as he moves to the bench. "I thought we'd answered that one already. I use my time well. I don't like to stop learning and trying new things. I suppose that's why I have the talents I do."

"I suppose so," I agree, drying my face and sitting on my bed as is my habit. "And you find unique places to use them."

"Well," he smiles, clasping his hands behind him, "my talents are no good to me if they aren't used to help others."

"Suppose not," I sigh heavily. I'm out of distractions.

"I'll go fetch your tea now." Damian smiles.

"Thank you." I smile as Damian leaves.

I try to figure out what to do to keep busy. I want to write to my mother, but I'm unsure what to put in a letter. So much changed so fast.

How do I explain it and not mistakenly spill it all to Dad before I'm ready? I miss them so badly. Mom would be so helpful in this heartache. I wonder if using the code of my apprentice will help me avoid Dad's eyes. I can only hope it will help patch up my heart too.

Chapter 32

I wake to my maids singing the cutest little trio piece. I'd never heard it before. I smile and listen for a while before I get up. They greet me happily and start our routine.

Damian walks in. "Good morning, ladies." He smiles, swinging his cane as he walks over to the workbench.

"Good morning," I wish him as the other girls chirp the same.

"Plans for the day?" Vivian asks as she finishes framing my curls with little twists of her fingers. I can't help but notice how she smiles at how easily my hair shapes the way she wants.

"Well, the ball is ever approaching, and we don't want it to sneak up on us," Damian smiles as he takes a seat. "So I think we'll start planning for that." He pulls out his notebook and shifts through the pages.

I swallow. "What were you thinking?"

Then there is a knock on the door. Odd, only the prince knocks. Flur is surprised and jumps to the door. A young man steps in.

I've never seen him before, but his presence immediately brings an air of warmth and peace, like how it feels to walk into a warm room with a nice fire after traversing the icy tundra. He has stunning, almond-shaped, vivid electric blue eyes that stand out. His black hair is a stylish, curling mess. He's paler than most Purerahians, not as pale as Damian, more like me.

There's something about him. I can't put my finger on it. He smiles a huge, inviting, charming smile. I swear even Vivian relaxes.

He keeps that huge grin in place as he steps over to Damian, holding a tea tray in one hand. "You forgot your morning tea. I think you're broken."

"Well, when you have other things first thing in the morning, some things get lost." Damian smiles and nods to him. I'd almost forgotten before getting ready for my date I'd ask Damian to post a letter for me. I'd debated writing Dad, but after how we left it when I last saw him, I don't even know what to say. "Thank you, brother," Damian smiles and nods to him.

I frown. Brother? This man isn't wearing a servant uniform. He is dressed casually, a white shirt, a blue waistcoat that matches his eyes, decorated with yellow scrollwork, dark brown trousers with black boots. It's nicely put together. It matches Damian's style.

"Your leaf juice." The man presents the tea dramatically.

I frown while my maids giggle madly.

Damian smiles and rolls his eyes. "It isn't leaf juice, Cedrick; leaves don't produce juice. We've had this discussion before," he says, but he can't help but smile at him.

"That's all it is," the man says. He looks around the room. My maids are almost staring. He smiles and even I blush. He has a dazzlingly charming smile. My maids giggle worse than before.

When I don't, his eyes go to me, and he grins. Oh, his grin is worse. I look to the sky, and my maids lose it.

"Are you satisfied?" Damian asks him, tilting his head.

"With that? Yeah," he nods quickly. "Look at you all sewing...y?" His voice goes up as he tries to find a word.

"Actually, we've not gotten to the sewing yet." Damian casually looks over his papers. "Just designing a dress for the ball."

"Ah, costume," he nods, looking over at Damian's notebook.

He is a pretty boy. My maids can't keep their eyes off him. They've paused their work. How could they be brothers? They're so different.

"Exactly," Damian nods and looks at him. "Did you really come all this way just to bring me tea?" He arches a brow with that knowing smile.

"Yes," the man nods. I notice something strange on his hand. A burn mark?

Damian lets out a sigh, "That bored?"

"Yup."

"Well, if you are going to interrupt, we might as well introduce you to the room." Damian turns to us. "Cedrick, this is Vivian, Ro, and Flur." He points to each in turn. "They help me and keep the room tidy. And this is Lady Kascia, the candidate I have had the pleasure of working for. Ladies, this is Cedrick, my brother."

I smile and nod as the others curtsy. Cedrick bows his head to each of them. "Pleasure. Are you done, or is she stuck in the chair?" he teases my maids, who jump as they recall their work. They have to wait for me to stop laughing.

Damian smiles, concealing a laugh, "You're distracting them, mate."

Cedrick clicks his tongue. "I know, it's terrible. I just can't help it. I'm so distracting all the time." The girls and I giggle.

Damian grins and looks at his brother, smiling through a sigh. "Well, I did always say you have a pretty face."

"You did," Cedrick nods.

"Well, as long as you're here. Perhaps you can help me," Damian says.

"Oh?" Cedrick raises an eyebrow.

"See, as I mentioned, the ball is approaching, and while Kascia is a dancer, ballroom dancing is a little different than ballet. I'm thinking a refresher course would be helpful."

That would be a good idea. But with him?

"Ah! Sounds lovely," Cedrick pauses. "Why don't you do it?"

"Because it is more beneficial and easier to give corrections when I can see both sides," Damian says, taking a sip of tea.

"Alright," Cedrick shrugs. "Sounds good."

"Dance shoes then," Vivian snaps herself to attention.

"She has breakfast first," Flur reminds her. Vivian flushes. "And maybe we can pick a more fun dress after."

"Oo!" Ro bounces on her heels.

"Then it is settled. We'll start after breakfast," Damian says.

"I," Cedrick says dramatically, "will warm up." And he grabs Vivian's hand and spins her around. She almost loses her balance, but Cedrick catches her.

"Oh, come off it." Damian walks over and pushes his brother's head playfully.

I smile. I've never seen Damian playful.

I go to breakfast. I smile at Lilly and the others.

"How was your date?" Azalea asks.

"It was good."

"He behave?" Lilly asks.

I catch on. "You had yours?"

"You were last," Jonquil complains.

I flush a bit pink. "Well, yes again."

"So how was it?" Lilly asks.

"Fine. I'm still here," I point out.

"Good," Bella beams. Dahlia rolls her eyes.

I'm halfway through my meal when the doors open, and Cedrick walks in.

The girls all stare at him. "Don't mind me. I just lost something I'm looking for," Cedrick says and starts peering around the room.

Every girl in the room is watching him, a few open-mouthed. Hanna's almost drooling, leaning over to get a better view, almost falling out of her seat. Dahlia closes her mouth and sits back grumpily. Ericka whispers to Forsythia, and they both nod.

"Who is that?" Lilly asks. "I've never seen that servant before."

"He's Damian's brother. He's not an attendant. He is a consultant for the guard," I say.

"If I lose, he's mine," Ericka says. Forsythia snaps no way in heaven or hell.

Finally, Cedrick stands upright. "Found it." He sits with Damian. I hadn't ever noticed he sat at the servants' table. It's hidden in a corner with decorative pillars blocking it. The girls are still trying to see him. Kamala almost falls out of her seat.

The king and queen's faces are anxious. I guess seeing their military consultant at breakfast is not a good sign.

The prince is watching us with a slight frown. Oh vene! Is Cedrick a test? To see if we decide a cuter boy is better? A princess is loyal, right? I blush.

The prince sees and smiles. I beam back, glad he noticed me over Cedrick then I flush. I shouldn't be so happy about it.

"What is he doing here," Jonquil asks, "If he's military?"

"He likes to tease Damian?" I guess.

"Your attendant?" Jonquil snaps.

"Yeah. He's Damian's brother," I remind her.

"They don't look alike," Jonquil says.

"Brothers don't always," Lilly points out. "They have the same hair."

"Color. Your attendant has straight hair, and the other one has messy curls," Jonquil says.

"Really cute ones," Lilly sighs, twirling one of her fingers. She's thinking about playing with them. I hit her arm. He's not that cute. He's cute, but not that cute.

Jonquil huffs, "He's a trick, you know. The king and queen see you drooling over him, you go home."

That gets everyone in earshot to start eating again. I look over at Prince Gavril. I hope it's a test, because if its not he just found out how quickly the girls will turn on him.

The prince sees me looking again and smiles then nods at the door. He wants to talk when we leave. I nod, impressed. We've not talked outside dates or formal meetings yet.

After breakfast, some stay to watch Cedrick.

The prince finishes a bit before me and gets up when I do and meets me in the hall. "Are you okay?"

"Yeah, why?" I frown.

"I just... after last night. I felt bad."

"It was a test. I know." I look down.

"Oh, well, it was, but that's why I feel bad. I... I feel like I used you."

"You did it to everyone. You say sorry to all of them?" I ask, last night's ache returning as I hug myself.

"Well, no." Gavril rubs his neck uncomfortably. "I just... I know you were scared, and I had to push. And I feel like a real jerk. I'm sorry. I shouldn't have dragged it out. I was trying to be polite about it. I..." He takes a deep breath and lets his hand drop with a heavy sigh. "I just... it was nice. I'm so sorry. I was so worried about wronging you. I kept struggling to keep my head in the game, and... I'm so sorry."

He is struggling too, sure, but doesn't he feel that way with all of us? "You should say sorry to the others then too. I'm sure you made them feel the same."

"I don't think so. I... I didn't..." The poor boy is struggling. He has trouble looking at me. He's stammering more than I've ever seen. "I didn't fear crossing the line with them. It didn't... With you, I thought I'd... and I really didn't... well, sorry." He's brick red.

"You wanted to do it?" He wanted to force me?

"No, no, I didn't want to hurt you. Not at all. I just... it was nice. I-I've never had anything like that before. It felt... it was..."

"What about Princess Zinna," I ask dully.

He forces an awkward laugh. "I'm told that didn't count. I only remember suddenly being unable to breathe and being pinned. I imagine that's what it feels like to drown or be smothered."

I manage a sad smile, but little more.

"So no, with her — and the others," he adds. "I didn't struggle to not enjoy it, if you know what I mean. I'm not used to being touched. I've only ever been hugged or hugged my parents. It was new and sudden and unfair to you. So please, forgive me. It was wrong."

So, though the test was why it started, his desire was why it was so uneasy for both of us. We both had wanted it. I nod, "It's alright. I was hardly better."

"So do me a favor and save the dress for later," he grins. I try to hide my anxiety at the joke, but his face falls at my expression. "Sorry, is that really bad? I'm sorry. It's the kind of thing my father jokes about, so I thought—"

"It's cute," I admit, "but with what's happened and is going on..." I glance back into the dining room where his twenty-seven other girlfriends are.

"Lady Kascia, I hope you know I'm not—"

"I should go," I cut him off as I notice Forsythia getting up. Several girls are looking back towards the open door. Some with glares I'd be afraid to give anyone. They saw I am the first to talk to him outside of dates. I flush as I get away from them, hugging myself tightly, hoping I can calm down before Cedrick and Damian arrive for dance lessons.

The lessons are actually rather fun. Damian teaches me the rules of ballroom etiquette. Cedrick is a talented dancer, better than I could have expected for a military consultant. Damian has to remind me a few times to let Cedrick lead, but even when I mess up, Cedrick rolls with my mistake as if it were his intention. Sometimes, he whispers corrections and repeats the move to help me master each cue to follow. It's unique. Between Damian's skill as a teacher, Cedrick's talent, and his warm, reassuring correction I catch on quickly. I'd rarely had better instruction, even if Cedrick is a silly goof who drives his brother mad.

Over the next few days, I catch Cedrick to practice and ease my stress. He doesn't seem to mind. He has a warmth about him that's peaceful. He and Damian both have a talent for putting me at ease when I'm stressed. Must be a family trait.

The only real problem with it is the other girls. They notice when Cedrick joins me in the practice room and start accusing me of "double-dipping" and there's hardly a girl who doesn't glare at me each time I come back after a dance. I do my best to ignore it, but Forsythia has a glare that could warp leather. Ericka's envy has her letting her mini dog Cuppy get into my things more than normal. Sometimes, I can't wait for the numbers to go down.

Chapter 33

Mid-week, a messenger comes into my room with a package as well as letters for me. I thank him excitedly and rush back out to the balcony to enjoy my letters.

I open the letter first, setting the box on the table behind me.

Mom's letter is full of worry after the attack even now, but she reminds me nothing I can do would make her not love me. She notes Dad has been anxious. Likely since he saw me. I am likely causing a lot of tension at home. I frown guiltily. I'll write her right after I see what she's sent me. I'll have to fight to find the words to say to her.

I put the letter into my pocket and pick up the box. I gently untie the string holding it together and lift off the lid. I smile. Perfect timing. It's a new pair of pointe shoes with a note reading:

Just in case, to protect you.

I frown. That's Dad's handwriting, I think. I at least know it's not Mom's.

I pull out the pointe shoes and examine them carefully, turning them over and checking the paper inside, but they look and feel normal. When I put them back in the box, I notice the box is heavier than it should be for just holding my pointe shoes. My frown increases.

I lift the shoes out and set out some of the protective paper on the table then put the pointe shoes on them. I take the rest of the paper out, but there's nothing else there.

The box is definitely too heavy. I put the paper down and feel around. The bottom of the box is crooked.

I carefully pick at it with my nail until I get a hold of it and carefully lift the false bottom to find more packed paper. I feel the pile; there's something hard inside. I carefully lift it out.

A leather line comes into view then suddenly a small cross guard pops out. I take in a sharp breath as I stare at what's in my hand. A white grip with brass or gold pommel and cross guard meets my eyes. The pummel sparkles in the autumn sunlight while the cross guard remains buckled to the leather sheath.

With a shaking hand, I pop the latch open. I hesitate a moment, my hand shaking over the grip, staring at it. Finally, I take a deep breath and pull it free.

A shining, sharp silver blade meets my eye. I take shallow breaths. My mind is reeling.

I'm not supposed to have this. This is what they want me to have. What Dad wants me to have. *Just in case, to protect you.* He thought I was scared of getting caught and being hurt. He sent this, so I can feel safe.

Something flutters in the corner of my eye. I look down and see a tiny slip of paper fluttering in the wind, protruding from the sheath.

Scared to let go of the dagger, I keep it in my hand and use my fingers to pull the paper out and open it with my free hand.

To save yourself and do the job if all else fails.

I drop the dagger and note, stumbling back. My back hits the glass of the door as I gape down at the thing resting on the floor of my balcony, shining innocently in the sunlight.

I am meant to kill Prince Gavril with it. I'm meant to take out the royal family that night if our people fail. He knows I'm scared, and his answer is to arm me, to make me the assassin.

There is a knock on the balcony door. I'm scared to move.

Damian slips out, looking concerned. "Kascia, are you alright?"

Taking deep gulping breaths, I manage to nod, looking back at the blade on the floor. "I-I'm fine," I gasp out.

Damian follows my gaze and frowns at the weapon. His eyes then shift to the box, and his head lifts slowly and drops in a nod, "I see." He raises his eyes to meet mine. "How are you really?" he asks with added concern.

"I-I'm alright," I nod, still gasping, "I..." How do I explain this?

Damian shuts the door. "Your father sent that, didn't he?" Though it's not really a question.

I nod nervously. I look back at the weapon. I don't want to touch it.

Damian stretches out his hand and bends to pick it up but doesn't as he looks at me. "May I?"

I nod and look to the side to check the sheath is there. Damian drops to a squat and snatches the dagger and sheathe, then carefully stands, placing one inside the other. He meets my eyes again. "Do you want me to hide this?"

"I... I-I don't know," I let out a breath as if that let all the tension go. "He... it was because I told him I was scared."

"I understand," Damian says. "What did he say?"

"The letter was from-from Mom. All he left were two little notes. First said 'just in case, to protect me' and... and-and the other..." I swallow. I half wish I hadn't dropped it, so I could show it to him. "To save me and... do the j-j-job if... if-if they fail."

"Nothing else?" Damian checks, arching a brow.

I swallow. "I-I didn't need more. He-he knew-knew I'd understand what he meant." Fear is slowly filling my eyes.

Damian sighs then wraps his arms around me. I accept the hug, and tears spring to my eyes.

"I can't do it; I'm scared." If Dad thinks this is the answer, what will he do when I refuse?

"I know. Shh." Damian strokes the back of my head. "It will be alright. I promise I will protect you. You don't have to do it. It's alright."

I rest my face in Damian's shirt to help me get my head. Just like I used to do with my father. Would I ever get to again? I could forgive him if I could just safely have him back. If he'd accept the truth. I regret how angry I was. I just want him back.

"I don't know how to tell him," I admit after a few minutes to get my shock under control.

"I understand. But be strong, and have courage," Damian says. "He may not listen at first, but if he truly loves you, in time, he will."

"So, is that it? I write him back and it's over?"

"Depends on what you mean," Damian says. "In theory, yes, you could write him and tell him you won't do it then not speak to him again. Or you could try to explain what is truly scaring you. That choice is up to you.

"Whatever you decide, stay strong in your decision. Show him that this does not change your request. Whatever you tell him, remember that you have the power to make a difference. Both to your family and this kingdom. And this weapon," he pulls back to look at it before meeting my eyes, "doesn't make you what he wants you to be. Swords and daggers are used on both sides. You can make this dagger as a tool to help your friends. You are what you decide to be."

I look at the weapon. "I guess that's true. I... I didn't expect that. He..." It's suddenly so real. I'd held the thing my father intended for me to drive into Gavril's chest.

I shudder at the idea and rest my forehead on Damian's shoulder. I don't dare say it, but I can't hurt him. I can't let that happen. I can't break like that again.

"I know." He holds me again, tenderly.

"This is going to hurt. What if I break? What if..." What if I can't do it? What if I can't let him go, or if I'm forced to and I tell my father and I have nowhere to go?

"Don't let him command you, Kascia," advises Damian. "Speak his language."

"What?" I frown.

"Show him that refusing to heed your request will bring more harm than good. There are still five born princesses his attack will put at risk, with no way to minimize that because all will be wearing masks. The only way to ensure their safety and avoid angering another nation to war is to either call off the attack until the numbers are down or at least agree to your original request."

My heart only sinks more. So I should find out what the girls are wearing to protect them, but then I have to pretend to go along with it. I grip Damian's shirt tighter. How could I do both? I hate my father for putting me into this place. I hate the Custods for doing this to me. There are so few people I don't hate right now. My lip shakes as fresh tears fill my eyes. What am I to do? And how do I manage to have the power to do it?

"Oh Kascia," Damian says softly. "You poor child." He shakes his head sadly. "I wish I could tell you it won't hurt, but it likely will. But that doesn't mean things can't get better from here. No storm lasts forever. In the end, all pain passes. This shall too. Until then, hold on, and know that you have friends that are willing to help and protect you. I will be with you every step of the way."

"Thanks." It's all I have to get through this. It would help if I knew what I wanted, but I only know what I don't want.

He smiles warmly. "Anytime. If you need me, just call and I'll be there."

"Will you get rid of it?" I look at the weapon.

"I can if you wish. But it may come in handy if there is another rebel attack," he points out.

In that case. "Can you get rid of something else for me?"

"But of course. What is it?"

I swallow and quickly step inside. I avoid looking up at all as I gather the impressions my father gave me and walk back to Damian, shutting the door again.

I offer the envelope to him. "I... I begged him for help to do this, and... he didn't want to, but he told me I could take these to remind me. I don't want two reminders."

Damian frowns and takes the envelope. His eyes lift to meet mine. "Mind if I look?"

"Not at all."

Damian reaches in and pulls out the impressions. One glance and his eyes widen in horror then close as he turns his head away in disgust. "Your father showed you these?"

I swallow and nod. "When I begged for help," I bow my head, "he said he didn't want to, but it's all he could think of."

Damian takes in a slow breath. "I have seen the horrors of war firsthand. With my brother's position, it was sort of... unavoidable." He slips the impressions back into the envelope without looking at them. Once they are concealed, he finally opens his eyes and takes a steady breath. "No one should have those images burned in their mind."

"Why I had to stop it." Or so was the logic.

He looks at me. "You can stop it without needing to see it." He taps his free hand with the envelope then holds it still. "I will, of course, destroy these for you," he says and bows his head to me, but he's more stiff than normal.

"Sorry, I should have... said something." I shouldn't have let him look without understanding. "I only meant to... Well, you understand," I sigh, hugging myself.

Damian softens and smiles gently. "Kascia, it's not me I'm worried about. It's you. He shouldn't have shown these to you, let alone let you keep them." He shakes his head. "Even if it was 'all he had'."

"We're just that desperate; it's... pretty bad out there." I suppose he wouldn't know.

"I understand. But seeing the horror of the battlefield only weakens or hardens the heart. And in many cases..." he sighs with a weighted sadness, "...it damages the mind. Sometimes beyond repair."

I look down. "Which is why it has to stop. That's why he kept them himself." I take a deep breath. "Why... why does it have to be me?"

Damian's deep green eyes rest on me with a warm, sad smile. "Because your mind is open and teachable. I feel there has been a lack of that in this kingdom for a long time."

"That is good, I guess." I take a slow deep breath, closing my eyes for a moment. "I just hope I don't mess it up or ruin it."

Damian's smile turns warmer, and he places a comforting hand on my shoulder. "I have every confidence in you. Now, come on. I think it's about time we get you ready for lunch."

I don't know how I survive lunch without incident, mostly no one noticing I am upset. I've almost gotten away with it when I notice the prince watching me. Oh no, not again. I avoid his eyes. I am not ready to talk to him.

I walk to my room with my head bowed, wondering how to word what I have to say to my father. I slowly go to close the door, but as I do, something slips past me. A meow cuts the air, and a black cat trots up to Damian and sits in front of him, large blue eyes expectant.

I frown. "You have a cat?"

Damian looks down and claps his face, shaking his head. "Oh, for heaven's sake. Really?" He looks questionably at the cat.

"He follow you home?" Ro asks excitedly, jumping over to pet the cat. The cat meows and leans into her pets.

"Must have. I believe it's a stray," Damian says with a sigh.

"Impressive stray," I compliment and try to call the cat over.

He trots right up to me and curls around my legs. I laugh. I sit on the bed and let the cat cuddle up. I giggle as he sniffs my ear and gives me a head bonk.

"Understandable," Damian nods. "You going to keep that thing?"

"Maybe," I tease, "if he'll let me or Ericka's dog doesn't get to him."

"Cats are clever. I'm sure he'll be fine," Damian says then eyes the cat and points at it. "Just no shedding."

The cat meows in complaint.

"I don't know if they can help it." I lean back on the headboard and stroke him. He purrs and curls around me then looks at Damian as if claiming I'm his spot now. I laugh.

"Sure, sit there all you want. Just don't come over here. I don't need fur coating my work," Damian tells the cat.

"He bothers you a lot," I gather from his tone.

"On the occasion," Damian says with a sigh.

"Well then, I can't keep your buddy from you," I tease as his purring grows louder. It is nice to just sit and pet his soft fur. It takes my mind off things. If only I had a toy.

"Don't do me any favors," Damian grins with a tease.

"Well, he'll wander off to you anyways." I see a ribbon bookmark and pick it up. The blue eyes become the size of moons. I laugh and tease the cat with it. He jumps for it. I laugh again. "I guess you need a name if you're going to tease us."

"Indeed. Playfully little thing, isn't he?" Damian smiles.

"He went right for it. How do you name a stray who is cuddly and playful and black as midnight?" I muse as he grabs my hands in his paws as if to pull the ribbon into his mouth. I laugh.

Damian smiles and shrugs, "He reminds me of Cedrick."

"I don't know if Cedrick is this easy to provoke." I pat the cat's head. He attacks my hand with velveted paws. "I guess you'd know better. But this one is cuddlier." I pat the cat again, letting him grab my hand and mock bite it. He then pulls up, watching my face with large eyes before he jumps up to give me a rather violent head bonk. I laugh, and he curls up on my lap to bat at the ribbon.

"Cedrick is cuddly. With his wife, anyway."

"He's married?" I raise a brow. "And still teases a room full of girls?"

"Well, that would mean that it was his intention to tease you, which it wasn't. He went in there to prove me wrong, which I was not," Damian smiles and sits back, arms folded.

I giggle. "Are you ever wrong?"

"Rarely, but it happens," Damian grins.

"At least you admit it," I smile and stroke the cat as he stretches dramatically, letting the ribbon tickle his nose. I laugh. He is a dork cat.

Damian smiles and shrugs, "Just don't give him catnip."

"Isn't that rude to the cat?"

"I have no idea. I only know people do it," Damian says.

"Maybe that's what we will call you," I taunt the cat as I pat him, "Catnip."

The cat shakes his head then tilts it like he's wondering if I'm sane. I laugh and stroke him down to his tail which wiggles itself free.

Damian laughs, "I'm sure he'll love it."

"Maybe just Nip for short." I pat him again. "Nippers." He's a good distraction from what I have to do anyway. He could "nip" that in the bud.

Damian chuckles, "If you like it, though you'll have to make sure it's a name he'll respond to."

"I get the feeling he'll respond to anything," I admit as I pick up the ribbon and pull it away.

Nippers chases after it at full speed. I laugh and pull it away. This time he almost slides off the bed, stopping at the edge before looking at me like he was saying "I meant to do that". I laugh again.

"Sorry Nippers," I pat him. "Maybe I can bring you to dinner, and you can make a show there and get some food."

I don't think he likes that idea as he meows at me when I pick him up again. "How did you get into the castle anyway?" I ask him as if he'll answer. He looks at me and flicks his tail. "Want to help me write some letters?" I ask him.

Damian looks at him then smiles at me. "Don't think he is going to answer you."

"I doubt it," I agree. "You run along." I pat the spot above his tail where his pelvic bone made a soft, flat-ish surface. "I have to get writing."

The cat huffs as if annoyed I asked him to help then told him to run off, but he jumps off the bed and walks over to the balcony where the sun is shining onto the floor. He stretches dramatically before flopping, just as dramatically, onto the carpet in the sunlight.

I smile a little before going to my writing desk. This is not going to be easy. I sit down and spend far too long getting comfortable, adjusting and moving the chair about before I finally pick up my pen, but then I fiddle with it as if I can't get a good grip on it. After a few minutes, I finally get out the paper to write on, but I freeze again.

How do you tell your father the mission you'd shared since you were born, that you cherished with him and believed in, turned out to be a big mistake? How do I tell him I don't believe it anymore? How do I tell him all we worked for was nothing? How do I break him like Jake did me?

But after I take a deep breath, I finally start to write.

My Beloved Father,

I find it hard to say on paper what I have/must say. I suppose that's why I felt the need to see you so badly. But I can't keep quiet anymore. I have to be honest with you. I'm so tired of playing the game, and I know that isn't going to end just because I voice it.

Being here has given me a close-up view of the royal family and the Custods they sent here. And I've had to do a lot of hard, painful thinking that has left me torn up. I know you did all you could to help me, but I no longer can ignore the truth.

I never thought the rebels would go so far, but what I saw was wrong. I don't care how good they feel their cause is, harming those who are honestly innocent is wrong. And I have realized I have done little to stop such harm in the past. I can't keep doing that.

I only hope I can put an end to the harm and fighting. I hope to ensure the future royal family does just that. That the mistakes of the past are undone by the rights of the future.

I guess I got all political there. You always were easy to talk to about these things. It's so hard to have these conversations one-sided when we used to discuss them so openly and with such passion before.

I don't know when I'll see you again. I hope when this odd game comes closer to the end then we can speak plainly and understand one another. I miss you and your guidance so much it physically hurts. I never realized how much I came to rely on it.

And on your question about the Harvest, I have no idea what anyone will be or what the guards do. We're not allowed to wander about. And the one time I saw the ballroom I didn't pay attention. Sorry.

I love you and pray we can talk safely face to face soon. I doubt I'll manage to make that happen, but I still hope and pray for it as well as your love and understanding about how hard this is.

All my love, your cygnet,

Kascia

A tear splashes onto my name, the ink still wet, and makes a kind of odd effect in the shape of the letters, but it's still legible.

I quickly wipe my eyes then the pen is knocked from my hand and a soft-surface bonks my cheek. Nippers had jumped onto the desk and is now rubbing my wet face with his dark fur, purring comfortingly.

I manage a weak smile. I'd had to scratch out, rewrite, start over, and pause to contain my emotions many times. And the words are still weak. But it's all I can manage. A pile of crumpled papers waits to be burned.

Nippers keeps purring and rubbing my face until I manage to stop the tears. I stroke him from head to tail in thanks. He likes that, curling up on the edge of the desk where the sunlight is.

I smile and let him sunbathe before I fold up the final letter and put it into the envelope. I set it aside to seal up after I finish the letter to my mother.

I express my fears without saying too much and assure her I'm safe. I want to say so much more, but it's not safe.

Nippers flops onto my lap as I set the letter out to dry. I laugh and scratch him behind the ears. "You're begging me to keep you," I tease him.

"Either that, or he thinks he already owns you. Cats do that, you know. Especially pretty kitties like him. Doesn't make him less annoying though." Damian gives the cat a bit of a smirk.

Nippers meows as if in protest.

I giggle and stroke him. "Well, I'm not going to make my maids feed you and all of that until you let me get a collar on you," I decide. "Then maybe, *maybe* we'll keep you."

The cat just purrs and settles into me as if to comfort me. I smile as I keep petting him. He's an odd cat, but at least, he's a good comforter.

Chapter 34

I enjoy petting Nippers. It's calming. I've just about calmed down when there is a messenger with a strange request from the prince. The messenger presents a very odd-looking dress. It's horribly out of date, and a strange mix of pink, green, purple, brown, and white. Once I'm in the outfit, I'm supposed to meet him in the practice hall.

I frown as I look it over. It's not a very flattering dress, but it's not exactly inappropriate. And I've looked worse. Those orange dresses come to mind.

I glance at Damian, but he smiles slightly, giving the dress a questioning look, and returns to his work.

I shrug and turn to the servant. "Of course, tell him I'll join him shortly."

The servant leaves, and my maids help me change into the dress. It makes me look quite funny in my opinion. Damian does not look up no matter what any of us says or does. I think he doesn't want to see.

I go down to the main room as soon as I can and find the prince waiting for me with a smile. "I can't believe you agreed to wear it," he says.

"What? You playing a prank on me?" I'm not in the mood. It's been a hard day.

"No, it was a test, shh." He puts his fingers to his lips.

"Test?"

"To see if you'd be obedient even if you didn't know why," Gavril replies.

A meow cuts into our talk, and I look down to see the cat following. "Nippers," I scold.

"Nippers? Cute, is he yours?" Gavril bends down to pet the cat. He trots up quickly and bonks his head against the prince's hand. Gavril laughs.

"No, he just showed up," I admit.

"Hm, well, we'll keep him around while we can," Gavril winks at me, "but now you get to learn about the next test."

"I thought I wasn't allowed to know about them," I frown.

"Sometimes they'll explain at dinner." Gavril keeps petting Nippers. "He's clean for a stray."

"I suppose, but what's the point of this?" I ask, folding my arms in annoyance.

"To see if you'd be obedient. Stupid, right?" The prince smiles up at me as he keeps petting the cat.

"I don't like most of the tests." I didn't like this one or the last one.

Gavril frowns as if in apology. "I can't deny that." He pats Nippers then stands upright.

"But it means I get to know about the next test?" I raise my brows.

"Father will explain at dinner," the prince assures me with a smile.

I nod a little. "So, we'll see some go home?"

The prince nods. "We're doing the last round today. This test was easy as I only need a moment of your time. Thank you for going along with it. I know it must have been... odd. Your attendant must have fought to keep his mouth shut."

"I look like a toddler's attempt to draw Little Bo Peep."

Gavril laughs.

I'm more than happy to change out of the stupid dress and let my maids take it away.

Gavril is right, several girls were missing at dinner. Amazingly, it leaves us at exactly twenty-five girls. By some miracle, we are down by half.

The servants don't serve us until all the girls are there and sitting. Princess Zelda closes her book as we all sit and the king stands up. "Thank you all for waiting. As you have likely noticed, we have reached the halfway mark of the Enthronement. I wish to congratulate you on making it so far." He pauses to cough into his sleeve. "Pardon." He clears his throat.

"This also marks the next round of rewards for getting this far. We know being a part of this can't be easy, and only one of you will get the full reward. You'll be given other positions of authority if you are dismissed from this point. If you didn't hold one." He bows his head to the born princesses. Only Princess Zelda and Princess Rose bow their heads in return. The others look nervous.

"And because of this and the popularity of this news about the Enthronement, we'll be having a public event to let the public get a look at you: a meet and greet, a small interview, not too large for obvious reasons, but it means a lot of preparation. This event, formally called The Presenting Ceremony, is already under preparation and more details will be given to you shortly. So please, if you need anything..." The king pauses again to cough, this time pulling out a handkerchief he keeps in his breast pocket. I'd never seen it folded neatly. It's almost always in a state of use. "...Let us know," the king finally goes on. "Also, with fewer of you, restrictions on time with my son are lesser and you are allowed more freedom about the castle, namely the conservatory and library are now open without an escort. Thank you all once again." He sits down and the meal begins.

"Wow, that is a big whoop," complains Jonquil. "Two rooms we could see with escorts."

"But that also means we can walk around more freely," I point out.

"True," Jonquil sighs.

"What kind of positions?" Lilly wonders.

I shrug. "No idea."

"Well, often it's mayoral," Princess Zelda says as she sets up her tablet again. How did she hear from so far up the table? "Most of all, if they plan on handing it to so many girls. But they may offer others the positions of advisors or managers of certain tasks. But your kingdom doesn't have many such programs to manage such as lost children, education, and the like, but I'm sure positions over farming or tourism are possibilities."

Lilly lightens up. "Like over rice farms?"

"Likely," Princess Zelda nods. "If it were in my kingdom, positions like ambassadors to other races would be most likely as you're young and pretty. But I doubt you have much need here."

"That would be neat." Lilly's eyes are far away. "Better than I'd ever get otherwise."

"What would you pick?" Princes Zelda asks.

Lilly thinks about it. "I guess over farming as I already know how to do that or maybe mayor over my hometown. I would like that."

"What about you?" she asks me.

"Um..." I lose, I have to avoid my father. "I don't know." What kind of job could I take? There aren't any art jobs in the courts. Just tax collector and that was not going to work for me.

"Lots of time to think," Princess Zelda shrugs. "I'd pick ocean research. It's amazing."

"But you don't need it," Lilly laughs.

"No, but it's fun to think about." She smiles at Lilly.

But my mind wanders to this upcoming event/test. "The Presenting Ceremony" sounds so ominous. I am not surprised some of the girls are anxious.

Our staff gets working preparing us. Over the rest of the week and into the rest days, the girls are nervous. Some do interview practice with themselves, Dahlia and Forsythia most of all. I think even Ericka is practicing with her little dog.

The day before, Hydie gives us a summary of how the event will go. The queen will introduce us then the representative of the press will ask us some questions that were sent in by the general public. They will allow some vetted people to come and be at the event in person and use live impressions to broadcast the event to every town hall and official gathering place in Purerah.

On the morning of the event, my maids wake me with one of their songs. It feels like opening day of a show. I'm nervous, yet excited, slightly outside myself.

I wish I'd studied more of the questions that Jonquil had highlighted in her newspapers. I sit there, trying to guess what they'll ask as Vivian works on my hair.

"Don't worry, miss. You'll do fine. So far, everyone you've met thinks you should win," Flur tries to comfort me as I close my eyes to let her put on my makeup.

It reminds me of when they put me in the midnight blue dress, but this time they go with a stunning green piece with gold around the hem. The top reminds me of a queen with a beautiful soft collar and gold designs making a V down the bodice to the middle where it blends into a golden belt. With my hair in a half updo, hints of gold around my eyes, and the Chosen mark perfectly outlined on the top, the only thing I lack is the crown. They finish with a perfect pair of golden heels. I look perfect as always. Now I just have to fill out the outfit.

The guards have the Chosen wait in the entrance hall as they prepare for the big event.

But we don't have to wait too long. Soon Hydie and her fellow attendants help us all step out onto the stage. Two chairs were facing each other at the front center stage. That's where the presenter and Chosen girl being interviewed will sit, I imagine.

Hydie is all bubbles and joy as normal. The twenty-five Chosen girls are spread out across the back in one line, but the royal family have thrones set center stage and elevated to be just behind the interviewer and interviewee. Hydie directs me to my seat where I'm closest to them, just to the right of the prince and a tad behind him.

I look over the other girls and realize something. All the girls are in varying shades of blue, most Purerahian blue. Some have national yellow with the blue as a highlight and others have blended them. I am the only one not wearing those two colors.

I wonder if Damian knew and wanted me to stand out. Is that a good idea? They look like they represent the country. What does that say about me?

The royal family comes out a few minutes later. The queen is wearing something not too different from me, but she went for the royal purple and silver. The king's jacket and royal cloak match her colors. Prince Gavril looks good in his lighter purple. He is the only one of the royals in gold.

The gold twirls in stunning patterns on his waistcoat bringing life to the jacket.

That's when I see it. For the first time, he's wearing the crown of the crown prince. The king's crown is solid gold with pearls and Purerahian blue and green gemstones. The prince's is similar, only it doesn't have the points. The queen's crown tiara is beautiful with the same pearls and gemstones as the other two, but had the look of blue and green waves rising to the pearls in a glorious splash.

The royal family takes their seats. The queen looks composed, sitting perfectly on her throne. She delicately places her hand in her husband's, squeezing it tightly. That's where I see the nerves. The way they rely on and support one another makes my heart melt. They look perfect for their people, but only because they have each other to hold on to.

Though the king and queen are nervous, Gavril is not. He isn't hiding how he's feeling in the slightest. He's wearing a huge smile, his teeth shining like the pearls in his crown. He's excited.

He takes his seat beside his father, leans over and whispers something to him that makes him chuckle, then cough into his arm.

The king chuckles a bit louder as he watches his son take it all in. The king leans over and whispers something to the prince who holds in a snort, but badly. The queen leans over. "Would you sit still? You're a prince, not a bird."

"Maybe we shouldn't cage him up like one then," the king teases warmly. "No one is even here yet; let him enjoy it." He covers a cough with his handkerchief.

Gavril ignores his parents' bickering. He takes a deep breath, sighs heavily, and sits back properly. For a boy who isn't allowed to do this often, he's containing himself better than I would if our places were switched. I can see more of his father in him than I'd ever seen with them sitting side by side.

A guard trots up the stairs and bows to the royal family. "The guard is ready, your majesty," he reports.

The king nods, "Let them in."

I see the king's hand go white with how hard his wife is gripping it. The king chuckles and whispers something to her. She nods and looks around as if trying to see someone, likely Sage.

I do a quick scan too. Godwin is standing behind us in the shadow of the overhang over the front doors. I spot two other people I'm not sure I've seen before. One is a man, dressed finer like Godwin. The man has an impressive dark beard with white cutting into the thick black coils. His hair is coiled too and on the shorter side for most nobles who like to show off their royal manes.

The other is an older woman, who wears a calm expression. From her dress, she's also a noblewoman. Were they the king's and queen's attendants? I'd never really thought about it before, but Godwin is standing with them and that would make the man the king's right hand and the woman the queen's lady-in-waiting.

I can't see Sage. I'm sure that's exactly how Sage wants it. I wouldn't be surprised if he's up high somewhere, ready to snipe out any would-be assassins. They set up the spot well. There is no place for an archer to get in their own sniped shot.

The gates open, and people begin to fill in. I can hear their chatter from here.

I take a deep breath. *It's alright. Sit like a queen.* I've played the roles. I know how. I fiddle with the ring on my right ring finger. I still haven't taken it off. I wish I had.

Sage appears and stands to Gavril's right, just behind his seat. He whispers something to the king. The king laughs, "Relax, you have it in hand. I trust you."

Sage narrows his eyes then looks at me. I smile and wave just to annoy him. He glares. I see movement to my right. I look over and see Princess Zelda doing the same. Sage rolls his eyes and looks back at the crowd. I'm sure he's memorizing each face.

Azalea, who's on my left, giggles. "He looks so serious compared to them," she whispers to me. "The prince and king are having a good time."

It's true. Both men are smiling and waving. The queen looks too tense. I think she's biting her lip, but on the inside, so no one can see. It's only her eyes that betray how nervous she is. She keeps glancing at her son. He and the king look like quite the buddies today. The queen's eyes disapprove.

The guards check over everyone before closing the doors. I should be looking, see if I know anyone.

A familiar face smiles and waves at me. I smile and wave back as graciously as I can, trying to mirror the queen.

It's the man who took my impression when I dropped off my application. He'd been in the impression of my fan club. I think, trying to recall his name which he'd signed on it. Adam or Allan, I think.

Relief floods me as I see no one I recognize other than that. No one to cause trouble today, no Dad, no Jake, no crazy castmates. I could live in my new world and focus on doing my best. I shut my eyes and say a quick silent prayer for help to do this.

I spot my maids off to the side, for once not in their uniforms. They wear cute little day dresses that make them look more girlish than I'd ever seen them. Ro is almost bouncing up and down in excitement. Flur is hiding her delighted smile.

Vivian is the only one who looks composed, admiring the setting, happy my dress matches the prince well and my seat position shows it. Damian is standing a bit behind the maids, watching the whole event with observant eyes, twirling his cane.

Soon, they have the crowd in place, and the king squeezes the queen's hand. It's her go. The queen lets out a sigh, glances at her son, and gets up.

She has mastered her art as a queen. She greets everyone and thanks them for their adhering to security. "It means more to us than you know." And I can hear she means it. "It is now my pleasure to introduce to you the girls who have earned their place among our nobility and one of whom will be your next princess." She then goes down the line of us, introducing our names along with a title they chose for us, where we're from, and our background. She introduces me as the Starlight Princess.

My breath catches, but I smile and nod graciously to the audience.

Starlight? Why am I the starlight princess? Jonquil is glaring at me. She is just the passionate one. Where did the queen get these names? She doesn't know us.

I look at the prince. Of course. He came up with them. That makes perfect sense. Princess Zelda, the curious; Lilly, the gentle; Ericka, the commanding; Isla, the faithful. These are all Gavril's ideas. I flush. Why is Jonquil the passionate? And why am I the starlight princess?

The queen finishes with "Caitlyn the bright" then hands the time over to a tall gentleman in a gray suit and a winning smile. His smile shines out from his face, contrasting his dark skin, making his smile and eyes stand out all the more.

They go backwards, starting at Caitlyn and working towards Princess Rose.

"What do you think of the prince?" "Gotten a kiss yet?" The questions are shot then flutter by like confetti out of a cracker. "What do you love most about the palace?" But now and then they'll throw in a hard one. He asks Rhonda, "How do you feel about being under constant attack?"

The poor thing stammers for a few good seconds, but it feels like a minute of stage time, before saying she feels sure the guards had us safe. But her answer convinces no one. The poor thing punched her ticket home.

I try to mentally prepare for the questions they are asking as well as any they may throw at me. I feel confident until they get to Azalea. I'm next. I forget all of my padded answers and scramble to find them. I think I have it just as Azalea curtsies to the crowd and returns to her seat.

I take a deep breath and stand as my name is called. I'm thankful for the heels and dress that help me walk like a princess and feel confident doing it. I sit down across from the master of ceremonies.

The big grin of the moderator makes my heart race. I miss my scripts. They kept me safe. There is no net on this stage.

"You look stunning," the moderator praises me.

"Thank you. You look nice too," I say, making him and the onlookers laugh. "But I have my attendant and maids to thank for that. They are the best."

"Not one of the best?"

"No. The best."

"Guess we'll have to run a poll," the moderator laughs.

I laugh with the crowd, "He'll like that."

"Hm, we'll have to make sure to get his comment." The moderator's smile grows. "But back to business. How is life at the palace?"

One heartbreak after another, but I'm getting over it. Of course, I don't say that.

"It's been wonderful. I adore my maids. My first attendant wasn't great, but my new one is perfect." I keep on that track. It keeps them away from harder questions. Deflect, that's what they say, right? "And I like spending time with them and going into the Ladies' Chamber with the other Chosen to play games or just talk or share talents."

"What kind of talents?"

"Well, a lot of the other girls play instruments or teach us about their former work. It started when Azalea," I nod over at her, "wanted to play the flute for me while I danced. It was a dream she'd always had. Some others came along and we made a party out of it."

"Sounds like a ball. You and the girls get along then?"

"Oh, of course," I smile. *Even if I want to throw the dog away.* "I love spending time with them. It's sad when they go home. It will be weird when more of us are gone. We still feel like such a large group. I am still trying to get to know them all."

"Sounds tricky. There are twenty-five. Who do you think isn't going to make the cut?"

That was a new one. I am not prepared for that. "Oh, I have no idea. They all seem so good," I say. "But I guess someone has to go home. I'm just glad I don't have to pick." I'm beating myself up for that first reply. I'm not sure saying "I have no idea" was a smart move.

"You sure no one should get the boot?"

"Of course not. I'm not the judge. I try not to do the job I'm not meant for."

"So, you think you can be the princess?"

Why is he asking me these harder questions? The others got one or two hard ones. Where did this come from? "I wouldn't be here if I didn't." I fight to keep the edge out of my voice. No reason to get combative.

"So, it's just a crown for you? Or do you like him?" the moderator asks the question he's asked everyone else with an edge to it.

I want to tell him to mind his own cursed business, but I handle it better than that. "Well, I wasn't sure if I would when I came here. But now, yes, I like him."

"Love him or the crown?"

I take offense to his tone. "I came here for my people," I state firmly. "I'm not here to make an idol of myself and take advantage of the position."

There's at least a beat, if not two, of complete silence. I try not to smirk. I'd shut him up pretty good.

"So, I take it he's not quite won your heart yet," the moderator gets himself back on track.

"I suppose that depends on what you mean. I certainly get excited when I have a date with him." I give a small shrug. How do I get the humor back? He feels too stiff now.

"Then perhaps you'll answer my question," he taunts me. "Do you love him?"

"Never ask a lady that. We'll turn your head in circles," I smile.

I feel the audience relax as they laugh. Confidence returns in a different way. I feel in control. I've gotten good at making an audience laugh.

This is just a unique improv game. That's all. I have this.

"Well, we only have so much time, so let's not do that," the moderator chuckles good-humoredly. "Have you kissed him yet?"

"I never kiss and tell. You can ask him," I say as a joke.

To my horror, the moderator turns to the prince to ask him. The queen's eyes become the size of moons as if just talking to him is a death threat. The king coughs into his handkerchief. I can't tell if it's to hide his nervousness or a laugh. Gavril's amber eyes widen but not too much as he tries to hold in his shock as the moderator turns to him. "So, you kissed her yet?"

Gavril looks at his father. "Am I allowed to talk to him?" He gets a laugh from everyone. The king is coughing his laugh so doesn't answer.

Gavril turns to the moderator. "You can ask, but doesn't mean I'll answer," His eyes sparkle as he looks at me.

"Oh, hiding secrets," the moderator smiles. "Everyone else said no. You two are being sneaky."

He's right. They all just said no. Did that mean they now all think we have kissed? I try to hide my blush.

"Have you kissed anyone?" the moderator asks to another laugh.

"Sure," The prince smiles, gets up, goes to his mother, and kisses her cheek. It makes her flush and calm down at the same time. She releases her tight grip on her husband's hand. That gets a laugh from the crowd too.

"Anyone not your mother?" The moderator gets himself back to seriousness.

"Maybe." The prince smiles as he sits back down. I frown to see his hands. They're shaking. I don't think he's ever spoken in a public setting like this. This is his first public event. And he just got pulled center stage without warning. Guilt bubbles in me. I didn't mean to. I owe him a serious apology for this later.

"So, was it with her?" the moderator smiles.

"I think I'm not allowed to tell," the prince smiles again.

"Well, that's all the time we have for Lady Kascia," the moderator turns to me.

"Are you sure you don't want to keep teasing him?" I mock, offended.

"Oh, she's a feisty one," the moderator laughs. "You'll be fun in the Enthronement going forward. Thank you, Lady Kascia."

I get up and curtsy to him and the crowd. I keep my head up, but I want to bow it. I feel terrible for dragging Gavril into the mud-slinging without warning. I also realize I am the first, and perhaps, the only girl to curtsy to the crowd and impressinor. Is that good or bad? I was raised on a stage, and you thank your audience.

As I walk past the prince, someone squeezes my hand. I glance down to see the prince pulling his hand back before it's spotted.

I smile a little. I accept his forgiveness. I take my seat, still wishing I hadn't done it. I take a deep breath and listen as the moderator tries the same tricks on Lilly. Lilly's biggest failure is she copies me, apart from turning it on the prince. But I don't think she failed. She just wasn't the strongest candidate.

Jonquil also aces this. She does a great job, even with those hard questions. She admits she hasn't kissed the prince without hesitation. Bella passes well, but with more nervousness in her voice. Dahlia, of course, handles it like a pro. As an athlete, I'm sure she does these all the time. The born-princesses fly by. Princess Zelda deflects by saying how much she loves learning about our culture.

I hear Gavril whisper something to his father. I look over and frown. His face has changed and looks worried.

The king is shaking his head and coughing as he often does. But the way Gavril looks, I can't help but wonder if something is wrong. I try to look away, but I can't help but look back at them as the next princess goes up.

Gavril takes a look at the handkerchief in his father's hand and hisses something. I try hard to hear. The queen then leans over and says something, but I still can't hear what.

The laughter of the crowd drowns out so much sound, they have to speak up. "Can you make it?" I hear the queen ask, but I can't have heard that right. Make it through what?

Princess Laurina impresses the crowd by talking about where she's from, where they work with the dragons in the mountains. I heard the princess even rode her royal dragon here. This distracts me for a moment.

Princess Neeraja also talks about where she is from, saying she'd love to have the royal family try some of her native dishes, most of all the king who likes to be adventurous with his food.

That brings my eyes back to them. It looks like I misheard. They're listening as if nothing had happened. Maybe they were worried about how one of the princesses did.

Princess Amapola talks about the rich history of her people and their ties to the first Potentate and the Merlin. That's when I hear the king cough again, but it sounds different. It's deeper; instead of just clearing his throat like it normally does, it sounds like he's fighting to get something deep in his chest out.

I frown and look over. The queen is squeezing his hand, facing forward to save face, but Gavril isn't as shy. He's watching his father with concern evident in his eyes. What's wrong? The king coughs all the time.

Princess Rose is finally up. I try to pay attention, but I can't take my eyes off the king. He's pale. He doesn't cough long, but I think I hear him wheezing. The queen snaps at Gavril to keep face, but even as he does, he keeps looking at his father. He puts a hand on his arm as surreptitiously as possible. What's going on?

Finally, Princess Rose finishes and thanks the audience, then the moderator asks all the girls to come up for an impression and a bow. I stand up, but my eyes are still on the king. The other girls walk past as the king coughs harder and bends over.

Gavril's face fills with renewed worry. "Father?"

"Aster, perhaps we..." the queen begins, but I see it first.

The king's eyes are vacant as he wheezes, his lips tinted blue.

"Inside now," Gavril says and helps his father up, almost picking him up with one arm. My eyes widen at the strength. I glance at the rest of the crowd. The line of the Chosen blocks the view of the royal family.

The queen tries to help support the king, but she has to let go to run around the other side of the throne.

Gavril is forced to pause as the king has another coughing fit. It sounds like he's having a hard time breathing.

I step in and move some chairs out of the way. Gavril's eyes meet mine for a split second. The man with the fine beard goes over to the king's other side. The lady goes to the queen, and Godwin opens the front door. Sage stands nearby, looking to be sure no one is watching.

They finally make their way inside, guiding the wheezing and coughing king. I follow.

Once we're inside, I close the door and turn to the family. The king is leaning against the wall, wheezing heavily, trying to get enough air, but it's clear he's not. His lips are definitely blue now. The man with the fine beard is kneeling close to him while the queen and Prince Gavril are doing the same on his other side. I'd never seen Gavril's eyes so wide.

Sage calls for two of the larger guards to take the king to his doctor. The two guards help get him to his feet with the king's man directing them. As they start to move, the king stops to fight another hacking cough.

"Carry him." The bearded man's voice is strong and full of authority.

The guards immediately follow the order and hurry up the main staircase.

Gavril and the queen go to follow, but Sage stops Gavril. "We need a royal to close out the event, or there will be questions."

"He's right, they are expecting final comments." Godwin's eyes dart after the queen and king before looking back at his prince.

"What?" Gavril sounds angry. "My father just had an attack. I think—"

"Which no one is to know about, Gavril," Sage cuts him off. "If all three of you aren't there, they'll think there was an attempted attack or maybe they noticed the king coughing and put it together. We need you out there to distract them." Sage grabs the prince's shoulders as he moves to turn away. "It's not the pretty side of being a ruler, but you have to distract them, Gavril. For your father's sake as much as anyone's. Not to mention your people. What if it got out?"

Gavril takes a deep breath and shuts his eyes. He nods, "Alright. Alright, let's get it over with." He adjusts his crown and goes out the doors again. His men follow. I quickly follow too.

A painful pinch grabs my shoulder and throws me around. "What did you see?" Sage demands, glaring down at me, trying to intimidate me.

"Uh..." I don't know how to answer, but the pull to help Gavril is overpowering. "I saw the king looked ill. Please, Gavril needs me, and they'll question why I'm gone." I meet Sage's eyes.

He releases me. "Keep quiet. I'll make sure it's explained." He pushes me away slightly.

I use the force to race after Gavril, and I take his arm when I've caught up with him. He jumps and looks at me. He smiles a little then frowns.

"I know," I say quietly. "Just stay strong."

He smiles at me in a way I've not seen before. He takes my hand and leads me forward as if in a dance. He even puts his hand behind his back.

The girls are still in line, taking impressions, a few are signing autographs. Gavril and I join the line.

"Ah, Prince Gavril." The moderator comes up to him. We let go of each other's hands instantly. "I thought your father was going to close the event."

"He asked me to handle it. A matter of state came up. It was urgent." Nervousness radiates off Gavril. I imagine how his heart felt bound and squeezed in fear towards where he wanted to be, and now he is giving his first official remarks to close out this event. His first, and he's going in blind without his parents' guidance.

Godwin suddenly comes up on Gavril's left and hands him a hastily scribbled note. Gavril looks at it, giving Godwin a look as if asking if he just wrote that. Godwin shoves the paper at Gavril before the prince follows the moderator. I notice Jonquil whisper to Lilly asking if Gavril was supposed to close it. They had told us the king would.

Prince Gavril handles himself well. He steps up to the center space looking perfectly calm and confident while I knew he is anything but.

"Thank you for coming. As my mother said, it's an honor to feel our people's support for once. I'm just happy to finally get to see some of you."

Gavril glances at me, and I give him a weak smile. "Thank you all for coming and getting to meet these lovely ladies," Gavril says with a small smile that always makes me smile back. "It..." he pauses just a moment, bowing his head with a small turn to the side, "...really has been my honor to finally get to see some of you." He looks the group over. "And I hope this isn't the last. I can assure you there will be many more events like this as the Enthronement continues. Thank you for your time, your loyalty, and your willingness to be a part of this. I know it's not easy. So, thank you," he nods at the crowd then looks over at us girls, "and you." He meets my eyes for a moment that freezes for a perfect second. He pulls away too soon. "Until next time, my people."

Gavril gives the impressionnor a quick nod, and they shut it off.

The crowd then presses closer. The guards keep careful tabs and stand between the stage and the people. Most want to go up to one of the Chosen and shake hands or get an autograph.

I don't look at the crowd. My eyes are still on Gavril. He looks like he's going to try to slink to the back. I glance at the moderator. He's watching him.

I walk over and gently block Gavril's path. "He's watching," I warn, smiling as if I'm apologizing for putting him on the spot.

Gavril looks at me a second before what I said sinks in. He nods so small I hardly see it. I use my skirt to hide the movement as I take his hand. I can't imagine how hard this is. For all I know, his father could be deathly ill, and he's here covering an event he'd not been prepared for.

Gavril gives my hand a quick squeeze back. I glance at the moderator, who's still watching. Gavril lets go of my hand as we join the line to meet the public.

A little girl races up to me. I beam. She's holding one of my old pointe shoes done up like Esmeralda. I bend down to sign it. Gavril beams at me. A few more girls run up for me to sign things, and I do. Some are just bits of paper or notebooks; others are more dance shoes I used to wear.

The first girl turns to Gavril. "Will you sign it?" She holds up the dance shoe.

"What?" He looks like he's never heard of such a thing.

"Give her your autograph, Prince Gavril," I laugh.

Gavril laughs and bends down. "Of course, Princess?" He raises a brow at the girl.

She giggles so hard her mother has to tell Gavril her name. "Layla."

"Layla?" I say as Gavril signs. "Like the first ballerina."

Layla beams and nods, hugging the pointe shoe the prince hands her.

"Well, I hope to see you dance one day," I tell her. Little Layla looks like she could explode with happiness before racing away.

I smile and finish with the others as fast as I can, so I can turn my attention back to Gavril.

Thankfully, other girls get more attention for autographs, so I make sure Gavril's okay.

He's watching with careful eyes as if it's up to him to make sure nothing happens.

"Hey," I whisper and touch his arm. "It's alright."

He huffs and shakes his head. I can tell he's thankful for my attempt, but his mind isn't here. It's back up in the castle. Who could blame him? I want to ask him what happened, but now is not the time. I try to hide it with my skirt once more as I take his hand and squeeze it. He forces a small smile. I watch him with concern. I wish I could do more.

Finally, the guards dismiss the crowd. I wave to them as they go with Princess Zelda and a few others, but after Layla is out of sight, I race inside.

Gavril is already on his way up the staircase. "Gavril!"

He stops and turns to look at me. I pause. I realize what I've done. I'd called him without his title. He smiles a little and shakes his head.

"Later. It's okay. I just... if you need me," I say.

He smiles, nods that he understands, and turns back up the staircase.

"Like he'd need you," Dahlia bumps into me as the girls come in.

"I can try just like you," I reply coolly, making sure they don't see the seriousness of the situation. They don't want anyone to know, I'll keep their secret no matter how bad it makes me look.

Chapter 35

We are sent to our rooms to "rest" the rest of the day, so dinner will be brought up.

"Um... can I ask an awkward question?" I ask my maids as they help me change.

"Sure," Vivian smiles.

"Does... is something wrong with the king?" I ask.

"Uh?" Vivian frowns.

"Like an illness or something?"

"No, miss," Vivian frowns.

"Oh, he just... coughs a lot," I say.

"Oh, allergies," Vivian laughs.

What I just saw wasn't allergies, but I'm not going to question it. My heart is pounding though I'm standing still.

Is he alright? I can't imagine what would happen if he suddenly died now. What was wrong?

Damian arrives partway through our eating. I invite him to eat with us unless he's already eaten. I'm enjoying the little evening without being burrowed in layers upon layers of satin. I even let my hair down. It helps my maids not see my fear and helped me cheer up, even if only a little.

Damian smiles and takes a seat. "You did exceptionally well today."

I flush. "Thank you. I was stupid though. I didn't mean to turn the attention onto the prince."

"It's alright," Damian waves me off. "It was good for him anyway. Better to have your first time be quick and relatively painless than to have it planned, long, and drawn out."

I chuckle, "I suppose."

"But really, you answered perfectly." Damian smiles and leans back in his chair, crossing one leg over the other.

"Well, theatre skills help."

We're finishing dinner when there's a firm knock. Flur nervously answers. Sage is standing there. He's alone. He looks around. He sees Damian but doesn't acknowledge him.

"Excuse the intrusion, but I need to speak with the lady alone," he says to my maids.

They look at me. I nod, "It's alright. You can bring up the tea in a little bit."

"Give us half an hour," Sage says to them.

They nod and curtsy before leaving.

I open my mouth, but Sage cuts me off. "He can stay." He nods at Damian. "You haven't told anyone what you saw?"

"No. No one."

"Good. Let's keep it that way," Sage walks over and leans on the vanity. "How did you notice?"

"I saw him coughing."

"He's always coughing."

"More than normal. And Gav... the prince, looked nervous. They had been joking the whole time, so I wondered if maybe someone had said something wrong in their interview. But then it got worse, and the queen looked worried. Then I saw his lips start to go blue before he had trouble breathing, and I just... jumped to help. I didn't mean to pry. I just..."

"You were in a perfect spot to see," Sage excuses me. "It was natural. And it was kind of you to help. But the best help now is to keep quiet."

"Is he alright?"

Sage nods, "Will be. He'll be back on his feet in a few days. He has these attacks now and then. They are getting worse with age."

"Is that why he's so thin?"

"Yes. It happened a long time ago. We have treatments, and he has a regular regime of therapies."

"Is it just a genetic thing?"

"No. Gavril doesn't have it," Sage says. How can he be so monotone about this? "It was rebel caused, actually. When Gavril was young, they tried a lot of means to kill the infant. Easier when they are delicate." I shudder at the idea. How could anyone... he was just a baby.

"There was an incident where the king was exposed for too long to a gas bomb. Clearly, he survived, but it left him pretty badly scarred. That's what causes his attacks. He has bad days, and sometimes, attacks like this. Stress or dry air seems to be a common cause. Today likely was both: the dry air, winds, and of course, having the first public event since the prince was presented as an infant. We should have expected something like this, but..." Sage sighs.

My people caused that? Anger rises in me. They were after a baby. I wish I could say they weren't my people.

I swallow. "Is Gavril okay?" I hug myself because it's the only thing I can do. I'd much rather hug him.

Sage narrows his eyes at me. Curse it! I did it again. "As he can be. It wasn't easy to deal with; it was the first he'd had to choose duty over anything else. At least, not like that. He and the queen are with the king now. I am sure he'll want to speak to you about it as well. Though for my part, I'm just glad you had the sense to help us hide it and get him in quickly. I hate to say it, but you were a help. Thank you."

I grin. Those words look bitter on his tongue. I smirk.

"You handled the crowds well, and you calmed him down. So you aren't a complete security risk today."

"Just today?"

"Don't push your luck. I still remember that day," Sage looks down at me, "And I still have questions." I swallow. "Just promise me you'll keep this to yourself."

"Yes. I won't tell."

"Well, you can talk to him," he nods at Damian, "but it doesn't leave this circle. It's not just rebels. Other kingdoms will take the chance to take over. The tourist trade is lucrative. Other kingdoms wouldn't hesitate to try to take it if they thought it could get rid of the rebel problem."

I nod, "So the other princesses most of all."

"Anyone most of all," Sage says firmly. "I don't like having to trust you, but you needed to know before you asked too many questions. Let me know if you have any others."

"Not right now," I state.

"Good. Until next time." Sage bows to me, nods to Damian, then leaves with a swish of his cloak.

"Such a pleasant fellow," Damian smiles after Sage, his hands knitted in front of him.

"Just to me," I sigh and get up. I climb onto the bed and hug my knees, thinking.

"Are you alright?" Damian's brows draw in concern.

"Just, taking it in." I look up at him. "You knew. Sage didn't send you away."

Damian nods, "When your brother is a military consultant, you get to know things. Truth is, I am different from all other attendants here. They were called for their talents for this contest. I, however, came here because Cedrick was called here. I merely saw an opportunity to use my talents while here."

"I got lucky," I smile.

"I'd say the same. Can you imagine if I volunteered, and Ericka was my assignment?" Damian makes a disgusted face.

I laugh, "I'd quit."

"Indeed," Damian grins then his face softens a little, "but I mentioned before, Cedrick and I hide nothing from each other, so yes, I knew."

"Must be nice to have someone like that."

But my mind is elsewhere. How could they do that to... he was just a baby. I fight hot tears. Tears of grief and burning ones for the anger at my people for being so cruel.

"To be understood is the best feeling in the world. Someday, I hope you have someone in your life that can get you that," Damian smiles gently.

I smile back. Then I swallow. "Damian, you've... Well, at least, your brother has seen war, right?"

Damian nods solemnly, "He has."

"Then maybe you can help me understand. I just... why? They did it to try to kill a baby. Why? When would that ever be okay? I don't understand." And it hurts. Did my father help? Did people I call friends do such a horrible thing? Was there any way it was okay?

"I'm not sure I can answer that," Damian frowns as his brows press together. "Frankly, I don't see an instance why that would ever be okay. But from what I heard, they have been after Prince Gavril from the day he was born. A babe, only a few weeks old, yet men fought at the presentation of his birth to break in and kill him. I can't imagine what kind of men they were to have such hatred in their hearts. I can only say the Protector must have been with him to have made it this far."

And for all I knew, my father was one of them. I shudder. "I can't understand. I just... I hope we can stop what we don't understand."

Damian meets my eyes with concern and nervous hope in his own. "I fully agree."

Chapter 36

We are confined to our rooms the next day, so they have our meals brought up to our rooms, telling us to just enjoy the rest days after such a stressful event, but I know better.

I worry about the king. I pray hard he's alright. I need a distraction.

I could try the library, but I'm not much for sitting and thinking. I'd rather be moving. The conservatory: it seems like no one is ever there, so I'll have the quiet I'm looking for.

I step inside and close the door quietly. Not because I have to, but something about this space just seems to ask for quiet. The cool, refreshing smell of the plants and running water is calming. The greenery is highlighted with more color now as we go into the fall. I walk around the main path, the one the prince used on the first date. It's easy to walk without thinking about it. I wander, looking at the little stream.

I'm so lost in thought, I don't realize I'm not alone until it's too late. I turn to where the river flows into a standing pool and jump. I'm not the only one. Prince Gavril had been leaning on the bridge rail.

"I'm so sorry," I flush. "I-I didn't know you were-were here. I just..."

"It's fine," Gavril sighs heavily. I can hear the frustration in his voice.

I frown. Was it worse than I thought?

"Really. I'm sure this is normally your one safe spot." If I couldn't think of a place to go to be alone, what about him? He likely still isn't alone. Sage is surely around somewhere, hanging off the ceiling like a bat or something. He's trapped and watched. He's hardly different than the poor fish that live in the pond.

Guilt bubbles inside of me. I forgot it's his safe space for the same reasons I had for coming here. I'd thought of running into him before. Why didn't I today? I'm so thoughtless.

"I don't have one safe spot," Gavril huffs and leans on the rail again.

I bite my lips as I study him. Everything about him is tense; his shoulders are drawn slightly up and close together. His hands grip one another tightly. His jaw is set as he stares off into the water without really seeing it.

I debate if he wants me to leave or not. He isn't telling me to go away, but he's not exactly inviting me over. "Have you ever?" I dare ask.

The Prince shakes his head. His eyes drop from the waterfall to the pond below. His eyes are open, but not seeing the pond or looking at anything. It makes my heartache.

"Are you okay?" I step closer to him.

"Depends on what you mean by 'okay'," the prince grunts and pushes himself off the rail, pacing from one side of the bridge to the other. Maybe I should go. I seem to be making it worse.

"Is 'okay' just being whole and in one piece?" He suddenly asks—of me, I think, but he might have just been addressing the air. "Or is more required." He stops his pacing and strikes the wooden rail before putting both hands on it, his shoulders rising. He shuts his eyes and lets out a heavy breath through his nose.

"I'll go with you're not okay," I try to lighten the mood.

"Someone does," Gavril starts pacing again.

"You want me to go?"

The prince pauses. "You're asking what I want?" His tone is full of surprise.

I blink. "Yes."

"You mean what I need?"

"No, what you want. Would you rather be alone? Well," I blush, "as much as you can, I mean."

He manages a half-smile and shakes his head. "No, I don't want you to go, but I won't make you stay. If you want to keep on your walk, I won't stop you. I know the castle can be confining. This is the closest to getting out you and I will get until something drastic changes."

I swallow, hearing the tension in his voice. I look around. "Is he alright?" I ask in a small voice.

"He'll be fine," Gavril sighs, "this time anyway. Or so they say, but they always give it with a lot of stipulations, like he has to keep up on treatments and all of that and avoid stress. But how does he do that?" Gavril demands. His eyes lose focus. "How does he keep doing it alone like this? When..." The tension returns to Gavril's shoulders, and he puts his hands on the railing. His fingers hold it so tightly I'm surprised he doesn't leave handprints. "When is it going to be too much?"

"Can... can't anyone help?" I ask timidly.

"In what way?" he snaps, but not really at me.

I shrug, "I mean with work and things. Isn't that what Damian's brother is for?"

"But it's not enough. He still leads alone." Gavril's jaw tightens, but I'm not sure why. There's a tension deeper than I can see.

"What about your mother?"

"She helps with what she can, but she's no strategist," Gavril says. "I doubt she can read a military report."

"Can't you?"

Gavril hits the rail so hard, I swear it cracks. I back away. I had felt his arms, felt him almost pick me up with one hand, but I didn't think he was that strong.

"I'm still not enough!" he snaps. "And to them, I never am going to be."

He paces again. Years of anger and frustration are in his voice, full of a powerful, hot, rushing waves. I hear the small cracks of pain and turmoil like dried-out soil. I watch as he paces, runs his fingers through his hair, tension in every bit of his body. "I just... there's nothing I can do. Do you have any idea what it feels like to be trained, groomed, told you'll have to do the work, and you're as ready as you'll ever be, but even when they need it, I... I'm just never enough. No matter how I try to prove it. 'It takes experience.' How am I to get it just playing at being a leader? How is running through endless fake situations going to get me anywhere? Why can't they just—"

Gavril tenses more, but he stops pacing. He puts his hands on the rail, taking deep breaths to control the tension. "If this keeps up, they're going to hand me the crown, and I won't have experience or help. He's go-going to drop, and that's it. They'll hand me a war-torn kingdom with no guide, no experience, no someone who's been there, nothing. I'll be going into this alone and blind. And I'm never going..." He sighs and drops his head.

"Sage told me to tell you I was an apprentice here. He thought it wasn't a lie. Well, it was. I've not once learned a thing about ruling a kingdom from either parent. I learn from tutors about laws, strategies of the past, swordplay, science, math, education all for what!? To have the best resume for the position in the world but no bloody clue what to do with it once I step onto that throne. Not one.

"I don't even know how it's going. I don't know if we're winning, if we're close. What we're even doing to stop these endless fights. I'm clueless, experience-less, helpless, and there's not a cursed thing I can do but watch the stress wear my father into nothing, and it's because of me."

I frown as Gavril stops, taking deep breaths that make his chest expand and collapse visibly.

I give him more time in case he isn't done before I dare speak, "Gavril, none of it is your fault. You didn't start this."

"He's this way because of me. He was defending me! That's why he was exposed for so long. The guard never let me forget it," Gavril snaps.

"Then... why aren't you as ill as him?"

"He shielded me from it more than himself. He was able to protect me. And besides that, I was young. It's easier for me to heal than him. It's my fault. Trust me. I've had guards who make sure I remember it," Gavril says bitterly. "I'm just... a-a diamond sword. Stunning and 'powerful' but too fragile to ever be used. What's the point!? The rebels are growing dangerously close to being right. I'm not able to rule better than whoever they want. I don't have a clue what I'm doing. And I'm not going to learn before it's too late. Time is running out for him, then what?"

"Have you asked?" I try gently.

I shouldn't have; Gavril hits the rail again. I see the crack in the wood this time. How strong is he? "I did! Over and over. I offer and what do they tell me? 'It takes experience in these matters.' How am I to get it if..." Gavril sighs, "...I'm not in the room. If I'm not even in the room to watch, how will I ever know?

"What can books written by experts who weren't even there do to help me? I ... I'm going to lose him before I've had him." Gavril's voice wanders close to breaking. "They're so busy protecting me, the last hope, that they forgot to prepare it for use. What am I going to do when it..." Gavril takes a deep breath. "...It's going to happen. It's going to happen with little warning. It's going to happen like it did yesterday. And that will be it. I'll be on my own to handle the longest-running war in history and be expected to end it."

Gavril shields his eyes with a hand for a moment. "I-I'm going to lose him out of nowhere, and I'll have to stand alone."

Last hope? Why is Gavril the last hope? That doesn't make sense. And why do they expect him to finally end it when they couldn't? Something sounds strange. But I can't worry about it right now. The answer will have little to do with helping Gavril.

"It's not all up to you to win this," I tell him. "It's not even up to just your father. It takes a team. His commanders, your mother, consultants, it takes a team. No war is won just on the leaders' shoulders. That's who gains the glory or takes the pain of defeat, but that's not how it works. You have to delegate. You'll have the same team to help you."

"The team that acts like I'm the toddler giving silly ideas?" Gavril demands. "How do I even earn that respect when even trying is considered disrespectful?"

"Is that what's bothering you, or the fear of suddenly losing your father?"

"Both!" Gavril snaps and paces for a few moments. "Without him bridging that gap, they'll never trust me. And... I-I need him."

I understand that pain all too well. "But he's alright?"

"For now," Gavril repeats, "but if they don't change something... How can I earn their trust when he won't let me?"

He has a point. I can't deny that. How can he prove himself when any chance to would just make it worse? I sigh, "I don't know. But that doesn't mean you don't have what it takes."

"What do I have? A lot of education?" Gavril challenges.

"One really stubborn attitude about wanting to try. You just broke that rail," I point at it. "What if you were able to actually channel that into helping? You're not as unprepared as you think. You're humble enough to listen to ideas others might not. You're observant. You've never met a rebel, but you nailed their personalities and tactics by looking at what they left behind. That's not a skill any of those advisors can teach you.

"You care about what the other side thinks. I about accused you of being a traitor for working for the royals, and you didn't get snippy with me. You wanted to know why I thought that way. You tried to understand. When was the last time someone tried to do that on either side? You're more prepared than you give yourself credit for. More than your parents or advisors give you credit for. They just refuse to see it. You'll prove them wrong. Just give it time."

"I'm running out of time, Kascia!" Gavril says. "He might not survive another attack. I'm never going to get through to them. I can't escape this without getting married. That's all they care about."

Why on earth does that matter so much? Does that "prove" he's an adult? And if so, why did they wait this long to run the Enthronement? "Sure that's not just a cover?"

Gavril pauses. He wants to say something. I know he does. But he doesn't.

He shakes his head instead, "No. It's not. It's been about that for a long time now. Grooming me, preparing me, then expecting me to magically change once I'm married. As if that's going to change who I am."

"Narrow-minded if you ask me."

"I sometimes wonder if they're not expecting me to actually do anything. If they just expect a true princess will step in and fix it all," Gavril mutters.

I laugh. That sounds so strange. So... backwards. "Isn't that how they felt about your mother?"

Gavril shrugs, "No idea. She never seemed to care to learn these more... violent parts of the job. She handles more of the budget for the war and casualties. But that's half the problem. When it happens, she can't help me. I'll be on my own with no guide on how to handle this."

"And you need one?" He's calmed down, so I dare lean on the rail next to him. I pray it doesn't break after how he's been beating at it. "You really don't think you can do this yourself?"

"No. I have nothing but a lot of books to throw at people." Gavril turns away. "I don't have a clue what to do."

"Well," I smile, "as Sage proved, books can hurt."

Gavril pauses then he laughs, really laughs. But it doesn't last long. His shoulders tense, and his eyes get lost in the water.

I watch him, my eyes flickering over his tense position. "You don't have any idea how to make a choice and accept whatever happens?"

"What if that 'whatever' is what finally brings my people to their ruin?" Gavril asks hopelessly. "I'm supposed to save it. But if I make a wrong choice, I'll surely kill it."

"Did they really not tell you 'you can do this'? Not once?"

Gavril thinks for a moment. "No, not that I can think of."

What is that like? Your parents not once telling you that you can be whatever it is you have to be? My father at least was sure I could do what I had to do and told me so. I was scared of letting his faith down. Gavril has no faith to let down, not in himself, not in his parents.

"Have you never had what you wanted?" I ask. *What you need?*

"No. Not really." Gavril shakes his head. "I just... waited until I would finally find it. And I've never found it."

"They've never given it."

"No."

I swallow, unsure what to say. This is not something words or even my actions can fix. How do I help when I'm even more powerless than he is?

Gavril isn't looking at me. His eyes are lost in the pond, not seeing it. There are shadows under his eyes. Was he up with his father all night? That likely wasn't helping. I swallow nervously and dare touch him, putting a hand on his arm.

Gavril starts and looks at me. I don't think he's used to being touched. But the tension in his shoulders starts to fade as soon as I touch him.

I heard you need positive touch to stay sane. Has he had enough of that to keep at least mostly together? With a mother so protective of him, I'd think he'd get too much positive touch. But perhaps now he's older, it's different.

"You'll find it. If they give it or not, it's not going to matter. I know you can do this. It won't be easy, but you have what it takes. Frankly, more than anyone any rebel or even Custod Council could choose. You're ready for this, Gavril. Know it or not.

"I understand you're scared. I'm sure you're hurt too. I know you love your dad, and he's still not even given you a chance. But he wants to. I can see that, but he's just as scared as you are. He wants to protect you. I'm sure that's annoying, but it's what dads do." Unless he's set on you helping him take over a kingdom. "Have you tried telling him you're frustrated?"

"Oh yeah, it went so well," Gavril sighs heavily.

"Well, you did your best. Just keep an eye open. You'll find your moment. And I know you'll succeed, married or not," I joke. "You could take the throne today, and I'd be sure you'd succeed. You have what it takes. Just trust it until you can prove it. I think the person who really needs to know you're ready is you. No one taught you what to do in that interview, and you nailed it. No one told you how to help your father; you did that. You were the one who was able to deflect the crowd after they were gone."

"You did that." Gavril shakes his head, "I don't know if I could have kept calm if you weren't there."

"So what? We all need help."

Gavril swallows and looks at me. "That is true." He smiles slightly then clears his throat, looking away. "Why, perhaps they are right about getting this whole contest right."

I sigh, "I didn't mean you couldn't do it on your own. I still fully believe you can. It's just not a bad thing to need help."

"How have I proved I can do this?" Gavril asks, watching me.

I sigh in a bit of frustration, "I just told you. I've seen it. I saw it in your interview yesterday. I saw it in your quick action to help your father while your mother panicked. I saw it in how you made sure we were all safe after that attack. I see it in how you question yourself. You aren't ever giving up on doing what's right by your people. A people you've never been allowed to know, but you are willing to endure this miserable life for. You could just run away, right? You could abdicate."

"Then where would I be? Food for rebels?" Gavril huffs.

"Or their new favorite son," I point out. He frowns, seeing my point. The crown prince rejecting the royals they hate so much? They'd want to adopt him before he could step foot outside the palace walls. My father would lose his mind in pure delight. "And you don't break the rules set for you. That's dedication."

Gavril flushes but nods, "I see your point."

"I believe you can do this," I say firmly. "I have no doubt."

"Even after you told me I'm terrible for working for myself?" he teases softly.

"I was wrong. I'm alright with that."

Gavril pauses, "I only got this far because of your help." His eyes return to my face.

"It's okay to need help," I smile. "Not like you've gotten much so far."

"Sage has tried. He's tried to make my 'education' more real as best he can, but he's an assassin Custod. He only knows so much, and it's not like my parents listen to him when he says I should join in," Gavril says. "I've needed a lot of help."

"Well, as long as you're not afraid to get help, there's nothing wrong with that. Not even the Merlin did it alone," I point out. "He had his brother and his wife. He had a network too. Perhaps the real secret is finding yours."

"I don't get to pick mine." Gavril bows his head.

"You will eventually. Just be patient and pray that it happens before you're alone." I take his hand. "Just wait a little longer. It has to be soon now."

Gavril looks at my hand then at me. Electricity fills the air as his golden eyes meet mine. My breath catches.

Finally, Gavril squeezes my hand back. "Soon, I hope," he agrees, looking down at our hands.

I take in a sharp breath at the pressure, my heart racing. I lose track of what we were talking about. I can't shake the feeling that fills the air when our eyes met.

We sit there a moment, in silence, only the trickle of the water breaking the quiet. It's comforting. Something is soothing about standing there, hand in hand with him, watching the water pass. It reminds me of late nights on the riverside with Jake. A knot forms in my stomach.

"Thank you," Gavril finally speaks, still looking into the water. "I don't know if anyone has ever spoken so openly to me about... well... anything."

That makes the knot in my stomach turn into a snake and slither around, making me feel ill. I am not. I am a liar. I came here to get my father off my back and make sure Gavril died in the process. I lied to him plenty. I hid why I came here. I hid how I know so much. I hid why I disliked him that first night. I hid everything. I'd turned my back on it, but I still am not perfectly honest with him. I don't know if I ever can be.

"I'm sure the other girls are," I cover.

"No, they're not. None of them care about the job or to talk to me about these things."

"I bet Zelda does."

Gavril chuckles, "Yes, but it's not the same."

"I'm sure she has faith in you. Everyone does." I can't look at him.

"Not everyone," Gavril looks at me, "and not everyone wants to help as badly as you do."

"I'm just more outspoken about it," I defend.

I finally look at him. He's really close. My mind goes to that night at dinner. I swallow. Is this just another test?

Gavril frowns, "What's wrong?"

"Nothing," I cover.

"No, it's not. What's with the face?" He sounds hurt.

Guilt pops in my chest. "I just... Please tell me this isn't a test."

"Oh," Gavril laughs, "of course not. How could anyone arrange this? Only you and I know about yesterday, and how would I know you'd come out here?" He pauses, "You were thinking of the chastity test."

I nod, "I just..."

"Thought maybe my intentions weren't real that night, and you're wondering if they are now."

Ouch, he hit it right on the head without a flinch. "See, you are observant."

"Don't change the subject. You like to do that." He smiles slightly. "I'm sorry it had to be like that. Trust me, it was not easy to try to ride that line." He flushes. "I... I knew you were struggling. I understood what you asked, and when you said it, it could have been over. But it wasn't over until you were in your room. I had to keep it up until we left, or they might have said I made it too easy. And it didn't help... I'll confess a small part of me wanted to. But when you said no, I didn't want to anymore. I wouldn't hurt you. It was harder with you than the others."

"Damian does a good job," I deflect, but inside, I'm relieved. He didn't want to push me. But he also did enjoy it a little, like me. That is comforting. Yet it can't be. Not yet.

Gavril suddenly tenses with anger. I stiffen in fear.

"How can you tell me off for not believing in me, when you love to hide behind 'Damian did it'?" Gavril demands with such anger I'm unsure how to react.

"What?"

"Honestly, I try to tell you you're good at something, and you deflect it to your attendant. It wasn't the stupid dress or your perfectly set makeup or any of that..." he struggles for the word, "...rot. It's you and always has been. You had none of that the night you snuck out, did you?"

"Well, no."

"And I doubt Damian sat you down for interview practice."

"No, not exactly."

Gavril raises a brow.

"Okay, okay, we never practiced," I admit. "I'd not have turned it on you if so." That would have been a good idea though. I should have asked.

"So how can you get so upset with me while you're using Damian as a shield and can't recognize you're good at this. Damian didn't help you get to the twelfth slot in the choosing. Damian didn't get that impressionist to vote for you. Damian didn't tell you to sneak out and yell at me. Damian didn't even tell you to help me yesterday, did he?"

"No."

"So why do you not trust that maybe you've gotten so far yourself?" Gavril asks.

"The tests aren't that hard," I defend.

"But this isn't about the tests. I said you were the hardest to try to trick into doing something wrong and you said it was Damian's handy work," Gavril sounds testy again.

I swallow, "Well, he did do a good job."

"But he didn't make it hard. Ericka could have been in that get-up, and it still would be easy to ignore her advance."

"I didn't advance," I counter.

"No, but I was afraid of what I'd do if you did."

"Why?"

"I..." Gavril sighs. "You really don't know?"

I'm terrified to know. Absolutely unwilling to admit it if it's true. "You don't have favorites."

"I'm not supposed to," Gavril shrugs, "but I clearly have ones I don't like."

"Who likes Ericka?"

"Her dog."

We both laugh. Gavril stops himself. "*You* need to stop changing the subject."

He's right. I do that without realizing it. "Sorry," I say. "I guess it's the actress in me. I deflect when I don't know."

"It's not helping."

"Sure it is," I smile.

Gavril groans and rolls his eyes. He squeezes my hand, reminding me that he's been holding it this whole time. "I'm not letting you escape this one, Kascia."

"Alright, so it wasn't the dress."

"Or Damian."

"Damian did set up the idea date."

"One time," Gavril points out. "And you aced the tests without him being in the room. It isn't him that's winning, Kascia. It hasn't been. You still caught my eye in that horrible orange." I laugh this time. "I saved you for last for a reason."

"I also yelled at you," I remind him.

"And I liked it. You were honest with me. No one is."

"I was not."

"More than others."

I don't like where this is going. I don't know how to deflect it. I look down at the water.

"Kascia," Gavril tries again, "you aren't just another one of the girls."

"I have to be for your sake," I remind him.

Gavril sighs, "There's no avoiding it. Sooner or later, I have to find some feelings for some of you or else I'm going into the strangest marriage ever, and really, I already am. I'm marrying whoever passes my parents' tests. Not mine. I don't get to choose."

"So why are we doing this?"

Gavril sighs heavily, "I don't know. Why not?"

"Because you don't get a choice." I have to remember that, or I'll go crazy.

What if I break him like Jake broke me? What if I ruin him for someone else? My heart is already shattered. I don't want to hurt him.

The prince sighs again, "Yes, I don't get a choice in anything. I don't get to help rule a kingdom, though I want to and have to. I don't get to pick which girl wins. I don't get to pick what I wear most days. Well, all days," he shrugs. I laugh. He beams, "And so, I shouldn't want anything?"

"Well, no."

"So, I'm not supposed to have favorites? I said early on I shouldn't. We're halfway through."

"That's still twenty-five girls."

"Less, a few more are sure to go home once my parents talk it over. I think I know who already. Not you," he says quickly. "So now it's getting down to choosing time anyway." Gavril starts to play with my fingers entwined with his. "Do you really not know? Even after that night?"

"It was just a test."

"Do you really believe that?"

I feared it. Now I realize the danger of the opposite. I'm afraid of being broken. What if I crush him? I already hate seeing him upset over yesterday. What will I do if I do that to him?

Gavril lets go of my hand and turns me to face him. I look up at him. He's watching me as if trying to decide something. His eyes flick down a few times before he makes his move. My chest rises and falls with my breathing, anxious, unsure I want to let this happen.

But he does it. He leans in and kisses me. He didn't hesitate once he made the choice. He pulls me in, putting a hand to the back of my head, tanging his fingers in my hair and pressing the other to my back.

It's what I wanted that night when he realized his mistake. His lips so firmly pressed to mine, holding them to his and sending sweet energy through me.

I shut my eyes and suck it in before I realize what he's done. He's so sure of his action, I'm not able to catch up. I put my hands on his strong arms holding me close before I return his kiss. The feeling sets me on air, my heart races in the thrill.

I don't know if Jake has ever kissed me like this. It's long, intent, and enough as it is. It isn't asking for more. But I get more anyway. Gavril kisses me again and again, and I let him, enjoying it. His arms around me tighten just a little as he keeps me close.

I can't help but smile before I kiss him back. He goes for it again. His hand on the back of my head teases my hair, loosening the already loose design my maids put into it. Some hair falls down my shoulders as he kisses me again and again, content with just that. To my surprise, I am too.

I can't help but smile as I feel my hair fall as if it makes me open up to him. He holds me more securely. Each kiss is deeper and more meaningful than the last as I return the kisses, over and over, each soothing and exciting me at once. Each filling my heart, silencing the fears it holds and bringing me to a happy place I never could have found again otherwise.

I don't know how long we're like that before he pauses. I take a breath. "We should stop." How long have we been standing here?

"Hm," Gavril sounds like he's displeased with my assessment. He kisses me again. I laugh. He is being a bit naughty, now isn't he? Who else has he kissed like this?

"It's not like I'm..." I start to say, but he stops me with another kiss.

"You're what?" he asks, his lips millimeters from my own, still holding me tenderly.

"Your only option."

My own heart shatters at those words. I'm not his to choose. I'm just part of his possible pool. In a very real way, I am just one more gem in his crown, another princess in his harem. He isn't mine. Jake was forced to be mine. My apprentice couldn't be mine. I grip his shirt tightly, not wanting to let go, but knowing I'll have to again.

Somehow, I feel more crushed and broken than I had when Jake told me to sell myself for the cause.

My words make Gavril stop dead, frozen, still holding me. I grip his shirt tighter. But I shouldn't; I should let go. But a part of me is scared to. His tension is just like it was before he hit the rail. What if he strikes me like that?

Oh please, don't get angry again.

I can say this for Jake: he never really got angry with me. At least not how Gavril does. I shut my eyes tightly, pinching them closed in fear.

"Is that really all you can say?" he asks. Oh no, the hurt in his voice is so much worse.

"Sorry. It's true. I just..."

He kisses me.

My brows draw together. What is he trying to do?

He frowns when my expression doesn't change. He bites his lip. Jake used to do that, but he bit them both and harder. Gavril looks more confused. He's watching me, trying to read what I want. His eyes flicker from one of my eyes to the other. The hurt confusion makes my heart slowly crumble like one of the worn walls in the burned district. "So did you want me to stop?"

No, not really. It was one of the best moments of my life. Jake had gotten me addicted and unable to stop before, but this is different. Gavril doesn't want more. This moment was plenty, and it was beautiful and wonderful for how little it demanded. It was filled with gratitude and contentment. It was pure. And... is it horrible I'm comparing the quality between them?

Gavril tilts his head when I don't reply. He's trying to understand. He reminds me of a dog trying to understand the new trick he's being taught. That makes me laugh. I almost forgot how inexperienced he is. Then I flush. Oh my gosh, am I his first?

"Are you going to say something?" he asks.

"What do you want me to say?"

"Um... anything? Get mad and push me off and call me a dog. Like it and kiss me back. Slap me and tell me to behave. I don't know. Something," Gavril swallows this time.

What do I want to do? Laugh and kiss him, but that might not be a good idea.

"I'm not sure what to say."

"Oh." He flushes a little. "I-I forgot. Was that too soon?"

"Forgot?"

"Yeah, like the day on the ship. Godwin told me off for being too close. I didn't even notice. He said with you being fresh off another relationship that was a bit rude. Did I just cross that line again? I keep forgetting," He sounds so apologetic and confused. I feel worse. This mess is not fair to him. And he doesn't even know why.

"Godwin is your go-to for girl talk?" I deflect, trying to figure out how I should react. What I want and what I should do can't be the same.

"Who else do I have to go to? Sage helps sometimes. And he's engaged, I'll have you know."

I laugh. I don't believe a word of it. I laugh so hard, Gavril lets go as I press a hand to my stomach. Gavril fights not to laugh as he watches me. He glances up.

I forgot Sage is there. I turn brick red and stop laughing. He just watc hed... oh, he's going to kill me, first for laughing, second for kissing Gavril so much.

"He'll survive," Gavril shrugs it off.

But will we? My face falls. I stand up and take a deep breath.

Gavril leans on the rail, this time his back against it. "Trust me. It's better to forget he's here if you can. I'll lose my mind if I don't."

But I can't forget he watched me doing that with the prince. I can't forget how he's watched me like a hawk, and he has every right to. I am a plant. Even if I am betraying the hand that placed me here, I am still exactly what he thinks I am. I can't play this game. I can't get Sage looking too close or I'll face the gallows.

"I should go."

"No, you just wanted a walk. I'll go," Gavril offers, "I'll take the bat with me."

I don't find that funny. I turn away. "This is your home, not mine."

I hear Gavril sigh deeply. I shut my eyes. He's disappointed. Why did he have to pick me? Why can't he just pick? But what if he did? I shake my head, hugging myself. I don't know.

Part of me hopes Gavril stops me, that he pulls me around, kisses me again, and declares he won't take any girl but me.

But he doesn't try to stop me. I go back the way I came, right up to my room. I try not to look at any of them and go right to the balcony to hide.

I feel like I should want to cry, but I don't. I just... I want to relive that moment and have hope. I want to feel free to love him and not fear ripping our hearts out and tearing them to shreds.

I bite my lips in desire. I let what happened play over and over in my mind, pretending I can still feel his lips on mine: so gentle, yet strong. He knows what he wants. I've never felt him be so confident, and I like it. I like it a lot.

A tear finally gets away. This game is so unfair. What will happen to me now? What will happen to him now?

Chapter 37

Two days after the event, Caitlyn and three others were dismissed. The table is arranged accordingly, and life goes on as if nothing happened. No one is the wiser to how close to a near national tragedy we'd come: only me and the royal family.

Bella and Jonquil in particular look happy to see the prince. I get a sinking feeling. Had he gone on dates with them in the last few days? Why not? It's not like the Enthronement isn't still going on. He has to be at least trying them all, right?

My suspicion is confirmed as we finish breakfast. Gavril asks Azalea if she'd like to join him for a walk. She accepts, and they wander off, arm in arm.

I hate how sick I feel. I hate what I've done to myself. I was right those months ago. This is a terrible idea. Dad was not thinking about what this would do. Not at all. I want to cry in frustration. I don't even have anyone to talk to.

I try to lose myself in music, dancing, whatever I could find. Dahlia complains I'm hogging up the practice room, but I don't care.

I find a distraction when Bella, laughing, shows me that day's paper. "Looks like you started a bit of a war."

My stomach fills with dread. "What?"

"The paper ran a piece to see if your team really is 'the best'. Look at the results," She offers me the paper.

They had, in fact, run a poll to see which Chosen girl's fashion the people liked best then followed it up with an article about the winning team. I frown and read the poll numbers. My team won hands down. There, in black and white, is an impression of Damian and all three of my maids with the caption "The Best Princess Team".

I laugh. "Mind if I take this?"

"Just make sure Jonquil doesn't come after it." Bella winks. I chuckle.

I go up to my room. Damian is working on... scales? Literal golden scales, I think.

"So, I heard you got your own interview," I hold up the paper. My maids burst into giggles.

"Hm?" Damian pulls himself away to look at the paper. After a moment of looking over the article, he sighs with a mixed smile. "So they did. Good grace." He frowns at the impression. "I look awful," he mutters to himself then glances up at my maids with a brighter smile. "You ladies look lovely."

"Oh, be quiet. You look just fine," I insist as my maids come over to take the paper. "I read it. So, you are claiming to be better than your namesake now?"

"I didn't say that," Damian says slowly, "I said he is my example and I try to test myself against his methods every time I do something new. I try to be like him and hopefully better."

"So he embellished?" I tease as the girls go over the article in delight.

"He did," Damian nods. "Perhaps I could get him for libel."

"I'm sure he was trying to capture your attitude. Your brother is right. You are a little vain." I can see his delight over outdoing the others by such a large amount.

Damian sighs dramatically, "And so it begins."

"What? You've earned the right to be a little vain. Your work speaks for itself and just look at these numbers. You could make any of us look this good," I insist. "This easily launches a lifelong career for you if you keep this up. You'll keep Adam in a job getting images of them."

"You think I'll find more contests to design for?" Damian arches a brow with a smile.

I laugh. "I mean selling the dresses you make. You'll make a fortune. Unless you're planning to stick around here your whole life." Which I doubt. Unless his brother stays, which I also doubt.

Damian shrugs, "I have no reason to settle down. As long as I have my brother with me, I don't need anything else."

I smile at him then sigh sadly, "At least you'll know how to make a living wherever you go."

The fame will help him and my maids for sure. But I can't help but wonder what's going to happen to me.

A messenger comes in, ending our conversation. I don't expect anything, but she comes over to me and hands me two letters.

I blink in surprise and take them. One is Mom's handwriting, thicker than the second. My gut clenches. It's my father's handwriting.

I dash to the balcony, wrapping a blanket around my shoulders as it is starting to get cold.

Why would Dad have written to me so fast? I expected another long wait. With shaking hands, I carefully pull the letter back out and unfold it. It's in code.

I spent the time until lunch decoding and still don't finish. I try to spend my time getting ready as if that will help me feel less worried about the letter.

My mood isn't improved as I go to lunch and find the prince and Princess Amapola are missing. He's really doing the rounds on those dates, isn't he? I shouldn't be so annoyed with him. He has no other choice, and I had to go and remind him of it. I wonder what the view from that dining room we'd used the night of my chastity test looks like in the day. I'm sure that's where they went.

I can't decide which is better. Thinking about that or thinking about the letter waiting for me upstairs. I have a hard time eating.

As soon as I can at least look like I'm finished eating, I get up.

My father used as few words as possible for the main message which actually makes the decoding more of a headache because I wasn't sure if I really found the right letter or just defaulted to that same pattern again. It's almost too similar to make deciphering it easy. I have a pounding headache by the time I decode the whole thing.

I sit back and rub my temples. Why does he have to make it so hard to communicate? Seeing my distress, Flur brings some tea to try to help with the headache. I smile and thank her. Flur blushes and retreats.

It's nice to just watch and not think about it, making my headache fade enough before I turn to finally get my answers.

Kascia,

We are running out of time. I've still not gotten a report back. What's wrong? Are they on to you? Do you need help covering? You got the weapon I sent you, right? Are you unable to get the intel? You can try more direct approaches. Flirting with guards goes a long way. Have you found the disguises for each of the royals yet?

Your father

My mouth drops open. I can't believe he sent this to me! Did he not read my letter at all?

Filled with anger and disgust, I check the letter one more time and even my code, but once I'm sure, I huff and throw the paper at the fire, feeling hurt, angry, and wanting to cry in pain at the same time. Tears blur my vision before I even finish making the throw.

He didn't address what I'd said. He pretended I said nothing. I know he understood. He ignored it; he ignored me. He didn't ask about how I'm doing, how I'm coping. He wants to know what was the hold up is on the intel. He still expects this of me even when I told him 'no deal'. He expects me to fall in line. I hate him. I hate him for it. He shoved me into this spot where my heart and mind are getting ripped apart, and he doesn't care.

I bolt from the room, unsure where to go, but I have to get out. I haven't felt this desperate and trapped since that first night, but then I could slip out. Not this time. Not during the day and not with security so high and where one false move will get me thrown out to my father who will do who knows what to me.

I feel trapped like the walls are trying to squeeze me in and stop me from finding the truth. But I don't want to do that. I don't want to be here, but I can't go back. I'm trapped. I'm trapped by all of them.

I fight to see through my tears, trying to wipe them away, but the constant action only makes it even harder to tell where my feet are taking me. I stumble as if ill, feeling lost.

I open the door to the conservatory. At least here, I can pretend to be outside the walls. With how little I can see through my tears, it isn't hard to forget I'm still, technically, inside.

After several minutes, I'm not sure how long, I hear a little tap on the conservatory post. I start and look up. Damian is standing there, watching me with a worried expression. I look away. I don't know what to say. I did just run out of there pretty quickly, didn't I?

Damian gives me a sympathetic smile. "I read the letter; it missed the fire. Don't worry. I made sure it was burned."

I swallow hard. "Oh." Well, that made my reaction seem even dumber. Hadn't I already said I am not going to do it? That isn't what is wrong. It feels like I just lost my father. He'd never been so cold, ever.

"Are you alright?" Damian asks with concern in his voice.

I sniff and hug myself tighter. "I guess."

"You don't look it. You look like your father just tore your heart out."

I swallow and try to wipe away more tears. "It's nothing. I should have expected it."

Damian nods to himself and presses his lips together before looking at me. "Should you have though? He's your father. He should care more about you than his mission." He comes closer. "You know I'll never force you to talk to me, but don't expect me to believe it's nothing. I've learned from working with my brother, it is never nothing," he smiles gently.

"What's there to say?" I try to wipe away more tears. "It shouldn't be a surprise."

"Doesn't mean it hurts any less. In fact, I would think it hurts even more because he's completely ignored you, repeatedly. Denying the hurt isn't going to make it hurt less. You have to let it out," he says and sits by me.

"But perhaps," he says carefully. "I'm not the best person to help with this."

"What?"

"You forgot something." Damian offers me Mom's letter.

He's right. I had forgotten. I force a smile, try again to wipe my eyes, and accept the letter.

My dear Kascia,

I nearly cried reading this. I suppose that sounds so strange. But all your life your father has driven everything. I had to make sure he didn't find either letter. I almost burned it, but it's a treasure to me. I always knew there was more to you, just hidden under the daddy's girl you'd become. It's why I knew signing up for the Enthronement was the right thing. Yes, he wanted you to do it, but it did what I prayed it would. It helped you decide for yourself. But with that gushing out, let me answer some of your questions.

Let's start by saying no matter how you understand my advice, follow your heart. I stand by what I said before,sweet girl,. If you run off with the prince, that's great., if you run off with the palace kitchen boy, that's great, If you come home to Jacek, that's great. As long as you want it. I only want you to be happy and to make your own choice.

Your father hasn't even told me about your requests. He's being as "sneaky" as ever. And that's about the long and short of it, and that's how it is with your father and me.

Just give your own heart a chance without those strings to anyone, the prince, Jacek, that apprentice, your father, me, just have fun. You can worry about more serious things later. Will I see you soon? It is almost November.

Keep hoping, keep dreaming, keep loving,

Mom

I smile a watery smile as I finish. She is happy with my choice. She is proud of me. And she's given me a way to say for sure to her, and hopefully through her to Dad, that I'm not letting the rebels in.

Damian smiles at my slight smile and hugs me. "I think you're ready to reply, don't you?"

I nod with another smile. Damian gives me an approving smile before helping me up and escorting me back to my room. It does help to sit down and write Mom back.

I tell her how unsure I feel, about how things are changing between the prince and me. But most of all, I express how happy her words made me. Someone I have known my whole life is happy with what is happening.

I smile as I set the letter aside. There. She is sure to do as I ask and tell Dad I'll miss him at the harvest. I have my maids post it right away.

Chapter 38

The prince isn't at dinner for a few days, but when I next see him at dinner, he looks exhausted. Or perhaps it's because his mother wants to have a meal with him because she spends the whole time speaking to him. The king sits with a small smile. He doesn't look any different than before his lung attack.

Just as we finish the main course, the dreaded ringing strikes the castle.

"How?" Jonquil demands.

"Is it normal for them to be this close?" Lilly asks nervously as we get up.

The guard goes to the wall on the opposite side of the doors and elbows one spot then press on another. A guard on the opposite side does the same and a passageway opens.

"In," Sage orders, quickly pushing the royal family inside then nodding at the guard to handle the rest of us.

Once inside, I stand near the opening and count heads. All the girls are here this time. The prince and his parents are guarded in a back corner while the rest of the girls retreat as far back as possible. Jonquil is standing with Lilly, both girls shaking in fright. Bella and Azaela are sitting on a bench along the wall, keeping close to each other. The "elite" are huddling together at the opposite corner from the royal family. Ericka looks particularly worried. I'm sure it's because her poor dog is out there.

I may not like the dog, but I feel sorry for her, so walk over once the door is shut. "Your dog is a fighter. I doubt they'll hurt him," I assure Ericka. "I mean, he nips at servants. Imagine what he'll do to the rebels."

That gets a laugh from her. However, Forsythia seems to take offense at my being so nice. "What do you care?" she demands.

"I'm sure I'd be worried if my beloved pet was out in the castle when those rebels are loose," I say. "Just being nice. You might try it sometime. May help with those grumpy lines."

I turn and smirk as Forsythia starts feeling her face. She turns to Dahlia and asks if she really does have scowl lines. I smile a bit more. At least I know they aren't infallible.

Lilly is shaking so badly, I can see it from here. I frown and join her and Jonquil. "You alright?"

Lilly nods, "Yes, just nervous."

"They rarely get inside," Jonquil points out. "Last time was their first. I don't think they'll do it again."

"After a first, it can be a lot more likely," Lilly points out. "Once a horse learns he can jump the fence once, he is more likely to do it again."

"I'm sure they pugged that hole," Jonquil comforts her. "Besides, they won't want to hurt us."

"Yes, they do," Lark speaks up. "They tried us last time. They think we're just part of the problem with the royals." She's shaking too.

"Well, they didn't find any safe rooms last time. They won't now," I try to assure both of them. "And we have double the guard."

Last time, they only left one. Now we have Sage, the captain of the guard, and five others. We're well defended. But even I worry the rebels will get in. They got in before. I am sure they will again. Someone let them in, but how? All the girls are here this time. Jonquil is with Lily. Florence is sitting with Isla, the latter of whom is praying with her hands tightly holding Florence's.

The girls trapped in the library together during the last attack were Florence, Ayesha, and Hawi. But all the girls are here apart from Ayesha who'd been eliminated. None of the girls could have let them in this time.

We're huddled in silence for a while. I'm not sure how long. Whispers fill the air. The royal family is talking in hushed voices. Gavril isn't included in the talk, apparently, as he begins checking in with all the girls.

Gavril frowns when he reaches the three of us. "Are you ladies alright?" He looks from Jonquil down to Lilly. Jonquil and Lilly nod. Lilly more frantically.

"Hey." Gavril bends to her eye level. "No one is going to hurt you. Promise," he says with more confidence in his voice than I've ever heard before. It makes Lilly smile.

The prince smiles back and then pulls himself up, and finally, looks at me for the first time in days. "Calm as ever?"

"I'm an actress. I hide it well," I cover.

"Of course," Gavril chuckles. "We'll talk soon." I hear the promise in his voice. He hasn't dropped me at least.

He walks away to check on the others, secretly brushing my arm. I smile weakly. I guess he just really wanted to do as I asked. Is that the only reason he's dating around? That makes it worse than if he just dropped me. He's looking out of obligation when he has no reason to be obligated to me.

Sage glares at me as he passes. I glare back. "It wasn't me," I say firmly but quietly.

Sage pauses and turns back to me. "Oh, if I thought that, you'd not be in here. Then we'd prove it for sure," he warns then follows his protectee.

I watch him go with a frown before I turn back to Lilly. "See? They know what they're doing."

She smiles bigger than she did before.

That's when the banging starts. Something hits the wall at full speed. Some girls let out cries. The guards hurriedly try to hush them. Jonquil covers Lilly's mouth to stop her scream. Lilly nods in thanks.

Dahlia and Forsythia dive to cover Ericka's mouth. All of the princesses cover their mouths just in case apart from Princess Zelda, who puts her hands on Princess Neeraja's shoulders to try to comfort her and stop her screaming too.

Kamala covers Hawi's mouth as Isla prays harder. Florence and Lark look at Nichol to get her not to scream. We all know they'll target that wall if they find we're here.

Sage pulls Prince Gavril back into the corner, keeping the prince's body behind his.

I hold my breath. We all wait, trying to not be too tense, so another bang doesn't set us off. There are four more bangs. One quieter, leading me to think they are trying other walls. Two as loud as the first then the fourth the loudest yet.

The guards hold their weapons ready. I wish I had a weapon myself. I keep close to Lilly to comfort and defend them. I tense. I should have accepted Damian's offer to help me be armed. The rebels haven't gotten inside yet, but if they do, I'd want to be armed.

I'm so lost in my thoughts, the next bang makes me jump. It's the loudest yet. The door bows. They found the door. A new sound makes Sage and I perk up in worry. Smaller taps along the wall, moving from one side to the other. Then two taps on either side of the wall.

They are looking for the two buttons that will open it. How do they know? Not even the Chosen know how to open these passages. How did they know two at the same time?

I look around the room to try to see if any of the girls look nervous or scared. They all look scared to varying degrees. None look like they knew this was coming. I guess if they got this far without Sage finding them, they had to be better than that.

But as an actress, I feel like I should be good at telling who's faking. Jonquil, Hawi, Marigold, Kamala, and Elice all look like they're putting on faces. But are they hiding fear or something else?

The tapping grows softer until it stops.

Then I hear one, two, three... four clicks.

My instinct drives me to push Lilly and Jonquil back and stand between them and the danger, bending my knees into a fighting position. I tighten my hands to be ready for a fight.

The fifth click strikes the air; the door unlocks then slides open.

The guards leap to the opening. I recognize some of the infiltrators. They are Loyalists.

They try to push past the guards. I see a Loyalist fall. His buddies don't care, shoving his body aside to make more room for them. It's like watching a bunch of rats try to escape a pipe all at once.

The center guard falls back. I don't think he's dead, just stunned. But that's all it takes for rebels to break in.

The girls burst into screams. The rebels look around; their mouths water.

I tense to fight. The captain of the guard snarls like a leopard and grabs the rebel in the lead and throws him back. "Keep them back!"

The two rebels look right at us. The largest of the men looks right at Lilly. I step between the two. He laughs and waves the other rebels to go for the royal family. As I look at him, I remember Dad always complained that Loyalists in battle were a pain because if their leader went down, they retreated. If this is the leader, I think I can end this.

But should I? I'd be suspected, found out. But what if word of what I did reached Dad? Would he finally accept the truth then?

Lie low. Dad had said. *Keep quiet.* I think the royal family would notice this.

The leader leers at us.

I snarl back at him. "You keep your hands off her." Both Lilly and Jonquil squeal in fright at my boldness.

"You're going to stop me?"

"Maybe." I tense, ready to do what it takes.

"Then maybe the partner I want tonight is you," he grins and goes for me. But I glance down and notice his feet. His feet aren't turned to me. They are still pointing at Lilly.

I pretend I think he's going for me by tensing and gasping in fright. It works. He moves towards me then at the last moment goes for Lilly.

In one instinctive, smooth movement, I slide my left foot in between the stance of the attacker. I push off my right foot and knee the attacker's left side, making his weapon arm come loose. I grab the weapon, still in his hand, flip it, then drive it into his chest. Just like I'd done a million times in drills.

It all happened in about two seconds, but I feel each movement is slow and drawn out until I hear the guttural gasp. He falls quickly but all the world has slowed for me until he hits the floor.

The other rebels see what happened. Just as I predicted, they rabbited away as fast as they could go.

It catches the guards by surprise. The captain of the guard barks orders for four of them to follow the attackers. She and Sage stay to protect the royal family.

I look up to see Damian standing there, ready to greet the fleeing rebels. He smirks as they scurry past him. He looks all too eager to chase after them, like a dog after a rodent.

Their sudden departure leaves the room silent. A flush steadily creeps up my cheeks as I feel everyone's eyes on me. I just single-handedly caused the enemy to retreat. That isn't very princess-like, is it?

It was instinct. I'd never done anything like that before. I'd never killed anyone. I am not even sure if I'd ever really hurt anyone before.

But now I did by pure instinct. Running a move I'd rehearsed so many times; it was muscle memory. Dad's weapon had been without a blade when we practiced, but regardless of the circumstances, the result lay at my feet.

Terrified I'm about to be arrested, I carefully look up. My eyes lock onto the prince's gaze.

Euphoria fills my chest as strong arms lock around me and soft, firm, warm lips press passionately to mine. Gentle, yet firm hands cradle my face, pulling me closer. All the tension drains in an instant as I return the expression, wrapping my arms around his neck and kissing him back, closing my eyes as I embrace the moment.

My eyes almost immediately pop open; I throw myself back. My heart thunders in my ears. I blink several times, gasping for air as if that will ground me back to reality. After a few blinks, I look up, and my eyes focus on the person in front of me.

Gavril looks back at me, brows creased in deep, almost agonizing remorse, a hint of a sheepish smile of an apology on his lips. "I-I don't know what just came over me," he confesses, his neck and ears red. It wasn't too bad.

But then my mind processes how bad this is. He'd not only just jumped me after he watched me kill someone, he did it in front of every candidate, Sage, the captain of the guard, and his parents.

Bile churns in my stomach as I fight to keep calm. The color drains from my face as I look around.

The room remains quiet as if rather than kissing me, the prince had jumped up to kill me. I don't dare look at anyone, but as the moment stretches on and on, I dare look over at Jonquil and Lilly.

They both are gaping at us. Lilly has a hint of excitement in her eyes. Jonquil's shock is harder to read. My eyes slowly scan the room. Azalea and

Bella are staring at me as if unable to believe I'm real. Ericka, Forsythia, and Dahlia look shocked and furious. Kamala, Marigold, Nichol, and Hawi wear similar looks of hatred. Isla gapes. Lark, Elice, and Florence look bitter as if wishing it were them getting jumped in front of the whole Enthronement.

But my eyes freeze when they reach Sage and the royal family.

"How did you do that?" the king finally asks me.

"What?"

"How did you know how to do that?" Sage's voice is accusing as he steps closer to me. Gavril tenses, but he doesn't move or speak.

"I didn't..."

"You can't just go around... is he dead?" the queen demands.

As one, the whole room looks down at the dead rebel at my feet. One of the guards checks. "Yes, Your Majesty," he says and drags the body away from us.

The other Chosen flinch away from it. I do too. I feel sick, scared, unsure how to react, but I don't have time to process my first kill because I am also being attacked.

"A lady just did that? That can't be in line with a true princess. She has to go," the queen protests. She looks at her husband in indignant horror.

I turn red and fight tears. What have I done? I ruined everything by just saving my friend. I look at Lilly, who looks ready to cry too, but she looks more scared than anything.

"What?" Gavril snaps. He finally pulls his eyes away from me and looks over at his parents. "Just because she knows how to defend herself? Where does it say a true princess can't do that? Shouldn't a princess be able to handle herself?" he's highly offended.

"It's not dignified. Of course not," the queen says.

"I don't think that makes sense," Gavril states bluntly. I don't know if they've ever argued like this with how the queen gapes at her son. She is looking at him like he's the one who killed a rebel instead of me.

"I'm afraid I agree with him. Why would that prove her not a princess? It's no different than... oh, being a sparkleball player," the king nods at Dahlia.

"Yes, it is. It's much more violent and... destructive," The queen looks at the body then at me then at Gavril.

Princess Zelda steps up, taking center stage without literally taking center stage. "Then kick me out right now." She sounds furious. She steps to my aid as if defending me from the royal family. "Because *all* the princesses where I come from are *required* to learn to fight like that. We learn combat magic too. Are you saying none of us are true princesses? Lady Kascia has done nothing but show her character. She was defending one of her friends from being taken. So, because I can do this," Princess Zelda makes a ball of light in her hand — I stare in amazement — and throws it into the wall where it explodes, leaving scorch marks, "I'm not a true princess?"

The princess stands tall, strong, shoulders square yet tense for battle. She looks ready to kill if I hadn't already done that.

After a pause, she lowers her hand and firmly places both hands on my shoulders.

"If you kick her out, kick me out too. If you drive her away and not me, I'm leaving this very night and she's coming with me to Hyvil to be made the proper princess you pretend she's not."

My stomach knots, and more tears come. She's not only defending me; she's making me equal to her.

I meet eyes with Gavril. His eyes betray his pain, looking from Princess Zelda to me. He'd lose two of the girls he likes in one. He's battling the turmoil in his chest as he looks between me and the princess.

The queen gapes at the princess in shock. The king smiles. He's trying not to laugh. Sage puts a hand on the prince's shoulder, looking between the two of us with new worry and suspicion. Perhaps he now doesn't trust Princess Zelda for liking me, or perhaps he's worried about this new layer of protection the Chosen "spy" now has.

"She has a point," the king says to his wife when she's speechless for so long. "Princess Zelda is a trained fighter. We knew that when we sent for her. She uses magic, sure, but is that much different?"

"I... well..." the queen splutters, "I..." She sighs and looks at her son who is still looking at us with that mixed expression. "I suppose you're right. Forgive me, Princess Zelda. I meant no offense to you, your father, your people, or your culture."

"I understand. It's a shock to see a lady you expect nothing of suddenly show herself powerful," Princess Zelda smiles graciously.

She turns to me. "That was amazing. I hope you can show me more of your technique one day."

I turn red but smile. Might I gain a friend in this princess? I'd never really thought about it. But she came to my defense without a second thought. She just swore to bring me into her family. I'm humbled and honored.

"Thank you," Lilly squeaks.

I blink and look at her. Her eyes are filled with sadness, unable to meet my gaze. She knows what defending her almost cost me.

"You're welcome. You're my friend; of course, I'll look after you."

Lilly beams in delight. Gavril smiles too.

The door opens again, and our guards return. "All the rebels have been driven out," he reports. "We will escort you to your rooms." Two guards go for the girls closest to the doors and see them out.

"Wait." Gavril runs up. "I want to go with you."

The guards hesitate and look over at their captain.

"Gavril, I'm not sure—" the queen begins.

"Sage is with me, and they have their guards. It will be fine," the prince insists and nods at the guards.

The prince and guards escort each Chosen girl back to her room in groups by those who share a floor. The king and queen are escorted by the captain of the guard, and two other guards stay with us in the room.

I fold my arms and look at the ground as I endure the long wait. I am the only one left on my floor and in my passageway. They'll likely take me last.

Finally, the prince returns and gives me a small smile. He puts his hands into his pockets nervously before looking up at me with his head still bowed, so he's looking up at me at a slight diagonal.

"So, you ready, or do you want to do drills in here?" he jokes.

I laugh. I needed the joke. "No weapons to drill with," I reply.

"Alright, come on then. I'm sure your attendant and maids are worried. It's getting late." The prince offers me his arm. I take it and glance at Sage. He doesn't react. I relax and let the prince escort me. Out of habit, I put my other hand on his arm.

Neither of us speak, walking in silence through the messy dining room. Smashed plates and food, broken chairs were thrown about. I expected far worse. But then I spot bloodstains and gore. I tense.

"Are you alright?" Gavril asks as we finally reach the hall. It's also a mess, but not as bad as last time.

I nod, "I wasn't hurt."

"I mean more than that. You alright? You just killed a guy." Gavril is watching me, concern and pity reflecting in his amazing amber eyes.

I swallow the bile in my throat. "I-I guess so. Your mother's attack kind of distracted me," I admit with a slight tremor to my voice.

Gavril sighs. "Sorry about that. She has a very... unique mindset. I notice Potentates as a family have their own biases that others don't. It's why I think she wants my hair to coil. It shows a more true Potentate bloodline, you see. I mean, she was fine marrying father, but she wanted her heir to be as Potentate as possible. And to them, that means that dark skin and thick hair. And they seem more... Their idea of a princess is different. They are more of an ornament in their... culture. To my mother, a princess who can fight would be too improper, too rough to be a real princess.

"But Princess Zelda is right, if you look at the code given to the Potentates at the beginning, not only is a lady being proficient in combat not forbidden but encouraged. Don't worry, she won't like it, but you did nothing wrong."

"She hates me now?"

"She doesn't 'hate' you," Gavril assures me. "She may get over it. She doesn't know you, remember that. She doesn't know any of you other than maybe Rose, but that's because she finds a bond with her. Princess Rose is the heir and 'purest blood' of the Potentates. My father isn't too fond of her as my bride, but that's also because then we have to sort out what happens to me then. I'd be married to the crown princess of Emilimoh and that means..."

"You'd become high king." The only person with authority over other kings, the purest blood descendant. Princess Rose was to be high queen; we all knew that, but it didn't click to me what marrying her meant for Gavril.

"You'd do well as high king," I say.

Gavril shakes his head, "No, I don't have the experience or the ability to command respect."

"You can get the first. You already have the second. Your guards didn't object to your order," I point out.

Gavril glances at them and the guards hide smiles. Gavril chuckles and looks at me, "Fair. Though I owe that to you showing me how."

"Sure." I roll my eyes.

"Surely," Gavril replies.

We're quiet again. "But you distracted from the point," he says after a moment. "If you're that freaked, I won't ask again. Just let me know."

The sick feeling rushes into my stomach, and tears come to my eyes. I swallow the tears.

Gavril frowns and stops when he sees my face. "You need me to shut up?"

I shake my head. "I've never done that before."

"Of course not, why would you have?" Gavril frowns, "Is it that bad out there?" In his eyes, I can see his mind reeling with the idea that most common girls out there have had to kill before.

"It's not that bad," I say quickly. "I avoided it all my life. Then I just... without even thinking. It was just..."

"You were defending her and yourself. Nothing wrong with that. You made a choice. It wasn't bad. He started it. It's his own fault for not taking you seriously," Gavril smiles, trying to cheer me up.

I let a small sob escape. "I didn't want to."

"I know." Gavril stops and hugs me, holding me to his chest comfortingly. "I know. It's okay. You did the right thing, even if it's hard."

I break down into sobs against his shirt, "I never wanted this." I'm a horrible Custod. I don't want to kill to defend. I feel sick doing it. Not like Sage who is able to just do it and sleeps fine at night. I never wanted this life, but I was born into it. It was finally my first. And I'm so scared of it. I don't ever want to do it again, but I'm sure I will.

"No one does." Gavril strokes my hair. "It's alright. I had a feeling you'd need a hug about now. But Lilly is fine and so are the rest of us because of you. Loyalists are cowards deep down, and without a leader, they flee. That's what they did. Your act stopped the attack. I know it's hard, but that has to be a little comforting, right?" Gavril sounds scared of being unable to help me.

I nod. It helps a little, but I ended that man's life, right or not. I wanted to take it back. No, I didn't want to undo it, but I wanted to give him his life back. I didn't have a right to take it.

I cry harder, and Gavril tightens his grip. "It's okay," he says. "You can cry all you need." he chuckles, and the movement of his chest is oddly comforting. "I want to hush you, but not to stop you crying. Feels like the comforting thing to do. I'm not great at this. I've never done it before. Is that alright? I mean, you need to cry, cry, but I want to comfort you. I really am an odd duck, uh?"

I think if his social awkwardness wasn't so funny, he'd have kept his mouth shut. I can tell he's using it to try to cheer me up.

It does make me smile a little. "No, it makes sense." I wipe my eyes.

"Hey." He takes my hand to stop me. "Until you're sure you're done, let them come. It's okay."

I take a quick breath and look into his firm gaze. He means every word. He's still holding my wrist strongly but also gently. He's studying my face as if discerning exactly what I need with his expression alone.

I'd never been told that before. Never had someone pretty much order me to cry if I wanted to. I half laugh, half cry, and bury my face in his shirt again.

Gavril holds me gently. "That's my girl," he comforts. "Shh, you're safe now. You can let it out. I'm not judging."

I hold tighter to him as I cry. Each sob hurts and heals at once. I cry over the sick feeling of what I've done. I cry over my stupid father, Jake, my frustration, my jealousy, all of it. I cry it out against him as he holds me in a way I hadn't ever done before. I cry it all out until my heart feels empty of the stresses and pains. It's still sad and down, but not as heavy.

Gavril can feel a difference; he strokes my hair and pulls back gently. "Better?" His eyes tenderly study my face. I love it. I want to nod, sob, and kiss him. Not a good idea.

I nod. I go to wipe my eyes, but he pulls the handkerchief from his pocket and offers it to me. I smile and take it to wipe my eyes. He smiles to himself as I clean myself up and hand it back to him. I avoid looking at his shirt. I'm sure I ruined it with tears and make-up.

"Good. Ready to go back to your room?"

I nod. He offers his arm. We're quiet as we walk. My room is much further than I realized.

"Well, in the fear of making things worse again, I still have to apologize," he says. "I didn't mean to just... go at you like that." He flushes.

"Why did you?" I'm afraid of the answer.

Gavril is quiet for a painfully long moment. "I don't really know. I saw you do that. And it just... made something powerful and..." he clears his throat, "It was like seeing you do that encompassed what I like about you. It made all those feelings rise and I just... I wanted it." He goes brick red, and I try not to laugh. "I didn't have time to think about it. I only got my head and pulled back when you did. I'm so sorry for whatever trouble it causes you." I can feel how deeply he means it in his tone. "I'm sure it made my mother even more scared. I embarrassed both of us, and who knows what else. I'm sorry."

"Forgiven." It's not like I didn't like it. I loved it. I feels what he means about the passion just overwhelming him. I'd tasted a bit of it. My heart is begging for another taste.

"I'll keep it in check from now on," he promises as we finally reach my room. "And thank you for not shoving me off. I know you're still unsure with your ex on your mind and everything."

Oh, if only he knew. I turn to him. "You're welcome."

But I can't just tell him I liked it too. He's being too careless with himself. If I lose, he'll be trapped. He has to be careful. I have to be careful.

"And... I didn't hate it," I try to ride the line, "but I won't say I loved it either."

Gavril nods, keeping an oddly neutral face.

He's getting good at hiding his feelings, or is he already good and just didn't bother until now?

"I understand." But does he? I'm terrified he does. "Well, rest well." He takes my hand and kisses it.

"I suppose they'll bring up breakfast again tomorrow, but rest assured, I'll be coming back to you in time." I hear the 'don't give up on me' in his voice.

I force a smile. "Until then." I don't know how to give up. If I did, this wouldn't hurt.

He smiles and stands. He looks into my eyes a moment before forcing himself to turn away. I take a deep breath and open my bedroom door.

Chapter 39

I step into my room and stop, my eyes widening in horror. Papers are scattered everywhere; tables have been knocked over and the bench at the end of my bed was tossed and stands at a funny angle. Containers of makeup, lotions, and perfumes, all scattered and spilled across the floor and debris. The bookshelf's contents litter the room. Bedsheets sit in a crumpled heap.

Flur and Vivian stand up quickly as I walk in. They'd been kneeling on the floor, cleaning up some of the spills. They bob me a proper curtsy.

"They... got in here?" I gape at the mess.

"Yes, miss," Vivian says. Her eyes are red, and her mouth is tense as if containing anger. "Our apologies. We should have had this cleaned up before you got back."

"No, no, it's alright." I rush over to help them, kneeling and collecting books into my arms.

"No, you're a lady. This is work for us to do," Vivian insists.

I look up at her, holding a book tightly in my hands. "Lady or not, I'm no better than you. We were all attacked. I want to help. This is too big of a job for you ladies to do alone."

"We're not ladies. We're your maids," Vivian retorts.

I pause at the harshness of her voice. "Vivian, that doesn't mean I think any less of you. You matter as much as anyone else."

Vivian shakes her head, pain and a hint of anger on her face. "That's not how it's done, miss."

"That's how I do it," I retort. "What's wrong?"

"What's wrong?" Vivian snaps, looking up at me with hot tears in her eyes. "What's wrong is those monsters still control our lives. They come in here, demanding to know where things are kept, and we're powerless to stop it. It's seeing those I care about disappear or die or worse, but we'll never know when they take them. It's being in one of the best jobs in the kingdom but not being able to be proud of it or enjoy it because the scum of the earth want to throw things at you or hurt you or get information from you. I'm sick of it and not being able to stop it."

My face loses color as Vivian speaks. They were looking in here? And worse. "You-you were still in here?" *Please, say you were in the safe room, please say you were in the safe room.*

"Vi, maybe now isn't—"

"Then when is?" Vivian stands up, wiping her eyes and throwing the rag she'd been using into the water bucket with a dramatic splash. "When do we get to say how we feel? Why are my opinions and feelings less valid because I don't hold the same opinion as the masses? When does what I feel become important or valid? When do we get a chance?"

I sit there, stunned, unsure how to reply. All I feel is the creeping guilt in my stomach. My people and I are part of what hurt her. Vivian is a controlled person. It takes a lot to push her into a rage like this.

"I-I don't know," I admit.

"They wanted your letters!" Vivian screams at me.

My head snaps up. "What?"

"They came in too fast; they demanded to know where your letters were." Vivian stomps her foot in frustration.

"You-you could have told them. I-I have nothing to hide." If it was that or my maids, I'd choose the letters any day.

"We didn't know where you kept them," Flur says in a quiet voice.

I look at her in horror.

"Why?" Vivian yells at me. "Why did they want them? What have you and your stupid rebel friends been up to? Please tell me you haven't been letting them in. What do those brixes want?"

I stare at Vivian, stunned that she, of all people, was yelling at me like this. I'd expect that of—

My heart stops. I look around in pure terror and jolt to my feet, knocking over the books. "Where's Ro!?" My voice cracks as the horror of that statement hits me.

"She was coming back into the room," Vivian's lip shakes, and tears spill down her face. "She saw the men had us and jumped on their backs to try to help us. The big one just... just scooped her up and tossed her on his shoulder like a sack of flour and walked away. They said if we wanted to see her again we'd give them the letters."

"But..." But Ro knew where I kept them. Why didn't she just tell them?

"They took her! Why? What do you have that they want?" Vivian demands, her voice shaking in grief and anger, hurt, and betrayal in her eyes.

"I-I don't know what they want," I stammer. "I-I have nothing to hide from them. They could read my letters all they want. Ro knew where they were. I kept them under the bottom of the drawer, so they didn't slide around. I ne-never meant for this to happen. They could have taken them."

"Why? Why do they think you do?" Vivian demands.

"Because I told them no!" I snap back. "Vivian, they kept begging me to help them. I told them no. I want Prince Gavril to take over and win this war as much as you do. I'd *never* help them stop that happening. I told them no. I... I-I told them no."

Tears of hurt and anger fill my eyes. If my father was involved, he'd pay for this. If it was Jake... "What did they look like?" I snarl.

"One was a big blonde man. The one who threatened us was a smaller man with darker hair," Flur says.

"Scruffy?" I ask.

Flur shakes her head, "No, actually he was surprisingly clean-shaven."

Alright, it wasn't Jake. But that doesn't mean he wasn't part of it somewhere.

"They... they re-really took her?" I dare ask.

Vivian nods and more tears fall down her face. "She fought them kicking and screaming, but we couldn't even go after her."

I fall back to my knees, angry, hurt, defeated. Is this my fault? What did they want in my room? I have nothing to hide. What could any rebellion want? Dad had my answers all he wanted. The Loyalists could ask my father. Would the Potentates do this? Why? Did they search the other rooms?

Does it even matter? They took my Ro, and that was the long and short of it. Would they kill her? Hurt her? Would she stop being her foolish self and just tell them what they want to know? I have nothing to hide. She has to be honest. But if I know Ro, she'll torment them by not telling them, teasing them.

I blink, but the tears fall down my face. "I-I'm so sorry," I sob. "I did-didn't want this."

"Did you really say no?" Flur asks.

I nod, trying to wipe the tears away. "I wouldn't let them hurt any of you. I-I..." I just risked it all to save Lilly only to come up here and realize I failed a different friend.

That's when the anger comes: hot, filling me like a tidal wave. They took my Ro. They ruined my life. They attacked us without question. They did whatever it took, hurting the innocent. Right or not, that did not excuse attacking those who did them no wrong.

"I don't know how, but I'll... I have to stop this." But I am powerless. Everyone I know is powerless. All but one who is not listening to me.

That thought angers me more. I get up and go to Vivian and Flur and give them a tight hug. "I'm so sorry." I wish I could say I'd make this better, but I don't know if I can.

"It's not your fault, miss," Flur says.

"Not her fault?" Vivian demands but doesn't break the embrace. "It was her rebel friends."

"I swear to you, I don't know who they were or why they wanted to see my letters. If you ever have to give them something, just let them have it. I have nothing to hide from you. Please, promise me if anything like this happens again, you will give them the letters or whatever it is." I hug them all the tighter. "I don't want any of you to get hurt. I don't know how, but we'll make them pay. We have to."

Vivian pulls away and looks me dead in the eye. "If you're telling them no," she glares harder at me, "keep telling them no. Win this stupid game and make them pay for this. Why do they think because the king and queen seem so evil that they can do these things? Don't they know if they'd stop, it would all end?" Vivian cries harder.

"Shh, Vi," Flur says. "You know we aren't to speak of that."

"What?" I frown. "Speak of what?"

"Nothing you need worry about, miss," Flur says. "In time, if you can just win this, you can stop them. Please, you have to win this. He likes you." New tears fill Flur's eyes. "You have to stop this."

I bow my head. "It doesn't matter if he likes me. That's not how a winner is picked."

"But that's why he likes you. You can help them stop this. If any of the ladies give me hope of that, it's you," Vivian says with such sincerity and tears in her voice it makes my heart melt. "We have to win this. You have to become princess. It's the only hope we have."

"I think the prince would be fine alone," I defend him.

"But he needs to know it!" Vivian snaps so sharply. I step back. "Lady Kascia, you don't know him like I do. That boy clammed up in himself, so scared to share, he shoved away anyone who tried. That man knows more about the rebels than me when I've been threatened, beaten, and had my loved ones torn from me by them.

"I worked on his personal team since he and I were teenagers. I know his struggles. He can do this, but he'll never believe it on his own. That's why he needs you. He opens up to you in ways no one else has *ever* gotten him to do. You know the ways of those monsters. You can talk their language. You accepted the truth when no one else would. You are his favorite because you're what he needs. He loves the hope and freedom and equality you give him. No one else has ever given him that. Not even those who should have," she bows her head, "like me. He's older, and yet, I treated him as a child as much as anyone else. You can and must win this, my lady. You-you have to." Fresh tears fill her eyes.

I gape at her, looking from her to Flur and back. I can't believe a word of it. I'm too stunned.

"We believe in you," Flur says meekly. "No one else sees hope in their girls. We ask. You care about us. You don't look down on us like everyone else. It gives us more hope than anything."

"So let us do our jobs," Vivian says. "Let us do the work and be our princess. Respect us and let us serve you, just as we hope you'll do far more in serving us."

The tears come so rapidly, I have to bow my head to wipe them away. I feel most of them drip down my hands. I'm honored. I'm humbled, and I'm terrified. What if I let them down?

"But the only reason they wanted me here was to use me," I confess.

"Well, they sent their own doom to stop them," Vivian says stubbornly.

"We just know you can help us. Please, just win this," Flur bites her lips, "F-for Ro."

I hug myself and nod as my tears drop to the floor among the books, papers, and smudged makeup. "I'll do my best," I promise.

Unable to hold it in anymore, I step forward and hug them both tightly again. They return it; we just cry. I cry for the pain these girls have known. What other pains do they hide that I don't know about? What have my people done to them? What more damage could they do? And even worse, how will I ever stop them?

When we've finally cried it out, they start cleaning again. Vivian doesn't want me to help, so I just stand there, feeling stupid as I'm not allowed to go anywhere.

Flur suggests Vivian clean up the washroom. Vivian takes the suggestion.

Flur makes my bed with fresh, clean sheets so I can at least sit on it. As soon as I'm sitting, she glances at the washroom door to be sure Vivian isn't listening.

"She didn't mean to let it out on you," she says. "She's just lost a lot." Flur makes me a cup of tea.

"Like what?" I dare ask as I accept it. "I thought the only ones hurt were out there. What has happened in here?"

Flur sighs tiredly, "A lot, miss." She resumes cleaning. "The attacks have rarely gotten inside, but when they do, they do a lot of damage. When Vivian was little, they took her older sister. Her father died shortly after trying to find her. Her mother worked herself out about a year ago. Her little brother was crippled by an attack about six months ago. They still don't know if he'll walk again. He was outside when they attacked.

"But the worst was about three years ago. She was out on the grounds. One of the men took her and beat her to find ways into the palace. She gets tense and angry every time she gets near one of those rebels. She fought the one who attacked us with all she had. She hates them. She'd do whatever it took to stop them."

I gape at Flur in horror. What kind of crimes were my rebel allies into? How did I blindly support this for so long? "Flur, I..."

"It's not your fault, miss. Only the rebels who did it are to blame. You didn't know. You'd never let it happen if you knew." Flur forces a smile as she finishes stacking the books now the makeup messes were cleaned.

"But it's wrong!" I snap angrily. "How could anyone let them—"

"They don't, miss. They do try to stop it. The king made camps for those driven from their homes by rebels trying to take over. He lets many come here to work. Like me," she forces a smile.

"You?"

She nods, "I was five. My parents immigrated from Gutchia when they were young. But they spent all their lives here. The rebels decided to try going for cities down south. I lived in a village near Magalleia. They burned crops and homes. My family was unhurt, but we had nowhere to go. The king brought us here to work. I don't recall much of it. Just nightmares of fires and screaming."

She shrugs like it's not a big deal. "But I get scared every time. My father passed away about two years ago, and my mother works in the kitchens. She makes up your teas." Flur gives me a warm smile. "I worry for her. She's not fast. Then I worry for Karrigan," My brows draw together and I part my lips to ask when Flur smiles and answers, "my fiancé."

"What?" My eyes widen.

She nods, "Just after Christmas. We're hoping the Enthronement is over by then."

"You can take time off anyway," I assure her.

"It's not that." Flur gives me another smile as she puts the books back on the shelf. "He was... hurt in the last attack. He won't be on his feet until then."

"No..." That makes me even angrier. What kind of pain did my people put these innocent maids through?

"It happens. He's a guard; he's in the line," Flur explains. "It's why I get scared."

"I-I am so sorry."

"Just win, then we can have hope again," Flur begs, her pale eyes shining in desperation.

I bow my head. I wish I could promise I would and that I could fix this.

"As for Ro," Flur reads the question in my eyes, "she grew up here like Vivian. She worked in the laundry until Vivian gave her a chance here. Why she's not so good with her mouth. Her parents died when she was young, and unlike most of us, she's not had many friends. She's rather used to it.

Why it was more of a joke to her than anything." Tears flood Flur's eyes. "I just pray she's safe."

"Me too." I hug myself tightly. "I don't know what I'll do if..."

"Win," Flur says firmly. "And make them pay for being the monsters they accuse us of being."

Chapter 40

When Damian comes in to start work the next morning, I'm delighted to see him. I want to embrace him, but he's reflecting all our moods. He's dark and grumpy. He doesn't speak to us as he sits at his workstation. Understanding the feeling, I let him have his space. ***

His hair isn't as neat as normal. He keeps running his fingers through it. He takes deep, even, forced breaths, pausing now and then to grip the desk as if trying to control the urge to do something, his knuckles white. It reminds me of when Gavril almost loses his temper.

My maids talk about last night, telling me they heard what I did in the saferoom.

"Amazing," Vivian sighs enviously.

Damian finally turns to us. He seems to have finally managed to calm down and has a proud smile on his face, even if his eyes still seem sad. "Indeed. You were wonderful yesterday, my lady." He stands and bows his head to me.

I pause in surprise. "Oh, thank you." I still wish it hadn't made such a mess though.

"You're welcome. I saw you take out the leader. It was excellently executed," Damian smiles.

I manage a weak smile. "Well, it was the only choice." I just wish I'd gotten there sooner to help Ro. Vivian and Flur glance at each other.

"True," Damian nods then sighs. "Ladies, I must apologize for my behavior. Last night, after I found out they had taken Ro, I went after those rats. I caught a few of them, but I couldn't get to her. I was furious. My brother had to stop me from doing something quite..." He raises his gaze to the ceiling, "imbecilic." He looks at us. "I apologize if I was sharp with you in my agitation."

I smile and nod. He hadn't said a word to me until now. I'm guessing this is for the maids. Flur and Vivian smile back at him. "It's alright. We all have been... different," Vivian says. Flur nods her agreement.

"Still, I do apologize," Damian says. "I know this is a blow to all of us. She will surely be missed. But the Father will watch over her. Ro, wherever she may be, is safely in His care."

That is a little comforting to think about. And my maids might be right. Perhaps if I win, I can fix this. But how will I know when they aren't being open with me? I wish there was more I could do.

Once I'm dressed for the day, there's a knock at the door. Princess Zelda is standing there in a short skirt, leggings, and boots. Her hair is in a tight but nice-looking French braid. Her tiara, for the first time, is missing. "Hello Lady Kascia," she smiles shyly. "I was... wondering. You could fight yesterday, right?" I nod. "Do you fence too?" I nod. "Oh good," she beams and pulls out two swords, blunted but still stunning. "My skill I'm afraid might be fading. Would you be willing to practice with me?"

I tuck my hair behind my hair. "Would I?" I turn, but my maids are on it. I beam.

"I'll let you get ready. See you in the practice room?" Princess Zelda asks. I nod.

My maids help me change into the gear with a really pretty and flattering button-up shirt, vest, leggings, and braid. Once I'm ready, I race down to meet with Princess Zelda.

Her smile is like a midday sun to see me. "Oh, you look so cute," she says. "I love it. The vest... we should do that in Hyvil. We just do these top things, called a bradice." She wears a white high collar shirt with a button on the neck. It's tight on her arms and body and tucked into her pants. There is the design of a phoenix over her stomach. Over that, covering just her arms and breasts is a kind of slip-on vest so to speak. That's the bradice. The sleeves of this only go to her elbows and make a feather design where it ends. But I like how the green color sets off her green eyes. She also has a nice wrap belt skirt around her waist that finishes off the outfit.

"But yours is stunning."

"Thank you. I like it too," she smiles. "Well, shall we get started?"

"Yes please," I grin. We bow to one another, as curtsying in pants looks rather silly, and both of us get into position.

Princess Zelda is fast, but she also is kind of loud in how she fights. I know breathing out and making cries with blows helps her technique but she has more voice to hers than I've heard before. I impress her with my agility.

"You're quick," she compliments. "Served you well last night. I meant what I said. If they kick you out for that, I won't stand for it. Promise," She smiles at me. "You've been so good throughout this. The way you help poor Lilly. And deal with the other brats. I like watching."

"I thought the princesses just ignored us," I say.

"They do. I would rather not. But they do make it hard to break out. They like to keep the clique, and as I can't alienate them as allies for my kingdom, I have to play along. But you girls have much more fun. I wish I knew more of that."

"You'd want to play with us?" I ask in shock.

She nods, "Oh, of course. I love Ostragie."

"We can play in my room. I have a set in there."

"Oh? How about we use my set," she smiles. "I can bring it to your room?"

"Sure. But would yours be more comfortable?"

"No. I think you have better maids to hang out with," she jokes. "And my room is almost too grand."

We change then Princess Zelda arrives with her set and a few other things she puts aside by the door. We lie on the floor on opposite sides to play. My maids watch with a smile as they work on my harvest outfit.

The princess's set is beautiful. It's made out of two different materials. One team's side is made of a beautiful blue stone. The other is made out of polished white stone. The board is also beautiful, made out of fine polished wood; I don't know what kind.

"You're very good," says the princess as we are about halfway through.

"You're better. I think you're winning," I frown as I put a piece into place. "So, these pieces have different names. Is this because this is what your people call them?" I ask.

The princess nods. "This set is the Hyvil and Sirea nation sets. You're playing as Sirea," she says, "Why your pieces have those characters. Sirea are part mermaid. Your base is their center, the wellspring of the Sirea Province. Their city is made from the same stone the pieces are. It glows in the dark. I love it. So that's why your base is called the Province. Your pieces are still king, queen, captain, and all of that though."

"Did they gift you this set?"

"No, this is a fancy set, but you can buy it from the Gargoyle craftsmen. It's not rare at all. They have different kinds."

"And they all have Hyvil as the other side?"

"Oh no, that's just the default. You can get the sets in whatever arrangement you want," the princess says. "I like the Hyvil/Sirea set, but sometimes when I play my brother, he'll use his Georo pieces."

"So, you normally play as Hyvil?"

"No, Sirea actually," she says. "But I figured you'd like to try that set first." She puts a piece on mine. "Battle."

"Six," I proclaim.

"Oh, four," she frowns and puts her piece in the discard pile. "I was completely wrong." I laugh. "But anyway, if you want to trade next round I don't mind."

"Sure, if you'd like," I say as I make an attack. "Battle."

"Seven," she grins.

"Ten," I laugh.

"Oh, I really misread that," she frowns.

"Did I take it?"

"Not yet," she laughs.

I end up winning the round, but she beats me in the second. We play a few more times, showing we are pretty evenly matched at this game too. We play over lunch then take the rest to sit out on the rail of my balcony, watching the waves.

We talk about all kinds of things. She shows me her unique tablet. It's not just an Imajoel. It's far more. As I'd guessed, she can read books that it scans as well as write notes on it. It also stores maps, pictures (though I call them impressions), even storing moving impressions. As far as I know, no one had figured out the magic to store moving impressions with sound like her tablet can. She calls it the Magus tablet.

She gets up the courage to ask if she can watch me dance on pointe and see my old pointe shoes. I laugh and agree.

"I'm so glad last night happened. I know it's sad, but it gave me a chance to be able to bridge the gap. The other princesses will see my act as a way of saying you're equal now. So, I won't be seen as a weakling or rude for snubbing them for you. In fact, they'll expect it."

I frown. Does that mean the other girls will hate me for it?

"Just deal with the drama as it comes. I know you have a very different style of girl fighting with the non-royals," she gives me a sad smile, "but you handle it well."

"I do not." I just avoid it.

"You do. But I guess as it's miserable you don't even notice you're good," Princess Zelda smiles. "Being royal is like that sometimes. You're good at something, but you don't know it because the job is so icky you don't know you're good at it because it feels horrible, good or not."

She talks like I'm an equal when I'm not. I try to ignore that and change the subject. We talk until dinner is brought up. We enjoy that over another few games before Princess Zelda finally has to excuse herself to bed.

"Thanks for hanging out. I had a good time," I smile and offer her the game set as she packs up.

"No, you keep it," she grins. "I can get a new one at home so easily, it's silly. Take it as a mark of friendship even after all this is over, no matter how it ends."

"What? No, this is too priceless," I insist.

"Replacing it is as easy as you getting new dance shoes," Princess Zelda insists. "Keep it. I want you to have it. You're good at the game and deserve a nice set. You can remember me when you play it no matter where you are."

I smile a little. I can't turn it down without being rude. I hug the set to my chest. "Thank you. I'll never lose it," I promise.

The princess smiles, "Maybe we can play more tomorrow after you show me how your dancing works."

"Alright," I smile back. "Good night, Princess Zelda."

"Just Zelda please, and you're welcome," she says. "And good night, Kascia. Until tomorrow."

"Good night, um Zelda." It feels odd to drop her title, but good at once. Who knew a friendship could form so fast.

That night, I'm alone, sipping my night tea when a chill flows over the bed. I put my cup down. I only recall one other time that's happened. Someone opened the balcony from the outside. "Sage, that better be you," I state firmly, tense to defend myself from a rebel if I have to.

"Hm, you're good at that," Sage appears next to the bed.

I sigh in relief but pretend to put on a brave face. The assassin still scares me. I wonder if that will ever go away. "It's been a long day; what do you want?"

"Answers." Sage bends down to eye level with me. "Those moves were impressive. I can put some off as dance skills, but not nearly all of it. I heard you gave Princess Zelda a sparring partner today."

"Yes. And?"

"Where did you learn to be good enough to be sparring partners with a Hyvian princess?" he asks, studying my face for deceit or lies.

"My father taught me," I state.

"And how is he so good?"

"I don't know."

"Why did he teach you?"

"Bit of a family tradition. He wanted me to be able to defend myself."

"Hm." Sage stands up and paces. "You know, you drive me crazy. I don't like you. You keep proving me wrong every time I want to give you the benefit of the doubt. I agree with the queen you should go, even if I disagree with why. I don't know how you let them in, but I'm sure you did."

I flush and stand up. "It wasn't me! If it was, they wouldn't have ransacked my room and taken my maid!"

Sage pauses. "They searched your room?"

I nod.

"And kidnapped your maid?"

I nod again.

"Why?"

"They wanted my letters apparently," I fold my arms, "or did you do that while they were busy?"

Sage glares at me. "I wouldn't steal your things. Even if I would like to," he huffs. "Your letters that interesting?"

"Not really. Just to my parents."

"You aren't writing anyone else?"

"No."

"Hm. Interesting. Why would they think there was more?"

"Your guess is as good as mine," I glare at him, "so stop acting like I'm not losing anything in all of this."

Sage nods, "I see. All that tells me is whatever rebel you are, it's not a Loyalist, which is dangerous. It makes you either the smartest Potentiate or a Custod. And I have no patience with that." He glares at me. "Betrayed their name and purpose in forming that rebellion." So, Sage doesn't know the secret orders. "You better hope that's not where you're from."

"I'm not." I am not one of them anymore. "Want proof?"

Sage frowns as I march over to my desk, pull out all the letters I kept, and shove them into his chest like I had the impression. "Read them," I dare him. "I am not a threat to the king, queen, or Prince Gavril. I'm as loyal to them as I can be. Maybe you can figure out what those cursed monsters wanted."

Sage nods to himself, watching me with interest and confusion. He takes the letters before sweeping out the door in one sudden, impressive movement.

The next day after lunch as I'm leaving the dining hall, I hear a small cough behind me I've grown to know well.

I turn to face the king and queen and move to get out of their way. But they don't walk past me. They walk up to me.

I freeze, glancing back towards the dining hall where every girl is straining and twisting in their seats to see what's about to happen.

"Lady Kascia," the king declares as if I was an old family friend they'd not seen in decades, "would you like to take a walk with us?"

"Uh," I can already hear the whispers of the other girls, "I would be honored, Your Majesties." I curtsy properly as my heart races, trying to find an escape. Would this be how they'd kick me out? I had never seen the king and queen, let alone the king *or* queen, asking someone to take a walk. Am I in trouble? The king's happy nature doesn't make me think so, but that's also just how he is.

The queen smiles, holding her husband's arm just a tad more securely as he nods me to follow. I walk alongside them, feeling like every eye in the palace apart from the prince's are on me right now, judging my step.

We walk to the front doors, and the guards open the doors for us. We're going outside? What in creation is going on?

We enter the rose gardens. They're in full bloom. Their scent is thick and lovely in the air. I can't help but enjoy a deep breath. It smells amazing. I'd never seen roses grow like this. They have the natural red and pink roses growing intermixed with the Purerahian rose, making a stunning display.

It makes my heart lift. But then it sinks in. This had been in Gavril's yard his whole life, and apart from the one night we'd been out here, I doubt he's ever walked this garden. He likely never has in the daylight. Would I get the chance to let him?

"You like the gardens then?" The king's voice jars me from my thoughts.

"Yes, your majesty," I say quickly, giving him a winning smile, the kind I use as a princess on stage that charms the Prince Charming. "They are the best I've ever seen."

"Our master gardeners have figured out the secret," the king smiles. "You prune them at the right time, and they bloom into this wild array twice a year. The workers deserve every gem they get and honestly more," the king sighs tiredly.

I force a smile, "Indeed, they do, my lord."

"You can drop the formality," the king waves me off. "We're not kicking you out."

"You-you're not?"

"No," the king chuckles and gives his wife a telling-off look as if telling her to stop scaring the nice Chosen girl. I can't help but smile, but I am too nervous to do more.

"Besides, who would wow me in talent shows?" the king grins a smile that makes me unsure if I should laugh or feel the awkwardness of his leering.

The king squeezes the queen's arm as if to soothe her. "Really, Lady Kascia, you're not in trouble. We just..." the king pauses as he searches for words, "...you've started to stand out."

I fight to keep my frown off my face. "I'm sorry, Your Majesty. I didn't mean to frighten anyone or cause a scene. I just... he was going to hurt her," I say lamely.

"No, no, it's not about that night," the king waves me off again. "You'll have to forgive my wife. She's a bit... traditional."

"Someone is too flippant about his duties." The queen gives her husband a look.

"You ever thought I'd be so stiff?" the king smiles at her.

"No, but I did think responsible," she sighs.

"I do that at least." The king turns back to me. "We were surprised. Your background doesn't seem to lend itself to being a fighter. We reviewed your application, the notes from your interview. We can't help but wonder how you know how to fight like that."

I swallow and look down as we turn around a corner to keep on the path. "My father taught me: a family tradition, and he wanted to make sure I'm safe."

"It's hard out there. I know. We try, but..." he sighs more heavily, "... it's just not easy with so many people out for us no matter what we say or do."

"Have you tried to negotiate with them?"

"Yes, but rarely do we get an answer. Not since the king before my time," the king says.

"My father used to rant about how little they would deal," the queen agrees. "It makes it hard to try to give them what they want."

"All they seem to want is your line to end. That must be hard. Why they hate the prince. It seems they believe if they get rid of him, all their troubles end."

The king and queen look at one another. "They've felt that way since I was born," the queen says. "They always say that."

"So, there's nothing particular about the prince that worries them?"

"Not that I know of," the king frowns. "Why? You hear rumors?"

I shrug. "Just what everyone else feels. It's dangerous out there."

"I know. We're trying," the king sighs. "So that's why you can fight?"

I nod. "My father thought it was good for me to be able to protect myself."

"You were very adept. Have you done that before?" the queen asks, nervousness shining in her eyes.

I shake my head, fighting the fear in me. "No, Your Majesty. I haven't done that before. Just with my father and stage fighting. That was a first for me." I fight the sick feeling I get every time I think about what I'd done that night.

The king frowns and puts a hand on my shoulder, making us all stop. "Are you alright?"

I smile a real smile at the concern in the king's eyes. Gavril's eyes may be sun-kissed brown, but their eyes were similar in shape. But even then, I didn't want to discuss or admit the nightmares.

"Are you sure?" the king presses me.

I nod. "Yes, thank you, Your Majesty." I curtsy slightly.

"Dear lady, you don't have to be so formal. We're alone in the gardens. Not even my son's guard can hear us out here," the king laughs.

The queen hits his arm to get him to behave. "Am I wrong?" he asks her. She shakes her head. "Well, anyway, don't worry. We came out here, so you can be free in what you say. No one but us will hear you."

"Thank you, but honestly, Your Highness, I don't have anything to say," I confess.

"At all?" The king seems surprised. "Don't want to give us a piece of your mind about all that's happening?"

I chuckle, "No, you are my rulers. I do not disrespect your thoughts, even if I disagree."

"But I'm inviting you," the king teases.

"Just because you're invited to say something doesn't mean it's the time or place," I say.

"See, she's better at this than me," the king says as if in confidence to his wife. I laugh. "Well spoken," he says back at me. "Then there is another topic I'd like to bring up."

I pause, anxious again.

"Thank you. You handled seeing my attack very well," he says. "And you kept it quiet after Sage spoke with you. I am thankful. I didn't expect you to be alright being silent. But you have and helped my son deal with having to keep the crowds busy. I don't take that lightly."

I blush, "It's nothing, Your Majesty."

"It's not," the king smiles. "Even if she rather I stay out of it." He nods at his wife. She flushes, and he smiles. "You earned sixth on the list for a reason."

"Not because I'm pretty?" I joke.

"Gavril deserves more than that," the queen smiles.

"Yes, he does," I agree.

I study them as we keep walking. Why couldn't they see the amazing, quite capable — though short-tempered — man they had raised? He might not be so short-tempered if they gave him a true chance. Perhaps...

"He loves you, you know," I say, looking at the king, hoping my eyes can express how much. "He wants nothing more than to learn from you and not have to wait until after you're gone. I know I may be saying more than I should, but nothing would mean more to him than learning how to run this war and protect his people by even just sitting with you through a report or even getting to learn by working with you. He may not like me saying it, but I know it's true. It would mean everything to him. So, give him more say in the Enthronement or not, at least give him that."

The king looks at me for a long moment, and the flicker of tenderness returns to his eyes. I'd seen it before. I get nervous and look away to the queen who looks sad and a bit confused. The king doesn't take his eyes off me though. "You really think so?" he finally says.

"I know it. He loves you, and he wants to learn from you, not anyone else. He wants to really be an apprentice monarch. Not just a puppet or a student." I smile a little shyly. "Forgive me if I step out of bounds."

"We did invite you," the queen says. "Don't worry about that." She gives her husband a look as if saying they shouldn't have let me have free speech. Heat rises to my cheeks.

"I-I don't mean to diminish your worry for him. He is your only son, and it must feel like the world is out to get him. But he's not a boy anymore. He fears never being able to show you he's capable of what you want. That's all." I flush.

The king smiles, "We won't tell him you said this." The queen frowns. "But perhaps you're right. We'll have to wait and see."

I bow my head. "Forgive me if I overstepped."

The king laughs again. "Relax, Lady Kascia. We don't bite," the king grins.

"Thank you for assuring a worried mother," the queen says. "Where does your family live? I may want to reach out to them."

I flush. "I'd rather you didn't."

"Why? Are they not trustworthy?" The king jokes.

"Well, Mom is fine. But Dad may be a bit bothered. He is protective too. He thought I should do this, but now he's having second thoughts."

"Why?" The king sounds honestly worried. "The attacks?"

"No. He feels I can handle that. I just... He's not very happy with me," I fight tears, "which isn't normal. In fact, if I get much further in this... " After the harvest, he's going to be livid. I'll lose him for good. That brings more tears.

"Hey, it's alright. Family is complicated. Look at us." The king makes a face and points at himself and his wife. His funny face does make me laugh. "No matter what happens, we'll look after you now. You made it to the top twenty-five. That's pretty good."

I suppose. Though for me, it might have just been hiding under the radar.

I think the king can tell I'm still not assured because he put a hand on my shoulder. "Would he not let you come home?"

"I don't know," I admit. "He just... has expectations I can't meet."

The king frowns and looks at his wife. She swallows, watching me, then nods at her husband.

He smiles and turns back to me, "Well, if they won't or you don't feel safe, no matter how the Enthronement goes, we'll ensure you have a place to go. Even if it means staying with us. If your father doesn't want you, I will."

My mouth falls open. Within a few short days, two powerful rulers had pledged to make me part of their household. Why me? I'm nothing special.

I glance at the queen, sure she can't be happy with that promise. But she just smiles tenderly at me.

I take a shaking breath to stop the tears. *You will not cry now. You're on their stage,* I berate myself.

"Thank you," I blink back my tears, "that means a lot." I put back on my "royal face".

The king sighs and surprises me with a hug. "You kept my secret. I can pay it back."

My lip trembles almost violently at his hug. I will it to stop. I return the hug, but I am scared to hold it too long.

I don't want to feel this way about them. What if this doesn't work out? Things are hard enough with the idea I'll lose Gavril, but I don't want to be this attached to them too.

"I don't deserve that much payback, but thank you anyway," I smile. "I wouldn't dare reject it, your majesty."

"Be sure we won't let you go without," the queen promises. "It's been tradition time out of mind. If there is space to spare in the palace, it's open to friends and family who can be trusted. You have proven you can be. When we can, we will help."

I smile. "You're too kind. I don't know how the rest of them can't see it," I say honestly.

"Your eyes are open," the king says. "Most people shut their eyes to what they don't understand. They prefer their own opinion to the truth." He takes his wife's arm again, so we can keep walking. "I'm just glad so many girls are as open as you are. We worried we'd be down to twenty in a day with girls ranting at us."

I laugh. Well, I am the only girl who had done that, just not to their faces.

We walk around the whole castle in one large rectangle. They even go through the royal beach.

The whole walk takes about an hour where the king mostly makes me and the queen laugh. When we go back inside, Gavril and Sage are crossing the entrance hall. Gavril frowns to see the three of us.

"Ah, just who I wanted to see." The king goes over to Gavril. Sage fades more into the shadows than normal. "We just had a lovely time with your fighting friend." Gavril gives an uneasy fake laugh. "And she had some interesting points I want to pick your brains about." Gavril looks at me like he wants to demand what I've done and why he's in trouble for it. I cover my mouth to hide my laugh. "Do you have a moment?"

Gavril turns a bit pink and glances at me before saying, "Um, sadly no, I have, ah... a date."

"Ah, of course, how about over dinner then?" the king asks.

"Uh, another date." The prince turns red.

"Right, right, you have a lot of girls to keep happy," the king grins like that's a huge treat.

"Yeah," the prince sighs and looks at me as if in apology.

"Well, let's do it over breakfast tomorrow," the king suggests, "then we can discuss it."

Gavril smiles, "That sounds like a good idea."

The queen kisses Gavril's cheek. "Behave," she reminds him.

"Mother," he groans.

"Well, you did kind of struggle the other night," I point out.

The look Gavril gives me could melt steel. The king laughs heartily and claps his son on the back. Gavril tenses at the touch.

"That's important. You need to let it loose now and then," the king says.

"No, a prince should be proper at all times," the queen corrects.

Gavril gives me a look that says "Oh here we go. What did you start"?

"Well yeah, in public, but he's dating. Be yourself," the king says. "Dumb but not too dumb."

"I don't think so, Aster." The queen shakes her head.

"I was," the king protests. "So why can't he?"

"Because he's got to find a girl less gullible than me," she says, taking her husband's arm.

"Take what you can get," the king stage whispers to his son. The queen rolls her eyes. The king just smiles. "Thank you for your time, Lady Kascia," he nods at me, and I curtsy to them both. They depart for their work.

"Why am I the one in trouble when you talk to them?" Gavril asks me.

"I don't know. I didn't say anything," I defend. "Not that should get you in trouble."

"I hope so. Dad *never* asks to talk to me like that." Gavril glances after them. "Well, I might be alive through the day, but if I pass that, you owe me."

I laugh. "Alright, I'm sorry if I did get you in trouble," I sigh. "Well... enjoy your date."

Gavril gives me another look as if the fact he has to date is my fault too.

I swallow and look away. If I hadn't reminded him that day, would he really have just devoted himself to me?

"You drive me crazy," Gavril shakes his head. It makes me laugh. It reminds me of how his parents' banter. Now I know where he gets his silly side.

When I finally return to the Ladies' Chamber, the girls corner me.

"How did you get him to kiss you?" Dahlia is the first to accost me.

I jump. "I didn't ask him to."

"He still did. Was that the first?" Forsythia joins in.

"I..."

"Let her breathe," Bella defends me.

"You getting tips from her?" Forsythia sneers.

"Maybe, if you want some you should be nicer," Bella says.

"What exactly is going on? First, he jumps you, now you're going on walks with the king and queen." Ericka pushes forward, her obnoxious dog on her arm. He growls at me.

"I didn't ask for that either," I state. "They just wanted to ask me about that night is all."

"They should have kicked you out. That's not proper. The prince shouldn't lunge at you like that with so many people watching," Ericka says.

"I didn't ask for it. He did that on his own." I push past them all to find a place to sit. The princesses are watching us as if we were a mildly interesting performance.

"How did you get him to?" Forsythia demands.

"By doing something he liked, I would assume," I snap back. "Maybe you should learn to fight."

"He does favor the two who said they can fight," Dahlia points out.

"So fencing lessons and get off my back." I look for a distraction.

"What about the talk? Was it just to tell you to stop kissing the prince like that?" Forsythia mocks.

"Maybe. I was asked not to say." I pick a book.

"How are you still in the lead? It's not fair," Ericka whines. "We behave, and you get all the goods."

"Maybe you can be nice to him, and maybe he'll kiss you," I say.

"How do you know he hasn't?"

I sigh as I sit down and try to hide behind the book. "I don't."

Dahlia looks around the room. "That's true. We should clear the air then. Maybe she isn't in the lead; she just is more visible. Let's just get it all out. Who has kissed him?"

I frown, "I don't think that's fair to the prince."

"I don't think Prince Gavril will mind," Dahlia sniffs.

I gape at her. I think he would mind having his private matters with his dates being up for display.

"We can keep track," Forsythia suggests.

"We can use this old board," Dahlia starts filling out an actual scoreboard with all of our names.

I turn red. "I don't think that's fair to him."

"It's rather barbaric," Zelda agrees with me.

"It's only fair. Then we all know where we are. Then if one of us is getting sent home, we all know," Dahlia says.

"That's against the rules," Lilly squeaks.

"Don't you dare," I stop Dahlia before she snaps at Lilly. "Do what you want, but I won't join in," I say firmly.

"Fine."

Ericka, Dahlia, and Forsythia work together to make the board and put it up in a corner mostly out of sight.

I look at it, unable to help myself. The left side has all of our names.

At the top, it says what the tick is for and how many points it's worth. And if you were the first to get something you got double points. My kissing him got me three points. There are also points for: holding hands, cuddling, dates, seeing him shirtless, seeing him in his bedroom, and even a section for getting him in bed. If anyone scores down there, they're out for sure. I turn back to my book to try to ignore them. Zelda does as well. Only she and I are brave enough to ignore the board.

Once they have finished as much of the board as they can, they round on us for answers.

"Come on, fess up," Dahlia demands. Lilly looks at us nervously. I think she's hoping we give in so this can all just stop. I refuse.

"I'm not dropping it until you confess," Dahlia stands firm.

I ignore her, but she keeps going from me, to Princess Rose, to Zelda, demanding the answers.

After an hour, Princess Rose finally snaps, "Alright, I kissed him once."

"Ah! So you were first," Dahlia puts it down.

"No," Zelda squeaks, "I was."

"Really?" Princess Rose frowns.

"Yes."

"When?"

"When was yours," Zelda shoots back.

"Late last week," Princess Rose frowns.

"Yeah, it was before that." Zelda pulls up her tablet.

"Alright, that tallies up the scores." Dahlia starts. "We just need dates. We'll go top to bottom. Florence is out with him right now, and including test dates, that makes four for everyone." Dahlia puts that down. "So, who has extras?"

They go through everyone. I'm still disappointed most participate, even Azalea and Bella. Jonquil, I'm not surprised, but the others bother me. Lilly joins out of fear. I know that. But I expected more of the others. I hate that even I want to look and see where I stand.

A few girls have a few more dates, Elise and Marigold have had five and Rose had six. When it's all done, I'm still in the lead. I am not highest on dates, but dates are required and only get one point, but my kiss got me three, plus my four dates, and Dahlia guessed I had an average in everything else. I hate that. I shut my book and go up to my room to cool off.

Chapter 41

I avoid the Ladies' Chamber for the next few days. Zelda agrees and plays more games with me in our rooms or we take up the far corner of the Ladies' Chamber where Lilly, Bella, Azalea, and sometimes Jonquil will sit in with us or play.

On the last workday, the king looks pretty smug at breakfast, grinning over at us, but not at anyone in particular.

"Do you think there's a test today?" I ask the others.

I spot Godwin, leaning on one of the pillars that separates the servants' area from the royal area, watching us with a similar grin. The prince isn't smiling though. He's been at meals more often later in the week, still going on a date or two a day but trying to vary the activities more.

"If so, he's looking forward to it," Florence frowns in confusion. "And I doubt we'll enjoy it if he's that happy."

"He's not that mean, is he?" Lilly asks.

"I don't know. The king likes a good show, and Godwin is another story," Florence glances back at Godwin over her shoulder. "He's got a twisted sense of humor."

Zelda, who was just leaving the table, giggles as she hears the comment. "He's not that rude," she assures us, "but... he has a sense of humor that would make the Faku creature happy." She smiles as she looks at the king a bit more nervously.

I frown, "That can't be good."

But after breakfast, no one is called, and we all go to the Ladies' Chambers. The tension makes us all jump when Dahlia lets out a scream of anger. I drop the book I was trying to be interested in. I spot Princess Zelda scramble not to drop her tablet, sighing in relief when she catches it.

"Who messed with the board?" Dahlia rounds on the whole room, her face red and fuming.

"What are you talking about? I thought you all were the only ones allowed to mark the thing." I don't hide my disdain for the thing in my tone.

"What's wrong with it?" Zelda asks as she checks her tablet isn't broken. "Apart from the fact, it, you know, exists."

"It's all changed! And there are new girls on it," Dahlia snaps. "Did you do it?" She rounds on me.

"No, why would I? If I wanted to dispose of it, I'd throw it off the balcony," I state honestly.

"And I'd bring it to the king and queen," Zelda backs me up.

"Then why are you winning by so much?" Dahlia demands of me.

"What?" I look down at the board in her hands where she'd been shaking it at me. The board is about three feet long and two tall. I'm impressed they made our names fit so neatly.

Heat creeps up my cheeks. She's right, if you don't count the new names, I am in the lead by more than I'd ever want to admit. My numbers are accurate... or are they? I frown. I have an extra date. My being the first kiss is corrected, and the fact I had two was also corrected. That alone shot me far into the lead.

"Hey, I'm not doing as well as the new names," I try to point out. But the new names are odd: Ashely, Dalilly, Sadie, and Godwinna. Wait...

"No way has anyone gotten him to bed over a thousand times!" Ericka snaps. She has a point. That slot shows a one thousand plus. The kisses section shows the same.

Ashely left early on. I think she failed her first interview with Gavril. And Dalilly? Isn't that...

"And who is Sadie?" Zelda frowns.

"And 'seen with shirt off' is also really high," Dahlia snaps.

That was it! "Why is the queen on here?"

"She is not," Ericka retorts.

"Yes, she is. Dalilly is the queen's first name," I point at it. "And both Ashely and the queen have high scores in everything but dates." Though Dalilly has a few. "So perhaps..." Did I dare say Ashley was a female version of the king's name? Who would do that? Someone with a great sense of humor.

I recall the king's smug face this morning. Did he?

"And why does Sadie have date points so high? It's like she's been on all the other dates," Forsythia says.

I recall Damian and I had a conversation about handwriting. He'd noticed my handwriting was a lot like my father's. I wonder if he could prove my theory correct.

"And who thought of adding the queen? That's not even fair," Ericka complains. "Of course, she's put him to bed a million times."

"It says 'gets' him to bed," Dahlia defends.

"Still, she put him to bed as a baby, right?" Ericka says. "That's not fair."

"Maybe the prince thought it funny?" I suggest. But then why add this Sadie? Oh, Sadie... "It's Sage!" I gasp.

"No!" Zelda bursts into the most unprincess-like laughter I'd ever heard. "It is! He's been on all of our dates." She sits down, holding her middle with laughter.

"He does not get a spot!" Dahlia snaps and starts trying to erase it.

Zelda stops her, "I need a picture first."

"You're not going to show him!" Dahlia gasps.

"I am too," Zelda laughs. "He'll be so embarrassed."

"But then who adds Ashely back in and the queen?" Forsythia demands.

"With so many points," Dahlia adds, "and they aren't allowed. No men without permission."

"Well, the handwriting doesn't match." I'm pretty sure Gavril added 'Sadie'. It is the kind of thing he'd do. "I bet my attendant could figure it out. He's good with handwriting. He won't tell, promise."

"You're sure?" Ericka asks.

"Positive. He's good with secrets."

"Fine," Dahlia agrees.

I send a messenger to get Damian, who strolls into the room, giving his cane a twirl as he looks over all of us. "You called for me, my lady?" he says as his eyes rest on me, having glanced at the board first with an arched brow.

"Yes, can you settle a debate for us?" I ask. "I think this is the prince's handwriting, but the rest doesn't match," I point it out.

"The rest of it is supposed to be there. Someone messed with it," Dahlia says. I sigh. It doesn't matter.

Damian glances at the board again then to her. "You do realize recording this means nothing, right?"

"That's not what we asked," Dahlia snaps. "Who messed with our board?"

Damian sighs and turns to the board, placing his hand to his mouth. He glances down at the name Sadie then back at the queen's and Ashely's names. After a few quiet moments, he smiles. "Seems like the prince found your board."

"But the handwriting for Sadie, or Sage, doesn't match Ashley or Dalilly," I point out. "So it was two people."

"Likely. Though Sage was likely trying to flatten the prince when he was adding this," Damian says. Some of the girls giggle. "But as for your second mystery writer, it is really quite simple. You can see a similar stroke of the prince's hand mirrored in the writing here in how the 'a' flows to the next letter. However, the prince's is more perfected than his predecessor. The second writer is freer in his curves but with a right slant to his lines. So, it should be rather obvious. Ashley, as it were, is none other than King Aster himself."

I knew it!

"That explains all his points," Lilly says.

"So, he added both parents. Then who messed with our proper tally?" Dahlia wonders.

"That was the prince, of course," Damian says, pointing to the added tally. "Each line is perfectly straight and if we took a ruler to this, I'm sure we'd find they are actually even."

"So this tally is more accurate?" Dahlia scans it with more interest.

Curse him. Why did he mess it up? Zelda even went down, giving me the first kiss point.

"Oo, you got more kisses," Dahlia smiles at me.

"He could be messing with us," I point out.

"I don't think so. He took points off," Dahlia notes. "Florence was lying about her date count."

"It doesn't matter," I point out.

"It might," Dahlia argues.

I sigh. I'm not winning this.

Zelda looks a little confused, likely wondering if I got the first kiss. Guilt bubbles in my gut.

"This is not fair," Dahlia complains.

"Maybe you should let him run the board," I say dryly. "Then you can know your real scoreboard."

"He'll mess with us," Ericka complains.

"He's not that much of a jokester," Lilly frowns.

"Yes, he is," Me, Zelda, and Jonquil say in unison.

"He added his guard to the board as a girl," Dahlia points out.

"She has a point," Damian smiles. "Though you are lucky it was the king who found it. If the queen saw this, she'd deem it highly inappropriate and unladylike."

"She can't prove who made it," Zelda sighs disappointedly. "Wouldn't matter if she did. She'd just have taken it out."

I sadly have to agree. "Maybe if she saw her name on it, she'd feel better."

"That is unlikely," Damian smiles sadly at me, "but Princess Zelda is right, which is likely the only reason why it remains. Keep it if you wish, but I can't make any promises that no one else will leave it untouched."

"I'll get it fixed," Dahlia sighs. "Though I'll need help."

I turn away as the "elite" girls and a few others start trying to translate the correct totals. Maybe it's how they try to feel in some kind of control of the strangeness that is now their life.

"Thanks," I smile at Damian, "but I'm guessing you have more fun things to do."

"You're welcome, my lady. Though I can't promise a certain brother of mine won't try to play with that," Damian smiles as he glances at the board they are trying to fix.

"He's welcome to it," I sigh. "It's just silly and annoying."

Damian nods, "Agreed. Well, I'll see you in the room later."

"Yes, enjoy," I smile. Damian bows to me then leaves.

Zelda asks for a game. I agree and set us up at a far table, using the set that's in the room.

She's quiet at first. I realize that she's likely wanting to ask something but is nervous, so I let us play in silence for a while.

Finally, she dares to ask, "Were you really first?"

I flush, "I don't know if I should say."

"I knew I wasn't. There was just something to it. I could tell. His mind wasn't quite there." Zelda moves a piece, "but I knew I had mine before Rose."

I frown. She doesn't seem unhappy with it. Just a little down. I pray his mind wasn't on me. I hope he wasn't comparing like I had. Oh no, could he tell I was comparing him to Jake like Zelda could tell he was comparing her to me?

"But mine wasn't my first either. I was just... trying so hard to know if I wanted it, you know?" She looks up at me. "Am I too logical about this?" I can tell from her voice she's worried about this for a long time.

"Too logical?" I am not sure what she means.

"I... quantify everything. It's how I handle being unsure about things," she's talking faster than I'd ever heard, "and I judge and ponder over every little thing. Am I overthinking this? Am I overthinking feelings? Is that why it's taken this long to find someone I'm compatible with? Is this even the right place to find it?"

I feel like I'm being sprayed with a fire hose. She's asking so fast and so much all at once. I wasn't expecting it. I just sit there, stiff as a board, blinking as she goes on.

"I mean, I'm older than my sisters were when they got married. And I didn't date as much, and it feels like I'm just evaluating each of them as I date. Then this came up, and I thought it was the answer. And now I'm doing it again and quantifying myself against all of you. And trying to 'feel it' keeps getting interrupted by worrying about the answer. You know?"

"Uh," I make sure she's done before I dare reply, "no, not really. I mean, I get overthinking it. But I can't say I've ever had the problem of being 'too logical' about it." I frown, "Are you saying you're not sure you want to say yes if you won?"

"I don't know," Zelda sighs and moves her piece, resting her cheek in one of her hands as she does so, looking morose. "But I'm not ready to exactly just say no and go home. I feel like I do need to be here. And I suppose I did promise my father and my people I'd see it through. This could bring the connection to our home nation we need. We've lost so much contact. I had no idea our cultures were so different. Just the way your people see a princess is so different.

"And that's not it. There are so many differences. You call him The Merlin more than we do. To us, he's Phoenix. I know it's a small difference as you call him that too, but it's like Merlin is the more prominent name where it's Phoenix for us but little things like that pile up. You're all so different here. I fear that only getting worse if we don't establish a firm tie here. I don't want my rule to be what ends the ties, you know? I want to make them stronger.

"But... does that mean I have to marry him? I suppose if I did, my sisters could take my place so there'll be no problem with an heir to my country's throne, but... do I even want that? I don't know. It was simpler before when it was just casual dating, and if you fell in love, that was that.

"This is different. And...what if there are girls better for him and his kingdom than me? I hate that stupid board because it makes me wonder." Zelda glances at it. "I wish I knew."

"That, I understand," I agree wholeheartedly. "I wish I knew too. Even just a direction to take." I move a piece.

"I know. But for now, I'm bound to see it through for my people. After that, who knows," she sighs. "Though if you beat me to it, ask Sage how he feels about being on the board." I laugh. "Really, I want to know," the princess smiles.

"He doesn't like me. He'd just snarl at me for asking," I smile back.

"Really? Why?"

I frown, "Well, he thinks because I had rebel friends, I'm a threat."

"Oh," Zelda pauses. "Well, I think he's wrong."

"Thanks." I manage a smile, moving my piece. "But that's why he doesn't like me."

The princess shrugs. "Sounds biased." She moves her piece.

"Maybe a bit." I move mine. "But I'm kind of used to it now."

Zelda looks up at me. "Well, I hope he gets over it. Because no matter how it ends, I have a strong feeling you're getting to the top ten." I blush.

"I mean it," Zelda insists. "Hanging out with you is like hanging out with any of my sisters at home. And they are true princesses too. I know you'll get far. I hope you do."

I sigh, "You're one of the few who thinks like that." I make my move, not paying as much attention, looking at it with a rather morose face of my own.

"Not according to Jonquil's papers!" Zelda cries. "Have you not seen them?"

I shake my head dully.

"Oh, you simply must!" Zelda cries, "Since the public event, the Enthronement is all they want to write about. And the polls show you right up at the top. Jonquil, Ericka, and Dahila are up there too. They don't want a foreign princess. They want one of you. And for many, you're the top pick." Zelda smiles gently, "For me too."

"What?" I shake my head. "There's no way."

"Oh, I forfeit. Hold on." Zelda gets up and starts going through a paper wastebasket. She brings me a few newspapers. "See?" She drops them on the table, scattering a few pieces as she does.

I frown and pick up the top paper. A weight drops into my stomach. There are polls from each week since the event. I'm in the top three for each one. I start flipping through them, feeling a strange feeling, like an out-of-body experience but only in my chest.

Apart from the polls are articles that try to dissect what's happening in the Enthronement. One states the prince had us all prove we can eat properly before being allowed to meet him. Another stated he demanded a strict dress code. That one was not even close to true. I can't believe I'm so high in the rankings.

I also wonder why Jonquil hasn't mentioned it. She had to know. And she too was always at least in the top five. Why wasn't she rubbing it in the faces of the other girls? She was the kind.

"On all this alone, you're in it for the long haul," Zelda smiles at me. "And I hope so. I don't want you to leave. I only just found a friend." She winks.

I laugh. Her joke helps alleviate the weight that dropped into my stomach.

"Well, I better clean this up," Zelda giggles at the mess she made of the pieces now scattered across the board as well as the floor. I get up to help her clean them up.

We start a fresh game, but I don't do well. I'm far too distracted.

We finish up just before lunch. I think she's going to ask for another round after lunch when Gavril comes over to ask her if she'd like to go for a walk. I smile and tell Zelda to enjoy herself, but it makes me a bit uneasy. He still hasn't asked me out. Not since our moment in the conservatory. He asks me not to give up, but then why is he all but ignoring me? I guess I'll just have to keep trusting him.

I keep wondering about it through the rest of the day. I see them both at dinner, but nothing seems off. I dare ask Zelda how it went. And she just smiles in a way that tells me it's the same as before.

I joke, "Do you need to add to the board?" She gets a good laugh out of that. I can see the king grinning. I smile. At least someone enjoys the board.

Chapter 42

But eventually, the thirty-first comes. Damian gives me some tea to help calm my nerves.

I smile my thanks. That was a good idea. I sip at it as I watch them, keeping in a comfortable robe while they work.

The room is filled with bustle and Damian sing-talking to himself as he does. I will sing along with him, often without him realizing it though he harmonizes with me, subconsciously singing with me.

My maids love it and enjoy it every time. Today he's really into the music as we prepare for the ball. Which puts my maids in a good mood as they love when I sing with my "Angel of Music", even if he doesn't notice. It's a good thing too, as both of my maids are still shy about the fact Damian insisted on making them costumes too.

Damian is just finishing Vivian and Flur's costumes. I'd offered to help but my maids had insisted it wasn't done.

Once Damian's finished, he asks them how they would like their hair and make-up. My eyes light up. That I can help with.

I help Vivian get her hair into a stunning updo. Flur's is a bit easier, getting it into perfect flowing patterns down her back. Vivian still insists it's not proper, but Damian and I win that argument.

But then it's my turn, and it's the most elaborate piece they've made yet. I take a deep breath and just enjoy the process. The pieces all together are stunning. I wear a simple bodice with the shell top over that, both a matching blue. I notice they went for the national blue, which is not a bad move as it makes me look like I should be part of the ruling of the nation, and it's a color I look good in.

Pearls highlight the bodice around the shells and a large collection of strung pearls make a beautiful shoulder necklace, which I love to play with. They're so smooth! I thought they were only faux pearls until Damian warns me they damage easily.

The skirt is stunning. Rather than just copying a mermaid skirt or skirt with a mermaid tail drawn onto it, I have a train that takes the shape of a seashell, making it look like the tail drapes behind me. The gems and masterful embroidery work create sections that look like golden scales and a seashell pattern along the skirt which flows like water down my legs with a ripple effect tied to my right hip. There's a slit that makes movement easy.

The flowy underskirt is golden sand with a larger scale pattern, so it's easier to see. The tight sleeves make it look like my arms have the same golden scales.

The makeup fits perfectly with my mask that's tied on with ribbon that I swear is real seaweed. They do my hair in beach waves, twisting the side part fringe into a headband of pearls, seashells, and little starfish. The final touch was blue lipstick to go with the eye makeup, mask, and the hints of "scales" they put on my cheeks.

"What do you think?" I ask, giving a twirl to show them the full effect. The train is amazingly easy to work with even though it trails behind me. It's like magic.

"Absolutely stunning," Damian says with a soft, warm smile, his eyes shining with pride. "You'll leave them all speechless."

I flush. "Thanks."

"Let's get impressions," Flur picks up the impressionnor. It makes me a bit sad. Ro normally manned the impressionnor. I wonder if the monster who took her will try to break in tonight. I half wish he does try to get in. We'd get the jerk then.

But I smile as if I hadn't recalled, "Alright, ideas?"

The girls and I have way too much fun, as always, getting impressions. And as always, we start with good ones, me strutting about the room and turning at just the right moment, not ever holding a pose long to help the pictures look natural, but it is only a matter of time before it gets silly and we are laughing and making faces at each other.

"Ladies," Damian smiles with a chuckle of amusement. "You two aren't ready yet," he says as he lays their costumes on the bed.

My maids flush. I laugh, "Well, come on then."

"No, I am not doing that." Vivian flushes.

"Fine, I'll help Flur," I agree. Vivian is really strange about me helping her.

Soon Flur's choice of hair and makeup makes sense. I help her get into a stunning dress, and Damian even surprises her with the last touch. She's Cinderella. She's so delicate and pretty. "They'll think you're a Chosen in seconds," I tease. She flushes in pleasure.

"Don't forget your slippers, my lady," Damian smiles as he brings over heels that look like they're made of glass. I wonder if her fiancé is healthy enough to be up tonight. He should match as Prince Charming. I wish I'd asked Damian about it. I'm sure he knows.

Flur flushes such a pretty pink I wish she'd left the impressinor in reach. Damian beams and kneels and slips the shoes onto her feet. She giggles in delight. I chuckle and look again for the impressinor.

I see Vivian has it and is already dressed. I laugh. I should have guessed. Yes, she's in a dress, but she's clearly what would happen if a guard had to dress in formal attire. It looks like Damian even managed to get her a proper sword. I like how her mask covers her face, but also looks like it's a crown too. I wonder if that's the job Vivian would really want. She does seem the protective type, but maybe too proper to try out for the guard.

"Perfect," Damian smiles as he stands back. "Now, how about we get a picture of all three of you?"

I smile and pull the girls over, making Vivian give up the impressinor.

We try to pose nice and follow Damian's directions, but not even he can keep us from getting giggly again after a while. I wish it was more like this in the Ladies' Chamber sometimes.

Damian does his best to take the images and even gets a few of Vivian and Flur individually before setting the impressionor down.

"I need copies for Karrigan. We'll keep the copier busy," Flur jokes.

"Indeed so," Damian grins then goes to the workbench and removes his waistcoat, exchanging it for a low-cut black one instead and his matching cravat for a white one.

"What are you up to?" Vivian smiles.

"What? He's not allowed to go?" I tease.

"They should have told me earlier if that was the case," Damian smiles as he pulls the ribbon loose from his hair then ties it back once more with a black ribbon, then throws a cape around his shoulders and secures the clasps. He turns to face us as he puts on his mask.

"Don't break the chandelier," I tease.

"I'll try not to," Damian smiles.

"So now I need your brother as backup?" I tease further as my maids start to get things cleaned up, so we can go right to taking everything off when we get back and who knows how late that will be.

"I promise not to steal any young women away," Damian says, smiling with a hand over his heart. "No matter how beautifully they sing," he grins.

"I'll just remember to be quiet then," I smile as there's a knock on the door, the cue saying it's time to gather in the ballroom.

As I'd not paid attention to it last time I was there, I'm looking forward to actually getting a good look at the ballroom this time. I know even if I wow the prince and get his attention, I won't be allowed to keep it all night. The best I can hope for is a good few hours, and that is being overly hopeful.

Damian picks up the impressinor. "Have to be sure to capture the evening," he smiles.

"Of course you would. You rather serve in the background than join the group," I tease as Flur opens the door to see us out.

"I forever will be where you need me," Damian smiles.

I roll my eyes, but I can't ignore the moment now. I take a deep breath and follow Flur and Vivian out of the room. Damian follows behind and closes the door. He offers me his arm to take me to the ballroom. I smile and accept his offer. He leads us to the ballroom. We're about to enter when, with his hand on the handle, Damian looks back at me. "Are you ready?" he asks.

I nod, "I'm ready." He nods back and pulls the doors open and steps aside. I take a deep breath and enter.

The first thing I recognize is the gold of the ballroom floor, decorated with ocean wave patterns across it in a light Purerahian blue. I look up to admire the ballroom as a whole. The pillars holding up the wrap-around landing are painted and carved with amazing skill to look like waves of water holding up the second floor. But the two most stunning views are right ahead and above. In the center of the room is a dome that shows the stars. It's as if it absorbs that starlight and reflects it to light up the huge ballroom. Ahead is a stunning display of gold and glass that leads out to a balcony that overlooks a view of the ocean I'd not seen paralleled. I thought the castle had stunning views. I suspect the sun sets right in the center of that balcony. It takes my breath away. How could I have missed it before?

The music adds a mysterious element to the room. They play classical dance pieces all with a spooky harvest theme, with a tinkling, musical, magical sound counting out the waltz beats. It's as good as any ballroom I'd pictured in our shows, if not better.

Damian beams and looks around the room then back at me. "Truly, there are few more beautiful sights."

"With a sunset, it might be," I say.

"Indeed," Damian says as he looks around again then gestures forward. "Shall we?"

A few girls are already here. Lilly looks adorable as a little fairy with wings that remind me of a butterfly. Her mask is simple pink with little flowers at each corner.

Zelda loves it. "You look just like the fairies back home, only bigger!"

"How big?" Lilly asks.

"Oh, four or five inches. Like little figurines." Zelda tries to show with her hands.

That's when I notice the unique ring and bracelet combination that goes with her costume. She wears a stunning white dress with a gold belt, flowing sleeves, and a golden glow about her. I wonder if she's using her magic for it. She wears a diadem with the golden symbol of her people. It blends perfectly with her golden mask. I guess she's Hyvia, Hyvil's founder. It looks really good on her. It makes her look powerful.

Florence gives me a smirk as she walks past. She's dressed as Ms. Daae, the character I am famous for playing, wearing a large white dress with stars and music notes done into the dress and her hair with silver marks. She looks regal next to Micalya who's dressed up as a cat.

"No, they're not stars; they're edelweiss," Damian mutters in complaint next to me.

"What?"

"Florence. Her costume is wrong," he says, waving a hand at it.

"Um... those are stars," I frown. The marks on her dress and hair are five-pointed stars for sure.

"I know, but they're supposed to be edelweiss; that's what's in the play," Damian insists.

"Oh, I've never seen real edelweiss."

"It's a lovely flower, and they should use it right," Damian states.

Damian has spotted who must be Florence's attendant; he excuses himself quickly. I laugh though no one around me understands why.

"We'll have to borrow him next time," Azalea jokes. She's dressed as a swan.

"But you look stunning," I object. "Those faux feathers are great; they look so soft and real."

"I was worried I'd look too much like the swans in the ballet. That would be terrible," Azalea laughs.

I laugh too. "I doubt Damian would come up with that. I do that for a living. That's pretty boring."

"Well, as long as we didn't clash. I don't want to copy you. It's important to stand out," Azalea says. "Unlike Ericka."

Ericka has gone for a ballerina look with a Juliet-style tutu and lots of sparkles. I would think it pretty if she'd wear it right. Even her high heels mimic pointe shoes.

All of the Chosen are here, but I don't see the king, queen, or prince anywhere.

I do see Damian now standing in a corner with his brother. I frown at Cedrick, trying to guess what he's dressed up as. His suit is mostly black with red and gold hints, like he is on fire with a soft flame, but then he has an impressive fiery cloak I'd never seen the like of before. Damian must have made it. The whole thing makes his blue eyes stand out spectacularly against his mask.

I spot Adam, the impressionist who was in my fan photo, ready and already working. Standing next to him is a man I'd never seen before, about middle-aged or perhaps a bit younger. He has blond hair, sharp yet warm eyes, and a ready big smile. He holds a notebook in one hand and taps a pen against it as he looks around, asking Adam questions which it looks like Adam is ignoring with impatience.

A trumpet call announces the royal family is about to arrive. We turn to the main entrance on the second floor.

The herald leaps up next to the doors and announces, "Their Majesties, King Aster and Queen Dalilly, and His Royal Highness, Prince Gavril." They step into the room together as the doors are opened for them.

The queen's outfit takes my breath away. I think it's supposed to be a sunset. The stunning orange, blues, and reds work with her dark skin and seashell tiara.

The king is dressed as a ship captain from his hat with the national gold braiding on it, the high collared jacket with braided shoulders, long buttons, and tails.

But it's when I look at Prince Gavril's costume that I have to cover my mouth to hold in a laugh. He is dressed as a sailor. He and his father must have decided to go for a theme. Maybe they're a couple of sailors trying to reach the sunset. Gavril doesn't look half bad. His shirt is perfectly white and crisp. I flush as I realize how low cut it is. Gavril has the national blue band around his waist, dark pants, and boots that match his father's perfectly. A dark cape is cast about his shoulders. His hair looks rather windswept as if he'd just stepped off the ship. His mask is different: one side is dark blue and the other is off-white with some kind of musical-themed scrollwork on it.

Good job, Godwin. He does look dashing. I swallow.

Now I've seen the other girls, I'm not sure I stand out as much as I hoped or thought I would. But perhaps that's a good thing. I'm not trailing stardust like Dahlia or mocking a fellow Chosen by dressing up as her day job.

Damian comes closer and smiles at me, "Well now, it seems the prince listened to you."

I jump and look at him. "What..." Then I realize what he said. "How did you know?" He wasn't there, was he?

"I have my ways. After all, no one pays attention to servants," he smiles and looks me in the eye as if seeing if I got the joke.

"And I trust you to take time off," I smile. "Who was the other servant with you, your brother?" I joke. Then pale at his smile. "You're kidding."

Damian chuckles, "It was Cedrick's idea. And I don't judge. But that is how I knew Gavril was struggling that night."

I give him a look. “You’re making it hard to have secrets. And you wonder why I forget you don’t know things sometimes.”

“I didn’t follow you out to the balcony,” Damian says. “Honestly, as silly as it sounds it was more about seeing how well the dress worked than anything else.”

I smile and shake my head. “Your brother's right. You’re so vain.” But that’s part of why we love him, right?

“Told you.” His brother appears. All the girls around us flush, but I ignore that. “But he did do a good job. He always does. You look nice.” he smiles, glancing over my head before looking back at me. “Looks like they’re getting ready for the first dance. May I?”

Damian arches a brow. “Brother,” he says in a warning tone.

“What? No one else has asked,” he points out. No one else had a chance. I giggle though. The other girls are envious. Ericka looks like she’ll break in her fake pointe shoes just by glaring.

Damian sighs and rolls his eyes then looks at me. “Your call, my lady.”

“Well, were you going to ask?” I tease.

“Not at the moment, but no one is on the floor yet,” Damian points out.

“I’m asking for the first dance when they start. They are about to,” Cedrick nods at the players getting ready to perform, and the king is getting ready to dance with the queen.

“Ah, very well,” Damian relents.

The herald announces the first dance. The king and queen get into position. A few couriers, other servants, and guards ask different ladies to join them. I sigh and accept Cedrick’s offered hand. He leads me onto the floor and into position.

He’s as smooth here on the ballroom floor as he was in my review lessons. I find it easier to dance with him just for fun than I did in lessons. He finishes the dance with quite a good dip for someone who isn’t used to doing lifts. He pulls me up just as smoothly, bowing and kissing my hand before leading me back to where he found me. I chuckle. He got it pretty much exactly to the spot.

Damian smiles as he leads Flur off the dance floor back to her spot then looks at his brother. “Excellent work. I think you make the prince jealous.”

I flush. “I don’t think so.”

“Oh dear!” Cedrick’s voice is dripping sarcasm. “Whatever will I do?”

Damian rolls his eyes. “You also earned some looks from a few of the ladies,” He says, glancing around.

“Oh, that one is a problem.” Cedrick follows his eyes. I giggle. “I’m too popular. What do I do?”

“Um.” I wasn’t expecting that. “I-I don’t know.”

"Hm, maybe I should ask the wise sage," he muses. I frown. Cedrick grins, "The wisdom cat."

I roll my eyes.

"Oh, good gracious." Damian rolls his eyes. "Why don't you just ask Vivian or Flur for the next dance?"

"That sounds nice," Cedrick agrees.

I smile. "It would make their night."

"Then that shall be the goal." Cedrick kisses my hand. "While you wait, you should try out the treats. They're really good. There's a fruit one, really sweet, pretty sure it's Hyvian." He winks at Damian before going to track down my poor maids.

Damian rolls his eyes again then turns to me. "Well then, do you think you need a break, or would you like to dance?"

I smile. "I'd love to," I accept his offer. He bows, offers his hand then leads me back out to the dance floor, where he glides me into a hold.

I smile. He's about as smooth as his brother but in a much more formal way. I step into the hold, feeling how precise he is in his position. He places his hands properly then begins the dance. His moves are like gliding on water, even when he leads me into turns, the hints are clear and his movements exact and sure. He contrasts his brother in that. Cedrick's dancing is smooth, almost perfectly blended. I can distinguish each step with Damian much more easily. I imagine Damian would be quite good in sharper dances.

To finish, Damian twirls me then drops me into a dip, catching me easily, then stands me up and pulls out of the hold, still holding my hand as he bows and kisses it.

I smile. "You are quite the gentleman."

"I try to be." he smiles as he straightens up and leads me from the dance floor.

"You were taught well." I smile. I look around. The prince is dropping off Princess Amapola, dressed as a rose dancer, with his parents, laughing at their conversation.

I'd planned to explore the ballroom while the prince is busy, but now I'm here, there isn't much to explore. Other than going out onto the balcony but who'd be able to see me out there? I'm starting to hate this weird game the Enthronement has become.

Damian leads me back to my spot, and he bows. "My lady, thank you for the dance."

"Thank you." I smile. "It was nice to dance with the man who keeps telling me how to do it right," I joke.

Damian chuckles as he straightens up. "Well, I figured I owed you at least one, after all, I put you through."

“Well, it’s been helpful. Thank you,” I bow my head a little to him.

“But of course, my lady.” Damian smiles and bows his head back to me then looks over at the royals. “The match there is rather uncanny.”

“You knew.” I roll my eyes.

Damian shrugs. “Not really. I never asked if he was following through on your joke. I just sort of... guessed he would. And I had no clue his parents would be following his idea. But you do match their theme rather well.” He smiles at me.

“The sailors maybe, but a sunset?” I raise a brow.

“You’re the mermaid playing in it.” he grins.

I laugh and shake my head. “Alright, if you want to put it that way.”

Damian grins again then looks over at the dance floor. “Looks like Vivian’s gotten her dance.”

“And she seems pleased.” I smile. They did look like they had a good time. I think Cedrick is complimenting her weapon.

“Indeed.” Damian nods then looks at me. “Can I get you anything, my lady?”

I smile and shake my head. “No thank you. I’m alright.”

“Very well. Call if you have need of anything.” He smiles and bows to me.

“I will. Thank you," I say that to him a lot, but he has earned it.

“You’re welcome.” Damian nods to me then leaves.

I sigh and look around. I’m not sure what else to do. I can see the prince is dancing with Zelda. Though their outfits don’t “match”, they look great together. Zelda’s white outfit flows around her, giving her the look of a goddess as Gavril twirls her around. I watch as he pulls her in and whispers something in her ear. She laughs.

I frown a bit. They look really happy together. He looks more natural with her than anyone else. I wish I could get myself to look away from them, but it’s not easy.

Zelda isn’t a brilliant dancer, but she’s good. Gavril’s surprisingly good, from what I can see anyway. They seem to fit. What if I’m wrong? What if they are perfect? What am I doing playing this game? She has the experience he lacks. She’d make a perfect princess for our war-torn nation. Why do I think I’d be of any help compared to her?

I take a shaking breath. How do I even know what is going on between us is real? I thought Jake was real. I’d have risked my life on it. But now... now he’s as unsure as my future.

Gavril had felt so sure in the moment. Even when we met, we clicked. I felt he understood me. I thought he felt the same. I was looking forward to seeing him again before I even knew who he was. A brief crush. My only crush before reality would hit. I am supposed to be with Jake. I wish he and

I looked half as good together. Zelda and Gavril just match. Not because they are the same, but because they are so different.

Zelda is the typical blonde of her nation. Gavril's milk chocolate skin and dark hair offset her so perfectly. I would cast them together if I were a director. I doubt I'd ever have put us together. I don't really know him anyway. After all, I didn't think he'd drop me after kissing me like he did. But that's exactly what has happened.

I wish I could look away. Gavril pulls her close in a back step, and he says something in her ear. Zelda smiles gently, and their eyes meet for a moment. Even I can feel the spark as they did. I want to look away, but instead, I watch as he kisses her cheek sneakily before sending her out in a twirl.

What am I thinking? Zelda is going to get over her unease. She is going to fall for those eyes, those kisses, the innocent power and passion that's hidden inside the prince who's so locked inside of himself. The pain bubbles up, and I fight tears. Who am I to even be hurt? So what if he kissed me first? I am not an option.

Gavril kisses her hand before escorting Zelda back to the treats table. I watch as his eyes land on Ericka and asks her to dance. He looks at her shoes and makes a comment that makes her laugh. Her eyes land on me, smirking. She was hoping I'd be watching. She thinks she stole my thunder.

I am not giving her that satisfaction. I smile as if in congratulations which makes Ericka extremely confused before I turn away. At least I'm good at something in this twisted game.

I take a deep breath and seek a different companion. Godwin is speaking with the man who'd been with Adam. Adam is walking around and getting impressions. But it's the second man my eyes land on or rather my ears. I know that voice. He is the reporter Godwin was talking to. I move over to try to talk to him, thinking I can use Godwin or the fact I know Adam as an introduction.

I have to wave through the crowd, losing sight of them for a moment. I'm almost there when Godwin appears in front of me. I try to step around him, but he moves in front of me. Is he blocking me on purpose?

"May I have this dance?" he asks, bowing to me and taking my hand, "You're the only one I haven't yet. I hate for you to be left out."

I hesitate and look over Godwin's head to the man I want to meet. He's taking notes in his notebook.

I look back at Godwin. I can't say no without drawing attention. "Guess you can't be left out." I smile back.

Is that relief that flashes in Godwin's eyes? He glances behind me then turns so I can rest my hand in his as he escorts me onto the dance floor. As we turn, I can't help but glance to my left to see what he is looking at.

The man who'd pretended to be the prince at the last ball is standing there, watching us with a strange look in his eye. I hold in my frown until I'm turning into position with Godwin.

I follow his lead without much thought, frowning. Why would Godwin be relieved? Or was he stopping that man from getting to me? I don't mind that idea. That man had creeped me out.

"Are you alright?" Godwin asks as he leads me into a twirl. "You're crazy. You look so distracted, yet you're dancing better than most of the other girls put together."

I chuckle as he leads me into a position where we're facing the same direction, my back against his right arm. "Thank you, I just have better body memory for it."

I glance over at the man in question again. Godwin follows my eyes as we return to a closed hold. "Know him?" he asks casually.

"Not really. He was pretending to be the prince that first night here."

"Did you like him?"

I hesitate. "Who is he?"

"Grand Duke Aldgrone." Godwin tries to shrug it off, but I can tell his choice of moves intentionally keeps me away from him.

"Should I like him?"

"Don't you get to decide that?" Godwin asks.

I roll my eyes. "You like to hide answers."

"I've dealt with the press. I have to, or get to, depending on how you look at it." He grins like thwarting the press is the most fun job in the world. It makes me laugh.

"What answers are you after?" He opens it up to me as we get onto the opposite side of the room from the grand duke.

"Why you're trying to keep me away from him?"

"Do you mind?"

"No, he was... Well, maybe it was because I thought he was the prince, but he was a bit..."

"Anxious? All over you? Oozy fake charm? Or just oozing?" Godwin asks.

I can't answer for laughing, which I have a feeling suits Godwin, just fine. "Does creeping me out and oozy go together?"

Godwin pauses to think, still dancing. "Sure, we'll call it the same thing."

"So why keep me away from him?" I ask.

"Well, do you want him to be creepy all over you?"

"I much rather not."

"Then you should thank me, not interrogate me. You and Gavril like doing that. It's rather rude. Do your maids ever complain?"

"No," I say through a laugh, "they like their jobs."

"I do too, but that doesn't mean he doesn't drive me nuts."

I glance over at where Gavril is dancing with Forsythia, dressed as a vampire. "You did a good job," I compliment.

"Aw, no one ever tells me that. Thanks." Godwin grins from ear to ear.

I roll my eyes. "Don't let it go to your head."

"Your attendant does," he replies.

"Does not; he's just always vain," I giggle.

Godwin nods. "Hm, I'll try that if it gets me more compliments."

I laugh as the song ends, and Godwin bows to me.

"Want another or shall I take you back?" Godwin asks.

"Is he still there?" I ask in a low voice.

Godwin glances over. "Yup."

"Can you escort me somewhere *not* near him?" I suggest.

"Sure, though that is breaking protocol." Godwin offers me his arm

"I have a feeling you and your team don't care." I accept Godwin's arm.

He frowns as he walks me over by where the king and queen's thrones are, the opposite side of the room from where we'd been. "What team?"

"You and Sage and whoever works on the prince's staff." I frown. "Are there not more? There should be."

"I never thought of it that way. I supposed we are, but if you could tell the prince that for me, so he stops acting like I'm the little brother tagging along and making things more silly and/or risky that would be great." Godwin gives me another one of his winning, joking smiles.

I roll my eyes. "That bad?"

"You have no idea."

I glance over at the table. The man I'd wanted to talk to looks ready to jump on the grand duke.

"Who is that?" I ask.

"I told you, the grand duke. I like to think of him as Sir Slimy."

"Not him." I give Godwin an exasperated look. "The man who looks ready to attack him."

"Uh? Who?" Godwin squints as he tries to see. "I don't see anyone."

Now I know he's hiding something. "The man you were talking to before you asked me to dance."

"I talk to a lot of people at these things," Godwin says as if asking me to be more specific.

How can I be without admitting I'd overheard them that day? "He came with the press."

"Only person who is here with a press pass is Adam." Godwin nods at him taking impressions of Gavril dancing with the girls. "I thought you girls met him already."

"The one who was with him," I insist.

"I told you; he's the only one with a press pass." Something in Godwin's eyes though tells me he's dropping me a hint. But if he is, I have no idea what this clue could be.

Perhaps I should try to find him myself. It would mean getting near the grand duke "Well, I guess you have other things to attend to. If you don't know him, I shouldn't keep bugging him," I sigh as if in defeat.

"Alright. See you around. Oh, and a great costume. It's my favorite." Godwin grins at me.

"Thanks," I reply, not caring much.

Godwin leaves me alone, still without answers. But I'd rather ignore the grand duke if possible after those warnings. I'll wait to see if the reporter gets away from the grand duke.

I wander to the front of the balcony as it stretches out into the starlit darkness. It's so peaceful, quiet.

An unwelcome thought crosses my mind. I think about my father and Jake, likely with their band, waiting for me to let them in. I don't know if my father took the hint, but I would presume he didn't.

The idea Jake is just outside, waiting for me like the prince at the bottom of Rapunzel's tower makes my heart ache. The poor thing is there, pining, expecting me to be madly in love and excited to see him. It hurts. Sure, he'd hurt me a lot, but that doesn't mean I'm overly excited to stab him in the back in return. This isn't fair to him any more than it is to me.

I hug myself, wanting to hide my face in the sudden shame that wells up inside of me. I haven't even thought about him in days or maybe even longer. He'd been a key part of my life, and I'd thrown him off. It wasn't easy. It took me a while, and I don't regret that. But I feel bad that it's all fallen apart, changed, broken, and ended, and he's still out there, clueless.

I suddenly wish I was anywhere but on this ballroom floor. I take a few more deep breaths and look back at the golden glass doors. and lean on the golden frames, watching the waves twinkling in the moonlight. It's not quite a full moon, but its strong waxing shape spreads powerful moonlight over the sea, the grounds, and the shining palace walls. I rub my arms as if cold, but I don't feel a chill. Just lonely and lost.

My eyes drift back to the ballroom floor but watching Gavril with the others makes me feel sick, so I avoid that at all costs.

Instead, my body sways to the music, and I count the steps in my mind. One, two, three; one, two, three. I join the dancers in my mind, accompanied by my dream partner: the one I made up long ago, knowing Jake was a hopeless dancer.

I look back out at the waves, my mind still dancing with the others but not out there anymore. I smile a little as I imagine dancing across those waves, on them, with the moonlight between me and my shadow partner and the waves as our enchanted dance floor. Sitting there, watching the waves, and daydreaming feels wonderful. I lose all track of time, just smiling. No one is controlling me here. For now, I am free.

Chapter 43

Someone taps my shoulder. I jump and turn to see quite the smiling face under his mask. "How long have you been hiding back here?" Prince Gavril asks me. "I've been looking."

I frown. "No, you weren't."

His face falls slightly. "What do you mean? You weren't even looking. You wish to dance among the waves?" He grins mischievously.

I laugh. He has a point. I am dressed as a mermaid and daydreaming about the ocean. "You caught me red-finned." Oh, wow that was a bad joke. What was I thinking? I turn red and look away.

Gavril laughs. "Well, I can't offer you an ocean yet, but will a marble floor done up as one do?" He offers me his hand. I give it a distrusting look. "What?" he frowns. "Don't want to? Your daydream that much better?"

"Maybe."

Gavril's face falls a little more. I should be kinder. It's not his fault I feel this way.

"I didn't mean to ignore you, if that's what you mean," Gavril apologizes. "I gave the other girls their turns first is all, I swear," he adds when I give him a look. "I'm not playing favorites and ignoring them. I wanted to save you for last. I-I liked that last time." His cheeks go slightly pink. "Come on. Just one? I'd feel like a jerk if I didn't give every girl at least one dance."

I fight a fresh flush coming to my cheeks. Of course, that's what he was doing. I should have realized. Then again, with how he'd ignored me, how could I expect any different? He'd been going down the list, hitting them all before reaching me like that first ball. Though I doubt that was on purpose with how I was hiding.

"Don't tell me you're hiding because you think you look horrible again."

That wins a laugh. No, no, that was not why this time. I feel ugly on the inside this time. I fight not to glance outside.

"Just one?" Gavril begs me. "I even did what you asked and gave all the others a fair shot. I really did."

"It seemed to work." I smile.

The prince sighs and bows his head. "So, is this how it's going to be?" He pulls his head up just enough to meet my eyes. "Even after I promised I'd be back for you? I only did as you asked. Not even one dance? You did tell me to not treat you like the only option."

I can't stop myself from frowning and looking away again. "You shouldn't have done it for me," I state. "You should have done it for you."

A slight joking smile crosses Gavril's face. "I did. I took a gamble and did what I wanted for once. I didn't dress up as a sunrise, thank you very much." I laugh at the idea.

"And I dated the way I wanted to. The only struggle was not asking you out again," he admits. "But you asked me to try around, so I did. Why punish me for it?"

"It's... not that."

"Then what is it?" Gavril asks, studying my face.

Oh no, I know that look. He's putting something together. He's getting angry doing so. I know that anger. It is the same one when he thought Jake had sent me something that upset me. And this time, he is right. How did I slow him down when he is right?

"Did he speak to you again?"

"No." But he's just outside waiting for me to open a door I never will.

"Then what is it?" he asks again. "Have I betrayed your trust yet?"

I'm going to have to distract him, even as part of my heart wants to scream and tell him everything. "You really did try?"

"Honest." His eyes carefully study mine. "Doesn't your board tell you that?" He gives me a teasing grin.

"It's not mine," I defend with a slight snap.

Gavril chuckles. "I figured. You didn't even admit you'd won the first kiss." His eyes sparkle as they meet mine again.

"I didn't know if I had."

"Well, you did. We just put it right. And helped take the edge off. You should have seen Sage's face when I added him," he grins. "Or did you not figure that out?"

"Oh, I did." I smile.

"Good, now come on. Every other girl got a dance. You can't accuse me of playing favorites for insisting you have one. You're the only one who hasn't," he says.

"You skipped me," I fake accuse him.

He grins. "You were hiding back here." I giggle at the reference to the first ball clear in his voice. "I told you I was looking, but there's only so long in the night. So please, just one dance?" he pleads a little but keeps that playful look.

"Well, I guess I can let my poor daydream take a break." I pretend it's the last thing I want to do.

The prince smiles as I give him my hand, "Maybe the real world is better."

He leads me onto the floor perfectly. I have to admire he even knows the proper tuck of his free arm before helping lead me into a closed hold. His hold is perfectly firm as he gives me that warm smile again. He isn't as perfect to form as perhaps Cedrick or Damian, but Gavril feels like his hold fits me.

I fall into a basic step with him almost subconsciously. He is really good. I smile a bit and give him a look.

"What? Don't tell me I'm not good. This is one of the few princely things I got to learn and be good at," he teases me as he leads me into a twirl. "Don't give me that look."

I laugh as we go back into a basic. "No, I'm just hoping you didn't go out of your way to impress me."

"I come with some good features included," he defends as he turns me into a sway in and out. I laugh at that. He smiles. "I don't have to fight for everything, just most things."

"Alright, fair enough," I say as we get back into a closed hold. "Well, I wasn't judging. You are good."

"True, but I'm sure you can. You do this for a living."

"Ballet and this are not the same."

"Could have fooled me." He grins. "Or is that also Damian's fault."

"Hey, that's not fair," I defend as we step in a turn around the room.

The prince's eyebrows go up. "So it isn't his fault?"

"Well, he did make sure I had a refresher."

"So, we're back to Damian is the master behind it all." The prince shakes his head. "Maybe it's him who should win and I should marry."

I miss a step, I'm laughing so hard. The prince easily twirls me a bit out of the way of the other dancers in traffic. "It's not that funny," he laughs too.

"Well, when you've got the disgust on Damian's face in your mind, it is." I am still giggling.

Gavril chuckles, rolling his eyes as he holds me. I like the feeling. I think he does too.

When I finally calm down, Gavril pulls me back into a closed hold. He's so confident and efficient it takes my breath away. "Well, that's not an option. I'm not asking him no matter how much you claim he's the real magic in you."

"You're really good." I didn't expect him to so easily pull us back in like that, and he got us out so easily. You'd think he did this every day, not me.

The prince shrugs, "No idea what you're talking about." He sets me into a thread of turns I don't think most men even knew how to do, let alone lead me into without warning.

"Now you're showing off." He's leaving me a bit breathless as we come back smoothly into the basic step.

The grin on the prince's face is contagious. "Are you sure you're a professional dancer? I thought that was a basic one." Oh, I can hear the taunting gloat in his voice.

I giggle, beaming back. "Are you saying I can't do more than that?" I give him a challenging, narrow-eyed look.

"Betcha you can't. You win... you get me the rest of the night. I win, I get to pick all your partners the whole night." The prince smirks.

That's a bet I have to take. "Done."

There is nothing he knows I can't do, I'm sure of it.

The prince grins. "Though remember this song isn't the best for some, so we may have to choose a faster song next time."

"Fair," I agree.

I love his playfulness. I love this game and the excuse to have more than just the one dance. I... love this magical time with him.

Gavril immediately starts a natural turn that is a bit more advanced, but nothing hard, and he leads it well, so I can't complain about that.

I raise an eyebrow at him. Is that the best he could do?

His grin is so big I'm thinking he's less of a sailor tonight and more of a pirate who's just found the treasure he's hunting. It makes my heart skip in excitement.

We don't do more than one or maybe two basics in a row after that. Each basic leads into something new: lifts, a few different kinds of sliding turns, even doing some turns where he's not even touching me, only to catch me right at the proper moment. I'd have thought he was taught this exact sequence just for this night. Maybe he had someone prepare him for it. It feels more like performing than anything I did in my refresher lessons. We challenge each other's footwork, turns, alignment, and Gavril impresses me by doing a few lifts as if I weigh nothing.

The prince finishes with a basic turn before dipping me the same way Damian had. He pulls me up easily, smoothly sliding his hand down to mine and kissing it. "Well, you gave me the first real workout of the night," he teases. "Who won?"

"That round?" I smile.

"Well yeah, only so many hard things to do in a waltz." He grins.

"Hm, I'll give you that one out of pity. I am the professional, after all," I state.

"Uh? It isn't Ericka? She's dressed like one." We both lose it laughing.

The next song is spooky and quick; the lights have dimmed to add to the mood. I quite enjoy it, and Gavril elegantly puts the moves together. We travel and own the room this time, taking advantage of the quick turns and slow steps to try each other's footwork and timing. I almost forget the competition, enjoying the flow of it.

Gavril is very good. We get off some impressive turns, and he even tries several fun dips, a few extensions, and even tests my trust with a lift and a turn with me bent back in almost a dip. The song ends as he pulls me up.

I can feel his chest rising and falling with his excited breath. I grin and dare look at him. The smile on his face makes me smile and laugh. Gavril takes the chance to kiss my cheek. Before I can react, the next song plays, the typical waltz the palace seems to like. He gets us right into it without missing a beat, but he uses more basics and simple turns to let us catch our breath.

"That was for Sage," Gavril teases. "He said I couldn't go from one dance to another. I just won a solo night." I laugh. "Seriously, he normally sits outside my door. I told him if I could do it, he'd give me a night where I don't have to worry about him at the door."

"He's just outside. What's the big deal?"

"Just nice to feel free." Gavril smiles and turns me, so we're in a position with my back pressing into his arm, facing the same direction. "So, who do you think won?" he asks in a low voice next to my ear, making my skin tingle.

"You're letting me pick? Isn't that dangerous?"

"You're the pro, better judge."

"Maybe we can ask Damian."

Gavril clicks his tongue as he turns me back into a rotation of basics. "I guess Damian knows everything."

"He creepily does. I swear to you."

The music picks up a little, and Gavril takes advantage of the tempo to have us travel the room, twirling me about and moving us to the outside of the circle of dance. I giggle as he pulls me in, back to his arm again. He steals another kiss on my cheek before twirling me back out then back into the basic.

I don't know who's having more fun, me or him.

But then he breaks it. He leads us both out of the circle of dance, behind a pillar, and stuns me with a kiss full on the lips.

Electricity shoots through me, making me feel excited, adored, and happier than I'd been in so long. I take a sharp breath of surprise, but I can't help but melt into his kiss and his hold on me.

He kisses me again and again, each one lighting a new rush of emotion and excitement that mounts upon the last. The tingle teases me from head to toe, making even the tips of my fingers tingle as he moves his hands up my arms to my shoulders.

When he finally pulls back, his eyes are still closed as if taking in the feeling, treasuring it, or perhaps examining it. Slowly, a smile lights his lips, even with his eyes closed. They open, and his amber eyes meet mine, making a fresh wave of that stunning magic wash over me.

"What was what?" I ask in more breath than voice. He's so close.

"I did what you asked. I'm going through all my options," he says, his eyes not straying from mine.

The moment is broken a little as someone runs past. I glance over to see it's Damian's brother my impressinor held defensively to his chest, at least I think it's my impressinor. A moment later, Damian runs past our hidden corner too.

Damian stops just short of running into us. The expression on his face highly embarrassed as he glances at us. "Sorry." He bows his eyes away then looks all around and spots his brother. "Cedrick, you little twit! Get back here with that!" he yells then moves around us and darts after him again.

Gavril and I both laugh as they pass. "Well, that wasn't odd." Gavril chuckles before looking down at me again.

"I get the feeling Cedrick does that a lot." I smile too. Then recall what we'd been caught doing. I flush. I'm not sure I am ready or if I even want this.

"Don't worry, we're going to get caught sooner or later." Gavril smiles. "I know you don't want the kisses you've won on the board. But come on then. I guess the safest place to hide is on the dance floor."

"But who won?" I ask.

"Doesn't matter." Gavril shrugs. "Either way it's the same result."

"What?"

"Well, you win, you get me the whole night. I win, I pick your partners all night. Either way, I get what I want," he says, taking my hand in position, so we could sneak back into the line of dance without anyone noticing we'd slipped off.

I open my mouth to protest, but he's already pulled me in mid-count to get us into step. "That wasn't fair," I accuse him.

"No, not really. But I've never bet, so I thought it better to defend myself," Gavril says. "But I'm on a winning streak, so might as well keep it up."

I sigh heavily. "Why would you even want me all night? You've not spoken to me since I threw the contest in your face."

"You weren't wrong," Gavril sighs heavily. "I was just busy doing what you asked. Trying to give the other girls a chance." He pauses as he executes a turn. "I felt guilty measuring them with the same stick. Did any of them make me feel like *you* make me feel?"

He meets my eyes, and I feel another shudder run through me. I'm aware of how close he is in our dance. "We all do it." I try to brush it off.

"Well, that's assuring." Gavril tosses it aside too. "And I suppose I did find there are others I'd be happy with, but it just wasn't the same. I don't get to make choices. And it felt really good to make one that day. And I'm not used to second-guessing those choices. The few I get to make, I just go for and live with," he tries to explain.

"Must be nice." I wish I were like that.

Gavril huffs, "I can count all those choices on one hand. And there's one I'm not at all proud of."

"What choice is that?"

I gasp in fright as Gavril tenses as if someone had struck him from behind, but there's no one there. As soon as his tension came, it's gone, and he sends me out in an outward turn. I can't see his face when he does that.

He pulls me back in, and I try to see his face, but he sets us off into a set of tricky turns before returning to basic where I can look at him.

He's smiling a little though. "No," he says, stroking my cheek a little before returning to position, "it's not you."

Relief flows through me, but the worry is still there. Why did he react like that? Is he alright? But his breath is on my skin, so close, distracts me. I move closer subconsciously.

Gavril does the same, but more deliberately. The hand at my back drops a little to make holding me close simpler as we move into a basic two step, which makes it easier to stay close. He does it so effortlessly. It makes my heart race. His soft but confident energy envelopes me, making me feel safe.

I lean my head on him and close my eyes for a moment. If I didn't know any better, I would have said we were dancing on those waves.

Gavril was right. The reality is better than my daydreams. I like feeling him there. His sure arm at my back, his hand tight in mine. His smooth cheek against my temple; his steady breath on my skin. His chest softly pressed to mine in a gentle rise and fall like an ocean wave.

"Trouble is," he whispers, "I seem to have made a choice without meaning to. If this was really up to me, mistake or not, I would have picked you."

My breath hitches.

Part of me rejoices and wants to latch onto it. The other part of me is in a panic. What if I break him like I did Jake? What if I can't win and he can't choose me? I'm not a true princess. I came here to stop that stunning heartbeat in my ears from beating again.

I hold tighter to him as if afraid that his heartbeat will stop.

What if I confess? Even if it's just to him. There is no way Sage can hear me. I can see him dancing with Zelda, though he doesn't look too happy. That means I am safe. Only Gavril will hear me. Can I do it? Can I follow Gavril's lead and just make the choice and deal with it?

My heart races with the desire to confess, to get it all out, to be brave just a moment, come what may. I'm sure he'd forgive me.

But the fear chokes that out and makes tears run to my eyes. Could my heart stand it if he did reject me once he knew the truth? It's one thing to have his parents toss me aside, but what if he did? Could I survive another heartbreak?

No, I should tell him now not to hope for me. Not to choose me. To try to keep his heart open still. It's the only way we'd both make it out of this.

I take a breath to explain that to him when the lights flicker out. Several screams of fright and surprise fill the air before the lights return just as suddenly. Was it just a part of the spooky night? It seems like a prank the king would pull.

When the lights return, a few people laugh in amusement, clearly thinking it was a show. My shoulders relax.

But Gavril's grip on me tightens before he takes my hand firmly. It isn't playful. He's tense as if for a fight.

Chapter 44

I frown at Gavril, "What?"

"I've seen that before," Gavril says tensely, "and if I'm right..." he looks to his left, and sure enough, Sage is suddenly there. He's as tense as Gavril, ready to spring and draw his blades.

"Oh no," I breathe. I didn't think Dad would dare try anything if no one let them in. I thought they'd all be safe! Fear and guilt fill me. I should have said something!

The lights flicker, but this time they go on and off faster.

"Saferoom, in the throne room. Now!" Sage orders.

Sage starts to yank Gavril on, but I grab his arm to stop them. "Wait." Somehow, my tone makes them both stop. "They're not going to come in the front doors. He's going to try to slip under you. It's faster that way. The lights are likely them trying to get past a guard post. He only has a few targets, remember? He doesn't have to take out everyone."

"Wait." Sage narrows his eyes at me. "Are you saying you know who's attacking?"

Sage lets go of Gavril and grabs my arm painfully hard.

I gasp in pain and yank free, but Sage grabs me again, even tighter, and shoves me into the nearest object. "What do you know?!"

Before I can answer, Sage is violently yanked off me. "There's no need to smack her around," Gavril snarls at his guard. I've never heard Gavril that dangerous or angry. I shrink back.

Sage doesn't back down. He retorts with his own dark anger, "She knows something. I told you she did from the start. I knew it in the garden!"

"I stand by what I said. I'm not letting you push them around," Gavril stands his ground.

The lights flicker once more, making us all look up.

"Um, as sweet as this is," I begin, "I don't think we have time for this argument. Yes, alright, I think I know who's attacking. I'll explain later." It's hard to go on as tears rise to my eyes.

It's over for me. I didn't let them in, so Dad will not let me home, but now I have to confess what I am, and I'm going to be imprisoned or worse. What could have I done differently?

My lip shakes no matter how hard I try to use all my acting skills to stop it. "I did-didn't think they'd do it." I take a deep breath.

I manage to look up at Sage, trying to ignore the hatred in his eyes. "I know which rebellion it is at least. It's the Custods, and if Gavril is right, they aren't going to bother killing guards or guests or anyone else. They're going to go right for the target." I look around the room. "Do you know all the guards here?"

"Yes, we checked them. Half of them are Custods," Sage says. "They couldn't get anyone in."

Why try the lights then? "Are the grounds lit?"

"Rarely."

"They know we'll be in the ballroom. They're coming here for sure. Is there any way to the saferooms outside the main doors?"

"The second level. The throne room can house the royal family and the side meeting hall should hold all the girls," Sage replies.

"Can't the throne room hold all of us?" Gavril asks.

"Perhaps." Sage shrugs and grabs Gavril's arm.

Gavril jerks away. "Then we should all go there. Splitting us up will..."

"Make it harder for them to get you. The ladies are in no danger from Custod rebels," Sage snaps. "They are going for you and your parents alone."

He grabs Gavril again, but Gavril has had enough and pulls free or tries to. Sage holds tighter. Gavril surprises me with his strength and breaks free.

"I can walk," he snaps and takes my hand.

That bothers Sage instantly. He opens his mouth to protest, but I let go of Gavril's hand.

"Sage is right. They won't hurt me." Or maybe he will, I don't know. I'm terrified, but I know this much. I can't go with him. I can't do this. I can't let this happen no matter how I want it.

"There's only one of you and twenty-one of me. It's alright."

Gavril's eyes widen in worry, and he shakes his head. He reaches out to me and puts a hand to my face, but I yank away. Other Custod guards have joined us and grab Gavril to pull him to safety.

He can't and shouldn't risk himself for me. I'm a Custod. This is my real job, not playing suitor to a prince.

I feel my heart cracking, ready to shatter into a thousand pieces yet again, but I hold it together. I have to. Because it's the one thing I truly am, even if I hate it. I'd have to wait to break later when I'm not needed. At least I can stop them from hurting the prince. Even if... I'll likely never see him again without chains on.

I will myself not to look back and step out onto the main ballroom floor. I don't see any free weapons, but I'm going to get one. I march right up to the main doors. My confident walk fools the guards, and I slip out without being bothered. If I remember right, there are a few decorative weapons around. I might be able to pull one free.

I don't see any in the hall. I listen for any signs of my former Custod rebel friends, looking to the places Dad would tell me to hide. That's the most likely place they'd end up.

My heart pounds in the fear of what I'll do if I run into my father or Jake.

"Look who's all pretty," a voice croons at me from behind. I know that voice, even if I don't like it.

I groan, "Can't you boys keep it to yourselves?" I shoot my elbow backward right into the foolish boy's stomach. I hear the grunt and feel his breath shoot over my shoulder.

It tells me exactly what position he's in. I turn and slam my knee under his jaw before I pull back and kick him in the throat, knocking him flat to the floor.

"Safer that way," I say as I walk over and look for a weapon, but he's not armed.

Stupid rebel. I turn and walk down the hall, happy my heels make a lot of noise. It should attract more of them.

The next set of people I walk into are castle guards. They raise their eyebrows to see me.

"M'lady, you should be in a safe room," one of them says. "I'll escort you."

She takes my arm, but I pull away. "I can help. They're coming through the side entrance," I point. "And using the main hallways as a means of getting in."

"How do you know?" The guard frowns at me.

"I... I don't know," I admit. "But I had friends in this rebellion, and I know how they think. They are using our tactics to fight full-on attacks against us. Which means they are likely trying to get into the safe rooms without facing any guards."

"Some do have servant passages, but how would they know about them?" the guard asks.

"I-I don't know." But I do know where I need to go. "How do you get into the throne room safe room?"

"Not even I know, miss. It's well defended," the guard shakes her head as we walk.

"Kascia." Damian spots me as we pass a hallway where he took out a rebel. He kicks the body down and approaches us. "I thought I'd find you out here."

"Why?" I am supposed to be in a safe room.

"Because you're you." Damian smiles then looks at the guard. "It's alright, I've got her. More rebels are heading up the left side. See to it."

The guard bows to him and races in that direction.

"Because I'm me?" I frown.

"Well, these are Custod rebels, are they not?" Damian looks at me, arching a brow. "So you would know them and want to do something."

I swallow. "It's half and half."

Damian nods. "Well then," he bends down and picks up a sword from the man he just killed, flips it around, then offers me the handle, "I expect you'll be needing this."

I smile. "Thank you. Is everyone inside a safe room?"

"Yes, as far as I could tell. I was trying to head off the attack when I saw you."

"They'll be going for the throne room."

Father would see they had cleared out the ballroom. His target from there would be the "royal's heart" as he'd call it.

"Then we should head that way, but first things first." Damian smiles then walks behind me, picks up my train, and pins it to the back of my dress so it doesn't drag on the ground.

"Thanks."

Damian grins. "You're welcome, my lady."

Damian shows me the way, heading to the core cylinder. For the first time, I go through the center doors.

It leads into a foyer. The moment we open the doors, six rebels turn and converge on us.

"On your call, my lady." He glances at me as we face the attack.

I smile and nod back at him. It's kind of nice and empowering to feel Damian sees me as equal in this fight. I don't think anyone has ever looked at me that way.

Damian gives me a half-smile with a quick nod then races forward and starts cutting through their ranks at impressive speed. I take my side, and we're able to take down several, but more are coming.

But that makes no sense. They are in stealth mode, right? Now they are charging full-on without care. That... something is wrong.

"Damian, keep them out!" I call over to him. "I'm going to check inside." I have a bad feeling whatever I find in there is going to explain their change of plan.

"Will do." Damian nods and kicks one of them back. "Go, I've got this."

I turn and run to the throne room doors, yank them open and race inside.

I pause on the threshold, the door swinging closed behind me.

The room is lit with the castle's enchanted lights. Part of the stunning glass dome covers the throne room, letting the starlight shine in. The two thrones bear the royal colors, but the golden plated seats' cushioning is on the floor. The seats for the court has been upended and tossed aside, tables knocked over and away from the walls.

Feeling along the left wall, muttering under his breath, is my father.

My breath catches as I look at him rifling through a drawer as if to find a key. My heart clenches in fear yet pummels itself against my ribs. Fear grips my throat. I tighten my grip on my sword.

I swallow past fear's painful grip on my neck and raise my weapon. "What are you doing?" I demand of my father, tears already stinging my eyes. "I told you no!"

Dad whirls around to face me, dropping whatever he'd been holding. But he relaxes when he sees it's me and beams as if I'm just demanding to know why he's late to my party.

Dad looks me over head to toe, a proud glint in his eyes. My heart tightens.

"Those impressions weren't wrong. You look stunning, my cygnet," he praises.

"That isn't what I asked," I state firmly. "I said no. I said I wouldn't do it. You couldn't even promise me my friends would be safe, then you ignored my pleas. The plan was off. What were you thinking breaking in anyway?" *Why would you break my trust? Did you ever trust me?*

"I figured it was too hard. I knew the party still offered a good distraction. But sadly, getting in set off the alarm. I know they're in here. Help me find it." Dad goes back to check the thrones again.

My mouth drops open; my hands shake so badly my weapon rattles. I grip it tighter. "Dad, did you even read what I wrote you?"

"Of course I did, cygnet. Now I'm guessing it's a set of switches. The Loyalists said that's how they got into the last safe room," Dad gabbles on as if he's teaching me a new technique on breaking into a secured building. "And they needed two people, so I'll need your extra set of beautiful hands." He gives me a quick smile over his shoulder.

I tense in anger this time. He completely ignored me and what I'd said. He isn't listening. He doesn't care. It's like he thinks if he acts like nothing changed, nothing would. I'm done letting him treat me this way.

I march over and grab his shoulder and yank him around to face me. "I said no!" I state firmly. "I told you what I saw. It's not like they all said.

Something is going on, and it's not what we thought, Papa. We can work it out with them. I know it. I'm working on it. Don't you trust me?"

I look up at him, tears finally breaking through my stubborn wall. That's what hurts. Not that he stuck to his beliefs or any of that. It's not even that he broke in. It's what it tells me. It tells me he doesn't trust me as his person on the inside. It tells me he doesn't listen to what I say when I disagree or don't understand. I was sure he had all my life, but right now, he is as far from it as possible. He doesn't trust me to be his girl on the inside with the right intel and understanding of the op. He broke in *despite* what I'd said. He didn't return even a little of the trust I gave him. And I gave him everything.

I gave him and Jake everything! I tense in fresh anger and push my father away from the wall. "You won't listen! Have you ever? You had to take everything from me for this, and when I ask you to trust me, you take it again and again."

"Because it's hard when you're deep undercover. I warned you about trying to be high on the score, but you did perfectly, my little cygnet, as always." He smiles at me with the loving smile I always adored and fought for. But there's another element to it I'd never noticed. It's a bit like how the queen smiles at Gavril when he says something that's smart, but she doesn't take it seriously. How dare he?!

"But this doesn't end until we show them the truth. The Potentates can't be trusted to rule with so little structure. You'll prove what a real queen should be." He cups my chin like he used to.

My heart quavers once more. I bite the inside of my lip to stop it from shaking. I miss this. I miss his sure love and protection. I miss being safe to trust him, knowing he always knows what is best and how to guide me to the next right step. I fight tears as a million treasured childhood memories flood my mind: Kassie wraps, dancing in the kitchen, nighttime tickles, stories, and kisses before bed, the nights he'd stay up when we realized I had a sleep problem. All of it strikes me at once as I feel how much I love him as the memories warm me inside. I shut my eyes tightly, a tear escaping.

It's all over. It takes all my self-will to pull myself away, slowly stepping back, eyes still shut as every inch of my body tenses in the anguish of what I have to do.

"But not this way," I say, opening my eyes and looking up at him through my tears. "It can't be done this way, Dad. We'll only bring more damage if we do this. We have to end it, actually end it. Someone has to step up and bridge the gap instead of trying to destroy the other shore. They will listen. They already have listened to me. We don't have to do this. Papa, please, don't kill them."

Dad's face drops. His brows furrowed in confusion, bordering on anger. I hold my weapon tighter.

"I know it's hard when you get attached, cygnet. But that's the price. Custods have had to do far worse."

"Like what!?" I demand. "They only did what was needed to people who had personally committed the crime. The prince hasn't done anything!"

"Yet!" Dad retorts firmly like telling off a child. "The Merlin warned us if we let him marry, it's over. This kingdom falls. We can't let that happen. It's our mission, Kassie. The only mission you've ever had. Don't you want to finish it successfully?"

My stomach drops. The Merlin said what? But I have to ignore it. I have to stay strong though my commitment waivers dangerously.

"Yes, in a way that protects the kingdom, not just our cause. Papa, I never wanted this! You knew that. I want this over for real, so *my people* are safe. This won't bring that, Papa."

"The Merlin said it will."

"Then why didn't you tell me?!"

"You didn't need to know. We kept it need-to-know for everyone's safety," Dad frowns. "What's wrong?"

My mouth falls open again. "What's wrong?!" I exclaim. "I already told you what's wrong! Us! We were wrong. You haven't listened to me. I told you I didn't want to do this, but you all pushed anyway. I told you no without a promise to keep the girls safe and you ignored me. You came in here quiet enough. You could have promised but you didn't!"

The anger rises in me like a sudden tide. "You wouldn't give me anything when you took *everything* from me for your cause. A cause that was wrong. And yet, I get to see and learn that, and you won't trust me when I trusted you. I trusted you enough to give up all I wanted when I was ten, and again, all those months ago. You couldn't even promise me!"

"I can't control them all. I can't make promises I can't hold up," Dad says. "And I did check on you."

"No, you didn't! You asked for more information. Your 'check in' sounded as empty as the raw data for a new code. That's not the same, you know it. You just found words that had the letters you needed that would pass the mailer's check. I'm telling you; we can do this without more bloodshed. Why not try? We don't need the Loyalists. We can still get what you want. I just have to win this."

Could I dare play this game? Dad wants *me* in power, not Jake. He wanted a Custod on the throne. If I win this, he'd get his wish. Can I dare pretend that's what I want to do? Will that protect Gavril?

"The king and queen aren't going to pick an actual true princess," Dad laughs.

"I've made it this far."

"With a bunch of other monkeys," Dad sighs in exasperation. "And that's the kind the royals want. These tests are for show. They'll pick Princess Rose, then things get worse. We get these corrupt Potentates on the High Throne? I don't think so. It has to be done. You knew this when you came here." Dad waves me to join him. "Now help me find it."

"No." I back away. "Don't you trust me to win them over? I thought I was your best asset. Your star actress, even in a live show," I repeat his words back to him.

"Their pride won't let anyone but who they want win, Kascia. Now we're wasting time. I'm sure we're hardly keeping the guards out of here. Help me find it. You're much more familiar with how they work than me." He turns back to the wall.

I grip my weapon tighter in my anger. "Yes, I do! So, trust me!"

"I said that's enough." Dad gives me a stern look. Mom used to look at me like that when I was small. Dad never had. This is a first, and it only makes me angrier. I'm not a child! *I'm so sorry I made fun of you for this, Gavril.*

"No, I want you out of this castle, now," I copy his tone.

"Kassie, this isn't a game. We're running out of time. Help me find it," Dad orders me in the tone he'd use to chastise me as a girl. "Kascia, now."

I shake my head. "No." I raise my weapon, fighting not to let it shake in my hand. "Step away from there, *now*."

Dad stops and turns to face me full on. It's his turn to have his mouth gape open. "What?"

"You heard me. Step away. I'm not letting you hurt them." I stand as firm as I can, drawing on all I know about looking strong and intimidating on the stage.

Dad blinks and gapes at me a moment longer before speaking. "Has being treated like a royal gone to your head? I'm your father, and you will listen to me. Now help me—"

"No!" I grip my weapon tighter.

Oh please, sweet Lord, don't make me have to fight him.

"You need to listen. I won't help you. I chose not to let you in. You're right, this isn't a game. I'm not just a piece on your chessboard. I'm not letting you hurt them. Get out. Now!" I square my shoulders in the hope of hiding how I'm trembling inside.

Dad's face darkens and grows dangerous in a way I only had ever seen on stage. "Kascia Custod, put that down right now."

"No." That word is starting to sound funny to me with how much I'm saying it. "I don't want to fight you. Please, Papa, please just trust me," my voice breaks. "I know what I'm doing."

But do I? I debated this exact question a million times. I deliberated over and over. But I made the choice. I have to live with it. And Gavril thought he'd not make a good king? He's better at this than me, and I am my Dad's choice.

"No, you don't!" Dad snaps at me. "It's not like with Jake. I know having to play him and getting close to him wasn't easy, but that was for your own good. This isn't for anyone's good. We can't stop what's happening with them alive."

"It *is* like with Jake! You dragged me into something for your cause. For *your* reasons! And I thought I got it to work. I gave him my heart because *you* told me I'd be happy if I did. It wasn't easy, but I did it. And you know how he treated it? He was happy to sell me! He was alright with whatever it took to win this. And if I had to sell my soul to the enemy to do it, then he told me I should. Do you have any idea how that felt?!

"He didn't love me enough to even want to keep me. He ripped all the love I put into him to shreds and threw them back at me like a barrage of blades! I gave him the power to do that because *you* told me to. That I'd be happy if I did. That was what a Custod should do.

"It was *you* who told him it was best, and he believed it. So, I trusted *you* again and what happened? I got torn apart again, and again, and again, and then you ignored my pleas for help!"

"I did not—"

"You forced me to look at images of tortured children and dying men! You made me feel guilty about my own feelings! *You* didn't care. It's always you, you, you. What *you think* is right and forget what anyone else says. And when I tried to think for myself, you ignored me. You didn't take me seriously. You came in here assuming I knew *you* were right. You've asked me to put my faith in *you* and what *you* think is best. I did, and where did it get me? Here! It got me here where I'm being ripped apart inside and forced to play a role with my neck on the line, not *yours.* I came in here trusting it was best, but it's only gone from bad to worse."

"So, what do you propose?" Dad challenges. "You knew being a Custod was hard. It hurts! Do you think I've not felt any of that pain? That I wanted to send you into the snake pit? That I wanted to give up what I was good at to pretend to be something I'm not in this backwater kingdom with royals who disrespect Custods at every turn? That I wanted my precious girl to have to fight in this ugly war? I had no choice. You're all the help I got. I don't want to do this, but it's all we have. It's our duty."

"And I'm doing it!" I scream back. "I said out, and I mean now!"

Dad pauses, looking at me. "What do you think you're going to do? Play the maiden in one of your plays and get the beast to turn into a true prince?" he mocks me. "Make a real-life fairytale?"

"Maybe it was I who was the beast," I reply, feeling the truth of that hit me hard.

I was wrong. I was the one who was biased and judgmental when I walked into this castle, not him. He accepted me, even with my bias. It was I who had been the beast, not the prince.

"What are they doing to you?" Dad asks in a gentle voice.

"Nothing you didn't do already," I reply, using all my courage to hold my heart up and keep my weapon on him.

"So, you've let them change you and not the other way around? Nothing has changed out there, Kascia. Those children are still suffering, starving, dying, and so are those unable to support themselves. More shops collapse; more jobs are lost. More people starving on the street. You've not changed them. You let them change you? You trust them more than me?"

"I know we can change it. Let me try," I try a different tact, trying to keep my heart together. I think the shaking is finally showing.

"You've had months, Kascia. Nothing has changed," Dad reminds me.

I struggle to find a rebuttal for that. Is he right? Have I done what I feared and let those charming eyes trick me? Did the view of someone who isn't even one of us twist me?

But I can't accept that. I try, and it just... it isn't true. I know it's not. I can't imagine anyone else doing a better job ending this pain than Gavril. Not Jake, not me, not my prejudiced father, not any of the girls who'd come here to try their hand at helping him rule. Not one of them.

"And it hasn't in five hundred years," I find my voice. "Not with your plans, with the Loyalists' or the Potentiates' plans for hundreds of years. And that suffering you made me look at in an attempt to try to stop it didn't do what you wanted."

I meet my father's eyes, the fire slowly returning as if someone or something was slowly blowing it and nursing it back to health. It only made me surer of what I have to do. End it at all costs. It takes great courage for a Custod to stand up to the enemy outside. It takes even more to stand against the enemy inside.

"I don't want to fight you, but I will if I have to. Custods have to do hard things. This is the hardest thing I've ever had to do! I hate saying no to you, Papa, so please, stop making me."

"So, you think you know better than me? What's your plan then? Win his heart? Get him to overthrow his parents, choose you, and you get the same happy ending with him, instead of Jake because he'd sell *his own soul* for the cause? Would your prince do that?"

"What?"

"You think he *wanted* to tell you to do whatever it took? Think he can't hide how it hurts him too? Do you have that little faith in his determination? You think you will do whatever it takes when your plan is nothing more than wanting to escape the boyfriend who didn't make you number one?" Dad mocks me.

His words sting. I feel a rising fear that he's right, but he made a mistake in mocking me with it. He caused my pain. He doesn't get to mock it too.

"Get out!"

"And what if your plan fails?" Dad challenges me.

"It won't." I'd make something work, even if it doesn't mean I get what I wanted in the end. I already swallowed that pill long ago because of him.

"But if you do?" Dad holds firm, staring me down. "What will you do if you fail?" he asks me slowly.

I take a deep breath. "I'll find another way."

"That way is right in front of you, Kascia! Just help me get in, and it's over. You get the life you wanted, remember? You'll be with Jake fixing this. You just have to get over your wounded pride that perhaps you aren't more important to him than the cause. I expected more of you. But you're young. It's completely understandable. I should have anticipated this. Don't you think he's hurting over this too?"

"Jake isn't the only answer. Assassination isn't the only answer. We can do this another way. And I've decided to take it." I'm holding to my faith by a thread. I'm trembling from head to foot as I finally lift my blade. "Now I asked you to go, I won't a-ask again." I take a deep breath.

Conceal it; don't feel it. I remind myself.

"What happened to you? What are they doing to you?" The anger on my Dad's face melts into pain. "You know better than this. What's caused this? Did the prince get to you?" He thinks a moment. "The Custods that don't know?"

"I said out!" I don't have an answer for him, but I can't let him hurt my apprentice. I can't. I am not strong enough. But am I strong enough to keep standing up to him?

"Kassie, you don't have to. It's alright, just put the sword down and go. You don't have to help if it's too much."

I shake my head. "No. Don't you understand? I don't want you in here. I chose not to let you in. You are not going to hurt them. I won't let you." I have no idea where the safe room is, but if I did, I'd make sure to defend it. I know it's here somewhere.

Dad stares at me open-mouthed. Tears start to form in his eyes. "My dear cygnet, what did they do to you?" my Dad's voice breaks. I fight my tears as I try to ignore his shining in pain.

My chest rises and falls rapidly as I try to contain all the turmoil, questions, aches, and fears tumbling inside of me like the pounding, spinning force of a wave's undertow. I feel like I might throw up.

I've done it. I've done what I feared most. I disappointed him. And that hurts more than anything. He was my hero, my papa, my best friend, my knight before I had one. He was everything to me from the first day I can remember. Now, here I am, throwing out what he holds most dear. He'd spent his whole adult life on this mission given to him. So long, even my birth played into it. Now his own daughter is stopping him. *Creator, forgive me.* I'm sure I've lost my Custod right by now, but I can't stand down.

I made the choice. And no matter how much I question it, and how my heart and faith wavers, it's not enough to let him hurt the only man who'd really given me pure love with no strings attached, without even the promise of my returned affection. The only man who'd taught me the truth and let me decide what it means. I can't betray either of them. Yet... how can I betray the man who'd given me who I am, my personality, my beliefs, my heart, my passions, who was everything to me my whole life? My papa.

"You're not serious," Dad finally says.

"Are you not listening?!" I snap, tears rolling down my cheeks. "I won't let you do this. Now get out." I point to the door.

"Kassie, no."

"Out!"

Dad's brows draw in anger. "Kassie, don't make me do this."

"You gave up that choice," I reply. *When I begged the same of you.*

"You know you can't stop me," Dad says, pleading with me not to make him.

"Do I?" I ask with a shaking voice. But then it gains strength as I say, "Do you?"

Dad lets out a tired sigh, "Alright, I suppose this one night we can let it rest. I've waited this long. Perhaps I'll have to let you fail to see the truth."

But he's not relaxing like he does when he gives up a fight. He's still tense. His sword is at his side, but I'm not ready to lower mine just yet. I know my Dad's tricks. He had me trained to deal with just such a move as I think he's preparing to make.

Please, I'm not strong enough to fight him. Don't make me do this, I beg in my heart, trying to hold firm, but I feel my sword shaking ever so slightly.

"But in time you'll see. He'll turn on you, just like all of his family has for generations. They only care about themselves and their image. You'll see what I mean in time." Dad's eyes are filled with pain at the idea of me having to suffer personally being betrayed by them.

"I already know what that pain feels like," I say, my voice breaking towards the end. "Now get out."

Dad gapes at me, trying to process what that meant.

"I still love you," he says. I don't relax.

Dad glances behind me. I read the look in his eyes a split second before he acts.

He dives towards my weapon. I block his blow and throw him back with a thrust. "It's not behind me!" I snap. Then again, maybe it is, I have no idea.

"Oh? Sure?" Dad asks.

"I told you out." I keep my sword up.

My heart is thundering so fast I can hardly tell when one beat ends and the other begins.

Dad puts his sword away and holds up his hands. "Alright, alright, if you're that set. You'll learn the truth soon enough. I'm sorry it will have to be so hard. And remember we got in without you once. When you find you're wrong, we'll be back. You just won't know when."

I already have a list of ideas on when. "Out." I need him gone before I break.

"Alright, alright. I'll see you soon, princess." He gives me a sad weak smile, "Know I'll be ready to accept you no matter your mistakes. I do still love you. I just wish you didn't have to learn the hard way." Dad studies me. He knows I'm struggling. He's waiting for me to break.

That makes the anger rise again. I grip my sword firmly, no longer shaking. "I said get out!" I pull that cursed ring my father made me wear off and throw it at him with all my anger.

It hits him on the forehead with impressive speed, making him stagger back. "Kassie," he frowns then looks down, rubbing the red mark on his head. The frown increases as he picks the ring up.

"I want you out! I want you to take that cursed thing with you and never bring it back!" I scream at him.

I am not going to let him use my pain as a tool to get what he wants. Not when he caused it. I am not sure I've ever loved and hated someone so much in the same moment in my life. I want him to be safe, and I want him as far away from me as possible.

"Alright, alright." He puts his hand on the door before looking again. But he sees the tension in my arm and legs. I will charge if I have to. He jumps, startled by that, and is gone with a snap of the door shutting behind him.

Chapter 45

I stand there, panting in trembling gasps, sucking in lungfuls of air as my whole-body shakes. I fight to keep myself in check. But after a minute or so, I'm sure he's not coming back.

I'm about to let my weapon fall from my shaking hand and collapse when there's a loud thunk behind me.

I jump a mile and turn to the door, weapon ready when I see it's Sage coming from the safe room.

My heart leaps into my throat. I try to drop the weapon before he thinks I'm actually about to attack him.

I'm not fast enough. Sage sees me armed but doesn't see the tears rolling downing my cheek. He moves faster than lightning and pins me to the far wall, putting a blade to my throat.

"What are you doing in here?" he demands in a low, dangerous snarl.

"I-I was getting the rebels out," I insist, fighting to recollect myself after I'd *just* been ready to cave into tears. *Help me, I can't do this.*

I shove Sage off. Either he isn't that afraid of me, or he's that surprised that I'm able to get him off.

"I knew they'd think to come into the throne room. I was trying to help!" Why can't Sage just leave me alone? Why do all Custods have to treat me like this?!

"By standing alone in the throne room with your sword pointed at the safe room?" the queen says, looking absolutely terrified as she and the king stand at the safe room door.

This is it. They're going to assume I was a part of a plot to hurt them. They'll never believe me. Sage has known from the start. I'm not going to get out of this. Or worse, Dad somehow rescues me, and I'm stuck with him and Jake again. I'll be forced to be Jake's toy as they eventually get what they want with the help of whoever is letting the Loyalists in. I'll be damned on the throne of a doomed kingdom at Jake's side. I think execution might be kinder.

"Yes," I reply in a meek squeak to the queen. "The last of the rebels just left the room. I was worried he'd come back."

"What he?" Sage snarls at me, holding me to the wall by one shoulder. "You said 'he' in the ballroom. You know who they are. You know them by name. How?"

I shut my eyes against the pain and anger. *I did my best!* I'm going through enough pain without Sage shoving me around.

"They were friends of mine, alright?" Tears escape my closed eyes, "They've been writing to me since I got here, asking me to let them in during the ball. I told them no over and over. I didn't think they'd try to get in without my help. I'm sorry I didn't say anything, but you're always on my case about trying to kill Gavril. I didn't think it was a good idea."

"And how do we know that's not a cover-up?" Sage demands.

I look up and meet Sage's stunning green eyes. They remind me of Damian's enough to give me the courage to speak. "I-I have no other proof but the truth." Another tear escapes. "You can th-throw me out, but it doesn't mean I lied. Does the fact I'm ashamed of my past make me less of a princess than anyone else?" I look at the queen. "Does my desire to want to help protect you in the ways I know make me less of a leader?"

The king and queen don't reply, watching me; the battle raging in their eyes, trying to decide what to believe.

"Since the first night, I knew something was wrong. What are you hiding?" Sage demands.

"I told you my secret! What more do you want?!" I glare at Sage.

Sage narrows his eyes, studying me carefully. "No, it's not everything," he says slowly. "There's more you won't say. Why won't you admit it? It *can't* get any worse for you."

"I have said. And even if I haven't, can you blame me? You've not wanted me here since that night. I'm not quite ready to give up just yet. Yes, I have a lot of close friends who are rebels. They asked me to let them in. I said no. What more is there to say?"

I don't know what's better: failed, accused and rescued by Dad, or being executed. Though making Gavril endure that might be enough to just make my heart stop on its own.

That's when I realize Gavril isn't there. I frown. Then my heart starts to race. Where is he? My eyes dart about the room. He has to be safe. I fight images from my imagination showing Dad having him cornered.

At that moment, Damian pushes the door open and strolls into the room. "A lot of commotion in here tonight," he comments. "The rebels have retreated. Their leader pushed past me on his way out."

"Did you know him?" the king asks.

"No, I've never seen him before," Damian lies smoothly. "He didn't bother much with me. He sounded the retreat and left."

The king nods then looks at the rest of us, "And the girls are all safe, so no harm done."

Sage looks at him like he's nuts. "Your Majesty, I must insist..."

"You don't get to judge the Chosen, Sage," the king says politely.

"Aster, perhaps..." the queen starts.

"It's been a long night. We're all a bit overwrought. We'll talk about this more when we're calmed down." The king's tone indicates that it is not up for debate.

What? He's just letting me go? Sage lets go, and I slide to the floor. I didn't realize he'd been holding me up. My shoulder throbs at the release of the pressure. I'm sure it's bruised.

I rub it as I look down, unable to believe this is happening. I'm not safe, but I have a space to breathe.I look up and see Sage's glare at me. He looks from me to the king with narrowed eyes. He is surer than ever. I'll never get past that. Sage has a lot more authority than me. I'll be sent home to my waiting father.

My stomach tightens. What will he do to me? What will Jake say? What life is left if I go home now? My eyes flood with tears. I'm lost.

Damian nods. "A wise choice, Your Majesty. If there are any questions, I can vindicate Lady Kascia's story. I was with her most of the time since the attack started, and I trust her." He smiles gently at me.

I manage a weak smile back. But how much can Damian do? Sage narrows his eyes at him. I can tell he wants to grab Damian and demand to know why he stands by me. I take a deep breath. They're wrong, but anyone on my side helps.

"Thank you. Sounds like proof enough to me." The king smiles and looks at his wife. She looks far more nervous. "Come on, we should all get to bed. Sir Damian, if you wouldn't mind." The king nods at me.

"Not at all, Your Majesty." Damian bows to him then approaches me and offers me his hand to lift me, as if nothing has changed. "My lady."

I smile through my tears and take it, fighting to control my emotionally wrought breathing as he helps me stand. Damian bids them good night then escorts me back to my room.

I hold it together as long as I can. I nod another thanks to him as we enter my room. I don't know how late it is. Damian closes the door behind us and pulls me into a hug.

I accept it and try to hold in the sobs, but it doesn't work. I finally break down, my knees shaking, trying to keep myself up as the tears stream down my face. The struggle to breathe finally is alleviated as the sobs and fear escape. What if he was right? What if he was right and I just made a huge mistake?

Damian sighs and brushes the back of my head. "It's okay. Just let it out. No one knows more than I how difficult that was for you."

I shake my head. "I'm scared, Damian." I'm terrified of what will happen once everyone calms down.

"I know," Damian frowns. "But I will do everything I can to protect you. You were right to stand up to your father, and I'm not going to let you be punished for that."

But what if I wasn't and he is right? That it's all me being upset that I'm second when I should be? His duty comes first. I would expect the same of Gavril, right? I don't know.

I break down, unable to hold my feet anymore. Damian catches me and just sits on the floor with me, hugging me, rocking a little as he strokes my hair.

"What happens to me now?" I ask. The terror makes it hard to breathe, though the sobs have abated for now. "They're going to throw me out at best, and it doesn't matter. He's going to fi-find a way to get me again. I'll be tr-trapped to him. E-enslaved again." No better than the slave girls in the shows I'd danced in.

"They are not going to send you back to him," Damian says firmly. "I will not let him take you again," His voice sounds dangerous. "You did nothing wrong tonight. Alright, maybe you should have told them earlier. But you didn't know, and really, what would it have done? They already enlisted the best guards there are, so it isn't like they could change anything.

"You did everything you could to own up and fix it. If not for you, sooner or later, your father would have found them. Gavril and his parents are safe because of you. Because you stood up to him. Tonight, you gave Gavril a chance to live long enough to prove himself. No one could ask for more than that. You were his guardian angel tonight. And I will defend that until my last breath."

But my heart still races in fear as I try to wipe my eyes. I didn't even see him there. He was… "He's alright, right?"

"Yes, he is perfectly fine. A bit frustrated with his guards, but he's alright." Damian smiles a little.

My lip shakes, and I nod. But no matter what Damian says, I was no angel tonight. What if Dad is right about why I'm here? That I was just upset for stupid reasons in the first place. Was I unfair in dropping Jake too quickly? Was that fair to him? Was that fair to me or anyone or even the right thing?

Like Jake's words once haunted me, Dad's are far worse. "What if they're right?" I ask. "What's going to happen to me?"

"What if who is right?" Damian asks, arching a brow.

"Any of them? Dad, the freaked out royals, Jake, what if they are right, and I just made a huge mistake, and I have just… been selfish?"

"Why? Because your father said Jake was willing to sell his soul for the cause?" Damian gives me a look like he doesn't believe that for a second. "If that was true, why wasn't he here? This was his mission too, was it not? Yet I didn't see a single man that even slightly resembled the Loyalist leader tonight. Which means he either looks nothing like his father, or he wasn't here tonight, which is more likely in my opinion.

"And regardless of whether he showed tonight or not, your father is *still* wrong. Jake wasn't selling his soul when he told you to do this; he was selling yours. And that is *much* different. No man who truly loves you would ask that of you, not even the Protector. So how can your boyfriend do such a thing and claim to love you? Answer: he can't. Not if he is being honest with himself and with you."

"It… but what does that say about me that I wasn't willing?"

Damian looks at me tenderly. "But you did, didn't you? You sold everything you had to be here. You were willing to do whatever it took, even though you hated it. Does that mean your sacrifice is less because your father disagrees with what the cause is?"

I swallow. "Only if I'm wrong."

"So, your father is more correct about the royal family than you, who has seen them every day for the past three months?" Damian arches his brow at the question. "Not to mention that is the same man who doesn't even know what the prince looks like. You really think he knows them more?"

"I doubt it." Not that I see the king and queen every day, but Gavril I felt more certain I know. And that's who my hope is really in.

"So how can he be right when he doesn't even know what he is fighting against?" Damian asks. "The Merlin knew Heklis was wrong because he saw him commit crimes against man and nature. What evil has the prince done?"

I shake my head, "Nothing I know of." A frown creases my face. "Dad just thinks the Creator says he will."

"Why is that?" Damian tilts his head.

"He said… the Merlin prophesied…"

Light comes to Damian's eyes. "I see. And what does he claim the Merlin said?"

"Just that if the prince marries, the kingdom falls," I shake my head, so unsure. "Then why didn't he tell me?" My lip shakes, I'm so mixed up and confused.

Damian shrugs. "Why he didn't tell you until now, I can't say. He could have a multitude of reasons. As for the prophecy itself, I wouldn't go believing it on the word of one man, no matter who he is. Prophecies are often misconstrued. The older they are, the more that is misunderstood about them. People develop their own beliefs about what they mean based on their own misunderstandings and biases.

"Even the prophecy of the Merlin was misunderstood in his day. The people at the time didn't realize he would come back after he died. So this prophecy, if it does exist, could have an entirely different interpretation than the one your father has deduced. The only way to know for sure is first determine if it is real and find the original source."

As I have *no* idea how to do that, I may have to log that away for more pressing problems. Like what's next. "I'm not sure how I'm getting out of this," I confess the fear.

"It is a bit of a shambles, isn't it?" Damian sighs and nods in agreement then meets my eye. "You still want to win, right?"

I swallow and nod.

"Then I will help you." Damian smiles assuringly. "You did nothing wrong tonight, and I will defend that with my whole being. I am proud of you, my dear night angel." He beams at me with that glowing happiness I once saw in my father's eyes.

I manage a weak smile and wipe my eyes. "I wasn't anything of the sort."

"On the contrary, you were strong tonight. It takes a person of true integrity and character to own up to their mistake like you did. And you were brave to stand against your father, when I know deep down that is the last thing you wanted to do. You are an incredible woman, Kasica. And someday, I hope you see what I see in you. You have strength you do not realize. Tonight, you proved you are a lady of compassion and heart. The royal family owes their lives to you."

"But... they-they saw me brandishing that sword, and I even admitted to Sage I knew about tonight."

"Knew about it but thought they were safe because the rebels couldn't get in. The only fault you carry is trusting in the palace walls and guard to keep them out, nothing more. That is not a punishable offense," Damian says as if reminding me.

"Hiding intel from the Custods could be." I swallow. "I'm so scared." I fight another sob.

Damian takes me into another hug. "I'll protect you, no matter what. I swear my life and power on it."

"I'm not sure that's a promise you can make." I hug myself. "I'm so sorry..." He shouldn't be trapped in the middle of this mess I made.

Damian smiles tenderly. "It's perfectly alright. It isn't your fault this is hard. And whether you believe it or not, I will do everything in my power to protect you. I stand by what I said in the throne room. I will defend your story. I won't tell them it was your father per se if you don't wish me to, but I know it was because of you that he left. I won't let them send you away for doing what is right.

"But that is for tomorrow. Tonight, I suggest you get ready for bed. I'll bring you your tea, and I'll be here if you simply wish to cry and let it out."

I nod. He's right. There's not much I can do. I get cleaned up, realizing at some point I must have taken off my mask, but I can't recall when. I think it was when I left the ballroom. Damian says he'll find it for me, but he hadn't seen it in a while. I chuckle at him reading my mind.

It takes a while to get all the makeup off. I'm sure in the attack my maids were told to take shelter in their quarters, but it would have been nice to have help getting all these pieces off. At least the pearls are easy, so they aren't damaged, and the action helps calm me down.

I finally am make-up-free, hair cleaned out, and ready for bed. I slip into the same old t-shirt and pants, as crisp and clean as ever, — the same I wore when I met Gavril —I've worn for bed this whole time. It feels like a lifetime.

But how much longer will I wear it? How much longer can I avoid being detected? I have a great team. My maids, Damian, the people cheering for me at home, but is that going to be enough? Can I win this? Will I somehow manage to get the king and queen to let me slip by, or tomorrow, will a whole new nightmare begin?

Either way, I have to be ready. Because like it or not, I'm in over my head. If I can manage to win or even make it any further is in the hands of providence and fate now. And I'll have to keep holding to that thin thread of faith I have left. In the meantime, I have to recognize I broke all ties with why I came here. I am no longer a plant. I am a true Chosen daughter of Purerah.

And if you enjoyed the book, help others find the book and join the community:

Ready for More?
You can download some exclusive deleted scenes collection for you to keep.
Simply sign up to receive the email with your free collection below.
Scan the Code

Character Guide

The Chosen

1. **Princess Rose**: High-Princess heir to the high throne of Emilimoh.
2. **Princess Amapola**: Princess of Spearim, elegant, fiery, and passionate.
3. **Princess Neeraja**: Princess of Sadeyu, gentle, kind, yet a tad judgmental.
4. **Princess Laurina**: Princess of Bruag, she loves her dragon, exploring, and is the boldest of the born princesses.
5. **Princess Zinna**: Princess of Dragia where they aspire to be like the wild dragons.
6. **Princess Zelda**: Crown Princess of Hyvil, curious, inquisitive, and will take any excuse to use her Magus tablet.
7. **Emmalina**: She's an excitable girl who's over the moon to be here.
8. **Bella**: A dreamer, high in the ranks but friendly with the other girls, most of all Azalea.
9. **Dahlia**: The most competitive of the girls. She's used to winning her matches.
10. **Jonquil**: Is one of the most friendly girls, yet judgmental of the others.

11. **Lilly**: Is the youngest Chosen. She's very shy and sensitive.
12. **Kascia**: Came here out of loyalty to her family but would rather be anywhere else.
13. **Azalea**: Tries to look after the other girls like she looks after her younger siblings at home.
14. **Ericka**: Is sure she's already princess and should be treated as such.
15. **Forsythia**: Is clever, and happily align herself with Dahlia and Forsythia in a click nicknamed "the elite".
16. **Violet**: She madly in love with the prince and is sure that alone will win his heart.
17. **Isla**: Is a woman of faith. She's shy and quiet with the other girls, often studying cannon.
18. **Kamala**: Is proud of her island home and sure she'll do them proud as princess.
19. **Latana**: Has been voted the most likely to get in trouble for trying to get the prince in bed.
20. **Marigold**: Loud and confidant, loves teasing her friends Kamala and Hawi.
21. **Hanna**: Is a tad vain but she's sweet with the other girls though a tad shy.
22. **Carleille**: She knows she's a unique beauty and talented. The others won't forget it.
23. **Nicholl**: quiet and mysterious though she's always asking everyone else questions.
24. **Hawi**: She spends all her time with Marigold and Kamala and enjoys intimidating the others.
25. **Ayesha**: Quite and nervous but she is known for demanding a lot of her staff.

26. **Daisy**: She's sweet but a tad ditsy and she'll talk to anyone who'll let her chat their ear off.

27. **Rhosan**: Is confidant in her own skin and the skill of her hands. She has the pride of a royal.

28. **Larin**: Is smart and eager to prove she's the smartest and the best choice for princess.

29. **Lark**: As her name implies, she loves music. She also loves the conservatory.

30. **Aqueela**: She's determined in all her work. And that includes winning the Enthronement.

31. **Jaine**: Is easily spooked. She wants to impress the other girls and fit in.

32. **Payge**: Is curious and mostly listens when others talk to learn all about them.

33. **Elice**: Strong and wants the power but not the rules of being princess.

34. **Heather**: Loves braiding the other girls hair though is a bit disorganized.

35. **Micayla**: She's friendly and likes to look after the plants about the Ladies' Chamber.

36. **Prisa**: She is a strategist, and it reflects in her personality.

37. **Florence**: Elegant as a princess and as a lawyer the best versed in law.

38. **Katy**: Is the boss. She runs her own restaurant, and her bossy attitude annoys the others.

39. **Rachel**: A bit of a tomboy. She had to handle all brothers.

40. **Rhonda**: She's an artist but doesn't speak much as she's nervous in large groups.

41. **Caitlyn**: She's sweet and quite the saleswoman.
42. **Cadella**: She has the stature of a queen and the confidence to do it.
43. **Ellie**: knows how to intimidate the girls around her. She loves the animals as she cared for for a living.
44. **Isobella**: Wants to bring justice to a suffering kingdom though she's a tad radical compared to the others.
45. **Lana**: Is a sweet little perfect girl and popular but perhaps she's a tad too "perfect".
46. **Cloue**: Sweet and excited to dress as a princess unlike the messy work on her family farm.
47. **Ashely**: Loves to make people laugh and is good at it.
48. **Pamia**: Is great with money but not her mouth.
49. **Veronica**: She's stubborn and though the queen likes her the king isn't so sure.
50. **Bellatrix**: Is humbled that she made it so far and is friendly with all the girls.

The Royal Family & Staff

King Aster: Is friendly and likes a good joke, but his borderline humor makes some girls nervous.

Queen Dalilly: The elegant queen who plays her role faithfully. Is an anxious personality.

Prince Gavril: Only son of King Aster and Queen Dalilly. The mysterious prince no one outside the palace has ever seen. Rumored to be hash to his servants.

Sage: The prince's Custod guard. Here on a six-month assignment.

Hydie: The castle's head of staff

Vivian: Kascia's head maid who keeps everything orderly

Flur: Kascia's second maid who is rather shy

Ro: Kascia's third maid who always is ready with a questionable joke.

Godwin: The prince's faithful and playful valet.

Maryum: The queen's faithful lady-in-waiting.

Porteous: The king's loyal valet.

Lila: Kascia's head of security. She's a Custod.

Other:

Peodrick: Kascia's loving father who pushes her to fulfill her Custod duty

Chryasinth (Chrisa): Kascia's loving mother who runs the theater and helps her daughter make her own choice.

Jake/Jacek: Kascia's fiancé in a marriage arranged when she was young.

Alsmeria: Kascia's best friend and first soloist at the theater.

Jashon: The cobbler who makes Kascia's pointe shoes and a friend of Kascia's.

Yarrow: Kascia's first attendant who wants to lead the cutting-edge fashion world.

Damian: Kascia's new attendant with an unknown past .

Adam: The impressionist the royal family trusts most.

Omran: The leader of the Loyalist rebellion. He's Jake's father.

Nippers: The black castle cat.

Marlon: Omran's falcon that has a soft spot for Kascia.

The Rebellions:

Loyalists: The oldest rebellion. The seek to put a common man of Purerah on the throne.

Potentates: Almost as old as the Loyalists rebellion. They want a properly endowed Potentate to take the throne, but not the direct Purerahian royal line.

Custod: The Custod rebellion seeks to have a Custod turn Potentate to rul

Other Books by Charity Mae

See full List Here:

About the Author

Lives near Mt. Shasta in Northing California and loves the nature there (though she'd like some more snow and rain). She wrote her first 700+ book when she was eleven-year-old and published her first book when she was twenty-one.

When she's not reading and writing, she enjoys making and watching YouTube videos, gaming, hiking, swimming, and sitting outside while working on projects.

Sign Up for her newsletters for updates and exclusive content:

Sign Up

And see sneak peeks, enjoy some memes, and more on her social media platforms.:

Instagram@charitymaeauthor

YouTube@mistressoflore

Facebook@charitymaeauthor

Pinterest@charitymaeauthor

Website:charity-mae.com

ISBN: 978-1-958797-17-4

The Character of Damian Lexus was used with the permission of Raye T. Watson.

Knighted Phoenix Publishing

Chairty-mae.com

www.ingramcontent.com/pod-product-compliance
Lightning Source LLC
Chambersburg PA
CBHW030541310726
48979CB00010B/1985/J

* 9 7 8 1 9 5 8 7 9 7 1 7 4 *